I0660519

Book One—*Deep Winter*, begins January Fourteenth

Book Two—*Shatter*, begins April Seventh

Book Three—*Remnant*, begins October Twentieth

REMNANT

rem·nant n
1. a small part of something that remains after the rest has gone
2. a small amount or trace of something such as a feeling or emotion
3. a small isolated group of people surviving from a particular culture or group

Copyright T.C. Sherry, 2005-2010, all rights reserved.
As if you wondered.

"PAY IT FORWARD, GANG."

ISBN: 978-0-615-40078-5

This is a work of fiction. Any names, characters, places and incidents are either the product of the author's wild imagination or are used fictitiously, and any resemblance to any actual persons, living or dead, events or locales is entirely coincidental.

REMNANT

1

The snowflakes outside the window, in a previous year, might have been beautiful. This year, the snows were early--three months early. Snow had been sticking, in increasing quantities, since October first. The first snows began right after Labor Day. Now, eleven days shy of Hallowe'en, the ground was white, with two or three inches of fresh snow. The ground was now frozen six inches down, as well.

I'd never seen any weather like this, so early, so severe. I remembered many years, digging potatoes this late. They'd been in storage for weeks now, thank God. Tons of them this year.

My hot tea, flavored with a little honey, waited for me on my desk as I moved back to the reports waiting for me. While most of my duties had been reassigned, there were some things that I wanted to keep track of, as if there were something that I could do to affect their outcome. I heard the barn door open in the next room.

"Dad? You OK?" Carl asked as I gingerly took my seat.

"Yeah, still hurts."

"Mom said that you were due for your meds. Here," he said as he handed me the pill bottle, filled with a locally produced pain medication. The bottle was recycled. New ones were impossible to come by.

"Thanks, bud. How're the studies going?"

"Good. Learned how to run the deep hole drill today. We bored a piece of that four sixteen stainless."

"For the next round of BAR's?"

"Who gets the first one off the line?"

"I think Anja's got dibs on that one."

"I'm sure Randy won't mind," I said. Randy and Annika Thompson lived down the road a ways, with a fully equipped gunsmith shop. Kevin Miller, manager of the community center, had partnered up with the Thompson's to manufacture new Browning Automatic Rifles, improved over the originals due only to advances in materials and machine tolerances. Carl and a number of other high-school age students were assisting them as part of their studies. I was a minority--and silent--partner in the business.

"Whatchya reading?"

"After action report. One of our trains was attacked."

"Where?"

"Southern Oregon. Had a load of equipment heading south. We were supposed to get food in return."

"They didn't make it?"

"Nope. Killed all of the security. Crew's missing."

"Oh. Anybody we know?"

"Don't think so, haven't read the crew manifest yet."

"I'll let you get back to it. We've got more classes this afternoon."

"What subject?"

"Food preservation. My favorite," he said with no small amount of sarcasm.

"You teaching or learning?"

"Mandatory, remember? Learning."

"Well, you might still pick up a thing or two."

"Right. Like three months of canning and dehydrating didn't teach me this stuff."

"Still things to learn, buddy."

"Yeah, I know. I better run. Mom says lunch'll be ready in about twenty minutes."

"K. Thanks. See you at three."

"Yep," he said as he left the 'office' I'd carved out of the former woodshop. I absentmindedly ran my hand over my still-sore ribcage. Six weeks out of the hospital, eight weeks after young Bob Henson and I crashed. Seven weeks after Henson's memorial service.

My desk, formerly an old drafting table, was stacked with reports that Pete Wolfson had provided me to keep me up to speed. I'd made an effort to do so, but I was slow in healing, and anything approaching real work wore me down quickly. It was frustrating to tire so quickly and to be unable to do what I knew that I could do...once. Pete had taken over nearly all of my 'administrator' duties since the crash. He'd told me on several occasions since then that it was a job that he'd be very happy to turn back over to me. And that from a guy who served in logistics, as a professional.

"Inland Empire No. 4 (former BNSF 7786, General Electric ES44DC), crew missing. Six Army Guardsmen KIA," the words said.

"Attack made with thermite reaction on rails in multiple locations to derail locomotive on low-speed grade. Armed attack made by multiple attackers using small arms and scoped rifles from fixed positions. Four troops killed before first magazines exhausted (Spec. Reynolds, Riverston, McKee, Lt. Wilson). Two remaining troops (1st Sgt. Calispel, Spec.Waddell) exhausted all ammunition and were captured. They both sustained GSW to the head at close range. Hands and feet bound with wire rope as evidenced by abrasions. Evidence on site indicated that up to fifteen enemy attacked the train, with at least six wounded or killed. No enemy bodies were present, although blood trails were found and a pursuit was begun, with mechanized reinforcements expected to arrive within six hours."

The writer—a former reporter for the Chronicle (the old evening newspaper) and now working for the Army, painted the battle all too clearly. The entire report was fifteen pages, double-spaced. I next read the section on the cargo...

"Eleven generating units were destroyed, stripped of copper, switchgear, and recyclable components. Appliance units (salvaged for trade) were similarly stripped. Notably, no weapons were taken, nor were personal effects of troops disturbed. Enemy apparently made no effort to collect used brass, and appeared to have substantial assistance to strip the cargo within the two hour time window before No. 4 was noted overdue."

"Crap," I said to Buck, curled up near the woodstove. He thumped his tail twice and closed his eyes again, happy for the warmth. I pulled out a map of the route, trying to glean any information that I could on where the attackers could have come from. I came away with no new insight.

The 'generating units' were irreplaceable and critical to the trade for citrus fruit and nuts from California. They weren't generators in the conventional sense; they were locally built producer gas generators designed by a local retired Department of Agriculture engineer. At their destination, they would have been hooked up to conventional diesel engines for stationary power generation. Some modifications to the engine would be needed of course, but the ability to run a diesel-type engine without diesel fuel far outweighed the modifications. And now, they'd been stripped for their copper piping and shiny parts. What was left wasn't worth bringing back north. The military guards rode along, in shipping containers that had been converted to mobile barracks. The Burlington shops in Yardley a few miles from downtown Spokane, was quite busy converting containers to multiple uses, all military. Day or night, the welders were running.

"Hey," the CB crackled. "Lunch is ready," Karen stated. I clicked to respond.

Our barn, including the one time craft room and a big portion of my woodshop, had been converted back into storage—much of it food storage on a relatively large scale. Each occupied home on the block—and in many areas of Spokane—had at least a minimum amount of food stored on site, ours exceeded the minimum by a multiple of five. Larger, commercial-sized food storage warehouses were distributed in the populated areas, and were under guard. Some large commercial warehouses, those that survived the Domino and the ensuing collapse, had been adapted for new uses.

I wondered pessimistically as I walked through the blowing snow if we'd stored enough. If winter would end when expected, or be longer on the other end as well. How long, or even if we'd make it.

Between our family, the Bauer's and the Martin's, we'd met and exceeded many of my goals to store as much food as we could. In most cases, more than a year of grains, fruits and vegetables, and we'd done fairly well on the steep learning curve of livestock on a limited basis. Besides 'the girls', our hens (not forgetting the roosters of course), we now had meat rabbits, and some hogs. I had along the way had to learn the difference between 'pigs' (under about a hundred-twenty pounds) and 'hogs', which were mature (or over two hundred-fifty pounds or so).

All of our food production however, depended on ways to harvest, preserve and store it for our coming winter. Karen and I had some limited experience with our garden produce, tree fruit and berries, but nothing on the scale that we were working with now. Karen's brother Alan's family, and our friends the Martins were learning everything from our library and from working with us.

Time was working against us. A verse from Ephesians was called to mind as I reached the porch.

"Be very careful, then, how you live—not as unwise but as wise, making the most of every opportunity, because the days are evil. Therefore do not be foolish, but understand what the Lord's will is."

"About time!" Karen said as I gave her a quick kiss and shucked off my coat. "You can't be late when there's soup on. Our son will take advantage."

"Couldn't blame him one little bit," I said. "Didn't he go back to classes?"

"Cancelled. Just came in on the radio. So he'll work on his assignment here. He's updating the inventory in the garage. Kelly's doing the same in the fruit room."

"Why?" I asked. "I mean why are classes cancelled?"

"Power's out at the school. Non-essential."

"One of my own rules," I said.

"Yes it is. I thought you'd remember that."

"Nope, that's why I write stuff down. Can't handle all the little stuff."

"Here's your first sandwich. Want a second?"

"I'm thinkin'," I said. "The first one's for dipping anyway."

"You plan on wearing that watch cap all the time now?" she asked.

"Forgot about it. Keeps my noggin' warm since I'm now sporting this new aerodynamic hairdo."

"Well take it off. You look silly."

"Yes, ma'am," I replied as I dutifully took off the cap. My hair was coming back in, but slowly, looking like a crew cut from my childhood. I thought I looked a little too much like my late father with this hairstyle. Of course, he didn't sport a twenty-nine-stitch racetrack on his head...

My lunch consisted of Karen's nearly famous tomato soup and a toasted cheese sandwich. In former days, that would've been a nice Tillamook cheddar and white bread. Now local cheese and homemade wheat bread. There was no question that this was better. One of the little things that made life these days 'better.' There were precious few of those.

The power situation was one example of the many hurdles we faced as residents of what was once a good-sized city now in a post War world. All of our electricity came from hydroelectric sources these days, our own dams on the Spokane River. All of the natural gas generating turbines were offline with the loss of the natural gas supply, of course taking with it all natural gas heat. The local dams produced only about thirty-five megawatts, only twenty percent of what the dam system had produced before. We'd lost the Nine Mile dam completely and the surge of water from Nine Mile compromised both the Long Lake and Little Falls dams. Grand Coulee, and all of the other dams on the Columbia, had been offline since the Domino. Coulee alone put out...well, used to, more than six thousand megawatts all by itself. The Columbia River dams that remained were being repaired, the distribution lines repaired, and most importantly, the SCADA controls replaced. (I also learned what 'SCADA' stood for: Supervisory Control and Data Acquisition, without which, power generation and regulation were impossible).

Three weeks after the misadventure that landed me in the hospital and killed my young pilot friend, I'd learned that the precious cargo he was returning to Spokane included new computer hardware and software to replace controls in the power distribution system for each dam and the Pacific Northwest 'grid.'

The surprise of learning of our cargo didn't fully hit me until a Bonneville Power Administration representative told me that a subcontracted firm in China supplied the original control system and software. The SCADA software and hardware were designed to be disabled upon a specific series of commands, and had succeeded completely. Four months of work went into building new boards and re-writing the software down in California. With the repairs, the Pacific Northwest hydroelectric system would operate again. Without it, probably never. Our little system was apparently too small to be of strategic value to the Chinese. Perhaps they'd forgotten about Fairchild Air Force Base, or perhaps they didn't care. I doubted that any of the decision makers in China were alive any longer to question.

At maximum operating capacity, the remaining dams could provide enough power for twenty-five thousand pre-War homes. However, the remaining dams either depended on managed lake levels at Lake Coeur d' Alene, or through free-flow of the river. In low-flow times (like this October), there was little water flowing through the river freely, reducing our available electricity to a little more than a quarter of 'theoretical' capacity. So, these days we were making do on nine megawatts, or sixty-five hundred homes worth.

The problem being of course, that we were closer to thirty thousand in number, and a fair percentage of people depended on electricity for heat.

"You aren't overdoing, are you?" Karen asked. "You've only been up and about for a week now."

"Ten days."

"Fine, if you count two hours a day sitting in front of your computer."

"I do."

"So? Are you feeling OK?"

"Ribs still hurt. As expected."

"Just don't fall. You've still got a couple weeks before you're out of the woods."

"Yes, Doctor Karen," I said with a smirk. She was not amused.

"Don't forget your meds. Here's your second sandwich."

"Had them already."

"OK. Alan and Ron will be here in a little while. Do you have time to meet with them?"

"Always. I'm done with my reading for the day. Pete's keeping me buried in paper. He should just put it on a thumb drive."

Karen sat down with her own lunch. "So are things going like you hoped?"

"No. They're worse. But you probably knew that."

"The weather?"

"Yep, but the overall recovery—I mean nationally—isn't happening at all like I'd hoped it would."

"Well, with the flu…you can't exactly set plans."

"No we can't," I said. "Yet we have to anyway. Doing something is better than nothing." To myself I said 'I hope.'

Karen and I had had many late night talks, when she knew that I was worried about something that I couldn't do a danged thing about. She'd heard my fears of the increasing shortages, of the stories of malnutrition in other parts of the region, of starvation. With the population crash caused by the flu, we had seemingly passed the threshold of being able to 'do things' that we used to do routinely. Manufacturing of many things we'd come to depend on, being one of the keys. Medical care being another. There were a half dozen other 'keys' that any one of which, when lost, would injure a society. When most of them were lost, we were in danger of losing a civilization. Or perhaps more correctly civilization as we knew it.

"Carl said you were reading about the attack on the train. Can you enlighten me any?"

"Yeah, I don't see why not. The train was deliberately derailed, the crew's missing, and the Army guards killed after a firefight."

"What was on the train?"

"Some of the producer gas generating sets that Chris Bellamy designed. We were trading them for fruit and nuts for this year and next."

"Were they stolen?"

"No, worse. They were stripped for parts. Copper. Stainless. Just parts."

"Anyone catch who did it?"

"Nope. Don't know if there's enough manpower down there."

"Where was it?"

"Southern Oregon."

Buck and Ada stirred, hearing the front gate rattle. "We have guests," I said. The dogs were at the front window, tails going like mad.

"The guys are here," Karen said.

I saw both shake the snow off their coats as they stepped onto the porch, where I met them.

"C'mon in, boys. Just in time for dessert."

"Hey, Rick. How you doing today?" Ron said.

"Fair to 'middlin.'"

"Save up your energy. We have a long backlog of Rick-only work for you."

"Thanks. You two ought to go into stand-up."

"Comedy's scarce these days. Get it where you can."

"Indeed."

"Pie's on the table guys," Karen said. "I've got laundry to do with Mary. Rick? You OK without me?"

"Never, but you're good to go."

"Trying to butter me up as always."

"Yes I am. Trying to stock up."

"I should be back by four," she said as she pulled on a hooded parka. It was a hike across the backfield to Alan and Mary's.

"Sounds fine. Take a radio."

"Remember to check in with Arlene by two."

"Thanks, I forgot."

"She doesn't. See you after while," Karen said as she gave me a quick kiss and headed out the back door. Arlene Lomax was the day-shift radio dispatcher for the County. I was asked to check in three times a day, and if someone needed to get hold of me, it would be at my convenience, not theirs. With my recuperation taking so long, naps were an often welcome and unscheduled part of my day.

"Let me take care of this first guys," I said.

"Don't mind us, we'll just polish off this apple pie," Alan said; only half-kidding.

"Right. I'll be sure to tell Carl that you ate his piece, too."

"Careful, Alan. That boy could probably take you."

"Yep, I know he can. Just don't tell him that."

I moved onto the still-unfinished back porch, where my county radio resided. "One thirty-seven to Spokane," I called.

"One thirty-seven. Please confirm availability for meeting your location at fifteen hundred hours," Arlene asked. This certainly piqued my interest. Alan and Ron were listening in as well.

"Affirmative."

"Spokane out, one thirty-seven."

"One thirty-seven." I was puzzled to say the least. I had had few 'official' visitors since my return home, and no 'meetings'.

"Wonder what's up with that?" Ron asked. He knew my schedule as well as I did.

"No idea," I said, and meaning it. "Hang around a while and you'll know as well as me. Meanwhile, let's talk."

2

"Ray Alden's place," Alan stated. "Any ideas on who we can recruit to move in?"

"No, got Casey Wallace's place, too," I reminded him.

Ray, his daughters, and another neighbor, Casey Wallace were going to relocate further west, toward what had been the heart of the downtown area. Casey had lost his wife, Martha, in late September to a septic infection. What should have been a minor injury killed her. He wanted to get out of the home they shared and start new. Ray would head up a new 'plant' of settlers in an area served by utilities, but severely under populated. He would recruit new settlers in a manner similar to his own recruitment into our neighborhood. The 'new' area had distinct possibilities for enhancing the overall region—it held the cities last stockyard and slaughterhouse.

Closed for more than two years, the meatpacking plant, built next to the main rail lines, was scheduled for cleanup and redevelopment as an industrial park. The St. Louis owners were looking for more money than the local market was willing to pay. I had briefly been involved with the project right after it closed, due to environmental cleanup issues on the site. The owners' reviewed our firms' fee proposal and decided we were too far out of their budget. I knew, however, that no one could meet the scope of work within that budget, and I wasn't about to give away the farm. The owners countered our proposal, and we declined. No cleanup work had been started, and the site sat untouched.

The quake had caused significant, but repairable damage to the facility, most notably the collapse of a shade canopy structure over part of the cattle pens. Vandalism of the plant was limited to broken glass on the upper two floors.

Ray's task for the last month or so, was to canvass the population of the Valley, then expanding into the City, for men and women with experience in working in slaughterhouses, as butchers, and meatpackers. These people would be asked if they'd like to relocate near the plant, with homes ready to move into, and signing bonuses as an incentive. Ray had been pretty persuasive apparently, as he had over fifty potential workers, not quite double what his goals were initially.

Coupled with Ray's task to re-establish a relatively large-scale slaughterhouse in the area, Casey Wallace had also been tasked with finding people experienced or willing to be trained in leather working, as a by-product of the slaughterhouse operation. Casey was a master craftsman in harness making, saddlery, and all other aspects of leatherwork; knowledge gained from his father and grandfather before him. With the anticipation of more working horses in our future, we'd need skills like these to be commercially available. I'd met Casey a few years before, when he'd re-strung a couple of my antique baseball gloves. Since that initial meeting, I'd picked up a new belt, rifle case, and tooled purse for Karen, just to see the craftsmanship.

"Ideas?" Ron said.

"I think we get a meeting together with the rest of the original settlers and run a straw poll. They might have ideas on folks that would be a good fit," I said. "We're also about ready to have the east and west blocks opened up, so we're looking at a much bigger issue here. Not two houses, but sixteen more, right?"

Alan responded, "Yes, once firewood is delivered. None of the places are 'wet' right now, either." Meaning, the water was shut off in all of the homes to prevent freeze damage.

With the spotty reliability of electricity, we'd made the decision to repair homes that could be heated reliably with wood only, with electricity as a backup. This was pretty much the opposite of the 'way things used to be'. We were now though, in a very new place.

In order to accomplish this, we worked with our neighbors around guidelines that I'd written in the spring for the entire area. Review the structural stability of the home. Determine if it could be heated with wood heat. Come up with a list of things that needed to

16

be addressed to put the home back in service. Of course, only homes within the Utility Service Area would be considered for repair. Homes outside the Service Area would be preserved for future repair if the utilities could be re-established, or salvaged for parts.

When the massive amount of work just to get ready for winter wasn't consuming all of our time and energy, our neighbors and some friends worked barn-raising style to repair and rebuild the handful of homes on the blocks east and west of our block. We'd usually work on two homes at once, with ten or so workers doing repair, cleaning, and testing. Of course, that would not have been possible without the help of our water and power utility crews. The company was originally a co-op, now that really had meaning to most residents in the area. It was always heartening to hear cheers go up when power and water came back on.

"OK. Let's put the word out. Can we meet at the store, and when?" I asked.

"Tomorrow soon enough?"

"Yeah, I was thinking next week, but if this snow keeps up, there's no way that it's going to be easy to get people into those homes, not to mention get wood moved in."

"Right," Alan said. "Which is why time is of the essence."

"All right, next on your Rick-only agenda."

"Just kidding about that. But we thought you'd be interested in how the stores are doing," Ron said.

"I am. Things going OK at the other sites?"

"Better than OK. We're thinking about opening up three more in the South zone."

I was surprised. Good news for a change. "Elaborate!"

"Otis Orchards, East Farms and Greenacres are all above expectations on trading levels and outright sales. Sullivan, Evergreen and Park are about on target. Trentwood and Logan are above projections."

"So you're looking now at south of Sprague?" I asked.

"Population's there. Again, once the weather turns really nasty," Alan said looking outside, "those folks will have a tough time keeping supplied on a regular basis with necessaries."

"Don't look now," Ron said.

"I know, we're there early," Alan replied, looking again at the snowstorm.

"Locations?"

"Altamont East is the riskiest, Liberty Park is almost ready and Havana at Sixth is two weeks out. That'll handle almost all of the serviced areas where there are shortfalls," Ron said.

"Those are the first three. All three sites near precinct barracks?"

"Or co-located in the case of Liberty Park."

"Right," I remembered. "Part of the old milling complex."

"Yep."

"They get all the structural work done?" I asked. "It was a mess the last time I saw it."

"Yeah, your structural engineer didn't like it much at first, but once Cavallini got done with it, he signed off on it. The last of the windows went in last Friday. Heating plant should be on line today."

"Good. How about staff?"

"Twenty-two officers at the barracks proper, with about half of them having homes in their precincts. Six spouses have signed up for shifts at the Liberty Park store. The rest are either teachers or medical staff at the LP clinic."

"K," I said. "Altamont is the problem child. The store is three blocks from the precinct house?"

"Yeah, and on the other side of the freeway."

"That area's always been rough. Are we considering 'now' or our historical bias?"

"Three dead in fourteen days says that we're not biased. Seven in the past two months."

"Causes?"

"Adultery in one case. Robbery in one, drug murder in the third."

"What's the status of the store?"

"Needs the most work of any of them yet."

"Remind me why we thought that location was a good idea?"

"It was free, remember? And in the service area and next to the school and the church. And has working gas pumps."

"Free isn't always a good deal," I said, thinking about options.

"We thought it might be worth looking into enhancing the precinct house in that neighborhood. Hence, the reason for us stopping by, seein's how you have some influence in that area."

"What, parking a Guard unit there?"

"That, and maybe taking the old school and using it for a militia center. Manned, of course."

I hadn't even considered that idea before. I seemed to be thinking slower these days though.

"That would mirror the Hillyard idea, and South Monroe," I said, looking again at the snow.

"Yep. And once the militia centers there opened up for business, problems dropped dramatically," Alan stated.

"Yeah, the magic influence of belt-fed weapons near by," I said.

"As long as they're in the right hands," Ron replied.

"All right, I'll talk with Mike and our liaison with the Guard. I think we'll be able to swing that. Might be tough getting the school put in good enough shape though, won't it?"

"There's work to do. Cavallini did the preliminary look-see," Alan said. "Six weeks minimum."

"It'd probably be smarter to co-locate the store and the militia center," I said.

"Yeah, if you can swing it," Alan said. "You know how much fun it was to prove to the locals that the militia or Guard units were good things to have near their stores."

"I do. Liberty Park was no fun. At least as far as the food distribution operation goes, Pete Wolfson says its working OK."

"Sure. But when you put a barter store in operation, it might be a different story."

"Agreed," I said. Ron, Alan and I talked next about the capital investment needed for each of these stores to get them initially established, and needed for on-going operations.

In our case, this meant an investment in the form of silver coins used for currency available to establish trade. At the barter stores we'd started, and therefore had a significant stake in, we had invested a portion of the pre-nineteen sixty-four silver coins in each operation. Along with our monetary investment, which I viewed as necessary to get real money into our new economy, other traders become stakeholders in the barter store system. For our return on investment, we bought goods that we thought we'd need, were 'rare', etc. These purchases were made with our share of profits that the stores generated, after expenses *and* after all other stakeholders had been paid. Most of the time, we ended up on the edge of being 'in the black.'

I also, nearly always anyway, paid the asking price, to put more money into circulation. For this, I was usually rewarded with thanks, sometimes more product than I paid for, or preferential treatment the next time I needed to buy something. Karen, Mary and Libby were asked to the do the same thing. Ron and Alan haggled a little for sport, but usually paid the asking price. I hoped that this would establish our reputation as being honest and knowing the value of items. If it didn't it would illustrate that we had more money than brains. Either way, my goal of putting money to work would suffice.

Our families also traded what we could produce or items that we saw as extra, hand-made items, or 'knowledge' in the case of many of my computerized files on primitive skills, food production and storage.

"Your company is here, Dad," Kelly hollered from the kitchen.

"Thanks, babe," I said. "You two wanna stick around?"

"Sure, curiosity being what it is," Alan said.

"That's Mike's Explorer," I said to Ron and Alan as I looked out the window. "No idea who the suit is though." Mike's new ride was formerly a civilian model, which had been upgraded with police radios, scanners and computers, and of course the Spokane County paint job.

Mike made his way through the stock gate and pulled into the driveway, while his passenger held the gate. His passenger also held a briefcase, shiny leather at that. He was also seriously overdressed for Spokane at least I thought that.

"Good grief," Alan said. "He's got wingtips on."

"Don't make fun of him just because he dresses like a lawyer."

"Not much use for lawyers these days," Ron said.

"Manners, boys," I said as they arrived on the front porch, which I still hadn't fully repaired after the Domino.

"Afternoon, Mike," I said as I shook his hand. "Getting much sleep these nights?" I asked, referring to his new twins.

21

"More than my lovely wife, but not by much, thanks. Rick, this is Chuck Severa," Mike said by way of introduction.

"Welcome," I said as I shook hands. 'Tall. Really tall,' I thought. 'Fortyish,' I guessed. "This is Alan Bauer, my brother-in-law, and Ron Martin, old friend and life-saver. That goes for both of them I s'pose."

"Pleased to meet you both," Severa said as he shook hands.

"Come in and have a seat," I said, motioning them to our rather scarred oak dining room table, inviting both to have a cup of elderberry tea which both declined, obviously wanting to get to business. "Before I forget Mike, here's a nice thick file for staff," I said as I handed him a heavy folder with police and fire staffing and equipment requests, most of which we couldn't fill. "Now, what's this about gentlemen?"

"Mr. Drummond, I'm the United States Attorney for this region, and I'd like to talk to you about the disposition of four prisoners in the county lockup."

"Don't need to guess which four," Alan said. Four ringleaders of an anarchist organization, which also happened to be tied into a criminal family, tried to dispose of me in a rather creative way. Mike's undercover task force had rooted them out, although nearly too late. I was quite happy to have missed that gun battle.

"Sure. Want to hang them now, or later?" I asked, only half kidding. "They did have a first class trial," I said, reminding myself of Brian Dennehy in the movie '*Silverado*.'

"Neither, actually, or at least not yet."

"Please explain," I said with a little irritation. "These people tried to have me killed. And did kill a few of our Guardsmen, and two deputies. What they did was unspeakable."

"We have reason to believe that they are part of a larger organization and we'd like to determine if that is in fact the case."

"OK, almost reasonable. Why a U.S. Attorney? I thought that you handled cases like 'United States versus John Terrorist.'"

"The office handles the prosecution of criminal cases brought by the Federal government, which this is one; prosecution of civil and criminal cases where the United States is a party; and the collection of debts owed to the Federal government which are uncollectible."

"That last item ought to keep your office busy until the end of time," Alan chuckled.

"Indeed. But this matter reaches well beyond this city, which is why I'm here. I'm asking for the County to allow the U.S. Marshals Office to take these men into custody."

"Why not just take them?" Ron asked.

"Protocol. Courtesy," Severa said, "and because these organizations were on the radar screen well in advance of the attempted attacks on your local officials, and the former Administration dropped the ball. They should have been apprehended long in advance of that time."

I didn't know quite what to say to that. Good thing Alan did. This had the added advantage of giving me time to think.

"Naw, I think we ought a just hang 'em here and save everyone the time."

"These men are anarchists first, criminals second. That puts them on my plate."

"With all due respect, sir, they are murderers first, and anything after that doesn't really matter around here. Once convicted of that, they're pretty much compost," Alan said.

"What organizations?" I asked flatly.

"We actually don't know all of their names or even their acronyms. There are actually dozens, nationwide. Or were before the War."

"Why here? Why now?" Ron asked. I wondered if this guy liked being tag-teamed.

"One of them is suspected of being the head of the Anarchists Union. They were big pre-War. More violent than not, which sets them apart."

"Again, why now?" I asked.

"Opportunity."

"And what happens to them then?"

"Interrogation, prosecution on Federal charges."

"And then they're hung?"

"If they're prosecuted and convicted of a Federal offense, it is customary for that sentence to be served first, if they are apprehended first. In this case, the Attorney General is willing to make an exception."

"No plea bargains?" I asked.

"Plea bargains no longer exist," Severa said.

I found that interesting to say the least.

"So," Severa continued, "they'll still get their hanging."

"Not a lot of incentive for them to give up information," Ron said.

"Giving has very little to do with it. Interrogation these days is….aggressive."

"Fine. Take them." I said. "But why are you asking me this?"

"Your interest is personal."

"It is at that."

"I'll have a cup of that tea now, if you don't mind."

"Not a bit," I paused. "Let me have my daughter round up a few other things as well," I said, and then called to Kelly, who produced a tray of delicate pizzelle cookies from a recipe that Joan Pauliano provided.

"Where you from, Mr. Severa?" Alan asked.

"Chuck, please if you would. Denver most recently. I served as assistant state attorney general down there, and was appointed to my current post on one October. Originally, North Platte."

"Appointed?" I asked, ignorant of how one was hired to his post.

"Yes sir. A Presidential appointment. The new Administration has been trying to fill a number of vacant posts, including the Pacific Northwest."

"Just how many positions are there? I'd have thought one per state. Is that correct?"

"Actually, there were ninety-three pre-War. There are forty-two districts in the continental United States at present, which is a considerable consolidation. It is likely that there will be a number of additional appointments in the Mexican Territory, and at least two more in the Canadian Territories."

"How long've you been in Spokane?" I asked.

He looked at his watch. "Two hours, six minutes."

"Welcome to town. Nice of you to bring Denver weather with you," I said.

"There's a good two feet of snow in Denver right now I heard, and probably several more feet on the way by the middle of next week."

"So what can you tell us about the East? We've heard a lot of rumors. Damned few facts."

"Where does one start?" Chuck said.

"The secession movement might be a good place to start," Mike said, as Ron, Alan and I shared a shocked look. Mike noted our concern. "I picked him up at Fairchild, so I'm a little ahead of the curve."

I looked at Alan for a moment. "Why does every day feel like a Twilight Zone episode?"

3

Friday,
October Twentieth,
4:15 pm

"We haven't heard much if anything about secession since...what, May?" I said.

"There was something on National Public Radio before they went under in July," Alan said. "That Senator. What was her name?"

"Cynthia Blackburn," Chuck said. "Flag bearer of the New Republic."

"That's the proposed name?"

"Affirmative. Not proposed. Real."

I felt as if I'd been smacked upside the head. "Since when?"

"September first. Their Independence Day."

"Who, exactly, is 'they?'"

"A hodgepodge of states and parts of states. They believe that their borders are not necessarily fixed things, and that those fellow travelers that believe in their cause are quite able to become part of their 'nation.'"

"Hogwash."

"Yes, but an effective way to create something from nothing."

"How effective?" I asked.

"Maine, New Hampshire, Massachusetts, parts of Pennsylvania and New York, New Jersey, parts of Ohio, Michigan, Minnesota, parts of Illinois and Iowa, West Virginia, Tennessee, the eastern half of the Carolinas. Not Florida, interestingly enough, but bits of it and Georgia."

"What, exactly, does this mean?" Ron said. "Sounds like a class 'A' cluster."

"It means that if you owned property in those states, that you don't any more. If you owned guns, you don't any more, and you are probably in prison if you're still alive. If you grow food, it belongs to someone else."

"Communism."

"Oh, communism would be a couple rungs above their philosophy."

"What's the government doing about it?" I wondered.

"They were waiting for it to burn itself out."

"And?" Alan asked.

"And it's not, or at least not fast enough. Raiding parties have been moving out of their 'territories' to get what they can't seem to grow, manufacture, or keep. That includes of course food, goods, and, workers."

"They're shanghaiing people?"

"Modern day slavery, yes."

"So again, what's the government doing?"

"Picking them off, little by little. They got Cleveland back, and most of Minnesota and Tennessee. And their local governmental units have been having trouble."

"What kind of trouble?"

"Families disappearing. Whole families."

"Dead?"

"No, relocated somewhere safe and prosperous. Which puts them in a bad spot, because if they don't cooperate, the U.S. government will be sure to let the New Republic masters know that their underlings have sent their families out of country."

"Slick," Ron said. "What about military?"

"They have what they could capture, repair and fabricate, which isn't a whole lot. We have a full naval blockade of course, so they have no trade by sea, as if there were any trading partners with that capability."

"So no active military actions?" I asked.

"Skirmishes mostly, from what I understand."

"So what about D.C.?"

"Under Federal control, but there aren't many people there anymore. The radiation will be a problem for decades."

"President still in Denver?" Alan asked, reaching for a second cookie.

"Undisclosed location, I think is the term of the year."

"Cabinet?"

"Ditto. You seem pretty hungry for information out here," Chuck said as he poured another cup of tea.

"Chuck, ever spend a couple months living in a barn?"

He chuckled. "Matter of fact, no. Three weeks in a bomb shelter was as close as I could get."

"Well, living in what is these days, the forgotten American disaster zone leaves us with a distinct hunger for intel. The sanitized news we get nationally is pablum. We want...no, 'need' better information."

"So I gathered!" Chuck said as the back door opened. Karen was home.

"Hon, c'mon in. We've company."

"Mike's family, not company," I heard her say.

"Yes, but I'm not," Chuck replied as he stood. "Chuck Severa. Pleased to meet you, ma'am."

"I'm terribly sorry. I didn't know we had guests," she said as she smacked my shoulder.

"Quite all right, ma'am."

"Karen, please."

"That's quite a sidearm you have there," Karen said, noticing something that I'd missed, hidden under his suit coat.

"Thank you. Don't leave home without it anymore," Chuck said as he removed a Glock from a hidden holster and placed it on the table.

"You sound like these guys," she said, not mentioning that she now had a compact .45 ACP of her own.

"May I?" Alan asked.

"Sure."

"We have 1911's mostly, but the mag capacity leaves a little to be desired.

"Which is why I chose the G21. Thirteen rounds."

"Light, too."

"It is at that."

"Chuck, we better get moving. Pete Wolfson's going to be heading out at five-thirty," Mike said as Alan handed the weapon back to Severa.

"All right. Rick, Karen, gentlemen, it's been good to get acquainted," Chuck said as he stood, re-holstering the Glock.

"Likewise. And thank you for this meeting."

"It seemed the right thing to do."

"In a world so wrong, it's refreshing."

"How's Pete holding up, Mike?" I asked as we reached the front door.

"He was wondering when you'd be back. As in, 'do whatever you can to get him back in this office and me out.'"

I laughed a little harder than I ought, and caught a stitch in my side. "I'll be a while yet." The snow was still falling, in small flakes that noted the cold. Alan and Ron were talking with Chuck about Denver and other parts of the country. 'Pumping him for information' was more accurate.

"So he's afraid," Mike said, also noting Chuck's conversation with Ron and Alan.

"The townsmen must be driving him nuts."

"They are at that. He's not cut out for bureaucracy."

"Neither am I."

"But there are a few townsmen that think big government is a good thing, and have been pushing for more of it since you've been away."

"Time to stomp that bug flat."

"Yes, it is. We barely have the resources to support what we have, which aren't enough in the first place."

"Agreed. We'll deal with this next week. I'll see if Dr. Karen will let me get into the office."

"Good luck with that."

"Thanks, I'll need it."

Saturday morning,
October Twenty-first,
1:10 a.m.

I'd managed three hours of sleep, and then was wide-awake for no good reason. I then thrashed around the bed for a few minutes and gave up. I almost managed to make it out of bed before Karen woke up. Almost.

"What's up?" she asked.

"Can't sleep."

"Take your meds?"

"Yes, that's probably why I'm up."

"You've got another three days of those pills. Gonna make it OK?"

"I need Art Bell to listen to. He always used to make me sleep."

"Well, he's retired."

"I know, still miss him."

"Whatcha going to do?"

"Listen to the radio for awhile. Maybe I can sleep in the recliner."

"Ribs still hurt?"

"Not bad."

"Well, turn the light on before you go downstairs. We don't need anymore hospital time."

"Will do. Sleep well," I said as I kissed her again.

My 'barn office' was a place to get away from the bustle of the house. In former days I used the computer out there for tracking stuff I needed to buy for projects and supplies. My 'basement' office I used on winter evenings when Carl or Kelly hadn't commandeered it for a game of Halo or Super Mario. These days, after the Domino, it was not quite a wreck, but really didn't resemble its former self. The two fluorescent lights, now minus their diffusers, flickered for a full minute before they stabilized. The rebuilt windows to the south and west were covered with heavy moving blankets, as much for insulation as for light control.

Most of our old furniture, which once included bookshelves, an old entertainment center and TV, and a monstrous Steelcase desk, were either damaged or destroyed in the quake. The desk remained, but everything else had been trashed. While we'd managed to put the rest of the house back together, the basement still sported studs and insulation, and exposed floor joists. The dented desk, which was the recipient of a two-foot diameter chunk of our fieldstone foundation, now held a new-to-me Apple laptop, and our higher-end radio gear. We'd run antenna cables up to the attic and outside, and with some help from Aaron Watters, had a passable ham radio setup. The temporary setup would be moved upstairs though in a few more days, once we cleared out a spot. The basement would be the recipient of new pantry shelves for more supplies.

I was more into listening than talking, maybe because I just didn't have that much to say, or because I found the process a little…intimidating.

I checked the uninterruptible power supply to make sure that it was powered up, and checked the line voltage on a pair of digital voltmeters 'upstream' and 'downstream' of the UPS. Our voltage had been more than a little flaky ever since the electric lines were repaired. Tonight, we had a nice, even reading on both gauges.

Buck decided to join me as I turned on the Collins, a gift from Aaron to Kelly on her birthday…and an extremely generous gift at that. The blower on the wood furnace—a modified pellet stove—kicked on to help take some of the chill off of the house. My wall thermometer read fifty-five degrees, which was about average for the basement. I wasn't really dressed for it though—and wrapped up in an old sleeping bag while sitting at the desk. Buck took advantage of the part on the floor, and promptly curled up on my feet.

The logbook that the kids maintained (with some adult input, but spare) noted times that they'd had luck picking up certain parts of the world. Even though we were back to some sense of 'normal' these days, they still kept up on their listening habits. We didn't deter them, except on school nights.

The changed weather patterns, Aaron told us, had dramatically altered shortwave transmitting and reception worldwide. I assumed that the changes were mostly due to the volcanoes and a historic decrease in solar activity. Some blamed it on the War, and thermonuclear pollution. It didn't really matter what caused it, except to those who blamed humankind for the woes of the planet.   For whatever reason, we could listen, and I suppose talk to, most of North America, a couple evenings a week. Once in a while, we could pick up Asian-language broadcasts, which we could not translate. Very, very rarely, we could pick up some broadcasts from England. We hadn't heard anything from the rest of the Continent since early August. Nothing from the Middle East or Africa ever.

Our world had again become a large place.

The radio suddenly came to life, left on the frequency that Kelly had on earlier. I expected words I heard only numbers, with gaps in the sequences that I assumed could only mean some sort of code. The frequency I noted was that of WWCR in the old days, which if I remembered correctly, was out of Nashville.

"Seven, forty-one, six, ninety-two, four, eight……one, thirty-three, six…." the pleasant female voice spoke.

If it was some sort of code, and it must have been, I would have no idea of where to start with it or what it meant. I did note that it began at exactly twenty-five past the hour, and ended at thirty-five past. Exactly.

During a prolonged pause, I waited, and reached to tune it to a different frequency, when a different voice spoke.

"Radio Free America broadcasting on nine point nine eight five. At thirty-eight past the hour, video from within rebel-held New York City has reached us that New Republic forces are seizing food supplies from the remaining population. Those resisting are being killed. Rumors of this type of brutality has been reaching us for weeks, but the video—secretly shot with a high-quality DVD camera—was smuggled out of the rebel zone by refugees to a RFA broadcasting unit."

This news really didn't surprise me one bit. The broadcast went on, with the broadcaster putting on an audiotape of the attack, with a narrative. For the world, I was reminded of a play-by-play. A macabre one in this case.

"The video has been copied and supplied to major media networks as well as the Federal government, with no comment since it was delivered to them two days ago."

"Rumors that the rebel government is near collapse continue to intensify, and I believe that this seizure of food and the wholesale executions we've seen in New York, Philadelphia, and Newark provide ample evidence that the New Republic must be close to implosion. Rebel leader Blackburn was last seen in Boston last Monday, and multiple RFA sources within the immediate area said that her motorcade came under fire at least twice during a fifteen-minute period of observation. Rebel guard forces then conducted a systematic attack on three separate locations, resulting in multiple fatalities. It is 'illegal'," I noted the dripping disdain of the commentator, *"to possess any firearms within the New Republic."*

The broadcast began to go into static, and then faded to a frustration point where I turned to another frequency. It sounded like a prayer vigil in an Islamic country. I noted the frequency, and looked it up in the logbook index. If it was correct, I was listening to Paris. Ten minutes of an utterly unintelligible singsong chant was enough for me. I shut off the Collins and turned on the big old Radio Shack multiple frequency radio. I wasn't able to pull in anything much, and shut it off finally.

I then moved to the banged up recliner, and reached to the small bookshelf next to it, and pulled out one of the oldest Bibles in the house. I read Paul's letters for two hours, before nodding off.

4

Saturday morning
October Twenty-First

"Hey, Dad. Couldn't sleep again?" Carl said as the creak of his door woke me, startling me for a moment. Buck and Ada both popped up and hurried over to Carl for a morning scratch. Buck looked for something in Carl's room to steal, and then bring him, which was one of his favorite dog games.

"Nope. What time is it?" I asked, noting it seemed still dark outside.

"Five-thirty. John and I are working the morning shift at the Community Center. Starts at six."

"Orphanage?"

"Yep. The kids seem to like me but they're all over John."

"Good for you guys. You have a talent there."

"Thanks. We're making breakfast today. Can I take your car?"

"Sure. You might need the four wheel drive."

"Are they going to plow if it's deep?"

"Arterials only. We're short on diesel…or will be unless we get things ironed out."

"What about the side streets?"

"That's going to be up to the neighborhoods. We don't have the resources to do all the streets, and there aren't that many cars running. People are conserving. We'll take care of the feeders to the train lines, roads to the schools and hospitals, nothing outside the core areas."

"But it's OK for me to use the car?"

"Yeah. Blue pass. Don't forget."

"Right. 'Community Center Staff.'"

"Yep. Don't forget to put it in four-by."

"K thanks. I better get going."

"Brush teeth and wash up first."

"Yep. I have a dentist appointment on Monday."

"Me, too."

"Where are the keys?" He asked as he loaded up his toothbrush.

"On the hook," I said as I got up out of the chair. I heard Carl brush as I opened the west curtains, looking out toward the barn, Alan and Ron's homes, and a good foot and a half of new snow.

"How's it look?" Carl asked after he finished up.

"Deep. I wanted to get some pruning done on the fruit trees down south. Not going to happen."

"You never seem to have a problem finding something to keep yourself busy."

"And everybody else, you didn't say."

"Figured it was a little early to take a shot at you," he grinned as he grabbed his daypack. I'd had each of our extended family members put together a miniature emergency kit, designed primarily to get them back 'home.' All of us now of course had larger backpacks as well…the get out of Dodge pack.

"Many thanks," I said. "Hey, drop this at the store for the day shift sentries," I said as I handed him some scones that Kelly and Marie had made.

"K. See you at two."

"Or sooner. Mom and I might pop by later."

"On foot?"

"We'll find a way. Might take the pickup since it's ethanol powered. We've gotta go anyway though I think. Aren't Kelly and Marie babysitting later?"

"Yeah, I think so. Libby, too."

"Drive safe."

"Always," he said as he closed the back door. I watched him through the darkness as he slogged along, both dogs quite happily bounding through the new snowfall, to the makeshift carport that held the little Ford Escape that replaced my big Expedition. The hybrid Escape was better on gas than anything else available at the time, but I sometimes missed the heft of the big SUV. I did however; truly hate the grey-brown-dark green camouflage paint on the little thing. It was the County's idea of 'blending in.' I thought it looked silly.

Carl drove the little SUV out of the carport, then remembered the gate, and had to get out to open it. Before he took two steps, I saw John slog past him to it, pushing it open through the snow, and in a few moments, they were gone. I decided to make some tea. The dogs decided they wanted 'in.'

After water was on to boil on the electric range, I lit up the woodstove, noting that it was only fifty-two degrees inside. No wonder I was chilly. At six, I decided to try to catch the morning news. I knew that there was a fair chance that the TV station might be up and running. A year ago we had seventy-five channels available. Today, we had one…most of the time, that is. Three radio stations though…some of the time. And one on FM. Always forgot about that one.

"…six oh-five, October Twenty-First. Thank you for joining us this morning on Television Spokane. If you've looked outside this morning, you'll see that we have our fifth official snowfall of the fall season, this one is expected to continue until eight a.m. local time, according to Air Force meteorologist Archie Brennan at his Mica Peak weather radar station. Archie? Is that right?" the newscaster, a twenty-something guy, was just a little too perky for Saturday morning this early. Maybe he was drinking real coffee in that mug, I thought.

"Yes, sir, Bryan. More tomorrow most likely."

"Thanks, Arch. We'll join you at twenty-five past for the complete weather forecast."

"See you then, sir," the impossibly young Air Force meteorologist replied to the stationary remote camera.

"Our winter weather conditions are obviously affecting essential transit, and will continue to do so until main streets to the Central Lines are cleared. Metro road crews are already out plowing the arterials at this hour, and expect to be working through the morning. A reminder, neighborhoods are responsible for clearing or packing side streets for at least single-vehicle passage."

"In local news overnight, Metro emergency response teams report that two additional deaths have been attributed to carbon monoxide poisoning due to faulty ventilation…" the broadcaster then repeated for the umpteenth time, the guidelines for indoor heat sources and the symptoms of carbon monoxide poisoning. We probably had a statistic lurking somewhere on how many people had died of CO poisoning since the Domino. It was dozens, certainly I knew.

I poured my tea, and sweetened it with the fireweed honey that Don Pauliano had traded for…then tuned my head back into the broadcast.

40

"Metro Interim Administrator Peter Wolfson in a press release today announced that weekly commercial air travel service to Spokane would resume in early November. National Airlines, the recent amalgamation of most major American carriers based in Denver and Salt Lake, has already resumed service in the central U.S., the Southwest, and in the Canadian Territories."

"And who, Pete, do you expect to have money to go on a commercial plane?" I asked the TV. I knew that this was part of 'recovery', but that it was also a double-edged sword. Part of our 'success' if it could be called that, was our isolation. More contact was more exposure to the flu or its mutation; more meddling from the Federals. Maybe that's what I was worrying about.

"...confirmation that the Metro shipment of biomatter electric generating units were destroyed in an attack on the California-bound transport by unknown forces. All personnel, including rail engineers and Northwest Command soldiers, are reported as killed in action. This shipment was the first shipment to Central California as part of a contract for continuing out-of-season food shipments to the Inland Northwest. No comments have been released by Metro Administration on how this loss affects projected food supplies over the coming months..."

"Not well, as anyone with a brain could figure..." I said.

"From the Seattle Zone, word that the Navy dredging operation has been completed from Edmonds south to the Puget Sound Naval Shipyard at Bremerton, where ships stranded by the uplift of the bottom of Puget Sound have been sitting since the Domino. Navy crews and shipyard workers have been returning two mothballed aircraft carriers—the USS Ranger and USS Constellation--to operational status, and preparing more than two dozen other ships to relocate to the Bellingham Naval Yard. Rear Admiral Louis Edwards refused to comment on the potential to restore the Bremerton Yard to operation, but dredge workers who have been working since March on the salvage effort commented that the channel has required almost daily work to maintain a sea lane, and that after the salvage of the stranded vessels is complete, the Navy will likely abandon the channel. Sixteen men were lost last month on a dredge that overturned in rough seas, bringing the death toll of the operation to twenty-nine."

"Finally, in Walla Walla today, Governor Hall is expected to announce the final phase for repairs to the former Bonneville Power Administration network, including restoration of control operations and electrification of large areas of the Northwest lost in the Domino and in the Third War. Substantial portions of both Washington and Oregon remain without electricity, and exports of power from remaining operational dams have been impossible. This as you know resulted in massive cascading brownouts throughout the American Southwest this past summer. FEMA officials estimate that deaths due to hyperthermia and lack of potable water in the region exceeded twenty-five thousand, but cannot be confirmed..."

"Hey, hon," Karen said. "Breakfast ready?" she said as she hugged me from behind and kissed my neck.

"Nope, but we have eggs, and eggs. And Spam. And some cheese."

"You haven't eaten yet?"

"Nope. Carl woke me up when he left for the Center. Just made tea and got the fire going. Omelet?" I asked as I poured her some tea.

"Sure. I'll go get dressed. You going to plow today?"

"I've been toying with the idea, yes. You reading my mind again?"

"I know you like playing on your tractor."

"Fact."

"Do you think you're mended up enough for that?" Karen said as she wrapped her hands around the coffee cup, and I stirred in some honey.

"Yeah, I still get a stitch in my side though. That's supposed to be 'normal' though. So they say."

"None of that phony Spam for me though. But a scone and some of the plum jam would be good."

42

"As you wish. Dress warmly."

"So I see. How cold?"

"Twenty-six, a little while ago."

"Lovely."

After breakfast, Karen roused our sleepy daughter to remind her of her babysitting shift at the community center, where Carl and John were hopefully cooking up a storm for the orphan population, which hovered around twenty, but sometimes grew to double that depending on in-migration and rates of adoption. Marie and Libby would also go for a four-hour stint, while Karen had this weekend off.

The orphan issue was on my part, utterly unforeseen. Too many variables came into play to predict it, although in hindsight, I should've at least thought of it once. A more-or-less complete collapse of the health care system we'd become accustomed to, or perhaps more correctly, a reversion to a third-world standard of available medical care; the devastating effect of the Guangdong Flu; exposure to weather; substance abuse. We survivors found ourselves serving as 'Uncles' and 'Aunties' and 'cousins' to children that ranged from days old to teenagers. We tried to work at least a few hours a week at our local center, and found that the continuity of familiar faces helped the kids adjust. Many children had already been adopted, and we thought that by this time, we were on the down slope of the problem. There were fewer kids being brought in or being dropped off. I hoped that this was a good sign.

The downside was the percentage of children with serious medical conditions, mental or emotional issues that proved in many cases, impossible for lay people to deal with. It was certainly more than I could deal with for any extended period. I was finding myself more fragile than I thought I used to be. Perhaps my age was catching up with me. Perhaps, I'd just seen too much.

"Babe, are you going to drive us over later?" Karen asked.

43

"Was planning on it. But five of us aren't going to fit in the pickup."

"How about Alan's truck?"

"How 'bout you ask him. I know he's OK on diesel for now, hasn't used his allotment by a long-shot."

"That way you can plow and not have to shuttle us around."

"That's OK, I'd like to go over later."

"We're leaving at quarter to ten if you're ready."

"I'll do my best," I said as I gave her a kiss and buttoned up my coat.

Outside, the little tractor was parked on the far side of the garage in another carport, built of one-inch diameter PVC pipe in a half arch, with a heavy brown military tarp for covering. I should have built something like this years ago, I decided as I fired up the ancient four banger. I moved slowly, trying and not succeeding to work the beast without any pain in my side. I decided that I needed to get used to it.

With a few minutes of warm-up, I had cleared out the driveway, the path to the barn, root cellar and the paths to Alan and Ron's places. An hour later, I'd moved north up our street and then made a swipe at all the streets that surrounded our block. I cleaned out the driveways of all of the houses that folks were living in on all four streets, too and turned down breakfast cakes and tea on several occasions. I did have a Pauliano coffee at Joe's though, where he was out getting his turkeys, pigs and chickens fed.

"How's Joan today?"

"Arthritis is bothering her. You hear anything about medicines coming any time soon?"

"Not much. I'll see what I can find out for you though."

"You healing up all right? You look a dang site better than the last time we saw you," Joe said, his Italian accent more pronounced than usual. They'd visited me the day after I made it home. I was still pretty much horizontal at that point.

"I'm getting better. Didn't hurt to plow at least. Well, not much anyway."

"Gettin' old's not for sissies."

"You got that right. Are you getting what you need from Alan and Ron?"

"They're good boys. They're doing just fine by us. Some of that arthritis medicine sure would be good though."

"I'll check into it. Let you know today."

"Appreciate it."

"I better get moving or I'll be in trouble with the missus," I said as I handed him the heavy mug. 'Darn that was good bourbon,' I thought to myself.

"Thanks, Rick. Your pig's lookin' good. Should dress out nice."

"Thanks, Joe. I'll be in touch," I said as I started up the tractor. It wasn't like Joe to hammer anything home like the arthritis medicine that Joan had had to use to keep pain in check. It must be getting bad.

I drove back home and found Alan's truck in my driveway. He must have circled around from the north I decided, while I was looping the block on the other end. I backed the little Ford into it's garage and shut it down, remembering to use the quick-disconnect on the battery and shut off the fuel.

"Mornin'" I said to Alan, clad today in insulated Carhartt bibs.

"Howdy. Thanks for doing the roads. You up to it?"

"Doin' OK. Better than sitting on my butt."

45

"I see you're traveling dangerously," he said, looking at me a little funny.

"Huh?"

"Sidearm. Haven't seen you without one since what, January?"

"Completely forgot it. I must be slipping."

"Don't worry, I won't tell my sister."

"Thanks. I'll…oh, too late," I said, looking over my brother-in-laws' shoulder. Karen was holding my ancient .45 in its holster, by her pinky finger. One of our hand-held radios was in the other.

"Forget something?"

"Yeah, sorry."

"I better check you before you go out the door like I did with the kids in grade school."

"Might not hurt," I said as Alan chuckled.

"You OK?" Karen asked.

"Yes, for the umpteenth time," I said with a little irritation. "Everyone waiting on me?" I noticed that Libby, Marie and Kelly were in the idling truck already, and waved at them.

"Ten more minutes and we would be. Do you want to get cleaned up before we go?"

"Absolutely. Give me a couple minutes," I said. "Hon, got a sec?" I asked quietly as I headed to the house.

"For you, all day," she said as we went into the house. "What's up?"

"Joe. He made it a point, like hammered on it, that Joan needs some arthritis meds. I don't think she's able to get around without something like the over-the-counter stuff from the old days. Do we have anything stashed away?"

"Yeah, some anyway. Mom used some during the summer but nothing lately. You clean up and I'll go check. I know Joan's hip was getting to be a problem before the War, especially when it was cold."

"K. Be right back."

I changed out of the somewhat grubby flannel lined jeans and two layers of work shirts, washed up and pulled on clean jeans and a rag wool sweater that I'd looked forward to wearing again, once I'd lost twenty pounds. I'd done that and then some, now down thirty-five pounds from my pre-War weight. I also managed to fit into a whole lot of jeans and slacks that I'd stored for far too long. I'd noted a few days before I weighed five pounds more than I did when I married Karen. It was good in a way to not be packing the extra pounds around. Tough way to do it though....

"Find something that will work?" I asked Karen, seeing that she had three boxes of something.

"Naproxen, two boxes. Two boxes of celecoxib."

"Cool. That's the stuff I used when my hip was bugging me, right?"

"The naproxen. I didn't know you had six boxes of each downstairs though."

"It was on sale."

"Sure it was," she said, knowing all too well that my 'it was on sale' statement was really, 'I'm buying it just in case.'

"I hope that'll help Joan. You ready?"

"Yep. Let me get my book bag though. I have some pop-up books for the nursery."

"K. Dogs inside?"

"Yeah, I don't think they're all that thrilled with the idea of being out most of the day."

"K," I said, making sure both were inside, and that hey had enough water. "I need to call downtown before we go."

"You better, or the weekend shift will come looking for you," Karen said.

A few minutes later, I was at Joe's door, and received many thanks in return.

"I'll see if I can find more. We have more at the house, but that won't last forever."

"Thank you Rick. And may God bless you."

"He has already, Joe. And you, too."

"He has at that," he said as I shook his hand.

5

Saturday
October Twenty-First
10:00 a.m.

Packed into Alan's truck, we made the familiar drive past our barter store, now christened Valley Metro Barter, over to the community center. The store was closed until noon on Saturdays, and only open until two p.m. Most of the time folks respected our need to do other things on Saturdays. Sundays, we were closed altogether. Our regular traders knew that they could reach us if they needed to on either CB or through law enforcement, if there was some sort of emergency.

"Alan, do you mind turning on the news?" I asked.

"Nope, not a bit," he said as he turned on the stereo.

"Thanks," I said. CBS was just coming on. Karen and Libby were talking about some dessert or other, while Kelly, seated between Alan and I, and Marie, in the back seat with 'the Mom's', were both reading paperbacks.

"CBS correspondent Drew Michaelson reporting from the Gulf Coast, where Hurricane Susan is expected to make landfall later this evening. Virtually the entire local population along the Coast, from about a hundred miles on either side of Mobile, have evacuated north in the face of this storm, which may be upgraded to Category Five by this evening."

"Landfall is expected around nine p.m., with the storm surge hitting the coast well in advance of that. FEMA evacuation centers

up to five hundred miles away, still strained from Hurricane Nellie four weeks ago are once again bursting at the seams."

"They just can't get a break down there," Karen said.

"Nope," I agreed.

"....salvage operation was expected to be suspended in anticipation of effects from this storm. Military authorities report that the population of New Orleans in the wake of Nellie is less than ten thousand, virtually all of who are without safe drinking water or electricity. Most, upon orders of evacuation, fired upon authorities, demanding to be left alone."

"The President announced that as of November first, recovery operations in New Orleans, will cease permanently—the city will be abandoned except for those that refuse to leave."

"Saw that coming after Katrina," I said as the broadcast continued.

"Why?" Kelly asked.

"Big chunks of it—like, half--are below sea level. Without pumps and electricity, the place goes under. Toss a few hurricanes at the place and you have a big mud flat with some human-built artifacts sticking out of it."

"Why'd they build there in the first place?" she asked.

"Well parts were above sea level. Those parts don't usually flood too badly. Flood, sure, but a foot or five. Not like the low-lying areas. Somebody figured out if they build dikes around the place and pump the water out, people would buy the former swamp flats and build houses there."

"Greed over common sense," Alan interjected.

"Yep."

"...last of sixteen platforms intended for the California offshore complex is expected to come on line by June of next year,

quadrupling offshore oil production over the first quarter of this year in the Santa Barbara Field."

"Well that's some good news," I said. "Domestic oil reserves. Who'da thunk it."

"Drop in a bucket," Alan said as we pulled into the unplowed, unshoveled parking lot. "Won't make a dang bit of difference up here."

"Probably right," I said. "Might allow some of that Wyoming gas back up here on a regular basis though, instead of the hit and miss we've had all year. I noted that all three of the vehicles in the parking lot, with the exception of the little Escape, had spent the night. The snow was untouched.

"Thought that the centers were on the plow list," Alan said as we got out of the truck.

"They are. But there's only four plows running right now in the Valley, four in the city limits, two up north. I'm sure they're working on the roads to the Central Line now. We'll get it eventually."

The Central Line—Red in the Valley, Blue from the north side to what used to be 'downtown', Green from the west plains by the Airport and Fairchild Air Force Base, were our commuter and cargo train lines. Red and Blue were built just this year, based on my recommendations that without them, most of us would be 'a-foot' as my late Dad used to say. Without gas to run our cars and trucks, we were walking. Train tracks, built on or in our former wide arterials, took months to lay. The Green line at least, operated on pre-Domino trackage. The Burlington Northern Santa Fe lines, the Union Pacific Lines that weren't wrecked, still operated when freight lines or passenger cars made it through, which was, infrequent at best.

"So long as they don't plow me in."

"You? You could climb a tree with this. That Escape can hardly get out of it's own way," I said, only half-kidding, as I took a load of books inside. Carl was there to meet us.

"Hey, Dad."

"Hey. How'd breakfast go?" I said as I set the box down on the counter.

"OK. Changed plans on us. I thought we were making pancakes. French toast instead."

"Easy enough."

"Sure, until you have to cut it all for the little ones. They can pick up a pancake. They don't quite manage with French toast."

"Why the change of plans?"

"Not enough flour."

"Since when?" I asked. This should not have been a problem. We had plenty of wheat, and the commercial mills were up and running.

"Since somebody swiped two hundred pounds," Kevin Miller, the manager of the center replied for Carl.

"From where?"

"From the delivery truck yesterday. We were unloading right here. Brought the hand truck inside with one load, left the step van door open, came back, gone."

"Report it?" I asked.

"Sure. Like it'll matter."

"It matters to me," I said as we went into Kevin's office. "You think staff?"

"No way. No one here would do something like this. I'm certain of it."

"Which leaves somebody in the neighborhood. I assume you didn't see any cars or trucks or anything."

"Nope, and we didn't hear anything either."

"We'll have to be a little more careful obviously."

"Remember, they had all of three minutes to do it. No way somebody did it on foot."

"I'll get some more flour down here today from the store. Or, maybe Alan will. Bucking flour bags might be pushing it a bit for me. Ron should be at the store at noon."

"Thanks. That'd be great."

"So how's the new BAR?" I asked, referring to his cloned Browning.

"Unbelievable," he said with a wide smile. "When you're all healed up, we'll have to try them out. It's like the difference between a stock V-8 and one that's balanced and blueprinted."

"Really...." I asked, wondering exactly how much better a rifle modeled after my original could get. I didn't have that much experience with mine, really, but mine was superb. In my opinion of course.

"As accurate as a .308 at a thousand yards."

"This isn't a one-off fluke?"

"First six in production, almost identical performance."

"Who was the shooter?"

"Two, Army marksmen. Two Air Force, two Marines."

"Bet that was something to see."

"It was at that. Yours will be ready in the next two weeks."

"Mine?"

"Couldn't have machined the trigger assemblies without your original. Tightened them up considerably with our better machining and better metal. I can rework your original trigger too, if you like."

"That's OK. I prefer to keep it the way it is."

"As it should be, I suppose. What brings you in today?"

"Thought I'd read some stories to the kids."

"Good for you. Practicing for grandfatherhood?"

"Don't put me in that category yet, Kev. Kids are a little young for that yet. Like, years and years. If I have anything to say about it that is...."

"Young John will probably get a head start on that."

"Could be. Sarah's a good egg though."

"She's all that. She'd be a first rate doc with a degree and med school."

"That's probably not going to happen, but she is a first rate EMT, or so the guys at Station One say."

"Hon, you coming? We have a full house," Karen said around the doorjamb. "Sammy wants you to read to him."

"Be right there, hon," I said. "Kevin, duty calls."

"Enjoy. Watch out for little Ina. She'll steal your heart."

"We'll be fine, see you before we head out."

"Thanks again for the flour, Rick."

"No problem."

After reading to little Ina, and changing diapers with Karen and Libby on six little ones, Carl and John bundled up the older kids for a

54

trip out to the playground, where the snow was just about right to build a snowman. I watched from the lone surviving original window on the east end of the center, and wandered down to the maintenance room to check on the heating plant that one of the mechanical engineers on Metro staff had cobbled up.

The original heating system was a relatively small natural gas fired boiler, which in turn fed radiant heat loops embedded in the floors. Without natural gas though, systems like this were dead. Thanks to Dale Rieger though, a workaround was created that consisted of a wood fired boiler. Either hand-feeding wood into the firebox, or the much more sophisticated auto-feeding 'pellet' system of wood burning would work…the key was not oversizing the boiler in the first place. In his former life, Dale worked for a mechanical engineering and contracting firm. So far, I'd discovered that what Dale wasn't able to figure out or fix, probably wasn't worth doing anyway. His first big repair and adaptation job was the heating plant for the Public Works Building that held the Metro offices. That took him, I understood, all of three weeks to repair and retrofit, pretty much all by himself.

This system had been on line for four weeks so far, with twice daily feedings of the hopper for the firebox. Kevin's staff loved the thing. Heat this year was not something to do without. The fire department safety engineers were far more skeptical, until Rieger built a system for Station One, and the department granted conditional approval…still, one accident was all it would take.

I heard my name being called from down the hall. "Down here," I replied.

"Mr. Drummond? You have a call on the radio," Lisa, Kevin's assistant called to me.

"Be right there," I said as I made my way back to the office. I heard John's voice, in an imitation of The Grinch, coming from the kindergarten room. I heard Karen, Libby and the girls try to herd the kids into the mud-room where I'm sure lots of soaked coats, boots and gloves would be residing.

Kevin's office held a county radio, much more elaborate than mine. I grabbed the plastic-wrapped headset and put it on.

"One thirty-seven to Spokane."

55

"One thirty-seven, be advised of shipment of four parcels to Fort Walla Walla. Sending party asked to provide you this notice."

"Understood. Anything else?"

"Unit one oh-seven is en-route to location 'Granite.'"

"Understood, one thirty-seven out," I replied. Karen was peeking around the corner, with 'that look' in her eye.

"One thirty-seven," the pleasant female voice replied. 'Not one I recognized,' I thought.

"Location 'granite?'" Karen asked.

"Here."

"Why's it called that?"

"Because that's where I am. That's my location code today. Security forces' idea to change a codeword daily, in case somebody's still looking for me."

"I hoped this was over now."

"It might be. I don't know, nobody does."

"What's Mike need?"

"Nary a clue. We'll wait and see."

"Soon?"

"Hon, no idea. I expect so. Need help with nap time?"

"Pretty quick. C'mon. Little Ina wants another story."

"K. I think *'Dinner at the Panda Palace'* this time."

"Good. I thought you pretty much wore out *'If you Give a Mouse a Cookie.'*"

"I like it—always have," I said as I took her hand and walked back down the hall.

"Softie," Karen said as she gave me a squeeze.

Once the kids were down for naps, the afternoon shift took over and Carl, John and the girls headed home for their afternoon of chores and precious little free time. Karen, Libby and Alan had headed down to the store, while I awaited Mike at the center. I'd hoped to have a few minutes to talk with Sarah, John's girlfriend, but she was in a class with two senior doctors on rotation from Valley General. Finally at two-thirty, a Humvee truck pulled into the parking lot. A light snow was beginning to fall. I met Mike and two camouflage clad Army guardsmen at the door. Both guardsmen had their M-16's at the ready, and were actively scanning the area.

"Mike, what's going on?"

"Inside, Rick. I've got some bad news."

"What?"

"Inside."

Kevin was packing up his papers and getting ready to leave for the day. "Kevin, mind if we use your office for a minute?"

"Sure, Sheriff. No problem," he said as he grabbed his suitcase and backpack and headed out. "I'm done here anyway."

"Thanks," Mike said as Kevin headed out. I took a seat.

"OK, enough of the secrecy. What's going on?"

"Pete Wolfson's dead."

"My God. What happened."

"Honestly, it looks like a suicide. We're investigating."

I was quiet for a few moments. "I don't understand this at all…"

"I don't either. That's why we're looking into it."

"His family…does he have…"

"Died in the flu. Wife, two daughters, one son. Lost his inlaws, too."

"I didn't know any of that."

"He preferred to deal with it privately."

"He was what, thirty-five?"

"Thirty-three two weeks ago."

I took a long pause, got up and looked out at the snow.

"I cannot imagine what it must have been like, losing them all like that."

"Yeah."

I stood there for a good couple of minutes, remembering the last conversation I had with Pete, him telling me that he'd 'keep things straight until you're back on your feet.'

"How are you going to break the news?"

"There'll be an announcement on the five p.m. news. That, 'he passed away while on duty.'"

"How's staff dealing with it?"

"Not well. Emma saw him just before it happened. She's under sedation at the triage center."

"Sh*t," I said. Emma was the second administrative assistant to fill that post since Kamela Gardner passed on.

"Rick, we could use you if you're up to it."

"I'll be there. Once you clear it with Karen. She'd likely have my head if I were to just 'tell' her that I'm going back to work."

"I can do that. Let's get you home," Mike said.

"Store, actually. We're moving some stuff about this afternoon. Or, more correctly, everyone else is. I get to watch."

"O.K. Let's go."

The conversation with Karen went about as well as could be expected, which was to say, she was disapproving with both 'the look' and her body language, seeing in the end that Mike wouldn't be asking her unless it was really his last, best option. Still, I knew that it would be a tough adjustment for both of us. I'd become accustomed to being taken care of at home, working when I felt up to it, as long as I remembered to stay out of Karen's way…

By five p.m., I was back home for a dinner of stew and some time with Karen and the family. I also had a lot of catching up to do, with some status reports that Mike had brought out. Most of the reading would wait until after everyone headed back to their respective homes, after dinner. There was one report, marked 'Sensitive but Unclassified' that piqued my interest. I excused myself from the pre-dinner bustle of the main floor, and headed upstairs to our bedroom to find a quiet place to read.

The report, about a half-inch thick, was one of the last things that Pete Wolfson had been reading. 'Was this a trigger?' I thought as I took it out of the manila envelope. I was still dumbfounded about Pete.

6

"Report on Future Logistics Operations
North American Theater

Prepared by North American Logistics Command (NALCOM),
Redstone Arsenal, AL"

The report was titled. I had no idea there was such a group, but then again, why would I? I had at least heard of Redstone Arsenal. I skimmed through the first few pages, trying to glean what I could before I took a serious read.

"The events of January through July, current FY have forced a reassessment of ongoing and future logistical needs for military and civilian operations in the North American theater of operations. Trigger events that precipitated this reassessment include:

•Collapse of the Middle Eastern oil field complex and depletion of the Mexican and Venezuelan reserves have decimated the worldwide economy and affected all major developed nations. As the United States largest consumer of petroleum products, the U.S. military is particularly affected by this depletion of resources and the collapse of the infrastructure to provide it.

•Multiple earthquakes and volcanic eruptions in the Pacific Northwest and northern California, disrupting commerce, military operations, and causing heavy civilian casualties and massive damage to the infrastructure.

•Military actions against M.E. nations, Russian, Communist Chinese, Mexican and other enemy nations. Military actions included

destruction of infrastructure and oil-producing geological features in the Middle East, Russia and former Soviet republics, coupled with destruction of refining and shipping capacities throughout combatant nations. "

This struck me as new news, the statement regarding the destruction of 'geologic features' in the war zone. 'They blew up the fields? How? Burying a nuke?' I wondered.

•Military actions against the United States resulted in the losses of key elements and resources formerly providing overwhelming dominance on the battlefield, within the seas, and in space. These losses, in addition to the physical losses of ships and personnel in battle, include the destruction of most U.S. shipyards capable of constructing, servicing and repairing SSN and SSBN fleet forces; loss of major contracting firms similarly responsible for Nimitz-class carriers, Aegis-class destroyers, and guided-missile frigates; and loss of space-launch capabilities on both coasts and within the continental United States.

'No statement about 'how many' shipyards were lost, just that we can't service our fleet? How could this be? Where did they refit our ships, anyway?' It began to dawn on me that what the report was saying in this brief paragraph, was that there was a very limited time left for the U.S. Navy to remain the dominant naval force in the world. Or more correctly, for there to **be** a dominant navy.

•Pandemic influenza geared toward specific genetic identifiers that is only at this time (15 October) reaching a peak globally. HXN-1 strains appear to have stabilized with regards to mutation, achieving a status of saturation in 70% of the First World countries within 90 days of onset. Losses in terms of human skills, educational resources, and societal stability have demonstrably affected local populations to terminal conditions within as few as 30 days after onset of the virus, with longer down slope affects projected to last at least fifteen to thirty years in most areas of the world.

'What does 'saturation' refer to?' Endless questions this report.

•Losses to United States civilian and military leadership have been comparable to all other developed nations, with critical losses at all levels of leadership and performance.

62

•Losses to manufacturing, service, medical, and food production capabilities throughout the North American continent have likewise achieved critical levels, reaching extreme levels in the most urbanized and areas most dependent on imports of food, energy, and goods.

"Firsthand experience there," I said aloud. I skimmed through more pages, finding a bit of a summary of the section.

These key events have triggered dozens of expected and unexpected consequences around the world, including:

•Secession of several parts of the United States led by communist forces under the badge, the 'New Republic,' and on-going conflicts between U.S. and N.R. military and militia forces.

"Finally calling them what they are, I see."

•Collapse of Communist Chinese government, establishment of interim democratic Free China government, and failure of that government within three months due to massive human die-off from influenza, starvation, and violence.

'Hadn't heard that on the news,' I thought.

•Establishment of the Islamic Caliphate, reaching through most of Europe and Asia, outside of Israeli held lands in the Middle East and North Africa.

'And I wonder what that sentence really means…' I wondered as I poured over the rest of the page.

•Collapse of the Canadian government into two governmental bodies, 'New Canada', which has asked for and received Territorial status from the United States; and 'Free Canada', which has asked for a 'strategic alignment with Rebellion forces within the United States.'

"That'll only end badly for someone," I said.

"What was that, Dad?" Kelly asked as she fetched something from her room.

"Nothing, babe. Talking to myself."

"You do that more and more these days."

"I'm a good conversationalist."

"Not."

•*Balkanization of Russia, including incursions from states bordering Russia on the south into the Caliphate, and from China. Chinese refugees appear to have captured the entire Siberian area without resistance.*

•*Isolation of Japanese islands from all contact to slow spread of influenza.*

•*Creation of a southern African totalitarian state not unlike Cambodia in the 1970's reaching from the former South Africa to the Congo, including the southern two-thirds of the continent.*

"Hmmm." 'Wonder who's in charge of that little nightmare,' I thought. Africa brought me mixed emotions.

Ten pages further on, the authors began to discuss 'recovery.'

Key recovery efforts within the N.A. theater include:

•*Re-establishing Constitution-based legal authority within areas unaffected by prolonged nuclear contamination, working within the State framework, with a strong State, weak central government model of operations.*

•*Collection of critical spare parts, resources, and otherwise irreplaceable technologies, and securing them in dispersed, fortified locations.*

'Fortified?'

•*Construction of new industrial facilities to maintain current infrastructure and supply mission-critical components to the U.S. military and key civilian industries throughout the planned interim period of adjustment.*

'And how long is this period of adjustment, fellas?'

•*Massive exploration and immediate action on new and previously exempt petroleum resources within the region, including the new oil fields off of California, Baja California, and Alaska.*

•*Construction and refitting of energy refineries in eleven coastal states and six interior states, seven territories, and two protectorates.*

•*Encouraging local governments to require individual responsibility for safety and security; production of subsistence foods; local production of goods and services; recovery and reconstruction efforts and entrepreneurship.*

•*Requiring State governments to enhance National Guard units from local populace for local needs.*

•*Distribution of medical resources to fortified regional medical research complexes.*

'Again, fortified?'

The next section was really what I was interested in.

Look Ahead—Year 1 through Year 10

Continental United States and North American Theater

"Beans and Bullets"

Key shortages in petroleum product availability at all levels will force a prioritization of available resources in a manner that will dramatically strain both the U.S. military's force projection capability and maintaining pre-War methods of food production and industrial capacity, until new oil sources come into production in late Year 3.

Critical to sustaining a peaceful population is the production of sufficient and varied foodstuffs to ensure health and maintain an environment in which the individual can thrive.

Projections of available fuel products within the CONUS and N.A. theater illustrate that it is not possible to maintain anything but a subsistence (survival) diet for the great majority of the population, working within the pre-War methodology of food production, transport, and processing. This will certainly result in civil unrest by the end of the Year 2 growing and harvest season, beginning again with certainty, in areas that are unable to sustain farming practices due to climate, urban density and lack of farmland, or lack of water resources. Example areas include Tucson and Phoenix, AZ, although dozens of urban areas exhibit similar unsustainable settlement patterns.

Regardless of whatever resolution comes from the 'New Republic' secession/rebellion effort near-term, long term survival of a large population in the Northeastern United States is not possible without fossil fuels to maintain a transitional economic and industrial model. Insufficient agricultural production currently exists within the region in an operational mode, without petroleum fuels. Additionally, on-going military operations between N.R. and U.S. forces will likely become increasingly one-sided as N.R. forces lose the ability to supply spare parts, fuel, and manpower to the rebellion effort.

Centralized farming operations and the loss of local knowledge of microclimate, advanced mechanization, and even simple farm skills have essentially doomed a large portion of the rural population to probable starvation until sufficient numbers of the surviving population learn how to produce enough food and goods to care for themselves as part of the transitional economy. Small scale industry, possible in the 1930's is likely all but impossible now due to the lack of knowledge, tools, skill, and heritage.

Petroleum production and refinery capacity in the CONUS will not appreciate and affect market conditions until late Year 2 or early Year 3, forcing USMIL forces to dramatically scale back operations in the Mexican territories and southern battle front, at the risk of not having enough fuel to grow food for both the military and civilian population. Oil fields off of California, although known in location, are unknown in capacity and longevity. Department of Energy sources state that three years minimum will be needed to establish new production wells in the California offshore area, including construction of platforms and transport abilities.

"Band Aids"
Medical care in the CONUS, formerly the highest in the world, has now dramatically declined in availability and levels of service. While it cannot be defined as 'third world' in a pre-War sense, routine medical care for minor ailments is all but unavailable, and we are now witnessing a dramatic increase in deaths of those citizens formerly on 'maintenance regimens' of medicines for many different diseases and afflictions. With the loss of key medicines and treatments for heart patients for example, losses due to heart failure and stroke increased by six hundred percent from January through July, with the peak hitting in mid-August. CDC staff stated that this was likely thirty to forty days after regular medicines ran out, with an assumption that many patients were taking reduced quantities at regular periods, in effect, stretching their medications out to last.

Surgical procedures have also been dramatically affected by the loss of technology, staffing, supplies and medicines. Post-surgical deaths due to infection have increased with the loss of European-produced medicines, as one example. Operable conditions pre-War are now far more complicated with the losses many advanced technologies due to computer chip and program failures.

CDC estimates that within the next seven years, the U.S. may regain up to 90% of pre-War medical abilities, assuming domestic production of pharmaceuticals through plant expansion; medical training programs are prioritized (including basic care and advanced diagnostic, surgical and post-surgical technique); and adequate individuals can be found for medical training..........

I skipped down a few more pages.

"All things shiny"
Re-establishing a national economy that is based on a recognized commodity or series of commodities is essential for all advanced economies. Formerly, and as required by the Constitution currency

*was backed by such commodities, until abandoned in favor of the fiat
economy. As all fiat economies, the former Federal Reserve Note
system failed utterly, compounding virtually all other issues the
world is dealing with at present.*

*Presidential directives to re-establish a Federal currency based on
gold, silver, nickel, and copper have been put in place, and new
coinage based on ounce-weights of gold, silver, etc. re-established as
well. Old, pre-1964 silver coinage (90% silver) is accepted at face
value, but post-'64 coinage, with the exception of some half-dollars
(40% silver) and pre-1979 copper pennies, are now being sold or
valued at the melt value of their base metals. Gold coins are being
minted in $5, $10, and $20 pieces, and paper notes will be
immediately redeemable for coins on demand. The base value of the
nickel seems to fluctuate in value from worthless in parts of the
CONUS, to face value, in selected regions.*

*Key issues related to the monetary system involve sheer lack of
metals for coinage. Silver, gold, and copper mines throughout the
North American continent have been acquired for the creation of the
new coins, but the Treasury Department expects at least some
coinage will be in circulation by the end of Year 1. By the end of
Year 2, there should be wide availability of silver coinage and notes,
and limited availability of gold coins. Until that time arrives
however, trading and barter will comprise the bulk of the local
economy.*

*Bullion removed from New York City and Washington prior to N.R.
occupation has been relocated to several secure locations well
within U.S. controlled areas.*

'Interesting,' I thought to myself. How much bullion? From where?
To where? And when did they figure out they were going to lose the
Northeast? How did they move it?

None of which really mattered, of course, except for my own
curiosity.

Deeper into the document:

*...Price controls were studied on a national basis, but deemed
unworkable as local economies, including barter, sales made with*

existing silver-based and gold-based coins, etc., were being created and acting with more agility than the Federal response could attain.

Of Credit and Debt
Federal taxation has been set at five percent of gross income, flat across income levels. Income is now collected by the local governments transmitted to the States, and to the Federal treasury. Limited information was provided for the generation of this report regarding the process, but it is the consensus of the reporting officers that this process has been fraught with corruption and mishandling of funds. Federal workers have been paid since 1 May in scrip redeemable at Federal commissaries. Military units have similarly been compensated at base and post exchanges. Purchases by the Federal government for such compensation have been made with physical commodities, such as silver or gold coinage.

National and international banking and finance concerns, since the onset of the Second Depression, have insisted that debt obligations be fulfilled per law. President Lambert under Executive Order abolished all debt obligations for individual Citizens effective 1 September. Debt obligations against companies, corporations and municipalities were forgiven on 1 August, after the Supreme Court ruled that lenders in the test case had breached fiduciary duty by attempting to collect on debt instruments that had been sold, and resold, until the true owner of the note could not be determined. In most cases, including the test case, the debtor company had in fact ceased operations within weeks of the onset of the Depression, with most physical assets being stolen, looted, or destroyed (Eurovian Finance Ltd. Vs. Detroit Motor Company).

Insurance concerns worldwide similarly, ceased operations within three months of the onset of the Depression and the outbreak of War. In more than ninety percent of all cases, no claims were paid due to the complete collapse of the investment portfolios held by the insurance firms, which were wiped out in the economic collapse. Individual claims against such firms, while certainly legally founded, will with certainty fail, due to the evaporation of the insurance firms from the new economic landscape.

The Domestic Political Future
Currently, national representation is in place from all fifty states, Puerto Rico, Mexican territories, Canadian Territories, and Pacific

territories, despite insurrections in several states. The full Senate was seated on 1 September, followed by the full House on 15 September. Interim appointees, selected by State governments, will formally run for office next November.

The stability of the current political environment is a direct result of the preceding Administration's Executive Order to immediately appoint qualified individuals to serve at the behest of the State leadership, should current representation fail to fulfill their obligation due to medical issues, etc. No major national legislative issues have been addressed, other than emergency and interim programs to maintain cohesive, Constitutionally mandated Federal control, and prepare for a dramatically smaller Federal government over the next five to fifteen years.

The success or failure of political leadership at all levels depends on people with integrity with a willingness to serve, sometimes in situations of grave hardship. Local leaders in particular, are critical to maintaining local order, control, and hope for recovery. Most successes locally have greatly enhanced the ability of the local population to cut dependency on the Federal response, which both frees up the Federal forces for other areas, and reduces the need overall, for involvement by the national government and military.

I heard the impending sound of dinner, and quickly flipped to the end of the report, not really knowing what sort of conclusion might be waiting for me. Nonetheless I was surprised by the ten-point text on the bottom of the final page:

'The preceding document is the consensus of six of eight NALCOM officers assigned to complete the assessment. Two dissenting staff officers withheld their consent signatures on the report, stating that the report was far too optimistic over the timeframe presented.'

7

Saturday evening,
October Twenty-First

"Hibernating up there?" Libby asked as I came into the dining room.

"Nope, reading up on some files that Pete Wolfson had."

"I'm very sorry. Karen told me a little while ago."

"Thanks. Pete was a good man. I'll be trying to figure it out for a long time."

"Some things we can't, ever. But you know that. Are they sure it was…suicide?"

"They found him at his desk. Mike said it looked suspicious."

"Autopsy?"

"Certainly."

"That'll tell then."

"Yes it will. Don't dwell on it."

"Thanks. I could use that," I said as Ron handed me a hot-buttered rum. "Ron, that's the best idea anyone's had all day."

"And the mix is from scratch."

"Even better. I bet the ingredients were tough to come by."

"Probably, but worth it."

"Who made it?"

"Sarah."

"She trade some doctorin' for nutmeg, cloves and cinnamon?"

"She isn't talking, so I'll leave that up to you."

"I'll not ask."

"Probably best."

After dinner, the kids got involved in a fairly serious game of poker, where Kelly's game face was as stoic as could be imagined, even more so when holding four of a kind. She'd won three of five hands, and was quite pleased with herself I saw, with a little glint in her eye as the adults talked in the living room.

"Monday back to the grind, huh?" Alan said.

"Yeah, duty calls," I said.

"What kind of schedule do you think you'll be working?" he asked. "Store stuff and all. Do we need to get some more help to cover for you?"

"Probably. I'm foreseeing myself spread mighty thin."

"We'll see what we can do," Ron said.

"I was thinking Randy," referring to Randy Thompson, who had a number of enterprises going, one of which, a bike shop, out of the back of our store.

"I was too," Alan said.

"Frankly, Alan, I'm thinking of being 'out' of the store business on a day-to-day basis. Maybe if there's some big issue I could remain involved, but I have a couple problems. One, probably a conflict of interest, now that things seem to be settling down and I'm back in this job. Two, I think there are better people to run things…but you already knew that."

"Yep. I know you don't like dickering."

"No, to be precise, I hate dickering," I said to emphasize my dislike for the necessary evil of a barter operation, or even a regular store with real money, and somebody wanting to pay less than the asking price.

"I was being kind."

"You were, that's fine. Karen, Libby, what do you think?"

"I think you think too much," Karen said with a smile as she finished off another rum. "And, you have too many irons in the fire at any given moment, and you have since the day I met you."

"Yes, but you married me anyway."

"I did. Naiveté being what it is…" she said laughing quietly. "You should quit the stores and let the guys run them. Your heart's not in it and probably never was."

"True enough."

"So find a general manager for each store, and have Uncle Alan and Ron run the whole operation. Duh," Carl piped in from the card game.

'Wheels always turning in that young man's head,' I thought.

"Play cards. Focus," John said. "We can't let the girls win again."

"Poker isn't a team sport, is it?"

"No, but the girls have won eight of twelve."

"Good thing you're not betting real coin."

73

"No kidding," Carl said. They were, however, using what passed a year before as real money, Federal Reserve Notes, non-silver quarters, halves, and dollar coins, with no real value these days. It was odd to see more than a hundred Old Dollars in green and colored bills and change, used for a card game. The money had been hoarded or saved or stashed away for a rainy day in one of the homes we'd salvaged, and had evaporated in purchasing power before we took over the house. We did though keep a couple of the mint-quality bills for posterity.

Karen could see I was preoccupied with something, and asked me quietly when we were bussing the dessert dishes to the kitchen.

"So, something in the files bothering you?"

"A lot of things in the file are bothering me."

"Can you talk about it?"

"Don't think so. Not yet, anyway. One of them was not quite classified, but was 'sensitive.'"

"Who's it about?"

"No one in particular and everyone in general."

"Oh, then it's a government file."

"Yeah, and how did you…"

"Generalities and no specifics. Unless I'm wrong of course," she said as she looked at me, hands in the dishwater. "But I'm not from the look in your eye."

"You're not wrong."

"Anything immediate that we need to worry about?"

"Worry, no, but there is a lot to **think** about."

"Great. My favorite."

"Not so much," I said. "C'mon. I think we have a movie to watch."

"We do. '*Sound of Music.*'"

"Dang. I was hoping for '*The Punisher.*'"

"Men," Karen said as we headed back to the living room.

Sunday morning,
October Twenty-Second

The nine o'clock service was sparsely attended with the new snow, which was fine with me, as I was slated to be a 'greeter', and to serve as the lay assistant to the Missouri Synod Lutheran pastor this morning. I was totally at ease in my own church, which was of the evangelical, Bible-based non-denominational variety. But in the much more ordered format of today's service, I felt like a school kid. I did at least have the fact that I was thirty years out of confirmation classes, and twenty years older than the minister, who was serving his first call at New Hope Lutheran when the Domino hit.

The eleven o'clock service more than made up for the light attendance at the early service, with a potluck scheduled right after the service was over.

The sermon theme was 'A Fruit Bearing Life', with the text taken from Psalm One, one through six.

Blessed is the man that walketh not in the counsel of the ungodly, nor standeth in the way of sinners, nor sitteth in the seat of the scornful.

But his delight is in the law of the LORD; and in his law doth he meditate day and night.

And he shall be like a tree planted by the rivers of water, that bringeth forth his fruit in his season; his leaf also shall not wither; and whatsoever he doeth shall prosper.

The ungodly are not so: but are like the chaff which the wind driveth away.

Therefore the ungodly shall not stand in the judgment, nor sinners in the congregation of the righteous.

For the LORD knoweth the way of the righteous: but the way of the ungodly shall perish.

With the dismissal after the sermon, I felt that I'd received more from this message than any other in months. Good preacher, this kid.

"Rick, you're almost the last in line!" Ellen Watters, Aaron's wife chided me.

"Part of the job, Ellen. Nice to see you. How's Aaron doing?"

"Well enough for a crotchety old man," she smiled. "He's over with the Thompsons."

"Thanks. I'll go visit."

"After lunch. He'll be here for awhile."

"How's his vision doing?"

"Doc says he's got about a year at the current rate of degeneration."

"We'll pray for him."

"Thanks. He's decided of all things, to take up painting."

"I probably would too."

"He's got a good eye for art. Too bad he didn't start sooner."

"Some lessons come late."

"The best ones often do."

"What do you recommend for lunch?"

"The gumbo that Lou Pecquet made. Start there---I think he brought five gallons of the stuff. Watch it though, might be a little hot for you."

"Sounds perfect."

"Your wife had a cup. Said it was too hot for her. Your friend Ron said it needed pepper though."

"Figures. Thanks, Ellen."

"You're quite welcome. Remember, you were warned."

The Drummond-Martin-Bauer family was seated over on the south end of the multi-purpose room, where I noted that they'd saved me a spot. I waved at them across the room and quickly dished myself up a medium sized bowl of the gumbo, and a small loaf of wheat bread.

- "You sure you want to try dat?" Pequet asked.

"It is legend, isn't it Lou? I've been hearing about it for a week or two."

"Itza secret, dat recipe."

"I won't ask."

"Watch out now. No shame if'n you can't finish."

"I'll take that advice to heart."

"Do dat now. No shame."

Lou came to us out of the woodwork, about mid-summer. He'd been living in Coeur d'Alene before the War, working as a temp electrical contractor on one of the big resort projects. After as much recovery work as could be completed was done over there, he decided to up and quit the City, and come further west for some better opportunities. He wasn't into salvage he was into building, fixing, and making things work. We got along pretty well. Pete had asked him to serve as the County's electrical engineer in charge of municipal facilities—that gave him a pretty big slate of construction, from the first day. I was still getting to know him. I did learn that he hailed from a little town called Hahnville, in St. Charles Parish, Louisiana, and that he didn't suffer fools.

"Ohmygosh. You're going to try it," Marie exclaimed as she saw my bowl.

"I am at that. I like gumbo."

"You really better take it slow. It creeps up on you," Alan said.

"The best gumbo usually does," I said, sitting gingerly down. My ribs still gave me a twinge now and then. I noted that Karen was looking at me with skepticism.

Lou was every bit right in warning me. Good grief that was hot.

It was almost half past two by the time the cleanup was done and we were ready to go. Carrying at least one firearm was of course 'regular' these days, but none were allowed in public buildings and most retail stores. One citizen of Colville, the county seat of Stevens County to the north, 'went off' one nice sunny Sunday this past August over some minor argument, and killed fourteen people before being shot by Army Guard soldiers who just happened to be there. I'd read the report before my Walla Walla adventure. I'd read that the argument had started over a half-pound of cheese, and a price that was arguably, too steep.

All of the visitors firearms were stored in the small coatroom now used almost exclusively for temporary weapons storage. No one entered the center without checking their firearms. The young Private assigned as guard inside the center, was attired in a set of BDU's more worn than this young man could have caused. I noted that he had an earpiece to listen in to the perimeter guards, and any other military traffic in the area. He also had a phenomenal memory, correctly retrieving all of the visitors' weapons without being prompted. I noted that all of our groups' adults had at least one weapon or another. I collected my newly-refurbished .45 (courtesy of Annika Thompson) in it's GI holster, and one of our AK's and its' magazines. This one now sporting a synthetic stock.

"Dad? Can I drive?" Kelly asked, about a year too early.

"Uh, no. You cannot. I'd be happy to have you learn on the tractor though. Lots of practice plowing snow."

"Too hard."

"It's in your future. You can learn how to run it, and graduate to the pickup." I could see Karen's smile out of the corner of my eye.

"How about something with an automatic?" she asked. "That's what Carl learned on."

"Different times. You need to learn how to drive a clutch," Karen said, beating me to it. I noted Carl was smiling and trying not to, in the back seat.

"I wouldn't be smiling too much, pard. You need some clutch time too."

"I know. It's still funny."

"Glad you think so. You get the next shift of plowing, which oughta start, riiiight about now," I said, as we pulled into the driveway. "Feel free to get started."

"I'll get my snowsuit on," he said. "What about Kelly?"

"I'd rather have her start when I'm up to it, which isn't today."

"'K," Carl said.

"Time, I think for a nap."

"Slacker," Carl replied.

"Not hardly."

"Kidding, Dad."

I napped for about an hour, and then went back to reading some of Pete Wolfson's papers, after getting a cup of Echinacea tea and clover honey. The second in the stack, after the Army report, was an interesting single-page recap of correspondence between farmers and ranchers in both Idaho and Washington, and Department of the Interior ecologists. The topic was 'wolves'.

"....acceptable losses of one human per year were deemed reasonable pre-War, in addition to unquantified losses of livestock. Since the outbreak of the War and the Guangdong Flu, total human losses in the Pacific Northwest have totaled fourteen however, in addition to four hundred and six documented kills of sheep, horses and cattle.

Pacific Northwest Army Command (PNWAC) expeditionary forces in the Grangeville and Salmon, Idaho areas noted that remaining civilian authority had (rightly) authorized bounties on wolves in that region, and that a uniform bounty in the PNW area of operations (AO) should be set. Department of the Interior ecologists strongly oppose this measure however, believing that the wolf population will soon stabilize. General R. Howard of PNWAC overruled the protest, and authorized both civilian and military use of force in eliminating the wolf population from settled areas."

At least we didn't have wolves to worry about...or perhaps our wolves were bipeds. The third report in the pile was an illustration of rising crime in Spokane and Kootenai counties, which began about the same time the weather turned. Increases in theft up thirty percent. Increases in robbery, doubled. Six murders unsolved. Fifteen attempted murders, with six alleged perpetrators killed in defense. Two drug labs destroyed, one by civilians, one by the Army.

The fourth report a similar criminal activity report in Stevens, Lincoln, and Whitman counties, the remaining counties with sizeable populations near Spokane. Several other largely rural Eastern Washington counties, Pend Oreille, Adams, Grant, Ferry and Okanogan, now had populations measured in the hundreds to a couple thousand. Drug and criminal activities were highest in Yakima and Kittitas Counties, despite the thinning out of most of the Hispanic population, and the relatively high military presence. Perhaps because of the high military presence?

The 'Six-Monther' syndrome began showing itself in August, actually about eight months into The Troubles. These were people, predominantly men and only rarely families, who had either evacuated to retreat properties or lived out in the boonies pre-Domino. After their stored goods were gone, many began to quietly filter back into remaining towns, or began trading trips in an attempt to stay at their secluded locations.

The 'six-monthers' were few and far between at first, because the weather was good enough for them to try to stay 'away' from settled areas, subsisting on their stored food and what they could hunt, fish, or, well, loot from abandoned homes. Most of the survivors of the flu that had 'bugged out' were good people, skilled in field craft and basic subsistence. Most of them.

Some of them however, were out-and-out predators or had become predators since January. Some of them were all hat and no cattle, or more correctly, all weapons and gear, and no knowledge of growing anything or feeding themselves beyond their MRE's. They took what they wanted, almost always at gunpoint. When they didn't get what the came for, they murdered for it.

Spokane really saw the influx start when the weather turned cold. This year, that happened on June sixth. Within two weeks, we had an additional five hundred families in town, and sixty-five singles. By the time the real cold hit in the fall, we had another fifteen hundred families…a population increase of six thousand.

Virtually all pre-Domino residents were living in single-family homes, duplexes, or in residences carved out of owner-operated retail or manufacturing buildings. Most had had some assistance in putting their homes and businesses back together; many had needed to move out of their former homes into 'new to them' houses within the utility service area. Six thousand newcomers, very late to the game, had to be housed, fed, and given something to do.

Pete Wolfson, standing in for me, led a big percentage of this effort, which was no small task. Salvageable homes and businesses needed to be found, repaired, connected back to the 'grid' of water and power, and supplied with firewood for the winter.

Of the fifteen hundred or so families, five hundred were able to be accommodated by the first of October. Two hundred more were expected to be housed by the end of the month. The remainder were housed in four community shelters near or in neighborhoods that had a good percentage of homes that could be adapted to reuse and were served by power.

What we didn't count on of course was the weather. Ninety percent of rebuilding efforts on the residential infrastructure was halted by the cold and snow. Many older homes that had been designed to be heated with wood or coal, and later converted to more modern means, had to be refitted with whatever could be found in the way of woodstoves or furnaces. Some newer homes were stripped to the foundations for their lumber, doors, sheathing, and roofing. What little work that did continue took far longer due to the difficulty of getting materials and working without adequate clothing.

Virtually none of the newcomers brought any substantial amount of food with them. Many were already showing signs of malnourishment, and their recovery would be difficult without proper medical care. The 'excess' food stocks that we had were adequate for the time being, but the variety of foods that were available to those who didn't produce it themselves was at best, boring.

You could live on wheat, rice, beans, lentils, and whatever other bulk foods we as a County could negotiate for, but meat products were scarce and expensive. The toll on the human body wasn't long in being illustrated. Malnutrition in those less well off came again in America.

The mental and physical condition of many of the newcomers wasn't good either. Many, in the words of my late father, were 'broken' in spirit and even I could see that some just didn't have the will to fight for themselves or their families. Some were walking shells, only doing what they were told and nothing more, faces and eyes, showing a thousand yard stare.

8

Monday,
October Twenty-Third,
5:30 a.m.

My first day back to work started rudely, with my alarm clock going off in 'buzzer' mode rather than with some...any...radio program or music. KDA was usually on the air at five, but today I didn't check, I'd probably doze off, which I couldn't afford to do. Karen though was already up and out of bed I noted, and both dogs were out of the bedroom I noted as I padded off to the shower.

After my short, hot shower, I dressed in a base layer, my well worn lined Carhartt jeans, rough-looking hiking boots, a winter shirt and a heavy shirt. If the office was cold, I'd at least be able to peel off a layer or two.

Downstairs, I found a crackling woodstove, real coffee brewing, a wonderful aroma coming from the oven, and no one in the house. Outside, I saw Karen and our kids, along with the Martins, were shoveling out a four-foot drift on both sides of the stock gate. The tractor would have been useless. I wondered if Karen called for help? I pulled on an old parka that we'd salvaged from our neighbors house, and went outside. Both dogs were on me immediately wanting to play.

"Good morning," I called out to everyone.

"Hi, Daddy. Nice snow, huh?" Kelly said as she gave me a hug.

"Sure, great snow for January. Not so much in October."

"See the drift? We could walk over the gate on the snow. It's really hard."

"And cold. What is it, fifteen out here?"

"Twenty. Just feels colder," Ron said.

"Called out the big guns, huh?" I said.

"Nope, had breakfast already planned. This is just our morning workout. After this, the whole day will be easy."

"Hope mine is," I replied as Karen came over and kissed me good morning.

"Good morning, sleepyhead."

"What time did you get up? I never heard you."

"Four. Had to get breakfast ready."

"It smells great."

"Should be ready. C'mon everyone, breakfast is up!"

The kids raced by me on the way back to the house, saying their 'good mornings' along the way. Libby pulled up the rear.

"You in on this too?"

"Of course. I made the cinnamon swirls. And some of the coffee is mine too."

"Quite a sendoff," I said as we reached the back porch.

"Just remember to come home this time so you don't worry your wife out of ten years....or another ten years."

"I'll be home, don't you worry."

"I know you. I don't have to worry. Karen does enough for everyone."

"Thanks. And good morning to you too," I said as I hung up the grey parka.

"You ready?" Ron said. "Been waiting a week this morning."

"Hush, you," Libby said. "Or you'll be last to eat."

"That's OK. 'The last shall be first.'" Ron replied, quoting the Gospels. "Shall we?" he said as we gathered around the table to pray.

I was directed to sit at the far end of the table, where my captain's chair now rested. Karen and the kids (I guessed) had spun the table ninety degrees, put two leaves in it, and gussied it up for my send off.

"And what is on the menu this morning?" I asked, just as it came into view.

"Christmas comes early this year," Karen said, placing my favorite breakfast meal in front of me. My mom used to make this every year that I could remember, an egg-bread-sausage-cheese-mushroom soup casserole. Why we only made it on Christmas I didn't know, it was pretty easy to make. I noted that this morning there were two of the nine by thirteen Pyrex dishes, packed full and steaming.

"Wow. I don't know what to say!"

"Then do us a favor and don't," Ron said. "Just dish us up."

"I can do that," I said as he handed me a spatula. "I am all about food…I do feel a little guilty though. What about Alan's family?"

"They'll be here for dinner. Little early for the kids."

"Little early for everyone," Carl said as I passed him his plate.

"It is. No argument. I'm doubting that the schools will be open today with this snow," I said.

"Late start. Open at nine. Out early too," Karen said as she brought out a pitcher of our Concord grape juice. "More wind this afternoon."

"So what's your new work schedule, Dad?" Kelly asked, between bites and her conversation with Marie.

"Don't know. I need to see what everyone else is working. Before my accident, we had everyone working flex-time. Forty hours minimum, forty-eight max. Some people were working twelve's and a short day, some were working longer than that and bunking in at the complex."

"They have room for that?" Libby asked.

"We had plenty of room for that, if you didn't mind spending the night in a jail cell. Three floors of empties, heated and powered up too, with intranet connections to the Metro network so you can do some work from your bunk if you have a laptop or workstation there. Also had one floor of one of the offices converted to a dorm. Pete had the other two converted this fall."

"But you're not going to do that are you?" Carl said.

"Hope not to. Rank has its privileges."

"Sleeping in your own bed is a privilege?" Karen asked.

"These days in public service, yes, sometimes it is."

The county radio crackled at me before I could take another bite of breakfast. "Spokane to one thirty-seven," a male voice said.

I made my way over to the radio and replied.

"Be advised, transport arriving your location by oh-six-forty."

"Understood. One thirty-seven, out."

"One thirty-seven."

"Transport?" Carl asked.

"I get a ride to the office."

"Can I use the car?" he asked, a predictable response from a sixteen year old.

"Nice one, Carl," John said, already knowing the answer.

"Not unless there is some really compelling reason for you to do so, no. That's up to your Mom," I said as I looked at Karen, sharing the same thoughts.

"Dang," he said.

"Told ya," John said to Carl as he cleaned up his first serving.

I had about ten minutes before my 'ride' would be here to shuttle me to the office. I'd packed an overnight bag just in case, under Karen's watchful eye, the night before. The kids were engrossed in a video game (at this hour?), and Karen and Libby were in the kitchen, cleaning up the wreckage of breakfast. There were no leftovers, we noted. That left Ron and I a few minutes to talk.

"You ready for this?" he asked me.

"Ready or not, not much choice it seems," I said.

"Any more news about Wolfson?"

"Nope. Still looks like suicide, the last I heard."

"Damned shame. He was a nice kid."

"Kid? He's what, ten years younger than you?"

"Right. A kid."

"What have you and Alan got on the calendar today?"

"We're going to meet with Randy Thompson about promoting him up to store manager at the Metro, and we're going to talk to Kevin about our vacancies. This afternoon I think we'll be trying to help Casey Wallace and Ray Alden get their stuff moved. Ray lined up a transport truck yesterday, and he's anxious to get moved."

"I'm going to miss those guys. They were good neighbors."

"Hopefully we'll have some good replacements, too."

"Kevin have any leads?" I asked, knowing that he'd run into Kevin after church.

"Some. He's pretty good at weeding through candidates. Like a pre-screening."

"Yeah. Let him know that I appreciate that."

"Well, you do own the houses. You ought to have some say in who lives there."

"I ought to. I know that some people think that I'm discriminating against them by not picking them to live in one of our houses. And they aren't just 'my' houses. We bought them, all of us basically for back taxes. The fact that I had some money to invest doesn't change that."

"Still hard to get through our heads though," he said as he sipped some hot coffee.

"It was better to get the money into circulation than let it sit there. Besides that, it's not like I had any better plans for it."

"Well at least we're in the black."

"So far, yep. Be nice if we stayed on the profit side of the line."

"Anything you can share yet, with all of your inside info?"

"Maybe. It's not that it's all that secret. It's that I need to digest it first."

"At least we're over the first hump. We made it to winter, have enough food to eat, and things have settled down."

"I'm really hoping you didn't jinx us there, Ron."

"Naw. You can feel it at the store. People are hunkered down, but they're actually not in a bad mood or as pessimistic as they might be."

"Right. But this is October. Give them a month or three of this weather, and get back to me on this in February. Cabin fever might be kicking in by Christmas for all I know."

"Maybe. We'll see," he said, then looked with more attention out to the gate. "Looks like your ride is here. Hummer."

"I miss my Expedition."

"I'm sure you miss its twelve miles per gallon, too."

"Not so much," I said as Karen, Libby and the kids lined up for hugs. Karen was 'last'. She got a kiss and a dip, like the sailor-nurse picture from Times Square or wherever, taken at the end of the Second War. I'd seen the picture countless times, and a sculpture of it in San Diego…was that only a year ago? Seemed like a lifetime.

"Off to the salt mines."

"You take care of yourself."

"I'll do my best," I said as I kissed her again.

"You better."

I was out the door and back into the cold wind. At the gate, a soldier was looking for the gate latch, and gave up when he saw me.

"Are you Mr. Drummond?"

"I am. Call me Rick, if you would," I said as I opened the gate.

"Yes sir. Sergeant Major Keith Enders. Nice to meet you," he said as we shook hands.

"Wasn't expecting this service today."

"One of the deputies heard our convoy was heading into town, and asked if we might drop you off."

"They get tied up?" I asked as I climbed into the front seat, and noted all the odd electronic displays.

"I think they're shorthanded."

"That's a fact. I'd be quite happy to drive myself. Sheriff overruled me."

"That'll happen," Enders said as we backed out of the driveway and headed south.

"Convoy should be a few minutes behind us. We might have to wait a minute or two."

"Convoy?"

"Supply run to the One Sixty First. They're getting ready for some action over east of Coeur d'Alene.

"Fighting? In this weather?"

"Could be. Got an issue with a little group of big-shots that needs to be resolved."

"Expound on that if you would, please."

"All this gear was cooked by some version of a portable electromagnetic pulse."

"I was going to ask about it. I've never seen the inside of a Humvee look like this one."

"Striker model. Surveillance, laser rangefinder and targeting, night vision, portable computers for dismounted ops, inertial navigation, lots of good stuff. Of course, its all just ballast at this point," Enders said as we picked up the convoy, near our darkened, locked and guarded store.

"So what happened?" I asked without looking at Sergeant Enders. I noted the two passengers in the back were both listening to iPods.

"One of our recon teams apparently got a little too close to the target for comfort. Fired a burst of something and fried it all. Our team never saw it coming."

"Anyone hurt?"

"Just their pride," he said, pointing to the two rear seaters. "Intel analysts, these two. Lots of well placed fire around the vehicle though. If they wanted our team dead, they'd be dead."

"Sending a message."

"Yeah. You could say that. Our reply will be somewhat more aggressive."

"So what precipitated this?" I asked, wondering why I didn't know about it already.

"Two Idaho State Police units were shot up on Saturday night. One officer dead, along with his wife, in their driveway. One wounded, alive only because he was in an armored Jeep. They were investigating livestock theft and intimidation of farms on properties adjacent to a gated community north of Harrison. They were scheduled to serve a search warrant this morning."

"Were there previous conversations with this gated community?"

"Apparently so. Idaho State prosecutor was ready to bring a slew of charges, based on what the search warrant showed. Wanted to have it nailed legally. The residents of this place are apparently very well connected."

"Hmm," I said more to myself than Enders. I looked again to the back seat, pointing at my ear, asking without words, what the left-rear seater was listening to.

"*Foo Fighters*," was the reply from the twenty-ish soldier.

'I used to have a Foo Fighters song or three on my iPod,' I thought to myself. 'A billion years ago. What was that song? Right. *Virginia Moon.*' I tried to play it in my head, remembered the tune, couldn't find the lyrics.

It had been two months and a few days since I'd been into the downtown core area, and I remembered how much of a mess the main streets in the central business district were. This day, we drove down Sprague, swung north to Riverside, with virtually no building wreckage remaining in the core.

I knew that Pete had re-organized both the north- and south-central salvage teams to quickly finish street clearing and aggressively salvage remaining building materials, supplies, and whatever, from the core before the winter hit. What I saw though, were neatly stacked pallets of used brick from dozens of wrecked buildings, stacks of terra cotta from the Old National Bank, stainless steel from the wrecked Seafirst building, pipe, ductwork and piles of unusable debris in every surface parking lot. There were very few vehicles left in the core. They'd been removed to locations unknown for storage, salvage of parts in a post-gasoline world, or recycling. Street lighting appeared to be back too, with wires strung above grade, pole to pole, for the first time since about nineteen-seventy. Odd.

"Looks a little different down here. I haven't been down here in two months."

"Yeah, it's been interesting to watch, not that I've had much time. It'd be nice to see stuff get built though, instead of torn down."

"Lots of work over in the U-District from what I've read in the reports."

"Gonzaga's starting classes in the spring I hear."

"WSU and UW too. Consolidated campuses. There's still a ton of work to do on the buildings though," I said. The WSU Chancellor's report that I'd read said that one of the five Spokane campus buildings survived the Domino with repairable damage. The others were burned out shells from the looting.

"Maybe someday, we'll see GU or the Cougars back in the Big Dance," Enders said, referring to both of our 'local' basketball teams past successes.

"You a fan?" I asked.

"Not of them. I wanted to go to U Conn when my enlistment was up. Went to Iraq twice though. College didn't seem to matter that much after the first tour."

"Huskies were good. Hope there still is a U Conn."

"Me too. Haven't heard squat since May."

"Family back there?" I asked.

"Not anymore. They were vacationing in Florida when it went up. Touring at Canaveral that day."

"I'm sorry for your loss."

"Thanks. Lot of that going around this year."

"Yep," I thought, thinking of my surviving brothers, at least I hoped they were still surviving. It'd been months since I received any letters from either Alex or Roger. They were quite well aged by the time I received them, as well.

We traveled rest of the way through downtown in silence, traveling to Monroe Street, and across the graceful arched bridge over the river to the County campus. The bridge hadn't been reopened until late September, when the wreckage of the Federal Building on the south end, and a half-dozen collapsed buildings on the north were finally cleared.

The anti-ram barriers were still in place, as were now-permanent enclosed guard structures, these appeared heated. 'Those woulda been nice back in January,' I thought to myself as the Humvee pulled up to the door.

"Thanks, Sarge. Take care of yourself," I said as I shook his hand.

"You too, sir."

Shouldering my backpack, I headed for the door. Surprisingly, one of young guardsmen opened it for me, standing at attention as I entered. It was a little embarrassing, as I said, "Thanks."

Inside a new reception area in the four-story foyer, with a young man awkwardly rising to greet me.

"Good morning, Mr. Drummond," the young man said.

"Morning. This is new," I said looking around. "You new here too?" I asked. He looked vaguely familiar.

"Yes sir, as of last week."

"Have we met before? You look familiar."

"Yes sir, briefly. We met at your home, with Captain McCalister."

"That's right," I said. "Akers, right?" I asked, remembering that evening last spring, in the barn.

"Yes sir. Dean Akers. I suspect you didn't know my first name."

"That'd be correct. What are you doing here?"

"Lost my leg in that dust up at the golf course with the Captain."

"Manito. Right," I said, remembering the last stand of the hired thugs of one of our former county commissioners, Earl Williams. Williams had been convicted of a number of murders and conspiracies, and after the sentencing for the first of the murders, there wasn't much point in continuing any further trials. I'd missed his very public hanging, which was held on September sixth. "Couldn't stay in the service?"

"Wanted to, but got a medical discharge sent my way."

"And you ended up here?"

"Someone figured that this would be a good job for me."

"You have any schooling, beyond the military?"

"Two years community college. Didn't really have much planned, which is why I chose the Army. Figured it would give me some options."

"What was your career track in the Army?" I asked, not really caring if anyone was waiting for me. There was something wrong about a kid like this being a receptionist.

"I was scheduled to go into Combat Engineering. After the Army, I thought that I might pursue civil or structural engineering."

"Still interested in that?"

"Yes, sir, but there isn't much chance of me getting a college education in it these days."

"Maybe, maybe not, but there are a few engineering instructors at Gonzaga, and we have our own engineering needs here at the County. Let me talk with whoever's heading up Personnel and I'll see what I can do about getting you re-assigned."

Akers didn't quite know what to say. "Thank, you, sir. I don't know what to say...."

"No problem. Just cover the front desk today, and I'll get back to you as soon as I can."

"Thanks. I believe that the Sheriff is expecting you, in Conference Room two, at eight-ten. I don't want to make you late."

"Mike'll understand. No worries," I said as I headed to the stairs. The elevators were still down...probably for good.

I passed a couple more staff on the stairs, shaking hands and exchanging greetings along the way. Mike was in the conference room, looking south across the wrecked and patched Public Health building to the river and the downtown area beyond.

"Hiya there, 'Dad,'" I said, dropping my backpack in one of the side chairs. "How're the twins doing?"

"Morning, Rick. They're doing fine. We almost made it through the night last night." Mike's twins, Suzi and Matthew, were born in early June, healthy, happy, and neither had slept through a whole night yet.

"Perils of the job. Neither of our kids slept for two years."

"Don't tell Ashley that."

"Not on my life," I said, shaking his hand. "What's the good word today?"

"Not really a good word, but news at least. First, Pete died from an aneurysm, not suicide. Second, the U.S. Attorney and his prisoners fly out today, although only a half-dozen or so know that."

"Some consolation about Pete. Small consolation, that is."

"Yeah. His memorial service will be this afternoon, downstairs in Council chambers. He requested a private burial."

"I'll be there. I assume that most everyone will."

"That's what I expect, yes."

"Mike, what can you tell me about this business over in Idaho? I had an interesting talk with my Army driver on the way in. Their Humvee got hit by an EMP burst?"

"We'll hear more about it from the Forty-First directly. C'mon. Get yourself some coffee and get ready for your briefing. You should have department heads showing up any time now."

"Great. Meetings. My favorite."

9

Monday,
October Twenty-Third

Once again, I entered what was 'my' office, feeling like a stranger. We'd lost Walt Ackerman, and now Pete. The desk, my desk, was too organized. I grabbed the stack of department summary folders though, from the center of the desk. Someone was looking out for my schedule.

The large conference room was at the end of the hall, with a view to the north, before the Domino anyway. Now the window frames were filled with insulated panels and unfinished sheetrock. Our department heads, and a few of the Townsmen, were chatting, waiting for me to arrive.

"Good morning, everyone. Thanks for putting up with my tardiness," I said.

"You're fine. We don't usually start until eight-thirty or eight forty-five anyway," Tonya Lincoln replied. "Nice to see you, again, Rick."

"Thanks, Tonya. You, too." Tonya was the acting head of our Commerce Department. She was hoping to get back to running a restaurant someday, as well. I made my introductions around the room, shaking hands with each department head and Townsman. 'Many new faces,' I thought as I moved back to my chair at the end of the scarred conference table.

Drew Simons, one of my former Recovery Board members, joined us right after I sat down. Drew was the head of the Utility Department, when he wasn't farming.

"Morning, Drew. Good to see you," I said as I shook his hand.

"You as well. You finally healed up?"

"Making progress, slowly."

"You did have about the closest call you could have and walk away from it."

"Walk was a relative term."

"Indeed. Ready to get to business?"

"Yes. Quicker we're done with meetings, the better. For everyone's information, I hate meetings. The quicker we can get through what we need to, the better. We've got more important things to do than sitting here."

"Good. I'm first up," Drew said.

"Sure, after the Pledge," one of the Townsmen reminded us. We all stood, faced the wall-hung flag that had flown over the Courthouse through the Domino, pulled from the wrecked flagpole that had torn lose from the tall central tower. It reminded me as I reaffirmed my loyalty to my country, of the World Trade Center flag hoisted by those three firefighters, years before.

We took our seats, and I shuffled my papers again. "Let's go then," I said. "Mike might have to interrupt our agenda, so let's get moving."

"Utilities. Expansion and restoration work in the urban area has been suspended for the winter on main electrical lines, but infill work within boundaries of existing feeds will continue until weather limits those operations as well. The good news is that with current work on the boards, we'll have just under six thousand more homes on line by New Years, including four thousand with backup wood heat, leaving two thousand, or a few less, solely dependent on electric heat—forced air electric in most cases."

"Wow," I said of Drew's report on electrical restoration work. "I had no idea your crews were able to get that many back on line."

"Power's back, but that doesn't mean the houses are ready. Water service is spotty in many areas within the electric boundary, and at least half of those homes still need some pretty serious work to be close to pre-War condition. Of the total number of homes, there's probably only ten percent that are ready to move into immediately. Those are almost exclusively in the Garland and Lidgerwood areas.'"

"How about work in commercial areas?" I asked. I noted that one of the Townsmen looked extremely bored, already.

"We're at ninety percent within the Service Area, which is probably over-served, area-wise. There are more buildings served with electricity than are being used for commerce...unless you count warehouses of salvage as commerce."

"So the next focus area, I mean when the weather turns, is what?" the Townsman who reminded us to take the Pledge asked. I looked at my notes, not remembering his name. 'Bruce Weathers— Rockford Township.'

Drew had several options available for us to consider. "Next year, I'd recommend restoring arterial power up to Francis on the north, from Assembly on the west to Market on the east; Division all the way up to the Newport Highway; and on the south side, power down the Hangman Valley to Hatch; Fifty-Seventh, all the way to Glenrose. That gives us a framework to work within, should we need to add more commercial and residential fabric back to the area," Drew said, obviously noting Weathers' expression of frustration.

"That's just in the urban area. In the rural districts, I recommend further restoration work to Mica, Valleyford, more work around Rockford," which I noted gained some satisfaction on the face of Drew's questioner, "and restoration to other hamlets through the south end of the County, within reason. There's darned little in the way of power, or population, within a mile on either side of Highway Two or Three Ninety-Five, all the way to the Pend Oreille and Stevens county lines. We'd like to get more done up there, but probably don't have the gear."

"How about water?" I asked.

"Everything north of Francis is off line, unless it's a private well. Too much damage in the Little Spokane River area to fix without more equipment. We're short of everything. Pipe, couplings, you name it."

"Thanks, Drew. You can head out if you need to."

"I do. Many thanks."

The Commerce Department was next, headed by one of my former Recovery Board teammates, Tonya Lincoln. Tonya provided us a ten-minute breakdown of the number of business operations in the County, although many were amalgamations of trading and bartering operations (ours included) and hybrid businesses that had many different offerings. Our businesses weren't unique, nor were they alone. Everyone needed multiple jobs to keep food on the table.

She surprised me by stating that the main problem that Commerce was facing was in keeping businesses in operation, because of the local 'banking industry.'

"Banking industry?" I asked, knowing there wasn't a real bank in operation, and hadn't been, since early spring.

"Sorry. Loan sharks is really what they are. They're tying up physical dollars, silver and gold, and taking it out of circulation. If people need physical money, they charge rates that would make the Mafia blush."

"I'm assuming there are negative physical consequences involved for those short on paying back?"

"Well stated in a clinical way, yes. "Unfortunately I really don't have a recommendation for fixing this though, Rick."

"Simple. We need a bank with real money."

"Sure we do. I need a nice tenderloin steak for dinner too. Both of us will be disappointed, however."

"Maybe. See me later today on this," I told Tonya, arranging for a later meeting to discuss it in more detail.

The Finance Department provided us a report, a grim report, on the ability of the County to continue operations beyond February, due to a lack of physical money to pay vendors, staff, and contractors. Most of the regular County employees were paid in a little silver and more Spokane County Scrip, which was only redeemable at Central Stores, and a slightly reduced price over 'retail.' This had been the brainchild of our former Assessor, who had put it in place and run Central Stores, until leukemia took him early in August.

Again, it came down to money. We simply needed more real dollars, silver and gold, in the economy for 'normal' operations. There wasn't enough in the first place, and with some people hoarding it (couldn't blame them one bit), what had been in circulation was being held for rainy days.

Transportation at least was a bright spot in the series of gloomy reports, with fully operational freight and commuter service running twice daily, soon to be three times daily, on the Central Lines. Former freight cars had been converted to handle commuter traffic, with the addition of windows and bench seating, in the old Burlington yards. Passenger stations were built along each leg of the Central, reminding many of the old wooden stations of the past. These were framed of dimensional lumber, roofed with plywood and sheet metal, and sounded like the inside of a drum when a train passed.

Snow plowing, also the responsibility of Transportation was limited to emergency routes, roads near hospitals, militia centers, and along the Central Line. Snow removal, clearing, packing, or plowing in residential areas was the responsibility of the neighborhoods. Several areas were building snow rollers, large wood or metal drums towed behind a hitched team, to pack the soft snow down. We knew that diesel fuel would be tight for using to plow roads, and had warned the neighborhoods early that they needed to make plans to deal with snow.

It was now approaching ten a.m., and I knew that our two remaining departments, Health and Public Safety, were eager to get on with the rest of their days. Both Rene and at least one of the Public Safety staff sat in through all of the meetings, to hear any discussions that might impact the general public. I appreciated their time. Two of our Townsmen had had to excuse themselves to tend to other Monday morning business.

"Rene, you're next," I said as she shuffled her papers.

"Good thing. I'm heading to Sacred Heart at eleven."

"Let's not make you late then."

"OK. First, you've read the status reports, right? No need in covering ground twice."

"I've made it most of the way through," I said.

"A quick summary then. We're on the down slope of deaths due to chronic conditions that pre-War were maintainable. Heart congestion, severe diabetes, asthma, some severe kidney ailments. Cancers that were being treated pre-War with chemo are now incurable, essentially, although homeopathic treatments have provided some relief."

"OK. How about the flu? Any progress on treatments?"

"None. If there is any good news on that front at all, it's that the CDC believes that by next spring, we will be at a saturation point across North America, with virtually all humans exposed to it by that point."

"Small comfort," Mike stated.

"Well, it might be. It will probably mean that survivors are either naturally immune or through some fluke, have survived the initial strain and the eleven identified mutations," Dr. Sorenson replied, fetching another report from her file.

"What support can we give you?" I asked, guessing what was next.

"This is our needs list. Not wants, needs," she said, handing a copy to Mike and I, and a couple others for the Townsmen, one who looked increasingly bored and restless. Weathers, seated next to him, looked over at him in some disapproval.

I scanned the list some of which I could actually understand, most of which, I could not. The pharmaceuticals alone were a page and a half on the double-sided single-spaced report.

"I'd like you to see what magic you can conjure to fulfill that list. We're down to triage levels of medical supplies in every single hospital in the region. Meds are virtually non-existent. I'm hoping you can work a miracle here...." she paused a moment. "If you don't, we'll be truly back in the eighteen hundreds as far as medical care goes, and that will take effect by the first of the year."

"I cannot say that I'm surprised by this. I'm assuming that all salvaged and stored medical supplies have been exhausted?"

"Nearly so, yes. And the Nova Pharma plant on the north side will be out of raw materials for their production, as of November one."

"I'll look into it. No promises," I said, rising out of my chair and shaking her hand. I didn't want to tell her that I'd already all but demanded that the County received a 'Priority Status' for medicine and consumables with Pacific Northwest Command. You don't get if you don't ask.

"None expected. I just don't want to see many more sutures done with fishing line."

"Understood all too well. I have a nice scar on my noggin that was stitched up with nylon monofilament."

"Right, because on August twentieth, we ran out of the real stuff."

"I'll see what I can do," I said as she turned to go.

"Thanks. And don't push yourself too hard too soon."

"You been talking to my wife?" I asked as one of the Forty-First command officers came in behind Rene.

"Nope, I can see it in your eyes."

"Sharp as a marble, that's me."

That brought a needed laugh. "See you next week, if not sooner."

"Thanks again, Rene."

I poured a glass of water as the officer, a Major, took his place at the table.

"Major Kurt George. You are Mr. Drummond?"

"I am the accused," I said as I shook the Major's hand.

"I've been assigned by General Anderson to serve as one of the new liaison officers to the Eastern Washington region." I'd met Bob Anderson only twice, the first time when he visited my hospital room, the second at home, a couple weeks ago. I'd had Carl fish out a couple bottles of a nice old Cabernet for him, after hearing that he'd be treating Governor Hall to a steak dinner in Walla Walla. I thought the wine might be appreciated by all in attendance. Anderson and the Governor had some history together.

"Welcome. And perfect timing by the way," I said. "Public safety report is up. Mike Amberson, I hope you've met? And our Townsmen representatives?"

"We have, thank you. Sheriff, good to see you again," he said to Mike. "Gentlemen, you as well," acknowledging our other county representatives and shaking their hands.

"You as well, Major. We're normally joined by one of our fire district chiefs, but they're recruiting today. I have a report for you on that, Rick," he said as he handed me a ten-page report.

"Lots to say here, apparently," I said.

"About half of that deals with proposed emergency response times and noted shortcomings in coverage. A few pages on shortcomings and equipment failures. Concerns about low water pressure in the Greenacres area, which affects a good-sized hunk of service area adjacent to the Red Line out there. The rest is…"

I cut him off. "Let me guess. Staff shortages."

"Yep. Which is why they're recruiting. They're approaching critical levels even in the all-volunteer stations."

"What's the key issue? Are we losing men and women, or what?'

"Not really, there were three more stations opened up in the Valley, and seven in the north and west areas over the past three months. All located in pretty well populated areas. We're just spread thin."

"I'm betting that you have the same issue."

"Not as bad, because I have these guys covering what I can't," Mike said as he pointed at the Major. "But it will be an issue we'll have to deal with soon."

"Thanks, Mike. Major? I have some questions for you regarding a certain problem spot over on the east side of Coeur d'Alene Lake."

"News travels fast," he said with some surprise.

"My ride today was a Humvee that'd seen some damage apparently from a directed EMP hit."

"Is that your conclusion?" he asked.

"From what the sergeant-major told to me, yep."

"That does appear to be the case, yes." ·

"I understand that a group over there killed a police officer and his wife in their driveway, and another wounded."

"That is correct, with the exception of the location of one of the attacks. That one was at a church. The deputy was picking up his wife on the way home. She was the pastor there. The wounded officer was coming on shift, and we think their shooters miss-timed their shot."

"Response?" I asked flatly, trying not to show how angry the preceding statement made me.

"No time like the present to brief you on this. One of the reasons I'm here today is to tell you that a large percentage of Army personnel will likely be assigned to this mission."

"Go on," I said.

"The subject property is quite large and terrain is pretty challenging. Individual homes are not readily observable from the lake, and recon shows that each subject property has constructed observation posts at key locations. The result is that there is a five hundred acre area that has overlapping fields of fire, with most targets fairly well hidden by terrain. The homes, and community center, from what we've been able to determine from scant records in Kootenai County, are pretty well hardened against attack. Cast in place concrete. Ballistic glass. Safe rooms, etc."

"I assume that Kootenai County had building plans on file for these?"

"Only one. The others managed to 'disappear,' along with most of the site plans, infrastructure plans, and accurate topographic surveys. Somebody got bribed to vacuum the files that well."

"You figure a ground assault?" Mike asked, knowing that the chance of success without casualties was almost nil.

"Almost certainly."

"What kind of opposition do you have?" I asked.

"Forty to sixty armed men and women, well trained, with top of the line equipment and the home-field advantage."

"Do they really think that...."

"We gave up trying to figure out what they are thinking," Major George replied, interrupting me. "At least half of the owners of these hardened homes have significant business connections on a national or international level. There have been several occasions where

106

political pressure has been placed on the armed forces units in the area to pass on action in this case."

"Bullcrap." I said, leaning forward, and noting that Townsman Weathers was most attentive.

"Yes, sir."

"How are they supplied power and water?" I asked, thinking about what I'd do if I were in the Army's shoes.

"Water is supplied through multiple wells and large storage tanks. Power is provided through Kootenai County Cooperative, although we know there are shielded diesel generators serving each home and common buildings."

"OK. We know what their response has been to outside authority, or at least some trigger-happy cowboys that might be running rogue."

"No sir. From what we've gathered through recorded radio conversations, these actions were directed by the leadership of Black Pine."

"That's the place?" I asked. "I've seen some of it. It was passably impressive. Been five years since I was out there."

"That's the place."

"They broadcast in the clear? You said their radio transmissions..." Bruce Weathers asked, before being cut off by the Major.

"Sorry, no. They're actually heavily encrypted radio transmissions. We deciphered them with some help from Air Force intelligence, while not raising any flags."

"Major," Weathers stated, "This ain't a ground operation. This is an air op. You've said that your civilian authorities were fired upon, some wounded, some killed. If that happened here in Spokane County, and it did, Drummond here would make a quick case of taking those sumbitches out, period. You've given them the opportunity to play on their ground. I say you play it on yours."

"You are, sir?"

"Bruce Weathers. In a previous life, I served on a -52 as a bombardier. If I may make a suggestion, you make a high-speed low level pass at oh-three-hundred hours and scare the sh•t out of the sentries. You then drop one GPS-guided bomb on a water tank or three from a nice, safe altitude, and give them fifteen minutes to surrender before your next pass to flatten the place. End of story, no ground-pounders at appreciable risk from hostile fire."

"Not to be critical of a really good idea, Bruce, but GPS is dead," I said. "War took out the satellites."

"Not entirely, Mr. Drummond. There is still a significant operational capability," the Major said, obviously intrigued by Weathers' idea.

"Major, I really don't want to lose the Army resources here in this county, even on a temporary basis, but of course that's not my call. I suspect that you don't really want to put your men and women at risk, any more than I do. If I may, I'd recommend that Mr. Weathers' suggestion be explored with your counterparts at Fairchild. Connections or not, political influence or not, we're not going to put up with this, I don't really give a crap who knows who."

"Frankly, gentlemen, it had never occurred to staff to consider this as anything but an Army operation."

"Where did your commanding General last serve, Major?" Weathers asked.

"Germany, from what I understand. One of the last bases to be evac'd," Major George replied.

"Ground pounder," Weathers said with a little friendly contempt. "Y'all have your General think out of the box a little. Give the Air Force a little something to do and keep your men and women outta harms way."

I had just enough time to grab a bite to eat at the cafeteria before getting ready for Pete's memorial service. I'd started to work through another pile of reports on my desk, and realized that time had drifted away from me. I noted outside, the snow was drifting as well.

The cafeteria was located in the old, ornate County Courthouse building, designed to imitate a French castle, and completed in the 1890's. The quake had caused significant damage, which would require far more resources than we had available to repair. The damaged portions were boarded up to keep the weather out, and power was off in about ninety percent of the building. If things remained on the course they were on, it would resemble Frankenstein's castle in another ten years.

The offices held a skeleton crew of staff for the mid-day meal, just enough people to keep information flowing in case there was some urgency that wouldn't wait until after lunch. Most of the staff had either headed to lunch in the cafeteria or over to their temporary quarters over in the Public Safety building. I grabbed a tray and was served a pasta-heavy casserole, with some ground beef and a creamed corn-looking sauce, along with a large wheat roll. A far cry from the pre-War days, when there were 'choices' of what one could have for lunch.

I recognized a few of the staff from my floor as I shook the snow off my boots, and headed over to their table. I noted that there was some whispering about 'who was coming over' as I approached.

"Afternoon everyone. Mind if I join you?" I asked.

"No, sir. Please do," one of the building department guys said. His name escaped me. Had we met?

"Thanks. I'm Rick Drummond. You are?" I asked as I set my tray down.

"Dub Henshaw," he said as we shook hands. "I think we met before your trip down south."

"Right," I said, remembering now. "Pardon me for not remembering. You're W.T., right?" remembering a lively discussion on his first and middle names, unknown to everyone, even the Human Resource department. Dub held multiple degrees, the most notable a structural engineering degree from Northeastern University, I recalled.

"Yep, that's me. And no apologies necessary for the memory. You've been through some tough times."

"I have at that, as have many of us," I said, deflecting the attention from my own bumpy past. "Since I have you for a minute, let me ask you a question."

"Shoot," he said, taking a seat.

"Snow loads on undamaged and damaged buildings. How much can they carry? Obviously it varies, but what do you think is a safe amount?"

"Pre-War undamaged buildings could take several feet of depth, it really depends on the moisture content. Forty pounds per square foot was the minimum requirement."

"OK, so real-world, say that we're in the third week of October and it snows, and we have eight or eighteen inches on the ground. And say, it keeps going off and on through March. What are we facing?" I asked, knowing the answer, as I took a bite of the casserole. Too much pepper.

"Without removing a sizeable portion of overburden, collapse, of course."

"Right. Can you figure out, based on some of the sloppy patchwork construction that has passed for interim repairs, when we're going to be needing to remove snow?"

"Commercial buildings will be the biggest threat. Flat roofs, no snowmelt," he said, thinking it over more thoroughly.

"Right. And those comprise the balance of our salvaged materials warehousing, food warehouses, and a slug of small industries and residences. Have you seen any problems of this nature yet?"

"None in permanently occupied shelters, but we've lost temporary shelters---basically beefed up carports, already due to wind and rain. Not snow, yet anyway."

"Can you get some staff to look into that? We can't afford to lose what we've got."

"I can do that."

"Need any additional bodies to throw at it?"

"Always," Dub said with a grin. "You've got a magic supply of structural engineers in your private stash?"

"No, but you might be able to put together a training session for some of our need-work people, and have a professional supervise a team of temp employees. Would double or quadruple your force," I said, taking another bite.

"That might work. Timeline?"

"Well, looking outside, I'd say sooner rather than later."

"I'll have a training outline put together by the morning. How many people can you supply for me as temps?"

"A report on my desk that I just finished, said that we have six hundred unemployed men and women looking for something to do in eleven neighborhoods around town. And that number is growing."

"I'm sure we can use at least some of them," he said. "Pardon me for askin', but how are you gonna pay them?"

"Working on that."

"Good enough. If you'll excuse me, I appear to have a new task to complete," Dub said, rising to go. I stood as well.

"I hope I didn't sidetrack your other work too much."

"We'll get by. Engineering for maintenance and bulk material storage facilities. None of them are at risk from what you've mentioned though. They'll wait."

"Thanks, Dub. Let me know when you're ready with your training outline. I'll set up training sessions in the neighborhoods and get some of these folks to work."

"Will do. See you tomorrow."

I finished lunch, chiming in a little on staff conversations of the train derailment that took lives and some of our hopes, correcting some of the rumors with fact. We wrapped up lunch and I headed back to the office to get cleaned up a little before Pete's service.

By five minutes of two, the Auditorium was full to standing room only. Mike Amberson had thoughtfully saved me a seat in the front row, near the rest of our department heads. Townsmen filled three rows, behind five rows of uniformed deputies and police officers.

We stood as the colors were presented by the Sheriff's Honor Guard, and only took our seats when the priest of Pete's 'home church', St. Aloysius, over on the Gonzaga campus, beckoned us to prayer.

As the service continued through hymns, eulogies and prayers, my thoughts kept returning to the many services that I'd attended this past year, and in years past, with each seeming to be more personal and poignant than the last.

Someone once said to me, that each loss we experienced was like the loss of a library of life experience, never to be retold, regained, or known again. I could not disagree.

By three o'clock, the service had ended and we slowly filed out of the Auditorium, and back upstairs towards our offices. I noted that as we did so, the law enforcement officers and military units in formal dress stood at attention and saluted a photograph of Pete, draped with a black cloth ribbon, as it was carried to the Public

Safety building. It would join fifty-six other photographs in the entry lobby, each officer lost since the first of the year.

Back in my office, I was greeted by a half dozen emails through the buildings' intranet system. Tonya Lincoln provided a nice summary on 'normalization of trade procedures with the eastern States' and 'pacification of rail corridors through Oregon and Northern California'. Her attachments appeared to show the locations of the attack on our train and on six interstate highway chokepoints, all allegedly under the control of a single 'entity.' I thought it odd that she didn't use the word, 'gang.' I saved the lengthy memo to my flash-drive to read later, at home. I wasn't up to reading fifteen pages of text, and three in the transmittal letter, and wasn't about to waste the paper on printing it.

The Personnel Department forwarded back their recommendation on accepting Dean Akers as 'Engineer in Training.' He'd be sharing time between Utilities and Transportation Departments. I fumbled with the keyboard, unaccustomed to the computer, as I gave them my thanks for addressing my request so promptly.

The next email, again from Personnel provided me notice that Akers' permanent replacement would be selected from the current County employee 'pool', and if no suitable candidate could be found, then the position would be opened up to the general public. I assumed that this was standard pre-War procedure. For the time being the position would be filled by a 'temp' employee selected from a pool of applicants who were not currently employed by the County. I suppose this was a way to get their foot in the door. As some would say, a way of 'sidling up to the public trough.'

By four-fifteen I was dragging, and I could hear the sounds of the second-shift—which I suppose I was on as well—getting packed up or meeting with third-shift staff to inform them of progress on assignments. First shift—midnight to eightish, would do the same for second shift tomorrow.

The whole two- or three-shift system was set up right after we found our feet in the spring, and was working fairly well. First shift was really a skeleton crew, about a third of our normal staff level throughout all departments. They were really there to handle continuing assignments on infrastructure, administration, supply and finance, and 'crisis management.' Second shift was the baseline against which first- and third-shifts were created, with full staffing in all positions, during a 'normal' workday, five days a week, although many worked six.

Pre-War, the County had about twenty-seven hundred employees. We now were making do with two hundred forty-one, about half of which weren't employed by the County a year before. The loss of institutional memory, let alone skills, was crippling. In order to make the infrastructure work better, or more consistently, or to repair damage, we needed more people. In order to provide a higher level of service in the 'peace officer' category, we needed more deputies. We needed more firefighters. Nurses. Engineers. The list would fill pages. The problem was, we didn't have enough money—real money—to hire anyone beyond the staff we already had, and we were flirting with not having any money on a monthly basis. Our governmental financial system was a cobbled-together mishmash of bartering, compensation in silver or ever-scarce gold, or payments of food or other goods. It couldn't last forever.

Our 'economy' would get to a point in the near future, where savings outstripped spending, taking 'real money' out of circulation, and 'traded and bartered' goods would not be able to fill the void.

'What then?' I wondered, as the desk intercom reminded me that my ride home was downstairs.

"Be right there," I said, grabbing my parka, putting on the black watch cap over my stubble, and stuffing some more files into my backpack. 'What then, indeed.'

Downstairs, there was a small group of folks waiting for the shuttle bus to the Central Line, huddled against the building, trying to keep clear of the light snow and out of the wind.

The shuttle bus in the County's case was an old GMC school bus that someone had begun to convert to an RV, then abandoned. A couple of County mechanics had put the interior back together, after a fashion, and tuned up the diesel as best they could. Still, it resembled a prison bus, similar to those the State used to use to transport convicts to The Big House in Walla Walla, the Washington State Penitentiary. My 'ride home' was already there, this evening a stock-looking Suburban.

"Anybody heading east?" I asked, as a couple staff took note, looking at each other, and then nodding. "I'm allowed, aren't I?" I asked my driver.

"No one's told me otherwise, sir."

"Six seats in this or eight?"

"Six besides the driver. Some of the back end is filled with an emergency kit."

"Let's go then," I said, beckoning to my co-workers. "No sense in taking an empty out east."

I took the front seat, with finance guy Bill Winkler, who just needed a ride down to Bridge Avenue—he'd be transferring to another shuttle heading north and east. Our three other passengers were all 'new' employees since the Domino, most of who lived within walking distance to the Red Line. One young man that I didn't recognize; the other two from Utilities, both women that I'd seen before, but couldn't remember exactly where.

"Thank you for the ride, Mr. Drummond," one of the ladies said, after Bill was dropped off.

"Rick, please. I don't think we've met."

"Susan Connolly. This is Margie Hunt."

"Nice to meet you both," I answered.

"I'm Jim Benker. I'm an RN over in Health, although I'm working in the Jail at the moment."

"Really? Staff assignment?"

"Dealing with a number of maladies in the prisoner population. AIDS and HIV among them, although without meds and in their weakened condition, most of that element won't be around this time next year."

"How's nutrition over there?" I asked, suddenly interested in the captive population.

"As good as we can do. Better than some of the general population in parts of the country, according to the rumors anyway.

Three meals a day, no work detail, not that any of them would be trusted for a New York minute out of their cells."

"How many prisoners total?"

"Fifty-five. Eleven with either advanced HIV or full-blown AIDS."

"Why aren't they at the hospital?" Margie asked.

"Too dangerous. Not the disease---the men."

"Oh."

We were passing again through the eastern end of Downtown, past the Intermodal Center where the trains were loading. It was nice to see streetlights on every block again, or almost every block.

"Streetlights. Nice," I said.

"You're welcome," Susan responded.

"Utility Department. Right."

"Not just that. We're linemen in real life. Or, line women, more correctly. Margie and I ran these lights, last month."

"Well thank you. You're in the office now though?"

"One day a week. Trying to round up record drawings for restoration work. The last of Sprague Avenue was hooked up last Friday, all the way to Greenacres."

"You work with Lou Pecquet then?"

"He's the boss. We're his minions," she replied.

"How is he to work for? Off the record, understand," I didn't want them to feel that they were ratting him out, I was just curious.

"Honestly, if I would have had had a boss like him pre-War, I think I'd have killed him," Margie said.

116

I laughed a little bit, which may or may not have been appropriate. "Sorry, I couldn't help it."

"That's OK. Lou's not the easiest guy to work for. He'd rather work with you, and be in the trenches, than tell you to do something. We do know how to run wire. We're all journeymen electricians. But if things aren't done his way," Margie said, "you'll never hear the end of it."

"I know the type. I've some of that in me, myself," I said. We were approaching Altamont, where I noted the collapsed wreckage of the old Safeway-store-turned-bingo-parlor had been cleared away. I was pleased to see Northwest Seed was still there, with lights on inside. I used to buy my garden seed there...before the War.

Not too far to the east, just beyond Freya, the streetlights were out, it looked like all the way to Havana, home of the Fairgrounds.

"Looks like your repairs need repairing," I said. The hair stood up on the back of my neck though, for some unknown reason.

"Stop the car. NOW!" Margie said before I could. "Back it up quick-like."

"Yes, Ma'am," our Army driver replied, perfectly happy to take orders from anyone who sounded like they were in charge.

"What's up?" Jim asked. "It's just the streetlights."

"Individual services are still on," Susan pointed out as we slid around to the west. "Somebody killed those lights, and that's not exactly easy to do."

"Head north, up to Broadway," Margie told the driver.

"You thinking ambush?" I asked, the obvious question.

"Highwaymen are out there. Why not pick the low-hanging fruit?"

117

"Because the Red Line is a hundred yards north of Sprague," I said.

"Doesn't mean a thing. Might as well be in Kansas," Margie said. "Not enough manpower to cover places like this."

We were now at Broadway, and turned east again. "Soldier, do me a favor and call this into dispatch," I said before addressing Margie again. "This happen often?"

"Coupla times a month. They'll pick off a stray, a car or truck or a transport, traveling alone, leave the driver alone unless he does something heroic, and take what they want."

"'They' you say."

"Thugs. Yes," Margie said. "Why do you think we're all armed? Who'd wanna shoot the guy or gal that's putting power back in your house?"

"The guy who wants your copper, that's who," Susan replied.

"This stuff showing up on the black market?"

"Eventually it will," Susan answered. "Ten percent of our parts inventory goes missing every week. To be re-bought again."

"That's gonna end quickly. We can't chase our tail anymore."

"Tell that to the thieves."

"I will see to it," I said as we passed the far end of the Fairgrounds, and then headed south to Sprague again, where the lights were still on. I rode the rest of the way pretty much in silence, thinking about this new little evil in our midst. Part of a verse from Hosea came to mind: '....*They practice deceit, thieves break into houses, bandits rob in the streets.*'

Monday evening,
October Twenty-Third

At home I was greeted by a largely darkened house. Not exactly what I was expecting. The dogs were glad to see me though as I opened the door.

"Anyone home?" I called, hearing Carl reply from downstairs. "Where is everyone?" I asked.

"Uncle Alan's. We're having dinner over there tonight. Aunt Mary decided that Mom needed a break. And Grandma didn't feel all that hot."

"You coming?"

"Nope. I volunteered to keep an eye on the place. I ate earlier."

"You monitoring the radios then?"

"That, and a little xBox."

"OK. Keep alert though. There's always something out there in the dark, you know. I saw some of that on the way home."

"What's up?"

"The old-fashioned term was 'highwaymen'...people who'd just as soon as kill you as not, for whatever they feel like taking from you. They kill the streetlights on one of the roads and wait for someone to blunder into their kill zone. Either kill you or not I guess, but you'll end up lighter of whatever you're carrying."

"Where did that happen?"

"I understand it moves around town, from what I hear. Tonight, there was a blackout down on Sprague, maybe a mile long. Plenty dark enough for somebody to hijack a car, and almost no traffic on the roads."

"The train..." he said before I cut him off, "...is north of there. And the passenger cars are lit, which doesn't really let anyone on the train see what's going on outside. Easy pickin's."

"What are you going to do?"

"It's already been called in. That'll mean it's in the lap of Mike and our friends in green. Just keep this quiet. Your Mom's worried enough about me without this tossed in."

"You're not going to be in the middle of this are you? Like out at the Samuel's place?"

"Nope. Not this time. I've had enough excitement for one year, or five."

"Good," Carl said, showing some relief. "It'd be nice to keep you in one piece."

"Truer words were never spoken, son. I better get going."

"I'll radio over if I hear anything important."

"OK. Make sure the County radio's on, too. Let me know if they're looking for me. What's my call sign today?"

"Wyoming."

"OK, and what's 'home' today?"

"St. Petersburg."

"Good enough. See you in a bit."

"'K," Carl said before he headed back downstairs.

I washed up a little bit and made myself a little more presentable before going over to Alan's, remembering to put the old .45 on before stepping out the door. Ada was curled up by the woodstove, perfectly content to thump her tail twice as I stepped over her, while Buck figured it must be time to go outside and find something to chase. He was disappointed that I left him inside as I pulled the door shut, locked behind me.

The low clouds were at least no longer dropping the light snow on the city, and I was glad for that. To the west, I could see across the garden and field to Alan's, Ron and Libby's, and Sarah Woodbridge's homes; her house through the ribs of the greenhouse, it's covering now stowed for the winter. I made my way down the steps of the porch and across the yard, the wood smoke from a hundred woodstoves on the cold east wind.

Dinner was wonderful, and a welcome mental break for me. A pot roast, potatoes, carrots and a burgundy sauce seemed like an extravagant dinner for the beginning of the week. More like one of our typical Sunday dinners.

"How was your day, hon?" Karen asked. I hadn't talked too much about specifics, with the exception of the memorial service.

"First half was meetings. Second half, paperwork, except for Pete's service of course."

"Probably too early for good first impressions on how things are looking then," Alan said.

"There is a lot to wrap ones' head around, yes. Although, it's not as bad as it could be by a long shot. Nor is it as good as it should--or could—be. The biggest problem it seems to me is that we just don't have enough money."

"Gee, there's wisdom for the ages," Ron said. "No one's ever had enough money."

I chuckled a little. "You know what I mean. There's not really enough money circulating—real money, silver or gold—to achieve critical mass. We're operating on fits and starts. Once money is acquired, it's stashed away and therefore taken out of circulation.

Hard to pay people in scrip or goods, when neither are universally accepted."

"What are you thinking?" Karen asked. "I mean..."

"I know what you mean, babe. I don't know. I can't fix this from within. There simply does not seem to be enough physical metal to keep an economy going."

"The silver mines up in Idaho are opened up though," Mary added. "And those mines up in British Columbia."

"Sure, but they're months away from really making any headway in production. Most of those have been closed for years, and they're scraping up equipment just to really open. No, I think this is something that we have to go to the outside to try to fix."

"Walla Walla? Or the Feds?"

"The former first, the latter only if absolutely necessary," I said, taking a deep drink from a home-brewed porter that Ron had traded for. "Dang that's good beer."

"Should be. Came all the way from Bonners Ferry."

"Nice. And how did the store do today? Snow keep things quiet?"

"Not really, although a few more days of this and I'm sure people will be staying in. Had about an average day I guess. We met with Randy Thompson—he's all over taking the manager position at the store, but he'd like to talk to you about getting that house to the east of it for a dedicated gun shop."

"OK," I thought. "I'll see what I can do. Why there?"

"The place is in OK shape after the quake," Alan said, "but the key is that it's reinforced concrete block, filled, and already has steel bars on the windows. Roof's metal, has electric heat, and probably won't take much to make it a go."

"Sounds OK to me. Did you help Casey and Ray get their stuff moved?"

"Had some help there. One load in a west-bound transport, and we were done."

"How'd'ja finagle that?" I asked with no small amount of surprise. Transports were expensive.

"Pint of Scotch and two cases of that porter."

"And that paid for the fuel too? Diesel's not exactly cheap anymore."

"I gave him five gallons of my own."

"Pretty gracious of you."

"Casey said he'd make me a new gun belt when he was set up and had the right hides."

"Good kid," I said. "Did you touch base with Kevin Miller on any new prospects for the houses?" I asked, as Alan's youngest came into the room, holding one of the little hand-held FRS radios.

"Uncle Rick, it's for you."

"Thanks, Sparky." I wondered what was up now, as I excused myself to one of the small bedrooms off the hallway.

"Wyoming," I spoke into the hand-held.

"Wait one," Carl said. I heard some radio chatter in the background. Carl would tell me what was going on when he was ready. Whatever it was, it was worth calling me up for.

"Wyoming, structure fire, third alarm just called in right after the first two, with building collapse, Sprague at Havana."

Smack-dab in the middle of the blacked out part of Sprague. "Anyone call for me?"

"Not yet."

"Thanks. Keep me advised."

"Rog. Out."

"Out," I said. 'That son of mine could be in dispatch, tomorrow,' I thought to myself as I headed back into the dining room, where Rachel was showing everyone a quilt that Grandma Grace had helped her make, with some assistance of course from Kelly and Marie. I noted the older girls were all but hiding in the kitchen, letting Rachel show off without distraction. This was her first sewing project, and she was quite proud of her work. Grace looked pretty pleased, too, but also, quite tired. I kept the radio close by.

"Anything wrong?" Karen asked me quietly as I sat back down, half-listening to the quilting procedure that Rachel was describing. Ron and Libby were listening in.

"Structure fire on Sprague. The old K Mart store it sounds like. Bad."

"You need to go?"

"Don't think so. Carl's got his ears open for me, though."

"Warehouse now?" she asked, watching Rachel's presentation, but keeping her attention on our conversation.

"Yeah. Mixed goods and supplies," I remembered. Pete had provided me a couple weeks back, a list of operational warehouses now located along the Central Lines, and what was generally stored at each location. "Food, too though there. Small store on the east end."

"You got that look in your eye, Rick," Ron said. "What's going on?"

"Not in present company," I said.

"Let's get dessert served then," Libby said, providing the excuse to take us to the kitchen.

"OK, out with it. What's up?" Karen said.

"On the way home tonight, there was a darkened section of Sprague. A couple of electricians that I was riding home with said that it was probably a trap set for travelers—and that the streetlights aren't shut off 'easily.' We called it in. The fire is probably right in the middle of that stretch of road."

"Trap, for you?" Karen asked with some trepidation in her voice, eyes fixed down on the apple pie she was slicing, but really focusing on me with all her attention.

"Not likely. More for anyone that set foot in the spider web."

"And the fire?"

"No idea. Coincidence? Probably not. Reasoning, again, no idea."

"You don't need to go over there, do you?"

"Not unless there's a compelling reason to, no," I said, even though she knew I was naturally pulled to such events.

"Back to business. Ron, did you talk with Kevin today?"

"Briefly. He has a list of six potentials for the vacant houses."

"That's a good start. We have what, sixteen total on all three blocks?"

"Yep."

"Impressions on his list?" I asked.

"Haven't had time to even open the files yet."

"OK. Maybe you and Alan and our lovely wives take some time tomorrow to vet them?"

125

"Works for me," Ron said. "I'm planning on being in the Otis Orchards store for about half the day. Then out to the Greenacres store. Should have time in there somewhere."

"Let's get back in there and have dessert, shall we? No point in alarming the natives," Karen said, referring to the youngest in the house. Both Rachel and Mark had just settled back down into normal sleep patterns, after months of nightmares. One of Marks' continuing fears was of small, dark spaces. No wonder I thought, after hearing about the wreck that his room was after the Domino, and Alan having to dig him out of the sheetrock with his bare hands. Good thing he had a stout bunk bed....and slept on the bottom. Rachel was greatly startled by loud noises, but not of gunfire. She hated thunderstorms now, but had been raised with the distant sound of her father's guns.

I was halfway through my carrot cake when Carl called me again.

"Wyoming, this is St. Pete." I excused myself and found another quiet corner.

"Go."

"Shots fired, multiple men down. Guard units being deployed."

"I'm on my way to your location. Out."

"Out," Carl replied.

"Dammit," I said quietly as I found my coat. Karen had tracked me down, and Alan and Mary were looking over her shoulder.

"I heard. You aren't going down there are you?"

"No, but I want to get back to the County radio and scanners. I wouldn't really be serving a purpose down there in any regard."

"That might be, but I know you."

"Yes, you do. I'll find out what I need to from the radio."

"I'll wrap up your dessert and one for Carl and bring it later."

"'K. Love you," I said as I kissed her lightly.

"You most."

"I'll radio back over if things change," I said to Alan. "Fill Ron and Lib in for me, OK?"

"Done. Watch that back step. Haven't had a chance to get all the ice off yet," he said as I headed out the back door.

"I noticed. If I fall, I'll know who to sue."

"Good luck finding a lawyer."

"Or an insurance company," I said, trying to make light of things. "Do me a favor though. Put a weather eye out. I don't like the sound of this."

"Think things will spread?"

"Don't know. But if the Guard troops and the police and firefighters are getting shot at, that means that other parts of the area have resources pulled. Which raises the specter of opportunity."

"Mind if I let the rest of the block know?"

"Nope, not even one little bit," I replied, thinking that it might be a good idea to really spread the word about what was going on.

I felt like I was becoming a propagandist, mulling over what sort of announcement might be made over the radio, telling the community that their policemen, firemen, and soldiers--all in reality, neighbors--were being shot at.

Home, Carl was bent over one radio, listening to two scanners, and handed me a note from County Dispatch that he'd just finished. I had a new call number, effective immediately. One Eleven.

"You need to call them now," Carl said almost in a whisper as he was listening on one side of a headset.

127

"OK. You transmitting?" I asked, seeing the Collins was powered up, as well as the scanners, the County radio, and our big multi-band receiver.

"No, just listening. Stuff's happening in the Northeast. Some stuff up in Canada, too."

"Fill me in later," I said, putting on a headset to call the watch officer in dispatch.

"One Eleven to Spokane."

"Thank you, One Eleven, be advised of structure fire with casualties, Sprague and Havana. Three firefighters down with GSW one fatal. Two missing in structure collapse. Looters on scene engaged in heavy action with Army and local police forces."

"One Eleven," I responded. "Dispatch, put me through to SIO immediately, please." The SIO—Sheriff's Information Officer—handled press releases and departmental communications. Time to get the word out.

"Wait one, One Eleven," was the reply as I waited.

"OK, what's going on back east?" I asked Carl, listening with one ear to my own headset.

"They're saying Senator Blackburn's been assassinated. There's open revolt in the New Republic. Three different sources, different frequencies, said that. There's also a lot of traffic coming out of Western Canada. Riots and stuff, but I can't track all of it. Sounds ugly."

"I'm sure it is. Take notes on what you're hearing?"

"Yeah five pages so far. Nothing, and I mean not a word, on the normal radio. All of this is shortwave. TV's been off since seven, so I haven't watched anything there. Then this fire happened, so I'm behind."

I wondered for a moment or two on if things were related, and then my headset came back to life.

"One Eleven, join One Fifty-four on secure channel one niner eight."

"One Eleven, Thank you. Out," I said before switching frequencies.

"One Eleven to One Fifty Four."

"One Five Four," came the reply. Unfamiliar voice female.

"One Five Four, you up to speed on the Sprague and Havana situation?"

"Yes, sir."

"I want a press release going out ASAP about this, including radio and television. I want to make it clear that firefighters and police as well as Guardsmen are under fire at that location, and that there is looting going on. I want to put the city on alert to watch out for any suspicious activities in any part of the area. Do-able?"

"Yes, sir, but we've not confirmed casualties at this time."

"We've confirmed wounded, and I've heard one dead. That's good enough for me."

"Understood."

"We're also hearing some shortwave traffic on a revolt in the New Republic territories and that Senator Blackburn has been taken out. You hear anything about that?"

"Yes, not through conventional media."

"Break the story as unconfirmed then. Get the word out. I want the vigilance part of this thing strong. I want people to be ready for whatever's going on, if there is anything going on. The timing is suspicious. Questions?"

"Curfew?"

"Not unless the Sheriff or Army want to put it back in place. Anything else?"

"You want to hear a brief of it before it goes out?"

"You're competent to do this job, or Mike wouldn't have assigned you to it. Right?"

"I like to think so, sir."

"Then go for it. Sooner the better."

"Understood. One Five Four out." She—whoever she was, sounded a little more confident after my reply back to her.

"One Eleven Out."

I took off the headset, and listened to the scanner traffic. Carl had two scanners listening in on the Sheriff's tactical frequencies, and one on the Fire Department incident frequency.

"Bud, make sure that the AM radio is up. KDA or KLXY. There should be an announcement coming over about this soon."

"K."

"So which are you listening to?"

"Police is pretty quiet. Sounds like they've switched over to Guard secure radios. Fire's a mess. Sounds like one of the Captains got hit, and two guys running hose to a hydrant. Then the hoses got shot up. Sounds like one of the pumper trucks, too."

"I'll tell Alan to get his ears on."

"K," Carl said, not lifting his head from the radios, still taking notes.

Alan had already put out a radio call to all of our immediate neighbors, who had in turn, called their small network of friends, over the CB radio. By the time I called him, there was a good chance that there was at least one armed person in every occupied house on our block, and in a dozen blocks around us, just keeping an eye on things. In the matter of another ten minutes, and the whole city would know.

I heard the dogs rustle and move to the back porch as they heard Karen and Kelly approach the house. I looked out the west window, and saw John and Sarah escorting them.

"Spokane to One Eleven," the radio spoke.

"One Eleven," I said as my wife and daughter came into the room. I heard John and Sarah talking on the back porch.

"Be advised, Northwest Command has instituted curfew for the entire command area, effective twenty-one hundred hours. No word on termination of curfew time for the morning, if any."

"Understood. One Eleven out."

"One Eleven."

Karen gave me The Look.

"You're staying home."

"Yes, I am. I'd just be in the way."

"Glad we're clear on that."

"What brings you two over here?" I asked of Sarah and John. Sarah was dressed in a deep blue wool coat and matching hat that looked of British design. John wore a camouflaged coat, in the old 'woodland' pattern, but this one was blacks and dark greys.

"Dad thought it'd be a good idea travel in herds," John said. I noticed his Remington 870 at that point, in the corner of the kitchen, leaning against the cabinet.

"Probably smart. You taking Sarah home next?"

"We'll be at Mom and Dad's tonight."

"OK. Despite the curfew, plan on a normal day tomorrow."

"Whatever that is," Sarah said. "I'm supposed to be at the Clinic at six."

"Meet us over here at quarter to. I can get you over there, unless like I said, you hear otherwise. Curfew starts at nine tonight. No word on when it'll end in the morning, or if it'll be lifted tomorrow at all for that matter. We don't know quite yet what the evening will bring."

"OK. Thanks, though. We're really short staffed at the clinic. I almost spent the night over there," Sarah said. "You have a good evening," she said as she squeezed John's arm and gave him a little smile, which said, 'Let's go!'

Another minute and they were out the door.

"Those two," Karen said. "They can't keep their hands off each other," she said out of the earshot of our kids.

"Wasn't that long ago and neither could we."

"Wait 'til later, mister," Karen said with that come hither look in her eyes.

"Promises, promises," I said, receiving a mitten upside my head.

Monday evening,
October Twenty-Third,
8:40 p.m.

The scanner traffic, what I could make out on the Fire Department channel, told me that both the warehouse and retail stores at Sprague and Havana were gone.

The firemen on scene had all but abandoned firefighting when the first shots rang out, leaving the salvage warehouse and whatever was in the grocery and retail stores to burn. I suspected though, that what was likely happening, was that the looters were pinning down the law and fire units, while taking everything they could out the back side of the stores. With the buildings being fully involved though, there was little chance that we'd find out through an inventory.

The situation for the looters got dramatically worse as I listened in on the Fire Department channel. From what I could glean, there were at least fifty looters, supported by riflemen at distance. Snipers.

That changed as what was described by the incident commander as a gunship--probably one of the A-10 Warthogs that I'd seen come into town--came out of nowhere with a strafing run from its' big cannon. I did wish in a perverse way that I could have seen it happen.

"Spokane to all units," the radio called. I hadn't heard an All Units call in months.

"All units, Pacific Northwest Command reports that secure radio communications within the region are believed to be compromised. No reply needed. Spokane out."

"Holy smokes," Carl said.

"That's an understatement," I said.

133

"Compromised?" Kelly asked. "That means the encryption procedures have been broken?" Kelly and Marie had both made pretty good students of the communications suite at the County operations center, under the tutelage of the director of the center.

"Maybe," I thought. "Way more likely they've just scammed some military gear."

I sat down and listened to the scanners, trying to visualize what was going on. The 'tactical' frequency on the joint police and military channel was dead silent.

"This is Spokane County Emergency Services Department broadcasting on all active AM and FM frequencies and television. Pacific Northwest Command is instituting a military curfew effective at nine p.m. tonight due to criminal activity in several locations in the Pacific Northwest region. Locally, this criminal activity includes an attack and looting on a large grocery store and warehouse facility at Sprague and Havana, with snipers shooting at firefighters, emergency service workers and National Guard troops. One firefighter is confirmed dead, and two wounded. An unknown number of additional casualties have been reported. County authorities request all residents of the region to be especially vigilant overnight, and to immediately report suspicious activity to your local precinct commander and local Guard units."

"Late word of criminal activity and direct attacks similar to Spokane's have also been reported in several other cities in the West, including Missoula and Kalispell, Montana; Bellingham, Ellensburg and Yakima, Washington; Bend, Klamath Falls and Pendleton, Oregon; Boise, Coeur d'Alene, and McCall, Idaho. Similar attacks are also reported in Edmonton, Calgary, and Vancouver in the Canadian Territories."

"It is unconfirmed at this hour, but reports have been heard over shortwave radio that 'New Republic' leader Cynthia Blackburn has been assassinated in The Hamptons in New York State. No word has been received from Federal authorities on the status of the New Republic rebellion or the rumors of its collapse. It is unknown if the widespread attacks are related to the status of the 'New Republic.'"

"Repeating in its entirety..."

"So Dad, do we need to be on watch rotation tonight?" Carl asked.

"And me on the radio?" Kelly said, an almost hopeful tone in her voice.

"Maybe so. I hadn't heard anything about the other cities, so that's news to me."

"You should talk this over with Alan and Ron," Karen said.

"I spouse so. Been months since we've had to spend the night in a camouflaged hole in the ground."

"Well, it is snowy outside again, so you're used it right?" Carl said one ear plugged into the shortwave.

"Not hardly."

"Will the Guard shack at the store still be manned?" Karen asked.

"Far as I know, yeah," I said as Carl and John called Ron, Libby and Alan on the CB.

The unasked question was obvious to me though Karen wouldn't ask it neither would John or Sarah. Carl was probably closest to actually asking, *'Are they coming for you?'*

Just because you're paranoid, doesn't mean they're not out to get you.

We were an hour into our first shift at our posts. Carl and Ron would trade off with John and I for second shift. John was on the west side of the block I was on the east. Alan took the night off—if this continued, I'd have tomorrow night off and he'd cover me. Two of our original locations were provisioned, and the block had help from other residents as well with their own posts further north and south. We were nothing if not well defended for one shift, maybe two…the problem with more area to defend was how quickly our resources were depleted.

Our lookout posts had all been upgraded over the summer with better protection as well as better camouflage. Each had a seat or bench of some kind; was better protected against the elements, and had the ability to have supplies stored in weather-tight containers as well. We hadn't yet found parts and pieces to hard-wire communications between the houses, the lookouts, or our neighbors' places….but we were still looking….along with, I'd add, a few thousand other similar-minded people. We had switched out our radios though to single-sideband CB's, which had plusses and minuses over our little FRS's.

Our better shelters allowed us to stay warmer and drier, but no less bored. How military scouts and watchmen kept alert was a mystery to me. Kelly had gone to bed at midnight, and Karen and Libby were taking over for a couple hours. Mary would work tomorrow night if needed. We all hoped that this would be a one-time event, though.

It was a nice December night…the problem of course, was that it was still October. We had a light wind out of the east, low clouds, and temperatures in the twenties. We hadn't heard any news of the various attacks since coming on-shift. My little Sony AM radio had nothing but static.

"Stainless to Rust bucket," the CB asked. That was me, 'Rust Bucket'. A holdover from my days of hauling home cars that ought to have been recycled, not restored. 'Stainless' was tonight's call sign for the base station, but only 'my' home call sign. Each post had a different frequency and a different call code name…unless we needed to speak to each other…common frequencies were then used.

"RB here."

"Northwest Command states that the Sprague and Havana situation is mopped up. Heard it on AM band," Karen said, knowing that I'd wonder where she heard it.

"Gotcha. Anything else?"

"Nothing I can say in the clear."

"Understood," I said as I noted headlights from a Humvee approaching. "Traffic coming our way. Military."

"Let me know."

"Will do. Out."

The Humvee pulled to a stop right in front of my post, partly hidden by a pine tree, and now partially underground. It really wasn't a secret where our posts were to the Army—I helped put a map together for them of the place. No point in trying to hide. Nevertheless, I'd already racked the shotgun and had it trained on the truck.

The driver got out of the truck, and called out to me. "Mr. Drummond? You out here?"

"Yep. And you are?" I replied from my location.

"Corporal Barnes, sir."

"And Corporal, I believe you have a key phrase for me."

"Yes, sir. *'Wise men lay up knowledge: but the mouth of the fool is next to confusion.'*"

"Correct. Proverbs 10:14. What can I do for you, Corporal?"

"Sir, my C.O. would like a few minutes of your time regarding a pending op. Thought you'd want to know, and sent me up here because regular comms are compromised."

"Where and when?"

"Well, sir, right now, and over at Valley Hospital. And sir? We have a full company ready to respond to any problem in this area. You really don't need to be out here, if you'd rather not."

"Good to know, but it never hurts to be sure."

"I understand sir. Do you need a few minutes?"

"That'd be best, yes."

I called in to Karen, and told her that I would be in the house in a minute, and to recall all of the lookouts that she was monitoring to our house.

I was wondering how she'd take this, and what 'pending operation' was so important as to round up a low-level bureaucrat like me in the middle of the night.

"Corporal, go ahead and park. I'll be right back."

"Very well, sir."

I stowed the shotgun, grabbed my pack and the M-16 in its' fabric sleeve, custom made by one of the armorers in the Forty-First, and climbed the steps out of the post. The Humvee had pulled into the driveway, just outside the gate.

"Be right back," I said.

"Sir."

Inside, both dogs were waiting for me, and Karen and Libby were looking for John out the back window.

"So what's going on?" Karen asked as she turned and gave me a quick kiss.

"Not sure. This corporal stopped by with orders to pick me up and meet his C.O. over at Valley General regarding a 'pending operation.'

"Why not on the radio?" Libby asked, before answering her own question. "Right. They're listening in. You sure they're on the level?"

"Yes. He gave me the correct password....you didn't know," I said to Karen and everyone, "but in the event that someone from the

Army came asking for me directly, that they'd be challenged with a key verse. I challenged, he answered correctly."

"Which verse?" Libby asked.

"Proverbs 10:14."

"Wise men lay up knowledge..." Karen said.

"So," I asked Karen. "Wanna go?"

"Me?"

"You," I said as John came in. Libby filled him in on what was going on.

"Let's tell the other watches to stand down. Army appears to have us covered."

"You sure?"

"Sure enough. Get your parka and boots. It's cold out," I told Karen. "Lib, would you mind keeping an eye on the place while we're gone?"

"I'll do it," John volunteered. "If I can play a little xBox while doing so..."

"No problem. We'll take one of the CB's with us. You ought a be able to reach us on it if needed."

"Cool. Thanks."

"You ready?" I asked Karen, now clad in her heavy coat, knitted mittens, and boots.

"Yep. And there's hot cider on the stove, and some cinnamon sticks in mugs. Help yourself."

"Thanks," John said.

"I'll stay here, too, Libby said. "The girls are upstairs, and that cider sounds good."

Karen responded quietly, "Don't forget there's some of that homemade apple brandy in the kitchen...."

"Thanks. I might partake."

Outside, Karen and I climbed into the back seat of the Humvee, with the Corporal driving and another soldier, literally riding shotgun. In ten minutes, we were standing in the Valley Hospital conference room.

"Mr. Drummond, thank you for coming. I hope I didn't disturb your evening too much. I'm Major Elaine Cross." The Major was dressed in her digital camo uniform and winter gear. Her striking red hair and freckles made her look much younger than she ought as a major...

"Major, this is my wife, Karen. Pleased to meet you," I said as I shook her hand. "I don't think I've met many female officers in the Forty-First."

"There are a few of us. I've just been assigned to Spokane after a couple months in Lewiston."

"Major, what brings us here tonight?"

"Sir, my daylight counterpart is Major George. I believe you met him today. Your Townsman, Mr. Weathers, floated a pretty good idea today. That idea has been ordered into effect immediately by General Anderson. That's one reason I needed to talk to you. There is another."

"What idea is that?" Karen asked. I hadn't filled her in on it, because I figured it had a snowballs' chance of actually taking place.

"An armed compound on the east side of Coeur d'Alene Lake has been raiding adjacent properties, and is responsible for the deaths of a half-dozen law enforcement officers and fourteen Army soldiers."

I cut her off. "Since when? It was two dead this morning."

"Since six-thirty this evening. The aerial operation will commence in less than an hour. Should the compound not surrender immediately, further aerial operations will eliminate the threat. Ground forces will then conduct mop-up operations beginning at first light."

"Good God. You're going to bomb them?" Karen asked with no small amount of alarm.

"Yes, ma'am. Hopefully, once. They have had ample opportunity to surrender, but they have instead acted with more aggression towards both civilian forces and the military. General Anderson agreed that it is a better use of resources in a combined operation rather than a protracted use of ground forces."

"This has been going on for a while, hon," I told Karen. "OK, I said. So why am I really here?" I asked the major.

"Your counterparts in Kootenai and Benewah counties were threatened directly by the leadership of this compound this morning. They are in protected locations at this time."

"OK. You think it's a problem for me, too? Security?"

"You have made some enemies."

"But you don't have any evidence that Rick or our family are in danger, do you?" Karen asked.

"No, ma'am. Better safe than sorry though. There are bigger issues at play here, with regards to the population of this compound. They are politically very highly connected to both the Federal and the Rebellion leaderships, as well as international banking cartels. They have been supplied by outside forces—outside of this region— since April. Those shipments, brought into the Coeur d'Alene airport as well as a private airstrip, ceased at the end of September. That is not public knowledge. Intel doesn't know why they have not acted like their eastern counterparts."

141

"Maybe they have, with all this 'coincidental' looting and whatnot today. Maybe today is their day."

"That may well be. In any regard, we'd like you to remain at your residence or under military protection until this is over."

"You think they have plants over here?" I asked.

"Yes. Most certainly. Those that have been identified through our local intel resources will be rounded up within the next three hours."

"How many?"

"I'm not at liberty to say at this point, and frankly, the numbers are fuzzy."

"All right. Let's talk about communications. Do they have military gear, and have they the capability to listen in on what are supposed to be secure communications? If so, that's going to raise Hell with normal police operations."

"That is what they believe, yes. It is not entirely true. One of our combat communications squadrons has seen to that."

"You're gaming them," Karen said.

"Yes, we are, Mrs. Drummond. You've seen the A-10 Warthogs, flying in over the past few days?"

"Pretty hard not to. They were at maybe, fifteen hundred feet," I said.

"You didn't see or hear, the Raptors. They've come in on the same flight path, at night though, and without anti-collision lights on, following above and just behind the A-10's. The A-10's were the diversion for the F-22's."

"You've been expecting this to come to a head," I said.

"There is a date that has been held pretty close to the vest, which is the second reason I needed to speak with you. That day is tomorrow, the day that new Federal currency is to start arriving at major population centers throughout the United States, in new Federal banks. The money is being delivered via Air Force transport aircraft."

"And about damned time. We can't have a functioning economy without physical money."

"Actually, Spokane and most of the Pacific Northwest Command is doing pretty well comparatively speaking from what I understand, if not for lack of adequate money to go around."

"My point," I said. "That's one concern that I can perhaps think less about…or more correctly, shift my concerns elsewhere."

"Ever the happy bunny, aren't you?" Karen said. "Major, exactly where are these 'Federal Banks' supposed to be? Most of our banks were sacked after the Domino."

"Fourteen locations within the utility service area have been identified as being viable for repair within ten days."

"Ten days won't cut it, Major. If people get wind that there's 'money' to be available for currency, you'll have riots unless you have some method to make it available and quickly."

"I have not seen the Federal plans for this, Mr. Drummond, only regarding the shipment, and that I could inform appropriate authorities within twenty-four hours of the scheduled arrival."

"When do I…sorry, 'we' find out about the rest of the plan?"

"I would suspect an announcement from the Federal level tomorrow. Word will spread, it's inevitable."

"It is."

"Mr. Drummond, I'll keep a squad on guard around your home tonight, in addition to the men already assigned. I'll have your driver take you home, when you're ready."

"Now's good," I said.

"A few minutes, Rick. I want to pop by the nursery first."

Major Cross looked at Karen, and was about to ask a question, but I responded first.

"My wife—baby magnet."

"I understand. I have two myself."

"Here in town?" Karen asked.

"Not yet. Still in Lewiston with my Mom. I haven't found a place to move them to up here yet. I lost my husband and my father down south."

"The war?"

"Yes," the Major said quietly. "They were at University Medical Center...my husband was working in ER that day, my dad in the pharmacy. Truck bomb went off. One of the first around the country."

"I'm very sorry," Karen said. Elaine nodded.

"Major, you come see us tomorrow at our place," I said. "We have a number of empty houses in the neighborhood that are almost ready to move into. You'd be welcome to choose, and we'd be happy to have you."

"I couldn't possibly," she said. "I'm sure that...."

"None of that now. You can certainly. I'm serious. Think it over and come by tomorrow. It sounds like I'll be home."

She was quiet for a moment or two, before she answered with a little waver in her voice. "Thank you. I will."

Tuesday morning,
October Twenty-Fourth

I woke up before sunrise again, my side hurting again, although sharper today. Finally I decided to get up, after thrashing around for half an hour. I heard the wind above my head, and wondered what magic weather system we were going to experience today. Karen slept soundly, even with both dogs doing their morning 'shake' and stretch. I could make it on a couple hours of sleep, it seemed I'd been doing it for months, with or without pain meds, prescription or improvised. Anything more than three hours of continuous sleep, since August, was something that I regarded as a very rare luxury.

I'd set my clothing out the night before in the bath, anticipating a relatively normal day. Looking out the bathroom window, I could see that we had a clear morning coming, even if it was windy. Some of the recent snow was drifting up around the fences, and our path to the woodshed was all but invisible.

After my shower, I made my way to the kitchen, and remembered our old tradition of breakfast for our soldiers guarding "our" store, or watching our backs for us right after the Domino. I decided that whatever troops might be watching over us might appreciate something other than whatever reconstituted or military chow they were eating these days.

It'd been a long time since I'd made a frittata, but today was the best day to do it, since it was the first day I'd thought of it. I stretched my memory back to remember how big a 'squad' was. Nine or ten guys...or gals...depending, I thought, on mission. Ancient knowledge from my early twenties came back to me. Knowledge that I'd just as soon not have memory of at all and had done my best to forget. Seven months, sixteen days in duration. An eternity to forget. It was three years before the nightmares ended....

The best thing about my frittata recipe is that it was pretty much built from whatever was on hand, whenever I decided to make it. Kind of a fluid thing.

"Three frittatas," I said to Buck, who was looking for breakfast. "No, probably four. Enough for us and our friends in green. Buck, do you know where Mom keeps those extra skillets?"

He looked at me of course, as if I'd asked him, 'Would you like a nice, fresh steak?'

"Didn't think so, thanks."

The recipe today would be a variable design of necessity. I knew we had dried peppers, whole and dried onions, eggs, Joe's proprietary Italian sausages, some bacon cooked up a day or two before wrapped up in the fridge, fresh milk and cream, dried parsley, oregano and rosemary, and some local cheese that passed for Parmesan. And some fresh wheat mini-loaves that Kelly had made yesterday…and some butter. The real thing these days expensive, but so much better than margarine from the old days.

I dug out the necessary gear, finding it after some searching. I'd never really figured out Karen's kitchen stashing methods after I'd remodeled the kitchen five years before, which had only changed again with new cabinets in half of the kitchen this year after the Domino.

A half hour later, I was loading the oven with two of the four cast iron skillets, the third ready to go, when Karen came in, complete with fuzzy slippers and thick robe.

"Forget to start the fire? It's freezing in here! Frittata? What's the occasion? It's been years."

"I was awake, and thought our local protectors might like something other than mil chow. Sorry about the fire."

"You like taking care of them," she said as she snuck up behind me and wrapped me up in a big hug.

"Reason to," I replied. "They keep us free," I said, remembering again to myself, a group of nameless men that saved me and a few others half a world away.

Breakfast was a little after seven, or a little before sunrise today, and we served our nine guardians in shifts of five and four. I didn't want to get anyone in trouble with their higher-ups, so some of them stayed technically 'on guard' while the others ate. Karen was her traditional self as gracious hostess, with Carl and Kelly providing outstanding service as servers and coffee-deliverers—the real thing, from a stash of Costa Rican coffee that went back to pre-War days. Once I had put the last skillet in the oven I'd prodded the kids out of bed and filled them in on our morning task, and what other surprises were coming our way this day. I was able to sit and talk to the young men and women, have some coffee and frittata, some bread and butter, and wait for the day.

Elaine Cross arrived just as the last of the guys finished up, all of who quickly came to attention as soon as their C.O. came into the room, one apologizing.

"At ease. You're off duty. It's oh eight-ten."

"Yes, ma'am," was the common response, but for one young soldier.

"Ma'am, there is a serving for you."

"Left me a little, Jenkins? You must still be cruising for that three-day." She was all command officer now sharp and determined.

"No ma'am, this is outstanding chow. That's all."

"Then I assume that you've shown your hosts proper gratitude. Grab your gear and get back to camp. You've enjoyed enough civilian hospitality for a while. Back on shift at sixteen hundred. Inside duty though—you get to be bank guards."

"What the..." Cross cut off her subordinate.

"Civilians present, Patterson."

"Yes, ma'am. Sorry."

"Move it. I want your report on my desk by oh nine-hundred."

"Yes, ma'am."

A few minutes later and the squad was gathered up and headed back to the old Industrial Park, where the Forty-First had a fair number of men and women billeted. Their 'air ops' unit, or what was left of it, was still at Felts Field. Only a few of the helos were used, and sparingly, due to spare parts issues—specifically, rotor blades and avionics. They had converted a fair number of fixed-wing private planes for observation platforms though, and we'd see them up once in awhile.

"Elaine, thanks for coming over. You seem to have a good unit there," I said.

"One of my best. Not that you should tell them that. I don't want them slacking off. You serve?"

"Nope. Diehard civilian," I said, which was technically true, I reminded myself. 'Why was I still thinking about those days?' "Let me get you a cup of coffee."

Karen and Elaine talked over breakfast, where both were able to relax a little. I dished myself up, slathered a half of the mini-loaf of wheat bread with honey-butter, and joined them. And then remembered coffee...

"Hon, why don't you show Elaine the yellow house after breakfast?"

"Funny, that's the one I was thinking of, too," I said. That house had had a young family that evac'd, and never returned. It was one of the last houses that was put back together, needing some foundation repairs and a chimney rebuild. I'd visited during the work, but it was too much for me during my convalescence to do anything but watch....which frustrated me no end.

148

"I actually have to pass on your offer, at least for today," Elaine stated. "I need Mr. Drummond to make a statement regarding the currency distribution. It's a prepared statement that came in this morning from San Francisco. State and local leadership is being asked to provide this statement at eleven a.m. local. You can record it ahead of time if you like. "

"Got a copy of it?" I asked. "I'd be happy to, if it's something that I can agree with. If not, well, then I'm not your guy."

"I have a copy. It's fairly tame, and appears legit."

"Not really worried about the statement, honestly," I said after thinking about my previous statement. "It's the after-effects that I'm worried about. What happens to any population, let alone the ten month long adventure that this part of the country has had, when you do something like this?"

"I have no idea. I don't think anyone does," Elaine said.

"We'd have to go back to other countries that tried this, but I can't think of one where a legitimate currency was introduced— meaning of course, one backed by silver or gold. Each time that, at least as I remember, a country issued 'new' currency it was still paper with different numbers. And you had riots. Argentina comes to mind, but I don't really remember that in much detail," I said.

"Elaine, I'm wondering if you have any news on last night's action over in Idaho. Heard anything?"

"Not officially. What I did hear was that they didn't surrender. First pass took out their command post, which resulted in hostile fire towards our ground units and active jamming of inbound aircraft. Second pass took care of the jammers and whatever EMP device they were using. Ground troops are mopping up, but have had no casualties so far."

"Small comfort," I said. "The older I get, the less I understand."

"In what way?" Elaine replied.

"How, in this country, we have come to this," I said, staring into my coffee mug more than I ought.

"Lust for power, greed, and control of others."

"Sure, those have always been around though. It just seems different now, in that there are those that see literally no consequences to their actions anymore, that acting outside of the law, any law, is OK."

"Absolute corruption, manifest in elements of the general population, on exhibit for all to see. Checks and balances are gone. All that is left, for them anyway, is the opportunity to expand their kingdoms," Elaine said.

"You seem to have experience here, dealing with this type of group," Karen said, forearms on the table, hands holding the coffee mug that Carl had made her in first grade.

"There are groups like this scattered all over the West. Command knows what they're up against. The quiet alliances that keep to themselves and stay within the bounds of the law hardly make the radar unless they did something pre-War to get on the list that Homeland Security had going. They went long on investing in weapons, raw materials, components that might be assembled into something greater than a pile of parts. Many groups though, have elements that are significantly hostile to the interests of the United States. Those groups ARE on the radar screen. Some know their days are numbered. Some groups, maybe like this one, I don't know. The leadership in this group seems to think that they were above the law on all levels. They found out otherwise."

"I think I heard yesterday that this group had connections—high connections," I said.

"They did. Intricate and deep connections to European and the old American financial system, insurance, real estate, Democrat, Green, and Republican party leadership positions on national and state levels. Connections in religion, industry, pharmaceuticals, and the military."

"The repercussions ought to be damned interesting to watch play out," I said.

"I don't know if I'd use the word 'interesting.' 'Dangerous' might be more appropriate. And we're smack dab on the front lines."

"Well we do live in interesting times..." I said, heading to the kitchen for cleanup duty, and to get another cup of coffee.

Elaine chatted with Karen as I cleaned up the disaster that I'd made in the kitchen. Alan and Mary joined us for late coffee, after hearing that the curfew was extended throughout the day, and Carl and Kelly had politely taken some of the last frittata, warmed it up in the dented microwave, and retreated back to their rooms on hearing that the curfew had limited their normal routine. I'm sure there'd be plenty for them to do around the house anyway.

Both of our kids had really applied themselves--I couldn't forget Marie and John though, as I knew that they were exceeding all expectations---in their home-schooling and their limited classroom time at the local composite school, excelling past where they would have with pre-War classes. Carl should have been in 'sophomore' classes, but in reality was midway through where a 'junior' would be, and would be near the top of his class, should University High School still operate as a twelve-hundred student organization, or Central Valley School District still exist at all. Valley Composite was akin to a small community school, with kindergarten through high school, as well as some college-level classes that were more real-world lessons in practical matters of medical care, food preservation and animal husbandry. Six composite schools in the Valley area, six more within the old borders of the City of Spokane, and scattered schools around the county in resurgent small towns. If we could get better transportation going on a larger scale without feeling we were risking life or precious fuel unnecessarily, we might actually get to have organized sports teams compete again. Wouldn't that be something.

The radio in the kitchen provided much rumor and little news of the overnight news blackout, yet no excuse or reason. There were reports of fighting gained through shortwave, in New York City, New Jersey, Richmond, Washington, D.C., and Philadelphia. No reports of fighting west of the Mississippi.

151

By nine, the kitchen had been restored to a semblance of its former self, although I'm sure Karen would be hunting for an implement or three the next time she cooked. Given the interruption in the daily routine, I decided to pack up the kids and head to the community center. They could spend a little time with at the orphanage, I could take care of the speech maybe I could end up back at the store in the afternoon. Maybe I could just goof off for a change and hang out. Karen and Elaine, as well as Alan and Mary were talking, although now in the living room, about all the work we'd done to put our house back together.

"Don't worry—your place didn't get hit as hard as this one did. And I didn't work on the repairs over there. So you have a better than average chance that things are done right," I said in my self-deprecating tone.

"Nonsense. You're a good contractor," Karen said.

"If slow equals good maybe."

"Quit now," Karen said.

"Anyway, it's a nice place. We can look at it later. Everyone ready?" I asked.

"Should be," Karen said. "We'll follow you over. I think you're supposed to go escorted."

"He is," Elaine said. "Although we can bend the rules a little."

"I'm good at that," I said.

I had an audience for the address, including most of the Community Center duty staff and my family. The speech was recorded by one of the "com Nazi's"—an Air Force communication specialist, as labeled by one of the Army captains. In the former state of the military, our recording engineer was assigned to a combat communications squadron based out at Four Lakes, west of Fairchild. These days he was reduced to recording a speech by a low level reluctant bureaucrat for the consumption of a probably disinterested public.

152

"Good morning, this is Rick Drummond, Administrator for Spokane County. I'm speaking to you this morning regarding several issues, the first of which comes from the United States Government. At this hour, a similar address is being made to the rest of the country by local officials, regarding the distribution of new legal currency that will begin within the next few days across the country. I am reading, by the way, from a prepared statement that was provided to me, and I have reviewed this document and if what has been provided to me is in fact true, I believe that this may be a significant step in the economic recovery of the United States."

"At this hour, transports are arriving in major cities with new Federal currency in the form of silver and gold coins, which have been designed as an update to historic legal tender in the United States and her territories. These coins include silver coinage virtually identical to ninety-percent silver coinage in wide circulation until Nineteen Sixty-four in standard denominations; and gold coins in general circulation until it was confiscated in the First Great Depression. Gold coinage will be provided in limited quantities in denominations from One Dollar to Twenty Dollars. On January First, printed currency redeemable on demand for silver or gold will be available in limited locations. By July first, these new currencies will be fully implemented nationwide."

"Within the next two weeks, a one-time distribution of two hundred dollars will be made to every man and woman over the age of sixteen years of age, across the nation and within territories and protectorates. It is the intention of the Federal Government that these monies be used to help jump-start local economies through the purchase of needed goods and services, and that these funds remain in circulation. These funds will be distributed through new Federal Banks that will be established nationwide. Specific distribution instructions will be distributed nationwide within the next few days. This ends the formal statement provided to me. I do have some additional comments if you would bear with me," I said, going off script.

"Everyone in this community has faced adversity. That adversity sometimes comes at the hands of your neighbors. Everyone in this community needs to be able to depend on their neighbor for their safety and security. We are really a mutual aid society. If you cannot do this, then none of us are really safe—I'm deadly serious here. You need to be able to trust your immediate neighbors with your life.

There are those among us responsible for looting, for theft, for robbery, for murder. As long as these people are among the peaceful and law-abiding citizens of this county, and of this region, you are not safe. These people need to be identified and held accountable. For some of you, these are your neighbors. You know where and who they are. Every neighborhood has a police or sheriff's precinct several have National Guard militia centers. If you need help, please use the law enforcement resources you have available. If you need to defend yourself, do so. But do so within reason. We need to work together to ensure that this County is ruled by law, not by fear, not by armed force, not by threats. I suspect there are far more firearms in the hands of the private citizen than either the police and the military, and that is the way it ought to be."

"We face a long winter obviously. We're rebuilding our economy, and we have sufficient supplies of food, even though it's not all that exciting in variety. There are more physical dollars in circulation. With physical money, and an understandable desire to keep it close and keep it safe, there comes increased risk for everyone. Be prudent, be cautious, be safe with your money. To those among us that see this as an opportunity to relieve your neighbors of their money, remember this: You may be paying for that mistake with your life."

"Every adult over the age of sixteen has been required over the past few months to undergo firearms training. The vast majority of adults 'carry.' Don't think for a minute that punishment for robbery or theft will be treated in pre-War terms. It won't. Punishment is severe and swift once law enforcement officers are engaged but more likely punishment might be meted out at the hand of your intended victim. A number of those caught in theft and robbery do survive though, to serve a lengthy sentence turning large chunks of broken concrete in to gravel, cleaning twisted rebar of concrete, and assignments in some of the most difficult or unpleasant areas imaginable. So please do consider your path carefully."

"Thank you, and as I stated earlier, additional information will be forthcoming on our new currency. Good day."

"Got it. Good job, sir. One take and you're outta here."

"I hate public speaking. Face for radio and all."

The airman laughed at that. "Me too, sir. Broadcast will go out at eleven hundred. Want a copy?"

"Nope. Not even a little bit. Thanks, though," I said as I stood to go.

"No problem, sir. Have a good day."

'That'd be a welcome change.' I thought to myself.

Outside of Kevin Millers' partially glassed office, my entourage waited, minus our kids.

"Where'd the kids end up?"

"Orphanage. Rousing game of duck-duck-goose," Karen said as we headed down the hall.

"We good to go, Kevin? Elaine?"

"Far as I'm concerned, yes," Elaine replied. "I need to go look at a house," she said, looking over at Karen.

"Kevin? Things going OK today?"

"No more thefts, which is a good thing. Might have something to do with fresh snow and tracks...."

"Or it might have something to do with the desert-camo Bradley in the front lot," Alan said with a chuckle, referring to the Bradley Fighting Vehicle parked in a relatively aggressive manner.

"Funny how that works," Kevin said.

"All Centers have a temporary detachment at least until curfew's been lifted. All storehouses too," Elaine said.

"That's gotta leave you stretched pretty thin," Kevin replied.

"Most are manned by neighborhood militiamen, so not to worry," Elaine said. "Let's go look at that house," she urged. She and Karen headed down to round up our kids as Alan and I waited.

155

"Kevin, let us know if you need anything," I said as I shook hands with him.

"I'll do that. I'll be talking with your cohorts later this week with some candidates for you. Got some good ones in the last in-migration."

"Good to hear. Made it through your pre-screening, huh?" I asked.

"Or I wouldn't be talking about them. Yep."

"Thanks. I…we owe you."

"No prob. See you later," he said as he headed back to his office.

"Ayup," I replied, echoing my late father.

Tuesday afternoon,
October Twenty-fourth,
3:00 p.m.

Bank of the West was now branded, 'Federal Bank.' Not exactly an imaginative name, but they did have a colorful logo, with a stylized profile of Thomas Jefferson. No idea what the symbolism was supposed to foster in the mind of the artist. I supposed they were aiming for 'trust.' It seemed to miss the mark, for me at least.

Federally-hired contracting crews were shipped in on Air Force transport early in the day, and were tasked with rehabilitating and re-branding local branch banks in more than a dozen locations in the redefined 'urban area.' Fourteen different crews, one per location, each equipped specifically to refurb their particular building as quickly and efficiently as possible.

It was a minor miracle of organization, certainly unlike anything that I'd witnessed in my experience with large government.

The McDonald Road building was constructed in the early Seventies, strong through its bulky reinforced concrete shell and large interior vault, weak through the triple glazed storefront. That storefront had now been almost completely replaced with ballistic and blast-resistant glazing and frames; doors replaced in a similar manner, and work had been organized to create a force-protection zone around a perimeter, similar if not identical to pre-War Federal buildings.

Our 'skeleton crew' workforce at County Administration was covering things for the day without any interference from me, although I could have gone to the office without too much trouble. Curfew operations weren't exactly routine, but there was a procedures manual in place now for the eventuality. Used a dozen times since the spring, refined a little each time.

I managed to find things to do out of the office that were still marginally within my scope of work, after dropping Karen and the gang off at the house. I was sure that Elaine would take us up on the offer for a new place to live, and I thought she'd be a good fit for the neighborhood and the house a good fit for her and her family as well.

I'd decided, after getting an OK from the Army and Karen (not in that order), to 'blend in' a little as a 'regular' County employee, and not 'the boss.' One of the maintenance shops happened to be located six blocks from the bank project, where the day-shift supervisor, also the caretaker who lived on site, checked me out a fairly well thrashed Chevy three-quarter ton diesel utility truck, and with a little negotiation in the form of some County vouchers for the employee warehouse, I paid for confidentiality. There was one work crew assigned to the bank, to ensure that utilities were operational and any of the needs of the Federal team were met.

I decided to assign myself to that team. I'd figure out a cover story along the way.

I arrived at the bank to find two Humvees with mounted machine guns on opposite corners of the property, providing a nice field of fire on all sides. The County vehicles were parked outside the perimeter, where I was directed to park as well. The parking area had been plowed all the way down to asphalt, a rare condition in this County this year. My truck was minus its two-way radio, so I went over to the Supervisors truck to 'check-in'.

"Afternoon. They got any work over here for us?" I asked.

"No, sir. Not a blamed thing. Everything's up and running, but we're not supposed to leave until they're done. Three hours we've been sitting on our asses."

"Swell."

"Aren't you supposed to be behind a desk somewhere?" a voice asked from behind. Mike Amberson.

"Sheriff, nice to see you," I replied, shaking his gloved hand. The supervisor nodded, maybe figuring things out, maybe not. I figured that pretending to be someone else was a bad idea, and gave it up. Mike was almost immediately distracted by a radio call, and moved back to his cruiser, a few feet behind my beat up Chevy.

"You a desk driver?" the supervisor asked.

"I have been accused of that, but I'm not in my chosen profession. Field work suits me more often than not, and I hate meetings. I'm Rick Drummond."

"Ryan Wizensky. So you're the head desk driver."

"Only when necessary."

"Well, I'll tell you, boss," Wizensky said in a matter-of-fact way, "these guys have their act together. After we activated utilities, they escorted us to the property line and we've just been watching the show. Those two flatbeds out front have everything they need to put this place back together. Those three semi-trailers over there have a job shack, kitchen and bunkhouse. There's fifty-odd men on this job right now, and none of 'em has made anything that looks like a wasted move."

"Escorted?" I asked.

"Yeah, as in, 'Get the Hell outta my way and off-a my job.'"

"Are they contractors?" I wondered.

"Well they aren't Army Corps of Engineers. First thing they did was set up a countdown clock. Twenty-four hours and this place is supposed be done."

"You heard that from the workers?"

"One of the glaziers, yeah, before those Special Forces boys shooed him back inside. Didn't look real happy to have one of their contracting boys outside of their comfort zone."

"Hmmm," I said. "So none of our guys have been inside since they got here?"

"Nope. But we haven't really any business in there."

"Maybe I'll take a little walk."

"Good luck with that," Wizensky said. "They get outta hand and we'll toss a wrench at them."

"You don't carry?" I asked in disbelief.

"Sorry. My 'wrench' is a 30.06."

"Gotcha," I said.

Mike had climbed back in his unit, taking some notes on a small pad. I decided that maybe a trip inside the 'perimeter' was a good idea when accompanied by law enforcement. Maybe not such a good idea when going incognito. I let myself in on the passenger side.

"How's your day going?" I asked when he was done on the radio.

"Lousy. Yours?"

"Better than lousy. What's up?"

"Four Regular Army dead last night. Patrol didn't check in. Found their bodies at thirteen-hundred. All their gear gone, and their truck."

"Where?"

"West Central. Also lost a State Trooper last night in Chewelah, and two reserve police officers in Pullman."

"Is it a stretch that these are connected?"

"No, since all of them were head shots at distance, and all of them were stripped of their uniforms and gear."

I stood there I'm sure looking like an idiot, trying to make some sense of it.

"You'll figure it out in a minute," Mike said. "Work the evidence," Mike said. "You will not like the answer."

"Somebody's gathering up current issue uniforms of law enforcement and military. They've already proven they're good enough or patient enough to learn the pattern language of patrol schedules and put together a series of relatively coordinated attacks. The only questions are 'who they are' and 'when do they act.'"

"Right."

"But the only important question is 'when.' Doesn't matter 'who.'"

"Right again."

"Well the only conclusion on 'when' is 'now,' or relatively soon. Nothing else would work, someone will put things together."

"Three for three."

"You think the banks are the target?"

"Honestly, I think the banks are the distraction. I think the murders are, too. Instill fear."

"What're the targets then?"

"Everything else. Step one, instill fear."

"What?"

"Do you think it's the slightest bit coincidental that nationwide within the space of a day or two, the socialist experiment finally collapses with the assassination of their 'president', that we have a new 'banking system' arrive just when we need it, and little riots and pinprick attacks happen all over the country?"

"No, not really. I thought that it was probably part of the New Republic sympathizers. But I'm having a hard time connecting all of this. You said 'step one.'"

"Right. Create fear in the population. We've had that in spades since January. Complete the decades-long destruction of their money. Threaten their health. Wipe out their food supply. Steal from them. Deprive them of security. Then come riding in on your white horse and save the day. The population will view you as their saving grace."

Mike was right. I didn't like the answer that was coming into view.

"And I delivered a speech that was playing right into somebody's hand."

"Since it was the same speech more or less all around the country, yeah. Probably correct."

"All right, let's play that angle. That can only mean one thing. That what is passing for the Federal government has tipped over into something decidedly ugly."

"That is exactly correct."

I sat there and looked at the dash, then outside to the bank.

"So how close are we to the heart of evil, I wonder?"

"Hundred and twenty feet, my guess. Problem being is that there are too many hearts to this beastie."

"What do you know about this work crew?" I asked, pointing to the bank.

"All the workers flew in on Air Force transports first thing this morning. Trucks came in on a special freight train last night, fully loaded and ready to go. Special Forces troops, and all their gear by the way, are from Eastern Command in St. Louis, not Northwest Command. They were on the train too, by the way. And they're not real friendly, I hear."

"Wanna see if we can test the perimeter?"

"Sure. I haven't been shot at in almost a whole day," Mike said.

A few minutes later, we were inside, after a casual, nonchalant walk past the sentries and into the glassed—bulletproof glass—vestibule.

"May I help you?" a black uniformed man asked as we entered the lobby space.

"I'm the County Administrator here. This is Sheriff Mike Amberson. Thought we'd see how things are coming along," I said as we shook hands. He did not give his name.

"Well enough," was the cool reply. I looked over his shoulder, and sure-enough, there was the 'countdown clock.' Mike was looking about, as if a tourist. I knew better.

"You folks really know how to move things along."

"We're under contract. Time's money."

"I'm wondering if you still need our county crews out there. They've been sitting around for a while now."

"We might. I'm not at liberty to give orders regarding local support."

"Well, here's the deal. I'm not paying them to sit on their butts in the cold. There's work to do elsewhere, and if you're not using them, they're outta here."

"Not my call," he said, before calling out to someone who may or may not have been his superior. An inverted pyramid of a man came out of the front office cluster over to us in the lobby.

"Problem?" he asked, with no introductions.

"They're pulling the locals," our first contact replied.

"No, you're not. We're not done with them."

"So three hours of them sitting in trucks is productive?"

"Don't really care about their productivity. I care about ours."

163

"We're done here," I said as I turned and headed for the door, with Mike getting there ahead of me.

"And you are who?" the Pyramid asked.

"The County Administrator."

"You're aiming to get arrested."

That got my attention. "You threatening me?"

"Damned straight I am. I'm not working for you locals, I'm working for the Federal Government."

"Well, then you oughta get acquainted with our local law enforcement situation. In this county, the Sheriff is the law. That includes superseding any Federal order or command if it's unconstitutional. Power comes from the people, not from the government. I take it you haven't heard that yet?"

"Don't really care what your rules are. I know what mine are, and mine win. Constitution's been suspended, and I'm getting paid to do a job."

Mike replied. "Since you've not provided your name, let me inform you of this: In this state, the Constitution is the law of the land first and foremost. That might not be the case elsewhere, but here, that's the way it is. Consider your actions carefully, sir, when in this County."

"What a load of crap. Get out of my bank."

"Your bank?" I asked.

"I'll be the manager of this branch when we're done with the re-fit."

"Then you'll be well shy of customers, if the so-called Federal Banks aren't operating under Constitutional law," I answered.

"When people get tired enough, they'll be here. Just wait."

"Where are you from anyway?" Mike asked.

"None of your damned business."

"Watch your step in this county, sir. You will not receive a further warning."

That received a string of expletives in reply.

"We're done here," I said to Mike and our difficult 'contractors.' "Let's send the boys on to their next job," I said, not knowing if they had any other tasks for this shift.

"Do that and our security forces will deal with you," was the reply from behind me.

"OK, fair enough," I said. "Mike, let's head outside and have a little talk."

Outside, it was beginning to darken with the lateness of the day and the increasing heavy overcast. It felt like snow again.

"You ready to take this on?" Mike asked.

"Call up our friends in the Forty First to weigh in on this before I poke them in the eye again."

"Condor," Mike said to his shoulder microphone, "You got that?" He tilted his head slightly, listening in on a very inconspicuous earbud.

"Good. Confirm ETA and force strength," Mike said to his radio. Mike was listening to the reply, without looking like he was listening. A full minute passed before I could interrupt him.

"You got all this on radio?"

"Had a feeling about it. Set it up before you got into my unit. Forty-First command was listening live. We'll know in a few minutes what kind of response we'll get."

"What do you think about all that 'Constitution's been suspended' talk?"

"Stands to reason if you're taking over and want a clean sweep, don't you think?"

"Clumsy strategy though," I said.

"Clumsy maybe, but we're still several steps behind them, and you can bet there are people—a whole lot of people—who are willing to let them run roughshod."

"Yeah, probably true," I said. "It does make one wonder, if these men are in fact military, or mercenary."

"There will certainly be a conversation on who's in command, and the nature of an illegal order, I suspect," Mike said as his eyes moved from one Humvee to the other. We were being watched, quite noticeably. Mike was distracted again by someone speaking in his ear.

"Affirmative. Holding in place with Mr. Drummond."

I stood there, waiting for his delivery.

"Ten minutes."

"Good enough," I said. "Do we dare go get in our cars?"

"Nope. That gunner behind you just tweaked his mount toward us. I think standing here is just fine," Mike said.

"Showdown."

"More like Mexican Standoff."

"We're a little outgunned. I've got my .45 and four mags, not a frickin' machine gun."

"Not for very long we're not. We have three general officers on our side, and their entire commands."

"That'll do," I said, more than happily surprised.

Mike and I made small talk, me kidding him about his twins and sleep deprivation, him kidding me about being an old fart with high-school age kids, getting wiser by the day. Less than ten minutes after we'd heard that the Forty-First would send a response, I could hear the echo of a Blackhawk...or two...which we hadn't heard in weeks. Helos just didn't fly much anymore due to the lack of spare parts. I looked over at Mike.

"Yeah, I hear it, too," Mike said, remaining non-chalant.

"Gunners don't seem to think anything unusual, though."

"Tourists," Mike replied.

I heard the A-10 only a moment before I saw it, popping up over the trees to the north, passing low over us, and immediately snapping into a tight circle as the startled Humvee gunners obviously wondered what to do. The Hog snapped back to level and headed further east, probably for a similar action at another bank. By then though, two Blackhawks were in shooting positions, and ground troops were moving into a perimeter across the street and behind cover on the back side of the property.

I looked over at the main entry to the bank as the 'manager' came outside, as he was ordered to stand down over a bullhorn. The western Humvee gunner made a false move and was warned off any further futile action with a burst of fire from one of the helos. I'd never seen anything chew up pavement like that before....

Mike and I didn't have much of a chance to move, let alone speak. When I finally came to my senses, I said to Mike, "I didn't know they put mini-guns on Blackhawks."

"Learn something new every day," was his reply. He was obviously as surprised as I was at the response that the military had forwarded. A moment later, ground troops passed us and took the bank. Mike was listening to something on his earbud again, for a couple of minutes.

"I think we can send the boys home now," I said.

"Yeah, and you better tell Karen that you're headed with me to a meeting."

"I am?"

"You are. We are required at Felts Field at seventeen-hundred hours."

"Let me guess."

"No need. Pacific Northwest Command is shuttling together the leadership in the region into meetings like this one. We're being teleconferenced together with the Governor to talk about a Constitutional crisis."

"Crisis?" I asked. "Heck. I'da called it a revolt."

Tuesday afternoon,
October Twenty-fourth,
4:50 p.m.

The 'conference room' was a hangar, with a video projection of the State seal showing on the sidewall, textured with rippled sheet metal, torqued in the earthquake. The entire hangar looked as if it had been twisted from the top down—the main doors didn't open after the Domino, and the side doors didn't seal all that well. The Guard, and later the Army, converted the big metal box to training space and set up some cubicles in the back end of the building.

"Coffee's ready, ladies and gentlemen," a young corporal announced. "And it's real coffee for a change."

"Good, I'm freezing," Karen said to me, poking me on my good side.

"Get some for me, too please!" Mary added.

"I live to serve," I said in a *'Princess Bride'* kind of way.

We'd stopped by the house on the way over to the base to tell Karen that I'd been summoned to a meeting with Mike. Alan and Mary were at the house getting some sewing supplies, and Mike extended an invitation to them to come along. Ron and Libby were tasked with keeping an eye on things while we were gone—which we hoped wouldn't be too long.

On the way over, Mike and I recapped the afternoon and the surprisingly forceful response from the Army and the Guard to what we thought might just be a local misunderstanding. Seeing the 'bank manager' and his associates face-down on the snowy asphalt, hands and feet zip-tied, and then roughly loaded into a military truck, told us that this was probably much more. We also didn't glean anything from the incident commander, other than being directed to be on time for the briefing.

Alan joined me in the coffee line, where I noticed that we had Styrofoam cups waiting for us, already filled but not 'dressed' with cream or sugar.

"Look it there. When was the last time you saw a foam cup?"

"Last January. Could be from old stocks, you never know."

A disembodied voice announced that the conference would begin in three minutes, booming through the overly large speakers flanking the video image.

"Mr. Drummond?" someone asked me from behind.

"Yes?" I said as I turned around to see who it was. "Hey, Dub. You got roped into this too?" I asked of Dub Henshaw, one of our County building inspectors.

"Well, sort of. I was out here looking at roof loads and wandered in."

"You took my question on snow loads yesterday to heart then?"

"Absolutely, especially after getting news about a dozen roof collapses in Newport, Priest River and Sandpoint this morning."

"How're we looking here?"

"Better, but just."

"Dub, I'm sorry. This is Alan Bauer, my brother-in-law. Alan, Dub Henshaw."

"Pleasure," Dub said as he shook Alan's hand. "Nice belt," he commented to Alan. Alan was sporting a new hand-tooled belt for his sidearm-of-the-day. Today, it was his Colt Anaconda.

"Thanks. Hired one of my neighbors to build this rig."

"I'll need to talk to him about some work," Dub said, still looking at the detail on the belt.

"I'll put you in touch." I said. "Sounds like we're about ready for the meeting."

"Don't get away until I talk to you about snow removal teams. Another six inches of snow here and we're gonna see problems," Dub said.

"No problem. Let's talk when this is over."

"Done."

Over in the third row, Karen and Mary were eagerly awaiting their coffee.

"This place is a meat-locker!" Karen said. She'd probably underdressed for the meeting. Mary certainly had.

"Sure it is. One little wood stove in an uninsulated metal building isn't gonna heat things much," Alan said.

"Who was that guy you were talking with?" Karen asked.

"Building inspector for the County. Structural engineer. He's looking at snow-loads on low-profile roofs in the service area."

"Worried they're going to collapse?"

"They sure could, yeah. It's October and we've got January snow. What'll we have in January?"

"How do you take care of that?"

"Clear the roofs off, by hand."

"Fun," she said as she sipped her coffee.

"Not remotely. But it might keep a few hundred or a thousand people working over the winter."

"Assuming you can pay them."

"Sure, there you go throwing cold, hard fact at me again," I said with a grin.

"Somebody's got to. And I have a license."

"Indeed."

Those still standing were being prompted to sit down, as a countdown appeared on the screen's lower right corner.

"Ladies and Gentlemen, Governor David Hall of Washington, Governor Mark Santiago of Oregon, Governor Earl Westra of California, Governor Samantha Merrick of Idaho, thank you for your presence at this briefing this evening. General Robert Anderson, commanding general of the Pacific Northwest Command, will make a short statement to those viewing this, before Governor Gregory's prepared statement."

"*Well, doggies,*" I said quietly in my best Jed Clampett imitation. That received a poke from Karen.

"Good evening," the General said from behind a lectern, one that I thought I recognized from Fort Walla Walla. "I am here to present to you information that will be made public within the next four hours regarding the discovery of information about pending Federal actions upon the populace of the United States and her territories."

"These discoveries were made by Pacific Northwest Command and shared with Central and Southern Commands, and can only be regarded as a direct attack on the Constitutional rights of the citizens of the U.S. I am here to provide an outline of the proposed actions of the Federal government against the States and the local population."

"Holy sh•t," someone behind me said. I agreed. Karen squeezed my hand.

"Within the past several days, announcements have been made hastily, regarding the re-establishment of a Federal currency throughout the U.S. and her Territories. The monetary system was presented as following similar or identical standards to those

172

historically in effect while the U.S. was on the 'Gold Standard.' What we have discovered, however, is that while the coinage is similar in size and denomination to older silver and gold-content coins, they bear little physical resemblance. Of more importance the rules under which the new Federal banks are to operate place unreasonable restrictions on the people. Let me first explain how this information was gathered, and then I will elaborate on the Federal banking plan."

"Intel," the General said as he looked down at the lectern. "Intelligence was gathered through civilian and military means within the financial industry and within the United States Department of the Treasury, Federal Bank division. Much of this information was unsolicited and forwarded to intelligence personnel for analysis. We have an exceptionally high degree of confidence that the material is in fact an accurate and comprehensive overview of the Federal plans. Multiple, independent sources have provided similar or complimentary components of the 'Central Economic Recovery Plan,' which is the official title for instituting and controlling economic transactions in the United States."

I looked around the few rows around and in front of me, where I noted both a degree of disgust and anger on the faces.

"On to the banking operations themselves. From our analysts, both in the military and independent and trusted members of the financial community, it appears that the Federal government intends to issue the initial 'distribution' of two hundred dollars, to be held on account at Federal banks, and only to be legally spent at 'federally approved' vendors at 'approved' prices. Existing silver and gold coins will be accepted by Federal banks but not 'approved vendors', and will be removed from circulation. By the end of the next fiscal year, non-approved silver or gold coinage or bullion will be illegal for use in the U.S. and in territorial states."

"Additionally, no transactions of any kind will be legal unless they are conducted with Federally-issued monies, effective on the first day of the new Fiscal Year, next July. This explicitly applies to retail, wholesale, public and private transactions of any kind. In short, if you want to trade someone a steak for two dozen eggs you can't do it legally. Nor can you cash a paycheck anywhere except a

Federal bank, and you can only have a limited amount of 'cash' from that paycheck."

"To summarize, the Federal government wants to control every dime you make and tell you where you can spend it and how you can spend it."

I expected that other video conference rooms were erupting in anger around the West about now. Ours was buzzing, but settled back down quickly.

"To continue, copies of the information collected through various means will be provided to every public official on a flash-drive, to be distributed as you see fit. The files are extensive and voluminous." Images of the documents the general referenced came up on the screen. They seemed quite authentic. Several were on White House stationery. One copy of an executive order bore the signature of the President.

"On to equally serious matters that are only a few weeks away, on the Federal calendar. An outline of planned Constitutional restrictions has surfaced in the last few hours, within the core of the Federal government, including milestones for their adoption by Executive Order and approval by congressional select committee. Recently-dated versions of this information have been discovered at abandoned or captured New Republic strongholds in the Eastern United States within the last three days, providing evidence of high-level collusion between New Republic and Federal leadership, long after known diplomatic contact had ended. These documents, originating within the Executive Branch of the United States Government, intend to abandon the principles on which this country was founded and seek to extinguish the light of freedom and liberty in the name of security and peace."

Now, our room erupted. General Morton ceased speaking to the camera, perhaps hearing the response in several of the feeds from various locations back to Walla Walla. In a couple minutes, our room had settled down, perhaps the others had as well with some prompting. Morton's intensity...or anger...was visible in his eyes if not on his face.

"These restrictions include severely limiting or eliminating many of our basic rights, including a free press, freedom of religion, the right to keep and bear arms, the right to assemble, and dozens more, spelled out in clinical detail. Copies of correspondence regarding this will be provided to public officials, again for publication and distribution as you see fit."

"Ladies and gentlemen, citizens of the United States of America and her territories, the joint United States military commands will not follow illegal orders to circumvent the protections provided under the Constitution of the United States. I would like to assure you that Army, Navy, Air Force, Marine, and Coast Guardsmen throughout the country stand fast and defend our oaths. We will not sweep aside the Constitution and the Bill of Rights as the Executive Branch proposes. To the contrary, we will defend them with our very lives and will tolerate neither fascism nor authoritarian dictatorships. A free and representative republic on this continent will be re-established and will use the Constitution and the providence of God as her guide."

"Ladies and gentlemen, I now present Governor Merrick from the state of Idaho. Governor?"

"Thank you, General Morton. Ladies and gentlemen, you have just heard a brief summary of information collected that represents the intent of the current Federal government to destroy the freedoms of the citizens of the United States. What we're not clear on is the depths of the connections between the New Republic leadership and the Federal leadership, and how events within the past twenty-four to forty-eight hours may be linked to a larger picture."

"I speak to you as the Governor drawing the short-straw. The Governors collected here in Walla Walla, as well as more than a dozen more are making similar briefings to the citizens of their states and territories. We are of a common mind however, in that the states will not stand for these planned actions by the Federal leadership and those pulling their strings."

"I am here to inform the citizens of my state, and those states represented here by their respective Governors, that our states will follow the United States Constitution as legally amended, in the preservation of freedom for our citizens. Actions otherwise by the

175

Federal Government will be regarded as illegal and subject to prosecution in the strongest terms. Actions to limit the movement of citizens, eliminate free trade, seize weapons or control state militias are unacceptable and will not stand."

"To the representatives of the Federal Government that are behind these plots and schemes. We know that you are listening to this or will have this information presented to you. You are being given an ultimatum. You are to resign your office by November first at the latest, and to be replaced by a legally elected replacement. Evidence of illegal actions and planned illegal actions is being gathered for prosecution to the full extent of the law. Refusal of this ultimatum will be regarded as an act of war against these several states."

"To our citizens, I would like to state this. The military forces within the collected states are formidable, and still perhaps the strongest in the world. We believe that the greatest percentage of our active and Guard units will uphold the oath to protect and defend the Constitution, and will not follow the shining path to dictatorship or fascism. State leaderships are united in this belief as originally stated by Jefferson, that the tree of liberty must be refreshed from time to time with the blood of patriots and tyrants."

"As of this hour, all military units under State control are on full alert, and will only respond to legal orders under trusted command and control authority. This applies to strategic forces as well, I am assured."

"None of us asked for this. None of us wants this, but it is here and we stand fast in our beliefs. The United States of America will not be ruled under fascist, totalitarian tactics. To the citizens of these several states, prepare and stand fast. A revolution is on your doorstep," the Governor concluded. "We pray that those of us that believe in the principles of the United States Constitution have the wisdom to see us through this. Good evening, and my prayers are with you all."

Karen was squeezing my hand harder than I thought she might realize. I looked over at her and a single tear rolled down her cheek. I put my arm around her, still seated, and pulled her closer to me. We were probably all in some degree of shock from what we'd just heard and seen.

"It's war," she said quietly. "It's a civil war."

We milled around for a few minutes before an Air Force major tracked me down, and asked me for a few minutes in private. Karen, Alan and Mary waited for me, talking with Dub Henshaw and a few other folks we'd had the opportunity to work with over the past few months. Karen looked worried for me as I was shuttled out of the hangar into an adjacent group of 'temporary' construction trailers. One still bore the name of a former client, Kingsley Construction. I was pleased to see Bruce Weathers in attendance, along with a half-dozen other Metro staff from various departments. Several of them stood as I entered.

"Please, sit. Or in the vernacular, 'at ease.'"

A moment later, General Robert Anderson joined us, minus rank on a digital-camo uniform. Anderson was the ranking officer in the Spokane region, putting him in charge of both ground and air operations. That sometimes didn't sit well with the Air Force side of the table, having a West Point graduate in the pilot seat as it were...

"Ladies and gentlemen, thank you for joining me. As you heard, we have interesting hours and days ahead of us."

"To put it mildly, General," I said. "I've not fought in a revolution before. Is there a how-to manual?" I asked with some humor to lighten things up a bit.

"We have the high ground here, obviously. But there are substantial challenges that we may see come up, which is why you're here. You heard the short version of the presentation, I'd appreciate it if you would take the time to review the documentation in full by the end of tomorrow, and share it liberally. If you didn't get a flash drive with the information yet, please see the warrant officer before you leave."

No one else was speaking up. "What kind of challenges do you see?"

"The Federals still have significant military assets behind them. We don't know to what degree they're willing to pursue this agenda with military force. If they act, we will react. If there is an imminent threat, we will use a pre-emptory strike against their forces."

"Bob, let me ask the zillion dollar question. Nuclear forces?"

"Nuclear weapons formerly controlled by the National Command Authority are now under the sole authority of the Joint Chiefs. Launch code protocols are in place under legal military authority with regional civilian leadership as well. We have complete control over remaining U.S. tactical and strategic nuclear weapons world-wide."

"You're sure."

"We're sure of what we have. Let me clarify. We're sure that pre-War U.S. nuclear forces are under our control. We're not sure of anything acquired black-bag or through New Republic operations on the Eastern Seaboard through smuggling. That might mean that foreign made nuclear weapons or delivery systems might be in Federal control."

I sat there for a few moments, before Bruce Weathers spoke up. "What flashpoints are on the map now, General?"

"Attempted seizures of the majority of Strategic Command forces in multiple locations this afternoon, a complete blockade of traffic into the Denver and St. Louis Federal Areas, and requirements for Federal identification for any travel across state lines or into Federal zones."

"Success on the Strat forces?"

"They took Barksdale, Whiteman, and Tinker Air Force Bases. They attempted to take numerous assets in Texas and were soundly defeated. What they didn't know is that the very few aircraft remaining at those bases are largely hangar queens or parts dogs. Ready aircraft were scrambled when the first illegal orders started showing up. There isn't much left on any of those bases that will prove to be of much use should real shooting start."

"Tinker had Materiel Command and one of the logistics centers...." Bruce said, thinking of the impact.

"Did. Until last May. Materiel Command was shifted to Ogden and Warner-Robins. Didn't want all our eggs in one basket."

"That include spares?"

"It did. Critical-needs parts for remaining weapons systems are no longer present at Tinker. They do have a pile of shot up parts and fried avionics however, marked as 'reserve ready.'"

"How long have you known about this, sir?" Weathers continued.

"I'm not at liberty to say. Longer than you might think."

"So what do they have in terms of military assets?"

"They have a very limited number of air assets, including rotary and fixed wing aircraft. F-15's, a couple –52's, C-17's, a couple AC130's. They have very, very little in the way of ordnance or parts. They do have at least five full divisions of Regular Army and Guard mechanized units, fully capable, and that means pre-War levels."

"What is that," I asked. "Fifty thousand men?"

"Easily that, yes," Anderson responded.

"Navy?"

"All United States naval vessels that survived the war are under control of the Joint Chiefs and regional commands. From what we can determine, the Federals have no viable naval assets. Again, though, we don't know what might be lurking in the East that slipped through U.S. naval patrols," Anderson replied.

"What's the sphincter-level here, sir?" Weathers asked. "These Army units firmly on their side or not?"

"We don't know for sure. We do know that a good thirty percent of them are, and that is certain. We think of those units in terms of the old Iranian Revolutionary Guards. They're the True Believers. It may well be that that thirty percent is making sure the remainder is staying in line."

"Anyone on the inside?" I asked, not expecting an answer.

"Absolutely," Bob replied. "Not everyone is on board with what the Feds are doing. They believed they had significant air assets that vanished quite suddenly. We have multiple sources in multiple units providing intelligence at the risk of summary execution."

"Fair enough," I said. "What's next?"

"Waiting game for the next few hours or days, to see how the Feds react to what the States are demanding. After that, things could go hot on us. We don't know."

"Expectations here? I mean, what do you need from us?" I asked.

"Things go hot, military units could be redeployed within hours. That means dramatic changes in security here locally, transport, infrastructure support and manpower. You know that as well or better than anybody else, Rick."

"I suppose I do," I said, turning over the implications in my head.

"One thing though, Pac Command doesn't suspect any military action in our area. They don't have the assets to come this far, and they have nothing in place up here according to our intel. That's the good news. The bad news is that you'll see a military draft. You'll also probably see refugees come into this area from other parts of the country if it lasts that long."

I heard a buzzer down the hall, reminding me of a cheap alarm clock. A moment later, a burly light colonel came into the room, and whispered something to General Anderson. He straightened up in his chair, if that was possible given his rod-straight posture, and looked out at the table before looking around at us.

"Ladies, gentlemen, I'm afraid we have a shooting war," he said. "Three petroleum refineries in Wyoming and one in Billings, Montana were just attacked and heavily damaged."

I felt as if I were six moves behind in a life-or-death version of chess. "Our fuel came from Billings and from Wyoming, in case anyone was wondering," I said.

"You'll excuse me," General Anderson said. "Apparently I have a war to fight."

1 6

Tuesday night,
October Twenty-fourth,
8:50 p.m.

We were all sort of shell-shocked I think, as we watched the local rebroadcast of our 'president' address the 'nation.' I wondered in silence how many viewers had seen this charade and believed it wholly.

My discernment, or newly formed prejudice, I couldn't decide which, was affecting what I was viewing. More than once I caught myself making snap judgments on half-completed sentences that the 'president' was delivering. Maybe it was fatigue, I just couldn't tell.

"...dominant force in the recovery of the world. We will be the leaders of this arduous task and ask the nation to support these efforts," he said as overly enthusiastic applause rang out in the Denver convention center. I wondered, how much of the applause was recorded?

"You buying any of this, Rick?" Ron asked me. Libby was watching from behind, giving him a shoulder massage.

"Sure. The same way the Italians bought Mussolini's schtick."

"....strong Federal leadership of state industry, nationalization of former major agribusinesses, redoubled effort in the revitalization of the honored military, and an American based economy that will operate independently of other nations, vigilance in the status of religious factions that are hostile to the ideal of the United States...."

"What a load. Nationalization of industry," I said, pondering the meaning.

"Just wait. I'm sure it gets better," Alan said, his son Mark asleep on his lap. "And it's not just industry. It's nationalization of business. You caught that bit, buried in the flowers of prosperity."

"And 'vigilance of religious factions hostile to our ideals,' don't forget that," I said.

"Those opposing the Federal mandates are misguided and fail to understand the depth of the crisis at hand, and that the only solution to the lack of progress in recovery is in the full support of Federal efforts to unify industry and national ideals. They will eventually come into the fold and understand the need for national and international recovery and unification..."

"Told ya," Alan said.

"He can't be serious," Karen asked.

"Dead serious. The true believers always are, to their adoring public at least," I said. "Re-education camps, I think China called them."

"...military forces are fully capable of protecting the strategic resources in the United States and her territories, and willing to use whatever force necessary in order to see recovery through...."

"Now the threat," I said. "Hitting all the bases tonight, aren't we?" I asked to no one in particular.

"...dissent is a vital part of a healthy, free state. However the dissent cannot be allowed to interrupt the mission of the state in the recovery efforts and future progress..."

"Thou shall not criticize the State, nor her minions, nor her policies, nor her actions," I said, more to myself. "Welcome to Fascist States of America."

Wednesday morning,
October Twenty-fifth,
5:40 a.m.

184

I didn't get much sleep, despite being bone tired and bothered by aches and pains. I knew that Karen didn't sleep much either. We spent a fair chunk of the night holding each other, occasionally whispering about all that was on our minds.

Buck finally decided that we needed company, and hopped up on the bed, soon joined by Ada. Welcome for a few minutes, but soon enough they were pushing us out of the way.

Neither Karen nor I felt the hard-charging enthusiasm to attack the day, knowing that 'working the problem' was far beyond our abilities to make much of an impact. After a hot shower, I anticipated an 'average' day. 'Average' of course, for anyone in the world whose country was coming apart at the seams...again. So many things were up in the air.

Karen made us some tea for an early breakfast, and a couple English muffins with real butter. Then, for me it was off to the barn for morning chores.

Egg production had fallen off fairly dramatically with the sudden cool weather, despite the lights we'd added to the henhouses, and our makeshift (ugly, but effective) insulation for the turkey and chicken houses and the pigs down at Pauliano's.

Our own food storage ('ours' being our extended family on the block and our new, hand-picked neighbors) met only some of the goals that I'd set forever ago, this past spring. Potatoes had been phenomenally successful, with almost ten tons harvested, all of them the hard way, by hand. Wheat was a disappointment, I'd expected far too great a yield, and had probably been fortunate to get a little over twenty bushels per acre. Old-time dry land farmers said that we'd done quite well to get that much. Corn did quite well, but it was a near thing. We harvested our last picking just as it turned really cold. The term 'we' was figurative. I was bedridden at the time.

Similarly, I missed the late grape harvest, Concords mostly. We enjoyed table grapes in early August, which didn't make it out of the neighborhood. The Concords furnished us juice and jam, from nearly a hundred gallons of pressed juice. The press was put together using a hydraulic press (in a former life used for pressing in wheel bearings in our neighbors' well equipped shop), a basket and pressing boards of white oak, and a stainless steel pot to capture the juice. I'd gone long on 'tools' of all kinds for more than fifteen years, along with more spare parts than we'd ever need. Only some had been used in the food production over the past year—it was clear that I'd overbought on many items. I did have a soft spot for forged tools, which was right up there with cast iron cookware.

Our tree fruit harvest was good, not great, but good. We couldn't keep ahead of it once it all started coming on. Still though, we'd dehydrated and canned more than we could reasonably expect to use in a year. Cherries, peaches, pears, apples. In the midst of dealing with a monster cherry and peach harvest (by our standards, monstrous, anyway, our tomatoes almost buried us. We traded hundreds of pounds of them, with our preferred traders and friends getting first pick. The rest, we sold in the stores.

The list went on and on. A hundred pounds of nuts- almost all English walnuts. Two tons of squash and pumpkins all needing proper storage and storage space. Raspberries, strawberries, blueberries (a disappointment!), melons....

We used all of our stockpile of canning jars, and then some. Next year, canning lids would be an issue.....along with looking for a new greenhouse skin. Our small greenhouse was in tatters, and we had a year or two on two others. Those at least were skinned with newer commercial-grade material.

"How many?" Karen asked.

"Fourteen," I answered, shaking off the cold. "Put them in the rack in the shop."

"Half of yesterday morning."

"Yeah. Remember way back when, with our first flock? We didn't get any eggs after the first snow?"

"I know. That'll be coming," Karen said. "You going into work today?"

"I expect so....but is the curfew still on?" I asked.

"Well, I don't know. Nothing on radio, AM, FM or shortwave. Nothing on TV. And I mean, nothing!"

"Hmmm. Odd. I'll call in," I said, already heading to the County radio. "One eleven to Spokane."

Nothing.

"Repeating, one eleven to Spokane." Karen was looking at me with the question-concern look on her face. She didn't like this either.

"One-eleven, be advised this is a compromised channel," Arlene Lomax replied.

"Understood."

"Spokane out."

"What was that?" Karen asked. "Compromised by who?"

"I have absolutely no idea. Nor do I have any idea of what to do next."

"Expect someone to show up in person. That's what I'd do."

I exhaled deeply. "I'm so damned tired of this drama."

"I'll get your things. Your boots are by the hall tree."

"Thanks."

Carl and Kelly were up and moving about the time the Humvee showed up in the driveway, followed by two more. I hugged the kids and gave them a few marching orders for the day, knowing that any plans that I had for a 'routine' day were out the window. A dozen soldiers dismounted and dispersed along the street, four more moved into the yard as a young Lieutenant came to the door where I met him.

"Mr. Drummond? Lieutenant Michael West. Would you mind coming with me sir?" I gave Karen a quick kiss and reached for my pack.

"You stay safe, mister," she said in a whisper.

"I will endeavor to do just that," I said before responding to the young officer.

"Expected you, Lieutenant. Where to?"

"Camp Overbeck, sir."

"Understood. Quite the detail you have here."

"Orders, sir. You should get used to it—I think we're your personal security detail from now on."

"Seems a little over the top," I said as we boarded the second vehicle, not the one in the driveway.

"Might be sir, might not be." The driver pulled out, heading north. Camp Overbeck, named for a local soldier who had been killed in the Mexican War. A posthumous Medal of Honor winner, he had held off more than a thousand enemy at Monterrey, giving hundreds of wounded a route of escape before being overrun. "The lead crew stays at your home location while you're away. Neighborhood patrols cover every occupied neighborhood in your city. Anyone gets out of line, it's not good for them."

"Where are you from?"

"Came in last Tuesday from Stockton on the train. Before that, New Mexico. Pre-War, Denver."

"Denver's a little different these days," I said, referring to the new 'national leadership.'

"Is at that. I'm pretty sure that won't last long."

"Could be. I think similar words were said in Eighteen Sixty-One, too, though."

"Right enough. The Cold Civil War is over."

"Cold Civil War?"

"All the bitching about how it's Us versus Them. Liberals versus conservatives. R versus D. All of it."

"I hadn't really put a label to it, but that sure works."

"Divide and conquer."

"Well, they've divided. The latter remains in question," I said.

We'd passed over the remains of the freeway, now a single plowed lane with no signs of traffic past two static Army guard posts. Ten minutes later, we were through the gates.

Inside one of the former industrial buildings, I was directed to a Spartan conference room, given some lousy coffee, and asked to wait. This building was on the south side of the old Industrial Park, a different building than one I'd visited back in May. This cavernous building used to house a furniture manufacturer, by the signs on the cracked walls.

A few minutes later, Elaine Cross and several junior officers joined me.

"Morning, Major," I said as I shook her hand.

"Mr. Drummond, thank you for coming. I've brought in several additional staff if you don't mind. Lieutenants Cambridge, Sugimoto, and Watts."

"Nice to meet you all," I said, shaking hands with each. Watts could've been a tackle at West Point, pre-War. The female lieutenants, Cambridge and Sugimoto, reminded me of college students too, but were seemingly more attentive than Watts. "Major, I'm hoping you can enlighten me on what's going on right now...."

"I'll try, yes. For your information, I've already briefed the Sheriff and his senior staff."

"Good to know."

"Since twenty-three thirty last night, there has been widespread disruption of all local communication frequencies with false alarms, false orders, and fake news broadcasts on shortwave frequencies, and some fake broadcasts overriding the local radio frequency signals, appearing therefore to be legitimate. We've shut down all local radio and television stations and all municipal frequencies in order to hunt down those responsible."

"How do you possibly do that?"

"I'm not at liberty to say, but I can say, we do it pretty well."

"When, assuming there's a when, can we get back to normal operations? I can't see the County operating with anything close to efficiency without good communications."

"Unsure at present. That's only one facet of the attacks we're undergoing at the moment. The others include attacks on infrastructure, including power distribution, petroleum distribution, shipping…"

"Pretty much everything then."

"Well, to summarize, yes."

"Responsible parties?"

"Federal forces have infiltrated non-aligned states and are carrying out attacks from within. Those states that did not immediately align with the new Federal bureaucracy have been hit hardest. Those that caved, not at all."

"Pre-positioned forces."

"Not only forces, but equipment, targets, and strategies."

"Local damage so far?"

"I can speak to that, sir," Lieutenant Watts replied.

"Please do."

Watts read me the details from a clipboard. "Explosives used on three substations served from Upriver Dam, resulting in minor damage to four feeder lines. Two municipal radio repeater installations destroyed by improvised explosives. Five separate attacks by small arms on municipal facilities including your office building, two shops facilities, and two community centers, neither of which were occupied....the attackers in three of the five cases were killed by local defense forces. The attack on the Montana and Wyoming refineries, which I believe you heard about last night, more of a regional impact of course, but certainly one that will be felt here almost immediately. Two severed railroad bridges across the Columbia River, and a third blocked due to an engineered landslide in Western Montana. Those are the ones we know about as of oh six-hundred."

"Casualties?"

"None in these specific attacks. An undetermined number of civilian municipal personnel—meaning firemen, police, state patrol—are unaccounted for."

"Unaccounted for?"

"Did not report for duty this morning. Military forces are checking on them at this time, but we're stretched pretty thin."

"Dammit," I said, looking down at my poor excuse for coffee.

"Mr. Drummond, I believe you met with a United States Attorney, by the name of Charles Severa recently?" Lieutenant Cambridge asked.

"Yeah, a couple weeks ago. He wanted to let us know that the Feds were taking four of our prisoners to Denver for interrogation..." I said, putting things together. "Now wait one damned minute. He was in on this?"

"No reason to believe so, although Mr. Severa has been detained in the Salt Lake area and is being questioned. After the prisoner

191

transfer to Denver, he was reassigned to Utah. We have reason to believe that several of those prisoners are back in this region and are deeply involved in the effort to undermine legal authority."

I sat there for a minute, rolling it over in my head. "You are certain that they are not in Federal custody...."

"We are," Major Cross responded.

"Then it's a safe wager that yeah, they're back, and whatever parts of their organization that we didn't wipe out is back and making hay. I assume you know who you're up against with the four that Severa kicked loose," I said, now not buying the plausibility of Severa not knowing what would happen to four sadistic murderers.

"We do, in detail."

"Then you also know about the threat that Ronnie Burkham and his pals represent. He threatened to gut Judge McNamara at his arraignment."

"Yes, sir."

"Well let me give you some more background. That sonofabitch executed unarmed soldiers, killed two veteran deputies, and was part of an effort to take ME out. He tortured the Guardsmen before shooting them in the heads, in front of their families."

"Yes, sir, we know all of this."

"Well, let me tell you one more little tidbit. I'm probably the one who killed his Aunt Rae. She was the ringleader of the whole deal. Pretty good chance that I'm the one that blew her head off out at their place at Newman Lake," I said. "So I'd be most appreciative of you putting a bullet in his head and letting me sleep a little better at night."

"We have three thousand troops on duty in the region, soon to be double that. We are confident that we will apprehend him soon," Cambridge said. Pretty girl, I thought, but naïve.

"Lieutenant, pardon my skepticism, but if somebody wants you dead, you're dead. There's not a damned thing you can do to stop someone who's determined to kill you." I turned my attention back to Major Cross. "Major, I know it's early in the day to ask these questions, but exactly what is the war plan that Northwest Command has brewing?"

"It'll come out soon enough, but expect more transportation and utility disruptions until the Federal government can be defeated."

"OK, already expected that. What are you planning for manpower and support from the civilian population? Draft? Food and housing? What exactly?"

"There is a significant chance of a draft or outright military conscription being put in place should initial counterattacks fail to bring the Feds around. I would expect that the age ranges would be between eighteen and sixty."

"Sixty? Good God."

"With the attrition we've had within the past year, I say that with a high degree of confidence," Elaine said.

"Mr. Drummond, in looking at your Federal personnel file..." Watts began before I cut him off.

"Lieutenant, I have no personnel file," I said, knowing that an ancient past was about to be unearthed, and there was nothing I could do about it.

"Excuse me sir, I obtained this through DoD databases showing your experience in...."

"Lieutenant, first, that was a long time ago. Second, it ended badly for all parties involved, and I was among lucky few to survive it. Third, I swore an oath to never, ever bring it up again. Period. No one I know now knows how I spent that first year out of college, and I have had no contact with any other party involved since my resignation. Understood?"

"Yes, sir, I understand. However, your file has been continuously updated since the events in the Sudan and the retrieval of your ground team."

"And you've reviewed the file?"

"That which was not redacted, sir, yes."

"Who in Hell would care what I've been doing for the past twenty-plus years?"

"The Defense Intelligence Agency, sir."

I sat there for probably a full minute before answering. "They do realize that I worked for them for what, eleven months? Exactly forty-two days in the field? The last nine of which are code-word classified for eternity?"

"I'm sure they do, sir."

"Lieutenant, what would possess you to even look for a file in my ancient past?"

"All public officials and responsible parties are being vetted, sir, to determine a confidence and trust level."

"This is not the Soviet Union, ladies and gentlemen. You do believe this though, that you need to background check every public official to have confidence in them?"

"There were some unfortunate incidents in other states where seemingly trusted officials handed over the keys to the Feds, Mr. Drummond," Lieutenant Sugimoto said. "We need to keep that from happening here."

"Well rest assured, Lieutenant, I didn't damned near get killed in some Godforsaken armpit valley in Africa well before you were born, just to cave in to the fascisti at this point."

"No, sir, I'm sure you wouldn't. I'm here however, to serve as a liaison officer during the vetting process of all Metro employees and volunteer staff."

"You're going that deep? That's what, eight percent of our population?"

"Yes, sir, approximately."

I inhaled, reflecting on the conversation. "Major, how do you intend us to operate as a public services provider without comms?"

"The bulk of public communications should be back up in twenty-four hours. I would anticipate numerous delays in restoring levels of high confidence in police, fire and municipal communications. We basically need to target them and catch them in the act. Problem is they transmit and shut down before we can find them."

"So can't we rotate freq's often enough to operate?" I asked.

"Yes sir," Sugimoto replied, "after your communications staff has been cleared."

"You know what this is going to do to morale, Elaine?" I asked, using her first name for the first time. "Everyone looking at everyone else like they're the spy?"

"Yes, but it beats the alternative. In the case of communication frequencies, imagine if someone's feeding the next days' freqs to the enemy?"

"Fine. I concede that there may be a need. I hate the idea."

Wednesday afternoon,
October Twenty-fifth,
1:15 pm.

"Spokane to one eleven," the County radio spoke, jarring me back to the present.   I was revisiting the ancient past, and close held secrets.

"I thought you said…" Karen asked, referring to our enforced radio silence.

"I did. Hang on a sec."

"One eleven, go."

"Be advised, rendezvous at location four niner-two, twenty six minutes."

"One eleven, out," I said as I wrote down the message.

"What was that? Karen asked, hands covered with flour from kneading yet another batch of wheat rolls. Kelly and Marie were even more decorated, although they'd been in the kitchen for far less time.   Libby was just coming up from the basement, with another stack of baking pans, for future batches of bread.

"Need to check my cheat sheet. It's code….twenty-six minutes translates to four minutes. Six minus two, second digit of the 'twenty' is disregarded. Location translates to….house thirteen on the street—four plus nine--disregard the last number." House thirteen is Ray Alden's place, I thought.

"SO?" Karen and Libby asked in unison.

"Meeting at Ray Alden's old house. Three minutes."

"Ron's up there now—He's working on that water filter in the basement," Libby reminded me.

"Good to have company. I'm sure our Army guard friends are all over it, too. Alan should be back up from Pauliano's any time. Hon, when he stops in, can you let him know I'm up there?" I asked as I pulled on my new-to-me chore coat, and my stumpy shotgun.

"Any idea what this is about?" Karen asked.

"Nope. Don't have time to guess," I said as I gave her a quick kiss.

"Watch yourself."

"Aye, ma'am," I said as I headed out the front door, Buck wanting to come along.

Ray's place was north of us a fair amount, and to make it on time, I hopped in the little Escape the Army had provided me and quickly drove up the road, round the permanent obstacles of black locust and green ash. One of the 'odd' looking Humvees was in Ray's driveway. This version had a larger turtleback, and was a forest of antennae. I waved at two sentries and parked in the deeper snow in what used to be the front yard.

"Yo!" I said as I entered the living room, my door opened for me.

"Mr. Drummond, thank you for coming so promptly. I'm Roger Wilson. I contract with the communications geeks around here. Army, Air Force and Navy."

"Nice to meet you," I said as I shook his hand. He looked like he would have been a video-game champ a year ago....too thin, scraggly beard...

"I'm working with Northwest Command to ferret out the comm problems in this region. I see the cheat sheet that Major Cross provided worked OK."

"Yep, no prob," I said, taking my jacket off and finding a seat in a folding chair. I heard Ron rattling around down in the basement.

"We're starting up, in about fifteen minutes, increased broadcasts from Metro communication to units stationed around the area. They're bait. All county staff at those duty locations are now accompanied by a couple soldiers, and we have nine triangulation units dispersed right now in the Valley. We know where our own transmitters are, and when fake responses come in, we have enough overlap to box them into pretty small cages quickly. Fast response teams will then move in at opportune moments, after some observation on the ground of course, and neutralize the offending transmitters. That'll probably happen during mid-shift, probably eighteen-hundred hours or later."

"OK, you sound like you've done this before."

"Yes, sir. I served six months behind the lines in Virginia, before the Feds decided they wanted to play both sides of the fence."

"All right, what do you need from me?"

"We'd like you to read a statement we've prepared, calm down the public, reassure…"

I cut him off before he could finish. "Mr. Wilson, you may or may not know this, but I've made the last announcement prepared by anyone else but me. I did that right before the BS banking situation manifested itself, and it made me look like a damned idiot. I'm not doing that again."

"OK, I guess I understand that. Do we at least have your permission to proceed?"

"Yep…as if you really need it. The sooner the better. We have work to do and the natives are gonna get restless. You find a quick way to end it, and a double shot of twenty year-old Scotch is yours."

"I'll take you up on that."

"I'll look forward to it. Question, though. Why are you here at this house? Why not just come up to my place?"

"We'd like to use this home as a base of operations for the foreseeable future. Pretty centrally located and non-descript. And decent security."

"Sure, other than that pincushion Humvee that screams 'communication vehicle' out front," Ron said as he came into the room, wiping his hands on a rag.

"Hey, Ron."

"Back atchya," Ron said.

"Ron, you have occupants for this place yet?"

"Could, needed to go over the candidate list with you first. They're ready though. Could put 'em in Casey's place."

"OK. Roger, right?" he nodded. "Sorry. Memory's not what it ought to be. You mind if I bring in some local talent?"

"What type of talent might that be?" he asked, cocking his head a little.

"We've got a friend of ours, active in the ham radio community. Frankly, I think he'd love to help out. Further, I think it'd be good for him. You mind?"

"Not a bit. I picked up this gig through my Dad's hobby. Might be fun. Bring him in. More the better."

"Ron, you got your hand-held on you?"

"Wife won't let me out of the house without it."

"Give her a call…" I said, before Wilson cut me off.

"No, sir. Just go get him when you have a chance. We'd prefer to keep operational security a little higher than a FRS broadcast over open frequencies."

"Understood. Sorry."

"That's OK. Nobody got killed," Wilson said. "This time."

"We done here?" Ron asked. "I've got stuff to do."

"Filters all set up?" I asked. Ron was rebuilding a slow-sand filter in the basement, in case our semi-reliable water system became less so.

"Yep. That's an even dozen. Five more to go."

"You're the pro. That's why you've got the assignment," I said, rising to go and shaking Roger's hand.

"Oh. I thought it was because I had a pulse."

A few minutes later, Ron and I were unloading the tools of the day in the big shop next door to our place. Our neighbors hadn't been heard of since the Domino, and it had only been in early August that I'd had the heart to even clean up the damage inside the building. Other than the early salvage operations in the house and boarding up the place after the quake, the house remained untouched.

The shop, split up into several bays, had been converted from auto restoration into an all-around workshop for work on 'the block'. Salvaged tools ended up here, and most of our fabrication work, whatever that happened to include, was done here. The best improvement or adaptation, had been a wood-fired boiler that provided heat for the in-floor heating system. The far end of the shop housed most of the office equipment, salvaged from my company, that I didn't have room (or use) for at present. Behind that, the wreckage of a little Model T speedster that belonged to the owner of the property, Pre-Domino.

"So what's this big stack of stuff for?" I asked, looking at a fair-sized pile of already finished, good quality interior plywood and hardwood. Used and salvaged obviously, but in excellent shape.

"New cabinets in some of the neighborhood houses, if we ever get to it. Some of the pantries and supply storage areas are pathetic. Our place in particular."

"Well, ours too from an organizational standpoint," I said. Our basement storage room had never really been thought out. We just used it as it was when we moved in.

"That's what your wife says, too. I think we'll end up with six big shelf units out of this stuff. There's more coming--hasn't been delivered yet, obviously. We're using your model that you used out in the barn, only enclosing some of them. Trying to modularize things."

"Who's the lucky carpenter?"

"We're just doing the cutting here. Assemblies going to be done in place. Sarah and John are going to do the slice and dice here, then building some units at her place, and two at ours."

"Where'd they get all this stuff? You guys do some creative trading?"

"John did, yeah. This used to be the employee exercise room ceiling at AgriLending."

I laughed a little, and felt a stitch in my side. "Nice to see that the exercise equipment for a mega-farm bank was housed in such nice surroundings."

"You should see the conference room if you think this is good."

"Do tell," I said.

"Five kinds of wood, I have no idea what, inlaid in all the walls, along with what looks like a bronze strip."

"What'd John trade?"

"Three downed Black Walnut trees, including stumps."

"Gun stock material!"

"Yep."

"Where were the trees?"

"On the block west of his place, right across the street."

"Sound like a fair trade to you?" I said, thinking that some nice looking plywood and other trim was much less valuable than the more rare walnut.

"He gets ten finished gunstocks out of the deal too, for whatever he wants them fitted to."

"Well, then, I think that's a fair trade! I wonder if I could buy one of those off of him…."

"I'm sure he's open to negotiations. We done here?"

"Yep," I said, shutting off the lights and locking the inner door.

"Let's see what trouble we can stir up at home," he said as we left the vestibule. It was snowing again.

"Dang snow," I said, just as we heard the muffled sound of automatic weapons fire somewhere far south of us.

"Someone's having a bad day," Ron said.

"To say the least." More gunfire, seemingly due west, more distant. Not an echo.

"Damn," Ron said as we got back in the Ford and drove back home. "Sounds closer than I imagined it would be."

"Me too," I said, once again instinctively putting my hand on the butt of the .45 on my hip.

Thursday evening,
October Twenty-sixth,
6:45 pm.

"Spokane to One Eleven," the county radio across the table crackled, disturbing my study of Romans. I fumbled a bit for the headset. Karen and Kelly came in from the kitchen, where they were finishing cleaning up from dinner.

"One eleven," I replied quietly. Karen moved to my side.

"Be advised, military announcement at nineteen-hundred hours, all active public radio frequencies, television stations, County frequencies and non-secure FRS and shortwave channels assigned to Pacific Northwest Command."

"Understood. One eleven out."

"One eleven," the female voice responded.

"What's up Daddy?" Kelly asked.

"I'm hoping, some good news for a change," I said, getting up to warm up my cup of Earl Grey. "How bout you wake up your brother and make sure he hears this?" Carl went to bed right after dinner. He was coming down with a cold.

"K."

"Think it's odd you didn't hear anything from the guys up the street?" Karen asked, followed a moment later by a knock on the front door.

"Not anymore, no," I said as I changed direction from the kitchen to the front door. Roger Wilson was shaking the snow off of his heavy wool greatcoat. Despite the Army's earlier beliefs of quick restoration of 'normal' business operations and a limit of curfew to nighttime hours, we were now almost through a second day of lockdown.

"Mr. Drummond, I assume you're ready for the next leg of the race," Roger said as he came in, shaking my hand, all smiles.

"We'll see, I guess. Roger, this is my wife Karen," I said as they shook hands. "And my daughter Kelly and son Carl," as they were coming into the room.

"Thanks. Nice to meet you all. I just wanted to say that the night shift will be taking over shortly, and to let you know how much I appreciate Mr. Watters joining us today. He's quite a character."

"That's good to hear. His eyesight's about gone, but he's as sharp as a tack," I said, then offering to take his coat.

"Can't stay, thanks. He is at that. Showed me a thing or five, and not to brag about myself, that's saying something."

"Indulge me on what's going on out there, if you would," I asked. Roger then decided to shuck his coat after all. Kelly handed him a mug of tea.

"Thanks, young lady. Fast action teams, twelve of them, squad-sized, have been in action most of the day. Opposition was light to medium on most objectives. Really heavy at one location. Turned out to be the control point for the whole region. After that, secondary objectives bugged out. Left their gear."

"So in English?" Karen asked. Roger looked a little lost for a reply.

"They didn't destroy their radios. They didn't burn their plain-text instructions. Didn't burn their contact lists. Or schedules. Operational security and compartmentalization is apparently foreign to these people. That means we're probably about done here. Every active transmitter has been eliminated. Brigade estimates that we have an eighty-percent kill."

"The ones that bailed?" I asked. "How about them?"

"Disappeared into the crowd."

"I believe a while back, over in Iraq, they called those kinds of people, 'insurgents.'"

Roger replied, "Yep. We hunted them down over there, too. We'll find them. It's not like they're making it hard."

"Chances of repeat? You said, 'active transmitters.'" I noticed Carl was looking on intently.

"There are almost certainly other hidden transmitters out there. Thing is, they'd have to be absolute idiots to try this again. We've got their playbook."

"No more airplanes into skyscrapers," I said.

"Right. It's been done."

"'Bout time for the broadcast, hon," Karen said. "And Roger, here's some apple pie. Have a seat there."

He looked a little stunned. "Thank you VERY much, Mrs. Drummond."

"Karen, please," she said taking a seat next to mine. Kelly had the radio on, and was adjusting the volume and shushing us.

"Rog, have a seat. I assume you're the author of tonight's broadcast?"

"Only supporting cast. I leave the really big decisions to Division," he said, taking a bite of warm pie, and savoring it as if he hadn't had a pie in years. Maybe he hadn't....

"Probably best that way," I said. "The military sometimes has an uneven tolerance for civilians during a war."

"Been there, done that," Roger said, as he took another bite.

"Ditto," I said quietly. Right on time, the announcement came on. We had the radio tuned to the TV band. We never thought to turn on the TV.

"This is Pacific Northwest Command with a special news broadcast. Today, combined units of Northwest Command and civilian law enforcement units eliminated numerous illegal Federal-

backed transmitters throughout the region. These illegal transmitters have disrupted authorized communications and were used to disrupt law enforcement efforts, emergency response, and civilian news broadcasts, resulting in the deaths of numerous citizens of the region.

A number of Federal operatives running these transmitters were taken into custody during the operations while a greater number were killed after firing on Command troops.

Pacific Northwest Command expects to continue these operations in the coming days until all unauthorized transmitters operating on authorized frequencies, or anyone impersonating authorized broadcasters have been taken into custody or eliminated. Any problems with false radio communications, false news stories, or false broadcasts of any other nature will be immediately investigated and appropriate punitive action taken.

Given today's operational success, Pacific Northwest Command is canceling the daytime curfew effective at seven a.m. tomorrow morning. All normal civilian businesses are expected to be open, as well as full municipal services.

A reminder to all citizens that official broadcasts happen only on 630 AM and 1510 AM at the top of each hour. Effective immediately, both of these stations will be returned to full-time operation.

This ends the special report. We will now return to regular programming."

"There ya go," Roger said.

"Well, maybe," I replied.

"So, Dad, school tomorrow?" Carl asked through a yawn.

"Should be, but maybe not for you. See how you feel tomorrow."

"'K. I'm back to bed. Nice to meet you Mr. Wilson."

"You too. Rest up."

Karen and Kelly cleared the dishes and then packed up another pie for Alan and Mary and the kids. "I'm going to run this over to Mom's, hon. Be back in an hour," Karen said. "Roger, nice to meet you."

"You too, ma'am."

"So formal. Karen, remember?"

"I'll remember now."

"Hey, don't forget to take the dogs with you," I said.

"I will, but John's here too."

"Pays to have hired muscle. Watch him though, he'll kipe a piece of that pie."

"Doesn't have to. Sarah made him one this afternoon."

"Like that'll stop him," I said giving her a quick kiss. "Watch your step out there. We haven't plowed out the path lately."

"I've noticed," she said as she opened the back door.

"Roger, I think it's time for that Scotch."

"That doesn't normally go with apple pie, but I'll certainly make an exception."

"Oban OK?" I asked, taking a bottle from the locked buffet cabinet.

"Sure, but that's not twenty years old. Fourteen."

"Well, you know a little bit about Scotch. Not this one, though. Thirty-two years old. Pre-Domino, this was a four-hundred dollar bottle of Scotch."

"You must've done well, Pre-War."

"Oh, I got this back in July. A little barter creativity."

Roger sat there looking at me as I poured two fingers of the precious liquid in cut-glass crystal glasses.

"What, exactly did you have to trade to get this?" he asked, looking at the golden liquor.

"I'm not at liberty to say, sorry." I replied.

"I hope it was worth it, whatever it was."

"It was," I responded. "Slaandjivaa!" I said as I took a sip, enjoying the smooth warmth.

"What was the toast? I mean, language." Roger asked, after taking a sip himself.

"'To your health.' Scots gaelic."

"Then I'd counter with, 'to our freedom.'"

"Amen."

We talked for a few minutes before the conversation found its' way back to the broadcast and the meanings of the days' work.

"I think we'll be done quickly. Ten days, tops," Roger replied to my questioning his progress, holding the glass in both hands, leaning forward toward the woodstove. In reality, my question was more an attempt to sound the depth of his understanding of the wider picture.

"That's all well and good to think that, Roger, but don't you think it was a little easy?"

"What do you mean? They did shoot back after all," the young man replied.

"Too easy, Roger."

"OK, I'm not dense, but I do not understand where you're going with this."

"They've played with our comms for what, two, three days? Your guys took them down in what, a day?" I said, stretching my back a little before I went on. "Rog, you've never heard of Frank Mikkelson. Guy I knew in a previous life. He made us memorize what are known these days as Murphy's Laws of Combat. Saved my ass more than once in a very short period of time. Get a pen and paper out."

"Uh, OK," Roger said, fishing out a little pad and a technical pencil out of his shirt.

"Good. Here you go," I said and then paused, remembering a million years ago in North Carolina, and an eternity of weeks I spent there. *"Number One: If the enemy is in range, so are you."*

"Of course."

"No, not 'of course.' Do not take anything for granted, ever. Number Two: *Incoming fire has the right of way."*

"Meaning?"

"Meaning keep your head down or get it blown off. Time your team response to minimize casualties," I said. "It's not as easy as it sounds. None of this is. Number Three: *Don't look conspicuous. It draws fire."*

"Sure…"

"No, not 'sure.' In too many situations just looking like you're in charge will put a target reticle on your chest or head. Don't get in those situations."

I was starting to get through to him. "Number Four*: There is always a way.* Followed by Number Five: *The easy way is mined."*

He wrote that down and paused.

"Now you see where I'm going?"

"Beginning to, yes."

"Good. Number Six: *Try to look unimportant, they may be low on ammo.* A corollary is that they are picking their target in their own time, and the merest hint that you are 'the man' just got you killed."

Wilson continued to write.

"Number Seven: *Professionals are predictable, it's the amateurs that are dangerous...*"

"Getting it."

"Are you? Are you dealing with professionals or with amateurs? You said earlier that they blew off all normal protocols for destroying their gear, their playbooks, all of it. Are you SURE you're dealing with amateurs?"

"You're making me think otherwise."

"Good. I'm not even to the one that drives it home yet. About that gear you seized. You sure it's clean? No explosives? No bugs that they're now using to listen in on OUR communications without us knowing about it?"

Wilson paused. "I don't think so."

"Better find out. Number Eight: *The enemy invariably attacks on two occasions: when you're ready for them and when you're not.* You might be getting played right now. You've exposed your mechanism for dealing with this communications interruption. You have to assume that they will now react in a manner that you're unprepared to deal with. Do not fall into the trap that an attack will be conventional."

"We hadn't considered...."

"That's an easy thing to do...the excitement of a solution, even if the solution is wrong but seems right, can overcome good judgment. Number Nine: *Teamwork is essential, it gives them someone else to shoot at.*"

Roger was writing again. I felt like I was not the one who should have been schooling this young man. Distinctly out of place. My mind felt sharp though, for the first time in months.

"Number Ten: *If you can't remember, then the claymore is pointed at you.* In your case, I'm not sure how that might apply. In most cases though, I'd say that if you've set a trap, make sure you're not the one caught up in it. I have some experience with that one."

Roger wrote without comment.

"Number Eleven: *The enemy diversion you have been ignoring will be the main attack.* You may consider that statement in light of the current situation."

"Understood."

"Number Twelve. *If your attack is going well, you have walked into an ambush.*"

Roger paused.

"Get my point?"

"Yes, sir."

"Good. Don't ever make the mistake of believing that you've defeated the enemy until they are dead and in the ground. And I mean all of them. If they're not ambient temperature, then they remain a threat."

Roger was mulling all of this over. I had succeeded in making him feel distinctly uncomfortable about the ease of the days' success.

"You know Roger, that successful battles don't win wars. We've seen the treachery that the organization passing themselves off as the Federal Government can descend to. They're not going to be defeated this quickly or this easily. Not by a long shot. Consider this the scouting mission. One more rule for you: *Drawing 'point' equals dead.*"

Thursday morning,
November Sixteenth
10:00 a.m.

We were finally on our way out the door, gathered up for the drive over to Fort Overbeck, now upgraded from 'Camp' status. Today was a milestone day. John Martin would take his oath of enlistment in the Army, along with dozens of other draftees. Their notices had been hand-delivered on Veteran's Day. Alan, Mary and the kids stayed with Grace, who was in declining health. The stores were manned today by our employees, and I took the day off from the Metro offices to attend. Elaine Cross, now a neighbor, had also asked me to meet with her after the swearing-in ceremony.

I was able to drive the family, today in an old tarted-up Suburban, complete with pinstripes, fender flares, and running boards. Pre-Domino, I'm sure this would have fit in nicely hauling a similarly painted golf cart to the golf courses at Meadowwood or Indian Canyon by a retiree who wintered in Palm Desert. We were escorted by a freshly painted, olive-drab Toyota pickup, modified for Army use. It looked like one of the African 'technicals', but better built and armored. I couldn't go anywhere these days without my PSD—personal security detail.

Our weather hadn't really improved a whole lot, with little snow left on the ground after a 'Pineapple Express' had melted most of our snow pack before re-freezing. That little adventure resulted in numerous roof collapses despite the efforts of the Metro staff and constant warnings through the media to building owners and squatters. Five people had been killed as a result, with several more missing in a building collapse and subsequent five-alarm fire, two blocks from one of our stores. Today, and for most of the past week, we had low overcast, temperatures in the twenties, and predictions of heavy snow that never came to pass.

At the Fort, formerly the Spokane Industrial Park, we found ourselves in a fairly long line of military and civilian vehicles waiting to gain access. The fort was at Threatcon Charlie today, and bounced between Charlie and Delta depending on the threats that Northwest Command perceived after the Second Civil War began on October Twenty-fourth.

Finally we were nearing the gate, and could see the entry process a little better. I'd been briefed on it as a part of the 'day job', but hadn't been to Fort Overbeck since the early days of the War.

"This looks interesting," Ron said from the right front passenger seat, looking at the emplacements flanking the main gate, backed up by secondary heavy weapons emplacements on the far side of the vehicle inspection area.

"No joke," I said, seeing a Chevy sedan in the inspection area being searched rather rigorously.

"They're doing every car?" Libby asked.

"Looks as if," I said. "Had some trouble down at a Guard base in Bend. Car bomb went off at the main gate. They upgraded security right after that, command-wide."

Karen, seated in the front-middle, looked anxious.

"It's OK, hon."

"If you say so. I have a hard time believing that though."

"Brave new world."

"Right."

We were waved to the left, rather than to the right with most of the other cars, into a separate marshalling area, this one screened off from the gate by what I recognized as a ballistic grade, anti-ram wall.

"Special treatment?" Ron asked.

"No idea," I said. "I'm pretty much new here, too."

The sergeant in our escort vehicle parked in a space as directed by one of the five M.P.'s in the lot, and directed us to park five stalls further in.

"Mr. Drummond and party?" a rather gruff M.P. asked as I opened my door.

"Yes, Sergeant. I'm assuming we were expected."

"You were, sir. Please leave the vehicle here and proceed through that sally port. Everyone is being screened for the ceremony."

"Uh, Sarge? Several of us are carrying."

"You can check your weapons at the sally port. Lockers are provided. Any long guns?"

"Well, yes."

"You can leave them in the vehicle. Once you are all out and the vehicle is secured, no one is allowed within this area."

"Understood. Thanks, Sarge."

"You're welcome, sir."

"All right, gang, let's get a move on," I said as the rest of the doors opened and we helped extricate our families from the back of the cavernous Chevy.

The sally port, a 'controlled access point' included a one-way ballistic-glass entry door beneath a large canopy, a hallway with 'bank-teller' like windows, again with ballistic glass, and formidable MP's at every turn. Within a few minutes, after providing proper ID, in my case my Metro Administrator pass and my driver's license, we were handed visitor badges and lanyards, and assigned an escort for our time at the Fort.

"Mr. Drummond? I'm Lori Sanders. I'll be serving as your party's escort for your visit today. Major Cross I believe has reserved some VIP seating for you and the Martins."

"Speaking of which, and thank you for your time today of course, this is Ron Martin and his wife Liberty, and daughter Marie. Their son John will be taking the oath today. This is my wife Karen, son Carl and daughter Kelly."

"Nice to meet you all," Miss Sanders replied, shaking the hands of each. "I trust you didn't have any trouble at the gate?"

"Not a bit, thank you."

"Please, follow me. The Induction Hall is this way. Unlike most visitors, we get to make the journey indoors." She reminded me of a pleasant tour guide. No uniform or rank given, I thought. Must be a civilian employee...

I noticed as we passed through a largish reception area, perhaps four-dozen cubicles to our left, fully staffed it seemed, with numerous computer screens lit up. No identification signs were present as to the function of the staff throughout the entire building, I noted. Peculiar...

We followed our guide along the labyrinth of halls, offices, and service areas, carved out of massive warehouses built during the Second War, finally arriving at yet another former warehouse, this one converted to a large and obviously temporary auditorium.

There, we were seated in the third row, behind Blue Star and Gold Star families. We shook hands with many of them, and I hugged a few of the Gold Star families, before we were prompted to take our seats.

The large, new flag of the Republic hung on the backdrop, smaller thankfully than that burned into my mind from the movie, 'Patton'. The organization calling itself the legitimate national government of course adopted the traditional fifty-star flag as its own, but had quite soon after the War began, started calling itself the State of America. No, 'United', no 's' at the end of 'States', truly telling all that their government was about centrality and control, rather than of individual and states' rights. The argument of exactly what we 'rebels' should call our government seemed to be settled more quickly than I would have thought, after we learned that we were in physical possession of the Declaration of Independence, the Constitution, and most importantly, the basic premise of the United States' founders. We were, the United States of America. 'They', were the S.A.

The flag however, was both new and old, modeled after the Union Army Guidon flag from the First Civil War, ours bearing twenty-seven gold stars, one for each state remaining in the Union as we recognized it. A wedge was cut out of the trailing edge of the flag represented that part of our Nation that was lost to us. This interpretation, and perhaps the creation, was from the Chief Justice of the Supreme Court of our own Washington State. Someday, we would hope to retire this flag, and have fifty or more gold stars to a blue field, with red and white bars extending to their full length.

I looked over at Libby, sitting on the other side of Karen, as we waited for the volunteers to file in. 'Oh, jeez. She's already to cry....'

"Toughen up, there, Lib. Don't embarrass your son now," I said, trying to lighten up the mood a little.

"Hush now, you. Wait your turn," she said, reminding me that my own son wasn't that far away from legal service either.

"Point taken," I said, as Karen wiped a tear from her own eye.

One hundred and six men and women, not all young, filed into the room, wearing 'utilities' not unlike workmen's coveralls. I learned much later that a good third of them didn't have clothing that the Army considered presentable for public ceremony, and as such rounded up these ill-fitting makeshift uniforms. John was in mid-pack, being in alphabetical order, and easy to pick out given his height.

We'd said our private farewells, or perhaps more correctly, gave him advice that we thought might be most useful to him in the coming weeks and months, four days before. He'd been given two days to report for the batteries of tests, physicals and other sufferings one was put through prior to being allowed to take the oath.

From what I knew, precious few people were being exempted in any case, regardless of condition. I wondered to myself how many would make it through 'basic' if it were being held to the standards of a year before, or if the Marine's 'Crucible' had similarly been toned down?

Major Cross, in full dress uniform, took the podium next to two other junior officers, and ordered the men and women to rise.

Spectators and inductees rose for the Pledge of Allegiance (unchanged), and remained standing as the men and women took their oath to defend the Constitution from all enemies, foreign and domestic. Within a few more minutes, we were milling about as photographs were taken. John came over in his undersized coverall and shook hands with us, giving his younger sister a hug as well.

"Do you believe this thing?" John said of his attire.

"Yeah, you like a big green burrito," I said, drawing a laugh. "I'm sure that the Army tailors will provide you much more suitable gear, any day now."

"It's one step above hospital clothes."

"You're being generous," Karen said. "Especially nice with the tan boots."

John moved closer and lowered his voice for privacy. "You should've seen some of the clothes these people were in! Dang near rags! One guy had mismatched shoes!"

"Maybe they figure they'll never wear them again anyway," Ron said to his son.

"I don't think so. One guy said this was the best outfit he's had in three months."

"Count yourself lucky then," I said. "What time you ship out?"

"Eleven-thirty," he replied.

"They figure out where yet?" I asked, knowing that there was some question as to where 'basic training' was going to be completed.

"Sierra Army Depot. Somewhere in California."

"Most of the others are too far east. Fort Leonard Wood's behind the lines anyway."

"Missouri?" Ron asked.

"Yeah. The others are all south east or too close to the lines for comfort."

Libby was too quiet. "Lib, you must be quite proud of your son," I asked.

"I am," she said in trooper form. "So is his fiancé."

"Well! That's news worth hearing about!"

"John, your story…" Libby said, now sporting a smile.

"I proposed the night after I got the letter. Dropped down on one knee and everything."

"Good for you. She's not here today though?" Karen said, looking around.

"No, she's on rotation at Sacred Heart. Emergency room this week. Pretty much impossible to get out here for this."

"Set a date?" I asked.

"Indeterminate," he replied. It seemed like only a few months ago we visited Libby and Ron in the hospital with their new little boy.

"That's OK," Ron said. Just leaves more time for your Mom and Sarah to plan something elaborate."

"Good to know, since you're the one on the hook to pay for it, since Sarah's alone now."

"I'm good with that. She's worth it," Ron said with a smile.

"John, I think they're saying that she's made improvements in you."

"I know that's what they're saying," he said as Major Cross made her way over to us.

"Private Martin," Elaine said in 'that' tone. It was good to see John snap to attention. I honestly had no idea if that was expected at this point or not, but it seemed appropriate.

"Major."

"At ease," Elaine replied. "I believe that some photographs for your fiancé are in order."

"You know?"

"My business. Sarah stitched up my elbow yesterday. Slipped on the ice and whacked my countertop. I prodded, she spilled. Congratulations."

"Thank you, Major," he said, shaking hands.

"OK, Martin clan, let's all get in the picture," I said, turning on the old Sony digital camera. "And let's all try to look respectable."

I took several pictures, including one with just John and Major Cross, and John and his folks. All too soon, John and the others were ordered back into formation, as the assembled spectators lined both sides of the hallway. They marched out of the room to the south and were loaded up on buses. I knew that the bus ride would be short, only as far as the train depot at north edge of the Fort. From there, a couple days on the train.

As the spectators filtered back outside, Elaine and her assistant directed us back to Elaine's office and the adjacent conference area, where we were provided hot cider or coffee.

"So Major, what's on our agenda today?" I asked. We'd had a few meetings over the past couple of weeks, usually routine business of scheduling the takeover of security patrols by civilians, as military units were called up and reassigned.

"I have a letter for you from Governor Hall," she said, sliding the sealed letter, complete with printed logo and my typed name, across the desk.

Without opening it, I thought I knew what it might contain, and I wasn't looking forward to it.

"From the Governor? My, aren't we traveling in rarified air!" Libby said, now recovered it seemed, and fully capable of firing appropriate barbs when needed.

I glanced over at Karen, seated in the other 'guest' chair in front of Elaine's desk.

I leaned forward, sliding the letter toward me, and then opened it. My eyes moved over the words, coming to rest on the phrase, 'request that you accept this commission in service to the State.' I noted Bob Anderson's signature as well, next to his title, 'Commanding Officer, Pacific Northwest Command.'

"Good grief," I said.

"What is it?" Karen asked.

"I've been requested to accept a commission as a colonel in the State Guard."

"Congratulations, Rick," Ron said. "You've been drafted."

"So it would seem," I said, squeezing Karen's hand. She looked like I felt.

"Major, this is for real?" I asked.

221

"Yes it is. The Governor isn't singling you out, Mr. Drummond. More than two hundred commission requests like this have gone out in Washington alone," Major Cross said.

"Elaine, you do realize that there is no possible way that I'd pass a military physical, let alone survive Basic," I said with a chuckle, mulling around what this letter had in store for me. For us.

"I believe that the request stems from your leadership abilities, not your current physical condition. Rick, you and Karen, and Ron and Libby of course, know the leadership vacuum we have right now. You've been tapped. The choice is yours of course," Elaine said, in a tone that did not imply that there was a choice available.

"Let me sleep on it," I said as I stood up.

"Don't you want to know a little more about the job?" Elaine asked.

"The job, as you call it, involves turning our lives upside-down again, just when we're really just getting back on our feet," I said, knowing that we weren't really getting back on our feet at all. We were as a city, *almost* getting by. Almost. I think what bothered me more than anything was that I was now 'comfortable' in our new personal and 'business' life. "I learned a long time ago when I was in government employ, that job descriptions really don't mean a damned thing."

Major Cross had read my non-redacted file, one of perhaps a half dozen people who had. I'd had a long talk with Karen, and later with Ron, Libby, Alan and Mary, filling them in on a less graphic version of my limited time and life-scarring experience as a fresh out-of-college, naïve employee of the Defense Intelligence Agency.

Three members of our team of sixteen survived it, all those years ago. We'd been assigned a 'cake walk' mission: Provide water purification plant construction techniques to local villages in southern Sudan using mostly indigenous materials, as 'part of a non-governmental organization.' The real mission was to provide on-the-ground geological reporting on strategic mineral and oil reserves in the region, along with incidental reporting on other tactical and strategic observations. Three weeks in, it was apparent that suspected oil reserves were far in excess of previous estimates. This earned us kudos from the higher-ups. To the much younger R. Drummond, that was a great accomplishment.

It blew up in our face on our thirty-sixth day in country, through no fault of our own we believed at the time. The president of the country imposed Shari' a law, and the firestorm of murder began their civil war. As the factions solidified, we found ourselves in the geographic middle. Soon enough we were hunted—we were different. By the time we were 'recovered', there were four of us left. I was the youngest. The senior surviving member of our team was nine months older. I remembered my friend, 'Mac', he was a good guy, always smiling, friendly with the village kids, respectful of the elders and all of the cultural customs. He'd graduated from the Colorado School of Mines, and was our geotech expert, as well as in knife-fighting. He'd been wounded during the first attack, a bad shoulder wound. For eight days, we'd evaded as best we could, losing team members all along the way despite our non-sanctioned, non-US manufactured weapons—NGO's weren't allowed to have arms. 'Mac' had almost made it out—he died on the floor of a shot-up Russian-made helicopter just as we crossed over into the Congo. Mary Elizabeth Wilson held his left hand. I held his right. Sometimes, I believe I still can hear her Carolina voice, with words that I cannot forget.

It was a few hours later that we learned that we'd really been hunted from the get-go because our cover had been blown somewhere from the inside. We had also been blamed for a series of massacres that oddly enough followed our evac route. The faction pursuing us simply killed everyone they met, and blamed it on us. Those substantial numbers that we'd killed were incidental to the massacre that was the tribal and religious civil war. That night we were on a C-141 back to Virginia. Six days in the infirmary and pounded by constant debriefs, and on day seven, I resigned. Twenty years it had been since I'd last hoped that the rat bastard who'd rolled over burned in Hell for all eternity, and one whole year passed a few years back, when I realized I'd gone a year without The Nightmare.

I'd never really gone through what might pass for Basic Training in anybody's idea of military service, although we certainly had our share of verbal abuse, during what was called a 'perverted version of Army basic,' with forty-eight hours of the Marine Crucible thrown in for the sadistic enjoyment of our Training Officer. Since those days, I had studiously avoided anything remotely like physical training, maybe more as a means of trying to forget, which was in retrospect about the worst thing that I could have done to remain in better health over time. Before the Domino, I was thirty-five pounds over my once-upon-a-time field-grade weight. Now, not a year later, I was only five pounds over the target weight of old, and that weight loss was not due to training.

Although I could still hit the target, my eyesight had declined over the years and I was now finding myself starting to play the trombone with the fine print. My two pairs of regular glasses sufficed for distance and were 'progressives' for reading, as both my ophthalmologist and optometrist had warned me at my yearly checkup, now eleven months ago, that this was coming. Back then I hardly wore glasses, just contacts. Now, contact lenses worked for distance, but no longer for reading. Libby provided me four pairs of reading glasses that she'd collected during salvage. They were a bother.

1 9

Friday morning,
November Seventeenth
5:00 a.m.

I had up to two weeks until I was to report to Fort Overbeck for my own induction. I appreciated that I'd get to spend Thanksgiving at home. I hoped it wasn't my last one.

Today would be 'another day at the office.' My first task would be to find my replacement and get them trained up. Somebody would be getting an awful shock today...I had a short list in my head of likely victims, er, candidates.

Ron and Alan had their hands full trying to round up special orders for Thanksgiving, now less than a week away. The easiest thing to come by: Green beans and dried onions. The most difficult (impossible) thing to come by: Marshmallows for the topping of sweet potatoes and yams. The stores in the 'more affluent' areas had heard of some extremely high offers...no one could furnish the goods though. It also appeared that farm turkeys (scarce in pre-Domino times in the region) would be supplemented by wild turkeys (scarce now due to over hunting) and geese. Our turkeys were being raised out at Don Pauliano's, with ample assistance from Joe.

Don and Lorene's farm was a profitable venture, and Don had hired two local kids, both orphaned, as hands for the place. They were quickly pretty much adopted as their own, with Joe and Joan serving as grandparents.

With the needed help out at the farm, the Pauliano's had decided to close up the city house two weeks before, moving the balance of the livestock out there as well. I'd located a semi trailer for moving the stock, bought it and it's tractor on the spot, and then after Don and Joe were done with it, put it out for rent to anyone who needed to 'double-up' their stock with anyone else's. It hadn't paid for itself yet, but it was pretty close. A few more runs in the spring, and we'd have our money out of it. Since the 'mission' of the tractor-trailer was related to farm production, we got fuel priority. If not for that, we'd have been better off renting the thing for far more than a one-time rental shot should cost. The former owner was more than willing to negotiate. I didn't press too hard, and I was able to hook him up with a job in the Metro motor pool. He turned out to be a pretty good wrench, the supervisor told me.

As soon as the alarm clock went off, Karen was up and going, giving me a quick kiss before she rolled out of bed to build me breakfast and lunch. I was getting an early start today, with the goal of trying to get a whole lot more work done.

I showered and shaved, enjoying for a little too long the hot water. It was a luxury that was sometimes a little too hard to resist. Dressing today in longjohns and Dockers, I also decided to wear a dress-shirt and tie. I could not remember when the last time I wore a tie. A while ago for sure. I picked a Black Watch plaid. By the time I was ready to find my boots, Buck had decided to play, and had taken the right one with him. I found him in the living room, boot in mouth, hindquarters raised, forelegs stretched out in front of him, his playful growl going full volume. Once I found 'the spot' on his right side, I managed to scratch him enough to get his hind leg going as he rolled over. The boot again was mine.

In the kitchen, Karen was stirring in some sun-dried tomatoes and onions into my eggs and hash browns.

"Mmm," I said as I snuck up behind Karen and hugged her from the back. "Smells great."

"So do you. You used my soap again, didn't you?"

"Coconut. Reminded me of Maui."

"You'll need that reminder. It's eleven degrees outside."

"What's the weather doing?"

"Fresh snow. Couple inches. Nothing on the radio though."

"Nothing-nothing? Or nothing worth listening to?"

"The former, sort of. Just a tone, then it repeats, KDA Spokane, fifteen-ten. What do you think that means?"

226

"Generally, nothing good. Anything on the County frequency?"

"Normal traffic. Shift change stuff by the sounds of it."

"Military?" I asked, referring to our newly installed mil-spec radio.

"Nada."

"OK. I'll zap downtown and see what's up."

"Toast'll be ready in a minute."

"K. Thanks," I said, as I got ready to call in. "One eleven to Spokane."

"One eleven," came Arlene Lomax's reply.

"Advise status on civilian radio station KDA?"

"KDA is down due to equipment failure."

"Alternatives?"

"Also down at this time."   That meant radio and television.

"Understood. One eleven out."

"One eleven," Arlene replied in her cool, clinical voice.

"What's up?" Karen asked as she brought me my steaming plate, toast, and grape jam.

"All civilian radio is down. And TV."

"Somebody take them out?"

"I'm betting yes."

"Shortwave?"

"Didn't ask. I'm assuming that's still up."

"Maybe give Aaron a call."

"You, my love, are brilliant," I said around a mouthful of eggs and potatoes.

"Yes, I have my moments," she said as she kissed my forehead, and then the scar on the side of my head.

Pre-Domino, to legally broadcast on ham frequencies, you needed a license. These days, you needed a radio, power, and somebody that recognized your 'handle.'

"Whisky-poppa four, this is Tango two-one," I said after warming up the Collins. I repeated my call.

"Whisky-poppa," came the reply.

"Good morning, WP. Hear anything unusual of late?"

"Plenty. Not the time or the place though," Aaron replied.

"Understood. Say fifteen?"

"Affirmative. Whisky-poppa out."

"Two-one out," I said, and then shut down the power to the KWM.

"Well," Karen said, "That was certainly cryptic."

"It was at that. I wonder what he's heard?"

"Sounds like you'll find out soon enough," Karen said, refilling my tea.

I sat there in the chair, staring at the radio for a few moments too long.

"You OK?"

"Yeah. I better get moving."

"Brush teeth. You're worse than the kids."

"Hazard of preoccupation."

"Don't make a habit out of it," she said as she found my one ticklish spot, just under the right side of my ribcage.

"Hey, now, play fair," I said.

"Better move it, Colonel, or I'll take you back to bed."

"There's an offer I could take you up on."

"If only," she said as she wiggled a little more than necessary on the way back into the kitchen.

Ten minutes later, I was out the door as my 'personal security detail' arrived to pick me up for the trip into town. I found that my .45 holster just didn't quite feel right with dress pants.

"Mike, good morning," I said as I climbed into the front seat.

"Morning, sir."

"Little detour today. Got a quick stop to make on the way in. Call it intel gathering." I gave him the directions to Aaron and Ellen Watters' home.

"Yes, sir," Lieutenant West replied. I'd gotten to know the young lieutenant a little on our occasional drives into town, along with two corporals and a sergeant who must've drawn the short straw with Major Cross. "Something special going on?"

"Maybe. Friend of mine is a ham radio geek. Wanted to talk face to face."

"Busy night last night for the comms guys we heard. Took out a couple of the civvies transmitters."

"I'm sure that's at least part of it," I said as we neared Aaron's place. "There on the right."

"Hard to miss with that mast."

"True. Sorry," I said as he pulled the Humvee pickup into the driveway.

"No problem. I'm pretty good at picking out the obvious."

"Right. Officer material," I said with a grin.

"Which, I understand, you will be soon."

"Right, so remember to respect your potential superior officer."

"All in good fun, sir."

"Be right back."

I had almost made it to the top step of the porch when Ellen Watters opened the door.

"Morning, Rick. How are you today?"

"Good, Ellen. How's that troublemaker husband of yours?"

"Boy, you've got him dialed. Come on in. He's in the radio shack. I'm heading out back to check the goats. I'll be right back."

"Thanks," I said as I made my way to the former bedroom in the back of Aaron's house. I found him with his headphones on, sitting before a most impressive bank of radio gear.

"Hey there, Whisky," I said to get his attention. He held up one hand to quiet me, as he took notes on the broadcast he was listening to. Two more minutes passed, and apparently the broadcast ended.

"Have a seat, Rick."

"Whatcha got?"

"Well, you already know that local radio and TV are out."

"I do, just from turning it on."

"Sheriff comms are on emergency backup, and your Metro frequencies are probably on backup, too. Railroad transmitters were hit last night, er, this morning. Sounded like rifle fire from what one of the tech's said."

"Hear any military communications?"

"Plenty, all scrambled. With that handy little unit you requisitioned though, here's the transcript."

Aaron was referring to an off-the-books transaction where I arranged to have a military receiver, capable of decoding encrypted transmissions, provided to Aaron 'for backup purposes.' As far as the Army knew, it just went missing. Without the encryption keys (provided), it was a boat anchor. With the keys, it gave us another window out of the box.

"Anything suspicious?"

"Red team is playing by the book. Blue team isn't."

Red Team was us, the United States. Blue Team was 'them,' the S.A.

"Summary?"

"From what I'm picking up, and that's well beyond the local area, S.A. forces are in a coordinated effort to disrupt transportation communications and civilian communications channels in all USA controlled states and territories. It's been marginally successful, apparently."

"Goal?"

"A bright guy once said without communications, you haven't got squat."

"We haven't had much in the way of comms for eleven months."

"Making what you have left, all the more valuable. And vulnerable. Other parts, Hell, most of the country has restored telephone service, or did until today."

"Ours isn't far away from working again."

"Don't advertise that too much. Rick, I think they're planning on some sort of offensive. I'm not sure with what, or when, but generally this type of action would precede some major action."

"Yeah. By a matter of minutes or hours."

"Certainly. And you haven't had a briefing from your Army comms contact today, and you might not."

"Roger?"

"Charlie patrol is two hours overdue. SAR units are looking for them now."

"Any idea where?"

"Browne Mountain. They were setting up a redundant transmitter up by the KDA site."

"OK. Anything else?"

"It's in the transcript. The S.A.'s putting up a helluva fight here and there. Shadowy. Sneaky. Dishonorable. You won't like what you read."

"I'm sure I won't. Your reception frequencies listed on here?"

"Yep. Feel free to share."

"I will. Once I find somebody to share with."

"Watch your ass, soldier. Somebody's likely to shoot it off."

"Thanks, Aaron, I will do my best. Joe get you that goose you wanted for Thanksgiving?"

"So he says. Good egg, that one."

"He is at that. I better run. Let Alan know if you need anything for the big day."

"We're fine. Ellen's a pretty fair quartermaster."

"I'm sure!" I said as Aaron rose and we shook hands. "Thanks for everything."

"Glad to do it. Remember what I said, Rick. You will not like what's in that report."

We were five miles closer to town, and five pages into the stack of paper, when I asked the Lieutenant to contact the PACNW liaison officer. He radioed to his command station, eventually tracking down Kurt George, Elaine Cross's counterpart. They'd switched shifts a while back, he normally handled the twelve-hour 'night' shift. I wasn't sure why he'd still be on duty.

After a few minutes of negotiating, we settled on a meeting at eight o'clock.

Aaron was right. I didn't like what I was reading.

By seven thirty-five, I'd settled into the office, cleared of the fair-sized pile of 'urgent' requests, and poured a cup of really bad coffee. The entire staff was on edge—everyone knew something was up.
Mike Amberson arrived just as I was punching up his extension.

"Sheriff. I see we're having another rough day."

"Ain't just us," He said. "You got the lousy coffee, too I see," he said as he looked at my chipped mug.

"Yeah. Who else? I got a report here from Aaron Watters that tells me all kinds of ugly from all over the country."

"Kootenai County's comms are completely down. And their power grid. Stevens, Pend Oreille, Lincoln, and Adams County got hit on their grids and on their domestic water pumping stations. Eight lines from Grand Coulee were dynamited as well," Mike said.

"This is happening all over the West, Mike. There must be hundreds of teams doing this, and they're right in our midst."

"Understood."

"Casualties here?"

"Some missing persons reports just coming in. Most of this didn't start getting noticed until an hour or two ago. Most people around there are used to outages. When the field crews went to track down the problems, they found way more than they bargained for."

"We're used to it. California, Nevada….Hell, most of the remaining states, they're not. We're barreling toward a bitterly cold winter and the SA just unplugged the grid. I'm betting the Army was caught completely by surprise by this."

"No one could have expected this."

"Sure we could have. We're still thinking conventionally," I said as Major George knocked on the doorframe.

"Major. I see we have a situation on our hands. Again." I said as I pointed to Aaron's notes.

"No offense, Rick, but that may be the understatement of the day."

"Have a seat. Avoid the coffee. Brenda?" I asked one of the office administrators, "Could you make us some tea?"

"Well, I could if we had some," she replied. Brenda held a Ph. D. in fashion and textiles. When there was a University of Washington, she was an associate professor. She'd found out quite quickly, when she was stranded in Spokane when Rainier went off, that an advanced degree in fashion was literally useless. She'd had to learn on the job, working her way up the ladder.

I reached into my desk and fished out a box of Darjeeling. "Here. Make plenty."

"Will do!" she said as she spun on her heel and headed to the lunchroom.

"OK, Kurt. I'm hearing from Mike we have big bad ugly all around us."

"Oh, here too, probably not quite as brutal as in other parts of the country."

"I'm assuming this was a surprise," I asked.

"We had no idea that something this widespread was coming."

"Not a complete surprise then," Mike asked.

"Not entirely, we'd heard some scuttlebutt but very little hard intel. Certainly no idea the SA had this capability," Kurt replied, leaning forward in his chair.

"I asked Mike this earlier. Casualties?"

"There are enemy dead. Locally, regionally and nationally. Most I'm hearing were taken out by civilian forces, not military," Major George responded.

"Different rules of engagement. You pull the plug on somebody's power in eastern Montana in the winter, and sure as Hell you're gonna be a hundred and sixty-eight grains heavier," Mike said matter-of-factly, referring to the weight of a rifle round.

"Kurt, I want you to read this through and tell me if this is accurate," I said, handing him the stack of paper than Aaron had provided. "What I just read on my way in tells me that there are more than a thousand dead. A thousand dead civilians. Maybe a third of them executed. A fair amount of that percentage were children."

"I can't say that's inaccurate based on what I've heard. I'm assuming this is from civilian radio traffic."

"Multiple bands. Not all civilian."

That sentence drew a raised eyebrow, but no further inquiry. We gave Major George a few minutes to read Aaron's notes. Brenda returned with a pot of tea, poured us all cups, and left us a small container of honey. I indulged, and added some to Kurt's cup as well as he nodded approval.

"Gentlemen, I can't dispute anything in that report. Since the S.A. moved their capitol from Denver to Chicago, they've consolidated regular military units to strategic locations well within what we'd regard as their frontier, with the exception of them bisecting U.S. territory along the Mississippi to the Gulf, and that's a narrow strip that's in constant flux. In the 'no man's land' between U.S. lines and their hard lines, they've got irregulars. Maybe military in civilian dress, a fair percentage of them ex-cons, and a fair percentage of that group downright violent. What we've seen in the past few hours is a taste of that. For sure, some of these have extensive tactical training, probably their team leaders, who may or may not be in the field."

"What's Austin doing about this?" I asked. Austin was now the provisional Capitol of the United States of America. Someday, we hoped we'd have D.C. back. Perhaps by then the radioactivity would be manageable.

"There will be serious reaction, I'm certain. One issue to consider here is the dispersed nature of the field targets. Many of the actions appear to be the result of very small teams, infiltrating deep into our territory," the Major replied.

"So hit some infrastructure!" I said in a mad-as-Hell tone.

"I'm sure that option is on the table."

"All right, Kurt. What's the plan for the day?" trying to calm my anger down. "I'm assuming our military forces are hunting bear."

"Affirmative. Don't expect to see any idle uniforms anytime soon. We have a battalion in the field today in six counties around Spokane. By noon, we'll have a brigade."

236

"Five thousand men hunting how many?"

"Figure a couple hundred, max. We'll get many of that number."

"What's this do to us in the metro area?"

"Figure that you'll have minimal coverage and backup from the military until this is handled."

"OK, figured that. How am I supposed to, sorry, how are we supposed to get the word out to our population that they need to watch out for themselves and keep out of trouble, because most of the police and military are otherwise engaged?"

"Are you supposed to?" Major George asked. "Maybe you don't."

"All right, I see your point here. Weather's cold, more snow coming, most commerce is running pretty slowly. You're saying let things self-police."

"By and large, yes. You still have about thirty-percent of the full complement of law enforcement personnel as residents in the various precincts, you have a largely armed population, and for the past two weeks crime has been pretty low."

"Mike, your thoughts?"

"We effectively have no way to really get the word out until civilian communications are repaired."

"And don't bet on that happening right away," Kurt George said. "Initial reports on damage to your TV transmitters look pretty bad."

"Mike, have you already increased security on our own power stations?"

"No, the power operators did that ahead of us. Private contractors, more than happy to be on sentry for three hots and a cot and a guarantee of work in the spring."

"Any other vulnerabilities?" I asked, knowing there were probably too many to count.

"Sure. Ones we can do anything about? Not many at this point. All we can do is get the word out to the neighborhoods, and let them handle it," Mike said.

"Dammit all to Hell," I said as I leaned back in my chair. "Major, anything else?"

"Not at this time, but we'll be in touch."

"I expected to see Elaine today. Did you two switch shifts?"

"She's at home today. Kids are under the weather, so I pulled a double."

"Anything serious?" I asked.

"Not sure. I got the word from one of my LT's."

"Maybe I'll have my wife check in with her."

"You're one of the few people in the County equipped to have that kind of communication, I guess," the Major said as he stood up. "Mr. Drummond, Sheriff, we'll be in touch later today."

"Thanks, Kurt," I said as I shook his hand.

I poured myself another cup of tea, now cooling to the room temperature of sixty degrees, and filled Mike's cup as well. Outside, the snow was coming down again, and the wind was coming up. "You ready for this?" I asked Mike as I watched the snow.

"No, but that's never stopped me before. It's here, and we're gonna get it, or it's gonna get us."

Friday morning,
November Seventeenth
11:15 a.m.

Mike and I had a morning interrupted by reports from his deputies county wide, who were barely able to communicate on their alternate radios—citizens band. We also put a rough draft of a press release for Mike's information officer to polish up and get out on the radio as soon as communications were restored, which happened around eleven. The announcement was pretty grave in its tone. Contrary to our earlier thoughts with Major George, we decided to spill it all. I wasn't one for concealing the gravity of things when lives were in the balance. Maybe some alert resident would come forth and rat out their 'neighbor' who liked to hunt police officers, radio transmitters, and electrical transformers.

"You think we're going to win this, Mike?" I asked as I stood at the window, looking out over the parking lot and its' guard shack, snow now drifting against the building. "The war, I mean," realizing that my question might have been in reference to the current battle.

He paused before he answered. "I don't know. If we have to sink to their level to do it, I wonder myself how much of ourselves we lose in order to 'win.'"

"Yeah. You heard anything new on the lines?" I asked, referring to states or parts of states held by the S.A.

"Not much. I was hoping to hear something from our military friends on that. God knows that those who pass for journalists these days don't open their mouths on the subject."

"Why should they?" I asked. "You saw what happened to that reporter in Denver when he questioned Lambert about an executive order to reinstate the Bill of Rights." Lambert was a former Senator, appointed President, who then decided to create his own version of American fascism. The first lessons they taught the nation was that it was 'their' way. Period. The second lesson was that only the first lesson mattered.

"Yeah. I heard it. His family, his friends. All of them." Fairly widespread coverage on Radio Free America had addressed the demise of William McDowell in some detail. His remains were found along with his extended family in a warehouse in East St. Louis, bound, gagged, and shot in the back of their heads. A few days later, additional discoveries were made, of his closer friends, co-workers, cameraman, and producer.

"Yeah. Not a real good incentive to poke your nose out."

"No, it's not. And that gal that worked for ABC in Los Angeles. She asked the wrong questions too. And they got her as well, way behind the lines," Mike said.

I was quiet for a few moments. "So how do we win this?" I asked, looking at an old sepia-toned map of the United States, one that had belonged to Walt Ackerman before me. "They've got the entire Northeast down to Virginia. Part of Virginia and West Virginia. Part of Kentucky. Part of Tennessee and that strip steak of Mississippi and Louisiana to Memphis and the wiggly line east of Little Rock. Almost all of Kansas. Half of Colorado. Big chunk of Nebraska, Iowa and that diagonal up to the Twin Cities. All of the Rust Belt."

"But not the Southeast. Not three-quarters of Canada. Not sixty percent of Mexico. Not the Navy, which I understand means the entire Pacific and most of the Atlantic. Not most of the Air Force. And of course, not the West."

"We're the Balkans," I said, knowing that wasn't quite right.

"No, we're the United States. We have a cancer though, that can kill us if we don't kill it."

"We have battle lines that are what, three thousand miles long?" I asked.

"Probably longer."

"So how do you manage a three-thousand mile front? How do you re-supply if you're inside that box?" I asked, knowing Mike probably wouldn't have the answers either. "C'mon. You're an ex-Ranger."

"Smart ex-Ranger. We left stuff like that up to the higher pay grades. We were more about where the metal meets the meat."

"Right. Now you're the youngest Sheriff in County history, with a pretty wife, cute twins, a new-to-you house, and a few dozen deputies to manage. And let's not forget our tens of thousands of neighbors. The war's only four states away, or next door, depending on what day it is."

Mike laughed a little bit at that. "We're fighting on a different front."

"So far, maybe."

"OK. If I were running the S.A. train, I'd consolidate my gains. Preserve the eastern seaboard for shipping. Hang on to the Mississippi. Create an air-cover umbrella over my territory. Problem for them is they seem to have no meaningful air force and we do. They appear to have no meaningful naval forces and we're probably blockading them. And yet they continue to posture that they are the stronger 'nation.' They basically have coal, and no oil. They have no way to import it without going through our lines. Terrorist tactics taken deep into the territory that they wish to win over by honey."

"Summary?" I asked.

"It makes absolutely no sense whatsoever. They're doing everything wrong, they do not appear to have adequate military forces to mount a meaningful offensive. They appear to have no means of sustaining themselves...."

"And yet, here we are, with men in the field, hunting ghosts."

"It seems to me that they cannot last."

241

"That's logical enough," I said.

"But you're thinking something else," Mike said, looking at me and not the map.

"I am. I think they've got an outside sponsor, they're planning something bigger and much more widespread, and are planning to BE the stronger nation as a result," I said, looking at the map, still not really understanding it.

"Gut feel," Mike said.

"Yeah. Nothing more. It's just that when nothing else makes sense, that one thought does."

We looked at the map again, as we heard the Emergency Broadcast System tone come up on the radio. We heard a more polished version of our words come out of the speaker.

"Let's get out of here for awhile," I said. "My brain needs a break."

"Old age, huh?" Mike said as we headed down to the cafeteria.

"Don't look now, but I'm not too many years older than you are, and when I was your age, my kids were already in school. You'll be, let's see, fifty-seven when they graduate from high school. Let's talk then about age, hmmm?"

"We should be so lucky," he said.

"Amen."

In the cafeteria, Mike and I found a table off in the corner, away from most of the other employees taking lunch. Today, we had what appeared to be a locally-made pasta, with some kind of meat—I didn't bother to read the menu, as it only had one choice—and corn in a casserole type dish. Beverages included water, or...water.

"So how's the new house?" I asked.

"Smaller than we're used to, which is just fine. Easier to heat."

"You got the old place secured?"

"After a fashion. We took everything we needed, or might need. Boarded up the windows, sealed everything else up as best we could."

"Well, it was smart to move. There wasn't any way those roads would let you guys stay out there, utilities or not."

"I know. Still, it was a shame leaving it. Ash must've had a hundred hours stenciling up the nursery for the twins." Ashley was Mike's wife, who was adjusting to life as a twenty-four seven mom.

"You've got more land now, a barn, and a good house going forward."

"And I have your brother-in-law to thank for that."

"Seemed like a good fit." Alan had been out at the Greenacres barter store in late September, trying to talk one of our 'regular' suppliers into staying. Brad and Jennie Rivers had a nice home and property, but had decided that it was better for their future to pack up and head south before the winter really hit. Through Alan's contacts, he'd managed to arrange travel for Brad and his family to Salt Lake, where they had extensive family. When asked about the house, and knowing there really wasn't any way to sell it, Brad told Alan to find somebody who could really use the place the way it was intended. Maybe someday, they could come back up to Spokane. Either way, Brian and Jennie didn't figure to get the house back.

"You'll have to give us some schooling on the garden thing. We just got a taste of it this year."

"We'd be happy to. I hear that most of your basement was set up for a pantry?"

"And a canning kitchen, which I was completely unfamiliar with pre-Domino."

"It'd be good to have a place designed on purpose," I said almost to myself. "Karen and I were married all of six months when we found our place. Moved in and filled it up with stuff. It's taken years to de-junk now, and only the quake made us serious about it."

"We're filling it up quickly enough."

"Cloth diapers and buckets of laundry slime don't count," I said. Laundry-slime was a concoction made from bar soap, washing soda, and Borax. The recipe for it was discovered in my stash of knowledge collected off of the Internet. At the Drummond house, we were stretching out our pre-Domino detergents, and using 'slime' to make up the difference.

"It's not all full of that, but you might think it. Lots of dehydrated stuff. Some home-canned stuff, lots of bulk food in the bins that the Rivers had built."

"While I don't agree with their religious beliefs, I cannot fault them one iota for food preparation philosophy."

"I'm not sure Ashley's going to be ready for all the work needed to keep that kind of system going."

"No one is," I said. "You remember that report put together by the Army—the Redstone Arsenal report?"

"Yeah. Some reason for optimism there, once we hit bottom."

"You think so? Are you forgetting the statements about 'fortified locations' for stuff? Industries, technology, medical…."

"I remember, didn't really make an impression, maybe because it just made sense. Why do you ask?" Mike asked.

"I'm just not sure that the bottom they've predicted, and the recovery timeline can be possible with a civil war raging."

"It can't. There's no way. Too much reallocation of resources and depletion of existing materiel to do both. Even so, it may be a delay, not a game-stopper."

I sat there for a few moments, thinking. What would our part be in the recovery? In the War?

"Spill it, Rick."

"We have a strategic industry here that's been idle since January fourteenth, and haven't done a thing about it."

"That would be…"

"The old Kaiser mill," I said. The Trentwood Plant had been shut down due to both the depressed aluminum prices and a plant refit when the Domino hit. I remembered the damage reports after the quake weren't catastrophic, and that mill employees had creatively secured the plant—windows were all barred anyway, and aluminum plate was welded over every single door. Since then, we'd just had bigger things to think about, no, more immediate things to think about, and this one got away from us.

"If vandals and thieves haven't gotten to it. No one's been guarding the place," Mike said.

"Let me get a crew on it. I'm wondering if we still have any plant engineers around."

"Bound to be a few. And speaking of replacements…."

"I know. Who's the lucky candidate for my job?"

"Yeah. You got a short list?"

"One Tonya Lincoln." Tonya had served with me on the old Recovery Board, and was now head of our Commerce department. 'Sharp' didn't begin to describe her.

"Good choice. Ask her yet?"

"Nope, got a meeting scheduled with her at two."

"Think she'll say no?"

"Doubtful. Bigger problem will be *her* replacement. I'll let her figure that one out," I said as I noticed an Army corporal enter the room, spot Mike and I, and make a bee line for us.

"Excuse me, Colonel Drummond?"

"Not commissioned yet, Corporal. At the moment I believe I'm still a civilian," I said as I stood. "What's up?"

"Report from Major George, sir. He asked that you review this immediately."

"My office, upstairs. Let's go," I said. "Mike, care to join us?"

"Sure. As long as I'm not getting drafted."

"I'll see to it that within my extremely limited powers, that you will remain a civvie."

"That'll make me sleep better," Mike said with a laugh as we hit the stairs.

On my desk, another notice that I had 'urgent' emails to review. Nothing new there. "Have a seat, Corporal," I said. "Where'd we lose the Sheriff?" I asked, just as Mike came in holding a sheaf of papers of his own. "Get sidetracked?"

"Report from West Plains. Seems our Airway Heights precinct got a few of the bad guys sniping at the flight line at Fairchild."

"KIA?" I asked.

"Four. Two wounded. Air Force security police and our guys are interrogating them."

"Losses on our side?"

"None."

"Good," I said, opening up the sealed envelope from Kurt George.

I scanned the requisition, then read it in depth, and summarized it for Mike and the corporal.

"Effective eighteen November, oh-nine-hundred, ninety percent of Spokane County's railroad stock is being requisitioned by the United States government for the war effort." I paused for a moment to let that sink in. "Corporal, is there some sort of acknowledgement that I'm to make here?"

"Yes, sir, second page. Your signature is required."

"Just for spits and giggles, what happens if I don't sign?" That obviously made the young corporal uncomfortable.

"Sir, I…."

"Corporal, the rail system is one of the keys to our recovery. Yanking that out puts us, to be kind, in a helluva spot. There's nothing here that says anything about continuing to supply Pacific Northwest Command and the civilian population through means of rail. Road traffic ain't an option. Get it?"

"Yes sir, but I…"

"I know. You're following orders to see that I receive these. I've received them. I will speak with Major George and the rest of Command regarding this. You're dismissed."

"Sir, I was ordered to bring back those orders, signed."

"Understood, corporal. I'm under a moral obligation to try keep Spokane County and most of the inland northwest alive. That means trade beyond our state for food we can't grow. Fruit that's out of season. Nuts. Stuff like toothbrushes and soap and paper goods hopefully someday. Supplying California wheat, peas, lentils, timber, maybe one of these days aluminum. Can't really do that without rail cars and locomotives."

"Understood, sir," he said, with resignation.

"I will speak to your superiors as soon as possible, Corporal. That might be a little while though. Feel free to make yourself

247

comfortable in the cafeteria or the employee lounge. I'll track you down as soon as possible," I said, all but telling him that it was no longer appropriate for him to be sitting in my office. He took the hint, and stood to go.

"Sir," he said at attention, spun smartly on a heel and headed for the hallway. I waited until he was out of earshot until I talked with Mike about it.

"Damn it," I said to the paper on my desk.

"You know, that request was a courtesy," Mike said with barely concealed humor. "They're going to take them regardless."

"Understood. I still want somebody to acknowledge that we're on the radar screen. We were all but ignored after the Domino. The Federal response was almost nil. I just don't want to be forgotten."

"Well damned sure you're going to get somebody's attention," he said. "Can you get by with ten percent of your rolling stock?"

"No idea. Not as well as we might have, but nothing works out the way you plan anyway," I said. "What's in your stack of happy news?"

"Nothing all that happy. Line crews getting sniped at while making repairs. Aiming to wound, not kill, and of course to take out the new transformers as soon as they're installed, wasting more time and resources. Got a report out of Whitman County that communications teams are being killed as well. Worse than that further out. Kidnappings of families of key people."

"To what end?" I asked, guessing the answer.

"Leverage."

"Of course...."

"I better get moving. Spent enough time indoors today," Mike said as he stood.

"Watch yourself. You could get used to it."

"Nope, too much time in the field. Not comfortable behind a desk."

"Remember, dinner tonight at our place."

"Six o'clock?"

"Earlier if you like—if I'm not there I'm sure Karen would love to spend time with the twins and catching up with Ashley."

"See you then," I said shaking his hand and looking at the time. I had less than hour until meeting with Tonya.

Time to rattle a cage.

I headed upstairs to the old Commissioners' office suite, which for logical reasons was now the home to our communications office. It was also the home to a half-dozen secure-frequency military radios that allowed us to easily communicate with our friends in green.

"Rayanne, can you see if you can get hold of General Anderson?"

"Yes, sir," the duty communications tech replied, nervous eyes downcast. I could imagine what she was thinking.

I was in luck. Bob Anderson was 'in.'

"Mr. Drummond, I bet I know why you're calling me."

"Bob, I'm sure you do."

"You understand the need we have."

"I have a pretty good idea, yeah. I want to know what assurance we have that we're going to continue to have commercial rail service to keep us supplied and keep trade active."

"You have as much assurance as I can give you, which frankly isn't much."

"Does anyone in Austin have the faintest idea of what it's really like up here? What it's been like since January?"

"Only as much as your senators and representatives can shout I suppose. Rick, we need those cars and locomotives. You know why."

"Sure I do. I also know that we've got substantial trade obligations with Oregon, California and the rest of the southwest that we need to fulfill. That might be dicey without dependable rail schedules."

"We'll do what we can, but I cannot make any promises."

"This will end up on my successors' desk. But let me tell you, Tonya doesn't take any guff from anybody. She needs something she will find a way to get it. She'll make noise. She'll make you uncomfortable."

"Sounds like my in-laws."

"Family comparisons aside, General, if we don't have reasonably reliable rail service, then we fail badly. I've done the numbers. People up here will die."

"Understood. Can't discuss this further right now. You have anything else we need to go over, Rick?"

"Not at this time, General."

"We'll talk next week. Good luck."

"Thanks. Talk to you then," I said as the line went dead.

Tonya was gonna love this, I thought.

Tonya was late, which meant that I had a few more minutes to read a recent status report on County service disruptions. Two more sniper incidents had taken out the engine blocks of County plows out in East Farms, out near the Idaho state line. Single shot, fifty caliber round. No one wounded. The loss of the truck, which was abandoned in place until scarce military units could arrive to go hunting, meant that both road links to North Idaho would be closed with the snowfall. I was still reading, and pondering how far away the sniper had to be to take out a moving truck, when Tonya Lincoln knocked on the doorframe.

"Sorry I'm late Rick. Problems, problems."

"Apology accepted, and I have some more bad news for you."

"Add it to the pile," she said as she shook my hand. She was smartly dressed as always, today in a cream colored business jacket that accentuated her African heritage and beaming smile.

"Interested in a new job?" I teased. She knew what was coming, I was fairly sure.

"If it comes with better pay and less hours, sure," she said with a little bit of a snicker. Tonya worked more hours at her job than anybody in the senior staff. And the pay stunk.

"It is what you make it. I've been asked to accept a commission in the Guard by Dave Hall." Tonya had met Governor Hall at a conference in late September, while I was still laid up in bed. "I want you to take over my position, with a starter course beginning right now."

"Kinda sudden isn't it?"

"I'm feeling pressure from above, it seems…"

"And things flow downhill," she said, cleaning up the analogy from the waste-plumbing version to something more civilized.

"They do. You have anyone to move up to fill in as Commerce Director?"

"My deputy director. He knows the system and what I expect of him, and most importantly knows what works and doesn't."

"Good enough. Now, to get you up to speed on some more bad things going on, we're losing most of our rail capacity effective tomorrow," I said, ready to gauge her reaction. She was unsurprised.

"We saw this coming, not that there's anything we can do about it anyway."

"You're taking that, well, better than I did. I was ticked."

"Armies move on wheels. When you have the wheels, you become pretty popular."

"Impact locally?"

"We're running a deficit for three more weeks, due to stepped up shipping from southern Idaho, Utah, Montana, and Oregon. We bought a lot of stuff in anticipation of losing rail."

"Stuff?" I asked, with more than a little surprise. We had as a standing order, doing everything in our power to run a 'balanced budget.'

"I apologize for overstepping, but we traded two months worth of lumber production for livestock, canned goods, cement, and dehydrated foods. We also have a request from the Idaho National Engineering Laboratory that we're not yet able to fulfill."

"What're they looking for?" I asked, dismissing Commerce's 'overstepping' their spending authority. It was prudent, assuming we could meet the production order for lumber. Our one working mill didn't exist in Spokane before the Domino, or not in operating condition. The mill had been shuttered and been slated for demolition. The earthquakes fixed that, though.

"Mil-spec aluminum."

"Your ears burning today?" I asked. "Mike and I were talking about Kaiser not two hours ago."

"Makes sense. It's a huge resource we've all but ignored," she replied. "Preliminary analysis by one of the former plant workers said it's four weeks from a return to operation, with the right amount of labor thrown at it and adequate raw materials."

"OK, then. You're ahead of me again. I was wondering if anyone had taken time to check it out."

"The Valley team did, last week. It's been on the list for awhile, but we needed to find somebody who knew enough about it to pronounce judgment."

"Who'd you find?"

"Ex-crane operator....that was his last job there. Retired three years ago. Started out sweeping floors. Did everything of consequence in the production line. Worked the hot-line up at the old Mead plant, too, before they shut that down."

"So back to INL," I said, using the acronym for the National Lab, "what are they looking for?"

"Request said they're looking for shaped mil-spec aluminum and specialty alloy products. Beyond that, they didn't specify. They did say that the other plants in Washington, like the old one over on the Columbia…"

"North of Wenatchee," I interrupted.

"Right. Alcoa plant, I think, was too badly damaged to produce for the foreseeable future. Longview plant is coming back, but it will be awhile too."

"They check with Columbia Falls? Over in Montana?"

"They've locked up production at that plant for the next two years."

Had I heard that right? "Two years?"

"That's what they told me."

"They want the same from us?"

"I would not be a bit surprised. This plant I think is more advanced than the Columbia Falls plant."

"Hmm," I said, thinking of the potential. "That's great news, Tonya. Good job."

"It'll be great news if we can make it happen."

"Hopefully from this chair you'll find a way to make it happen. Some advice though…"

"Absolutely," she replied deferentially, which was not necessary, I thought. She had a good head on her shoulders, or she wouldn't have the job she had. There were a lot of days that I thought that I ought to be working for her, not the other way 'round.

"Stay close to the ground here. Don't get desk bound, get out in the field with staff and the field crews. Run away from the power mongers. Better yet, put them in places where they can't muck anything up. Do the job, and get out. Don't let it run you, because given the chance, it will."

"Sage advice."

"There are things you can do. There are things you can't, even though you might want to. Do what's necessary. We've seen too much of the former and not enough of the latter for too many decades to count. Necessary is unpopular, sometimes ugly, and quite utilitarian. Necessary is cheaper though for the population, but won't make you all that popular."

"Sounds like you've been in this job for thirty years."

"No, but there are days that it feels like it. This is one of them," I said. "There's a stack of electronic paper that comes in every hour, more than you can take in, which then affects your decision-making. One task though that you cannot delegate is recovery planning, and that really needs to be the highest priority."

"We've been busy just keeping things going," Tonya said, correctly.

"Right. But where are we going? If we just focus on the now, the immediate, the next meal, and blunder along that way, we're likely to never really progress. Just exist. That isn't succeeding."

"Suggestions?" she asked. "You've obviously been thinking about this for a while."

"Gave me something to do while confined to bed, as well as retraining myself to think."

"Got it---you don't seem the type to ever rest," Tonya said with a smile.

"Like I used to tell one of my pastors, 'I'll rest when I'm dead,'" I said as I stood up to stretch, and look out at the snow and the east wind. "Recovery doesn't come from an office and it isn't imposed on people. It has to come from them and they have to want to be engaged. They need to be part of their community locally and feel that their voices are heard. We've tried to do that, but it's been more of trying to help them and less of trying to get them moving forward," I said, leaning back on the windowsill. "Sometimes I think we're failing them," I said with some frustration.

"Without being part of the whole process, they'll never be engaged. They need to relearn the cost of freedom, the price of it, and that complaining about their elected representatives can only be fixed by putting the right people in place and keeping them accountable," I said, "and that's not what we have in place throughout most of the State, and probably most of the country. Sure as Hell not in the S.A."

"Agreed, but what did you have in mind? I mean here? I'm not sure I know where you're going with this."

"I'm not sure I know myself. I think at a minimum though, the population in the urban area is under-represented. The Township system works fine for nice, even representation in rural areas, but it's unfair to the more dense areas—we haven't really paid enough attention to moving forward. And the townsmen keep loading up their relatives in jobs they're not qualified for. Find a way to differentiate the two, but provide balance, and deal with the rural and urban issues fairly," I said, finally coming to my conclusion. "I think the point I'm trying to make is this: Get the neighborhoods to use their voices. Have them elect a representative, make sure they're having scheduled discussions, votes, whatever, to make sure that you're hearing what they want you to hear. Term limit them too, so you don't have the same three percent running the show all the time. What you're really doing is grooming a generation of new leaders, from the ground up."

"Teaching them to lead."

"Yep. You can't force it on somebody—they have to have the spark to want to make a change. I think once that process is really going, the workload of the person in that chair," I said, pointing at the chair she'd be occupying shortly, "will go down precipitously. As it should."

She thought about my statement, which was not really something I planned on talking about in the slightest. It was just on my mind.

"So, you still interested in the job?" I asked.

She looked at me for a moment, "Perhaps now more than before."

"Good. Right answer."

By four p.m., Tonya was at the saturation point, and I'd talked myself hoarse, reviewing Metro-wide organizational issues, reviewing staffing needs, reviewing procedures for our new 'flash traffic' alerts to Metro supervisors and line crews. I then gave her one of the laptops with more gigs of information than she could consume for her evening read. She shook my hand, thanked me for the opportunity, and headed back to her office. I was sure she had a pile of work to do herself, and to get her replacement up to speed.

I could tell she'd be a good fit for the job, perhaps permanently. Maybe come next fall, we could have new elections for a new leadership structure that depended more on equal representation and less on the shoulders of one person. She'd be a good candidate, I thought as I sat back in my chair.

"Mr. Drummond? This just came in. Flash traffic again, sorry," one of the communications staff said as she handed me a canary yellow piece of paper.

"Everything's an emergency," I said. "Thanks," I said as dug out my reading glasses. Central Command. 'Great', I thought. 'Another missive from Austin.'

16:01:00 HOURS

FLASH TRAFFIC ALL COMMANDS

Tactical analysis of attacks against civilian infrastructure has been identified as functionally identical to swarm attacks used in Iraq and Afghanistan against US forces. 'Swarms' in those cases are small groups of three to five acting autonomously to disrupt and destroy targets of opportunity within a specific region over a period of days or weeks. The groups may work together or may be working individually within previously identified regions.

Swarm attacks are intended to demoralize the population through constant harassment and disruption of infrastructure, communications and basic services. Personnel are not typically targeted unless they have been identified as crucial to repair and reinstatement of services. Enemy agents conducting the swarm attack may blend into the civilian population, may pose as military, or may be concealed during part or all of their operations. Weapons include common-caliber rifles, handguns, and improvised devices.

All commands are ordered to pursue swarm agents with all resources available. It is noted that no swarm agents have been captured alive during current operations, and have killed EMTs and civilians trying to treat their wounds.

CENTCOM recommends civilian leadership inform the civilian population immediately of the current threat and tactics of the enemy.

End transmission, 16:01:03

"Swell," I said to myself, reaching for the phone.

By the time I was heading out the door, with my security detail in front and flanking me, the notice was being broadcast to the general public on both public radio stations, AM and FM. TV was gone again, with the transmitter taken out I'd read, by an armor-piercing round from a 30.06. I had a case of those myself, squirreled away. I wondered how many others were out there.

The ride home tonight was shared with a couple of our community center directors and staffers from out in Liberty Lake, who'd catch the Line at Fancher Road.   The wide-ranging conversation covered most of the plausible scuttlebutt about the War, with me holding my tongue when I ought to have.

"So, Mr. Drummond, who're you rooting for this basketball season?" Liberty Lake center director Jeff Bronson asked. A change of topic was welcome. I was weary of war talk.

"Central Valley Combined," I said. "But Jeff, I'm prejudiced. I went to the old CV. Kids were at University High before it hit the fan." The combined Central Valley district, far smaller than before the war, conducted specialized high school classes at one of the former middle schools roughly in the center of the Valley. Most academic classes were held in neighborhoods, at elementaries that were universally in walking distance.

"You don't think North Valley or one of the City schools can make a show?"

"You sound like an alum of one of the former schools in those districts."

"No, I went to Ferris just after the last Ice Age. I just hear a lot of talk on that sports channel on CB." One of the single-digit CB channels had been taken over in a local version of sports talk radio. When there was no dependable television or radio, or when the network coverage of the War, or the inane sitcom reruns were too much, there was always Fat Mickey and Rabbit to keep the locals entertained. I'd discovered them myself right after getting out of the hospital. They had a pretty good following, with comments coming to them on the adjacent frequencies. Three hours a day, they gave people something else to focus on. I'd like to meet those guys. I wondered what they did for a real job. Hopefully something legal.

"Kerry Jacobson will clean up," I said. Kerry was a classmate of Carl during grade school. He was now six foot five, I'd heard. I'd seen him play league ball against Carl, and Carl learned to his dismay that basketball wasn't in his future. "Phenomenal shooter, saw him hit from half-court three times last year."

"Yeah, but North Valley....they got that kid, what's his name....Aveolela. That Samoan kid," Jeff's assistant said.

"Haven't heard too much about him."

"I heard that one of the Cal schools was recruiting him before the War," Jeff replied.

"Well, if they were, they were probably violating more than a few rules," I said. "Like that matters."

"We'll all be home in time for the game, and we'll just wait and see," Jeff said as we pulled near the train platform. "Channel three, I think. Starts at seven."

"Where are they playing?"

"The old Trentwood middle school, I think."

"I might have to listen in," I said. "Be a nice change of pace."

"Take care, Mr. Drummond. Thanks for the lift outbound," Jeff said in thanks. "You saved us an hour."

"No problem guys. Take it easy," I said as the door closed.

"I'll tell ya, sir, no disrespect, but City Central's gonna mop up when the Valley schools play 'em," my driver, a buck sergeant contributed.

"Speaking as if you know, Sergeant?"

"Yes, sir. Our unit was billeted at North Central where they practice. They've got five starters that could be playing college ball anywhere. The smallest of them is six-six. My money's on them all the way."

"Good to know when it comes to wagers," I said.

"Sir, I don't bet unless I'm dead sure I'm right."

"Neither do I, Sarge. Neither do I."

Fifteen minutes later, the Sarge dropped me at the gate, where Buck decided that my glove looked like a chew toy, despite my hand being inside. He was playing tug of war, 'talking' with me as we wrestled up to the porch. I looked up the street, and saw lights on up at two of our recently vacated homes.

"Buck, we've got new neighbors. Looks like Alan and Ron made an executive decision. Good for them, huh?" I said, giving him a tug and a smack on the top of his head. That served to encourage him all the more.

I unlocked the front door, and heard a kitchen full of noisy friends and relatives. Kelly ran up and gave me a hug.

"Hiya Daddy. How's your day?"

"Pretty average. Yours?"

"Great! We learned how to make jalapeno cheese today, and can it of course, and I got an 'A' on my advanced placement exam."

"Good for you! My day wasn't quite so exciting."

"Do you have to go in tomorrow? To work I mean."

"Nope. Monday. Which should be my last day." That let the air out of her balloon.

"Are you going in the...Army then?" She looked worried already.

"No. I'll go in on Monday for awhile, but that'll be it. Tonya Lincoln, you remember her? She's taking over for me next week. I'll go in after Thanksgiving," I said, as Ron and Libby noticed me.

"Friday night, and you need a drink," Ron said from behind Lib.

"How's your day?" Libby asked.

"Too early to tell. Maybe after I decompress with whatever Ron's going to serve me...." I said as I stowed my pack and shucked off my shell and shirt-jacket. "Where's Karen?" I asked.

"She's over at her Mom's. Should be back in a bit. Sarah's over there with one of the Doc's. Mom took a fall this afternoon," Ron said.

"And Alan and Mary are with her too," Libby added, passing me the drink that Ron was cradling.

"She OK?" I asked as I took a drink. Bourbon. Very, very good bourbon.

"Might be a concussion. Might be a hip, too. Maybe, more," Ron said with appropriate gravity.

"When did this happen?" I asked. I don't think it had hit me then.

"About an hour ago. Karen didn't want to call you—she knew that you couldn't get here any sooner anyway. We're helping out with her canning, and by extension, dinner. She was processing a bunch of meat for canning when Mary called over. She called us to finish up."

"Thanks. Should I go over?" I asked, probably a stupid question.

"Probably a good idea," Libby said.

"Hence, the drink?" I asked.

"These days, yes. This might not end up well," Ron said.

"Thanks. Where's Carl?"

"Down in the radio room. Sounds like the fighting in Colorado's getting pretty intense," Ron said. "He came back over a little while ago."

"Yeah. Heard a little of that myself," I said, taking another swig.

"What does the S.A. have in Colorado worth fighting for?" Lib asked, perhaps rhetorically.

"Pride. I can't imagine what else," I said honestly.

"Especially in the winter. I can't imagine what that must be like," Libby said, obviously putting her son in the position of the replacement ground soldier in a winter offensive.

"John will be OK, Lib," I said, taking her hand and giving it a squeeze. "I better go across the field."

"I'm ready, Daddy. Here's your heavy coat," Kelly said, handing me my Eddie Bauer parka.

"Your job to shuttle me over?"

"After giving you a minute to decompress, and have Aunt Libby and Uncle Ron get you that drink, yes."

"You're what, fourteen going on thirty?"

"Some days, yep. C'mon," she said. "Oh, and Mrs. Amberson won't be able to make it. The twins are coming down with a bad cough. Carl got that on your County radio from the Sheriff."

"Darn," I said. "Probably just as well all told." I said. "You put her up to all of this?" I asked Libby.

"Nope, this she came up with all on her own."

"Ron, you and Alan get the new houses filled up?" I asked.

"Yeah—we'll go over that later. They're good choices."

"Karen and Mary and I made the final choices," Libby said.

"Well then, I'm sure we're good. Be back in awhile," I said. Thanks, you two."

"Glad to do it. Now get moving," Libby said, giving me a hug.

Across the 'back forty' as we called it, the house was fully lit up. Kelly and I walked without much talk across the field, without Buck or Ada to scout.

We entered through the back door, and Karen met us there.

"How's she doing?"

"Stubborn as a Kansas mule," she said. "Not great."

I could hear Sarah and one of the doctors from the clinic down the hall in Grace's bedroom. "Is she going to be OK?" I asked as I embraced my wife, who was starting to tear up.

"They're stitching up her head. Cut her scalp when she fell. Landed wrong on her chair too, and might have broken her hip or her pelvis. She has a lot of pain in her back, too."

"Dang. Any idea how she fell?"

"No. She doesn't remember it. Mary and Rachel heard her. They were downstairs when it happened. Mark was outside."

"Hospital?"

"Probably soon. Ambulances were all busy. Doc Abernathy made a call though."

"Can I go in?"

"Sure. I had to get out for a minute."

"OK. Be right back."

"Kel, give your Mom a hug. And say a prayer for your Grandma."

"Done."

Back in the bedroom, I quietly entered the room, where Grace had been mildly sedated, and relatively immobilized. Sarah was finishing up the sutures as Sandy Abernathy looked on. Alan was staying out of the way, and Mary I noted was in the room across the hall, keeping the little ones out of the way, but keeping an eye on Grace, too.

"Hey," I said softly to Alan, "How's she doing?"

"I heard that, and I'm fine," Grace said, with eyes closed.

"Mom, hush now. They're going to take you to Valley to check you out."

"Waste of time. I'll be fine tomorrow."

"Don't argue, Grace. You're outnumbered," Sandy said. "And I'm tougher than you are."

"Fine general practitioner you turned out to be," Grace said with a wince as Sarah tied off the last stitch. "Not so tight, dear, unless you're trying to take the wrinkles out."

"Sorry, Grace. Kinda new at this."

"I noticed," Grace said as I heard a vehicle out front.

"Bus is here," another unfamiliar voice said. I heard the voice, talking to a radio, "Transport in five...."

"Look at it this way, Mom. You get breakfast in bed for awhile," I said, trying to put a cheery spin on it.

"In a pig's eye. You ever had a catheter?"

"Why yes I have, and recently," I replied. "Maybe they'll get you a nice male nurse," I said as I heard the gurney enter the living room and unfold. I stepped out of the room, and called over to the house on Alan's hand-held radio, and made a quick request of Ron.

"Grace, we're going to move you now," Doctor Abernathy said calmly. "I want you to relax and let us do all the work, OK?"

"Like I have a choice?"

"Tensing up while we move you might cause some more problems. And pain. If we do this, you'll be more comfortable, OK?"

"All right, let's get this over with," she said.

"Clear the room please," Sarah asked, quite officially.

We filed out of the room as the parameds moved in.

"You going to the hospital?" I asked Alan and Karen.

"I think so," Karen said. "Alan?"

"Yep."

"Ron's bringing the car around," I said. "Kel, are you OK to stay here with the kids and Mary?"

"Yep. We'll be fine."

"You need anything, call Ron or Libby. OK?"

"We'll be fine. We'll play some games and make some popcorn. Just let me know how Gram's doing when you can."

"Thanks, babe," I said as Grace was moved out the front door. "We'll find a way to call over soon."

"K. Love you."

"You, most," she said as I gave her a hug.

Another fifteen minutes, and we were camped in the ER at Valley General.

2 2

Karen had tossed and turned most of the night. Unusual for her; not for me. We'd made it back home around eleven, Grace admitted for the time being. She hadn't broken a hip or pelvis, but that was conditioned on the disclaimer, 'no obvious break.' She did however, have numerous compression fractures in her back. The orthopedic specialist said that a full recovery was unlikely, given her age. Within the space of a few hours, she'd transitioned from an active and relatively healthy senior citizen to being in almost constant pain with the slightest movement. Even pre-War, this would have been a difficult situation to deal with, both for her and the family.

Now, in the midst of the Second Civil War, in this place and time, the resources we once took for granted were no longer available in any fashion. Skilled nursing for the elderly, once so common, now flat out didn't exist.

In these days, here and now, people of Grace's age were rare. The lack of medicines that had extended the lives of so many were all but gone. As a result, so were those that had depended on those miracle compounds.

None of us knew how we were going to take care of Grace, try to keep her out of pain, try to extend her life. I wondered, as I lay there on an unheard-of, sleeping-in-on-Saturday morning, listening to my wife sleep, how Grace would handle the pain once the diazepam wore off.

I heard Kelly and Carl downstairs, making breakfast. Even though the blinds in the bedroom were drawn along with the heavy drapes, I could tell we had one of those brilliant sunny days, setting off the fresh snowfall. Once upon a time, less than a year ago, we'd have been awakened by the newspaper guy, delivering the morning yesterdays' news at five-thirty in his beat-up Subaru, and then some poor soul having to be at work before seven.

As I lay in bed, I was thinking that I couldn't remember the last time that a car on our street disturbed my sleep. Even the Army patrols didn't drive down the street in early morning. Maybe once a night—the majority was on foot. In the outlying areas, or the suburbs that had been abandoned, the cavalry was back. The demand for horses and tack for Army use outstripped any reasonable expectation of delivery. One of the new Army Mounted Cav units was in training at the old Fairgrounds, under the watchful and direct training of members of the Backcountry Horsemen. To say it was odd to see a modern horse soldier, with the new Forest Green digital camo and headgear, was an understatement. Some enterprising quartermaster had also come up with a way to create modern saddlebags equipped to handle MOLLE gear attachments or in some cases, the older ALICE gear. Leather was still the preferred sleeve for the rifle, although the newest main battle rifle, the M16C, nicknamed 'California', was quite different than the -16's of old. Super-light and strong alloys used in the receiver and barrel, relatively large in profile, but providing a finished product that was a full three pounds lighter than a -16A4 with a thirty round magazine.   I hadn't seen one of the new rifles, and I'd heard they were still quite rare, still using a common M-16 round, manufactured at a new factory in Long Beach.   California must be a very different place these days, I thought.

After a shower, shave and dressed in clean work clothes, Karen and I found our way downstairs for breakfast.

"Good morning, Daddy," Kel said as she gave me a squeeze. "Hugs for Mom," she said to Karen as her turn came.

"What wonders have you created this fine day?" Karen asked as I looked at the fully decked out breakfast table, including one of my parents fine tablecloths and our best Sterling silver. "And look at that table!"

"Raspberry scones, Carl's working on the hard-boiled egg, ham and cheese breakfast casserole, coffee, and....orange juice. And English muffins for Dad, because I know he likes them."

"Where on earth did you get OJ?" I asked. We hadn't had that in more than six months.   Oranges weren't just a luxury, they were unobtainable.

"Uncle Ron got a case in that last shipment that came up through Boise," Kelly said. "We were saving it for the holidays."

"I'll bet that was a complicated trade," I said. "Good for him."

"Hon, you want to check in at the hospital?" I asked Karen. She was a little choked up as she hugged both kids again.

"Can you do that?"

"I expect so, yeah," I said. "Don't know until I try."

"Sure, I guess."

"How long until breakfast?" I asked.

"Maybe fifteen," Carl said. "The casserole's not bubbling yet."

"OK," I said, "Any other news this morning?"

"Colorado—fighting's pretty intense there. KLXY is back up, TV I mean, and they had some footage. Sounded like they're fighting over the Denver airport."

"Hmmm." I said, getting some coffee, and looking at the small TV in the kitchen, repeating the same loop of tape. It looked like mechanized units on both sides, the 'enemy' finally being taken out by what had to be an aerial bomb, and then 'our' ground troops advancing. In the distance, I could make out the distinctive shape, or more correctly, the remains of the distinctive shape of the Denver International Airport terminal. It looked a wreck. I'd been through there dozens of times.

I decided to check in with 'the office' for the frequency of Valley Hospital, and see how many rules I could break by using County radios for personal reasons.

"One eleven to Spokane," I said.

"One-eleven," a male voice replied.

"Request radio frequency for Valley Hospital, general communications," I said, as if this were something that was done every day.

"Wait one, one eleven," the dispatcher said, either checking to see if there was a frequency, or getting permission from someone higher up for this odd request.

"One eleven, you'll need Med Sixty-three, which is found on page thirteen in your desk reference manual."

"Thanks, Spokane. One eleven out."

"One eleven," dispatch replied.

I tuned one of the other radios to the assigned frequency, after flipping through the many pages of the Metro user manual. The manual had daily change frequencies for many of the departments, which rotated around the capability of the many Metro radios in service each day. Finally I found it, and punched it in to the digital tuner.

"Metro one eleven to Valley," I said, trying my best to sound official, and probably not succeeding. I repeated the call.

"Metro one eleven, go ahead," a female voice, replied.

"Valley, I'd like to check the status of a patient. Is that possible?"

"Yes, Metro. Name please," she said, and I replied with Grace's full name.

"One moment, one-eleven. Are you a relative?"

"Affirmative."

"One moment while I retrieve that information."

"Karen, c'mere for a minute. Valley will be back on in a sec," I said. Karen had poured a cup of coffee, and was cradling it in her hands, and warming before the fire.

"You got through?"

"Yep," I said, putting an arm around my wife, and flipping on the desk speaker for Karen to listen in.

"One eleven, patient status is unchanged, stable but serious condition. Patient is lightly sedated at this time, but is awake and having breakfast."

"Understood, Valley. Thank you. One eleven, out."

"You're welcome. Valley out."

"There you go," I said quietly to Karen, as I smelled the shampoo in her hair. "We'll go over after breakfast."

"Sounds good. What'd you have on your list today?" Karen said with some relief in her voice. She'd had more than her share of stress this year, much of it because of me.

"Thought I'd get filled in on the new neighbors."

"Well, I can do that. What else?"

"Figured we'd run our turkey down to the butcher today."

"Did that yesterday. The butcher and his family were looking for a place. Kevin had them on his list. They're moving in this afternoon."

"Okay," I said. "That sounds good....who're the rest?"

"Breakfast, in five," Carl called from the kitchen.

"A pharmacist who works at Valley; two families that work on the Red Line—I mean, engineers and mechanics, they're taking the two houses on the west block that are side by side; and a couple of contractor types working for the school district, they're sharing a house. Your Army folks also want a house, across the street to the west of the store."

"It's not ready. We didn't even do any work on that one. Too far gone."

"They didn't care. They're planning on moving the guard shack from the parking lot at the store, and moving it there."

"Fine with me. It won't be Army anyway. It'll be Guard, which means local, in theory at least."

"Breakfast is served," Kelly said as she pulled her Mom's chair out for her. For the first time, I noted that Carl was wearing a white long-sleeve shirt, dark slacks, dress shoes, and a tie. Kelly was in one of her best dresses.

"I feel underdressed," I said.

"You are, but we'll cut you some slack this time," Kelly said. "Orange juice?"

"Absolutely," Karen said, moving one of the crystal glasses closer.

"What's with the big bag of scones on the counter?" I asked.

"Some for Gram, the rest for the hospital," Carl said.

"Good job, both of you," I said, with justifiable pride.

The kids made sure we were served first, and then we forced them to join us. It was a wonderful meal. Months later, I'd still remember it, going over the details in my head, when such luxury became again, unheard of.

"This is KLXY Spokane, it is now ten a.m., Pacific Standard Time, and this is the news," the announcer stated. Karen, Alan, Mary and I were in the little Escape, on our way to the hospital for a short visit with Grace.

"U.S. Army units in Colorado yesterday made the grisly discovery of several small towns where all civilians had apparently been murdered as S.A. forces withdrew from the battle area.

Spokesmen for Company A of the Fifteenth Oregon stated that the civilians appeared to have been rounded up and shot before the building they were in was burned. Several hundred victims were found in each of three towns, which as of yet have not been identified."

None of us commented.

"Other news from the Colorado front was the public admission that European-built heavy armor is being used by State of America mechanized units. Civilian consultants identified tanks as modified versions of German built Leopard main battle tanks, produced beginning in the late Seventies, and used by seven countries before the Third World War began. Department of Defense spokesmen believe that the tanks were purchased in northern Europe and shipped to the Eastern Seaboard during the reign of the New Republic. No comments were made regarding the possible number of tanks, or other military hardware brought into the country. D oh D and Administration spokesmen have continued to decline to comment on statements made that the S.A. has been receiving direct support from European nations. Sources within the Air Force and Navy have stated that air superiority and a total naval blockade have remained in effect since the start of the War. Air Force sources also report that U.S. aircraft have destroyed several strategic industries in the Midwest, including the former factory where Abrams tanks were built and refurbished."

"Navy and Coast Guard units, backed by a large, but unknown number of Army units, are now in control of the Mississippi River, from the Gulf to Vicksburg and Jackson, Mississippi, north of the U.S. Highway 20 corridor. Running battles along this corridor over the past weeks, have now successfully isolated the S.A. forces from the Gulf of Mexico, shutting off any chance of shipment to S.A. held territory."

"In regional news, the City of Coeur d'Alene today announced that power restoration along the Highway Ninety Five corridor will resume in the spring, with restoration of power along the west side of Lake Coeur d'Alene expected by next summer. This will complete the restoration of basic power around the lake."

"That'd be nice to have done," I said. "Been a long time now."

"I'm more interested in phone service," Karen said.

"You didn't hear this from me, but we'll have cellular service back up by Christmas in the metro area."

"You keeping that a secret?" Mary asked. "That's huge!"

"I just saw the progress report from one of our guys. Testing is going on right now on the cells within the Valley. Most needed some serious work," I said as we pulled into the unplowed parking lot, getting a wave from one of the perimeter guards, to a closer lot, due to my 'car badge.' "Don't want to get my hopes up, or anybody else's, either. Got it?"

"How's that going to work?" Alan asked. "Different carriers, different towers, providers, services, whatever. They're not bringing them all back, are they?"

"Nope. One carrier. Not sure who. They were the only one left after the crash."

"So much for competition," Alan said as we trudged across the parking lot.

"Doesn't really matter," I said. "They're pretty well regulated by the government, as in, all but owned by. They're actually planning on creating one entity, then splitting them up within the next three years."

"How'll that work for phones?" Karen asked.

"Not sure. Something about replacing the SIM cards with new ones that would let any phone be activated and put in service, once it's registered."

"Coming up with money for that will be interesting," Karen said. "Phones for everyone were common. Now, even having one is a huge luxury."

"Imagine. Calling me at work!" Alan said to Mary as he took her hand.

"Idle chit-chat," Mary said in reply. We passed the Guard station, with three attentive soldiers, and moved inside to the sign-in desk.

To get admittance to the hospital, we needed to sign in, check our weapons in a weapons locker, and go through screening like we used to have in airports and other 'secure' buildings.

The upgraded security measures were put in place after a series of robberies and attacks, most of them before the War really got going. Many were for drugs, at least at first. After that died down, supplies were being stolen at gunpoint. Much of the stolen goods were then sold on the black market.

We only had one situation recently, where someone obviously 'new' to the area had tried to relieve a hospital pharmacy of its' contents. The popular tale included him serving as an organ donor. I knew for a fact that he didn't really have any salvageable organs left after a Guardsman using a BAR clone, was done with him.

Our visit was relatively short, with the nursing staff just helping Grace finish up breakfast—saving her scone for later--and then she would be due for a sponge bath. We traded barbs, as we usually did in one form or another, although by the squeeze of her hand I knew she didn't mean any of it, and of course neither did I. I gave Alan and Karen a few minutes alone with her and Mary and I tracked down the on-shift doctor, through the duty nurse.

"Excuse me, are you Mr. Drummond?" the doctor asked as Mary and I waited outside of Grace's room.

"Yes. This is Mary Bauer," I said in introduction. "Grace is our mother in law."

"Rudy Cole. Nice to meet you both. Well, she had a good night. That was a bad fall she took, injury wise. I believe that Doctor Richardson gave you his prognosis?"

"He did. I was wondering if you have any suggestions for long-term care," I asked. "She was pretty independent, despite her age."

"How's her home set up for accessibility?"

"Not great," I said. "She lives with Mary and her family," I said. "Doc, I'm wondering if there is a possibility of hiring nursing staff to help out. It's not like we have much in the way of either nursing homes or assisted living facilities anymore."

"No, we sure don't. There are days when we almost have first-world medical care. Almost, that is," he said. "Let me check with the nursing staff. I know there are at least a couple of nurses who bunk here at the hospital. There could be a possibility of a live-in nurse, part time."

I thought about that for a second. "Doc, how many staff do you have that are, well, homeless?"

"Fifteen, easy. Why do you ask? You think you can do something about that?"

"Maybe, yeah. In my neighborhood we rehabbed a bunch of the houses that could work without natural gas or reliable electric. Heat with wood, that kinda thing."

"Well if you could do that in this neighborhood, that'd be somethin'. Let me check with staff. There some way I can get hold of you?"

"Sure. Here's my business card," I said, handing him my Metro Administrator card, which was at best, rarely used. "That ought a be good for about another week. Then I'm going to be wearing green."

"Well, I must say I'm a little surprised," Doctor Cole said with a little grin. "You don't strike me as the Administrator type."

"I am dressed in my typical farm attire, true enough. That's probably why I'm getting drafted."

"I'm quite glad to meet you, Mr. Drummond. I didn't make the connection. You managed to wrangle a priority status for us back in October. I think without that status, this place would be closed."

"You can credit Dr. Sorenson for that. She asked I just put it in motion, with...some appropriate emphasis. Sacred Heart and Kootenai, and that small hospital up in Sandpoint got their priority, too. Besides that, having been a patient at two of the three hospitals, I have a distinct self-interest."

"Those that act, usually do."

"I'll take that as a compliment."

"As well you should. I'll let you know what I find out."

"And we'll see what we can do about some housing. Thanks, again," I said as I shook hands.

"Mrs. Bauer, a pleasure, although Mr. Drummond and I monopolized the conversation."

"Doctor, thank you for everything."

"I just hope we can do more someday," Doctor Cole said as he headed down the half-lit hallway with a wave. Karen and Alan were heading to meet us.

"Everything OK?" I asked Karen.

"Ornery as ever," she said as she gave me a hug. "We gave the bag of scones to the nurses—they said the patients would get them, not staff."

"Ever to serve, these people," I said quietly.

"You talking with one of the docs?" Alan asked as we headed back toward 'reception.'

"Yeah. They're housing-short. And I was checking on care for Mom. Maybe a live-in nurse."

"Rick, we don't really have room."

"I know. What happens though if we rehab the house next to us, and set that up as Grace's place with a live-in nurse or two? It's a rancher, doors are wide enough for a walker or a wheel chair, and it's already got half of the accessible stuff needed."

Alan was thinking this over as we retrieved our sidearms, and as Karen and Mary signed us out.

"Not a bad idea," Alan said. "That place is gonna need some work though."

"I know. Now onto the other idea. Nursing or staff housing for the hospital. A bunch of them are bunking at the hospital. What would it take for you to get some home-improvement types together and put some houses together?" I asked as we headed back to the car.

"You know the answer to that as well as anybody. 'Depends.'"

"I mean supplies. Can you get stuff to put a typical place back together?"

"Sure, from stripped and salvaged buildings. How much you wanna spend?"

"As little as possible as always. Horse trading is my preferred method, as poor as I am conducting those transactions."

"You're good enough at them, you just hate the idea of them," Alan said, sizing me up correctly.

"Yeah, that's true enough."

"Let's take a little drive through the neighborhood and see what we have to work with," Alan said. "Besides that, there's a little place over on Sullivan that we need to go visit."

Saturday
November Eighteenth

The neighborhoods around the hospital had been originally platted and settled first as truck farms, then as subdivisions, from around nineteen hundred through the sixties. By the time the hospital opened in the mid-sixties, the homes were 'mature' in the sense that many of the original owners had passed on or the homes had become rentals, opening up the neighborhood for transition. Transition meant three decades of medical offices and the occasional nursing home replacing the single-family homes, or poorly built apartments popping up on arterial streets.

In a post-Domino Spokane, very few of those buildings could be serviceable without full pre-Domino utilities. Many, if not most of the post nineteen-eighty construction, had simply collapsed as a result of the earthquake or the snow loads or the combination. Some had been salvaged for useable parts; most were abandoned heaps, the most notable being a three-story apartment complex south of the hospital.

We found about ten houses that just by 'drive by' told us they 'could' work if they weren't damaged too badly. It was odd to see entire streets within the utility service area without a single occupied home. Nineteen-sixties all-electric architecture was to blame. You just can't heat a rancher, all spread out, as efficiently as a 'box' house. Unless of course, you have a wood-fired furnace or the capital to build one.

On Sullivan Road, once a seven-lane arterial filled with strip shops and box stores, Alan directed me to what was once an old sports bar. I remembered that it had been built during my high-school years, and that it was something of a scandal when it opened. My mother in particular, was not impressed. I'd never darkened the doorway of the place. It looked, well, nasty. It also had developed a reputation as being one of the places where the steelworkers let off steam after going off-shift from Kaiser.

"Alan, you can't be serious," I said.

"I am. Don't judge the book by the cover."

"I'm not. I'm judging it by its reputation. This is a pretty rough place."

"Used to be. Not anymore."

"Where's the sign? What is this place?" Karen asked.

"It's called 'Dad's Place,'" Alan said. "And you'll like it. Trust me."

"This oughta be good," I said a little under my breath.

There were a half-dozen 'normal' vehicles in the parking lot, thus making it a highly popular place. Not too many people could afford gas, and not much gas was available. I parked in what would have been a 'second row' of parking, if there had been more traffic.

Inside, there were probably forty people, seated at the bar (completely full) and at some scattered tables. A waitress (!) seated us at a reserved table near a fireplace. Above the fireplace, a big-screen TV played a tape of last years Purdue at Notre Dame football game. There were a number of guys (and a few gals) cheering for the Irish, despite the already-determined outcome.

"Thought you might enjoy a trip back in time," Alan said as a rotund, ruddy-faced older man with an apron made his way over. His thinning red hair was almost outdone by his sizeable pork-chop sideburns.

"Good day, everyone. I'm Danny O'Malley. Or, 'Dad,' as you prefer. "Alan, good to see you. Where's that scoundrel Ron today?"

"Minding the kids and the farm," Alan said, before introducing us all.

"Pleased to meet you all. Now, I know what Alan's favorite poison is, but I'll do my best for you all. Mary? What can I get you love?"

"It's a little early in the day…"

"Nonsense. Sun's over the yardarm. High time," O'Malley said. I liked the guy right off.

"OK, then, a Lemon Drop."

"And you my dear?" he asked of Karen.

"No question. Sex On The Beach."

"And a fine day it is for that, ma'am," O'Malley said without missing a beat. "And you sir?"

"I'm sure you won't be able to fill this order, unless you've got a direct line to the ancestral homeland," dropping a large hint of my favorite porter.

"Not Guinness by brand, but I'd bet a twenty-dollar gold piece that you can't tell the difference."

I thought about taking the bet, and then thought about it twice more. "If I had a fresh Guinness to sample it against, I'd take that bet."

"Then an O'Malley's it is. Here are your menus, and I'll be right back with your libations."

"Quite a guy," I said to Alan. "How'd you find this place?"

"See that big walk-in refrigerator in the back?" he said, pointing to the kitchen, "Three way trade got Danny that, and got us three wood-fired boilers. They're heating two of the barter stores. Third one we haven't put to use yet. He's a regular at the Veradale store—supplier and buyer. He's got lines on stuff nobody else has. Stand up guy."

"Where's he from? What'd he do before Domino?"

"You wouldn't believe me," Alan said.

"These days, yeah, I probably would."

"Bank president. Chicago First Federal."

"OK, maybe I was premature," I said. "How in the heck did he end up here doing this?"

"Dan was on a pre-retirement ski vacation, RV'ing his way across the country. He'd just spent a few days at Silver Mountain, had already hit Schweitzer, was going to try out Mount Spokane for something a little less intense. Bingo."

"So why'd he stay? I don't get it. Bank president, should've evac'd."

"Forced-retirement bank president," O'Malley said, bringing our drinks. "I was being shown the door, at the ripe age of fifty-five, after telling the Federal Reserve—or Feral Reserve as I called it---and the board of directors to go stuff themselves. That didn't really endear me to them a whole helluva lot, especially since I'd been there for thirty-five years and was one of the last people that knew how to run an honest bank. I had six weeks of vacation, so I took it. They were about to name a replacement for me when it hit the fan." O'Malley pulled up a chair, spun it around and sat down, arms folded across the back.

"So, again, why'd you stay here?" I asked. I noticed that Mary was halfway through her drink. Karen wasn't far behind.

"Why not? All my money was electronic, I'd sold my place on the Gold Coast in about three days, had a pile in the accounts, heard there was good snow out this way. I figured that I'd start new, after the quake, maybe seize an opportunity. Just never figured that all my electronic money would vaporize before I had a chance to convert it to gold or silver or land or guns or whatever. So I sold what I could, bought this place, and worked the deal for putting this place together."

"So what'd you tell the board to get yourself canned?" I asked, probably prying a little too much.

"Let's just say we had a philosophical difference in return on investment," he said. "Ladies, how're your drinks?"

"Perfect," they both said in unison, and then both giggled.

"Fractional reserve overshoot…" I said.

O'Malley smiled at me, knowing what I thought. "Also known as, 'leveraging', back in the day. We had a nice, stable bank, regulated poorly by the Feds, and we could have gotten away with murder. We didn't. Against my grain. I was getting pressured from the board on behalf of the investment arm of the bank to step it up, you know, take it from ten to one to one-fifty to one like the big boys. Make the big money. Short good companies and destroy them in the process, but make a killing on the stock. Dive deep into the black holes that were the derivatives lottery. Take the money from the Fed as part of all those bail outs—we didn't need it though. I went to the mat, and was shown the door."

"Greed does funny things," Karen said. She and I had had numerous talks about our own finances, and keeping a safe haven for most of them. Only my brother ended up saving our bacon in the end. I used to think that precious metals were too speculative. Hard to believe I was that naïve back then.

"You in the business back then?" Danny asked us.

"No, only in the sense of seeing the potential for an avalanche and getting the heck out of the way," I said. "I never had a good feeling about the whole bubble economy. The Fed just made it worse."

"Then you and I have something in common, Rick. Now, about lunch. You decide yet? Ladies, your second round is on the way," Danny said as he waived to a young man behind the bar, who nodded and immediately went to work.

"We'll end up pouring them into the car."

"As long as they're not driving...I'll give you a minute more to look over the menu."

"Thanks, Danny," Alan said. Danny made his way to another table and took an order.

"Incredible," I said as I looked over the menu, instantly deciding, and putting it down.

"Told ya you'd like the guy."

"He's got quite the place here, starting from scratch."

"He does at that. His microbrewery is in the old grocery store across the street. That's also where he lives." The young barkeep arrived with the girls' second round, yet they weren't quite finished with their first.

"This oughta be an interesting afternoon with the wives," I said.

"Yeah, if it was dinner instead of lunch, we might've gotten lucky," Alan said.

"You might get lucky in the middle of the day," Mary said with a smoky little glance.

Karen and I both ordered potato soup, with small loaves of rye on the side. Alan was apparently a regular, and had a corned beef sandwich on wheat, with a local cheese. Mary had an open faced chicken sandwich with a thick gravy. After their second rounds of drinks, a pitcher of water and two large glasses appeared. By the end of the hour, we were all stuffed. Notre Dame had beaten Purdue, again, and the fans, some wearing their team colors, celebrated perhaps a bit too much.

It was well after noon when said our goodbyes to Dan and his staff, and got on about our day. I made a mental note to mention O'Malley to Tonya Lincoln. While I appreciated his public house, it seemed a shame to me to have that potential mental talent go to waste.

We headed north to Sprague, and crossed the Red Line, and headed back towards town and home. The weather had warmed up considerably, and rain was starting to fall. It was depressing in any regard, driving down what had been one of the cities busiest streets, and seeing no other cars, and only a dozen or so pedestrians. We did see though, numerous storefronts converted to home businesses. Wood smoke was thick in the air as we made the drive, mostly keeping quiet as the well-worn wipers smeared the rain around.

Most of the more successful businesses were located within a half mile of the rail lines, and you could tell where 'trouble' was going to be by the distance between precinct houses along 'the line.' If there was a trouble spot, chances are it would be as far away from one precinct house as another, usually on the edge of the utility service area, and when the police or Guard responded, drugs or 'shine or some other form of illegal entertainment were almost always found. None of the pre-Domino vices were encouraged, neither could much be done to stop them. Once raw materials for the synthetic drugs vanished, more dangerous chemistry found its' way to light, with often fatal, sometimes tragic results.

Most of those involved in the uprising against--well, the rest of us--were in those fringe areas. Most of the 'fringe areas' that had participated in the October riots had lost a fair percentage of their population, either to neighbors protecting themselves, others deciding to 'get even', or Guard and Army units, who shot anything that fired at them.

Before our lives were turned upside down, I'd almost always had some major pre-occupation with an upcoming far-flung business trip or assignment, sometimes to the point of losing sleep, wondering what I'd missed, forgotten, or would be blindsided by, once out of touch with 'home' or 'backup'.

Now, at home and few days before Thanksgiving, I was at it again, wondering what I would find myself doing in a little over a week, once I would be assigned to Pacific Northwest Command. Virtually no new information had been provided me since the initial commission request from Governor Hall. I had no idea what the State wanted me for.

Saturday afternoon was spent with Carl, Ron and Alan, over in the Valley General neighborhood, checking abandoned homes for refit. We'd dressed in our outdoor gear and rain shells, boots, flashlights and a couple of clipboards, as well as the obligatory sidearm, shotgun, and rifles.

The shotgun was really the weapon of choice for this type of work, assuming that we might run into close-quarters work. Through my friendship with Mike, I was able to procure 'law enforcement' loads for our twelve-gauges. They were pretty destructive to human or animal flesh. Once upon a time, we might have had various shells in a shotgun, from a number seven, to a number four, and then double-ought buck. The lighter, first shots might scare off someone who wasn't really serious about killing you. The heavier loads were for the more determined. Anymore though, the loads were set to kill from the get-go, if they were in range.

I'd once seen a shell called 'Dragon's Breath,' used by an Army unit to both light up an area with an 'objective target' downrange, which also succeeded in creating a most impressive flame reminiscent of an artillery shell being fired. An unfortunate result of that type of round (for the objective) was night blindness and perhaps, being set on fire by the many-yards long fireball. I would expect that that type of shell, used indoors, would be a great way to burn down a building.

I'd called in to Dispatch to let them know what our objective for the day was, and had a brief talk with the Sheriff's dispatcher, just in case someone didn't like the looks of us. The Sheriff's office then let the local precinct and the Guard command structure know that we weren't a threat. It'd be mighty embarrassing to get shot up while trying to find somebody a place to live.

Standard operation procedure for entering an abandoned house started with recon. Animal tracks into any entry in the home, whether the animal was two- or four-legged, automatically told us, 'weapons out' and 'cover', until the point man and his cover cleared the building. Once the building was cleared to enter, three of us would enter, one remaining on guard and concealed as much as possible.

I had naturally, a father's trepidation about putting my son in harms way of any kind, even though I'd done it several times over the past year. It never made it easier though.

Each house, we had eleven to look at, had been ransacked after whatever salvage operations had taken place in the early days after the Domino. In three cases, it was plainly evident that the occupants had either been badly injured or killed in the quake, due to the black stains that were dried blood. Some houses had been merely stripped of copper wire and anything of any black market value. Others had been all but destroyed from the inside out.

Four houses, we deemed were worth repairing, having the required provisions for wood heat in a centrally located fireplace or chimney; having repairable quake damage; and having literally weathered the past eleven months without catastrophic results.

We'd redone enough houses to know what it would take to get the houses back in shape, even without the help of materials takeoffs and computerized spreadsheets. Work could begin within a few days, if we were willing to bust loose the capital—meaning real money—to expedite the purchase of salvaged materials and hired labor. We might be able to have the prospective tenants or owners of the homes contribute, but typically med staff was working twelve hours on and twelve off, six days a week. That didn't leave much time for a life outside of the medical community.

Our pre-Domino savings, wisely converted to silver and gold by one of my older brothers, had been sparingly used to buy properties for back taxes adjusted for new currency values; to finance rebuilds; and to provide operating capital and 'cash' for our barter stores. So far, we hadn't used a quarter of it. With that money, we owned most of the property on our own block, half of the property on two blocks on either side of ours, and more business relationships than we could shake a stick at. The barter stores by and large operated in the black, with any excess set aside for the opening of other stores or expansion.

This expansion of 'our' housing concerns wasn't located near anything we owned, had control of or really, had any interest in except as a benefactor of some kind. Property in our home neighborhood had been acquired because it was contiguous, had a strategic position, or because it presented a good opportunity in some fashion or other. This was different. As a result, I was reluctant to really get into the speculative nature of the thing.

Alan suggested that we coordinate the work and the payment of the rehab work, and that we buy the properties. Essentially, we'd have a closely held corporation where we 'owned' the property, organized and coordinated the work, but didn't have to pay for all of the remodeling. For those that wanted to perhaps invest in something without having to take on all the risk, this might be a good opportunity. I thought this was a good idea too, as did Ron. I don't think any of us, especially me, were all that hot on taking on the whole thing ourselves. Since there was only a slight chance that I'd have any time at all to invest in it, I left the decision and the organization to the guys.

By the time we wrapped up, we had pretty steady rain coming down, making those streets that had had any traffic at all a sloppy mess or a sloppy mess on top of ice. Before we headed for home, we checked in again at the hospital, and found Grace sleeping soundly. The nurses said she'd had a pretty good afternoon, but could tell that she was in pretty healthy pain. We skidded and slipped all the way home, listening to the local news. We heard on the way home, as had been rumored, that cell phone service would be available 'soon', for the first time since January fourteenth. Instructions then followed for procedures expected to re-activate cell phones, which I thought would probably put a serious run on salvaged cell phones and chargers. I remembered that we had a garbage can full of them at our first barter store.

Saturday evening,
November Eighteenth
5:40 p.m.

By the time we got home, dinner was simmering away in two big slow-cookers. Our wives had taken my idea about the house next door to heart, and had spent some of the afternoon looking it over in detail. They'd decided that we'd have a big dinner to discuss it with all of us. Carl and I were enlisted to get the extra dining room table leaves, round up more chairs, and a couple more tablecloths. Karen's grandmother's sideboard, converted from an old Kitchen Queen, was decked out with plates, silverware, and a bunch of glasses.

Karen had given me the notes they'd made for the work on the former home of Nate and Ginny Woolsley. She knew that I liked to think things out before diving in whole-hog, and with my imminent military commitment, this would be less about my direct contributions, and more about supporting the project. It seemed that we were about to get into the extended care business.

The home to the south of us had belonged to a retired couple who'd never returned from Western Washington after the Domino. We'd never heard if they'd died in the quake, the ash fall, or had evacuated somewhere 'else.' Other than some minor salvage work at their home, mostly involving very little stored food in the place, securing a damaged water line, and checking the power before we shut it off completely, we hadn't really been in the house. I'd boarded up broken windows right after the quake, patched some holes, and that had been about it.

The home had been retrofitted before our neighbors bought it, for an elderly couple in their last years in the home. The kitchen was designed to be accessible to a wheelchair bound chef, bath facilities, ramps and handrails installed, and doors widened. With some repair work, the house could be reused and could serve as a better alternative for Grace to get around, without having to deal with stairs, traditional tubs, and narrow doorways. This home could also be big enough for another resident or two, as well as live in nursing staff, just on the main floor. A couple of basement bedrooms were options too, but of course weren't accessible.

The biggest negative was the 'rancher' layout, and the lack of a fireplace in the middle of the home that might help heat the place with a woodstove. The all-electric home didn't have a great option for a wood-fired furnace either. It could be done, but not all that easily. For these reasons, we had decided months ago just to keep the place 'off the grid' for home rehabs.

A few minutes before six, our dinner guests arrived, Libby carrying in both hands clutched before her, a canary-yellow paper that I immediately recognized by the official seal. Sarah, Ron and Kelly followed and then Alan's clan behind. The house went from relatively quiet to quite noisy in a flash.

"Good evening all! Come in!" I said, playing the welcoming host, and ushering everyone inside.

"Lib, I see you've heard from John," I said, referring to the Northwest Command paper.

"They made it to California. Just got this from Elaine!"

"Good to hear. Personal message, or just the facts?"

"Mostly the latter, unless you count the cryptic message he sent Sarah," Libby said, looking out of the corner of her eye at her future daughter in law, with a little smile.

"Sarah? Care to elaborate?"

"Nope, not even a little, thanks," she said as she gave me a hug. "Thanks for the invitation to dinner. It seems like it's been ages."

"It does at that. Apple and pear cider are there on the buffet. Make yourself at home," I said, finally taking their wet jackets and coats.

The guys, including Carl and young Mark, gravitated to the living room, where Carl had moved his video game console. Rachel,

Kelly and Marie headed upstairs to Kelly's room, for a few minutes of goofing off before dinner.

"Hon, here's the apple-jack," Karen said, putting an old-fashioned brown jug on the buffet.

"Thanks—Nice container there," I said.

"Seemed appropriate. That stuff must be eighty-proof!" she said. The antique moonshine jugs must've been pre Second War. I picked up a half dozen of them at a garage sale when I was in high school. They'd decorated various cardboard boxes ever since. Only one was ever displayed as an 'antique' and that one was lost in the quake.

"Now, now," I said. "Not a smidge over seventy."

"Pauliano's?" Alan asked.

"Yep. Don managed to resurrect the family's ancient still," I said. "I snagged a small amount of scrap copper for Don in trade." I poured each of us a tall shot glass. The copper included sheet, tubing, and some piping, left over from one of our gas producer units.

"Holding out on us, huh?" Alan said, taking an experimental sniff, then sip, of the concoction. "Holy smokes!" he said after his sample.

"Not bad, huh." I said. Ron tried a sip, and declined more.

"A little much for me," he said. "As in, not for consumption around open flame."

"True enough," I said, taking a larger sip.

"Is Don going into commercial production with this?" Alan asked.

"Maybe next year, he said. Not a huge priority for him. He just wanted to see if the old recipes were still good. Joe said Don did a better job on the finish than he did, which is pretty high praise."

"Rick, would you call the girls down? We're about ready to dish up."

"Done," I said, and then took another sip, before summoning the giggling girls. Rachel was four years younger than her cousin, but was fitting right in with whatever inside joke was running.

"OK, you boys, have a seat," Mary said, directing us to the far side of the dining room table, away from the kitchen.

"Yes, SarMajor sir!" I said, taking my place near, but not at the head of the table. I figured correctly that Karen would take that spot.

After we had devoured most of the stew, all of the wheat dinner rolls, and some applesauce, the ladies outlined what 'we' needed to get done next door before Grace would be released from Valley General, this coming Wednesday.

"Whew. Is that all?" Alan asked with a little humor.

"Can you do it?" Karen asked her big brother.

He and Ron gave me a look, I nodded very slightly, and then he responded. "It'll be a push. Rick, you been in there lately?"

"Not since the summer, no."

"We're going to be working some serious hours to get this done," Ron said, looking over the notes. "And this is a busy week at the stores, Thanksgiving and all."

"So let's hire some bodies," I said. "I'm not sure what kind of hours I'll have this week anyway, and next week's too late," I said, without saying, 'And I'm wearing a uniform then.'

"Can you get it habitable, even though it's not all finished?" Karen asked us. I noted that Sarah was taking in the discussion attentively, but hadn't contributed much.

"Yeah, if you hold a loose definition of that word," I said. "You made a good list, but I also know that in addition to that, we'll need to go through the circuits one-by-one, like we did here; we'll need to check the plumbing again; and the electric furnace. Problem is of course when the power goes down, that place freezes. We need a backup source of heat, and that's where a fair hunk of work is, over and above the sheetrock, broken glass, and getting the place weather-tight again," I said. "Ron, you have that list of skilled tradesmen available from the main store's want-work list, right?"

"Yeah, it's at the store."

"Maybe we ought a run down there and get it. We can probably get some labor lined up tomorrow at church, if they attend."

"Most do," he said.

"You trust them?" I asked, knowing that some of the men and women on the list of 'I'm for hire—I can do these things' were really there to case houses for strong-arm break-ins or invasions.

"They aren't on our lists unless we do. We've vetted them all."

"OK. Let's go that direction. Maybe we use the same forces for the houses near the hospital, just finish up next door and move on to the next project," I said. "Now, knowing what you know about those other houses, how much money do you need?"

"Probably two-hundred cash. We can trade for quite a bit of what we'll need. Cash is faster though, although it shows our hand," Ron said.

"Yeah, it does," I said. Anyone using a fair amount of cash, and two hundred dollars was certainly above that threshold, would invite unwanted attention from those who were cash-poor. Regardless of connections to law enforcement or military, if you had those kinds of resources, you became a target. You couldn't watch your back all the time. Having several thousand dollars in precious metals was all well and good, if spending it didn't get you or a family member kidnapped or killed. "I wonder if we can maybe work something out with the hospital that might deflect that a little," I thought out loud.

"What do you mean?" Mary asked. "I got the impression that they're all but broke."

"Maybe we buy the houses. We coordinate the refit. In exchange, the laborers who put them back together get some sort of break on medical care. I don't know, something like that."

"Might be worth talking about," Alan said, thinking this through to himself.

"Sarah, you've been pretty quiet. What do you think?" I asked.

"I'm a newbie to all this."

"Well, if you were a caregiver, which you've done over at the clinic and the hospital, put yourself in that place and comment."

"Security," she said without pause. "People figure out that you have a care facility and therefore you have meds. You have meds, and they're not protected, you get robbed. Even the home-grown meds and the manuals for holistic medicines—they take everything."

That put a new spin on things. The Woolsley's house had a very low fence around the front yard, an open driveway, lots of hiding places around the home, and just looked like a soft target. Alan and Ron both took notice and leaned forward attentively. Karen, Mary and Libby listened on.

"You also need a safe room, separate from the medicine storage area. People aren't the targets. Drugs are. Separate the staff and patient safe room from the drug storage, and things are far safer for everyone."

"Or go the 'Harder Homes and Gardens' route and secure the whole facility," Ron said.

"Sure, but your residents then feel like, and they are, living in a prison," Sarah said. "It's like the rooms over at Valley that face on the courtyard. The patients that are in those rooms just don't do as well as those that have a view to the real outside, without a big honkin' security fence."

"Hmm," Alan said. "We'll look at the place. Rick, aren't the bedrooms all on one end?"

"Yeah. Living and dining room in the middle, kitchen and family room in that order, moving away from the bedrooms."

"Shouldn't be too hard to separate functions then, and meet Sarah's goals."

"They're just ideas," Sarah said.

"Sure, they're good ideas," Alan said.

"Anyway, let's get the first project off the boards and see what goes next. It'll be your baby soon enough," I said to the collected adults. The kids had made themselves scarce as soon as the last empty spoon hit the last empty bowl.

"Don't remind us," Karen said. "Let's get going on these dishes. Boys, it's all yours. We ladies are going to put our feet up."

"Fair enough. I just hope you can find your dishes when we're done putting them away," Alan said.

"Rick will…"

"Oh, no. Don't bring me into this. It's our house. It's your kitchen."

"Men," Libby said. "Ladies, come join me for a cider over ice, with a little cinnamon."

After a dessert of apple pie, we took turns playing Sequence, working as couples. For a change the Drummonds took a commanding lead, and ended up winning. The woodstove cracked quietly as the 'losers' fought over last place. Sarah had headed back home with Ron and Alan escorting her, before they'd returned to fight over last place. Buck heard something, stood up a fraction of a second before Ada joined him, growling at the door.

"Gents, we may have company," I said, reaching for a shotgun. Ron and Alan took up arms as well, as our wives collected Mark and Rachel, and moved upstairs until we could see what was coming our

295

way. For an opposing force to get this far, they'd have had to have come through the neighborhood guard. Doable, but messy.

The doorbell rang. Not the modus operandi of an attacker, unless tactics had changed dramatically. Buck and Ada both took a step back, and barked, fur on the back of their necks raised.

"Do me a favor, boys, and cover me here," I said, cradling my modified 870, now sporting a handgrip and folding stock. This shotgun was loaded with double-ought, except for the last round, which was a law-enforcement slug round.

Ron had his own sidearm out and trained on the door, listening for anything amiss. Alan had one of our AK47's. I moved past the door, unlocked the deadbolts, and found Elaine Cross on the other side. The dogs went into 'sniff mode' immediately, with buck grabbing an old toy and wagging his tail furiously.

"Major, this is a surprise. To what do we owe the honor?" I said, ushering her in as Ron and Alan quietly stowed their weapons. I safed the Remington and stowed it behind the door.

"I have a couple of things for you. For all of you, actually, but there are some briefing papers in here for you as well, Rick," Elaine said as Karen, Mary, Libby and the little kids came back into the room, and resumed watching their movie. Such interruptions were not seen as irregular by the kids, and both Rachel and Marky were turning out to be pretty good shots with single-shot .22's.

"Hi, Elaine. Come in for some pie. Sorry for the armed reception," Karen said.

"That's OK. I understand. You do have two squads on patrol in the area though. Not much is going to get by them."

"Good to know, still…." I said.

"I know, better safe than sorry."

"How're the kids doing?" Karen asked.

"Jenny's getting better. Now Bobby's coming down with it."

"Sarah got you that elderberry concoction, right?" Libby asked, serving a nice sized piece of pie to Elaine.

"Sure did. That stuff's magic," she said. "Aren't you curious about that packet?"

"Yes, but I'm willing to wait," I said.

"You shouldn't. Seriously," Elaine said with a wink.

"That does it. Give it here," Karen said, tearing open the large manila envelope. The contents spilled onto the scarred dining room table.

Four cellular phones, identical in manufacture but in different colors spilled out, along with their charging units. They slid out along with a smaller envelope, about a half-inch thick, stamped with the logo of the Pacific Northwest Command.

"Oh, my," Libby said first. "Are you serious?"

"Yes!" Elaine said. "You're among the first to get them. They're already activated. Look on the back for your names and your numbers."

Everyone started talking at once at the prospect of being able to make a phone call again. I was wondering, who would I call?

The packet addressed to me, I opened after our guests had left for the evening. I'd asked Elaine if she knew anything about the contents, and she suggested that they were probably an outline of my command responsibilities.

They were all of that. On their face, the documents illustrated a complete reorganization of the United States Army and the Guard. Many of the historically centralized training locations had been eliminated by the Second Civil War, and the ability to ship a soldier from Washington to wherever for basic training, and then back to a unit, and then to the "front", wherever that was, had been recognized as wasted motion and time and resources. For young John Martin, this would have meant training closer to home. Unfortunately, it came a couple weeks too late. He would likely though join a Washington State infantry unit.

The three-page Command Summary document outlined my intermediate future. In a few days I'd be a brigade commander, a minimum of a thousand troops under my command on day one, up to three thousand when full strength, the Third Washington Engineering Brigade, or Third Washington Engineers, part of the Forty-First Division, Transportation Command. Our brigade had an interesting assignment, being to support the front line troops with materiel, repairing rails and roads on the way to the War, mostly rails, alternating between rear-area support and repair of transport potentially under fire. We'd help out communities along the rail corridors as we could, to support our primary mission, that being to get men and machines East to meet the S.A. forces. We'd be rail-mounted from Spokane, and head east, fixing things along the way along with BNSF train crews, eventually pulling in behind the line in the snow that separated United States Army forces from those of the S.A. The War was bogging down to a winter slog, along ragged lines crossing Colorado, Nebraska and Minnesota, as well as across Kansas, Missouri, and through northern Kentucky, parts of West Virginia, slicing neatly along the North Carolina state line to the East Coast. The Air Force had a role of course, but this was mostly a ground war. With the war in Mexico and then the turmoil at home, there was a serious shortage of airborne munitions. The historic stockpiles had been used up or abandoned and blown up overseas, leaving very little in North America to fight a modern air-superiority war.

Everything in the Northeast was S.A. territory, including of course the irradiated Washington D.C. They held the Great Lakes, parts of Ontario, the St. Laurence Seaway. The State of America forces had been beaten back north from the Gulf of Mexico on up the Mississippi. They were blockaded by the Navy in the Gulf, along the East Coast, and along the Canadian Maritimes. They held Memphis, and roughly a third of Tennessee. Alex and Amber were there, last spring, with their young children, Luke and Jaime. It had been more than six months since I'd heard from them. Almost as long since I'd heard from my oldest brother and his family. Jack at last word had been north of the Twin Cities. Both of my surviving brothers and their families were behind the lines, if they were still alive.

I studied the next document, fifty-pages or so long, to see the depth of the changes. The reorganization would be literally from the ground up, harkening back to units created during the First Civil War and before, from local areas, organized by the States, trained together as units and sent in service of the national war effort. Each state would have their own 'basic training' post. Ours would be at Fort Walla Walla, and would be in operation by the Monday following Thanksgiving. Oregon would have their post in Walla Walla as well, since they had no active military bases pre-War. Idaho would train at Mountain Home Joint Military Center.

I was thinking to myself, what I needed was a copy of *"How to Command an Army Brigade For Dummies."*

Karen snuck in behind me, as I was buried in further Army bureaucratese, giving me a bit of a start as she snaked her hands around my ribs.

"Bedtime, my love," she said, nuzzling my ear. "It's late, and, we're alone."

"I like the sound of that," I said, finally noticing her quite transparent gown. "I like the sound of that *a lot!"*

Sunday,
November Nineteenth

"You think the phones will work today?" Karen asked as we lay in bed, lounging before the alarm told us to get moving.

"I'm betting it's hit and miss. You just got the 'all circuits busy' last night, right?"

"When I got anything at all. You didn't find numbers for Alex and Jack, did you?"

"They didn't give them in their letters, and even if we had them, they're behind the lines. No idea what's working back there, if anything. I don't see a single reason why there should be a working phone line that crosses battle lines."

"Sure, be logical about it," she said, just as Buck decided it was time to steal one of my boots and announce his importance to us.

"Who's preaching this morning?" I asked. We had a rotation of pastors around the Valley, among the many small venues.

"That young kid right out of Bible college. He was over at Faith Christian last week."

"Hmmm," I mumbled as I got out of bed. Back in the old days, our church would progress through books of the Bible, in a sense of order. We could study upcoming verses, context, and prepare a little bit. In the current situation, we were flying blind each Sunday. I liked the variety. I didn't care for the lack of structure. Maybe that was a lesson that Someone was teaching me.

After a hot shower and finding some church-worthy clothes, I got the woodstove going for heat, and cooked up some steaming oatmeal with cinnamon and sugar. It was just about ready when Carl and Kelly made their sleepy way to the table.

"Seconds are up!" I said as I dished them up.

"Seconds?" Carl asked.

"Kidding. You're up. Mom's drying her hair and getting her makeup on."

"What's the order of the day?" Kelly asked.

"Breakfast. Church. After that, I'll think about the rest of the day."

Kelly looked at Carl with a furrowed brow. "You always have your day planned. Especially on the weekend. And that means you have our days planned, too."

"In a few days I'm in the Army. They plan the days for me. I'm trying to adapt."

"Right," Carl said. "Let's see how long this lasts."

"There'll be plenty for you to do around here without me shepherding you around. There's a list on that clipboard. Don't worry, it's only ten pages, double sided."

Carl picked up the ancient clipboard that had belonged to my Dad. It'd been stashed away in one of his old footlockers, found when we cleaned out the house. "Good night...." He said.

"Don't bother counting," I said. "There's two hundred and fifty-five items on that list. Some repeat though," I said.

Carl took a bite and flipped through the pages.

"How to run the house, property, equipment, garden and animals in one easy afternoon of reading. Remember, that's just the summary. The real how-tos are what you need to learn in various binders, shop manuals, and inside your Mom's pretty head."

"What's this?" Karen said. "My ears were burning."

"I gave the kids The List."

"Hardly a fair way to start the day. We'll be lucky if they don't enlist."

"It'd be less work," Carl said, flipping another page.

"No argument there," I said. "Anyone up for some dried apples?"

The List was admittedly, pretty brutal in length. Most of it I'd kept in my head before the Domino, and it was as natural as the seasons for me. Since things Got Complicated, there was much more to juggle, even if supplies and parts and seeds and dependable power and water were available. I'd basically sat down with a calendar and did a brain dump into the computer, trying to arrange first the equipment maintenance, house maintenance and gardening and farming items, then putting them in some sort of calendar order. I was sure that I'd missed things, but at least the important stuff was there. Between The List, and the help of Ron and Alan, Carl would do OK. I hoped that I would come back some day to relieve him of that big fat burden.

As we had been doing for months, the Drummonds and Bauers caravanned over in our SUV and today in Alan's diesel Ford pickup, making our way through the unplowed streets. Ron and Libby both stayed home with sore throats and mild temperatures. Sarah had a shift at the hospital, so Marie stayed home to tend them both. The church service was standing room only for the first service, and looked to be again for the second service. We checked our long guns with a soldier posted at the door of the community center, and picked them up again after the service. My sidearm and two spare magazines remained on my belt.

The sermon theme, and probably most of the hymns reached back to the first official Thanksgiving, created during our First Civil War by Abraham Lincoln. The young pastor, who was perhaps twenty-three years old, recited Lincoln's proclamation, and then spoke on Psalm 65, where the psalmist gives thanks for the freedom and providence with which God has blessed Israel; 2 Corinthians, where Paul asked the Corinthians to give to a collection to benefit starving Christians in Jerusalem; and the gratitude given Jesus by the lone Samaritan leper, in Luke 17.

The sermon and its' supporting verses had seemingly little to do with our current situation, with the War, with our losses and the things that we were really thankful for.

Maybe that was the point. It bugged me at the time perhaps that's why I still remember the verses covered.

After a visit with Grace at Valley General, and finding her more heavily medicated than we expected, we headed back home. She'd had a very bad night, and the staff had upped her painkillers to keep her more comfortable. I said a prayer for her as we passed a horse-drawn snowplow, keeping two lanes of Pines Road clear. I noticed that one of the buildings that had collapsed in the Domino was stripped even more than it had been a week before. For firewood, it appeared.

"You OK?" I asked Karen, who'd been silent since we left Valley.

"I'll be all right. It's just hard seeing Mom like that," she said, looking at the abandoned shops and offices on the west side of the street.

"I know," I said. I didn't have much more to say. Carl and Kelly were silent in the back seat.

"Dad, can you turn on the radio? News should be on," Kelly said.

"Sure," I said as I reached over and punched the power button.

"......and Florida are rumors only, while the Department of Defense confirms that the Colorado attack was in fact a chemical or neurotoxin attack. While casualty numbers were not provided by the spokesman other sources requesting anonymity confirmed that the losses were heavy. Communications blackouts currently are in place in Phoenix, the greater Dallas-Fort Worth area, Miami and Tallahassee, Florida. These blackouts are at present, unexplained by the Federal government in Austin."

"Dammit," I said to myself.

"They're using chemical weapons?" Karen asked. "Those are illegal," she said, before remembering whom she was talking about. "How could they?"

"Poor man's nuke," I said, listening further to the news. Both kids were leaning forward, listening.

"...reported that civilian populations were also targeted in the scorched-earth retreat by S.A. forces. Early relief efforts in Colorado were called off in the wake of discoveries by Golden State Army units, where it appears that civilians in every city and town between Interstate Seventy and Interstate Seventy-Six in northeast Colorado are missing and presumed dead. Cities and towns within this corridor, and potentially additional cities and towns in western Nebraska and south toward Guymon, Oklahoma, may also have been attacked and destroyed by State of America forces in retreat. Reporting from Colorado, Jim Paulson reports for Radio Free America. Jim?"

"Thank you, Charlie. For security reasons, I will not identify where we are reporting from, and indeed, this is a tape-recorded report, that has been cleared by the Defense Department. The reports just don't do justice to what we're seeing, following both Lone Star and Golden State units in the slow advance across Colorado. There is not a single building left in the towns that we've passed through that has not been burned or destroyed in some other manner. No homes. No outbuildings. Anything burnable has been burned. Anything that might be used by United States forces has been stripped or destroyed. There are no livestock. There are no pets. There are literally no civilians in any of the areas that we have seen. Units from Arizona—the Third Cardinals—and from New

305

Mexico, who we met up with as they were heading back to rear areas, report that the devastation we see here stretches for at least a hundred miles east, likely much farther."

A lengthy pause present in the broadcast indicated something the Army censors didn't want released. This made us all the more curious. Carl was about to say something when the reporter picked up again.

"Reporting from eastern Colorado, this is Jim Paulson."

"Chemical weapons consultant Doctor Stanley Laufer is joining us from a remote location. Doctor, from what we're hearing from Colorado, some of which has not been publicly reported, does this sound like a chemical attack?"

"Charlie, I cannot answer that based on what I know right now. It could be either chemical or neurological. Until the agent is identified, it isn't possible to know."

"How long might that take?"

"I'm sure that Army chemical weapons teams are on location at this time, and will begin analysis."

"From what National Radio initially reported before they went dark, this sounded like it came upon them without any warning. Thoughts on this, Doctor Laufer?"

"It is an arguable point, for many reasons best of either type of weapon—chemical agent or neurotoxin—is delivered without warning. No scent, no appreciable physical reaction until a concentration high enough to disable the victim is achieved. This type of weapon leaves the victim no time to don protective gear, may immobilize him within moments, and kill in minutes."

"No time to react. And the attackers are already in protective gear by that time, or out of harms' way."

"Correct."

"And the S.A. denies any knowledge of this attack," the host said, with barely concealed contempt.

"Of course...."

The radio station cut to the Emergency Broadcast Signal, ending the report.

"Now what?" Kelly asked, saying it before I could.

"Please stand by for an Emergency Broadcast Message from San Antonio, Texas," an unfamiliar, almost mechanical voice said.

"Ladies and Gentlemen, President McAllen will be addressing the nation in a few moments. Please stand by."

"This can't be good," Carl said.

"Nope, it can't," I replied. Former Senator Ryan Robert McAllen served briefly as Vice President under David Lambert, before Lambert's administration went rogue. McAllen was one of a handful of patriots in the truest sense of the word. He and a few others had escaped Denver as the true plans of Lambert and his handlers were revealed. With McAllen in the now-mythic escape, came the Constitution and the Declaration of Independence, carried by Secret Service agents and four members of the Supreme Court. The President's address began.

"My fellow Americans, upon the recommendation of the Department of Defense, I am imposing a curfew, effective immediately, nationwide. This is not done lightly, but in the wake of a series of devastating nerve gas attacks by enemy forces within our borders."

"These attacks fall on us less than a month into the Second Civil War, both on the front lines of battle and deep into states formerly untouched. Civilian populations have been targeted in seven cities in the United States, including Atlanta, Miami and Tallahassee, Phoenix, Dallas and Fort Worth, and Los Angeles. It is unknown at this time if additional population centers have been targeted. The method of delivery for these attacks is being investigated but is unknown at this time. For this reason, I am requiring you to return

307

home or to a place of shelter immediately, and remain there until we can determine if this attack is over, or is the first wave of a larger offensive."

"From what I am being told, there is no warning to these attacks. The evil that is the leadership of the State of America has proven that there is no limit to what they will do to eliminate freedom in this nation and enslave the population to serve their twisted ideal. Many soldiers have died today in the service of this country, fighting for our freedom. Civilians have been murdered in their homes, their stores, their places of worship. These losses are heavy. The payback will be equally heavy. We will defeat this evil. The United States of America and the ideals of this nation, set forth upon this continent by men who cast long shadows, whose greatness cannot be underestimated, will prevail."

"Please know that I pray for you. Know that the peace of God is with you, and that His strength follows you. Good night and may God bless the United States of America."

During the address, we had turned toward home, but hadn't quite made it yet. I instead turned toward the Metro store. I noted that Alan followed me. Within a minute, we were both parked. I noted that the Army guards were coming toward us, all business.

"Sir, I'm afraid we're under curfew effective immediately," a corporal said from forty feet away, moving toward me, hands on his battle rifle. "You'll need to return home or to shelter immediately."

"Understood, corporal. Wanted to grab a few things before we're sequestered," I replied.

"Sorry, sir. I didn't recognize you. Thought you were a customer."

"No problem. Thanks for bending the rules. You guys need anything before we lock her up?" I asked.

"We're good sir. Thanks though. The real eggs are much appreciated."

"Should have some smoked bacon one of these days, too," Alan added.

"Don't tease, sir. That's not kind," Corporal Cannon said with a wave. "Don't be long in there. Don't want a run on the place."

"Neither do we," I said.

I waved Karen and the kids to come inside the store. Depending on how long the curfew lasted this might be an important trip. If not, some stock would be shifted back to the store when it was over.

"Order of the day?" Alan said.

"You heard the address, what do you think?"

"I think not here, but what the heck do I know?"

"Then anything perishable goes now. Anything that there's even a hint of being short on, or high demand later, get it."

"You have a feeling about this, Rick?" Mary asked as she herded the kids inside.

"I dunno. Maybe."

Ten minutes later, we were done. We'd cleaned the store out of perishables and a few dozen other items of high value, all of which we'd completely taken for granted a year before.

As a culture, we now understood the complexities of creating, packaging, and shipping items that we once saw as 'common.' We used to think nothing of picking up any sort of item at any convenient store, paying next to nothing for it, and going on about our pre-occupied existence. Along the way of course, we were being transported in vehicles made of thousands of parts manufactured on multiple continents, fueled by gasoline or diesel from the other side of the planet, because 'their' fuel was 'cheaper' than 'ours.'

Within a month or so of the earthquake, the highest demand non-firearm, non-food item in Spokane County, Washington, was toilet paper. After initial on-hand supplies were exhausted, newspapers, catalogs, and then any available paper-like material was treated as powerful barter material. After T.P., feminine supplies soap and cleansers of all kinds. Surgical and N95 masks, with the Guangdong Flu. Anti-virals and antibiotics of course. Then elderberry extracts. Cigarettes, then any kind of tobacco. Deodorant, and that was gone, perfume and cologne. Waterproof matches. Batteries. Winter boots, parkas, gloves and mittens. Salt. Sugar. Flour. Yeast. Liquor. Beer was gone almost immediately. Anti-bacterial hand gels. Nuts, jerky, trail mix, peanut butter. Anything that looked like 'factory food': Crackers, chips, cookies, canned goods. Popcorn. Plastic zip-lock bags. Canning jars, lids, rings, pectin, paraffin, pressure canners. Cooking oil…and of course, chocolate. Summer items, discarded in those first few weeks, grew dramatically in trade value when the summer hit, some things unexpectedly. Dust masks, sun block, 'farmer hats' that shaded the head and neck, leather gloves, cargo shorts, garden tools. I'm sure the lists of scarcities varied from city to city. In the depths of our first full winter, post-Domino, some things seemed to have disproportionate value.

The perishables included a hundred pounds of potatoes, some squash, as well as twenty pounds of beef jerky, a dozen paper-wrapped hard sausages, a case of local hardtack, and a few pounds of dried apricots and apples. Other good stuff included home-made soap, similar to but not as good as that we used to buy from a vendor down in Portland, before the quake; some locally made pear brandy; and a dozen pairs beautifully made leather gloves from Casey Wallace. He'd made me a couple pair early in the year—the first pair wore like iron but were the softest work gloves I'd ever worn. I'd ordered up a mess of them for the whole family for Christmas this year, as well as new boots for the bunch of us, with the quality of White's, again, before the Domino.

"Got everything checked off the manifest?" I asked Alan. We had three copies of the stores' manifest: One on a clipboard in a counter near the register; one electronic version on a thumb drive, that was then copied over to an off-site computer; one with the store manager when they left the store. Anything sold during the day was updated on the multiple copies and verified for inventory. It cut down on losses due to poor inventory control—meaning, theft on the part of shoppers and employees. Our 'main' store never had a problem with that, probably due to the Army presence. A couple of other stores did though, but with co-location of stores and Army Guardsmen, that was winnowing out, too.

"Done," Alan said, hanging up the clipboard.

"Anything you wanna toss to the Guard?" he asked as he locked up the door, and slid a lever on the side of the door, dropping a heavy cross-bar across the inside—an invention of one of our customers to keep the place more secure.

"Got anything in mind?" I asked. "Hadn't thought of it."

"There's a dozen young men over there who'll be eating MREs or whatever the military calls 'food' for Thanksgiving, and they're a long way from wherever 'home' is."

"No locals?"

"Not a one."

"We'll take care of that. I'll dig out a gallon of that pear brandy. We'll see what we can do about Thanksgiving when we get home."

"Meet at the house in an hour?" he said as he reached the driver's door.

"Works for me. You need any help with that stuff?" I asked. He had at least as much stuff in the covered back of the F-350 as we did in the little Escape.

"Nope—I'll just back the truck up to the garage and offload there. We've got just about this much room left in there."

"All right—see you soon," I said, opening Carl's door. "Carl—hand me one of those shoe-boxes."

"The brandy?" Karen asked.

"Little off-duty wind-down for the Guard."

"As long as they all share," she said.

"That'll be up to them," I said.

"Well, there are two of them out there now, so you have witnesses," Carl said as I closed the door, box under my arm.

"Sergeant, Corporal, a little something for your down time. Share with the rest of your squad, if you would," I said, handing the box over.

"Thank you very much, sir," the Sergeant replied as he opened the box, a surprised look on his face. Maybe twenty-two years old. Maybe.

"Command got anything coming your way for Thanksgiving?"

"Not unless they can find a way to resurrect the NFL, sir," the corporal said.

"Well, no chance of Detroit playing in any regard. I have heard a rumor that Dallas will play San Diego."

"Packers fan, sir."

"Maybe someday," I said. "We'll see what we can do about rounding up some better chow. What's your headcount?"

"Baker's dozen, sir. Four on duty at all times."

"Done. You guys have a TV, in case there is a football game?"

"Secure data-link, sir, and a twenty four inch monitor."

"That'll do then I guess," I said. "Anything you can share about Colorado?"

"Saw the attack, near-real time. Infantry dropped like flies. *Free America* cameraman and reporter started running like Hell, then it got them. Camera stayed on after they went into convulsions. Wasn't pretty. They'd a danged near puked out their lungs. Whole lotta blood. Lotta red snow out there."

That didn't sound line a nerve agent, but I wasn't exactly up on either chemical or neurological agents. "I'm thinking that wasn't on regular TV," I said.

"We kinda hacked into a direct feed from the satellite, before it went through editing. Happens a lot when you're bored and you have a quarter-million dollars in communications equipment to play with," the corporal replied.

"Thanks—I better get going. Few more days of civilian life and I'm under orders myself."

"Our condolences, sir," the sergeant replied with a smile.

"Not at all. I may end up being your C.O."

"Nobody's that lucky, sir. We're a long way from the real shootin' war."

"Hope it stays that way. We've seen our share of action here, though. Things change fast," I said as I reached the driver's door of the SUV. "Pays to be awake and suspicious. You don't want to be a target for some antsy civilian. They're better armed than you guys are."

"Might be, but we own the night."

Sunday evening,
November Nineteenth

It is, and should be, something that will forever alter your view of humanity, seeing lifeless bodies in the street, either in person or through television or still photographs. On this night, with intermittent power and television signals, we were watching commercial television news of the attacks on American citizens, caused by American citizens. I think the Drummond family was more in shock and sadness, that this could happen, that this should be, 'on purpose.'

The Los Angeles attacks might have been the worst, or most graphic, I could not decide which. The commentators, constantly warning that the images should not be seen by younger viewers or that they were particularly shocking, eventually ran out of adjectives as the hand-held, and helicopter mounted cameras showed block after block of dead in the streets, most wearing the customary California casual wear. Three major theme parks were hit, just two weeks after reopening for limited runs. Four other major outdoor shopping areas, and one shopping mall, were hit, nearly simultaneously. It appeared to me within a few minutes that there had to be multiple delivery methods to deliver whatever agent was used, with the common factor that it was an airborne agent, or perhaps several agents.

Many of the bodies had burns and blisters of some kind while in other locations the bodies were relatively unmarked.

In L.A. alone, there appeared to be thousands dead. Little television footage was shown of the attacks in Dallas, again at an outdoor market; no visuals from Phoenix or the attacks in Florida. I suspected they were at least as effective as what we had seen in California. Very little was said of the attack in Colorado. I assumed that this was due to censorship, rather than for lack of available information.

I got up from my spot on the couch, sandwiched between Karen and Kelly, and cleared the dinner dishes from the coffee table. Carl shut off the television. I think we'd all had enough.

Before I reached the kitchen with my armload of soup bowls and mugs, Buck and Ada were up and moving toward the door, just as I heard the front gate rattle.

"Easy, you two. Carl, see who might be on the way in, please," I said.

"Got it," he said as he reached for the twelve-gauge with his left hand, holding back the window blinds with his right. "Army...It's Major Cross."

That got Karen up and moving. She'd been staring a little too long at the blank television screen after it was shut off. I'm sure she was thinking the same kinds of things that I was.

"Carl, Kelly, you two take care of the dishes. And there's laundry to fold downstairs," Karen said as she opened the front door for Elaine. Both dogs then lowered their guard and went into attention-getting mode.

"Good evening, Major," I said as I came back toward the door. "Come on in."

"Thanks," Elaine said, taking off her Kevlar helmet and non-Army scarf. The bitter winter winds were coming back in from the East.

"How's Bobby doing?" Karen asked of Major Crosses' young son.

"He's doing OK. That elderberry stuff is great. He's just being a pill now, is all. Jenny's back to almost full steam and starting to drive my Mom up the wall," she answered, before a pause. "You've seen the news."

316

"We have," I said, saying with two words what many might not adequately convey.

"Come in for some tea," Karen added. "You must be frozen."

"I'm OK. It's pretty tough to keep up a good attitude when you're stuck outside all night though," she said as she took her camo parka off and sat at the dining room table. "Our neighborhood patrols tend to do their watching from inside warm buildings."

"Can't say I blame them. We had enough nights out in the snow last year to last a lifetime. Any problems? I mean other than the obvious."

"No. Cold's keeping most everyone inside. That and the word is out that breaking curfew will get you killed for your effort."

"Seeing what's on TV, that shouldn't be a surprise," Karen said, pouring a cup of steaming tea.

"It shouldn't be," she repeated. "That's why I'm here. Rick, they want you early," Elaine said apologetically, looking more at Karen than me. Karen did not seem surprised. "There's an outfitting session for your unit tomorrow at oh-nine-hundred. Have you wrapped up your transition at the County?"

"As much as need be, yeah. There'll always be loose ends," I said. "How soon before we ship out?"

"No more than a week, I think. Can't really go into it in detail, more because I don't know anything in detail. They're aiming at a big call-up. The Army is expanding dramatically, more than I would've ever expected."

"Here too?"

"Yes. I don't know if Mr. Bauer or Mr. Martin will get called up or not."

"I doubt either would be accepted," I said. "Ron's got a heart condition, and Alan's not exactly a kid," before adding. "Of course, neither am I."

"Honestly, Rick, if they're breathing and can carry a gun, they're pretty much eligible. They might get lucky and get passed over as performing an essential civilian function, but this will be huge."

"What about the kids? How young are they going?" Karen asked.

"Not sure. Eighteen at present. I doubt they'd take anyone younger unless they were orphaned or emancipated or something."

"How bad is Colorado, Elaine?" I asked, referring to the cryptic information we'd heard over the radio, and the story relayed to us by one of the Guardsmen down by the store. We'd heard updates on all of the civilian targets, but nothing more about the lead story, since it was first broadcast.

"I don't know much more than I knew this afternoon. Nothing's being broadcast, which should tell you volumes," she said.

"Size of force attacking? Size of target? Casualties?" I said, getting a little impatient and frustrated, yet knowing that she probably didn't have any more information than I did.

"Rick, honestly, I have no idea. I suspect we were hit very hard. I'm sure that we had a large force in the field."

I paused for a few moments and leaned back in the captain's chair. "There really won't be any going back from this. Even after the betrayals that we've seen in the past....this sort of atrocity demands no prisoners."

"I cannot disagree with that," Elaine said. "I doubt that anyone in uniform tonight would."

"How did the United States of America come to this?" Karen said rhetorically. "The Founding Fathers must be spinning in their graves."

"And have been for quite some time," I added.

The Founders expected all of our troubles of course, and gave us ample and repeated warnings in the Declaration, the Constitution, and many other pieces of correspondence that made up the history and anecdotes of the founding of the United States.

Laying in bed, hours after Karen had drifted off to sleep, my mind went back to a time before the war, to electronic discussions with other like-minded men and women on 'the future of our country.'

It was apparent to everyone that the whole system had become a fraud; that political parties only existed to increase their power; that banks and insurance companies and rating agencies and talk-show hosts were in out-and-out collusion to sucker the American public and the American business into a lose-lose game of gambling with the financial future.

I'd counted myself among a large handful of people ready to start a new political party, once based solely on the beliefs and guides given us by the Founders, a return to Constitutional guidance and uncommon, common sense. Unfortunately for the 'Federationists', time ran out before common sense could prevail. The backlash of nearly a hundred years, maybe more, of erosion of State's rights, our personal rights, our financial engine, our international entanglements, were all spelled out for us in advance.

We refused to learn those lessons we now faced the harshness of remedial education. We'd grown as a culture too complacent, too dependent, too lazy to stand up. Maybe it is true that people only learn from personal experience, and that history is too abstract.

I wondered how many years, (or perhaps a generation or more) before we would return to the definitions, the respect, and the obligations of freedom and accountability?

It was tough getting to sleep, and once I finally did, it was a very short night.

Monday morning,
November Twentieth
5:50 a.m.

The alarm rattled me awake, followed by the ascension of both dogs onto the bed.

"Well, good morning to you, too," I said as Ada licked my face, Buck jockeying for position next to her.

"Morning," I said to Karen, still snuggled under the covers.

"That is a matter of debate," she said, sneaking over between the dogs and giving me a kiss. "What time are you going in?"

"Right off. I figured seven."

"Get much sleep?"

"After a fashion, no."

Karen snuggled closer, nudging Ada out of the way. "How old would your Dad be today?" she asked out of left field. That's right, it was Dad's birthday. I'd forgotten.

"Ninety-three," I thought after doing the math.

"He'd be proud of you, you know."

"No more than me of him," I said cuddling her close by, despite Buck's desire to take over the bed. "You going to be OK?" I said, before thinking a moment. "I mean…"

"No, but we'll manage. I just don't know what I'd do without you."

"Remember what I said, before my last misadventure. I will come home to you."

"Maybe I need to be more specific," she said with a little laugh. "'Come home in one piece and undamaged.'"

"That'd be good, too. Someday when we get through this, I owe you a trip someplace nice. I'm thinking Maui."

"I can hardly think that far ahead. I don't think you can either," she said.

"I can hope. This can't last forever."

"No, but it can last a long, long time," she said. "What if this is eighteen sixty-one all over?"

"What if it's eighteen sixty-four?" I answered.

"Elaine looked worried. She knows something."

"I imagine a lot of people looked scared, after seeing what happened yesterday. They're targeting anything. Everything."

"Your unit isn't supposed to be near the front line, though…."

"No, we're not, but this is war and things change."

"You are too old to be doing this," Karen said.

"Better me than our children, hon. You know I'm not exactly one to go looking for trouble."

"What these people did was unthinkable…and you *are* going after them."

"Yes, because it needs to stop. If I weren't already being called up, I'd volunteer."

"You can't be serious."

"I've never been more serious. My wife and children and my future grandchildren mean more to me than I mean to myself. If I can help stop these bastards, I will. Heck, if they 'win', I'm dead anyway. There's no way they'd tolerate someone like me, someone who'd stand up to authority. And from what I've read, by extension, any of my relatives."

Karen didn't have a response to that.

"Honey, I'm going to do whatever I can, work with whatever men I can, to make sure that isn't going to happen. With God's help, we'll win."

"Don't forget your gun this time. Take your Dad's with you."

"Planned on it. Army might frown on it, but it hasn't let us down yet."

"I have a surprise for you…well, the kids and I do anyway," Karen said, finally giving up and letting Buck have the center of the bed. It was time to get up anyway.

"What's that?" I said, finally putting my feet onto the cold floor.

"We'll show you after you shower. You better get moving. I'll get the fire on and get breakfast ready. Move it, soldier," she said, giving me a kiss as she put her heavy robe on.

After my shower, I dressed in decent work clothes, figuring that I'd be wearing something in green by the end of the day. I'd also taken some time the night before after Elaine had left, to pack up some civilian clothes and other items to take with me during my time away. All of that fit in a medium sized pack, leaning against the damaged oak buffet in the dining room.

Downstairs, Karen had the fire in the woodstove going and Carl was trying to coax some more heat out of it. Kelly and Karen were making pancakes and eggs in the kitchen.

"Morning, you two. How's our day looking?"

"Great if you like cold, dark, and cold," Carl said.

"Carl, you're such a grouch," Kelly said.

"Not so much into cold, no," I said, tousling his hair as he fed more maple kindling into the firebox. "Any new snow?"

"Didn't look like it. More news, or I guess, more of the same on the TV. Local radios had just the curfew notice and weather. Rest of the time it's network."

"Hmmm," I said as Karen handed me a big travel mug of tea. "Thank you my dear," I said as I gave her a hug.

"Ready, kids?" Karen said.

"Sure," they said in unison. "My get," Carl said.

"We hadn't really planned on giving you this until Christmas," Karen said. "It's hardly a traditional gift."

"OK, now I'm intrigued," I said. Carl emerged from his room with a long, well-finished wood case, complete with brass corner protectors, four latches, and a tooled leather handle. "Well now, what do we have here?"

"I think you'll like it," Carl said.

"Definitely a guy present," Kelly said, amused but eager to see me open the case.

Carl placed it on the table in front of me. The case looked like furniture-grade cherry I noticed as I snapped open the latches.

"Merry Early Christmas," they all said as I opened up the top. Inside the padded case was a beautifully restored and reworked Springfield 1903A3, and matching personalized leather pouches for ammunition and accessories.

"Wow...I don't know what to say....other than thank you!" I said as I picked up the weapon. "Is this my grandfather's?"

"No, we liberated one of your shooters. Annika did all the work except the stock. She's got a guy in Greenacres who did that."

"Black walnut?" I asked.

"Yeah," Carl said.

"Like it?" Karen asked.

"Absolutely. I'm going to like trying this out," I said, hoping I had time to do so before I shipped out.

"That one's the fancy version," Kelly said, coming back into the dining room from the kitchen. "This one's more for work," she said, handing over a second case, this one of stained plywood and painted steel fittings. This one was much heavier.

"TWO?" I exclaimed. "Unbelievable," I said, opening up the second case.

"Pretty much the same custom work on both rifles. Synthetic stock on this one obviously. Anja called this a 'serious, bad-ass sporter'," Carl said.

"The scope tells me that much. Holy smokes," I said, picking up the weapon. "Man this is light."

"That one's not one of your originals," Karen said. "Anja built that one pretty much from scratch."

I noticed there were more custom leather pouches in this case.

"Ammunition. Half of those are black-tip," Carl said.

"Where on earth did you get that?" I asked incredulously. Black tipped 30.06 was armor piercing, very scarce pre-War and very, very expensive. My private stash had cost me several hundred dollars, pre-Domino.

"Actually, our old friend Scott McGlocklin sent that. Said you'd appreciate it."

"This just gets better and better," I said. Gunny McGlocklin was now down in Oregon, out of the Marines, and trying to keep a lid on things in the Oregon Zone. I hadn't heard anything from him directly since the Spring. He took a distinct liking to my treasured Garand, and an equal amount of interest in my three Springfields. "It's not every day a guy gets armor piercing ammunition and a finely crafted lead slinger, let alone two. These had to cost a fortune."

"That is none of your concern," Karen said, rubbing my shoulders. "And you need to quit drooling over your new presents and eat up. It's getting late."

"Yes'm," I said. "She could be a drill instructor," I said to the kids, who both grinned a little.

"I heard that," she said from the kitchen. "And no, I couldn't. I couldn't stand dishing out or taking that kind of abuse any more than you'd like taking it."

"Duly noted," I said as she put a heaping steaming plate in front of me.

"Now eat. Enough chatter," she said as she turned, whacking the back of my head along the way.

Carl pretty much monopolized our breakfast talk as he told me more about the re-worked, former 'shooter.' Built to National Match standards, including extensive trigger work, a hand-fitted stock and many hours of fine machine work to truly bring out the best possible performance. The 'sporter' had a composite stock, all the same machine and trigger work of the beautifully finished walnut-stock model, a custom-built Weaver-type scope mount that didn't mess up the original firearm, and a Zeiss Conquest scope, that I was completely unfamiliar with. A scoped 1903 in general, I'd be unfamiliar with, I thought to myself. The stock '03 had a pretty good accuracy out to a couple hundred yards, at least for me and my aging eyes, and probably an effective range of not more than five hundred yards overall, but I hadn't experience with that. A 'new and improved' 1903....the possibilities were interesting, to say the least.

The morning's activities included my formal swearing in, with Karen and the kids attending, in a private room at Camp Overbeck, administered by none other than General Robert Anderson himself.

Karen told Bob, "You keep him out of trouble, General, or I'll hunt you to the ends of the Earth."

"I will do my best ma'am."

"You better," she said, before turning to me. "See you tonight?" she asked me.

325

"Hope so. I'll let you know. I have your number now," I said, giving her a quick kiss and hug. I noticed Bob talking with Carl, from what I could overhear, about my 1903's.

"You two take care of your Mom. I'll call you later," I said, giving both a hug and a kiss. With that, they made their way out, and back home.

"You have a delightful family, Rick," General Anderson commented.

"Yes I do, sir. They tolerate me far better than I deserve."

"What's this about an -03 your son tells me?"

"Two. One was a casual shooter that they had rebuilt for me, more like transformed. Beautiful to the point of artwork. The second was, for lack of a better phrase, created out of thin air. I haven't had a chance to use either of course. The second is more business. Synthetic stock. Big scope. Complete with AP rounds loaded up on strippers."

"Bring it with you when you go. You might have a chance to use it."

"So if I may General," I said before being interrupted.

"Bob is fine, Rick," he said, introducing a more casual conversation. "Let's walk. I have an office in this maze somewhere."

"OK, Bob it is, in private. What is it that brings you to Spokane on this cold, snowy day, right before Thanksgiving? And why am I being called up early?" I asked, as a couple of young Air Force airmen passed us in the hall, saluting in a bit of a surprised manner.

"In the office," the General said, waiving me into a smaller-than-average office, at the end of the hall. Major Kurt George came out of the office just as we prepared to enter.

"General, report's on your desk, current as of fifteen minutes ago, including comments from other commands, five minutes old," the Major said. "Colonel Drummond, good to see you."

"You, too, Major. I expect I'll have a uniform one of these days to go along with my rank and command...."

"You will, I'm sure. Lieutenant Banks on the left there will set you up," he said, pointing to a cubicle down another aisle. The General was right. It was a maze of a place.

"Major, convey my thanks to Communications in getting this so quickly," the General said.

"Will do, sir."

"Colonel, close the door," he said moving to the desk chair, and flipping open a red folder. I closed the door and...waited for orders. "Take a seat."

I moved to the chair opposite the desk and sat down. 'This will take getting used to,' I thought.

"You up to speed on that Command Summary that Walla Walla sent up?" Bob asked as he read the file, not looking up.

"Yes, sir."

"Good. Now file it. Things changed yesterday, a lot."

"Understood."

"Well, you think you do. That's OK. Sixth Army was wiped off the map yesterday in Colorado. I mean, gone. Fifty-three thousand two hundred and six men and women, dead."

"Holy sh•t." I said, a chill going down my spine.

"Yeah, pretty much what I said, too," he said, finally looking up from the report. "That isn't all. Air Force and Navy air units were hit with similar effects, on a much smaller scale just due to population concentration, at seventeen installations all around the country. Alert facilities were locked down immediately and most of them had environmental controls that slowed the attack. Ground personnel didn't have that option. Dead."

"How…"

"Neurotoxins. Odorless, colorless, no symptoms until lethal concentrations are achieved, then its death within minutes as you suffocate. Dispersal through the use of UAVs in some cases in most there were remotely detonated canisters set in and just upwind of troop and population concentrations. Silent release, sometimes at night, kills as you sleep, exposed to the airborne agent. Within thirty minutes of release, the agent neutralizes itself within normal atmosphere. Some key agent combines with airborne nitrogen and becomes inert."

"So the enemy needs to be more than thirty minutes downwind," I said, thinking about the clinical detail, rather than the up close and personal. "Which is why they found miles and miles of empty in Colorado. They were out of range."

"After the agent became inert, the Statist forces moved back in, stripped communications gear, food, weapons, ammunition, armor, in some cases uniforms. And moved back West. We watched this on satellite and on UAVs. Our dead army is still on the ground, in the snow, where they died."

"Jesus Christ. That means they've got open access to us. They can infiltrate us at will…"

"They think that, yes. It's not quite that easy, although they don't know that."

"How's that? They've got gear identical to ours."

"Everything is RFID chipped, quite covertly, and is easily tracked. Uniforms, weapons, ammunition magazines. Tanks. Everything. The Statist commanders don't know that. We can also remote detonate the tanks when we're of a mind to. Goes for some other key gear, too."

I didn't have anything to say.

"Rick, your new assignment will eventually be as it was described, just as it was before you walked in this building. First, you'll be doing that in addition to shuttling men and gear to the line. Going in, you're running supplies and troops. Your orders are to help create a forward support base out of the wreckage that the S.A. forces have left, whatever the Hell that means, so that we don't fight over the same ground twice. That piece of Colorado has already cost us more Americans than Gettysburg did on both sides."

"Bob, how do we fight this? Our troops could be going right back into a trap."

"Working on it. Air Force is bombing the sh•t out of them right this minute. Anything that had an RFID tag on it that moved west beyond Sixth Army's position won't be an issue. The line will be reestablished, with our troops in full-on chemical gear, shortly. Anything that crosses a predetermined frontier is taken out from the air."

"You said earlier, that 'going in' we're running troops and supplies.' What about coming out?"

"After you first arrive, your transported troops will secure the battlefield. You will have media with you—press release on the attack goes out tomorrow morning. Your Brigade's first mission will be to bring Sixth Army back. We are not leaving them there," he said, looking at me, and through me, at the same time. "Questions?"

"No, sir. Not a one."

"Godspeed, Colonel."

Monday afternoon,
November Twentieth

Never having been in the military, I had no idea how much crap you are responsible for in the way of uniforms, boots, manuals, gear, and stuff that would never realistically be used. By fourteen hundred hours, I had more duffel bags of stuff than any soldier, or anyone in charge of soldiers, ought. Dress uniform (as if there should be an opportunity to wear one) fully equipped with nameplate, colonel's birds, uncomfortable dress cap. At least the utilities were comfortable, the winter gear seemingly well made, the boots comfortable. I'd never seen digital camouflage in whites, grays and black. I hoped never to see red on any of it.

The surprises were the twin .45 caliber side arms, complete with small Picatinny rails and suppressors. All built around a relatively familiar frame, this one the Colt XSE. And of course the M-16C. I could not get over how light the weapon was, similar to the feeling the first time I picked up an unloaded Glock, versus my 1911. Unreal. Same mag as the standard M-16, which is where the real weight was for the ground troops, hogging all that around, using it a bit at a time.

One of Camp Overbeck's master armorers walked me through both weapons, as well as general familiarization with many others that we might encounter in the field. I think I surprised him by being able to field strip a half-dozen of the Communist-bloc weapons without instruction, reassemble them, and in the case of the SKS, point out the fact that a spring-loaded firing pin and a recoil buffer would help improve the weapon, especially the firing pin using American-made ammunition. The soft Western primers behave differently than the 'hard' Russian primers. It'd be embarrassing for two or three rounds to go off at once with the American made stuff. The spring-loaded pin helped prevent that.

With twenty minutes in the hundred-yard indoor firing range on the assigned weapons, all rounds from the California were in the black, but three of sixteen from the Colt were outside the black or on the edge. If I had time to practice, I might again shoot as well as I did at twenty-two, I thought. 'Never mind the fact that your eyesight sucks,' I said to myself.

"Pretty good shooting for a...a newly minted officer," Chief Warrant Officer Tim Vanhoff commented. "Generally speaking, officers can't hit the paper, let alone the black."

"Thanks, Mr. Vanhoff. That rifle is amazing," I said, ignoring his stumbling for words as I placed the weapon on the cleaning bench. "I haven't had to qualify on anything in, well, let's say a long-ass time."

"You're not Army trained though. You've got some idiosyncrasies in your stance, your form, and your targeting. Too late to make you unlearn it though. It seems to work for you."

"Let's just say my training was more, freelance in nature. My form's a little rusty because I can't quite move like I did when I was a kid. I've been driving a desk for too long." I didn't mention the fact that my ribs hurt like heck.

"You'll do OK with this outfit. God-willing, you won't have to see much action."

"Thanks for the instruction. I'd love to spend another week on these," I said as I put one of the range-room's Colts, and the empty magazines, on the cleaning bench.

"So, level with me if you would sir, where'd you pick up your background on firearms? That Glock in there, you stripped like you'd been doing it all your life. And the AK, and SKS..."

"Frederick County, Maryland."

"D.I.A." Vanhoff said, referring to the Defense Intelligence Agency.

"Yeah, just after the last Ice Age."

"I didn't really take you for a spook," he said, before adding, "sir."

"I was quite young. I had a very short tenure. I got the Hell out. End of story. And, I never considered myself a 'spook', either."

"Well, a lot of that training stayed with you. It'll serve you well, Colonel."

"Thanks, I suppose. Frankly, I'd hoped all that was long-forgotten. And I'll never feel that I've earned that title."

"Not your choice in getting it, sir. Therefore no point in fussin' over it. Anything else you need, see me before you ship out."

"Will do. Thanks, Mr. Vanhoff."

"Oh, and sir? If you have a chance, pass on my compliments to Annika and Randy Thompson. I've got their fifth B.A.R. off the line. I understand you're neighbors."

"True enough. My original was handy for them in modeling up the trigger assembly on the computer, so they could re-engineer it." I then remembered talking with Kevin Miller about the shoot-off between Army, Air Force and Marines, using the first six Brownings. "Were you one of the shoot-off competitors?"

"Guilty as charged, sir."

"I assume you've fired a stock B.A.R. before?"

"Yes, sir. One that saw service in Vietnam. Heavy bastard."

"So are the new and improved models that much better?"

"Unbelievable. It's my new favorite classically engineered weapon."

"Colonel?" I heard from behind me. "You have a call from Walla Walla holding," one of the office secretaries said.

"Be right there," I said as I shook his hand. "Tim, you're a Renaissance man."

"I just appreciate great engineering."

"And you probably treat January twenty-third as a holiday," I said with a grin.

"John Moses Browning's birthday ought to be a holiday, sir."

"Can't argue with that," I said as I headed toward the door. The secretary, whose name I had yet to memorize, was waiting, a little impatiently.

"Sir, I apologize—it's not a phone call. It's actually a teleconference that's scheduled to start in less than five minutes. Most of your senior staff will be attending, either here or in Walla Walla. Sorry for the short notice."

"No problem. Lisa, right?"

"Yes, sir."

"Do you have that list of my command staff? I think I left mine in the office," I said, entering the large conference room where I was promptly saluted by two young enlisted men. I returned it, somewhat awkwardly and added "As you were," as if I knew what I was doing. I felt like a bad actor.

"It's in your folder. Your staff should be here any minute. You're missing your S2 and S6, medical and chaplain. Everyone else should be here," Lisa said as she ushered me into the room,

I struggled for a minute to remember what the S6 officer did, finally gave up and looked it up in my briefing folder. 'Communications.' S2 of course was intelligence.

About a minute later, the room was full, and I rose to meet many of my new staff, informally.

"Please excuse my lack of military protocol. Until this morning I was a chicken rancher, storekeeper, and jack of few trades."

"Sir, that goes for about a third of your senior staff, up until a month ago or so," my executive officer, Lieutenant Colonel Jim Schaefer said. "As far as my own career, I left the army after the Gulf War. Didn't look back until six months ago."

"I know we only have a minute before this starts, but I'd appreciate your keeping me on the straight and narrow."

"Sir, we're ready," one of the enlisted men announced.

"Seats, everyone. Here it comes," I said, not knowing of course what 'it' might be. The screen was filled with the Pacific Northwest Command insignia, overlaying the 'new' United States flag. I thought for a moment, does one salute an officer on television?

"Afternoon, everyone. For those that do not know me, I'm Brigadier General Rodney Howard. This is a briefing across the entire command, regarding the attacks on the United States by S.A. forces," the General began.

"As has been reported, both military and civilian populations were hit with a neurotoxin delivered through various means. Unmanned aerial vehicles. Manned aircraft, crashed into targets of opportunity. Car bombs. Bombs planted within structures, underground, or otherwise concealed. These weapons were coordinated largely without an extensive communications network therefore, they have been planned well in advance of the attack. We lost more than fifteen thousand civilians. We lost the entire Sixth Army—that alone was more than fifty thousand men. We've lost much in the way of airborne capability due to the deaths of more than ten thousand off duty pilots and mechanics, electronics technicians and weapons techs. Our airborne capability has been seriously affected."

"Within the next few days, you will see a general call up of all former retired military personnel, regardless of age to fill the gaps and train new soldiers. You will also see dramatic clamp downs on movement of refugees—many of the attacks have been traced to transient movement through porous battle lines and those enemy mingled freely in civilian populations....." I thought about that for a

moment. We'd seen a significant inrush of refugees as the weather grew cold. Did we have that element among us?

"....were made using unmanned aerial vehicles, smaller than a single-engine plane in many cases; truck and car bombs in market areas; or in the case of Sixth Army, the weapons were concealed along a line within a thousand meters of the Army. The Sixth was manipulated by numerically insignificant S.A. forces to be where they were when they were attacked. What seemed like a dominating position for the Sixth Army turned out to be a massive trap. S.A. forces had evacuated the area to a safe distance, calculated to be thirty minutes downwind of the detonation points. The devices were also silent, according to sources who survived long enough to report. Think, compressed air, released in a high volume low pressure manner. It also came when most of the Sixth Army was down for the night."

"Once Sixth Army was attacked, all units were put on alert. The problem of course was that no one knew what to be on alert for. Within six hours, the entire attack wave had been completed. As a note, we do not know if follow-on attacks are in the offing. There, at this point in time, is no way to know."

"To our men in the field, there is not enough MOPP gear to go around. There is no warning for this airborne agent. No odor, no sensation, until lethal concentrations kill. No warning whatsoever. No antidote."

"Elements of the Texas Guard are now on site at the location of the Sixth Army massacre, and will hold this position until reinforcements arrive in the next eight hours. Airborne elements from California, New Mexico, Arizona, Alabama and Georgia are in transit at this time to reinforce the line. The One Seventieth and One Seventy Second brigades will be in place in twenty four hours. Pacific Northwest Command will deploy front line and support personnel in the effort to secure the line and reinforce the front line troops. Two brigades of the Forty First Division will deploy within thirty-six hours. The Fighting First Washington under command of Colonel Todd Hauser. Third Washington Engineers under command of Colonel Richard Drummond. First Washington will deploy in support of the One Seventy Second's mechanized battalions. Third

Washington in support of the One Seventy Second's combat engineering battalion and other units as needed and as available."

"Gentlemen, what I am about to tell you will not sit well. Word will filter out in the media, but the brutality of the S.A. attacks is by no means contained to military forces or civilians far behind the lines. The S.A. is taking no prisoners. The S. A. is executing civilians. They are putting them in buildings and burning them alive. They are doing this to men, women and children. Their tactics are to terrorize, to utterly shock their opponents into submission. Anyone who does not comply immediately will either be summarily executed or shipped off to slave labor. Satellite intelligence show mass graves." The general fell silent for a moment, and took a drink of water before continuing.

"This is what you are up against. You are now being passed more detailed briefing packets on your assignments. I wish you Godspeed in your persecution of justice. That is all. Good day."

With that, the screen switched back to the flag, and then fell to black. Sealed packets were passed out to everyone at the table. Before we opened them, I decided to address the officers and men in the room.

"Ladies and gentlemen, as I said earlier, until this morning I was a civilian. My most recent employer was Spokane County, where I served as County Administrator. I've not served in the military. I have had some government service, quite a while back. I appreciate the confidence that Governor Hall puts in me by honoring me with this commission. I would ask you to indulge my civilian manners as I learn the ropes here. I will do my best to make sure I don't do anything stupid and get us all killed." That at least, brought a couple of snickers.

"Now, on to business. We've all seen some evil at work over the past year. I think that what we just heard tops it all. How we react to this as a nation will help define us for many decades to come. I might sound like I'm some politician on a stump speech. I'm not. I'm as far removed from that as I can get. My gut reaction is that these bastards need to die, and that I want to help them along that end. I know that we're a support brigade. I know that we're not supposed to be on the line. I also know that plans are perfect until you implement them. I want everyone in the outfit fully armed just like a combat brigade. This brigade needs to be ready for whatever shit storm comes our way. Questions," I stated, not asking. None came, but there were a number of glances exchanged. "Very well," I said as I stood, picking up my packet as the staff rose to attention. "I want everyone back in here at sixteen-hundred, up to speed on these orders, and no, I haven't read them," I said as I slapped the packet down on the table. "And readiness, staffing, and schedule for departure. Dismissed."

In a few moments, the room was empty. "Private," I asked of a young man just outside the door, "Can you find me my office?"

That made him smile. "This way, sir. It's just this side of Communications."

"Thanks. Work to do."

"Yes, sir. There is at that."

The Communications room was a darkened maze of computer servers, monitors, and perhaps thirty personnel working on a myriad of problems. The room had been carved out of the massive warehouse, with framed in, heavily insulated walls, ceiling, and fat bundles of network cabling behind the racks of computers. I was pretty impressed.

My office was an eight-by-eight square, one high window on the inside wall facing the open cube farm populated by Camp Overbeck's command staff, desk empty except for my initial briefing packet. My hastily dumped gear bags resided in the two non-matching side chairs. Before I dug into the file in any depth, I thought I'd give Karen a phone call. I actually remembered the last time I called her at home: Friday afternoon, January thirteenth. I always called to let her know when I was leaving the office for the day. I called the new cell number that Elaine had given me.

"Well good afternoon," I said, pleased to hear her voice.

"How's it going?" she asked. "I miss you."

"You most," I said. "Going OK so far. I have another meeting to get into in a little while, and some paperwork to go through first."

"You home for dinner tonight?"

"Should be. Probably around eighteen hundred before I get free though."

"We'll be ready. Pork sausage and rice."

"That'll make me hungry if I think about it long enough. Everything going OK?"

"Weird without you, that's all."

"Yeah, I'm in a *Twilight Zone* episode of my own."

"And nothing you can talk about."

"Affirmative."

"That's OK. I probably don't want to know."

I thought a moment before answering, which was enough of an answer for her.

"Thought as much. Back to your paperwork. Dinner will be ready. And Alan has a nice bottle of wine for us too."

"Good for him. See you in awhile."

We finished up with our customary 'love yous' and I set about to reading.

The trains Third Washington would take would be pulled by militarized versions of General Electric-built Burlington Northern locomotives. Militarized, in the form of armor being installed over exposed radiators and hydraulics, with provisions for ballistic glass installed in the cabs, along with shuttered windows. On the railcar immediately behind each engine, an Abrams tank would reside, fully crewed. Once the 'command' units, supplies, tanks and bunkhouses were offloaded, the locomotives and empty flats would move back west, be reloaded with the rest of the Brigade and gear, and meet up with the first shipment on the ground. Fifteen hundred men per load.

Our soldiers would ride in lighter armored converted shipping containers. Pre-War, several companies specialized in converting shipping containers into transportable office or disaster relief units, with wide ranging options in their design and construction. Some of the units were set up as strictly 'transport' units, with rudimentary seating arranged for maximum capacity with limited passenger comfort. Most were set up as triple-deck bunkhouses. We'd have a couple 'office' units, two command and communication units, a pair of medical/surgical suites, laundries, bathroom and shower units, power generation units, two pharmacies, and a substantial amount of supplies, far more than our brigade would need, it was hoped. The occupied units would be stacked on half-height supply cars, cut down from full-height cars. The half-height cars would contain most of our provisions, including fuel, water, food, ammunition and supplemental weapons, and relief supplies. Resupply trains would follow along behind us in theory, carrying more men and gear for 'the War Effort.'

We'd be second in, after a Marine Expeditionary unit secured the Sixth Army battlefield.

DEPARTURE: 11/23 0700 hrs. depart Spokane for points east. Transit time estimated at four days to destination, Sterling, Colorado. Upon arrival, set up temporary HQ for retrieval operations. Second train containing remainder of Third Washington will arrive within four hours. 249th Engineering Battalion, Company B, 'Prime Power' will be on station within twenty-four hours of arrival. Third Brigade will assist in retrieval of KIA, support of MEU, and restoration of utilities to Sterling. Further movement east will follow line units in similar duty.

"So much for Thanksgiving dinner," I said to myself.

Tuesday morning,
November Twentieth
15:50 Hours

"Uniform suits you. Not," Mike Amberson said from the doorway, pulling me out of the mental exercise of all the things that could go wrong on our mission.

"What are you doing here? And out of uniform at that?"

"Out of Sheriff's livery, for sure. Active duty, effective eighteen-hundred. Sam Waybright's the new head badge." Sam was a couple of layers junior to some of Mike's staff, but knew how to command, from what I knew of him. I'd only met him twice.

"Snagged your sorry butt and pulled you back in," I said as I shook his hand. "Working for me again?"

"Not hardly. Real working unit, unlike your soft rear-echelon pukes."

"Don't look now, but three quarters of my brigade served in line units in Mexico, Iraq, and Afghanistan."

"Good. You called it 'my brigade.' You passed your first test. Not bad for your first day."

"Thanks. But seriously, where are you headed?"

"Like I said. Fighting unit. Rangers again. Second of the Seventy-Fifth," he said, referring to Second Battalion, Seventy-Fifth Regiment, formerly of Fort Lewis.

"How's Ashley taking this?" I asked. I could imagine the answer. New mom of twins, too many family lost over the past year, husband back in harm's way.

"About like your Karen, I suspect."

"Not that well, I think. You in some cushy staff job? Intel? Personnel?" I said, kidding. I knew perfectly well where he was likely to be.

"Hell, no. Operations."

"Light Colonel?"

"Yeah."

"Good. I still outrank you."

"That's fine. I don't mind doing your heavy lifting," he said with a smile.

"I'm heading into a staff meeting. You free in an hour or so?"

"Should be. Got a call in a few minutes with Regiment in Walla Walla."

"Had one of those earlier. You hear about Sixth Army?"

"Yeah. Right after Major Cross shanghaied me during a little dust-up in East Central. I stopped in at the house, grabbed my gear, gave Ash the news, and here I am."

"A little harsh way for her to find out, don't you think?" I said, surprised.

"She knew before I did. The Major took care of that," Mike said.

"Funny how she operates," I said as Lisa, last name escaping me, beckoned me back into the conference room. Keeping me on time, I noted.

"I better run. Meet me in the Commons when you're wrapped up," I said, referring to the 'official' name of the cafeteria and lounge area. It must have been a machine shop of some kind, pre-War. It had a twenty-ton bridge crane, just over the buffet line.

At seventeen-fifteen, we wrapped up the briefing. I thought that now that everyone understood everyone else's needs to meet our departure schedule, now less than two days out, the deadline was real, the provisions needed to be aboard NOW, the time for training was OVER and only the last minute stuff—which is usually equipment or stuff we'd miss most if we forgot it—was about all we had time for.

My Tuesday would start in Yardley, where our trains were being assembled component by component, in guarded train yard. Once loaded, the trains would have more firepower on them than any other moving thing in the state, aside from the dozen B-52's we had in residence at Fairchild.

And here I was, less than twelve hours in the Army, in command, with a staff who had every right to be completely skeptical about my abilities. I was certainly skeptical myself. Sitting in the commons, reviewing everyone's personnel summary documents, I waited for Lt. Col. Amberson to show up. 'Lieutenant Colonel Amberson' would get some getting used to, I thought.

In the Commons I was out of my staff's way, reading yet another stack of paperwork—this one, the personnel manifest for the entire brigade. I'd have hours going through most of this.

"Mr. Drummond? What are you doing here? And in uniform?" Sarah Woodbridge asked, quite surprised. She was dressed in scrubs, carrying insulated coveralls and her parka and her backpack, I assumed for the trip 'home.'

"Likewise, kiddo. What are you doing here?"

"Training in the infirmary. Two days a week here, one at Valley General, the rest at the community center."

"Well, I pretty much got drafted. You heading home?"

"Waiting for the shuttle."

"Don't bother. I've got wheels, well, Mike Amberson does. You come home with Mike and me."

"Cool! Now, I have to ask. Are you going to seen John? Are you going to California?" John Martin was just a few days ahead of me, heading off for what passed for 'basic' these days.

"Afraid not. Heading someplace colder," I said, being deliberately vague.

"Colorado then."

"Can't say, and you shouldn't ask."

"OK," she said, before noticing my insignia with some astonishment. "You're a Colonel?"

"Brigade commanders are apparently Colonels. Therefore, when in Rome...."

"You're the new commander for Third Brigade then. You're the talk of the post."

"And plenty of snickers, I'm sure."

"Well, some griping, but that's probably normal from what my Captain says. Mostly, that you're shipping out like, Wednesday. And, that Third Brigade's former commander is now a two-star."

"That's not quite right. He's just a brigadier. That's one star."

"Fast track, either way. The career people are, 'miffed' I guess is a good word."

"I'm sure. They may well have a right to be."

"Word's out that you were some kind of spy in your younger days."

"Oh, not that crap again," I said, suddenly angry that my ancient history, MY history, and a handful of other people who might still survive, was now being dredged up, embellished, discounted, distorted.

"So there is something there," Sarah said with a furrowed brow. "Sorry I brought it up. Sounds like this bothers you."

"It does, and it's been twenty-four years."

"I'll not bring it up again."

"It's OK. Things you bury eventually come back to haunt. This particular part of my life was buried a long time. Sometime I'll tell you about it. Call it a learning experience."

"I'll take you up on that," she said, finally sitting down at the table, just as Mike appeared behind her. He was carrying two overly large duffels.

"Looks like our driver is finally here. About damned time," I said with fake irritation, looking at my watch.

"Sorry Colonel, real soldier-business to attend to. I'm sure nothing you've ever troubled yourself with," Mike said, shaking my hand.

"Probably right, Mike. You ready?"

"Yep. Your bags in the rig?" he asked

"Yeah. You need a hand?" I'd brought my new gear bags out earlier, and stashed them in Mike's newly-assigned Humvee. This one, according to the motor pool sergeant, actually had a heater that worked. And, I noted as I tossed my two bags in the back, freshly painted, riveted-on patches covering a stitch of holes from automatic weapons fire on the driver's side.

"Let a superior officer haul a Ranger's gear? When Hell freezes solid around David Lambert's tortured soul," Mike said, referring to the former United States President, now President of the State of America. Many creative insults had been fashioned about Lambert, some making hay on the 'lamb' in his name, many disputing his parentage, the only thing in common was the universal hatred.

Sarah laughed a little at that. "I was expecting another sheep joke, maybe with Secretary Canlin being the shepherd this time," she said, referring to a popular string of jokes and cartoons about Lambert being on the receiving end of a lonely shepherd. Canlin was their Secretary of State. Usually, in the versions I'd heard, it was the ISC being the shepherd. Lambert was universally on the receiving end though. The Internal Security Cooperative was even more hated than Lambert. ISC was the modern, North American equivalent of Hitler's SS.

"C'mon. Let's get moving before my cell phone rings again," Mike said.

"Ashley?"

"Yeah. She said she had a surprise for me when I get home, and wanted to time it."

"Food," Sarah said. "Gotta be."

"Maybe," I said, thinking it could be something else. "Might be something both aerobic and horizontal in nature," I said, deadpanning it.

Sarah thought about what I'd said in my matter-of-fact delivery, before she realized what I meant. "You're *awful!*" she said after a moment, turning red and laughing uncontrollably. *"You men!"*

A few minutes later we were off post, winding our way home behind a string of heavy trucks moving gear from the fort to God-knows-where.

"This thing ever going to heat up?" Sarah asked. "It's freezing in here."

"About the time we hit the driveway," I said. "Mike, is Ash going to stay in the place while you're gone? That place seems a lot to manage."

"We've got help there now. I've got a retired State Patrolman and his wife helping out while I'm gone. And to boot, he's a pretty good farmer. Had a place north of Newport, but his wife needed more medical care than he could get up there. Seemed a good fit."

"You do have the room for them, that mother-in-law suite and all," I said before getting back to Sarah. "So, Sare, what are you picking up at the infirmary?"

"Tons of stuff. Holistic medicinal practices for depression, even aromatherapy, which I used to think was a bunch of hooey....except it works. Working my way through the thousand pages of the *Physicians' Desk Reference for Nonprescription Drugs, Dietary Supplements and Herbs*. Wound trauma is kind of a continuing theme, but we're also learning about use of colloidal silver, and purifying elderberry extracts for influenza and a bunch of alternate uses for other common stuff. Iodine is pretty cool."

"All sounds pretty good to me," Mike said.

"Plenty of downsides. Cancer victims can't do much for them. Heart patients, lots of congestive heart failure. We can medicate a little with some diuretics, but not much more. Organ recipients are going into rejection without their anti-rejection meds. Asthma has skyrocketed....and then there's the lung scarring from the flu, plus no meds. Hepatitis patients going into end stage liver failure...."

"I take back my comment," Mike said in reply. "I didn't think about that stuff."

"We really saw the first wave...losing patients, that is...back in the spring when the really medically dependent people lost their regular meds. Most of those we're losing now were on maintenance drugs. Some were undiagnosed."

"Let me ask a hard question. Maybe you've talked with your instructors about this. 'How long until you lose the majority of these patients—and you, ahem, have a stable population?'"

"Hard question. Much discussed. No more than a year."

"Wow," I said. "That has to be unbelievably difficult to deal with."

"I think the staff is used to it, honestly. I know I'm not. Some days are really tough. I can't do the kids cancer ward anymore. I just can't handle it."

"Sarah, I'm sorry I brought this up," I said, turning to face her in the back seat.

"It's OK. It's good to talk about it. I kinda bottle that up inside."

"I'm guilty of that too. It's not all that healthy."

"Villa Drummond, on the right," Mike said as we slowed to turn into the driveway.

"Oh-six-hundred, Colonel. Do you need a wakeup call?" Mike asked, laying it on a little thick.

"Not hardly. We're heading over to…"

"Security, Colonel. Need to know and all…" Mike said, reminding me to shut my mouth.

"Sorry. Thanks for keeping me out of the stockade."

"Somebody's got to."

"C'mon, Sarah. Mike's got a hot date."

"Or a nice dinner, I think."

"I'll not wager," I said as I grabbed my bags from the rear seat, piled next to Sarah.

"C'mon. Stay for dinner," I said, inviting her in.

"Thanks. That'd be nice," she said as Mike's Humvee pulled out and headed back up the road. She took one of my bags watching me struggle a little bit. "So, before we go inside, can you answer a question for me?"

348

"Sure, unless it's classified. Of course, I could forget it's classified...."

"Do you think we'll win?"

"Yes," I said. "No doubt about it."

"How can you be so sure? They're drafting more people I hear, starting like Monday. And we heard about a recall of all former military, no exceptions. Is that real?"

"Probably, yeah. On both counts. I'm probably an example of some of that, despite the fact I wasn't in the armed forces. And I'm no kid," I said as we reached the front porch.

"Will John come back here? Will he be in...your command?"

"I don't know the answer to that. I do suspect that he's going to be one of the last to get shipped out for 'basic.' They're going to have to start training locally," I said, not really answering her question. "Sarah, I pray that he'll stay safe. I don't know that he will. I've seen a lot of crap in my life that has shaken me to the core. When John was born, Libby and Ron were scared for him then, he had some issues at birth. I knew that he'd be OK though, and I don't know how I knew that, I just did. I hope that he still will. I just don't know."

"Thanks for being honest."

"Some things need to be said straight out. These are those kinds of days."

"Let's get inside. Karen's watching us," Sarah said with a little guilt.

"She's a mind reader. I suspect she knows you needed to talk. You need to take advantage of her listening ability. She'll be there for you. And you should take the same opportunity with your future mother-in-law."

"I will. Thanks," she said as she opened the front door. Karen was setting the table. Buck and Ada were waiting for me, sniffing my new uniform, bags, and rifle case.

"You two have a nice talk?" she said with a smile.

"Yes we did. Thanks," Sarah said. "How are you, Karen?"

"Good now that my hubby's home. This news is depressing," Karen said as I gave her a kiss, taking off my Army issue parka.

"Where from?" I asked, seeing Buck snag one of my heavy gloves from the parka pocket.

"Los Angeles, Texas, you name it," Carl said from the kitchen. "And Colorado, but they're not talking about that on TV. Plenty on shortwave though."

"Hmmm," I said, looking at the dining room table, now extended to its full length. "OK if Sarah stays for dinner?"

"Absolutely. The Martins will be here any minute. Alan and Mary are over with Mom. Rache and Marky are upstairs with Kelly."

"Great! Sarah, make yourself at home," I said, "but that does not mean you're peeling potatoes."

"Right. She can help with the beets instead," Karen said with a wink.

"How's Mom doing?" I asked.

"Ornery. Wants out as in 'right quick.'"

"Nothing happens that quickly these days," I said.

"No, but the Woolsley's house plans are coming along," Karen said. "Thanks to Ron and Alan and their contacts."

For some reason, that struck me as a statement that excluded me. I didn't like it.

"Do tell. They had a busy day I'd bet."

"Lots done. I won't spoil their thunder—they'll tell you over dinner. Now, spill it," Karen said. "What's the word?"

"Wednesday morning."

"East?" she said, obviously having listened to the radio broadcasts, official and otherwise.

"Yep, although I'm not at liberty to say where."

"I can guess. The guys figured as much, and with Mike shipping out too, and this new draft coming…"

"I'm not in a combat outfit, hon," I said, knowing that really didn't matter, and not caring that Sarah and Carl were in the room.

"Right. And that long-gun is for what exactly?" she said, pointing to my 'California' in it's slip case.

"Varmints," I said with a smile. That really didn't soothe her deep concern. "Now, what's that nice smell coming from the kitchen?"

"Baked chicken, and you know that very well," Karen said with a 'tone' in her voice.

"We are nothing if not regular in poultry, Sarah," I said, further trying to lighten her mood. "Sometimes to the point of distraction."

"Sorry, Chicago deep dish pizza wasn't available at Costco."

"Costco isn't available at Costco. And when, seriously was the last time you had a decent pizza?" Sarah said, laughing.

"About the same time I had a really nice shrimp scampi," I said.

"Now let's not go down that route," Karen said. "We'll all just end up depressed and hungry, rather than just depressed."

The dogs ran to the back door, hearing our dinner guests crossing the yard, despite the snow cover.

"I'm going to go change quick," I said, moving to get into civilian gear.

"Oh, no you're not. Not until we get pictures with you in your uniform," Karen said.

"Jeez. Like Easter when I was a kid. 'Stay in your dress clothes until we get all the pictures done!' It's not like it's my dress outfit," I said. Digital camo isn't exactly chic."

"Holy smokes. You look like you're wearing a slipcover," Ron said as he saw me.

"Better to blend in to the local living rooms, watch a little TV, and move on," I said.

"Securing popcorn and ESPN for all," Alan said.

"Well, that and freedom," I replied, shaking his hand.

"At least you now have clothing to match that haircut," Ron countered.

"You two really ought to go into standup. I could probably arrange that with the local draft board…"

"Don't you dare," Libby said. "I'll have your….oh, I better not say that."

"You just said it without saying it, Lib," Ron said to his wife.

"One piece of good news for you both though: Your chances of getting drafted aren't that good. Too soft," I said, kidding of course. "And you're classified essential, for some reason known but to God and General Anderson."

"It's our general contracting ability," Ron said to Alan. "I told you word'd get out."

352

"Stellar barter negotiations. That's my bet. Half the county'd starve without us."

"The mutual admiration society factor is definitely kicking in," Sarah said. "And me without my hip waders."

"Lib, this young lady has your husband and my brother in law pegged."

"She does at that. Only took me five years!" Libby said with no small amount of love.

A round of home brew and fifteen minutes of digital photographs later, I was able to change into jeans and a flannel shirt, my native garb.

Over dinner with the grown-ups (Alan's young ones had been excused to watch *Brave Little Toaster*), everyone studiously avoided asking me about my orders. That was appreciated, but it was handled almost to the point of ignoring the obvious, even that stuff that had been publicized, officially and otherwise. Only over dessert did the discussion nose into areas that I couldn't talk about.

"You going to Denver?" Ron asked. I could see that Carl wanted to ask that.

"Can't really say. Doubtful. Now do me a favor and don't ask. Next subject."

"I spoke with one of my cousins today in Fresno," Mary said. "So there's your next subject."

"You did?" Alan asked, obviously shocked. "And you're keeping this a secret?"

"Some good news, some not. I wasn't quite ready to share."

"Is Diana OK?" Alan asked.

"She is—but she wasn't home. She's working at the Fresno Army Terminal. She lost Pete to the flu," she said. Pete was her husband, I remembered. "She remarried two months ago. Everyone else down there—our aunts and uncles, all of our cousins except Jeanine, went back to Texas right after the market tanked. My Uncle Clay had a big ranch down there. They figured it was safer."

"Did you get their phone number?" Alan asked. I watched and listened.

"Tried it. No answer."

"How're things in Fresno?" I asked.

"Jeanine said things were pretty bad, but not like up here. Most of their problems at first were labor related—as in, no one to work the fields and farms—all the Mexicans left when the economy started going down. Things have gone to pot since then."

I thought about that for a minute. "Funny how that sounds better than up here, so much better I mean."

"Other people's troubles always sound better than your own, until you try them on for size," Libby said.

Mary had more details of course, one of the more interesting to me anyway, was of the mega-farms that produced single crops mostly for export out of the region, failing due to the lack of market. How many million acres of nuts do you really need, when what your body needs is a balanced diet? The factory farms of the Central and San Joaquin Valleys as I remembered them were anything but diverse. The failures were spectacular, with walnut groves going up in flames after months of no irrigation; massive dairies slaughtering milk-cows for lack of feed and water. I wondered in a morbid way, what were the artifacts of the factory farm, and would lessons be learned or just as quickly forgotten?

We talked until quite late that evening about how the Metro stores had evolved, the barter network had expanded, and of the many shortages that were now appearing as more and more wear and tear on everyday necessities caught up with precious supply. The growing problems of security, of seed for next years' crops, of failures of food preservation.

Our own crops would sustain us, but the labor to produce the food was staggeringly high. The storage effort, along with everything else just normal 'life' in these depleted times demanded, was wearing on us all. There were so many around us that had so little to live on, really, that our own security felt inadequate.

The problem with sharing, is that there are some who see you as rich, when you have merely saved; that you have plenty, but what you really have is a closely held belief to help; that you have more than you 'deserve', even when some—those that will not work to save or provide for themselves—never have enough.

It was easy for the lot of us to see that we might be able to make it another year before some event or other—a breakdown of a water system at the wrong time, a change in local leadership, a crop failure, whatever—made our 'recovery' effort fail. Our damaged infrastructure and our devastated distribution system and our crashed economy would do us in without some dramatic 'good news.'

That 'good news' had to be the war. If we won and a restored United States of America were able to devote the resources of the nation to true recovery, then we might be OK. If we lost the war, there could be no recovery. There could only be further collapse, balkanization, tyranny, more death.

It was a half-hour before midnight before we were talked out and tired, but did take time for another bite of dessert before bedtime. I thought that Karen probably understood better at that point why I was called up, why I was going, why it was so important.

Everything depended on us winning.

Tuesday morning
November Twenty-first
05:30 hours

"Coffee's on the table, Daddy," Kelly said as I came downstairs. Karen was working in the kitchen, making something with a wonderful aroma.

"Thanks, Babe. And what are you doing up so early?" I asked, as she looked over my digital camo uniform, with mixed approval.

"Figured I better so I can see you before you take off tomorrow."

"Saving up then," I said.

"Sort of, yeah. Carl's downstairs—he's getting some stuff put together for you before you go—don't let him know that I told you that though."

"Surprise for me, huh?"

"Care package in advance, Mom said."

"Nice. I'll appreciate that I'm sure."

"Is it true what they're saying on TV about the soldiers?"

"I don't know. I haven't seen it," I said, being technically correct, as Carl came into the room.

"They said that fifty thousand died in Colorado," Karen said, interrupting, before I gave her another good morning kiss. "That was on the national news."

There wasn't much point in denying it. "True. The number is fifty-three thousand two hundred and six, or so I was told. More than were lost in Gettysburg on both sides."

"And you're going into that?" Kelly said.

"Actually, and I'm breaking rules here, Third Washington is going to bring those men and women home. We're tasked with setting up and recovery."

"How close to the fighting?" Kelly asked.

"Honest answer, no idea. It'll be farther east of us, I'm certain. Not sure how far," I replied. "We are not a front line unit. We're support."

"Sure, and we live in a safe suburb," Karen said.

"Honey, I will try to be as safe as I can within reason. I will also keep my men as safe as I can within reason," I said. "You know what it's like out there now, all three of you. Nothing is sure, nothing is secure. We're on permanent Condition Yellow all the time, and half the time on Condition Red. Maybe someday we'll go back to Green. I know that if we don't win this war though, if attacks like this continue, things will go downhill from where we are now to someplace just this side of Hell on Earth. Stuff I've read about the Statists would turn your stomach."

I picked up my coffee, and Karen went into the kitchen, returning with a platter of pancakes. Carl brought out a pitcher of milk.

"Raspberry pancakes. Thought you might like these," Karen said. "Sorry for the tone," she said quietly.

"I think you're justified. And I'm a little surprised you're holding up so well with all this, and your Mom on top of it all."

"Resignation. I can't make you stay. I can't do that much for Mom."

"Getting her close by, and into a situation where she has the right amount of care is much more than you might think," I said. "C'mon, you all sit down here and have breakfast. There's no way I'm eating all of this," I said. "And Mike'll be here any time."

"OK," the kids said in response.

"Now listen up, and listen good," I said, putting some butter on the hot pancakes. "I'm going to do what I need to do. I'm doing it because they asked me to, and given what we know today, I'd be more than half-tempted to volunteer anyway. I do this to try to keep that evil from coming here. Stop it now. Ron and Alan feel the same way, but they're probably more important here than in a uniform just to keep things running. A whole lot more men and women are going to get drafted. Service is going to be compulsory. People are in this for good versus evil now, and I think they're finally starting to realize the stakes involved."

None of them said anything. "I can't remember who said this, or something to this effect: 'Let the troubles come in my time, rather than in the time of my children.' Well, the troubles are here. You'll see them for quite some time. Maybe your children will be free of them."

They finally dug into breakfast, the radio broadcast and interviews droning on in the background. Yet another curfew notice repeated, as the dogs stirred and went to the door, knowing it was someone friendly on the other side. I finished my last bite of pancake as Carl got up to unlock the door, finding Alan on the other side.

"Well, good morning!" I said as both dogs sniffed him up and down, and Karen gave him a hug.

"Back atchya. Big day today, huh?" he said as I shook his hand, noticing the fresh snow on his coat sleeve.

"Meet the troops, check out the gear, put on a show."

"You know your guys are all over TV today, right?" Alan asked.

"Uh, no," I said. "I haven't had it on."

"Crew's over at Yardley with some PR flack from the Army."

"Nice operational security we have going," I said.

"Well, things change," he said, turning on the television. The big former Burlington Northern locomotives were in the background, behind the talking head.

"This looks like a repeat from a few minutes ago," Alan said.

Sure enough, the reporter said that this was Third Washington's outbound train, heading east for 'the War Zone,' they were calling it.

"Now, let me ask, what are you doing up so early?" I said to Alan. "Curfew's still on, right?"

"Your Army boys down the street asked the Metro stores to be open at six, closed by noon."

"All of the stores?"

"Yep. The lance corporal said that by having the stores open early, and closing early, they'd probably throw off the troublemakers."

"Sure, they're probably still in bed. That'll work until they get used to a new schedule."

"Right, unless the Army…or Guard, or whoever is running the show, constantly changes the schedule," Alan said.

"Sounds like something you'd find in Russia. 'Trains are always on time' and all."

"Well they were, since the schedules were never set," he said with a little grin.

"My point."

"And I need one more thing, before you head out," Alan said.

"What's that?"

"I need you to read this through sometime today. It's a proposal to set up a private bank," he said as he handed me a thick envelope.

"Whose idea is this?" I asked. "And why me?"

"You'd be the primary investor for one thing. As in supplier of physical capital. Ron and I've looked at it, it seems to make sense. And, it came from Dan O'Malley."

"I won't find the words, 'fractional reserve banking' in here, will I? Or 'fiat currency?'"

"You won't find anything in there that resembles any bank that has operated in the last fifty years, that I know of anyway. As a stockholder you'd get a portion of crops, product, whatever, is being produced with invested capital."

"When did you have the time to look this over? Why didn't you bring this up last night?"

"Got it yesterday at lunch. Honestly, we both forgot about it. Too much on our plates. Same thing today, with the store and work next door."

"I'll see what I can do," I said. "Breakfast?"

"Already had some. Just wanted to drop that off."

"One more thing. This curfew and getting the Woolsley's house done. How're you going to manage that? How're you going to get the labor here?"

"Bribes. Works just fine, not too expensive."

"Careful with that."

"They're just the post down the street—and all the labor's within walking distance anyway. Tools are plenty, materials are a problem, but not enough to keep us from making do."

361

"Right man for the job," I said. "Just be careful."

Mike showed up just after Alan left in the old, ethanol powered Ford pickup. We'd picked up another couple inches of snow overnight. It was still coming down, now like light feathers in the still morning.

"Spring in your step today, Colonel," I said as I invited him inside.

"It is a lovely morning," Mike said, sharing the inside joke. "Good morning, Karen."

"Morning, Mike. Everything OK?" she asked, a little suspicious of his broad smile, as the kids said their good mornings.

"Just fine, thanks. Ashley said that she'd take you up on your offer for the baby clothes when you get a chance."

"Thanks. Figured she could use them," Karen said. "Here's a couple travel mugs of tea. Sorry, coffee's all but gone."

"Much appreciated, thank you."

"When did you talk with Ashley?" I asked.

"Yesterday. Phone, remember?" she said, holding up the cell phone.

"Yeah. Right. I remember phones….they used to interrupt me at all hours."

"And shrink the world," Mike said.

"That too," I said.

"You ready?"

"As much as ever," I said before turning to Karen and the kids. "See you this afternoon. Should be home around five."

"We'll be ready for you," Karen said as she gave me a fairly intense kiss. There was something she wasn't telling me, but I didn't want to pry.

"You two," I said to Carl and Kelly, who were expecting orders, "Go easy on your Mom." With a hug, I grabbed my day bag and hit the door.

"See you tonight."

On the way out to Yardley, we were stuck, oddly enough, waiting for a train to pass moving all of a mile an hour, and it was probably a mile long.

"Good thing we're early," Mike said.

"That 'drop in and surprise the troops' tactic isn't exactly going to work at this rate."

We had a good chance to talk about how we landed where we were now, covering a wide swath of the past decade.

"….no, I didn't vote for him. I voted my conscience," I said. "Thought you knew that."

"Figured you voted the party line."

"I haven't really believed that there were differences between the two in almost ten years. I mean look at what we've had in the last few years. The worst of Chicago politics. One termer booted out along with all his minions, but not before the damage had been done. Pendulum swung too far the other way, with that joke of a Texas cowboy, trying to resurrect the glory of Imperial America, a lot of patriotism and spending more money we don't have, obviously didn't learn a damned thing from his predecessor's mistakes. We lose him to the flu, end up with a phony conservative who's actually a fascist."

"Can't really argue with any of that," Mike said, with a bit of a chuckle.

"The facts are self evident, unfortunately," I said. "You know, I hope one day when we're on the other end of this, we can sit on the front porch as old men, with grandkids on our knees, and tell them how screwed up things really were before the War."

"You think this can be taken care of in a generation? I mean, undoing the brainwashing?"

"At least there are still some of us that realize that we've had that for the two generations ahead of us, and that there actually can be something better," I said, not saying, 'if we win.'

"Rick, the depth of belief in what is not real, or what wasn't real, looking back on it now that it's gone, is just astounding," he said.

"No argument. There were just damned few of us before the War that knew it and we were all looked on like we were Grade A chrome plated nut jobs. I felt like one more than once, too, bringing home a case or two of ammunition, storing it, building lists of things, for the 'just in case.'"

"You weren't a conspiracy theorist, though, or at least I don't think you were," Mike said.

"No, Sheriff, I was not. Maybe I ought of have been. You look back at the way that debt went from evil to being marketed as something that you had to have to be one of the successful people, you know, 'take that vacation, you deserve it! That home equity, it's just sitting there! Put it to work for you! That new boat! It can be yours! The cancer spread of course across anything financial with insurance companies getting into banking, mortgage companies buying off underwriters and selling class C junk as AAA bonds. Banks getting into everything, convincing the public that they deserved that new house that they couldn't afford, that new boat, convincing us that our home equity was just a wasted bank account, and since everything was intertwined, put at risk and collapsed when the fat lady sang.'"

"Pack of lies."

"Sure it was. But it was an exceptionally well marketed pack of lies, that's what made it successful. And the financiers loved every

364

minute of it. Think, a population too stupid to figure out what the meanings of 'assets,' 'liabilities' and 'equity' really mean. They voted for bread and circuses and bankrupted us all."

"You're doing OK," he said, looking at me with a bit of envy.

"Through little fault of my own. I mean, I had some money in the markets, sure. My brother saved our asses. Not just mine, but all of our brothers—through bailing us from equities into physical commodities, silver and gold, as things came unspooled. If I'd put enough thought into things, I would have done that myself at far earlier and better prices than he ended up paying, and had way more than I do now," I said. "Now let me ask you something, you don't have to answer. How are you and Ash doing financially? You doing OK?"

"We're doing all right. Things get tight from time to time. We have a load of credits at the Metro commissary, but that doesn't cover everything. It's not like they have anything anyway."

"You know if you need anything, you just ask. Or, if you don't ask, I'll make sure that an anonymous donation ends up in your lap."

"Rick, we're doing fine."

"Mike, I have, well, the Drummond-Martin-Bauer group has accumulated a fair amount of working capital. We loan out some, start businesses…"

"I know," he said before I cut him off.

"Mike, we're really not in any of this to make out like bandits. Fact is, we just break even. Money we earn over and above what we need to keep up the place and try to keep stocks up gets plowed back into something else. It's an unorthodox way to invest, but it's investing in the people and the enterprise, rather than in the machine of making money for money's sake."

Mike was quiet for a moment. "Let me ask a stupid question."

"Perfectly all right. I've heard you ask plenty in your time," I said with a laugh, "Like, your bachelor party. You asked that dancer, 'Are those real?' and she answered,"

"'Real expensive,' I remember that part of the night." Mike said, a little smile on his face. "Rick, you could've ended up owning this city with the money you have. Why haven't you gone down that road, even a little bit?"

"Simple, although it sounds simple minded. I'm not wired that way. I have more than I need now. There's a whole lotta folks that would think that I'm an idiot for doing what we're doing," I said. "Mike, I've seen what twenty dollars can do in places where two hundred dollars is a years wage. Miracles. Changes peoples' lives. They have reason to work, employ others, grow, change economies, make their villages and towns better. Gives them hope. Money's just a tool, a store of labor. We're just using the toolbox."

"Helluva philosophy."

"In the old days, we had an abandonment of reason, from what was good and honest and wise, to latch onto whatever passing financial fad came through. Remember the price to earnings ratios that were double or triple digits to one? How many people really realized that you paid two hundred dollars, in the case of the triple digit P/E, to earn ONE dollar of earnings? How stupid were we?"

"Your words, 'self evident.' We're sitting on the edge of a civil war, caused by the financiers."

"Yep, and their greed for more," I said, seeing the trailing car of the train approach. "Last car, finally."

"Good thing, this tea's starting to freeze up."

"I thought this had a heater?"

"Occasionally, it does. I'm not sure what it takes to get the magic back to run the fan."

We pulled ahead, getting into the queue for the Yardley train yard, where dozens of light towers lit up the yard like a circus. It had to be the brightest place in town.

"So what're you ordered over here for?"

"Same as you, more or less. Except we're on the next train behind you. We'll leapfrog you at some point. You have a chance to read the operational plan for deployment?"

"That which wasn't Greek. Why in God's name does the Army insist acronyms when words suffice?"

"Question for the ages," he said, finally getting the move-ahead to the vehicle search and storage lot. We'd be afoot from there on in.

"Any idea where I'm supposed to go?" I asked.

"Building Twenty-one sixty. Over there," he pointed as we parked the Humvee, under the watchful eye of a body-armored soldier.

The deployment plan was to stage a series of trains, like our own, which were being constructed and assembled by the small army of yard workers, running twenty-four seven. Hundreds of transport containers had been converted already, more transport railcars than I'd ever seen collected in Yardley, being loaded by the yard cranes and the self-loaders. We would advance along the cleared lines east, and we'd determine on the fly where the Brigade would stage for 'recovery' of the civilian areas.

That plan of course would be after the initial push to Sixth Army. My late-night reading showed that our first train would have about half the brigade aboard, followed immediately by the remaining men and gear. Both trains would carry thousands of body bags and remains transport cases. A third train would carry still more cases. It would take all three trains to provide enough transport ability to return Sixth Army to a to-be-determined final resting place.

"Don't forget your gear bag," Mike said. "Hate to have a newly minted Colonel have to beg for a pad and pencil."

"That's what supply sergeants are for. See you for lunch?"

367

"Sure. Warning though stay away from the stew. I hear it's mixed meats."

"Good to know." Mixed meats could mean almost anything.

3 0

I'd stopped at the first car with lights on, figuring it was the Command Car. I was wrong, of course, but only missed it by one car. Below the car number, One Oh One, was the cardboard label 'Primary Command Car', taped on with duct tape. Good to know that someone else needed a map....

I shook off the snow and stomped my new boots free of the snow and ice, and stepped inside, tossing my gear bag in the first available chair.

"Good morning, Colonel," our logistics officer, Major Gary Ryder said in greeting, rising from his desk and saluting smartly. I returned his salute. An un-natural thing, saluting. At least for me anyway.

"Major, good morning. Managed to find my way through the maze after all." Gary was a former Reservist, now gone full-time. In 'real life', he'd been a lawyer, and 'sharp' didn't begin to describe him.

"They're making good time getting us put together. Our first train's maybe half assembled, should be fueling tonight by twenty-two thirty. Heat in the occupied units kicks on tomorrow at oh five-thirty, departure at seven hundred."

"Thought we were at six?"

"Government railroad."

"Yeah, gotta remember to factor that in. Major Morrissey in yet?"

"I think he's in the secondary Command Car, sir. Car number Two Oh One."

"Thanks. I'll be back in a few."

I headed to the rear of the train, walking along a plowed path, passing the dozens of cars that composed our train, looking for the right car.

Each Command Car would eventually be closer to the middle of the train, separated by eight or ten cars from the locomotives. I'd seen the floor plans for each type of car, along with its' capacity and equipment compliment, along with the train's defensive capability. Six cars in each train held the defensive capability unlike anything I'd ever heard of, let alone seen. Outwardly each was similar to the observation cars of years past, but these had ballistic glass in a few key places and a most impressive selection of weapons. Ports for individual battle rifles which were the lightest weapons available. Four M242 "Bushmaster" Chain Guns, pride of the old McDonnell Douglas, per car. Anti-tank guided missiles. Anti-aircraft missiles. It was a wonder there was any room for the weapons crews in the cars. The plans also included low-boy rail cars set up to handle tank transporting. Tanks would be manned during transit, and ready to fight should the need arise.

The command cars were set up with incredible communication and data suites, complete with encrypted land and satellite links, fully integrated links to armored units and individual ground commanders from squad-size on up. My 'office' was housed in the first of the two identical cars. The second unit was at the opposite end of the train for protective reasons. My second in command would be in that car, with command staff split between each. When we arrived at our destination, both cars would be linked together, and remain at whatever 'post' we landed at, until we were told to advance.

Morrissey was the Brigade's personnel officer, who owed me the rest of the staffing plan for Third Washington. We were going out minus a deputy commanding officer, although Jim Schafer would serve there as well as in the XO position; no legal officer; a fair amount of third-tier command structure was in place, but ragged organization throughout the rest of the Brigade, at least according to the file I was provided the day before.

Four cars from the end of the assembled train, the secondary Command Car sat with a portable staircase running up to the middle of the unit. I saluted a Private guarding the unit. He looked younger than Carl.

Inside, I heard Morrissey rattling around the far end of the car. It was almost five degrees warmer inside the car, which would make it about forty.

"Major, good morning."

"Morning, Colonel. Report's on the desk there, to your left, sir."

"Mind reading your specialty?"

"No, sir. Just knew this'd be the priority of the day."

"You knew correctly. How's it look?"

"Opinion, sir?"

"Yes, an honest one."

"Patchwork quilt would be generous. A full third of the men are under twenty years old, half of those just out of Accelerated Basic. All the sergeants though, have battle experience, most recent, down south. Junior officers, well, green as grass."

"I can relate to that," I said. "Numbers?"

"Total ready to deploy tomorrow should be twenty-nine fifty-five."

"Better than I thought," I said. "You're regular Army, aren't you, Major?" I couldn't remember. I'd been reading too many files.

"Yes, sir. Served in Tenth Mountain Division, Fort Drum, deployed to Wardak Province Afghanistan. Eight months there before they pulled the plug. Two months in Mexico. Dinged up twice down there."

"How'd you end up here, in Personnel of all places?"

"General Anderson figured you'd need somebody who knew what they were doing, to be a little blunt, sir."

"Blunt is appreciated. And he's right on," I said. "Now let me be direct myself."

"Yes, sir. No problem."

"Can this Brigade defend itself? If called upon, can these men fight?"

"Accelerated Basic covers everything we used to do in Standard, but in six weeks. If anything, if they've made it this far, they're maybe a little too focused. It's been all they've been able to do for a month and change. After the initial shock of actual combat wears off, they'd do fine, sir. Everyone's been trained in the new rifles, and the old '16's will go to local armories or be used in reserve."

"Our Guard Armory was stripped out long before we had a chance to really mobilize. We received the California's right off."

"Now that there are enough coming out of the factories, consider the unit lucky, sir. By One January, all front line units will have Californias, all older M-16's will be reserve weapons only, Colonel. Probably, when this all ends, they'll de-militarize them and sell them off."

"Coming out of the civilian universe, what do you really think of our capability? Again, be direct."

"Given the losses that the fighting forces of the United States have suffered in the past ten years, let alone the last ten months, I'd say in last year's terms, it's almost up to a three of five possible. Almost."

"Fair enough. Now, if I remember correctly, your last assignment was opposing force analysis work."

"Yes, sir," he said as a courier entered, left some files, and left us. "Extensive experience. They're meaner, more ruthless, more brutal than I could believe possible out of Americans. That's the first thing that'll surprise a newbie. They aren't your brothers or cousins or whatever. Half a chance and they'll slit your throat. They're not badly armed, they're not great tacticians. We bungle this we can lose. No recovery once you've got a boot on the neck and a barrel in your ear, sir."

"That's all I needed to hear," I said as I stood, getting ready to get after the day's work.

"And sir?" Major Morrissey asked, "Glad to have you. I hear you're one tough nut."

"Nut, maybe. Not exactly what I had planned for the year, but none of us is living the life we had planned. And who's talking about me?" I said with no small amount of curiosity.

"A Ranger. A Lieutenant Colonel Amberson, sir."

"The Colonel and I go back a ways," I said. "Thanks, though. Oh nine hundred over at the assembly hall. See you there."

"Yes, sir. See you then."

Back outside, the snow had picked up, from flurries to downright heavy snow. One thing I had to give the military credit for, and was quite pleasantly surprised, was in the new grey/black/white digital camo winter gear. Warm, dry, and visually effective. I noted they'd changed the camo pattern to a 'larger' scale, based on some comments about the 'green' and 'tan' versions blending together at distance, eliminating the effect of the camouflage.

I was walking next to the train when I heard a horn behind me, sound twice. I turned to see a patched together crew cab truck slow, and the passenger window glide down. It looked like the pickup was composed of at least a half-dozen donors.

"Need a ride, Mac?" the driver asked.

"Much appreciated, thanks," I said. "Just up to the other end," I said as I got into the warm cab. I hadn't realized how cold it was outside until the blast from multiple heaters hit me.

"No prob. Just going to pick up another crew for the outbound. This'n yours?"

"That'll be our home for the foreseeable future, yeah."

"You get back there and kick some ass. I got family down in Nebraska. What I heard from down there ain't good."

"Yeah. That's a fact."

"Name's Bender. Frank Bender," he said. He looked about sixty, maybe older. Deep lines in his face, close-cropped hair under a heavy cap.

"Rick Drummond. Nice to meet you, Mr. Bender."

"Ain't you the County guy? The one runnin' Metro?"

"Not anymore," I said.

"Well, you did a helluva job while you were. Put together a pretty good outfit. My day job is maintenance on the Lines," he said, referring to the local train system that was cobbled together from scrap. "Be nice to have rail service permanent-like."

"You guys did a pretty good job with what little you had to work with. Never ceases to amaze me when I see those trains running, and on time."

"Lotta good people. Makes all the difference."

"Yes, it does," I said. "Thanks for the ride, Frank."

"Watch your ass back there, Colonel," he said as I closed the door and nodded.

Inside the Command Car, I'd barely opened the door when I noticed the car was nearly full of workers. A team of

374

communications workers was running diagnostics on the multiple flat panel multi-function displays.

"Ten-hut!" someone said from the rear of the car.

"At ease," I said, thinking that I'd never get used to the protocol.

"Colonel, good morning. I'm Captain Greg Shand. Communications."

"Nice to meet you, Captain. Just back from Walla Walla?"

"Yes sir, as of about ten minutes ago. The inbound train."

"Welcome to the primary Command Car. I understand that you're in charge of all this gear?"

"Yes, sir. It's a beauty."

"Run me through what I'm looking at. My briefing packet was conspicuously missing this section."

"Code-word classified, sir, and the files weren't to be distributed until everyone's been briefed. All these techs are cleared, as is the rest of the command staff. First suite over there on the left is dedicated uplink to central command. Second suite is assignable, but both it and third suite are set up at the moment to link real time with our own field units. Every unit commander will have direct real time link back to us, as well as links to each other, air assets, whatever they want that we can give them. Every squad sergeant has a helmet cam. We can see what he can see, maybe more depending on how we enhance the uplink."

"Impressive doesn't begin to cover it," I said, pondering the network, the technology, the problems that could crop up.

"That stuff's all pretty standard, sir. The really impressive breakthroughs are in suites five and six."

"Suite four?" I asked, noting he'd skipped it.

"Redundant, but really serves as the master coordinator between all others, as well as links to the second Command Car, for increased capability."

"All right, so, suites five and six."

"Suite five will be set up to track friendly and enemy forces, including location, speed, real time. Suite six tracks disposition of friendly equipment including equipment that may have been captured, sir. I forgot your suite, sir, down on the end. The Command Suite can monitor all of the battleground information real time, and you can direct assets and adjust tactics either from there or direct the communications officers to execute your orders."

"How do you track the individuals, and separate between friendlies and enemy?"

"Friendlies have RFID chips in their dog tags, MRE containers, weapons, uniforms, boots, you name it. The RFID's are trackable and programmable on the fly, and each chip links to each other as well as to the assigned soldier, unit, group, or command. There are common 'calls' between friendlies as well, so if gear gets swapped, that doesn't necessarily trigger an alert. RFID's update once every hour in standard deployment. In battle once a minute. The 'California' model of the M16 reports rates of fire and ammunition levels as well, although without more capability on this end, some of the more detailed data are only useful for after-action tactical analysis. Thank God we're changing out all the front line units to the California's, and retiring the old rifles. If gear is captured, we can track it based on proximity to enemy. If we get confirmation from a field commander that he's lost troops or gear, we can track that gear, find out it it's been captured, track it, and assign an enemy tag to it, and then track it, sir."

"What if the enemy has no RFID equipped gear, Captain?"

"Even easier, sir," McGowan said. "We track their heartbeats, if we're close enough, or close enough for a transmitter and bounce unit to pick them up. Five mile range, narrow frequency that picks up on heart rate and the electrical frequency of the human heart. Can also be adjusted to discriminate between animals and humans of course. If a bird is in range, we can uplink to satellite for a broad view of the battlefield and adapt accordingly. Combined with RFID protocols, we can also determine if friendlies have been captured and are among enemy, sir," he explained. "Questions sir?"

"No, that's about enough mind-blowing information for one day, thanks," I said. "Although, I'm curious to know if this has been tested in battle."

"Yes, sir. Black ops for the past five years at least, all over the globe. They used it in taking back the lower Mississippi Valley. And secured the Mexican Frontier with it."

"Cross it and die," I said aloud, not really meaning to.

"Absolutely, Colonel."

"Incredible," I said, thinking of adding, 'frickin' video game." "Thanks, Captain. Although I don't really look forward to seeing it in action."

"Way of the future, sir. "

I spent the remaining time before our oh-nine-hundred assembly by reading and studying. Far too much material to cover and too little time to take it all in. Too much info too much detail. That weighed on me as I was driven over to the Assembly Hall. I decided to improvise my portion of the morning.

The 'Assembly Hall' was a converted warehouse that had held a pole building manufacturing center, before the War. The enormous, unheated volume was large enough to hold the Brigade, many of them spending the time in heated tents, within the building shell. Hundreds of non-matching folding chairs, mismatched light fixtures, and a makeshift presentation screen and podium spoke to the state of our infrastructure. I knew that our gear at least matched, more or less.

The brigade was brought to attention. I was introduced by a senior staff sergeant and took the podium, along with the rest of the brigade staff.

"Please join me in the Pledge of Allegiance," I said, before leading them through the pledge. Our 'new' flag hung from the steel rafters above us, as well as on the plywood stage on an unfinished pine pole.

"At ease," I said to the ranks, before beginning. "Thank you all for your service to our nation. Be seated," I said, scanning the collection of men, young and old, all in grey camouflage fatigues and outerwear. All, I noted, armed.

"If you've had the opportunity to see the morning news, you men are all over it. In less than twenty-four hours, this Brigade departs for eastern Colorado. You have all been briefed to the nature of what Third Washington's operational mission is supposed to be. I'm here to tell you that there is more to it than that. Our first mission will be less than conventional."

"It is now becoming common knowledge that Sixth Army has been wiped off the map. More than fifty-three thousand dead remain in the field. More than were lost at Gettysburg. Total losses in the past few days surpass the American casualties in Vietnam by a sizeable percentage. Attacks on Air Force facilities nationwide have crippled our air capabilities. A new draft, quite widespread, will be starting within days. Many units across the country are moving in to fill the void caused by this massacre, including units from Texas, New Mexico, Arizona, California and two brigades from the Fighting Forty First. Third Washington will be first tasked with the recovery of the remains of Sixth Army, and transporting our dead from the battlefield. Our follow up task will be support of line units and recovery of civilian infrastructure, utilities, and transport."

"You are obviously now aware that there are no women in the ranks within Third Washington. All women line soldiers have been reassigned after events in Colorado, across the entire United States military, effective twenty-two hundred yesterday. These women are now running training units and responsible for a large amount of basic and advanced training. It should be known by all, and you will be briefed on this in more detail today, that numerous patrol units and more soldiers in forward observation posts were captured prior to the attacks on Sixth Army. The male soldiers were executed. The female soldiers were tortured beyond any recognition over a two hundred mile long front. This was not an isolated incident, nor the result of a lone group. It is systemic. Every soldier in this room will review the recon reports. That is an order."

"Most, if not all of you, know that I'm not a regular soldier. Most of you until a few days or weeks ago weren't either. In this part of the country, for most of a year now, we've been living in what could best be described as primitive conditions, and yet we've prevailed. Despite fears to the contrary, we didn't tear ourselves apart. We adapted. We've survived. There is though, a real danger that we could lose this war, that the Statists will prevail, that we will be at best enslaved, doomed to live under the heel of a fascist dictatorship. That more women and children and the helpless would be burned alive as the residents of Siler, Colorado were. That places like Sunrise Springs, Colorado not have the mutilated bodies of that farm community piled in front of their City Hall. Our troops have searched across entire counties, where farms ought to be, where people ought to be and have found burned out buildings and bodies. This is what your enemy does, how they operate, and what they believe in. We're assuming that they've captured at least a portion of the civilian population and transported them East. That assumption might be optimistic. They may have just killed everyone instead." I paused for ten or fifteen seconds, to let all of that sink in. The things that I'd read in the recon reports and scouting reports from Colorado made me sick to my stomach.

"We, all of us here, we citizen soldiers, all of our families, all of our futures, are at risk. Everything is on the table. I say this not to strike fear, not to be a pessimist, but to show you that I believe that, and that knowing that failure is possible, to do everything you can do to ensure that we do not fail. There is too much at stake."

"This Brigade is labeled a support unit that was four months in the planning and assembly. Don't bet on staying a support unit. Plan on using your weapon. Plan on working in fire teams. From squad to platoon on up the brigade chain of command, including the command company," I said, looking over at the Brigade command unit, "plan on doing your job and learning the job of the guy next to you, above you, and below you. This train ride we have will take a couple of days if we're lucky. Use that time wisely. We just might find a hot zone on the other end."

"You will spend the rest of today, until seventeen-hundred hours, with your battalions, reviewing your assignments, and training. You will also read the same after action reports that I've been reading for

379

many hours. You will not like what you read. If there remains any question as to the nature of the enemy, there will not be after you read those reports. Tomorrow, we hit the rails. The next portion of this briefing will be presented by Major Gary Ryder, covering load out of the Brigade. Major?" I said, giving the podium over.

"Thank you, Colonel. All right, First Battalion, commanded by Lieutenant Colonel Shawn Miller...."

Each battalion was trained with more or less identical skills in terms of supporting the needs of the overall Brigade, rather than assigning a single battalion to specialize. The Army apparently decided that specialized battalions and brigades weren't the way of our future, and tapped the ways of the past in this reconstituted military force. Perhaps the reality of doing what really worked, rather than what merely sounded good, was finally starting to permeate. So, we had, at least on paper, the ability to generate power, clean water, work to restore damaged civilian infrastructure, supply medical care, and many other capabilities. In addition, we'd defend ourselves, feed the front line troops or civilians....an endless list.

Our battalion commanders all had 'line' experience, and recent at that. Many were junior officers who'd been promoted one or two grades within the year, all up to the rank of Lieutenant Colonel. Most had been decorated in the Mexican War. First Battalion, with Shawn Miller in command, a newly minted light colonel, had also served in Afghanistan. The Second had the six foot-four Trayvon Chappel, a tank of a man, ramrod straight but with an absolutely disarming smile. Chappel had played on the defensive line for Grambling State before going into the Army right after graduation. Six years in Iraq, two in Afghanistan, with specialty schooling on top of that, and messy work in Tucson. Third Battalion was headed up by Hugh Epstein, who'd served in Germany, Iraq, and Korea, along with major action in the Yucatan. Jesse Casselis, a proud product of South Philly, was Fourth Battalion's top dog. Casselis served at Fort Bragg, in Kosovo, and Kuwait before numerous battles in Los Angeles and on south. Bryce Atwood was Fifth Battalion's commander the lone command officer with Pentagon experience, although he'd redeemed himself of that unpleasantness with cave searches in Afghanistan, roadside bombs, and urban and rural warfare. Atwood was from Ocean Shores, on the Washington coast. He'd only been in Spokane for two days, after visiting his remaining family at home, his first trip home in three years.

The briefing for each battalion covered final loading of equipment and men, duty schedules, training schedules, and final assignments of unit commanders down to squad level. By the end of the hour, each battalion was ready to get moving and get some work done. I had my own list of tasks ahead of me, and precious little time to get through it.

Back in the Command Car, I found myself in the way and the place too busy to get anything meaningful done. Right behind that car though, was the car that I'd be billeted in, along with one of the command staff. Peace and quiet at last...until my cell phone rang.

"Hello?" I answered.

"Hiya, lover. How's your day?" Karen asked.

"Uneventful so far, which is a pretty good thing. What's going on at the homestead?"

"Alan and Ron have the house next door powered up. There're about twelve people working over there. Heat will be in this afternoon."

"Wow!" I said. "I'm more than a little shocked."

"Me too. Things are coming together."

"Your Mom know she's moving tomorrow?"

"Not yet. We'll tell her this afternoon," she said before pausing.

"Everything OK?" I asked.

"Yes. I had to sneak upstairs and into the bedroom. I need to know if you're going to be on time tonight."

"Yeah, barring the unexpected crisis. Got something planned?"

"Keep it a secret and act surprised, OK?"

"Sure. I'm good at that. Had to be with your family," I said. The Bauer's were always trying to keep little secrets about birthdays, parties, and presents. Most with little success. "Now, what's up?"

"Thanksgiving dinner a couple days early. Ashley and the twins are here, along with a houseful of help."

"That sounds perfect," I said. "Hon, I'm missing you already."

"Don't get me started, or I'll be bawling."

"Sorry. We going to be able to fit everyone in the house?"

"It'll be a tight fit. We'll make do."

"Nice. I don't know what to say."

"Then don't say anything. I'll see you tonight," she said quietly. "I love you."

"You most," I said in reply, hearing her click the phone off just after.

I'd already forgotten that it was Thanksgiving week, caught up in my new future.

Tuesday
November Twenty-first
12:30 hours

The morning had gone quite quickly, despite the cold wind and the typical snafus that define military operations in general and this one in particular.

Every soldier's gear consumed far more space than the space allocated by the designers of the working cars and the transports— winter gear was the reason. A quick meeting with the battalion commanders, and then orders to the men, forced the soldiers to gather the gear they'd need at hand during transit, including their rifle, their day pack, their cold-weather outerwear and a few personal items. The rest of their gear would be stowed in the overheads where possible (not likely) or in a pile at the end of each passenger car.

The tone of the Brigade throughout the morning had changed as the Colorado reports were read per my orders. The reports across the battlefield were provided in multiple copies, included photographs, identification of the victims (as possible), and forensics. By the end of the day, everyone would understand.

Lunch was taken in shifts, although many men ate on the go within the train cars, mowing through the stew, hard cheese, coffee, wheat bread or rolls, and apples while hardly taking a break. I wasn't used to the schedule or the stress, and decided to head to the mess hall—another banged up warehouse building, this one unheated but at least lit. I was tired, and it was too early in the day to be tired. I shared a table with Frank Bender who I'd met earlier. Frank had also seen me trudging around in my Army-issue cold weather gear, and scrounged up a valuable, insulated Burlington Northern jumpsuit to wear over my Army gear. Bulky but warm. Two of Frank's Green Line engineers joined us first, then a couple of diesel mechanics, and finally a sergeant from Third Battalion and his squad. His soldiers were not sure what to make of sharing a table with an officer. Only after much prompting did they relax a little.

"Colonel, you're gonna wanna see this," an Air Force airman said as he tapped me on the shoulder, placing a laptop in front of me, running streaming video from Fox News. I'd just taken a big bite of the Golden Delicious apple in my lunch.

"Whatcha, got, Airman?"

"L.A., sir. Again."

"Gather round, all," I said. "Crank up the volume on this." The young airman did as asked and then hurried back across the room.

"...-oratory site has been hit by the same type of weapons used over the weekend at multiple theme parks, shopping centers and military installations in the L.A. region and in other critical areas in the United States. The Statists quickly took credit for these attacks, unlike the delayed response over the weekend. It is unknown at this time if Lawrence Livermore was in lockdown mode at the time, or how many casualties there might be at the University campus. Many, if not all buildings, are heavily climate controlled due to the nature of the research, including isolated air-handling systems...."

"Sir, command is looking for you," the Airman said as he returned to the table. "Is your cell phone working?" he asked as I stood up, the men under my command moving to attention.

"Was earlier," I said as I fished it out. "Five bars.... Gents, best get a move on with lunch. Sarge, take care."

"Sir!"

I did my best to run over to the Command Car, hitting the phone's speed dial along the way, and getting an 'all-circuits busy' signal.

"Sir, Walla Walla direct on Suite Four," one of the techs said as I entered the car.

"Thanks," I said as I shucked off the top half of my jumpsuit and peeled off the coat underneath.

"Headset's on the console to the left. You're on VOX with the green button, sir."

"Got it," I said, putting the Bose-manufactured, ultra-light headset on. Once on, it didn't feel like it was there at all.

"Colonel Drummond here," I said to four LCD screens with the Division logo on them.

"Colonel, General Anderson will be with you in a moment. He's currently en route to Lewiston."

"Understood."

"Colonel Drummond, you on line?" Bob Anderson's voice was instantly recognizable.

"Yes, sir. Sorry for the delay."

"Cell phones are crap. You've seen the news out of Livermore?"

"Yes, sir."

"Bellingham as well. Pac Fleet was hit, and there was an attack at the San Francisco Naval Yard, too. Bad." Within the space of less than a year, a massive construction effort was building a new naval yard to service the fleet, years after all the old bases had been closed, sold off, abandoned.

"Threats locally?"

"None that we know of, but we didn't know anything about these, either. Consider your location a primary target—every concentration of military equipment and personnel and every major concentration of civilians is a target."

"Understood. They use the same delivery system?"

"Container ships in the port attacks, aided by favorable winds. The Livermore attack was upwind, outside of the secured perimeter. Multiple releases."

"So our upwind is our target area, sir?"

"Affirmative. We cannot discount that you've been infiltrated. Alerts to the civilian population are going out in about five minutes, although all businesses are closed due to the curfew. This'll be all over the news whether we like it or not, by fifteen hundred."

"Understood. We look for anything suspicious upwind of us, ASAP."

"Correct. Good hunting, Colonel," General Anderson said, before I heard a click in the headphone. He was gone.

"Captain Phillips, get me my battalion commanders, five minutes ago. Conference room in the next car down."

"Yes, sir!"

Three minutes later, the five commanders were crowded around the small conference table in the next unit. I'd been busy barking orders to the command staff, who'd gathered quite quickly once summoned.

"L.A.'s been hit, nerve gas again it looks like, along with San Francisco and Bellingham. General Anderson thinks we might be a lucrative target. I need patrols in the field two hours ago, looking for anything suspicious. We're closer than the Guard units at Fort Overbeck—Five hundred men are on their way, but it'll be a while. Here it is: Upwind, up to Greene Street, south to Sprague. Winds are pretty light, so that'd force any gas release to be very close. There aren't many, if any, viable businesses or factories in that zone. Evac anyone within that perimeter. The only critical transit link of course is the Red Line, which might be a really good way to deliver a weapon, if I hadn't shut it down a few minutes ago," I said. I'd called Metro and ordered it off-line, not that there was any real demand, with the curfew in place. "What can you get moving?"

"Five companies, sir," Trayvon Chappel replied. "One from each battalion. Transport would be handy to have, but ours is loaded. We can get there on foot, nice little run."

"There's fifty up-armored Humvees and twenty five Bradleys over on the Havana Street side of the rail yard," I said, "along with a slew of old M35s that have been refurbed for local use. There's brand new steel plate armor on the Thirty-Fives for about the same level of protection as the Humvee. Paint's still wet, I hear. We can have a dozen of Overbeck's Bradleys here in an hour, but I want boots on ground before then."

"You got it, sir," Chappel answered, with nods from the other commanders.

"I want at least a company to go through the yard, too. You'll have assistance from the yard workers in searching the trains, comparing manifests, the works. We've had three inbound trains today. One from California, one from Oregon, one from Montana. Rail cops have secured those trains already," I said.

"Gentlemen, at best this is a real-life run through of your comm gear and small-unit tactics. At worst, you run into a great big bucket of shit. Questions?" I asked as I stood, triggering the rest to stand. "All right then, let's move. Dismissed."

The men filed out quickly and with purpose, and I grabbed my parka from the corner chair, and headed back to the Command Car. By the time I was inside, I had a hot cup of *real* coffee waiting for me in the Command Suite, and A Company, First Battalion was checking their equipment and moving double time through the yard to ensure its' security. In fifteen minutes, all five companies were well on their way to being deployed. Two M35s stubbornly refused to start, along with one of the refurbed Humvees. Typical.

I decided it prudent to make a phone call to Karen, to let her know that the unexpected crisis was rearing its' ugly head.

"Hi. Guess what?" I said as she answered the phone.

"I know. I'm watching it on the news," she said.

"And….."

"You're going to be late."

"Not just me, likely."

"Any idea on when?"

"Not even a little one. Do me a favor though. Just keep your schedule. I'll get there when I can."

"We're planning on serving at seven, just in case you can make it."

"I'll try to let you know. Snow let up over there yet?"

"Yep. Carl's out plowing the driveway and the path over to Libby's house."

"Good for him. Bet he's having a ball."

"He makes it sound otherwise. I think he's having fun though. Kelly and Marie have been absolute fiends making apple pies, so the place is a mess."

"But I bet it smells great."

"It does. It'll just make you hungry thinking about it…"

"True," I said, hearing some commotion from one of the communications suites. "I gotta go, hon. Love you most."

"You best. You take care of yourself."

"I will. You take care of yourself and my kids."

"And the dogs, always underfoot…."

"I'll call later," I said as I hung up, putting on the headphones. "Mr. McDowell," I said referring to a young corporal in Suite Two, "what am I listening to?"

"Sorry, sir, we tapped into one of Division's tactical channels. They're in pursuit of hostiles over near Bellingham."

"Good, but let's make sure all *our* players are in *our* game. Status report in five minutes, every platoon."

"Yes, sir."

"And keep me apprised as to what's going on over on the coast."

"Yes, sir. Done."

I wasn't about to cut off the communications link—it got the adrenaline flowing in my own staff as much as the information getting passed along to our own companies in the field. Blood in the water, so to speak. I flipped through the various feeds received by each suite, as well as drilling down through each company to the sergeants. It was like watching the soldiers' helmet cams in *'Aliens.'*

By fifteen-thirty hours, Third Washington's field companies had secured the perimeter around the Yardley train yard per my orders, and Guard units were moving up to relieve them. No threats had been found, including through the laborious search of the incoming trains. The crews scheduled to off-load the inbound trains were sent back to their holding areas until the all clear could be given. Any crucial loads needed around town would be loaded later in the day, with military or police escort to its' destination. Guard units were also securing a perimeter to the north and east. A big slice of the Valley would be within secured perimeters, including air operations at Felts Field, the train yard, and Fort Overbeck.

Over on the coast of Washington, three hundred plus miles away, we listened to the pursuit of three groups of suspected Statist agents, who'd been traced to the Bellingham Naval Yard through their vehicles and video surveillance. The pursuit down Interstate Five ended just north of Burlington. The first two vans tried to shoot it out with the Navy units pursuing them. An air unit took out both in a single pass. The third suspect vehicle, took a few pot shots, and sped straight into a concrete bridge abutment. No one survived the crash and subsequent fire.

While all of this excitement was going on, the loading of the train continued, with sentries keeping watch over the entire yard as their fellow soldiers finished the task of the day. By seventeen-thirty, everything except the day-of-departure materiel was loaded. The numerous engines (I didn't take time to count them) would be fueled just prior to departure. At eighteen hundred, the balance of the Brigade was either back at the rail yard, electing to spend their last night near their gear (this seemed to apply to the communications geeks), or just north at Felts Field, in one of the barracks. I made a pass through inspection of the entire train, surprising more than a few soldiers who were settling in, and finding little amiss with the load-out. What little I did find, was quickly brought right at the command of a senior master sergeant, who I found pretty intimidating. A few of the privates were shaking in their boots.

Mike was waiting for me when I hit my Command Car, a few minutes shy of eighteen hundred.

"How's the first day on the job, Colonel?" he asked.

"Busy. You?"

"In spades. Third Washington ready to roll?"

"Damned close. Last minute stuff goes on two hours before departure."

"You ready to get out of here? Advice, though, before you answer: Get out while you can. Let your staff handle things."

"Sage advice," I said, before turning my attention to the overnight duty officer, Captain Gerry McGowan. "Captain, you good for the evening?" I asked as I gathered up my parka, gloves, and a new mil-spec backpack for the inevitable crap to haul around.

"Yes, sir. Take the Colonel's advice."

"I'll do that. Have a good evening. You have my number."

"I'll try not to use it, sir."

"Much appreciated."

Outside, Mike's new-to-him Humvee was running, with a sentry keeping an eye on it, I thought.

"Corporal, get in if you would, and quit freezing your ass off," Mike said.

"Sir!" the young man responded, and quickly climbed into the back seat. Mike climbed in to drive, and I joined him up front.

"Corporal Cory Burrus, meet Colonel Richard Drummond, C.O. of Third Washington."

"Sir, pleased to meet you," the young man replied. I could hardly see him under the big Kevlar helmet.

"Likewise, Corporal. You assigned to this man's Ranger unit?" Mike threaded his way through the yard and barricades, towards the exit.

"Yes, sir."

"Do me a favor and keep is ass out of trouble. I won't be able to do that like I've been doing for the past year." That caught him off guard. Mike just laughed.

"I'll, um, do my best sir."

"I invited the Corporal to dinner for the evening. He's from out in the Palouse. Where is it, Burrus?"

"Endicott, sir. Just outside."

Who did I know from Endicott? Something clicked. "You know any of the Morasch family?"

"Yes, sir. You know them?"

"Dan Morasch and I went to W.S.U. together. Roomed next door to me freshman and sophomore years. I don't think I've thought of him in twenty-five years."

"He's been pretty busy, sir. Eight kids if I remember right. Big farm west of town."

"Good for him. Ag Econ major, if I remember right," I said. "Mike, those your units?" I asked, forgetting they weren't Mike's units any longer. There was literally a new sheriff in town. Four Sheriff's Department Suburbans were headed east, strobes flashing no sirens.

"Used to be. Wonder what's up?" he said. "There's a lot of firepower in those four rigs. That can't be good."

"What's the freq for dispatch?"

"Won't matter—those four are on tactical and won't respond except on the scrambler, and dispatch won't respond to us, unless we have the daily code key. Too many contraband police radios out there. Had to change procedures to keep false traffic from messing with us."

"No way to find out?"

"Nope. Not until whatever is going on is all over."

"Even you?"

"If they respect protocol, yeah."

"Well, damn. I liked getting inside info."

"You're going to miss that Metro radio, aren't you?"

"Almost as much as the 'all-access' driver pass and the company car."

"What's Karen going to drive while you're away?"

"She'll have the Expedition, sporting a new flat gray paint job, a newer grille, nice brush guard, and steel wheels. Looks like Hell." It was a little too risky I thought to keep it in the original color scheme after last summer's aborted attempt to get me killed while driving it.

"Probably smart."

"Thanks. I'll remember that you think that, when Karen sees it."

"She hasn't seen it?"

"Nope, but she knows something's going on. She'll get it tomorrow after I head out. Hoped to have it delivered today, but the guy doing the work for me didn't think he'd have it done in time."

"You actually farmed something out? Didn't do it yourself?"

"Nope, dang near killed me. Kidding. Guy down on the next block needed some work, I didn't have time then, don't have time now. Worked out."

"Fire up ahead," Mike said. We could see the glow, more than a mile away.

"Big one. They don't have fire flow up this far. This'll be a burner," I said. We could see the fire department's collection of trucks around the site as we pulled closer. "They're just gonna contain this, not fight it," I said as we pulled to a stop. The Sheriff's Suburbans—two of them anyway—were holding traffic. We were the first in line.

"That's Deputy Schmitt coming our way. You remember him?"

"Yeah, been a long time," I said. "Paul, right?"

"Yeah," Mike said as the Deputy came up to the driver's door, and Mike unbuckled his harness and got out.

"Deputy, what's our holdup here?"

"Boss, good to see you again so soon," he said. "Mr. Drummond, as well. Arson fire. Seventh one this afternoon."

"Even with the curfew?"

"Yep."

"So they've pre-placed materials or they're carrying them in on foot," I said.

"Yeah, we've got two other units in pursuit, heading up the hill. In the old days we'd be tracking them with the helo. Now it's four by fours, guys on horseback and tracking dogs."

"Wish we could send you some help—got our own issues right now," Mike said.

"Paul, you get the word out about these fires on the radio?" I asked.

"Yeah, every fifteen minutes. They're hitting any target of opportunity. Houses vacant or not in the first two fires. Number six was a warehouse down by Gonzaga. Now this one," he said as the fire flared in an orange, then gray mushroom cloud above the store site. The roof had collapsed. The firemen were stationed around the block, hoses ready but little water flow available, in case they needed to knock the fire down as it spread. With the snowfall, that wasn't likely.

"Then you've got quite a number of suspects operating, coordinated attack, with an unconventional communications network," I said.

"Pinned that right," the corporal said, before adding, "sir."

"Something to add, Corporal?" Mike said.

"Yes, sir. Up until the curfew, civilians had unrestricted access to just about anywhere. Easy to set up a network, schedule, coordinate placement of weapons, whatever, sir. You're just reacting at this point. Nothing you can do, sir, unless you cap the enemy."

"No argument with that," Mike said. "Paul, you watch your ass. This feels a whole lot like an ambush."

"Yes, sir. Like they're sizing us up. We do have men in the shadows, sir, but they're only going to be able to react. You should be able to proceed as soon as we get that hose line secured," Deputy Schmitt said. I was wrong, they *did* have water up this far.

"Paul, one thing…" I said, thinking it over. "Are the fires getting further from town? Further out on the edges of the Service Area?" The service area was the limit of water, power, and municipal support. We'd been forced to 'contract' the suburban area after the Domino. We had neither money nor materials to fix all the damage.

"Well, now that you mention it, they seem to be."

"Then pull your guys back, and deploy only a minimal firefighter effort. They're drawing you out for something. Concentrate in the service area. Don't take the bait," I said. I saw the hose line that was blocking us go flat, as a firefighter disconnected the line from the hydrant.

"Works for me. I'll pass it on to the Sheriff," Paul said. "With of course, appropriate attribution. Looks like you're good to pass."

"Take care, Deputy," I said. "Buy you a beer after the war."

"I'll take you up on that."

Mike started the engine, closed the door, and we steered around the pumper truck.

"Nice call, Corporal," I said.

"Thanks, sir. One more thing, if I may," he said.

"Go for it."

"Further out they get, easier they are to pick off in a big way. IEDs. That kind of thing, Colonel."

"Hmmm," I said. "We'll pass that analysis on up the food chain." 'What were they planning?' I thought to myself as we drove on along the darkened street. 'Who is the, 'they?''

Ten minutes later, we arrived outside the gate, where Carl had just finished clearing the road in front of the house and the driveway.

"See you in the morning, bright and early," Mike said, unaware of the dinner plans obviously.

"Not hardly. Your lovely family is inside. Be surprised," I said. "You, too, Mr. Burrus."

"What's going on?" Mike asked.

"You like turkey, right?"

Tuesday evening
November Twenty-first
19:15 hours

"Pastor, would you give the blessing?" Karen asked.

"I'd be most happy to, Mrs. Drummond," the young pastor replied.   Peter Gottschalk, a very recent graduate of Concordia seminary, was serving as a vicar in one of the local churches before the Domino. With the loss of his senior pastor, his on-the-job training provided him more education than he might have had in ten years as an associate pastor.

We joined hands, making a large and uneven oval between the dining room and living room, across three tables.

"Father God, we give thanks today for the food you have given us, prepared by loving hands and hearts, in a welcoming home. We give you thanks for the lives you have given us, the freedom of this nation, and those that would defend her. As we partake of this food, we pray for health and strength for us and for those in our hearts that could not be with us this evening, to proceed through the challenges and difficult days ahead of us, and to live as you would have us live. This we ask in the name of your beloved son, Jesus Christ. Amen."

"Amen," all responded.

Karen's 'surprise' was carried off well, until we hit the front porch and the aroma of turkey and dressing had hit us like a two-by-four. We had a houseful, with the Martins and future daughter in law Sarah and her new roommate, the Bauers, Mike's wife Ashley and twins Suzi and Matthew, and of course the pastor. I'd quickly come in, with as much honest surprise as feigned, and made a quick trip upstairs change into (comfortable) civilian clothes.   My 'departure' bags were mostly packed, but I'd have another hour or so to get those finished.

"Nice job carving, Ron-boy," I said. I wasn't kidding. There wasn't much meat left on the carcass, just enough to toss in the pot for turkey chowder…which I'd miss.

"Thirty-eight pounds of the best turkey you'll ever drool over," he said. "After of course, the tax due to the chief carver."

"He had help," Libby said. "So don't let him take all the credit."

"Alan?"

"A-yup," Ron said.

"Hon, will you pour the wine?" Karen asked, sneaking her arms around me from behind, being careful of my left side.

"It's what I live for," I said.

Tonight, unlike many Thanksgiving dinners in years past, the kids were included all around the table, but close enough to each other to get into the expected mischief and associated entertainment. Carl was busy entertaining both Suzi and Matthew, who could not quite understand the concept of 'peek a boo', yet followed him with full attention, until the butternut squash appeared, and the game was sacrificed in favor of food. Rounding out the dinner menu with 'Birdzilla' being the featured entrée, were our Yukon Gold potatoes, rutabagas, beets, beans, dinner rolls, canned pears, butternut squash, peach, pumpkin and apple pies, and ice cream.

Kelly and Marie were already engaged with Mark and Rachel, in a game that was all but indecipherable, but it had something to do with the shape of the dinner rolls, from what I gathered, the game at the dinner table was an outgrowth of crafting the rolls earlier in the afternoon.

Within a few minutes, everyone had a plateful and the adults wishing to partake, had a glass of wine. Despite the 'poultry' and the traditional 'white' wine, we weren't standing on tradition and I had four different vintages going. Dinner chat was mostly about the food, which was spectacular. Seconds and in my case thirds (I paced myself, small portions all around).

"Mrs. Drummond, this is quite a meal," Pastor Gottschalk commented. "I can't remember the last time I've seen food like this."

"There are plenty of things to be thankful for, even these days," Karen said. "And that bird, despite how tasty he is, will not be missed." Karen didn't like Earl (the kids had named him), and Earl didn't really care for Karen, either. Never did figure out why.

"Come about Friday, I'll be missing the leftovers," I said.

"Any idea where you'll be?" Alan asked.

"Not really. Depends on what we find down the line," I said.

"How about you, Mike?" Ron asked. "You going to keep Rick safe and sound?"

"Rick's brigade can more than do that. We're headed elsewhere. Can't talk about it. We'll head out tomorrow too, though."

"Ron, how'd work go next door today? You guys get things shaped up?"

"With a sizeable crew, we did. Grace should be good to move in, sometime after noon tomorrow," he said. "I'd like to take all the credit, but your brother in law was the ramrod."

"I'd like to see that after dinner," I said. "Good job."

"They did a great job, hon. I couldn't believe it," Karen said.

"And we did it without my little sister ordering the contractors about," Alan said, only half kidding.

"Watch it, pal, or that peach pie goes to everyone but you," she said, smiling, but meaning it the way that only a sibling can.

"You didn't hear the other big news of the day," Karen said. "Pastor will be house-sitting at the Pauliano's for the winter."

"Congratulations, I think," I said. "There's a fair amount of work to go with that place."

"Not a problem. I grew up on a farm in Iowa," he said. "And do please call me Pete."

Dinner had wrapped up, except for dessert, by eight-thirty, and the kids had retreated to Carl's room, where they'd put in a copy of *The Wizard of Oz*, piled on the bed and the bunk above it, and watched intently. As many adults as possible (about four, it turned out) populated the kitchen in the big cleanup, rotating through putting away leftovers, working over the pile of dishes, and eyeing the pies. The young pastor was banished from the kitchen, along with Corporal Burrus, Sarah and Brooke. Cory had lost enough times, badly, at a game of 'manipulation', a card game I'd never had much time to get good at.

Alan, Ron and I had a few minutes to sit and talk, in relative quiet, before the onslaught of dessert.

"You guys really about done with the house?"

"Cleanup, a little wiring in the basement, and some more work on what'll be the pharmaceutical closet. Fencing will have to wait until the spring, but we'll come up with something to create a better perimeter in the meantime," Alan said.

"You guys gotta be thrashed," I said. "I know how much work that place needed."

"Twenty workers, fast work," Ron said. "Your mom-in-law will have company. Three of the families from church have elderly parents in need of full time care. They helped out a ton."

"Staff?" I asked.

"Rotating staff from Valley Hospital, in exchange for priority in the next round of housing rehabs. Staff of eight in the rotation," Alan said.

"I should get drafted more often," I said. "I think you got more done in the last couple days than I'd have been able to do in a month."

"Providence, that's all," Alan said. "You doing OK? You've kinda gone from zero to ninety in not much time."

"I'm handling it better than I thought I would. I'll tell ya, guys," I said in confidence, "I've seen some things done by the S.A. today that will haunt me to my grave."

"Shortwave alluded to that, too," Ron said. "I told Marie to not listen anymore. Pretty graphic."

"You have no idea," I said. "And while I've known you both a very long time, there are things I've seen, long ago, that I still can not find words for," I said, before taking a sip of brandy, made by one of the trading store clientele.

"We're supposed to be a support unit. We're going to retrieve the remains of Sixth Army. Once done with that, it's anybody's guess. I told everyone in the Brigade that I expect Third Washington to be able to fight. Honestly, I expect them to be able to kill every God damned Statist soldier that is anywhere close to being in range."

"It needs doing. We'd go...we *will* go, in a heartbeat," Ron said.

"No, you won't," I said. "I saw your files. You're hi-pri here. You can volunteer, and you'll be denied. Your jobs are to keep things running on the commerce and civilian side of Metro."

"Rick, you have any idea how long this'll last?"

"Honest answer? No. From what I know that I can talk about, we have extremely diminished war-fighting capability. We're faced with asymmetric tactics including every conceivable option used by the enemy, virtually all of them 'illegal' in the classic sense. Civilians surrender after a siege. They're rounded up, put in a building and burned to death. Civilians cooperate with the enemy, they're exploited in ways I won't describe, and put to death. Enemy agents infiltrate us far behind the lines and use chemical and nerve agents on civilian population centers. Ditto viable military targets, but again the agents are dressed either as friendlies, as civilians, as delivery people, whatever. Didn't matter. They show no mercy, they strip everything of any use from wherever they are. They burn everything they possibly can, in their wake. They kill their seriously wounded. They kill their deserters, and the families of their deserters. They contaminate the water supplies. They slaughter livestock they cannot transport…they're just destroyers."

"Sherman had nothing on the S.A.," Alan said, looking over at the kitchen, where the pies were being sliced and the card game was wrapping up.

"And it's a matter of debate on whether Sherman was on the right side of that war," added Ron.

"Well, there's no debate on these bastards. If I get the chance I'm going to send every single one of them to Hell to roast on a spit," I said.

"Pie, gentlemen. If you would be so kind to pick one, and only one slice," Libby said. "In other words, leave enough for the cooks. Soldiers first, Mr. Bauer and Mr. Martin."

"The one time it pays to have a uniform," Corporal Burrus said.

"Oh, I don't know, Cory," I said quietly as I lined up behind him. "That young lady over there seems to have been eyeing you most of the night."

"She is a *looker*, sir," he said as he leaned back a little to reply.

"Corporal, there are opportune moments. You might consider this one of them," I said. "You ship out tomorrow. Time's a wastin'. Consider that, not an order, but advice."

"Yes, sir. Consider that done."

"Hey, Kare? What are these other pies doing, uncut?" Alan asked.

"Two are for the men guarding our store. The other apple pie is for Elaine Cross, the other pumpkin is for Aaron and Ellen Watters."

"How about that cobbler?" I asked. It looked better than some of the pies.

"Anja and Randy."

"Yikes. The oven must've been going all day," I said.

"Use it or lose it," Mary said. "Stuff doesn't keep forever."

By ten, things had really wound down. Alan and Carl carried Alan's little ones home across the field, and Marie was spending the night with Kelly. Libby, Mary and Karen were going over 'move in' details for the new convalescent home, right next door. Pastor Gottschalk had headed home around nine, leaving Sarah, Brooke, and the young Corporal to chat, and to return to base by the witching hour with the Humvee. Mike had taken his family home in Ashley's personal SUV, with Mike's 'military' pass in the window. The curfew in our part of the Valley was a loose thing, with searches of cars rarely completed. Two or three miles west, and it was anything but.

Ron and I took a tour of the day's work next door. The transformation was pretty amazing. Even the cleanup of the construction work wouldn't take more than an hour or two.

"Whose bright idea was this safe room?" I asked. They'd built a pharmaceutical closet within a newly framed shell. On the outside, salvaged wood paneling. The door, three layers of plywood, with three layers of quarter inch steel, and the biggest, gnarliest hinges I could imagine. From the outside, what appeared to be a normal, lever-type door handle, and a nice oak plank pattern, appearing to be a little cheap. On the inside, sheet steel, needing some paint, and an overly complicated for me to quickly understand, latch and lock system. The room shell would need to be paneled on the inside, as two by sixes and three-quarter inch reinforcing steel, both vertically and horizontally, were tied together with heavy duty wire.

"Guy named Darrel…last name escapes me. His mother has Alzheimer's. He ran a contracting outfit before the War. Built foundations, so that's where all the bar came from."

"There's a small fortune in steel in this shell. Still, I guess no one's getting in here easily," I said.

"They're bringing in two layers of salvaged plywood tomorrow—it's out in the shop out back now. Overlapped and screwed together at twelve inches on center. Someone wants in here, they damned well better have the key," Ron said.

"Where'd that door come from? I just noticed the frame. Wow," I said. The frame extended eighteen inches on each side of the door opening, and likewise, above the door.

"Salvaged. No idea where it came from. Took six guys to move all of that in, in pieces, and bolt it all up. Came right in through the front door. You haven't seen it yet, but there's a significant amount of new framing downstairs to hold all of this up."

Moving out of the pharmacy room, and down the hallway, I noticed four hospital-type beds stored in one room, along with piles of bedding and linens. "Hospital stuff?"

"Nursing home, over on Adams. It was abandoned right after the quake. Scotty Wallace set us up with this stuff, and much more if we need it."

"You guys really done good," I said with a country-boy twang.

"You never know, we all may be living in a place like this some day, our kids taking care of us."

"Should we be so lucky," I said.

"You all packed up?"

"Mostly. Need to get my old Springfield and a thousand rounds to go, some comfort items. Some stuff for bribes, you know, the usual," I said. "You guys seem to have your stuff together. I'm sure things will run just fine without me."

"You have any more thoughts on this banking idea of ours?" Ron said.

"Honest answer? Haven't thought one iota about it. Libby and Karen are on board with it, right?"

"They are if you are."

"The only conditions that I'd put on it are the same conditions I'd put on any business: Operate fairly and honestly. Don't screw anybody. If you have a bad feeling about somebody, then don't do business with them."

"The usual," Ron said.

"The usual. Oh yeah, try not to lose money."

Karen and I talked, long into the night that night, after I'd finished packing, about many things and nothing. She fell asleep snuggled into my shoulder long before I drifted off.

Morning came far too quickly.

3 3

Wednesday Morning
November Twenty-second
06:00 hours

I'd been up since before five, Karen as well, helping my with my last-last minute packing and making me corned beef hash, eggs, toast, and apple juice, none of which I'd likely have again, any time soon. Both dogs thought they were entitled to some too, but I wasn't about to surrender.

She'd roused the kids at five thirty to spend some time with me, and both were pretty sullen—I couldn't blame them, I wasn't exactly chipper myself. Kelly was doing her best to keep from crying. Carl probably was too, but was putting up a better show. I'd had long talks with each of them about my new role. Neither of them liked it, but understood, sort of, it seemed.

Outside, the Expedition was parked in the driveway, ready to shuttle me to the rail yard, and for continued service after I'd left—it had appeared overnight as the surprise that I'd hoped for. Karen would have a 'farm' pass for the use of the Expedition, no more unrestricted driving with my Metro pass, now turned in. Many other things would change with me 'gone', along with my pass, went a priority for security, the Metro-frequency radio, and the considerable influence that I could wield, if I were of the mind to.

Loading my gear out to the Ford, Carl took one look at it and immediately called it, "bad-ass."

"Not bad, huh?" I said from under my parka hood. It was really cold, but I hadn't bothered to look at the temperature. Sometimes, it's best not to.

"Hate the wheels though. They're ugly."

"Yeah, but they have new all-season Michelins on them, that before the war would've cost three-hundred apiece," I said. "Get used to them. You'll be driving this thing about too, you know."

"Sweet," he said.

"Go get your sis and Momma. We should be good to go."

"We're already here," Karen said. "And you forgot your day-pack."

"I did at that," I said. "Want a job as my porter?"

"No, just as your wife and lover."

"Done. Get your bags," I said as I gave her a kiss.

"I'll have to clear my calendar. Sorry, no go."

"Next time, then."

"As long as there's no war, it's a date."

"You driving or me?" I asked.

"You are," Karen said. "Show me the routine. That way I won't get us in trouble."

"You'll be OK, just follow the plowed roads, and don't tick off anyone with a gun."

"Easy for you to say," she said. "I don't pack a forty-five."

"You should. Get that compact model out and start wearing it. I'm serious."

"I have it, it's in my purse."

"Needs to be in reach in a moment's notice, babe."

"I know. Alan's getting one of his harness makers to put a holster together for me."

"Good. And that will apply to the kids any time now," I said.

"I don't really like that," she said. "And you don't either."

"No, I don't. Unfortunately it's our reality right now," I said as I started up the Ford, the first time in months. It felt odd. The CD player blared to life, with Roger McGuinn's Rickenbacker and the Byrds version of Bob Dylan's *My Back Pages* sending me way back in time.

We crossed over the freeway to Trent, past the wreckage of the previous night's structure fire. With a skiff of new snow, there was little to see that couldn't have been there for six months. There were no vehicles on any of the roads we drove, and scarce evidence of vehicle traffic overnight.

The few cars that were about were all headed to the rail yard checkpoint, with full searches going on for every vehicle entering the drop off area. We'd be in that group.

"Is this normal? Did you have this yesterday?" Karen asked.

"No. Honestly, I'm not sure what normal is these days," I replied. We had three cars in front of us, and armed soldiers moving down the line, weapons ready. I rolled down my window, and made sure my Army I.D. was out, and my insignia showing. I also turned up the heater…and noticed that we had a full tank of gas. I hadn't thought to check that.

"Identification, please, sir," the corporal, with an unranked armed soldier behind him asked.

"Here you go," I asked. "What's our security level today?"

"Red two, sir. You're Third Washington?"

"Colonel Drummond, commanding."

"Thank you, sir. Please pull over to the left for additional screening."

"Thanks, Corporal."

I pulled ahead of the two cars ahead of us, both of which were being searched. They appeared to contain full loads of rail yard workers, mechanics, and engineers, carpooling in. Each car was being thoroughly searched.

I parked the Ford where directed, and was directed to step out of the vehicle, along with all other passengers.

"Good morning, Colonel. You and your passengers can step over there under cover, if you would," an Air Force Security Policeman asked.

"No problem. Thanks."

"Sir, can I inquire as to your baggage?" a sergeant asked before I walked over to the shelter, looking over my regulation load, the heap and my personal gear.

"Full and Combat load in the packs on the left. My California's in a hard case to the right. The ammo cans at the front have one hundred rounds of armor piercing 30.06, twenty-five rounds of tracer, the rest is match-grade ball, along with a thousand rounds of ammo for my .45's. They're all labeled if you want to look. My personal gear is on the left, the usual contraband. The long case is a Springfield 1903 sporter, cleaning kit, and more ammo in pouches."

"Not exactly regulation, is that?" he said before adding, "Sir."

"Not in this war. Several wars previous though. It was kinda tough deciding to take that one or my Garand."

"Thank you, sir. Dog'll be over in a minute to give the car a sniff, along with the underbody inspection. After that you'll be directed to the marshalling area near Charlie Six."

"Charlie Six?"

"Sorry, sir. That's your trains' designation."

"Got it. Thanks again."

Under the 'shelter', in reality six sheets of corrugated metal nailed to a light wooden frame, my family waited patiently.

"Lot of security for this," Carl said.

"It'd be a coup for the S.A. if they took out a troop train behind the lines, don't you think?" I said as a large German Shepherd and his handler approached the Ford.

"Yeah, I guess," he said.

"They'd do that, too, wouldn't they?" Karen said.

"Hon, they would do anything and everything imaginable to achieve their goals."

In a couple minutes, the dog and the underbody mirror inspection were complete, and we were allowed to continue on to the parking area near the train, about fifty feet from the Command Car. Other than two Humvees, we'd be 'it' in the parking area. The locomotives were already running at idle.

"This is your new home?" Karen said.

"No, my home is my home. This is my train though."

"How many men and women aboard? How many are with you?" Kelly asked as I got out of the Ford.

"Fifteen hundred men, no women. Second train will have roughly another fifteen hundred. We're a little shy of the three thousand we're supposed to have." Carl was already out and had opened the rear hatch.

"Why no women?"

Without getting graphic and giving Kelly the real reason, I said "This war is no place for women. The Statists have already proven that."

She got the point. "Oh."

"Carl, second car back, this end. That's my bunkhouse. The other end is one of the other officers. The Command Car is that one over there," I said, pointing it out. "That's where I'll spend most of my time," I said, not adding, 'If I'm damned lucky.'

Karen wasn't saying anything...I don't think I was expecting her to, either though.

"Morning, Colonel Drummond," a voice greeted me from behind.

"Good morning, Major," noting he did not salute me. Salutes out of doors in active battle areas tended to get one killed. "Major Gary Ryder, this is my wife Karen, son Carl, and my daughter Kelly."

"Nice to meet you all," he said. "Moment, sir?"

"You bet," I said. "Karen, head on over to my car and I'll be there in a minute." Major Ryder and I stepped a few feet away to talk in private.

"We're an hour fifteen from departure-ready. Three quarters of the compliment are already aboard, the remainder will be aboard within the half-hour, sir."

"Good. Please assemble the brigade senior staff in forty minutes for our morning brief, and the battalion commanders at ten hundred in the conference car. Any issues with transit between cars when we're underway? I hadn't thought to ask that."

"No, sir, with the exception of the defensive carriages. Any other car can be accessed up to those," he said. "Sir, I didn't mean to interrupt. My apologies. I'll let you get back to your send-off, sir."

"Thanks, Major. No problem."

Carl and Kelly had ascended the outboard ladder to the side door of my car, and let themselves in. Karen waited for me at the bottom of the stairs.

"This is it, huh?" Karen said, looking at the former Chinese transport container, now modified for Army use.

"Yep. Go on up and take a look," I said. We could hear Carl say, 'this is cool,' as we reached the top of the stairs.

Inside, my half of the eight foot wide, twenty foot long container included a full size bed, desk and chair, side chair and a fold out table, a closet and small galley (including a refrigerator, bar sink and microwave), and a small bathroom with a raised floor (to make room for the plumbing and on-board tanks) that had a stainless steel sink and vanity, medicine cabinet, toilet, and corner shower unit. Each unit was equipped with towels, bedding, first aid supplies, and the regulation vitamins and minerals that someone in the Army deemed 'required'. The interior walls were a fiberglass-reinforced panel, which covered up a layer of light armor up to mid-height of the walls.

"Well, this is pretty nice," Karen said. "Way better than I expected."

"This is a two-bedroom unit. There's the command unit, which is double the size of my unit; there's laundry and galley units; shower units; ten- and thirty-man bunkhouses; generating plants; water and sewage treatment units, the whole schmeer." I didn't mention 'armory', 'machine shop', or the 'defensive units.'

"All built from sea-crates," Karen said.

"Yeah, pretty much."

"And you have heat?"

"And air conditioning. And the whole train is pretty well self sufficient, really, each car, as long as we have diesel."

Carl had hauled in one of the Army packs. I'd grabbed one of my personal bags. One more trip and we'd have the bags, and then a couple more for the rest. We made pretty short work of it, and then....it was time for our goodbyes.

"You remember the last time you left me," Karen said.

"Of course. I promise I will try to return in one piece, this time."

"Good. I'll hold you to that," she said as she hugged me and moved to kiss me. "And you hurry home to me."

"I will do my best," I said. "And take care of my kids."

"I will. I'm going to miss you," she said as her voice started to crack.

"I know hon. Remember how much I love you."

"I will."

"And you two," I said to the kids, hovering uncomfortably and not knowing what to do, "Make me proud and be there for your Mom while I'm gone."

"Come home, Daddy," Kelly said as they both hugged us.

"I will, babe. I will."

Carl and I had a private moment after Karen and Kelly got back in the Ford.

"You take care of them for me, Carl. I know you think you're too young to be the man of the house, but I know you can do this. And you should know by now how proud I am of you. You've learned a lot this year, and I think you know how much you still have to learn, just like me."

"I've got a pretty good idea, yeah," he said, embarrassed.

"You'll do fine. Ask Alan and Ron for advice. Frequently," I said. "And keep up on your work with the kids and at church, OK?"

"O.K.," he said. "And Dad? Will you be able to call us?"

"I hope so, yeah. I really don't know, but I'll try."

"O.K. We better go. You've got a couple guys over there looking at you," he said.

"I'm popular. Drive safe on the way home. Get straight home. Follow any Army or Guard or Sheriff's directions. We're still under curfew."

"I know. And we have Grandma to move today. That'll be interesting."

"Yeah. As if your Mom and Alan don't have enough stress. Try to make it easy for them if you can," I said.

Too soon thereafter, they were on their way home, me standing there waving goodbye, wiping more than one ice-cold tear from my ice cold cheeks.

"Coffee, Colonel?" one of the Privates asked, carrying a handful of mugs and a stainless steel thermos.

"Absolutely. Blacker the better," I said. "And thanks."

"No problem, sir. There aren't that many people aboard who're interested in staying awake."

"I can't blame them," I said. "If I had much of a choice, I'd be sacked out myself."

We'd headed east-northeast out of Spokane, sliced up through North Idaho, across the north end of Lake Pend Oreille, and into Montana. I'd taken an Amtrak train once on the same route, moving closer to sixty miles per hour on that trip. This trip though, was sometimes half that. It was heartening to see streetlights in Sandpoint, Idaho, and businesses open.

Our train, Charlie Six, and Dog Six behind us containing the second half of the Brigade and much more equipment, would slice diagonally across Montana, entering Wyoming on the 'Colorado' leg of the BNSF rail lines, rather than the 'Powder River' lines, which would take us straight into enemy territory. We'd either arrive at our final destination by skirting Denver, or hitting Denver and then heading east from there.

We'd finished up our senior staff meeting relatively quickly, with everyone reviewing work to be completed in transit, which sometimes required me to ask for less detail than more. I really didn't care how many troops would be responsible for meal preparation during the trip, who was running what shift, etc. In only one case did this draw a look similar to panic. The officer in question seemed to only act with initiative and approval provided by others, rather than acting on his own under the authority given him. This would be a continuing issue during my entire time with the Army....a culture of order-takers and followers rather than leaders and thinkers.

I left the communications area of the Command Car in charge of Jim Schaefer, the Brigade's deputy commander/XO. The communications suites were busy with testing of the satellite uplinks, scans of multiple radio and broadcast frequencies from the Mississippi west, and continued civilian broadcasts of further details on the most recent attacks. One of the suites was dedicated to providing entertainment choices for the troops aboard, with a half-dozen selections of movies available to the flat panel displays in the troop transport cars. I found it interesting that more than half of the video requests were for the Eighties classic, *A Christmas Story*. The tongue-stuck-to-frozen-flagpole scene, along with *'I triple dog dare you'* will always be favorites of mine.

In my office area, adjacent to the command communications area, was cramped with equipment well before any human was inserted into it. Inside though, I had a dedicated data link to any of the communications suites, as well as the ability to link to any military data feed available. I chose to review Sixth Army's tactical analysis and supporting data, hoping not to repeat their mistakes.

By three in the afternoon, we were approaching Columbia Falls, Montana, just outside of Glacier National Park, and met our first delay of the trip, caused by a freight derailment between there and Shelby. I realized, in pre-War thinking of course, that I could have driven from Spokane to Columbia Falls and most of the way back in the time the train had taken to get us this far.

"Excuse me, Colonel. This delay looks like about three hours duration, conservatively," Greg Shand said as he interrupted my review of the Sixth's videotaped demise.

"How far behind us is Dog Six?"

"Forty-five minutes, sir. Engineers say they'll go ahead and handle some maintenance work during the delay."

"Leaving us to decide," I said, before correcting myself, "rather, me to decide what to do with three thousand troops during the delay."

"That was the next question to be posed you, but that was going to come from the XO, sir," he said with a smile.

"If I recall, the total population of Columbia Falls, pre-War, was about four thousand. Seems a little much to inflict on a small town," I thought. "How about you try to get the local Sheriff on the radio. I'll have a talk with them."

"I'll see what we can do, sir."

"Thanks, Captain," I said. He soon had assigned one of the techs to the job, and in five minutes, had Chief of Police Gary Davidson on the line for me. I didn't ask how they did it, the answer would have probably been over my head in any regard.

"Chief, this is Colonel Rick Drummond. Thanks for taking the time to talk."

"Well, Colonel, it's not a problem. If I can ask, how did you get a hold of me? I'm in my patrol rig."

"My staff as some electronic magic. I'm wondering if your city can handle some visitors for a couple of hours." There was a fairly long pause on the other end of the conversation.

"Well, I'm not sure. How many are we talking here?"

"Just shy of three thousand, for about three hours."

"Holy smokes! I don't know about that, Colonel. There's only fifty-five hundred in the town!" he said. Jim Schaefer was leaning on the doorframe, listening in on his own muted headset.

"Understood, Chief. We've got a delay due to a derailment between here and Shelby, and it'll take some time to clear, I understand. If there's the chance to let the troops off the train for awhile, I thought I'd ask."

"Don't get me wrong, Colonel. I'm sure they'd be welcome, especially if they had some spending money or things to trade," he said with some enthusiasm. "We just don't want or need any trouble."

"Nor do I, sir. We'll be pulling in within about twenty minutes, I understand. I'd like to give my troops the option to see your city, if they'd like."

"I'll spread the word, Colonel. I'll meet you myself at the station."

"Thanks, Chief. See you soon," I said as I terminated the connection. "Captain Shand, patch me through to this train and to Dog Six if you would," I said.

"Yes, sir," Greg said. I could hear the smile in his tone.

"This'll be interesting, sir," Jim said in the doorway. "Riding herd on three thousand troops in a small town."

"They aren't all going to go. First, it's eleven degrees out there. Second, as I remember it, there aren't that many things to do, eat, or see in this town. Of course, I could be wrong. It's been five years since I was here last."

"Patch is ready sir, Select station twelve on your base unit, and you're on," one of the techs said, pointing out the right button on the console. The lettering was probably easily read by the twenty-somethings, but not so much for us on the north side of forty.

"Good afternoon, this is Colonel Drummond. We are approaching Columbia Falls at this time, where we will have a delay of approximately three hours due to a derailment ahead of us. I have spoken with the local Chief of Police regarding our stop in Columbia Falls, and request your attention."

"The Chief has informed me that Third Washington troops are welcome in the city, but the city is quite small and will certainly not be able to accommodate a massive surge of soldiers over a three hour period. He'd also invite you to spend your money or conduct some trades. I'd also like to make sure that everyone knows that it's all of eleven degrees out there, probably pretty deep snow, and if you elect to leave the train during this delay, you will do so with the knowledge that if your train leaves without you, you'll be charged or hunted accordingly. Visitors to Columbia Falls will travel in groups no smaller than squad strength, and squad leaders are responsible for their squad during this stopover. Battle rifles are to remain stowed aboard side arms however are required. That is all," I said.

"Not bad, Colonel," Schaefer said. "Not bad."

Wednesday Afternoon
November Twenty-second
15:40 Hours

"Chief," I said to the parka-clad form in front of me, "Rick Drummond. Thanks for accommodating us."

"Glad to do it, Colonel. I've got three patrols out to direct your men into the downtown area. Your train's pretty long, so I expect we'll be herding them around a little."

"Second train will follow us in, and it's about the same length. It's been a few years, but as I remember it, most of the downtown area is a fair ways further south, is that right?"

"Used to be, but there's been quite a bit of development up here on the north end. Streets are pretty well cleared as you can see," he waved to the southwest a little, showing single-lane side roads and the cleared state highway which was the commercial artery of the small town.

"I'm not sure how many men might want to go for a walk. Pretty brisk out here today."

"Good thing you weren't here on Monday. We almost made it above zero. Colder'n last February, and that was damned cold," he said. "So, where you from, Colonel?"

"Spokane. Born and raised," I said as I gave the 'all-clear' to our railcar leaders, beginning the offloading of some of the men.

"You there during the big shake? Army and all?"

"Oh yeah. I wasn't Army then. Matter of fact, I've not been in the Army a full week yet."

"Well, you must've been on some body's shit list to get drafted at your age, no offense."

"None taken. They tell me the opposite. Leadership of any kind is a little tough to come by right now."

"I hear you there. There are a lot of towns out east of here that don't have any kind of peace officers left. Either they run off when things got tough or they're nothing like what you'd expect in law enforcement, 'cept maybe in bad dream. I hear the further south you get, the worse it is."

"Let me know where those towns are, if you would, and we might be able to do something about that, sooner or later."

"Where you headed? This is one helluva big train. Biggest we've seen in months."

"East, then south." I didn't need to say more, nor was I about to.

"Good for you. I hope you cut them bastards' nuts off and feed 'em to 'em. Then put a bullet in 'em. I saw what they did to them girls down there. They put it on TV this afternoon. Warned everyone what they were gonna show, so the kids could get outta the room, but by God the things they did...I never thought I'd see such a thing in America."

"We've got our work ahead of us, Chief. No doubt about it."

"Colonel, up ahead there on the left is a little restaurant...the Blue Dot. They've got the hottest coffee—the real thing—and the best pie in three counties. Spread the word. They'll take care of you. Owner served in Gulf War One, lost his boy in Tucson last spring."

"We'll send some business their way. Thanks, Chief."

"Glad to do it. You remember, Colonel. You fry their asses," he said, almost spitting.

About a third of the men on Charlie took the opportunity to disembark, and found within a few minutes, that dozens of pickups and SUV's were more than happy to ferry Third Washington around town. Word spreads pretty fast in small towns.

Before heading down to the restaurant myself, I made sure that the Command Car crew had a chance to get out, staying behind with a skeleton crew until they got back. While I was waiting, more information came our way regarding the Livermore attack, with detailed losses, more classified information, force deployments in Colorado and Nebraska, and confirmation that nerve agents were the culprit in the majority of the attacks. Russian in origin, the report stated, and didn't speculate as to how such quantities and delivery vehicles found their way into the hands of the Statists.

"Mr. Kennedy, you have one of the untraceable cell phones handy?" I asked. We had a number of cell phones available for use, as long as they routed through the trains internal communications network, and as long as nothing remotely close to classified or containing anything about positions, strengths or tactics was discussed.

"Yes, sir. Here you go. Calling home?"

"Surprising the wife."

"I'll listen in per protocol, sir. And there's a slight delay."

"No prob." Private Kennedy could kill the call should anything sensitive get out.

I had to dig out Karen's cell phone number, and punched it in. It rang twice before she answered.

"Hiya, babe," I said, noticing the slight delay caused by Kennedy's equipment.

"Well this is unexpected!"

"How're things on the home front?"

"Good. We just got Mom and two other ladies settled in, and two nurses, and their meds. It's going very well. Can you talk? How're you able to call me?"

"I can sneak a call now and then, as long as I don't go into areas where I shouldn't."

"Where are you?"

"Well, I'm right here. That's about as definitive as I can get. Things are going OK for my first real day on the job. Troops are doing well, too. How're the kids?"

"Liking this week-long curfew, except the work they've got to do."

"How strict are they calling the curfew? Everything staying shut down?"

"Stores are running weird hours, which is irritating, and everything's shut down at dusk, no exceptions."

We spent about ten minutes on the phone, mostly small talk on the surface, more being said between the lines, before the rest of the communications crew made it back. It was good to hear her voice.

"Heading down to the Blue-Dot, sir?" one of the techs, Private Wheeler, asked.

"Got something to recommend?"

"Pecan pie sir. Killer."

"That'll work. Thanks."

Another voice stopped me before I headed out the end of the car and out.

"At least another hour, sir. Just heard from the combat engineers working up ahead."

"Swell. Thanks. See you in a few," I said as I hit the door.

I'd packed my thrashed Eddie Bauer parka for using when I wanted to blend in a little better than the new winter Army camo. I found, unexpectedly, the spare tractor key in one of the pockets.

The main street was much more developed than I'd remembered, with signs that showed boutiques, salons, and antique stores on the storefronts. Many though, were different stores than the expensive signs identified. Used clothing, small appliances, a harness shop in an old coffee bar, a bakery now housed in what was a nail boutique. I was surprised at the number of Third Washington on the streets and spending some of their limited funds in the small shops.

I made my way up to the Blue Dot, a pre-War diner-style restaurant that could've been a clone from the Fifties. Above the doors, I recognized a partial trunk and rear fenders from a nineteen-fifty Ford sedan, taillights equipped with blue dots in the style of the old rodders. The place was packed with Third Washington's men. I opened the door and someone immediately called, 'Tennnn-*hut*!

"Whoa, at ease already. I hear they've got pecan pie here."

"Yes, sir, Colonel. Come on up to the counter here. Sarge, make a hole," one of the lieutenants directed.

"Arch, got any of that pecan pie left?"

"Oh, yeah. Saved one for your C.O. This him?"

"Yes, sir."

"Colonel, nice to meet you. Arch Rivers. Made sergeant once upon a time. This's my joint."

"Thanks for the hospitality, Mr. Rivers. It appears the men are well taken care of."

"If I had a few more lovely ladies to wait on them, I'm sure they'd be even more so."

"Not hard to peg the entertainment value of a piece of pie…"

"…when it's another piece they're interested in," he said, finishing my thought for me, making me laugh immediately.

425

"Got that right," I said, taking a forkful of pie. Sinfully good almost described it. "Wow, that's good," I said.

"Thanks. My late wife's recipe."

"And how did you get pecans?" I asked. "We haven't been able to get them since before the Domino."

"Creative trading with folks down south. Took some doing though."

"Sounds like home," I said. "We do a lot of that," I said. "I understand you served in the first Gulf War?"

"Yeah, lost my foot there. Ground pounder for ol' George. Caught an RPG."

"Thank you for your service, Sergeant. And for your son's sacrifice as well."

"Thank you Colonel. I miss that kid every day. He was a better soldier than I ever would've been, and he never saw twenty years old," Arch said, before asking me about my service.

"Civilian. Governor decided that my time was best spent in service of the State. I'm not exactly what you'd call a regulation career-path officer."

"Good. Then you still have some brains. Here, have some coffee," he said as he poured me a huge mug. "Don't know what it's like now, but when I was in, they seemed to breed out the guys who could think on their feet and take initiative, at least in the Army. Focused on 'diverse experience' and 'performance initiatives' and endless classes. Keep that crap up long enough and you end up with a brainless collection of zombies who cannot think for themselves."

"I think you just described the S.A."

"Yeah, could be. Problem is that right or wrong, you've gotta have men that can think."

426

Arch and I spent a few minutes talking as I finished up the pie (which was outstanding, I left a clean plate) before he beckoned me behind the counter to the inner workings of the Blue Dot for some private conversations.

"So, Colonel, do you have any medics aboard?"

"Of course. I take it that you've got a need?"

"No doc's, no dentists, no meds for three months. Yeah, we have a need. The hospital's all but boarded up—no one to staff it, no meds. Anything you guys can do to help out?"

"Depends on how long we're here. Once we open up the medical car, there's no telling on how long the lines might be as much as I'd like to. We've got a schedule to keep," I said, hating the words as I said them.

"I hear ya. How about anything more permanent -like ...or maybe a traveling clinic. You guys got anything like that in Spokane?"

"We set up neighborhood clinics with rotations of docs from the hospitals and permanent clinics. Works out OK, but medicines are scarce or homemade."

"Well, we've got nuthin', and even the basic health care isn't possible. Maybe put the word out to the Army?"

"I'll do that. I assume you have EMTs or some folks with basic skills," I said.

"Yeah, a few, but they're overwhelmed and honestly, they don't have the resources, the reference material, can't really make good diagnoses...let alone supplies."

"C'mon back to the train. We'll hunt down our doc and see what we can do in the interim."

"Much appreciated, Colonel. I've a couple of grandkids I'd like to see live past age ten."

Arch and I, along with a dozen soldiers from Third Washington climbed into the back of a converted pickup truck to make the trip back up to the train. The truck's box had been removed, a flatbed installed, steps added to the back like a trolley, and a sheet metal top and partial sides added. The rest was open air, no lights, and the benches were two by twelves, facing the center aisle. The truck was branded with the City's logo. The men, once they realized whom they were traveling with, quieted down to a more military level and attitude.

I had Rivers wait in our conference room car, while I gathered up some stuff from the Command Car and had staff track down our medical officer, Dr. Jeff Willitson.

"Arch Rivers, this is our chief medical officer, Doctor Jeff Willitson. Jeff, Columbia Falls has next to no medical staff left. I'm wondering if there's something we can do, or get some help coming in."

"We can try, Colonel, but there's a global shortage of medical professionals that are not assigned to the war effort and as such, are near line units. We can pose the question to Command, certainly."

"I realize this is closer to home than we thought, but are there supplies you can provide?"

"Sure, we can help out to a degree. Once we reach destination, we'll have resupply trains coming through regularly, barring something truly unfortunate," Dr. Willitson said, referring to another attack.

"I'd appreciate that greatly, I'm sure the whole area would," Rivers said. "Exactly what kind of supplies? It's not like we have a lot of training."

"First, reference materials geared to the lay person. You have computer access? Not internet, just computers?"

"Sure. Those still work."

"OK. Part of the gear we anticipated providing towns like yours include a series of CD's with extensive reference libraries. Load them up on the computers—and I'd make copies if I were you and

428

share them widely—and those'll get you a head start. Some is military some is civilian—all if it is good stuff. There's a couple that I'd recommend starting with, like *Where There Is No Doctor* and *Where There Is No Dentist*. Those two will cover a bunch of your basic needs. Then there are more detailed references on a series of CD's called *Operational Medicine*, those were produced by the Navy and Special Operations Command. They have photographic and video demonstrations of wound care, really too many other things to cover," the doctor said.

"Now, supply-wise," he continued, "are you ex-military?"

"Gulf War. Second of the Sixteenth, Dagger Brigade, First Infantry."

"O.K. Basis of understanding—You'll get med supplies equivalent to a line battalion. That'll have to last for awhile, until we get a steady stream of resupply and you get some more skills on the ground." Willitson then, from memory, ran through most of the equipment complement. Most of it was over my head.

Arch was a little stunned. "You have that stuff, today?"

"Yes. We can have it delivered to a location of the City's choice in an hour. How's that?"

"Better than I ever hoped, Doc."

"Mr. Rivers, we will need to make sure that this equipment and the supplies go to the parties in charge of the region. Can you contact your leadership and put them in contact?"

"Doc, I'm the Mayor. I have a city council of five. I have eleven deputies and one Sheriff. I have six other city employees doing the work of twenty, one police chief, one combo EMT/fire chief. Volunteer fire department. That's it."

"Sorry, Mr. Mayor. You're entirely sufficient for the transfer."

"No apologies necessary, Doc. And my eternal thanks."

I found myself pleasantly surprised at twenty-one forty-five hours, that everyone was aboard the train, fifteen minutes ahead of our scheduled departure. The fast reports requested from each squad leader up through the chain of command reported all accounted for and double checked. No problems in town, of any kind. 'I thought, it probably doesn't get much better than this.'

The medical supplies for Columbia Falls had taken about a half hour to unload from one of the supply modules on the train, into six pickup trucks, lined up and headed back to the hospital. Word of the supplies spread quickly throughout the town, and people were clamoring for them to be released almost as soon as they left the train car. I thought that it might be a long night for Chief Davidson and Arch Rivers, and especially those with limited medical skill who'd now be pushed to provide more care than they were reasonably able.

I'd settled back into my 'office' a few minutes after pulling out of town, looking over the schedule for the rest of our trip. If all went according to plan (and of course, we all know that plans are perfect until they're implemented), within twenty-four hours we'd arrive at our destination, Sterling, Colorado.

East of Sterling, we'd find Sixth Army. Somewhere further east of the Colorado state line lay the S.A. army, scattered between Grand Island, Nebraska and Manhattan, Kansas. U.S. Army intel stated that a corridor stretching from Interstates Seventy to Eighty, and some miles beyond, was being treated to the same scorched-earth tactics we'd heard of in Colorado. Aerial reconnaissance was all but impossible due to dozens of shoulder-held surface-to-air missiles fired at any target. Reports from Sterling stated that the munitions were Russian in origin.

Satellite reconnaissance and data collection was a different matter, I was learning. We'd been led to the understanding that all GPS satellites circling the earth had been disabled in the early days of the Third War. My own GPS displayed a screen stating, 'No Signal', and the little icons showing circling satellites were missing. It had resided in the desk drawer at home since that time, stripped of its' batteries, a useless electronic gadget.

Air Force Space Command, however, had breached the innovation frontier, and launched via aircraft and unconventional space launch methods (meaning, converted U.S. Navy ballistic missiles) enough replacement satellite equipment to provide continuous targeting capability. The 'next-generation' GPS satellites used signals unique to new, proprietary targeting software, which

430

had been integrated into all U.S. acquisition and targeting hardware. If the 'new' hardware or software was captured, it could be used only until the next cycle of codes were integrated into the operating system....which happened randomly. This in theory, could prevent the use of United States military equipment against United States troops....in theory, anyway. I was skeptical, because I know that there's always someone out there trying to find the weak link and exploit it to its' fullest.

With the losses of Vandenberg Air Force Base and Cape Canaveral though, there was no way to launch, as of yet anyway, anything close to the capabilities of the National Reconnaissance Office's now-dead KH satellites. The lightweight recon satellites launched from converted B-52's were though, better than nothing. The relatively poor quality images of Sixth Army on the LCD screen in front of me were completely adequate for counting the dead however, or locating the Marine and Army 'front line' units further east of Sixth Army, serving as the picket line for the dead.

Thanksgiving morning,
November Twenty-third
05:00 hours

I'd enjoyed a far better night's sleep than I had in months. The rocking of the train at a slow and steady pace put me right out. My internal clock though knew it was time to get up, and at half-past four I turned on the bedside lamp. We were somewhere in southern Wyoming, if our schedule was true. Still dark outside of course...I cleaned up for the day in the bathroom before donning my uniform and taking the bitterly cold walk from my car to the Command Car.

"Good morning, Colonel. Early day for you," Major Pat Morrissey said.

"Morning, Major. You drew the short straw for the overnight?"

"Best time to brush up on all this hardware. Like the bridge of the starship *Enterprise*."

"Yeah. I can run my own console, with help. These tech's are pretty sharp." Two comm specialists were monitoring the trains internals, as well as information from the National Command Authority. "How's our status?" I asked.

"Better than Dog Six," he said. "Four cars lost power overnight, troops had to relocate to other quarters. Posed a bit of a problem in one car, where on-board water started to freeze. Charlie Six only lost heat in two cars, still had limited power. Hundred men inconvenienced a bit, sir."

"Location?"

"Still headed east…halfway between Casper and Cheyenne, more or less, sir. Not far from Gillette, Colonel," he said as he pointed at the route map on one of the Suite Four displays.

"How're we for arrival in Sterling, Pat?"

"If the weather holds, we'll be an hour late. New storm front moving in though, straight shot, west to east. We might get lucky and arrive before it hits, no way that Dog Six will clear Denver and make it to the terminal point, and given how shaky the tracks are, they may be eight or ten hours delayed. Call it twenty-one hundred hours for Charlie, more or less, sir."

"Disposition of the Marine Expeditionary Unit?"

"Sitting tight, sir. Forty-four hundred men, even, deployed along this line," he said, scrolling over to the Sterling area, showing the green indicators of 'friendlies.'

"Twice what they told us?"

"Eleventh MEU from Pendleton, Thirty-first, used to be over in Okinawa, most recently from Fort Worth Naval Air Station, sir."

"O.K. Do we have an E.T.A. on remaining forces?" I asked as a private entered the room with a contractor-sized thermos of coffee.

"Texas, New Mexico, Arizona, and California will be on site within three hours. Marines will then advance east, Colonel."

"Total men on the ground?"

"Should be in the neighborhood of twenty-thousand, sir."

"I hope someone's thought about that as another target, Major."

"Yes, sir. I've read the intel already. Report's on your desk," Pat said, catching the young man's eye. "And Private, see what you can do about rounding up some breakfast for the Colonel."

"Sir, will do. Colonel, the mess has a pretty limited menu."

"I'm good with anything, thanks, Private."

"Very well, sir," he said as he headed back out the end-door to the small galley car.

"O.K., Pat. Senior staff meeting at oh eight hundred, brigade commanders at oh nine hundred. Do you know if the mobilization plan is all ironed out?" I poured a cup of coffee, and topped off Pat's.

"Yes, sir, down to assignments for the next ten days," he said. "Had a dozen men from the brigades work it over into something workable. That should be on your computer desktop now."

"Thanks. You off duty at oh six-hundred?"

"Yes, sir, and back on at noon."

"Sleep's overrated anyway," I said as I headed toward my desk.

The mobilization plan, as it was termed, would direct how we were to go through recovery efforts for the bodies and equipment of Sixth Army.

We had yet to get an answer on how to deal with the bodies, now frozen together, frozen to the ground, to their equipment, in their tents. Temperature at the location hovered in the teens in the daylight hours, below zero at night. The early reports from the lead Marine units reported scavengers already working over the dead. It appeared that the Army had no idea on how to remove the dead. I found it difficult to believe that in all the planning that must've happened over the decades, that no one could lay hands on body retrieval in a winter war.

It appeared that we would go into the field with the gear on hand, with whatever means of removal we could devise, and work from there. I reviewed the "plan", which was more of troop assignment and retrieval of equipment and munitions than a 'how-to' manual. I perhaps, was asking too much.

I would need to address the entire Brigade on the process, to help mentally prepare them for the gruesome task at hand. Three thousand men would retrieve fifty-three thousand dead from a frozen battlefield, remove their weapons, retrieve their useable major equipment, and transport them to a burial location that wouldn't be determined until "later." The salvaged equipment would then be cleaned, checked, and sent out for re-use by other troops.

I doubted that there was a more difficult task than body retrieval. I fumbled for words to say, and found myself writing down what had to be said.

"Sir, breakfast for you," Private Gullickson announced politely, carrying an insulated container.

"Thanks, Mr. Gullickson. What's the galley serving today?" I asked.

"Grapefruit juice in a box, a breakfast sandwich that's not quite an Egg McMuffin, but close. Reconstituted eggs, but real ham, and something not too far from an English muffin, and some reheated cubed potatoes. Two OK sir?"

"That'll do nicely, thanks," I said. "Is this standard fare for the Brigade, Private?"

"Yes, sir. There a problem?"

"No, I don't want anyone, including officers, to get better or different food than the rest of the troops."

"Not a problem, Colonel. There aren't many options right now, sir."

"Thanks, Private. Dismissed."

"Sir!"

The food was pretty good, all things considered. The galley car I'd read, could prepare a thousand meals per hour on average. I wondered how many a fast-food operation could serve in the old days?

I moved through the available intelligence, now obsolete but not by much, and through the mobilization plan, reviewing the credentials of those who'd prepared it along with their edits to the outline provided by Division. Most of the best changes (my opinion)

436

were put forward by the non-commissioned, mostly sergeants. They were forward-thinking enough to prepare support options for the line units, including hot-bedding the sleeping quarters to allow line units to get warm and some real rest as well as rotating Third Washington into 'line' positions; and expanding the field kitchens from the line units with prepared food from the trains' twelve galley cars.

I was quite impressed.

The eight a.m. staff meeting was crowded, with ten of us crowded around a table designed for eight plus a couple of junior officers stuffed into the back of the room. We were tossed another curve with a cryptic memo from Texas, reassigning 'Prime Power', Company B of the 249th Engineering Battalion to metropolitan Denver, rather than meeting up with us in Sterling. No explanation given.

We reviewed the days' training schedule, crew assignments to repair heating and power units that had died overnight, and the methods to remove our frozen dead from the battlefield.

Our supplies, in addition to humanitarian and support equipment and materials, included sixty thousand body bags, split between both trains. The retrieval process would be outlined by Jeff Willitson to each Brigade during the day. Upon retrieval, we'd be transporting Sixth Army to Fort Carson, just south of Colorado Springs.

Jeff and our senior chaplain, Captain Adam Fillmore, also discussed the mental effects on the soldiers assigned to retrieval. If there was any good news in this aspect of our task, it was that our men could see an end to this duty....it boiled down to simple math. Eighteen dead men and women to be retrieved for every man in Third Washington. Nearly four thousand of the Sixth Army dead were women.

The individual Brigade briefings covered the specifics of clearing the battlefield of potential booby-traps, improvised explosives, and Sixth Army weapons and gear. Boxcars were scheduled to arrive sometime after Dog Six, to load Sixth Army for their final destination. Third Washington brigades would then focus on refitting Sixth Army equipment and have it ready for reuse.

We had no real idea of how long any of that would take.

The day passed slowly, with little in the way of 'work' to do for many of the men. The repairs on the power and heating units could not be completed while we were in transit, due to the nature of the repairs. With each Brigade commander briefing their men with the schedules, the nature of the work coming at us, and the chaplain's briefing as well, most of the men found themselves some sleep while they could. After a walk through a number of the cars and losing at a few hands of poker with the enlisted men, I managed some sleep myself, while the communications techs monitored chatter from all over the country. I knew that we'd probably have a busy night ahead.

We learned by seventeen-hundred hours that the 249th Engineer Battalion had been reassigned to Denver proper, rather than meeting us east, because the entire Denver grid was off-line, and had been for some time. Their ability to set up and generate commercial-grade electricity was obviously needed more in the urban center than in rural areas further east. The S.A. had apparently sabotaged large parts of the infrastructure when they'd evac'd, according to rumor anyway.

We'd rendezvous with the One Seventy Second's combat engineer company at Sterling, which was a surprise to me. I'd expected to have the two brigades, the One Seventieth and the One Seventy-Second on the ground there....but they'd been reassigned further east. I expected their reassignment was in support of a ground offensive. By 'dinner' time, I was ready for another walk, and decided to eat with the men, rather than in my quarters or the Command Car. I was joined by Fourth Brigades' C.O., Jesse Casselis, who'd found me an empty seat in the middle of one of the Spartan transport cars, before rounding up dinner himself. Many of the soldiers didn't quite know what to make of me joining them.

"Evening, sir. Anything we can do for you?" one of the lieutenants asked as I sat down and took a bite of the ham sandwich.

"No, Lieutenant. Just got tired of the scenery in the Command Car and decided to see how the working men travel," I said, seriously. That garnered a quiet laugh or two.

"Any news you can give us, sir?" A private asked.

"Not a helluva lot," I said. "Dog Six is running late. Probably won't get in until tomorrow morning, with the weather. Most of the two brigades we were supposed to meet have already moved out further east," I said before taking another bite. "Marines are already on the ground and further out yet, no contact with the S.A."

"Any new attacks, sir?"

"Atlanta. Hartsfield Airport, fifteen hundred hours. Not too many casualties, and they actually captured a couple of the bastards before they set off the gas. Killed a couple of civilians though."

"F---ing bastards," I heard from behind me.

"Got that right, soldier."

"So," another voice asked, "Food any better back here sir?"

"Same stuff up in command, guys. Seriously. Leaves a little to be desired for Thanksgiving dinner, though. But, this coffee's actually hot. We don't get fed until after you guys do."

"Yeah, but your quarters are better. You don't have to sleep with guys who ate cabbage and beans for dinner last night," someone from a few rows ahead of me said, before adding, "sir." The men had a good laugh over that.

"True enough. And I do have my own bathroom. With decent toilet paper."

"Must be nice to be an officer," somebody said.

"Not really one by choice. But as long as I'm here, I will do what I can to send every sonofabitch in the S.A. straight to Hell," I said. "I assume you have all seen the photographs that the Marines and the Texas Guard sent up to command?" I asked to no one in particular.

"Yes, sir. They put them up on the monitors."

"OK. What you saw there were those soldiers of Sixth Army who weren't killed in the gas attack, tortured to death, some skinned alive. Some burned alive. Many were mutilated. Many were women. They've done the same shit to children....they've done worse," I said, before having some more coffee. "I've seen that happen in

439

other parts of the world, up close and personal. Never thought I'd see Americans do that to Americans," I said as I took the last bite of my sandwich, and then stood up with my coffee mug, looking around the car.

"The work we have to do over the next few days and weeks will not be easy for anybody. Everyone in this brigade will pitch in. We will recover the bodies of our men and women, we will do what we need to do, and then we get on with more work that needs doing. And that, officers and men, is to do what we can to put every S.A. soldier under the sod."

"You call them soldiers? Sir?"

"They think they are. It's OK with me to let a higher power sort that out, once they're off this rock."

Lieutenant Colonel Casselis a few minutes later took me aside. "That was quite a speech, sir."

"No speech, just the way it is," I said. "You think otherwise, Colonel?"

"No, sir. I think it was probably something that needed saying. There's a few men in the Brigade who think this is all some big setup. Pictures faked...or that the S.A. isn't really real. Or that they're not really soldiers. That we're doing this to get them out of the state."

"Boots on the ground long enough will tell them otherwise," I said as I looked at my watch. "Inside of three hours this trail will be on location, split up and parked on sidings, defensive perimeter set. Inside of three hours and twenty minutes, we start unloading and getting to work. If they still believe this is some sort of conspiracy this time tomorrow, send them to me. I'll explain the concept of 'critical thinking.'"

Colonel Casselis grinned at that. "I should just save us all the time and send them now."

"Seeing is believing. No better way for these men to learn."

By nineteen-hundred hours, we'd slowed, then stopped, in a railyard north and a little west of the Downtown area. By looking out of the few windows that weren't blacked out, you'd never know it. I climbed out of the car with a couple of the communications techs for some fresh air. Not a single light on, no signs of life at all. High overcast, no snow. It felt much colder than the twenty degrees indicated.

The train crews and the men in the defensive positions rotated off duty as fuel levels were topped off, I noticed from an adjacent tank car rather than from a fixed fueling point. We had about a hundred miles, as the crow flies, to Sterling. We didn't stay outside long.

"Sanders, give me the latest intel on Sterling if you would," I said as I poured another cup of coffee. I'd need it. It'd be a late night. He pulled up real-time satellite data of the Sterling area.

"Clear over the target...sorry, sir, destination area. Warming fires in these locations—orange is a heat bloom—and not much else. Clusters of farms in the outlying areas east are all dark—no one there. A few out west, but we're ten to thirty miles out of town before you see any sizeable civilian population. Marine air unit is at the airport just east of town, there's a latent heat signature of a couple of their birds," he said. "Our rail sidings parallel Highway One Thirty-Eight, crossing underneath the Highway Six overpass. Interstate Seventy-Six is about two miles east of our jump off point. That big heat bloom over east of town on Highway Sixty-One is what's left of the Sterling Correctional Facility. I understand it's been burning now for the better part of a week, sir."

"Any idea on how many inmates were housed there?"

"Twenty-seven hundred and some spares, last record sir. Level Five, meaning highest level security."

"Any idea where they are?"

"Report from ten minutes ago are that they helped sack Sterling, and then vanished with the S.A. ahead of the massacre, sir," one of the other specialists added.

441

"Shit," I said. "All right," I said. "That green line's the Marine expeditionary force, correct?" The computer system could tag different units RFID transponders with different colors, as assigned by the communications software.

"Yes, sir. Deployed from Highway Sixty three two miles east of Interstate Seventy Six, to four miles north of Highway Six, joining up at Seventy-Six at the bend, here, sir. These transponder signals are units from Texas near the interchange; New Mexico, Arizona south of Sterling; and the Georgia unit north on the west side of the Platte. Marines though, sir, will probably be pulling out and moving east before we arrive."

"Wouldn't expect them to wait for the fight to come to them," I said. "Now pull up the transponders for Sixth, please."

He did so, and the RFID chips of the Sixth Army filled the screen all along Highway One Thirty Eight, straddling the Platte River, up to Interstate Seventy Six, glowing purple.

"Good God," I said. No one else spoke.

"OK, Sanders. How much of Sixth's gear can you track?"

"Assuming the RFID's weren't damaged, most of the major equipment has already been accounted for. Maybe a thousand uniform pieces are in enemy hands, a couple thousand -16's, magazines, some heavy weapons. It's scattered from Goodland, Kansas to North Platte, Nebraska, and east all the way to Grand Island, sir."

"Following the interstates, east."

"Yes, sir."

"What are these icons, west of Sterling?" I asked. Triangular red icons, flashing.

"ICBM silos, sir. Deactivated in the Nineties. Used to base Titan II's out of them."

"Hmmm. Peculiar they're tagged, don't you think?"

"Hadn't thought much about it, sir, but…yeah."

Thanksgiving evening,
November Twenty-third
Sterling, Colorado

We'd made decent time from Denver to Sterling, arriving at our designated siding by twenty-one twenty hours. Twenty minutes before arrival, I'd given the orders to get have the men prepare for arrival. In the case of most of Charlie Six, that'd mean stowing personal gear and preparing for overnight duty outside, some further work on malfunctioning equipment, and going into 'Service Mode.'

Charlie Six would have a full complement of overnight guests for meals, showers, laundry, and much needed rest. The Texas guard had been engaged in fighting the S.A. since the 'formal' start of the Second Civil War on October twenty-fourth. Regular Army units from New Mexico and Arizona had been in the field for just over two weeks; the newcomers to the western fight were the Georgia 'Dogs, who'd just come west from near Vicksburg, Mississippi. They'd stuffed the S.A. forces north from Baton Rouge north through Natchez to Vicksburg, before heading east to Jackson. Units from Mexico had then freed them up to reinforce the Western front against the S.A. I imagined that the cold weather was quite a shock to their systems....

Our men would deploy, set up temporary shelters outside, and rotate through the night with the other units, maintaining security throughout the night. At first light, the real work would begin.

The galley crews and on-board support crews would also rotate out, serving meals, providing medical care and performing any equipment maintenance that was needed before going off-shift and getting some rest themselves. Most of Charlie Six would start the day with four or less hours of sleep, if they were lucky. As expected, the Marine Expeditionary Unit had moved out.

Within an hour of arrival, temporary shelters were set up and Third Washington was moving into the field. Charlie Six was parked on a siding not far from Northeastern Junior College, or what was left of it. I'd read sketchy reports on what we'd find in Sterling, but we'd wait until daylight to size things up. I was getting ready for our first operations meeting, and camped out in the conference room car with a live link to my command-car computer.

"Excuse me, Colonel. Brigadier General Garcia is here," one of the lieutenants said. General Garcia was the commanding officer of the Texas National Guard, and had been in the field since the start of the War.

"Thanks, Lieutenant. Please show the General in," I said. A moment later, a parka-clad form appeared in the doorway. I'd only read the name...there was no dossier provided.

"Colonel Drummond, General Angela Garcia. Pleased to meet you," General Garcia said as I saluted and then shook her hand...of course not knowing what protocol was required...She looked like she was about fifty, about five foot six, with piercing brown eyes and similar demeanor.

"General, it's a pleasure. I wasn't aware that Texas had a brigadier in the field until a few minutes ago."

"Or a woman, no doubt."

"That is a fact, ma'am. How're your troops holding up?" I asked as she sat down.

"You cannot train for what this is, Colonel. Sit-rep on Third Washington, please," she said, all business. Her outer shell and winter pants were as dirty and stained as I'd expect to see from a line soldier.

"Charlie Six will be fully deployed in about an hour. Temporary shelters in twelve locations; Second Brigade is reviewing clearing operations with the Engineering Company of the One Seventy-second. The balance of Charlie Six, with the exception of maintenance and galley crews will be relieving the Texas Guard units by twenty-three hundred. Dog Six should arrive by twenty-two hundred, follow a similar deployment just south, then relieve the New Mexico and Arizona units overnight, Georgia Bulldogs are in good shape overall and will need minimal rehab. We were expecting a pretty good storm to slow Dog Six down…that looks like it's passing to the south, ma'am," I said as a corporal brought in a pot of coffee and a second, containing hot chocolate.

"What's your total Brigade strength, Colonel?" she said as she looked, and chose hot chocolate. I couldn't quite tell if the expression on her face was surprise, disbelief, or something else entirely.

"Twenty-nine fifty-five, ma'am."

"How long active? Third Washington, that is."

"The unit as deployed, about three days, General. The unit has a substantial amount of men with combat experience in multiple theaters, however."

"Shit. That is *not* what I wanted to hear," she said with irritation. I could tell where this was going. "How long have *you* been in the Army, Colonel Drummond?"

"Since Monday, ma'am. Prior to that time I was the county administrator for Spokane County, Washington."

"No military experience," she said, nearly spitting the words. *"What the Hell are you even doing here?"*

Getting a little hot under the collar, I replied. "With all due respect, General, a year ago I was a private sector consultant. Last January, we were caught up in the middle of the Domino, and then all but ignored by the rest of the nation as what passed for civilized society decided to take a breather. Over the past eleven months, we've put Spokane back together, after a fashion. During that time, we've removed a local government gone rogue; fought a significant number of gang problems…many of which were probably created by the S.A.; negotiated trade agreements; fed and watered ourselves, generated our own power; supported our military units as best we can. I serve as requested by Governor David Hall. You have a problem with my experience or leadership, General," I said with an increasingly raised voice, "and you can…."

447

"Enough, Colonel," she said, waving her hand to stop me from finishing my rant. She sat back her chair and considered my statement. "My men and women have been in the field for a month. On the run, hit and dodge. Six hundred dead, twenty-six hundred wounded, walking or otherwise. No real shelter. MRE's for every meal, except what we could scrounge. Gear breaking down daily. Playing by rules when the other team has none. I don't have time for amateurs."

"General, how many people have you personally killed in the last eleven months?" I asked.

She didn't quite know what to say. "None, Colonel."

"General, I can give you a list of who and how many I've killed, and by and large, what they looked like as they died by my hand. Some were kids, high school age. Some were thieves, some were out-and-out murderers. Some in my own neighborhood, some on my own land. Some we went hunting for. That'll cover the past eleven months. I can go back to a time when I was fresh out of college and give you a similar list for some unpleasantness that I had in the Sudan. I will never forget what any of them looked like as they died, whether they were in uniform or not. Just because I haven't been in the armed forces of the United States of America doesn't mean I don't know how to kill people or help our forces kill them."

She paused for a full minute before answering me. "Colonel, I owe you an apology....there are days that I turn into a chrome-plated class 'A' bitch."

"As long as you have a good reason, General, and you do, no apology necessary," I said. "How good has your intel in the field been?"

"When it works, it's decent. It works though, about thirty percent of the time. Usually, the thirty percent of the time we really don't need it."

"Hardware problem, General?"

"Probably not. Probably active jamming."

"We haven't seen any issues with the information coming in…yet."

"I saw the command unit. Our stuff doesn't hold a candle to that. If they made it portable, that'd be something, but if we lost one of the data packs, they'd have the keys to the city," she said. She was losing the battle with fatigue. I noticed for the first time how tired and worn she looked.

"General, how long has it been since you've had a decent meal and sleep?"

"Too long," she said.

"Your troops are being taken care of with hot food, showers, clean uniforms. Take advantage of that, General. My quarters are at your disposal."

"Thanks. And you have real food. I can't remember the last time I had hot chocolate."

"My car's next door, far end. Desk drawer, left side bottom, bottle of bourbon, and one of Scotch. Feel free to partake, ma'am."

"I don't drink. Against my faith."

"Probably smarter long term. Let me grab a few things and it's all yours. I'll have some dinner sent over. No turkey and dressing unfortunately. Stand down for awhile, General."

"Turkey?" she asked.

"It's Thanksgiving Day, General." I said.

She sat there for a moment before realizing she hadn't said anything. "Sorry. That….honestly that's so foreign to me and so far removed from where we've been that it never would have occurred to me."

"I've had weeks like that myself, ma'am. Never a full month though."

I escorted General Garcia and her second-in-command through the Command Car, and had one of the duty specialists walk through the many layers of information immediately available to Third Washington, and by extension, anyone we were able to communicate with via secure frequency. I could tell, even through the fatigue, that they saw this level of information as a game-changer in our favor. While she was focusing on the information at hand, I arranged to have fresh clothing delivered to my car for the General. The sergeant at hand wouldn't be held accountable if the sizes were wrong, I assured him.

Once we were done with the six-bit tour, I grabbed my parka and we headed out of the car, down the exit stairs to the snowy ground, and over to my car.

"This is quite a production, Colonel," she said, looking at my troops prepare for the arrival of Dog Six, along with the steady stream of Texans heading into the galley cars, showers, and berthing units. "Again, my apologies for tearing you a new one."

"General, I've been known to go off on occasion, especially after too many days without sleep. I discovered there's actually a term for it, other than 'battle fatigue.' 'First Responder Fatigue,' in the civilian world," I said as I opened the door to my quarters and stepped in.

"Same effect in the end….impaired judgment and decision-making."

"Sure, that and occasional irritability descending into outright bitchiness, General," I said with a little grin. She chuckled a little at herself, which I think she needed.

"Nice quarters, Colonel," she said, looking around. "Your family?" she asked as she saw the photograph of the Drummonds, Bauers and Martins, from last New Years Eve on what passed for my desk.

"Yes, and some friends. My wife and kids on the right, me with significantly more hair; my brother in law and his family in the center, and our friends the Martin's on the right. For the past year, we've been rebuilding," I said, and then explained briefly how our year started, as I packed up a few things for the night.

"You've had quite a year, Colonel," she said. "Without getting too personal, did you pick up that scar in the quake?" she asked, referring to my quite noticeable 'skull zipper,' as Carl had coined it.

"No, I picked up that along with some broken ribs in an accident back in August. Almost healed up," I said as one of the galley crew delivered dinner in an olive-drab insulated container.

"Private, just put that over on the table, thank you," I said.

"Certainly sir. I've also delivered your dinner to your office in Command," he said, looking nervously between General Garcia and I. "Dinner this evening is ham, mashed potatoes, green beans, and apple sauce, and tea. Anything else, sirs?"

"No, thank you, Private," I said. "That sounds fine."

"Ma'am, sir," he said as he made a hasty exit, obviously uncomfortable with our ranks.

"Jeez, he's all of what, eighteen?" I said.

"If that. He doesn't look old enough to serve."

"Might not be by old regulations. We have a fair number of orphans without records who've enlisted. He might be one of them."

"This smells great," she said, "But I think I'll get cleaned up first."

"We can get your gear cleaned up overnight. That uniform bag on the bed should contain a change of clothing, although we don't have anything in the way of clothing for female soldiers, General," I said.

"Damned shame, Colonel. But no one's getting me off the line, or any of our other women."

"I can appreciate that, but after what we saw with Sixth Army, Washington has decided otherwise."

"So has Austin, but I told them to shove it."

I laughed out loud. "I bet you did just that. General, have a restful evening. There's an iPod in that bedside table...should be charged up, and some headphones. Many different genre's if you are so inclined. And a portable DVD player and a wallet full of movies, forgot about that. Goodnight, ma'am."

"Thank you, Colonel Drummond. Good night."

Dog Six was clearly the cursed train of our two. Four more heating failures between Cheyenne and Denver and two additional from Denver to Sterling. Communications problems between the cars were also an issue, including a complete failure between both Command Cars in that train and both defensive cars. Charlie and Dog Six crews would spend most of the night trying to figure out what was wrong.

Our conference room car had been taken over for the night by three rows of Texas Guardsmen, now showered and fed. I caught a couple of hours of sleep in the Command Car, with the lights dimmed.

Black Friday,
November Twenty-Fourth

I'd woken without any cause at about one-thirty a.m., and gathered my winter weather gear for an impromptu early morning inspection. Sergeant Major Chet Travis was heading up the midnight to oh-four-hundred shift, giving the officers some much needed sleep before things got moving in the morning. I'd learned that Travis was one of those blessed individuals who could function on sleep gained a few hours at a time. I was not so blessed.

"Sar-Major," I said, entering the main part of the communications bay of the Command Car. "Anything newsworthy?"

452

"If anything, sir, it's been too quiet," he said. "There has been absolutely no change since twenty-two hundred. No enemy troop movements, no contact on perimeters anywhere across a five hundred mile front. Austin's pretty puzzled by this too," he said, referring to the big brains calling the shots in Texas. The Department of Defense had to be somewhere, I supposed. Texas was as good a place as any.

"Communications intercepts?"

"Literally, nothing, sir, since twenty-three hundred." one of the communications techs said.

"What's our baseline case? Is this typical or not?"

"Atypical, sir, but we are talking about the S.A. They're not exactly conventional. There's always some chatter of some kind. The S.A. has radio silence in place, and it is highly disciplined at that."

"Tracking of Sixth Army's equipment shows no movement, correct?"

"Correct, sir," said another tech in one of the other suites.

"Riddle me this then," I said. "Do we have the capability to determine if the S.A. has moved, is moving, covertly, except with the RFID chips in Sixth Armies' gear?"

"Not at this range sir, and the satellites are tasked elsewhere until oh-eight hundred local. They retasked about twenty-three forty-five."

"Can we determine if there has been incidental movement in the RFID's, I mean, what is our tolerance of measurement?"

"With the sensors available via satellite, we can tell within a half a meter, sir. The last airborne sensing mission was called off. The S.A. sent up a blizzard of SAM's at them. Becoming standard tactics, I'm afraid." I'd read a report that said that a single aircraft was targeted by no less than forty shoulder-fired surface to air missiles....French and Russian in origin...and a dozen long-range SAM's from towed launch trailers. The best stealth technology available couldn't beat sheer numbers. Math always wins.

"When did the gear last show movement?" Travis asked.

"I'll….I'll pull that up Sergeant Major."

"You think they're doing an end-run, sir?" Travis asked.

"Maybe. It's not like I'm a tactician, Sergeant," I said. "But if it were me, trying to get out of a tough spot, or if I'd want to go on the offensive, now'd be the time to do it."

"That'd imply that they know about the RFID chips and our tracking schedules for the satellites."

"Yep. Which means we have a spy or twenty inside of the command structure, or they're damned smart, or just lucky," I said.

"Not really one for luck, sir," Sergeant Travis said.

"Yeah, me either."

"Sir, the last trace that we have of United States Army equipment in motion begins at twenty-one thirty-six hours. Time lapse imagery from satellite is on monitor two."

The loop passed through twice with us looking at the images. "Look at that," I said. "Normal motion, see that? Then from these three points, motion ceases in a radial pattern. It's viral. They know. Has this been uplinked to Austin?"

"Yes, sir, data went up real-time as it was being tracked and monitored by Third and uplinked to Austin and from Austin to Space Command. No response though."

"Get them on the horn for me. Now."

"Yes, sir."

"Sarge, how long for the S.A. to get here?" I asked as the Private made his way through the security protocols to get through to Command.

"In force, maybe six hours, weather and transport permitting obviously, Colonel. You don't think…"

"No, I don't. But there is always the 'what if.' And if we don't have a satellite retasked to tell us otherwise, we might be in for a surprise come dawn. Am I wrong in thinking that?"

"No, sir. Frankly I should have thought of this myself."

"Sir, Major Stephanie Everett will be with you in a moment. Your headset, sir," the tech said as he handed me the wireless headset.

"This is Major Everett. Colonel Drummond, are you on line?"

"I am. Major, I believe we have a situation brewing," I said, and reviewed the information, sending her the time-lapse view of the S.A's movement of the Sixth Army equipment, and it's sudden stop.

"Colonel," she replied with a concerned tone, "We've seen no such data come through to Command. Our data continue to show movement."

"Then I believe, Major, you have someone who's parsing your communications links. According to my communications staff, the satellite providing standard imagery of the S.A. location was retasked at twenty-three forty-five per our direct-linked images. Are you certain you are getting current information, Major? This smells damned funny."

"One moment, sir," the voice in my ear said. Everyone in the communications suite was listening in. "Our satellite link shows current time."

"OK, it shows current time," I said. "Is it current date?"

Silence on the other end of the transmission. "No way to verify that, Colonel. That's not on the screen. I need to wake up some people."

"Do that, Major. Because on my end, I have a time AND a date," I said, then hearing the link go into a light static.

"Sir, any orders?" Sergeant Major Travis asked.

"Not quite yet, Sergeant. Maybe soon though. Find me all five battalion duty-officers. Don't wake up the commanders yet. Time will tell if we need to."

"Done, sir. Give me ten minutes," Travis said as he hit the door. "Some of them are scattered to Hell and gone."

"OK, gentlemen," I said to the communications staff. Find us some relevant intel, and get it moving right now."

"Sir, we can probably swing an Air Force recon mission if needed," Specialist Ayers said.

"Sure, if we want to kill a perfectly good pilot and aircraft," I said. "Three in six days shot down. Let's see what Texas has to say first, Ayers."

"Yes, sir."

Each of the communications suites was fired up and whatever information available from the past eight hours was now on-line on-demand, and orders were put in for re-tasking of any available satellite to cover the central United States. The soonest a bird would be in range would be oh four-hundred. Ten more minutes passed before a voice came back on line, just as Sergeant Travis and the five battalion officers came into the communications suite. Things were now pretty crowded.

"Colonel Drummond? This is General Yancey. We have confirmed your data is correct."

"Find out who's responsible for keeping you in the dark, sir?"

"Yes, Colonel, and we're now going hunting for them. More than one. They went off-shift at midnight."

"Sir, this leak appears to have given the S.A. the heads up on the RFID tracking."

"At the very least, Colonel. In fifteen minutes we'll have data on line showing the S.A. position at present."

"We were under the impression that we weren't going to be able to get that for a couple hours, sir."

"These are unconventional times, Colonel."

"They are at that, sir."

"Be back in a few. Go get yourself some coffee, Colonel."

"Way ahead of you, sir," I said as one of the battalion duty officers, a Captain Brooks, handed me a cup.

"Gentlemen, we may have a problem," I said to the gathering before me. "Get yourselves some coffee."

Friday,
November Twenty-fourth
0250 Hours

"They're in retreat, Colonel. S.A. troops are a hundred miles east of their last known and moving east," the General said.

"Do you have a high degree of confidence in this, General?"

"As good as it gets, Colonel Drummond. It does not appear that your position is being threatened."

"Thank you, sir. Catch your spies yet, General?" I asked.

"Affirmative. Two survivors, six dead."

"I'm sure the survivors are being treated with all appropriate care."

"Indeed they are. Colonel, good luck in your mission. We lost a lot of good soldiers up there."

"Yes, sir. Tough few days ahead."

"Take good care of our men, Colonel. Yancey out," he said, and the transmission ended.

"All right, battalion officers. Sounds like we can lower our adrenaline a little. We'll keep you in the loop if anything changes. Get your field communications gear on, and pass the word for command-level staff to be wearing theirs while on duty—should've done that this time. Oh-five hundred and the Brigade's up and moving for a long-ass day. Let's be ready for it. Dismissed."

The five 'night-shift' officers filed out and back to their respective units, scattered along two miles of railroad frontage, three of them providing additional supervision to Dog Six and their continued setup and staging.

I grabbed another cup of coffee and decided to continue my original plan, to go for a walk and check out our Brigade. I needed some fresh air.

Outside, I went for a walk through the staging area for Dog Six's motor pool, Humvees and trucks unloaded and parked and waiting for the day. Several guards noticed me and nodded my way as I passed through the area. Further south, one of Dog Six's machine shop cars was open for business with stacks of the Texas Guard's rifles under the watchful eye of two guards. There were thousands of weapons. The Texas Guard had almost five thousand men and women in the field. I decided to visit the local gunsmiths in uniform and see how things were going.

"Good morning, gents. How's business?" I asked, entering the nearly warm machine shop.

"Morning, sir, is still a matter of opinion," said a first sergeant from one of the Georgia units, barely looking up, but finally noticing my insignia. "Sorry, Colonel. Thought you were..."

"No problem, first sergeant," I said, noticing the workbenches and nodding at the other men working on the disassembly, cleaning, refit, and reassembly lines. They were working on a series of M249 SAW's, the machine gun of choice since the old Browning Automatic Rifle was retired decades ago. I looked over some of the discarded parts, tossed unceremoniously in a series of plastic bins. "This typical wear? These are a mess."

"No small wonder, sir. This is what wear looked like in the 'stan after a few months. If we had enough new 249's to issue to those Tex boys, we'd scrap the whole lot. Lotta field changes messed these up but good. Barrels switched, weapons pieced together. A bunch of these've also seen max rates of fire for too long. A thousand rounds a minute. Overheated them. Can't dissipate that kind of heat."

"Are the -16's in this bad of shape?"

"Looked over a couple dozen so far, and some of the M4's. We've got our work cut out for us, no doubt about it. Probably ten percent unusable as-is. We can fix the rest and get them back to spec. Replace the others with new-issue. Not going to mix up the unit with old style -16's and the new Californias, Colonel….although our Bulldogs could surely make use those C models. Not enough to go around though."

"I'm sure they're coming your way, sergeant. I'll get out of your hair. Thanks, all," I said as I headed for the door, receiving a *'sir!'* in unison.

Further south, Dog Six's perimeter guard units were quietly watching south and east, over the darkened terrain where the last of Sixth Army lay. I turned around and headed back to the Command Car. I knew that I'd need some rest for our first day in the field.

At oh five-thirty, the alarm on my watch roused me from an unpleasant dream, more so than my current reality. I pulled out my soft earplugs and emerged from the make-shift darkened cubicle into the fully staffed communications car, and smelled burning coffee.

"Somebody trying to convert coffee to carbon?"

"Sorry, sir. Been a little busy."

"Reason for not waking me?"

"Yes, Colonel. You needed some sleep," said my deputy C.O., Jim Schaefer. "My orders."

"You're almost as bad as my wife."

"Wait a few days. This duty schedule will catch up with you— you'll see it, sir."

"You're probably right, Jim. Status overnight?" I said as I turned off the coffeemaker, noting the many different types of information on each communication suite screen.

"S.A.'s pulling back east, as well as moving major forces back up the Mississippi Valley."

"Hmm. How far east of us?"

"Leading edge is U.S. Eighty-Three, damned near a straight line through Nebraska and Kansas, but they're keeping well clear of the Oklahoma line. Seems like they're consolidating along an evac route on Interstate Seventy."

"Reason?" I asked.

"Air Force socked 'em with a few high yield cruise missiles up in North Platte, seemed to take out command and control for this northern group. They're running like hot butter on a skillet, sir," Specialist Ayers said.

"Seems a little dramatic for a little punch in the nose," I said. "How's their communications? They still maintaining silence?"

"Not as of an hour ago, sir. They were yelling 'incoming' as the second and third wave dropped on their ears."

"Got a BDA yet?" I said, referring to a battle damage assessment, which drew some looks. I apparently wasn't supposed know that kind of thing.

"Uh, yes, sir, Colonel. We're not privy to the ordnance package that the -52 was using, but radar uplinks showed twenty cruise missiles in flight. Single delivery aircraft did that. I'll pull up the satellite images and put them on Suite Four. The rest of the suites are monitoring their retreats and trying to assess their numbers and capabilities."

"Monitor two shows the greatest concentration of KIA's. The wider views show vehicle and equipment kills across a pretty wide area," Schaefer said. "Fair percentage of their personnel transports are scrap."

"Hmm." Jim said, looking at the carnage on the monitor, a ghostly grayscale image. "You sure cruise missiles did this?" Schaefer asked.

"Yes, sir."

"This kind of damage reminds me of cluster bomb impacts," he said. "There's an odd 'shotgun' look of the impact damage, and the debris scatter. Air Force must have something new."

"Could've been worse. Could've been a hyperbaric weapon," I said.

"Civilians still present in the area, sir. Probably drove the weapons package."

"The S.A. left them alive?" I asked.

"Yes, sir, although a significant number evac'd before the S.A. pulled in. They're now filtering back into North Platte. Vehicle signatures, trailers, horses. Following pretty much every road into the area…from the north, that is."

"What's Austin saying about moving that way?"

"Airborne units will deploy up there first, probably on the ground within the next couple of hours. They're deploying from Helena and Cheyenne. Troop estimates, five thousand men."

That surprised me. 'Fair number of men,' I thought. "Enemy headcount?"

"To the nearest thousand, Colonel, sixty-one five."

"O.K." I said, while thinking, 'Damn that's a lot of enemy.' "Third Washington ready for the day?"

"Reveille at oh-five hundred. Mess is running full steam with our visitors and light support for Third—our guys are mostly on MRE's today. Elements of each Battalion will rotate into and out of the field for the day, with obvious support personnel remaining with the trains. First and Fifth Battalions will be first in the field, followed by Third and Fourth. Second will be handling loading of the remains collected by the field crews. Each battalion will have combat engineers ahead of them to make sure there aren't any surprises, sir. All per the schedule."

"How're the other units? They getting everything they need?"

"Could always use more room, sir. About half of the Texas unit spent the night in temp shelters outside, their choice. Got the heaters running in there, and they're passable. Third Cardinals are mostly down in Dog Six. New Mexico's going to rotate in when Texas vacates."

"Our guys keeping up with the load?"

"Laundry guys aren't, sir. Mess hall's been running non-stop, but the lines are pretty short."

"How're the guys in the armory doing? They had one helluva backlog last night."

"Not bad. Nowhere near close to being done though. Those Georgia boys are pretty damned good, sir."

"How long until re-supply is needed?"

"Three days at this rate. We've already told Cheyenne to step on it, sir." Our re-supply train was already on the siding in Cheyenne, packed with non-perishable food, ammunition, uniforms, medical gear, and fuel. We were expecting to need a re-supply every two weeks....we weren't planning on supplying this level of fighting men, or the levels of depletion we were faced with.

"All right. Battalion commanders can handle the morning deploy. Let's get senior staff assembled as we can for a look ahead at oh seven hundred."

"Yes, sir. Not a problem," Schaefer said.

"Ayers, what's the civilian chatter today?"

"Sir?" he asked, a little surprised.

"Mister Ayers, don't tell me you haven't been keeping an ear and eye on the civilian side," I said with a little smile.

"Yes, sir. Didn't think it would matter all that much to be honest," he said. "Specialist Briggs has most of that, sir."

"Briggs. Give me the skinny."

"Some shortwave, bunch of traffic across the all amateur civilian bands, mostly family members looking for each other from behind the lines, no civilian AM or FM radio broadcasts within three hundred miles. I got the impression that the S.A. had been hunting down people that were broadcasting…what I picked up were short bursts of talk, some primitive codes, some foreign languages, but the S.A. didn't pursue them this time, it seemed. Outside the zone, more chatter on the S.A. attacks around the country. Nothing we don't already know, sir."

"Any word on our arrival?" I asked.

"No sir. I doubt anyone in the local area has broadcast anything."

"Very well. Thanks, Briggs. Now who's handling weather?"

"That's me sir, Private David Kittrick," the young man said. I looked at him in some surprise. He looked as if he'd been playing video games, rather than a multi-million dollar communications suite.

"Private, good to meet you. What's incoming?" I asked as he pulled up the weather imagery for North America.

"Weather front…the bulk of it, sir, is passing south and west of us. We'll get arctic air within eight hours, holding for at least thirty six hours. We'll probably get some snow, but from the east, not the southwest. We'll be in single digits every night, maybe up to the high teens if we're lucky. Second front is heading east and north of us, we're between systems, sandwiched. That eastern system is the one that could give us some snow."

"How about further east? What's coming in on the S.A.?"

"That second system, just crossing into North Dakota, will hit them in the next twelve hours. The cold of that system, when it hits this warm front coming up from the south, could really bury them, sir."

"Bottles them in, with luck."

"Yes, sir."

"Thanks. Back at it," I said. "I'll head down to the mess for breakfast, and back here before oh seven hundred. Jim, where are we meeting? Our conference car is now a dorm, right?"

"We'll be in one of the big tents, Colonel. Setting it up as we speak."

"You are nothing if not a mind reader, Colonel Schaefer."

"Just forward thinking, sir."

"Good. Figure out a way to bottle that and you'll be a millionaire."

Outside, the eastern sky was growing lighter, with sunrise in an hour or so. I headed 'down' the train to the southwest toward the mess car, passing many men along the way, and a few women, who were the targets of some attention. I met General Garcia on the way, she'd already taken breakfast.

"Good morning, General. Did you get some rest?"

"Yes, and thank you, Colonel. Thank you for the hospitality. I'll be out of your quarters shortly."

"Not a problem, General. I'm heading down to the mess for a bite. Lieutenant Colonel Schaefer can give you a full update on the S.A.'s current position."

"Coming at us or running away?"

"The latter. Air Force whacked them up in North Platte not quite two hours ago. They're running hard, east."

"Back to the chase."

"Yes, ma'am. Looks like."

"Thanks, Colonel. I'll see you after breakfast," she said as we exchanged salutes in the near-dark. "I'll be over in Lone Star command, that a'way," she said, directing me toward a tent south of our Command Car.

"Ma'am."

I took my place in line, heading into one of the mess cars, again receiving some looks from the men on my presence in the chow line.

"We must be screwed if the officers are eating this stuff," I heard from behind me.

"To the contrary, soldier. I figure if we eat this stuff, nothing's gonna kill us. It's done wonders for y'all," I said, getting some laughs. The breakfast was actually pretty good, with scrambled eggs, bacon, bread and canned fruit. As I ate, I chatted with several of the Guardsmen from Texas, New Mexico, and Arizona. Only about thirty percent of them were Guardsmen a year ago. All had lost family and friends in the flu and in the invasion from Mexico. Virtually all had been in battle in both Mexico and against the S.A.

Our senior staff meeting was brief, all of twenty minutes. My staff got the point that I liked short meetings, and we all had a mountain of work to do. With our crowded quarters, we had to rotate staff through, releasing some to get back to work a little ahead of the others. The big surprise was coming from the west, not the east. Civilians by the hundreds were coming east, according to intel provided by the Colorado National Guard. The CNG was trying to pick up the pieces after the occupation of the heart of the state, first by what seemed to be the legitimate United States government, then, what became the S.A.

The Colorado Guard, before the War, had maintained a company-strength unit in Sterling, part of the One Hundred Forty-Seventh Brigade Support Battalion. The battalion was based in Boulder, and from what we were able to glean from the advance units, the local installation was largely intact. A recon team would assess the condition of the facilities and any other structures that might be used to house the current military needs. We expected to meet with someone from the Joint Force Headquarters, as they advanced east from their base in Centennial. One of the many intelligence briefs that I'd read recapped the re-assignment of many of the Colorado units to the Mexican War, and then quiet reassignment and evacuation out of the state as the intentions of the 'Federal' government became clear to the military leadership. There was little left for the S.A. to gather from the military as far as supplies and equipment went…at least as far as the intel knew.

At oh seven-thirty, anyone not working on an essential function was ordered to stand at the perimeter of the Sixth Army battlefield, as all the chaplains led a brief prayer service. Along with my senior staff and five battalion commanders, I stood at attention as the twenty-seven star Guidon flag was raised, then lowered to half-staff, on what was left of a utility pole, stripped of wire. From somewhere east of us, we heard *Amazing Grace,* on bagpipes. Our senior chaplain, Captain Adam Fillmore, had organized this, along with men from each brigade and from the other state units.

I dismissed the senior staff to their duties, quickly changed into 'work' wear in my quarters, and headed over to General Garcia's command tent.

"Ten-*hut!*" a lieutenant said as I entered. I'd never get used to that.

"As you were," I said. "General Garcia available?"

"One moment, sir," the lieutenant said.

It was more than a moment, but I was OK with that. The Lone Star command staff was pretty busy. It was good to see a well-organized, smooth running operation. That perception always hid the complete chaos lurking just under the surface. I noticed that everyone in the command tent had an M-16 or M-4 within arms' reach.

"Colonel, you may come in now," the lieutenant said. She was a stocky young woman, maybe twenty-three or so. I could tell by the look in her eyes that she'd be tough in a fight.

"Thank you, Lieutenant," I said as I entered the second bay of the tent.

"Colonel, thanks for coming by. I'm going to cut to the chase if you don't mind. I want to get my unit reprovisioned and back in the fight. Honest estimate. How long until your crews are done with our gear?"

"Just got out of our staff meeting, General. Weapons refit will be done by twelve-hundred hours. Your crews are working as hard as ours are, across the board. Provisioning for the individual soldiers is taking probably more time than it should. We'll be done with Lone Star by fourteen-hundred. Late in the day to be making an advance, my opinion, especially with weather moving in."

"Don't really care about the weather, Colonel. I do care about picking up some mileage for our Texans, and getting us up to North Platte. Which is why I need a couple of your locomotives....and slug of those boxcars coming in."

This surprised me, it was probably obvious. "We had intended those to be used for transporting the Sixth, ma'am," I said. The transport trains would be around a hundred cars apiece. In theory, we could load the remains of the Sixth Army in two trainloads...in theory.

"Understood. But I know that you have more cars than you're going to need before your resupply unit gets here, and I've already arranged to have more cars sent up ahead of the supply train from Denver. I don't believe this will change your operational plan or schedule at all. Two trips up to North Platte and back and the personnel are done. A hundred and forty miles."

I thought for a moment. "OK, General, then we'll spin up the schedule. Some of the refit work can be done in transit; we can make up some time on the provisioning side. The crews have been re-supplying each soldier's packs assembly-line style....we can just toss the bulk supplies in and have your troops do it themselves. Probably pick up a couple hours."

"No argument. I appreciate that, Colonel Drummond."

"I'm beyond arguing. The sooner the last S.A. sonofabitch is under the sod, the sooner we can all go home."

"Agreed. Thanks for your cooperation, Colonel."

"No problem, General," I said as I stood to leave.

"And Colonel? Thanks for the use of the iPod. It's been a long time since I had a chance to listen to a little Stevie Ray Vaughn."

"Pride of Texas, that one," I said. "Magic with a Stratocaster."

Friday,
November Twenty-fourth
0840 Hours

I'd had a couple of options on my mornings' chores. I could sit in the Command Car, and absorb information as it came in; I could head out into Sterling just behind the advance units from Third Washington, who were conducting an inventory and assessment of the town; or I could help with the basic mission for us in Sterling, retrieval of Sixth Army.

I chose the last.

The portion of the battlefield we'd first clear reached from Factory Street south to County Road Twenty Six, an open field that had been some of the heaviest concentration of Sixth Army's central line. South of Twenty Six, the land had been subdivided into smaller parcels with small hobby farm sized lots. The Sixth had some units scattered in that area as well, mostly west along the South Platte River.

We'd work from the wreckage of the sugar beet mill to the south--the mill had been burned, quite recently. A squad from the Second Battalion stood patiently, waiting for the Combat Engineers to clear the area for our team to start retrieval. I hadn't asked to join a squad, I looked over the ten squads tasked with the mornings' efforts and picked one.

"Sir, something I can do for you?" A First Sergeant named Jones asked me.

"Come to lend you a hand, First Sergeant," I said, pulling on medical-grade gloves before putting my outer gloves back on. "Everyone in the Brigade will be doing this. Figure I'd lead by example."

"Very good, Colonel. Engineers should be ready for us in about ten minutes. You might want to look this over, though, sir," he said, pointing to a concentration of his squad, looking at something on the ground.

"What is it?" I asked as we walked over, the men making room for us.

"One of the canisters that released the gas. The Engineers figured that it's a converted propane tank—big bastard, too. Remote control and release valve is there on the side, Colonel."

"How many have they found so far?"

"So far, one every two hundred yards or so. That translates into a shitload of them, sir. Engineers are checking for any that didn't go off, in addition to booby traps and IED's that the S.A. might've left us. No reports of any of that. One undetonated device, a couple miles north—that's where the prisoners were captured, Colonel."

"Pretty impressive use of tactics and unconventional weapons. I hope we have the chance to pay them back in kind."

"I think everyone's of the same mind, Colonel."

Within a few more minutes, we were given the all clear to begin retrieval operations in an area a couple hundred yards deep.

Sixth Army had been hit in the early morning hours, probably around three in the morning, from the reports I'd read. Those that were roused by the sound of the venting nerve gas had a chance to get outside of their tents and shelters, in time to have the gas hit them and drop them where they stood. Those that were not in earshot were killed where they slept, as the colorless gas saturated the atmosphere.

Initial analysis showed that the weapons were triggered not quite simultaneously, working from west-to-east, with a light prevailing wind. This directed the majority of the gas concentration from the release points—mostly along U.S. Highway Six—toward the South Platte. Sixth Army was between the highway and the river, where the brush and terrain prevented any escape. A well-planned attack, calculated to kill everyone.

The first victims we found were outside of their tents, not dressed for the cold weather, obviously warned that something was going on. I'd never seen a frozen body before, translucent skin, hands gripping an M-16 and a belt of spare mags. All ranks. All races. Men and women, dead on the frozen field.

We worked quietly, a few men working together, to identify each soldier, remove him from the frozen ground and thin snow cover or frozen tent or sleeping bag, and other men retrieving personal effects. The dead were placed in body bags, with much effort and using means that would offend an 'average' person, further indignities inflicted upon the dead. The final rotation of the process included weapons and ammunition removal. Further clearing would remove tents and other equipment, destined to be reused by soldiers who wouldn't know the history of the equipment in their hands or over their heads.

Three hours of this work left the squad drained emotionally and physically. We were all ready for a break when our relief team showed. The morning field squads would rotate through cleanup, then the mess cars, and then on to other work apart from body removal. I had enough 'command' issues to deal with to occupy my time, if not relieve my mind from the mornings' work.

I cleaned up, took lunch in the Command Car, as my eyes moved over the words and images on the screens in front of me. By thirteen hundred, it was time to get moving again. Outside of the Command Car, a steady stream of dead received last rites from the chaplains gathered from various units. The first Lone Star soldiers were loading on boxcars, getting ready for departure.

"Colonel, we're going to have visitors," Captain Shand told me as I put my parka back on, getting ready for my next task.

"What've we got, Captain?"

"About a thousand civilians, moving up from Denver and coming south out of the hinterlands, sir. About an hour and we'll start seeing the first of them."

"I hope they're bringing their own supplies."

"Yeah, I was thinking that myself, Colonel."

"We have any idea where they're going? Are they from Sterling?"

"Don't know for sure, sir. Colorado Guard has cleared them, so I'd bet CNG knows what they're carrying, sir."

"With all this commo gear you can't get an answer?"

"CNG's equipment is pretty thrashed, sir. Calling it a patchwork would be generous. We actually got the relay direct from Austin."

"Great. All right, are they at least coming in on a couple of roads? We can at least checkpoint them there," I said.

"New Mexico's already got that covered—and every other entry into the area, Colonel."

"All right, we've got an hour. What's the status of the recon through Sterling?"

"Thirty-six dead civilians so far. Pre-War population was around thirteen thousand. There's about two hundred residents still here, Colonel. Second and Third recon teams are moving toward the middle of town. They should rendezvous at what's left of the Logan County Courthouse within about twenty minutes, sir. I believe that Lieutenant Colonel Chappel should be here any minute for your trip into town."

"Any report on the status of the CNG facilities here?"

"Not yet sir, not by Third Washington, anyway. We've seen some digital pics from the initial recon sweep, which aren't good for anything."

"Good chance we're not here long enough to make use of them anyway. It'd be good to have an idea though for staging materials for the forward areas," I said, as Lieutenant Colonel Trayvon Chappel came inside.

"Colonel Drummond, good to see you sir."

474

"You as well, Colonel. I wish we were watching your Grambling Tigers playing Southern today, rather than this."

"Yes, sir, that would be a pleasure. I understand you were in the field this morning with Sergeant Jones squad."

"Yes, I was. I'll do that when I can. Good men he's got there. I think they're working on the last of resupply for the Lone Stars this afternoon. Pass on my compliments to them. They worked their asses off."

"I'll do that, sir."

"Captain, keep me apprised of the civilian approach. I'll meet them out at the outer checkpoint when they come in. Gotta see this for myself."

"Yes, sir. Your radio's on the rack over there, with the headset there on the left."

"Thanks," I said as I grabbed the light radio unit, checked the frequencies of the day, and power. The headset was matched to the unit, and wireless. Pretty slick. "OK, Colonel, let's go to town."

Outside, I noticed that the Lone Star command tent was now down and being packed, and General Garcia personally overseeing the loading of her men and women and all their gear, getting ready to get back in the fight. The wind was blowing a little harder, and the overcast seemed to be lowering. My ribs hurt.

"Colonel, let's go give our regards to our friend the General," I said. "I'd like to shake her hand before she heads out."

"Hear she's a real firecracker, sir."

"Fair assessment, I think," I said as we approached General Garcia, and caught her eye.

"General Garcia, this is Lieutenant Colonel Chappel, commander, Second Brigade. Thought we'd pay our respects before you head east."

"Thank you, Colonel, and Colonel Chappel, I believe that I saw you help beat my alma mater a few years back."

"Been more than a few years ma'am, since I played," he said with a grin.

"San Diego State. I think you stopped our team from scoring three times that day. My husband yelled until he was hoarse."

"That was a good day, ma'am, thank you."

"Looks like you're getting close, ma'am."

"We are, Colonel. Third Washington is a compliment to your state. I have a tough time believing these men haven't worked together as a unit for months."

"Most've seen action of a different kind, General. We've already had eleven months of survival of the fittest, with the occasional skirmish thrown in to keep everyone on their toes."

"Understood. Thanks again to you and your men. I look forward to seeing you down the road."

"Ma'am," I said as I shook her hand. "It's been an honor. And good hunting."

"To the ends of the Earth, Colonel," she said as Chappel and I saluted her smartly, and left her to her duty.

Two men from Chappel's brigade joined us on the trip 'into town', one backseater armed with his M-16C, the second manning the top-mount machine gun, in the cold. I believe that he drew short straw.

From Factory Street, we headed west to Division Avenue, and headed north. We passed several blocks of burned out business on our right, abandoned homes to the left. A Catholic school seemed to have drawn particular attention, with numerous cars and trucks driven into the building and grounds, and burned. There wasn't a wall on that building that wasn't pockmarked with bullet holes.

At Fourth Street, we turned right slightly, following the angled road, and saw the wrecked and smoldering Classical Revival building. I suppose it once had a domed roof, now collapsed, and the source of a fair amount of smoke.

"Damn. What'd these people do to deserve this?" I asked.

"Escaped inmates probably did this, sir," Chappel replied. "We found a fair number of dead dressed in prison jumpsuits this morning. Civilians didn't go down without a fight."

"What's this town got left that's not destroyed?" I asked.

"This area's really the worst of it. Some of the business district is untouched. There's hardware store down by the highway that looks like they just locked it up and walked away. One broken window, no looting, I couldn't figure that one out, sir. Most of the residential areas seem OK, other than lack of power."

"How about water?"

"It's in the pipes, sir, but no power means no pressure. We were expecting Prime Power to assist us with tracking down problems like that. There is electricity on the outskirts, so things look repairable."

We met up with the recon sweep units, who briefed me on the locations of civilians and their status, the overall condition of Sterling, and of course, the threat analysis as viewed from the ground. When we'd wrapped that up, I ordered additional troops to provide regular patrols throughout the town and to relocate a couple of the poorly located observation and security posts. I also ordered that our troops direct civilians to our location if they needed any supplies until outside connections could be re-established.

Checkpoint Able, off of Interstate Seventy Six, was composed of four Humvees, one Bradley, and twenty men from Charlie Company, Second Battalion. Chappel and I arrived just after the first civilian vehicles had been seen by long distance spotters.

Within a few minutes, the rag-tag caravan from Denver was at the checkpoint. The vehicles—mostly SUV's and three-quarter ton four-by-fours with canopies—were each searched, along with the civilians. The first truck flew the Colorado state flag, along with a homemade version of our 'new' national flag.

Chappel oversaw the search process, while I spent some time with the driver and passenger from the first truck. He looked about sixty, barrel-chested, close-cropped hair.

"Good afternoon. You've got quite the caravan here, sir," I asked. "I'm in command in Sterling. I'd like to know your business in this area."

"I'm Jess Armstrong, Colonel. Twenty years, Air Force. Can't serve anymore due to a new heart, and I'm sixty-six," he said. "Colonel, most of us are from Denver. Some from Colorado Springs. We've come to help bring these soldiers home. They helped get us free of the S.A. in Denver. We owe them. We know some of them. I had a couple stay at my house."

I hadn't expected this, of course. We had a whole other plan in place, and I wasn't sure how to integrate a civilian volunteer element into the equation.

"Mr. Armstrong, we are charged with this task. I realize you've traveled a fair distance, but this really isn't an operation for civilians."

"Colonel, I have five hundred and sixty people who'd respectfully disagree. We don't need anything from you or your men. We do need to do this though, sir. Not want to….need to."

I could understand his sentiment, and as the sweep team moved to the third vehicle in line, I realized that sooner or later we'd need to work with civilians, either here or somewhere down the line.

"Mr. Armstrong, I assume you retired out?"

"I did, Colonel. Chief Master Sergeant."

"And they haven't found a duty station for you?"

"Like I said, Colonel, I'm not in the prime of health these days."

"Chief, I'm betting there's still a wealth of knowledge up there," I said, pointing at his head. "I also know I'm going to lose this situation, Chief. Teams still have to clear your vehicles and the civilians. I'll figure out a staging area for you. We'll need you to have team leaders go over protocol, same as our men."

"We can do that, Colonel. I appreciate it."

"I'll probably catch Hell, but in won't be the first time."

"Good officers know where they can bend the rules, sir."

"I'm new at the officer business, Chief, but I agree. Be back with you in a few minutes."

"Thank you, sir."

I walked back around the Humvees and told the Command Car to start planning on a logical staging area for our civilian grave detail.

"Best place, Colonel, is over at the junior college. Big parking lot, easy to secure, short walk to Command. We can probably swing some power generation over there, too," Captain Gerry McGowan, our logistics guy, said.

"Sounds fine, Colonel. Figure out a traffic cop for them, or five, and get them set up. It's starting to snow down here, and we only have about two hours of daylight left and we're pretty much out of the field for the day."

"Done, sir."

The snow was starting to pick up, along with the wind. We'd get some weather yet, it seemed.

Dusk brought more wind, turning the battlefield into drifts of light snow around the bodies, tents, and equipment.

The Combat Engineering teams made faster progress than the retrieval operation, and by the cessation of work for the day, half of the battlefield had been cleared for body removal. Most of the on-duty command staff was pre-occupied with a snowstorm of their own, real-time battle data coming in on a major firefight on the southern front of the S.A., in retreat from northern Oklahoma, moving towards Wichita. Two of the Georgia Bulldog officers were listening in as well, commenting on tactics and pondering the enemy.

I'd listened in for a half-hour or so, finding much if it over my head, although the tactical side was intriguing. I was also unaware that the S.A. had as much armor as was engaged along the line: If the satellite imagery was to be believed, the S.A. had more than three hundred tanks and hundreds of other vehicles moving north in a controlled pullback, against the five hundred M1A2 and A3 tanks of the Army. They apparently had more armor, further north and east.

While the tank battle was tipping in favor of the U.S., without air support in the form of the A-10 Warthog and the depleted uranium shells, the fight was much more evenly matched than our previous fights in the Middle East. We still had A-10's of course, but there was no defense for them against dozens of SAM's fired each time they approached. I wondered if the Air Force had other ideas, other ordnance that could be used without wiping out civilians behind the lines.

There was no 'routine' to the day; perhaps there wasn't one in the position I was now in. When most of Third Washington was pulled from the field and other units working toward moving east, to follow the Texans or to head straight east in their own engagement. Their respective commanders were anticipating a jump-off within the next twenty-four hours, after the expected orders were given from Austin.

I decided to go see how the civilians were settling in, as directed by some of Bryce Atwood's Fifth Brigade. Fifth was currently tasked with night operations, with shifts coming on line overnight to keep the Battalion in operation while the rest of the men stood down. The rotating schedule would have them on 'day shift' in a couple more days, for their time in the recovery operation. I was joined by Chet Travis, for the short trip over to Northeastern Junior College. Chet wasn't scheduled to be on duty for hours yet, but nonetheless was in the Command Car.

"Chet, you had a look around town yet?" I asked.

"Yes, sir. The college in particular. Quite a bit of it is pretty messed up. Left their big arena alone. Trashed the library and most of the offices. Didn't burn them though."

"You've had a chance to read through the initial recon reports," I stated. "Do you think this is typical of what we're going to see the S.A. leave behind?"

"Frankly, Colonel, no. There aren't enough bodies left here to make it 'typical'. What I've read about southern Colorado, and parts of Denver for that matter, they killed anyone in their way. Some for sport, it seemed," he said as we approached the college campus, parking lot lit with some jury-rigging from our electrical engineers. Chet pulled the Humvee into the parking lot, and I pointed out Jess Armstrong's truck and camper.

"Nice to see some lights," I said. They said to me, 'civilization.'

"Engineer group said they'll be a week or so finding all the damage locally, sir. Problem is though, there isn't power coming into town from the main grid. Nothing we can do about that, which really means that we shouldn't even try to fix most of the local stuff. Might be different if the power was actually coming into the town."

"I'd come to that conclusion myself. Not really in my nature to leave a job half-done though."

"More support behind us to take care of that, Colonel."

"Probably so, long time in coming, I'd bet."

Friday,
November Twenty-fourth
1730 Hours

Chief Armstrong was helping others finish setting up their temporary homes, and saw us pull in. We met not far from his camper set up, where he was helping another volunteer with their trailer jacks.

"Good evening, Chief. Getting settled in?"

"Doing fine, Colonel. Thanks," he said. "Nice having shore power, such as it is."

"We've got a lot of capacity, Chief," Chet Travis said. "Not much in town worth powering up without a population."

"How many civilians left here?" Jess asked.

"Not many," I responded. "Virtually all of them will be housed over in one of the dormitories tonight. Williams Hall, I think it is. Engineers will have power back up over there any time, Chief."

"We've seen a lot of that in this state," I said as I noticed Chet getting a call in his ear. He stepped away for some privacy.

"Chief, I'd like to invite you to dinner this evening. I'd like to hear about your time in Denver, if you'd care to tell."

"I'd be most happy too, Colonel. Mind if my wife joins us?"

"Not at all! I didn't know your wife came along," I said.

"She was traveling a few trucks back with some friends. If you don't mind, let me catch her before she gets our dinner on," he said as he headed for his camper.

"No problem, Chief," I said as Chet came back to the conversation. "What's going on, Chet?"

"Texans are safe and sound in North Platte, Colonel. Train's on the way back, with three hundred and sixty-one civilians. All from Sterling, sir."

That surprised me, perhaps it ought not to have.

"All right, we've got a couple of hours at best to get them a place to stay. Not real fond of the idea of turning them loose to their own homes until daylight. What's the status of the refit on that dorm? Can we get the other dorms up and running?" I asked.

"We'll have most of the campus up within the next couple of hours, sir. I think the dorms are all part of one, big complex."

"Let's get some men working on cleanup. I'm also betting they're going to need a hot meal."

"Mess is already on it, sir."

"Chet, remind me again why I'm here?" I said.

"To take all the flack from above, sir," he said with a smile. "Actually, the comms guys passed on info to the duty staff, and they started getting ready almost immediately. We should have about two hundred men making a sweep through the dorms to double check them, and a hundred or so on cleanup. Security will be there overnight, and will also have to check our men to make sure no looting's going on."

"Assuming anything's left worth stealing," I said. Looting and theft weren't just limited to the S.A., unfortunately.

"One more thing, sir. That train's carrying an Army media crew, been on the ground since before the Sixth went down. They apparently have a fair amount of video of the S.A.'s operations up in North Platte, the Air Force hit, and their evacuation. There are orders back in the Command Car for both Third Washington and this crew."

"Media crew. Swell," I said. About the last thing I thought we needed was a bunch of photographers.

"Yes, sir," Chet said as Chief Armstrong approached, his wife on his arm.

"Colonel Drummond, my wife Gabrielle," Jess Armstrong said, presenting his bundled-up wife.

"Ma'am, pleased to meet you," I said. "This is Sergeant Major Chet Travis."

"Sergeant Major, Colonel. Thank you for the dinner invitation. I wasn't looking forward to another can of stew for dinner," she said as she shook our gloved hands.

"I hope we can do better, but honestly Mrs. Armstrong, no promises." I noted that she had a slight accent, perhaps German.

"That's fine, Colonel. We're happy just to be here."

"Let's get out of this snow. Looks like our weather predictions are as accurate as ever," I said, directing them over to the Humvee, and radioed ahead, making provisions for my dinner guests.

We made the short trip back to the group of Command Cars quickly, despite the clogged wipers on the Humvee. There was too much noise to carry on a conversation between the back seat and front, unless we wanted to shout. Once we disembarked, it was more civilized to converse.

"Colonel, I have some business to attend to over in Command. I'll have a report on your desk by nineteen hundred on your desk regarding the incoming train and accommodations for that incoming crew."

"Thanks, Sergeant-Major. Remember to get some dinner yourself."

"One of the benefits of being in the Command Car, sir. Delivery service."

"True. Cold food, but it is delivered," I said, drawing a smile. We did have a microwave though, so it could be warmed over, instead of merely ice cold.

We headed down the train a couple of cars to our conference room, which had been restored to its planned use, with the departure of the Texas unit.

I'd asked for Captain Gerry McGowan to join us. As our intel officer, he might be able to get some info out of our dinner conversation that I'd miss, or ask a question that I would not.

"Are you entirely based on this train?" Gabrielle asked.

"Of sorts, yes. Primarily for travel, and then we setup and expand. We're not a front line unit—meaning, we're not really geared for combat, ma'am."

"Please, call me Gabby. Everyone else does."

"It's quite civilized," Jess said. "I didn't quite know what to expect, Colonel."

"Call me Rick, if you please. I've been 'Rick' far longer than 'Colonel,'" I said. "I've asked one of our officers to join us for dinner, if you don't mind. He's our intelligence officer. I thought he might learn a thing or two."

"That's fine. It's been a helluva place, Denver. Never thought we'd see anything like that happen here," Jess said.

Over dinner, we compared notes on our experiences in dealing with the collapse. Jess and Gabrielle lived in Littleton, rather than Denver proper, in a retirement subdivision. Their home backed up to a small lake though, and Gabby quietly turned their back yard into a farmyard as homes around them were foreclosed and vacated. They raised chickens, goats and sheep, and had discovered 'permaculture' through a website created by an Oklahoma City resident, called *'Better Times Almanac of Useful Information.'* The lake proved valuable over the summer, as the 'Federal Government' cut off water to most of the urban area at varying times of day, for no apparent reason. It demoralized the civilians, probably encouraging them to relocate out of the Denver area.

Fewer people to complain, which is what the 'Federal Government' wanted, I thought. The Armstrongs and their small group buckled down, stayed off the radar, and waited.

"It was apparent right quick after they relocated from D.C. that things weren't what they should've been," Jess said. "Even with the dirty bombs going off, the war and all that, it just didn't feel right. They locked everything down within their 'Federal District'. Took whatever they wanted from the stores, the shops and groceries. Accountable to no one."

Gabby added in her beautiful accent, "It was understandable at first, but it just grew and grew. We welcomed them at first, encouraged everyone to make their transition easy, and that seemed to just fuel their sense of entitlement." I noted that Gerry was thinking hard on that statement.

"What'd the local government do? Or the state government for that matter?" I asked.

"State couldn't bend over backwards fast enough, which compromised any attempt at resistance from the get-go. They were neck-deep in it all. Probably half of the state government left with the S.A. when they pulled out. Some of the state workers up and left. Anyone that showed any backbone was 'reassigned to benefit the recovery,' which meant they disappeared. A bunch...no one knows," Jess said.

"Our local police department was ordered about by the Feds, right and left," Gabby said. "One of the officers said that they'd seized all of the police rifles and shotguns, and left them with only their handguns."

"What about your own weapons?" Gerry asked. "Were they seized?"

"They would've been, had they not been stashed away. I did have a couple of sacrificial weapons for them, to make it look good. Old Savage deer rifle with a cracked stock and a rusty .32. Oh, and a crumbling box of ammo each, just to make it look good," Jess said.

"A few days after the seizures were wrapped up—which was found out word of mouth—they jammed all the normal broadcast frequencies, and burglaries and home invasion robberies started. Too organized, knew what they wanted and tore the places up trying to find it. Silver. Gold. Diamonds. Jewelry. Food. Took whatever they could load up and left. And they had the guns."

"Were you robbed as well?" Gerry asked, taking notes as he did so.

"Let them in, saw them coming," Gabby said. "We just stayed out of the way."

"Knew it was coming though," Jess said, pouring another cup of coffee. "Most of our stored food actually ended up in the walls of the house well in advance of it all."

"What'd you do with your livestock?"

"They had no idea what to do with it. Left it untouched. If it didn't come in a can, box or bag, they left it," Jess said.

"So, I've got to ask, you don't have to tell of course, where did you stash your weapons?"

"Buried PVC sewer pipes, dummy drain pipes in the house, dummy ductwork and a fake air conditioner. With the exception of the buried pipe, all of it was in plain sight," Chief Armstrong said with some pleasure.

"Don't forget my little .38 and some of the ammunition was hidden in the entertainment center," Gabby said.

"Not exactly, hon," Jess said, explaining further. "We had a twenty-seven inch TV set that died a few years ago. I gutted it and put an LCD in the case. Left lots of room behind it for contraband."

"What about fuel for your vehicles, and restrictions on travel? Can you tell us how that went?" Gerry asked.

"Once the guns were gone, you only got enough gas to get to your 'imperative employment location.' If you didn't have a job that 'FedGov' deemed 'imperative,' you were screwed," Jess said. "No job, no food vouchers. That said, I had about a hundred gallons of diesel stored for the GMC. They walked right over it when they came into the house. It was in a little area I remodeled, right under the front porch. Coupla nice big metal tanks."

"Did you have 'imperative employment?'" I asked.

"Gabby did. Critical care nurse. I've been a kept man since retirement," Jess said.

"Don't let this Yank pull the wool over your eyes, Richard," Gabby said…she never did call me 'Rick.' "While I was tending the sniffles of the Statists running the place, he was working against them every step of the way."

"Do tell," Gerry asked. "If you don't mind. I'm interested in learning about your resistance methods, if you don't mind."

"Not a problem, Captain," Jess said.

"Call me Gerry if you like."

"Will do," Jess replied. "The area has a substantial population of retirees from all branches. Anyone who's served more than a tour and has some life experience behind them could smell that something wasn't right. Most everyone, with a little fair warning, dropped down low years back. Cash purchases of firearms, ammunition, supplies, and bought at various locations. Nothing bought in one lot, at one time, nothing on credit. Multiple locations of stored product."

"You knew this was coming?" Gerry asked.

"Sure, kid. You're what, about thirty?"

"Thirty-two," McGowan replied. He seemed older to me, I thought.

"Son, I'm thirty-four years older than you are, saw action on three continents, heard and saw stuff I wasn't ever intended to see. This country's been in a downward spiral for the better part of forty years, my opinion. Probably longer than that, it's just that I've been paying attention that long. One thing I learned way the Hell back was that government eats to survive. It destroys. It does not create. When the U.S. government forgot how to fight wars, but got really good at prolonging them, I knew it was a matter of time. A whole lot of us

489

did. By the end of my first six years in, I could see the writing on the wall. General Eisenhower said it back in the Fifties. Military-Industrial complex. He forgot the Financial side of the triangle, though. Started developing a network back then. Lost some members, gained others."

"Network?" I asked.

"Consider it, Colonel, a mutual-aid network. Cell based, small enough to not draw a lot of attention."

"Leaderless resistance," I said, all too familiar with the concept.

"Yes, of course with the common goal at mind at all times: The preservation and defense of the Constitution of the United States of America."

"How big is your typical cell? Gerry asked.

"Three. No more or less," Jess replied. "Recruiting happens rarely, generally from people who've sworn to uphold the Constitution, and then proven their willingness to do so."

"Usually military then," I said.

"Almost universally. Maybe three percent are law enforcement, non-military recruits, damned few politicians," he said. I noticed Gabby was keeping very quiet.

"I won't ask about your operations, unless you'd care to tell."

"Sure, I don't mind. Operations are done around here anyway," Jess said. "Our cell and our sister cells are going inactive again, and no one could find 'em if they tried."

"We don't want you to compromise anything, Jess," I said. "Honestly, this is probably more for my own curious nature. It's fascinating."

"I'm immune from prosecution, I assume," Jess said.

"Anything you care to say stays in this room," I replied.

"There were a number of operations carried out, once the S.A. exposed themselves. Before that, generally information gathering and generation of contingencies, some of which was fed to the legitimate military. Whole lot of intel happens that way. The operations that I know of decapitated the S.A.'s Court of Equal Justice, and the removal of a dozen or so other officials from this mortal plane within a matter of hours. That didn't happen until after we'd heard they'd decided to pull back to Chicago, so the natural chaos of an evac was an opportunity to exploit."

"I'll bet," I said. "I'm very impressed, Chief, to put it mildly." The 'Court of Equal Justice' was the S.A.'s version of the Supreme Court, and dispensed anything but 'equal justice' from what I'd read of their 'Judgments for the People,' which included sixty summary rulings handing all power to the State, along with most property that wasn't already controlled by the State Board of Industry.

"Colonel, they made it absurdly easy. Within an hour or so of the operation starting, word got out of course, they got all panicky and bailed on most of the more sensible security protocols. Making it even easier and lower risk, of course."

"How many men did you lose?" Gerry asked, assuming that in any operation of this nature, some would be captured or caught.

"None. Two close calls. The work was all done, shall we say, at a distance. After that operation, everyone faded right back into the fog."

"Formidable opponents," I said.

"Those willing to give their lives for their beliefs always are, sir."

"Chief, did you see that kind of dedication in the faces of the S.A? Are we fighting against 'true believers' or opportunists here?"

"The opportunists cut and run, they're the balance of the leadership of course. Bunch of self-serving bastards. The true believers stand and fight, with the exception of their high command. Here, in Sterling, this was an action of true believers. Well-planned, well-executed, minimal casualties of friendlies from what I hear. The opportunists are in Chicago by now. Those in the field—those that did this—they'll go to the mat. Doesn't matter the cost, they'll pay it with their men's lives. They've shown time and again no sense of mercy, and they should be shown none in return. Do you disagree, Colonel?" Jess said, leaning forward on the table.

"Not remotely, Chief. I've dealt with both types you've described over the past year."

"'They're everywhere,' we used to say, 'and they vote,'" Gabby said. "Colonel Drummond, I saw Europe, I watched citizens rights get whittled down year over year; I watched the nations dissolve and the E.U. emerge, always taking more than it gave. I watched as 'movements' became 'religion.' I watched what happens when mediocrity rules and when compromise reigns. Those that are true believers take over, fractionally at first, too small to really notice as the people are distracted with famous people having scandals. When the changes approached a singularity—and the rate of change reached a round number—say the number hit one—and the changes then doubled, and doubled again, the cascade happened too quickly to stop and too quickly to influence. And, of course, too quickly to ever understand. Soon enough, Europe could not recover," she said with passion. "I may have been born in Schweinfurt, Colonel, but I am an American first. I will do what is necessary to protect my country."

"Very well spoken, Gabrielle, thank you. I'm assuming you had a role in the resistance as well?" I asked.

"I did. I will not speak of it, however. You simply do not need to know, Richard," she said with both words and piercing green eyes.

"Understood. But I thank you, nonetheless," I said, which gained unspoken approval on her part.

"Colonel, I think it's time we headed back to our chateau on wheels," Jess said as he stood up. "It has been a pleasure though breaking bread with you and Gerry here, though."

"You as well, Chief. We'll do what we can to help you out while we're here. We should be seeing that train arrive with our returnees any time now. I'll have you taken back over," I said, shaking their hands. "I have to say, I don't really have words to tell you how proud I am that there are people like you both out there."

"One day, Colonel, they'll say, 'they're everywhere, and they vote.'"

"I hope so, Chief."

Friday,
November Twenty-fourth
2030 Hours

"Here's one of the worst sections, sir. Pretty sure this won't see network time," Lieutenant Susan Kirchener said. The lieutenant and her platoon were trapped in North Platte when the S.A. front line troops arrived en masse. Our senior staff along with all five battalion commanders were watching the digital video, taken over several days of occupation. The bulk of the data was being uploaded to the communications centers' computers, and then compressed and sent to Austin, unedited and without comment.

"Colonel, these were taken from one of our remote cameras, we had six. We were in the basement of a warehouse a half a click from their headquarters. Good thing we were underground, or the Air Force would've cooked us for sure. We deployed the cameras around our position just before the S.A. moved in—too late to get out safely. The cameras kept us aware of what was going on around us."

"They didn't search, Lieutenant?" Captain McGowan asked.

"Spotty, Captain. Our warehouse had a big 'foreclosure' sign on it, so they probably figured, correctly, that there wasn't anything in it."

"You and your crew did well getting this, Lieutenant," Gerry said as we watched a dozen S.A. troops change magazines. They then opened up on around fifty civilians backed into a corner. None appeared to be a particular threat. Something bothered me about it, more than what I knew must be coming, even as I watched it unfold. I couldn't put my finger on it though.

The camera, although small, picked up every detail, and the muffled screams of the massacre.

"This is what we're fighting, sir. There are piles of dead up there, or were when we left. We have three massacres like this, within two hundred meters of our location. We were outnumbered a thousand to one," she said, starting to break down. "Everyone...the civilians knew we were there. They didn't tell the enemy. They died ......not telling them."

"Lieutenant, that's enough for now. Let's get you out of here for a while," I said. "Captain Fillmore will see that you get set up. Adam's also our brigade chaplain, Lieutenant. Go get some hot food and some rest."

"Yes, sir. Thank you, sir."

"Thank you, Lieutenant," I said, shaking her hand before Fillmore led her out of Command as the video continued, then switched scenes, shocking everyone.

"Christ Almighty," one of the specialists said without thinking. "That guy just shot a kid. Just walked up and shot him!"

"Briggs, rewind that...no, get me the first massacre."

He found the scene, coded on the hard drive, and played it. There it was again.

"Get the next one," I said.

"Sir?"

"Do it, Briggs," I said. "Anybody else see something about these that doesn't add up? Briggs, get me Austin. I want to talk to my boss about this."

"Holy shit. Look at that," Epstein, Third Battalion's commander said.

"Yeah. You figured it out, Colonel Epstein. Good for you," I said.

496

It was all of five minutes before Briggs was able to connect me to Austin, where their staff was just starting the review of the images.

"Major, I assume you've seen some of this video from North Platte?"

"About three minutes of it, Colonel Drummond. Intel is going through it all. It'll take some time even with two dozen staff working it."

"You plan on putting this out, Major?"

"For the public? That's a call for General Yancey, the Joint Chiefs, and the President, Colonel Drummond."

"Major, you can bet money that this isn't the only imagery of a five year old being executed. Have you seen that?"

"No, I haven't, Colonel," he said, sounding as disgusted as any human ought to.

"You better, Major, and damned quick. The soldier carrying that out was carrying an M-16, and was dressed in Sixth Army gear and insignia. They all were. There's a videographer filming the whole damned thing. He's ten feet behind the guy that shot the kid."

"Propaganda."

"Damned right. They're setting this up to make us look like we did this. Seems to me the sooner we get out with the facts, the better."

"Sir, I'll get this up the chain of command as soon as I can."

"Much appreciated. Third Washington out."

The Command Car was quiet as my transmission ended. I didn't know what to say next, and I doubted that anyone else did either.

"Damn it all to Hell," I said. "Ayers, Briggs, get an honest, condensed version of Lieutenant Kirchener's video put together. Third Washington is going to see a version of this. Have it ready by reveille. Everyone sees this tomorrow, everyone. Everyone gets a briefing. Whole Brigade. Got it?"

"Yes, sir," Ayers said.

"Battalion commanders, fifteen minutes after reveille, every man in Brigade watches this, then back to assigned duties. Spread the word. Dismissed," I said. Minutes later, the Command Car was empty, but for duty staff and two additional computer techs, who'd take over the duties of Ayers and Briggs. I sat alone in my command cube, thinking about what I'd seen.

"Sir? Communication from Colorado Guard. Joint Force HQ rep has been delayed. Says they're coming on the resupply train, sir."

"Very well. Thanks," I said. "Kennedy, grab me a phone."

"Yes, sir. One moment."

It'd been only two days since I spoke with Karen. It felt much, much longer. Private Kennedy came back in with the phone.

"Comm protocol same as last time, sir," he said, reminding me that he'd be listening, and that there'd be a slight delay on the call. I dialed Karen's number.

"Hello?" Carl answered.

"Well, my son, how're you doing?"

"Hey, Dad! Where are you?"

"At work. Can't tell you where. Everything OK?"

"Yeah, things are pretty good. Everyone misses you. Me included."

"You, too, bud. You shouldering my load?"

"As much as Mom and Uncle Alan and Ron will let me. Which isn't all that much."

"They'll lighten up a little. Give them time. Just don't push too much. How's Kelly?"

"She's over with Grandma and the ladies. She's helping with the home-care. Doesn't like it, but she's helping."

"Perfectly understandable," I said. "Is your Mom home?"

"She's just coming back in from the barn…evening egg round-up. Here she is—take care, Dad. Love you."

"Love you too, Carl," I said before Karen took the phone.

"Hey! This is a surprise!"

"Had a spare minute," I said.

"You don't sound good. Are you OK?"

"Not a great day. Everything up there going all right? Grace doing OK?"

"She has her moments, that's for sure. Couple more days, I hope she'll settle in a little bit better."

"Curfew still in place?" I asked.

"Yep. Until Monday at least, the news says. Ron had the store open today for a couple of hours. All of the stores were open at some point, but not at the same time. Staffing and supply nightmare for the guys."

"I'm sure the buyers don't care for it a whole lot either."

She was quiet on the other end of the line for a moment. "Can't talk about it, can you?" knowing that I wanted to, and couldn't.

"Nope. I'd like to though. Some day."

We spent a few more minutes on the line, and said our 'I love yous' and 'goodnights', and I promised I'd call again when I could.

I think in the end, I felt worse after the call than before.

Saturday
November Twenty-fifth

Saturday was filled with recovery and body removal, done in shifts as the cold winds took their tolls on the field crews.

I'd risen before reveille, shaved and showered, and spent the first couple of hours of daylight in the field with Fifth Battalion in recovery. Jess Armstrong's civilian volunteers were spread throughout the three field operations. When the Volunteers weren't in the field, they were assisting Sterling residents to get back to their homes and try to settle in. I'd assigned Forth Battalion a house to house sweep operation, along with the Combat Engineers, once they'd completed the sweep of the battlefield.

By eleven hundred hours, I was chilled to the bone and ready to spend some time studying the attack on Sterling. Army tacticians assigned to the Colorado Guard were piecing together the events on the battlefield, but I didn't understand and didn't know of any one looking into why the S.A. didn't burn Sterling to the ground like every other small town in their path. Things were different here, and I wanted to know why.

There were key differences here. Only some of the commercial zone was looted, some not even broken into or damaged in any way. Civilians were alive when the first recovery units arrived, although in hiding. It was a break in the S.A. pattern. I didn't understand it, and wouldn't understand it any time soon, it seemed.

"Colonel, there's a Major Conrad Long here to see you, from the CNG Joint Force HQ."

I thought, 'and about damned time,' but said, "Send him in, Private."

"Good afternoon, Colonel. Sorry for the delay. I'm Major Long," he said with a swift salute.

"Major. How was the trip out?"

"First time I've made a train trip next to the engineer. Interesting, sir."

"Major, what brings you out here?"

"CNG will re-occupy the Sterling facilities within the next forty-eight hours, sir. We expect to have several hundred troops arrive with the return train from Colorado Springs." The train to Colorado Springs held the remains of Sixth Army's soldiers.

"Major, are you supplied well enough to do that? We have a fair number of civilians just arrived from North Platte last night, electricity is dependent on Third Washington's rail-mounted generating plant, and everything out here depends on that. No power, no water, no heat."

"Arrangements are being made to ship several temporary generators in from Arizona, sir. I'd like to know though sir, how long you anticipate being in Sterling."

"By the end of the day, we should have sixty percent of the body recovery complete and those recovered will be on their way to Colorado Springs. Anticipate a quick turnaround of that train, and expect completion of body recovery by the end of the day tomorrow. Recovery and refit of equipment, probably another twenty-four hours. I'm expecting orders from Austin tomorrow on our next destination. So, by Sunday, we should be out of here and on the rails."

"I've noticed that the New Mexico and Arizona units are packing up, sir. Anything you can share on their schedules, Colonel? I've been in and out of touch with Command since last night. Actually, the State Command Center is pretty much in the stone age, sir. Nothing like the capabilities you have here."

"End of the day they're supposed to be on the road. We shut down recovery operations at dusk, by and large. Not enough portable lighting to go around. Their forces will move east to the US Eighty Three corridor in Kansas, using their own vehicles and quite a bit of gear from Sixth Army. Texas has the north end; Georgia's Bulldogs will follow Texas tonight on the empty supply train that you came in on. Some of the flatbeds will be used for Bradleys and Humvees from Sixth. Texas and Georgia will split those up. Georgia will depart as soon as that train's ready. You gonna have power units up here by the time we move out?"

"We should have something by Monday, sir. Our new Governor said that we should do anything possible to assist our fellow states in the prosecution of the War. We don't have much left though, sir. The S.A. cleaned us out."

"And I see they paid your former Governor back by putting a bullet in his head."

"Yes, sir. Whole family. Wife and five kids."

"Standard S.A. tactic, it appears."

"Yes, sir."

"Major, I think the CNG can help us out by getting the citizens of Sterling back in their homes and instill a sense of peace in them, that they're safe. Get power and utilities back up, get the community back to a productive town. It looks like most of the economy here was farming. That right?"

"That and the prison, sir. I understand that the prison was burned."

"Along with several hundred prisoners, and probably all of the guards, yes. The Marine units first on scene reported that. When Colorado is back on her feet, then send some fighting men. Meanwhile, it seems to me that the other states will take this fight home," I said. "Anything else, Major?"

"No, sir. Thank you for your time, sir," he said as he stood.

"Not a problem, Major," I said, standing and returning his salute. "Let us know if there's anything CNG needs that we can provide. Dismissed."

For three more days, far longer than we'd estimated, we removed Sixth Army from the battlefield, two days of the work done in blinding snow. One of the least pleasant parts of that experience, for me at least, was the documentation process. Lieutenant Kirchener and her video team filmed the recovery process, interviewed the removal teams, interviewed the chaplain, and interviewed me as the commanding officer. I suppose there was a need for the process, I just didn't see it at the time.

Wednesday,
November Twenty-ninth

As with any project that I've ever experienced, clean up and de-mobilization always took longer than the initial setup. That applied as well to getting three thousand men and their equipment stowed, only on a much larger scale. I was discovering that with command, the best place for me was to stay out of the way of my men.

The Colorado Guard made good on their schedule to re-occupy Sterling, and Third Washington crews assisted the CNG in getting their temporary power system up and running. They had a massive amount of work ahead of them.

The returning residents of Sterling were shocked to find so much of their town intact, but of course devastated to learn as we did that most of those that stayed behind were rounded up and forced into the high-security prison just west of town and then burned alive. Lieutenant Kirchener's crew again documented the finding. The body retrieval for Sterling would be done by the Colorado Guard and the civilians. The recovery process for the towns wrecked by the S.A. would be long in coming, but this town at least was now behind the battle lines.

We learned through one of the survivors who'd stayed that the destruction of Sterling was only interrupted by the rapid approach from the west of Sixth Army. Sixth though, didn't press hard enough or fast enough to put the S.A. troops immediately to flight. They had reason—Sixth was outnumbered at least two to one. The delay let the S.A. plant their weapons and stage their departure so that the Sixth would stay in Sterling until morning, when the pursuit would resume.

The fatal decisions were made by Major General Michael Wright, his mutilated remains found by the advance Marine unit. If anything was to be re-learned, it was to fight the war of your choosing, not the war that your enemy has chosen for you. I'd hoped that all products of West Point would know that. The well-equipped Sixth Army delayed the approach to Sterling to assess enemy troop strength that was already well-established and then didn't elect to pursue the S.A. until the assessment was complete. By the time they mobilized, it would have been too late to save most of the remaining citizens of Sterling, although we didn't piece that together until much later. Sixth then camped in exactly the same place that the S.A. had camped in during their occupation, hours after the S.A. evacuated east, taking most of the prison population with them. When the S.A. was far enough east to avoid the nerve agent, they detonated the devices, resulting in a kill-rate of more than ninety-eight percent. The terrain was in their favor; the troop concentrations ideal; the weather perfect. After the nerve agent attack, a small percentage of the S.A. force then moved back into Sterling. Survivors were tortured and killed, equipment, ammunition and uniforms taken. Had the Marines not had a rapid-deployment force available, much more equipment would have been taken, and Sterling would have been burned to the ground anyway. The S.A. might have then moved back toward Denver, or with their new gear perhaps gone on a major offensive south. With a hundred thousand men and Sixth Army's equipment, a possible attack south to Texas might have the United States government on the run again. The many might-have-beens in any war, I also pondered.

Army Command required us to return approximately half of Sixth Army's rifles, handguns and ammunition to Fort Carson; oversee the shipment of the remaining heavy weapons, ammunition and armor east; and refit line units east of us with the remaining recovered equipment. These orders in turn, drove other issues: Our two initial trains were designed to transport and support the Brigade and the basic equipment load, not spares for thousands of others down the line; and our trains were completely unsuitable for the transport of the Abrams tanks, Bradleys, and dozens of Humvees in various configurations. We'd need another train, crews, and railcars designed for the purpose. Third Washington did have a handful of men checked out to operate the tanks and Bradleys, as well as a few former gunners, and loaders. No tank commanders however, and no surprise.

The Colorado Guard was exceptionally helpful in helping round up transport cars for the heavy equipment, six more locomotives and Army rail crews who would now be assigned to our Brigade. The engineers and rail mechanics who kept the locomotives running numbered less than fifty men, without them we were stuck.

Before we departed Sterling, I had one more visit to make, after our long morning meeting with the CNG command and keeping tabs on the load-up.

I borrowed one of the Colorado Guard's Humvees and made a quick trip over to Jess and Gabrielle's camper, where I knew they'd be packing up for their trip back to Denver. Jess met me as I got out of the truck.

"Chief, I just wanted to stop by and give you my thanks for all your help," I said.

"Rick, this was a terrible job for anyone to do. None of us will ever be the same by it, I think. All the same though, it was a singular honor for everyone."

"I believe you are correct, Chief. Please pass along the thanks of Third Washington to your Volunteers. You have a good group, there."

"You have a fine command. I pray that it stays intact until this mess is over. And look us up when you get a chance. You and your brigade members are guests anytime."

"Thanks, Chief. Much appreciated," I said before saluting him, as a junior officer might a senior, when in fact the roles were reversed. He returned it smartly, and we shook hands before I left.

4 1

Saturday
December Second
North Platte, Nebraska

North Platte had suffered far more in much less time than Sterling.

Twenty-six hundred and fourteen civilians were killed by S.A. forces in less than a day. United States Air Force bombardment of the S.A. command-and-control center had also killed at least fifty-six indentured citizens...or 'slaves.' Ten percent of their pre-War population, from the last census....probably a far greater percentage after the flu had ravaged the population. Among the dead was the entire leadership of North Platte, and every preacher, fireman, teacher, and of course, police officer. A few prisoners were taken by the S.A. on their departure--all females, under twenty years old. The survivors in North Platte were mostly in shock from what I could tell. I couldn't find any semblance of a 'command authority' anywhere. Anyone who'd stood up to authority was killed for the favor. After a fruitless day of trying to find someone to lead the city, I ordered essential infrastructure repairs to be made, and headed back to the train. I had other work to attend to, including mapping out transit to our next destination, getting recon crews out ahead, and looking over rail lines east to see where else we might be headed. Trains would be following us along and we didn't have a whole lot of time to waste.

The Air Force targets needed to be cleared by ordnance experts before remains could be safely retrieved, as one of the young Marines first into the city had the bad luck to discover. His remains however were recovered not long after Third Washington arrived. The S.A. dead could be estimated, but not confirmed until any unexploded ordnance was addressed. It was a relatively safe bet that five to six thousand enemy dead lay in bits and pieces within the blast pattern.

Our trains were staged on the rail lines that bisected North Platte and in the old Union Pacific Bailey rail yard on the west side of town. Troops from Dog Six worked to repair the rail lines between the city and the small airport. The missiles blasted a jagged path through the yard and cut the lines to the airport and points east. The airport was also heavily damaged, although we didn't investigate in depth. There wasn't time.

The men from Charlie Six were working with the civilians to repair the damage to the infrastructure caused by the S.A. and isolating the bombed areas. In three days of work, the Brigade had restored power and water to half of the city, albeit with makeshift repairs. As the wreckage was searched and 'safed', the civilian remains were recovered and identified as much as possible, with many unfortunately going to a mass grave in North Platte's cemetery. S.A. weapons and materiel were recovered, cleaned and stored for potential use. Interesting discoveries were forwarded up the chain of command. The S.A. dead were unceremoniously collected via front-end loader and dump truck, trucked out of town to a location east of the regional airport, and buried in a mass grave carved out of the ground with a bulldozer. We thought about sending an honor guard to the burial, and then thought better of it. Most of the S.A. had no identification of any kind. Those that did were isolated and buried at one end of the trench. One of the brigade's chaplains and a few of the command staff and I were present as the last of the S.A. were buried, and brief prayers said over the grave.

"Helluva thing, Colonel," Major Ryder said as we stood in the blowing snow, the bulldozer driving from the burial ground.

"A price to pay, certain to grow much higher, soon, Major. These men may some day be honored by their families, wherever they are, and at a point in time where what they did fades away. They will certainly never be honored by those here."

We never did get an accurate body count for the S.A. dead as no one was interested in piecing them back together.

By late afternoon, the weather had turned clear and cold again, after days of overcast. The vast majority of Third Washington would stand down from sixteen hundred until oh six hundred, Sunday. By late Sunday morning, we'd head further east. Lines east of us were being cleared and repaired. IED's under a highway bridge somewhere between North Platte and Grand Island had taken out the line, not far from the old Cornhusker Army Ammunition Plant. A highway bridge was brought down on top of the tracks.

With our security patrols keeping an eye on things around the train (not that there was an issue, the residents of North Platte could not have been more kind to us), I took some personal time along with Sergeant Travis for some time with my early Christmas present. Chet had a bone-stock 1903A3 when he was growing up, and we'd talked a little about the custom '03 that Karen had commissioned for me.

Within five rounds, I was shooting three-inch groups at a hundred yards...unfamiliar scope and all. Within five more, sub two-inch groups. Chet bettered me, but he was also fifteen years younger, better trained, and a professional. I still counted that as a win. It was not satisfying though, despite the accuracy of the weapon and the craftsmanship that went into its engineering. The ought-six was just another tool used to kill.

"Thank you, Colonel. That brought back a lot of good memories," Chet said as we drove back to Charlie Six.

"Thanks. They did a fine job building that weapon. Impractical as all get out, though."

"Everything has a time and a place, sir. There might be a time and place for that 03 one of these days," Sergeant Travis said.

"Only if the S.A.'s within a few hundred yards of me...which means the organic matter has really hit the fan. Time for some coffee," I said as we parked the Humvee. "And time to clean this rifle. Chet, you spent most of the day in town today. See anyone in the way of a leader? I came up dry. Pretty frustrating. I'd like to know that someone can get this place back on its' feet."

"A few, sir. Lot of folks came into town this afternoon trying to help out. Lot of 'em looking for family. Seems like there are a couple of folks from down south who're naturals."

"See if you can round them up. I'd like to talk to them about the recovery after we head east."

"Will do, sir," he said with a salute. I headed into my quarters to get my cleaning materials for the Springfield. I decided to clean it in one of the work-cars, rather than in my quarters.

A few cars further back, a Third Washington crew was finishing up cleanup of captured and salvaged weapons, even though they'd been given the order to stand down.

"Ten-hut!" I heard as I entered the converted shipping crate.

"At ease," I said. "You men do know that you're off-duty, right?"

"Yes, sir. Anyplace more entertaining than a room full of weapons, sir?" Master Sergeant Schrock, one of the weapons specialists asked.

"None come to mind off hand," I said with a smile. "Need to clean this old Springfield. Mind if I use a cleaning bench, Sarge?"

"Not a bit, sir. You pretty much own the place."

"Not hardly. I'm just the chief custodian," I said as I opened the rifle case and pulled the rifle out of a protective 'sock'.

"Well, now. That's quite an antique, sir," one of Schrock's men said.

"Family had it built for me before I deployed. Just took it out for a walk with Sergeant Travis. Pretty nice work," I said.

"Mind if I take a look, Colonel?" Schrock asked.

"Not at all," I said, handing him the rifle taking out my cleaning solution and tools.

"This is a beauty, sir," he said after some close examination. "I've got two of them myself, back home in Klamath Falls. None anywhere near this nice. I've never seen a stock like this. Carbon fiber composite, nice fitting work. Custom hand made scope mount; good scope. Damn. You ought to be able to take out a robin's eye at three hundred yards with this, Colonel."

"Well, given my aging eyes, I'd settle for hitting a man in the chest at that range."

"Never underestimate one's ability, sir."

"I make it a point never to overestimate it, either, Sergeant. I'll live longer that way."

"True enough, I suppose, sir. Cleaning solutions are in the fireproof locker, over there, along with the swabs and cloths."

"Got my own. Homemade concoction."

"Seriously sir?"

"Yeah. Found it a few years ago…the recipe anyway. The bore cleaner is called 'Ed's Red.' One part Dexron II automatic transmission fluid; one part K1 kerosene; one part aliphatic mineral spirits; one part acetone. And some lanolin. Keeps things from rusting for quite a while. Works pretty well. Cheap, too."

"Might have to scrounge some of that stuff, Sarge," one of the younger soldiers said. "We went through a ton of cleaner on those Texans' rigs."

"Yes we did, Heinrich. Make yourself a list. Maybe see if we can start rounding that stuff up before we ship."

"Yes, sir." I repeated the list for the young man as he took notes.

Twenty minutes of cleaning and conversation later, the 03 was back in her case. I then had a chance to look around at the weapons that Sergeant Schrock and his men had been cleaning.

"This is the one you were telling me about?" I asked, regarding the bin of captured weapons stowed after the blast area was cleared.

"Yes, sir, Colonel. Intel's already had a look," he said, referring to one of my senior staff, Gerry McGowan and his lieutenant.

The lower rack held hundreds of weapons, many damaged to the point where they were only good for parts. I recognized many types, although I was puzzled by the vast variety of calibers. "What a mess," I said.

"No joke, sir. Just about every caliber you could think of."

"By percentage, what's on top—the most common?"

"Easy. 7.62x39, followed by .223, then 7.62x54R."

"Thought I saw a PSL in there among the AK's."

"Yes, sir. And these are just the ones that were suitable for parts. Whole lot more are in the bin there in the back—maybe fifteen hundred. Need to be cleaned but serviceable."

"How was the ammo count?"

"Maybe fifteen thousand rounds across the entire spectrum, Colonel. Never saw more than three mags on any body close to an AK. Guys that were slogging the Mosins and the PSL's had maybe fifty rounds max. Sixty rounds max for anyone with an AR."

"Pretty thin," I said. "And as much as love my 03, it's heavy. So's the ammunition. The Mosins and the like are much heavier. Our men, packing the same weight, can carry hundreds of rounds more per man."

"Yes, sir. And that's good for us."

At nineteen hundred, I was shuttled over to North Platte High School, ten blocks or so south of the rail lines occupied by Charlie- and Dog-Six. The place was packed with survivors and refugees, most looking like one would expect after getting caught in a war.

Sergeant Major Travis and Lieutenant Colonel Miller had helped get the refugees organized and directed to three feeding and warming stations we'd set up, which overall seemed a woefully inadequate response.

"Colonel Drummond?" a corporal asked as I entered the cafeteria. I noticed about fifty Third Washington men were serving food, passing out blankets, coats, and directing civilians towards medical care down one of the hallways. The building was powered by two of our big portable generators.

"Corporal? What's the good word?" I said, catching him by surprise.

"No one's shooting at us, sir," he said after regaining his composure. "Lieutenant Colonel Miller asked me to direct you to his table. I believe he's gathered some of the civilian leadership."

"Very good, Corporal," I said. "Relax, kid," I said as we threaded our way through the room. What I saw, I didn't like. These people were malnourished, which was not just something that had happened through the actions of the S.A. locusts as they passed through town. This was a long-term issue. They hadn't been eating right for a long time.

"Yes, sir. Sorry, sir." I noted he did not yet relax. This kid looked scared.

"If I'm next to you in a firefight, I don't want you freaking out because you have a senior officer next to you. I'm just as full of shit as the next guy," I said, getting him to lighten up a little bit.

"I'll remember that, sir."

"Good. Pass it around while you're at it. And this too: If I am next to one of my men in a firefight, and they're not doing their job, as in, keeping the team alive because they're scared of screwing up in front of an officer, they are as likely to get shot through inaction as through action. From our side or the enemy side. Clear?" Meaning of course, that I'd likely shoot them myself if they were endangering my life.

"Yes, sir," he said with the appropriate amount of respect. "Right over there, sir."

"Thank you, Corporal Johnson. Carry on." I didn't know why I was so edgy.

I made my way through the last couple of tables over to Shawn Miller's table. He was joined by one of his Majors and a Captain assigned to his battalion. Two civilians rounded out the table. All stood as I approached.

"Colonel Rick Drummond," I said, shaking the hands of both civilians.

"Jim Kreinbeck," the first said. Well fed, but thin, dressed appropriately, about my age.

"Chuck Varleson. Good to meet you, Colonel." Tall. Really tall, I noted.

"And thanks for bringing the United States back to North Platte," Kreinbeck said.

"I think the Marines and the Texans did that. And our boys in the Air Force," I said.

"Regardless. It's pretty much been Hell under the S.A.," Varleson replied. "Although we hear it's been worse the farther East you go."

"Haven't heard that, but good to know," I said. "I understand that there isn't anything left here in terms of civilian leadership. Is that accurate?"

"It is. They're in a common grave over by the Country Club. S.A. rounded 'em all up and machine-gunned them," Chuck Varleson said. "They'd have got us in time. Some of them won't be missed, though."

That puzzled me a little. "What did you say?"

"Sorry. We had an asshole who took charge of the place after the S.A. occupation. About the time they moved to Denver. Bruce Devlin decided to be the big fish. The Mayor went fishing one day, never came back. So'd the Police Chief. Devlin put his brother in law in charge in the city, his cousins in the police department. Things went to shit from there," Jim said. "All guns were declared illegal and seized. Almost all the fuel was seized. Radios seized. TV's smashed."

"Colonel, pre-War, these guys thought they were God's gift to the planet. Well, Devlin did anyway. Big shot banker, into real estate, trophy wife, all the most expensive toys. Moved back up here before the real-estate market collapsed a few years go...made a bunch of money down in Tucson. Built a big-ass house.. Bought off anyone who got in his way, unless they were too stupid to take the money, and then he'd just destroy them. Once the S.A. came in, he welcomed them with open arms. Mayor and Chief disappeared about two weeks in. We had a local currency—scrip-type system—set up before that happened. Of course any precious metals went his way, too, and then the guns went away. He took it over, took cuts off the top, ran the bank. Got to the point where the regular Joe's couldn't make it...he was taking from everyone. Commerce basically stopped. People gave up. If they were able, they escaped."

"I see significant evidence of mass malnutrition here," I said.

"You do at that, Colonel. Devlin and his thugs took all the stock, any grains that were being harvested, down to banty hens and milk-goats. Stolen at gunpoint, a lot of it. Nothing most folks could do about it. Fed themselves, sold the rest to the S.A. Too many guns, too many men, always watching."

"So what happened to this bastard?"

"S.A. popped him and his friends along with all the others. I hear he begged for his life at the end. Offered up all his silver and gold, which they took anyway and then shot him. I just wish I'd have been the guy to kill him myself. I'd have done it slower."

"I can understand that," I said, remembering our own tyrannical local leaders. "Let me get to the point here. Are you from North Platte proper?" I asked.

"No, sir, Colonel. Few miles south, I run a feedlot down there, or did before the S.A. took all the cattle," Kreinbeck said flatly.

"Chuck here ran a resort in the summer down on the lake south of town, and farms as well."

"Pardon me, if I'm repeating anything that Colonel Miller might have told you, but we need to establish a civilian leadership structure to make sure that the town gets back on it's feet. More support of course will be coming from the U.S., but we're not long for this town. Resupply trains and new generating units will be here before we leave. We don't want these people suffering anymore than they already have. It's important that we get a few men and women to take the reins here. Are you two interested?"

"We're not politicians, Colonel. I think I feel safe speaking for Jim here," Varleson said.

"Chuck, neither am I. A year ago I was a civilian, just living and doing my job, raising my kids, bitching about paying taxes and listening to whiny employees. Our state got hit by a big-ass earthquake and not long after, I'm running the county. Then I get drafted, at my age. And here we are."

"Colonel, we wouldn't know where to start."

"You'll have help. We'll get some folks in here to give you a hand. Not sure if they'll be from Nebraska, or Boise, or Sacramento or wherever. I can say that they're not interested in running things. They are interested in North Platte running itself. You'll get communications back. You'll get weapons back. Soon," I said. The captured weapons didn't have any use to Third Washington. The citizens of North Platte might as well have them.

"Fresh approach in these parts," Varleson said.

"Yeah. Expect to see a lot more of that," I said. "Remember the Constitution? The real Federal Government actually pays attention to that these days."

Jim replied, looking at his friend, "Will wonders ever cease?"

"Hopefully not. Before we head out, we'll do what we can about getting you a schedule on supply trains and resources that will be available," I said. "So, can we sign you up?"

"Heads I'm mayor," Chuck Varleson said. "Tails, dogcatcher."

"I'm in on that," Kreinbeck said. "It's not like there are cattle to mind these days."

Sunday
December Third

We'd departed early, earlier than I might have liked. I'd hoped to attend the first worship service in North Platte since July, not long after they were occupied by the forces that became the S.A. Services would be held in several locations, but none of the churches, temples, stake centers, or worship centers were left. Charlie and Dog Six left at oh seven hundred, in the near dark, in blowing snow. I'd been up since four-thirty, and took forty-five minutes to get back into physical conditioning in one of the crew cars. Weights, a couple spinning machines and treadmills helped burn off some of the pent up energy as well as keeping....or in my case, obtaining, increased physical ability. Breakfast was coffee, some biscuits, and more coffee, taken at my station in the Command Car.

A half hour out of North Platte, we received a radio signal—coded—that S.A. units remained active in the area ahead of us, despite the area being overrun with Marine and Army units. It would seem that the S.A. filled the vacuum after the U.S. units passed through, and pushed further East. Without stable support and 'occupying' forces, the S.A. just melted away, and then moved back in. Within a half-hour, were barely moving.

"Colonel, track report coming in from up line," Greg Shand said. "Still decoding."

"Thanks, Captain."

"Sir, we're also getting some chatter on the S.A. frequencies. Trying to get it cleaned up."

"Let me know when you have something. Anything from our friends from Texas? They were in Grand Island yesterday, correct?"

"Yes, sir. Expect they're still there. Weather's ugly. The Texans and the Marine units are bogged down on one side of the storm front, the S.A. main force is on the other."

"Sir, we've got a blocked track ahead," Private Kittrick said.

"How far out?" I asked as I stretched my side. Ribs still hurt.

"Town called Cozad. The auger unit cleared to that point and is returning. Said they also took some small arms fire as they reversed."

"Distance to Cozad, Mister Martin," I asked.

"Fourteen point two miles, sir. Auger unit will be parked on a siding at Gothenburg."

"Gothenburg status," Captain Shand asked one of the other techs.

"Marines report six hours ago said no one alive, sir, within five miles. And IED's all over the place."

"Affirmative, sir. Remote sensing coming on line, should have a sat picture any second now," Corporal Martin said as the screen flashed white and then went to the 'blue screen of death.' "Holy crap! Comm failure on the sat link. Kittrick, Get Dog Six to verify uplink status."

"What's going on?" I asked as everyone scrambled.

"Bird just died, sir. S.A. just took out the satellite," Kittrick replied, and then waited for confirmation. "Confirm that, sir. Central U.S. satellite is down.....Sir, San Antonio reports Air Force is tracking multiple launches from S.A. territories. Have to be anti satellite missiles. Dog Six confirms and is tied into Air Force tracking radar."

"Get the word out to all units ahead. Now," Shand ordered. "While we can."

"Yes, sir," Kittrick said.

"Martin, get a status update to both trains. Might be warm up ahead," I said. "Tell the engineers to park us five miles outside of Cozad until we're ready to proceed in."

"Yes, sir. Could be losing comms with Command pretty quick, Colonel."

"Things have been going a little too well, Captain. Counteroffensive had to happen sooner or later. Looks like sooner. Gents, get every position of U.S. forces downloaded to the protected server. They pop an EMP this gear's in a world of hurt."

"Done, Colonel. Automatic trigger and isolated, protected data storage," Kittrick said. "Western U.S. satellite down. Dammit. Inbounds heading toward Eastern satellite.....one point five minutes max."

"Kittrick, where are they launching from?"

"Detroit region, sir. Can't tell for sure. Two different profiles. Mid U.S. satellite was definitely an airborne launch due to the speed of intercept. Other two were ground launch for sure."

Nothing that I'd read or seen spoke of anywhere near this kind of capability. If anything, I thought that Command had overstated the case, hammering on the lack of technological sophistication of the S.A.

"Any other ballistic launches?"

"Can't tell sir. All satellites within line of site and single point relay are gone."

"AWAC's?"

"None in range sir. Preservation of assets, I believe the Air Force is calling it."

"So U.S. forces could be on the receiving end of a ballistic missile attack and we'd have zero warning," I said.

"Afraid so, sir," Kittrick replied.

"Charlie Six, I want you putting together a work around for distance communications with the field units. Dog Six on analysis of the attack pattern and communications options with Command," Greg Shand ordered, "With the Colonel's approval."

"Don't wait for me," I said. "We don't have time."

Ten minutes later, we were in mid-conversation with both Austin and San Antonio, when the signal went dead.

"Gone, sir. Not sure we can get them back," Martin said, fiddling with his computer, as the other techs scrambled as signals disappeared.

A few moments, later, Kittrick stated, "We're in the dark, sirs. Systems operational, no data out there to collect."

"Alert all battalion commanders," I said. "Things will be interesting when we hit Cozad. Bet on it."

Signals officers from Dog Six prepared the attack analysis against U.S. communications systems, and had it ready for a hurried Brigade briefing at nine-hundred hours. All Brigade commanders were attending either in person or electronically.

The outlook wasn't favorable.

All civilian and military bands were affected, with multiple small EMP detonations in near space. Hardened military satellites were destroyed through direct impact, with airborne launched anti-sat weapons and several small ballistic missiles.

None of those capabilities were in the capability models created by the Department of Defense. The airborne launch alone proved that the S.A. had high-altitude fighter or other high performance aircraft capable of launching a missile able to target a satellite. The ballistic capability of course proved that they had the ability to drop a nuclear weapon wherever they pleased, assuming advanced targeting capability.

522

Charlie Six signals teams were testing on-board communications gear, finding no faults, and testing the typical battalion communications gear. Thus far, everything was working. The secondary communications suite was trying to communicate with anyone not aboard either train.

"We're not quite back in the stone-age, Colonel. We can see it from there, though," Captain McGowan said.

"Last knowns of U.S. forces. Major Ryder?" I asked.

"Marines are inbound to Grand Island after a detour up north, numbering thirty eight hundred six, down from forty-four hundred. Lone Star is in and around Grand Island, fielding forty-three nineteen, sir."

"Between them, they've lost twelve hundred men. They're down thirteen percent in less than ten days," I said.

"Affirmative, sir. No counts on the New Mexico or Arizona units. They're south of us. Haven't heard from them since oh three hundred."

"Georgia. Where're the Bulldogs?" I asked.

"Due south of Grand Island. Town by the name of Hastings. They're down to thirteen hundred and twenty, Colonel."

"Down about two hundred since Sterling. Between the units that you've listed, and the known killed-in-action, we're out of men in a few weeks....or days. All these units have been doing is a harassing campaign as the S.A. retreats. We need reinforcing units. NOW," I said. "There is not one damned reason that the S.A. couldn't mop us up right now. All right. Last known on the S.A. forces...Major, headcount."

Gerry was hesitant to answer. "Well in excess of fifty-thousand, sir. Probably closer to seventy-five thousand. At least forty-thousand are split between Omaha and Kansas City, with the balance in the field against U.S. forces as they pull back east, sir."

"So our units are down thirteen or more percent, fighting the stragglers," I said. That comment was met with silence. "We continue on like this, and we're done. We need serious manpower in this area and we have nothing."

"Recommendation, Colonel?" Third Battalion commander, Lt. Colonel Hugh Epstein forwarded.

"Absolutely, Colonel Epstein," I said.

"If we can find a means to communicate to the other Guard and Regular Army units, we need to consolidate in defensive points and stay there, until the U.S. can muster enough manpower to counter the S.A. There's more men out there, they're just in the wrong place. In light of our communications breakdowns, continued movement east without reliable intel is suicide, sir."

"Thanks, Colonel," I said. "Can't really argue with that. Once we hit Cozad, we'll have some time to plan while we figure out how to clear the tracks. Battalion commanders, expect an update on comms enhancements as soon as we get some news. In the meantime, First and Second Battalions, we're five miles from Cozad and we're taking Charlie Six in first. Dog Six hangs back a country mile in reserve. First and Second will deploy as soon as we approach the blockage, barring something unforeseen. You will secure the area and we will assess the damage to the tracks. If Cozad is anything like what the Marines said about Gothenburg, there probably aren't any civilians left, or left alive. And probably IED's as well as hostiles. Saddle up. Dismissed." I said and the video feeds to the other railcars went dark.

"All right, communications boys, let's have you work some magic," I said to the staff in the communications suite. "Sergeant Travis, double our crews in the defensive cars. I want a dispersal map for First and Second with real-time positions plotted on the last satellite maps we have, uplink feeds from platoon leaders and leaders on up to battalion level. Got it?"

"Yes, sir. No problem," Private Briggs replied.

"You say that now, Briggs. Shooting hasn't started yet."

At eleven-thirty hours, Charlie Six began the advance into Cozad. The Defensive cars were fully manned and weapons-free, and both assigned battalions were in full gear ready to deploy.

Within a half-mile of our intended stopping point, both the engineers and the communications teams said that they could see the blockage ahead. Almost simultaneously the train came under scattered small-arms fire. The Command Car was better armored than much of the train, and we could hear the occasional rounds *'spang'* against the superstructure of our car.

"Briggs, any word on damage to the train?"

"None so far, sir. Small arms at significant distance, according to the crew in the forward D-car," he said, just as the resounding *'whump'* rattled through the train. Briggs answered before I asked.

"Ours, sir. Abrams just let one off," he said to me before directing our defenders to other likely targets.

"Shooters atop the grain elevators, right above us to the north and east on the other side of the downed bridge," Briggs said, quickly switching video feeds to serve as spotter for our crews. "Sir, forward Abrams just targeted another tall structure just south. That one's gone, sir. Screen feed sixteen," Brigs said.

With a few keystrokes, I could select any one of two dozen video feeds from aboard the exterior of the train. Most were fixed view, but some had the ability to zoom in on the image. Feed Sixteen showed the collapsing remains of a five or six-story concrete tower, hit mid-way up by a round from the rail car mounted Abrams tank. Feed Ten showed, with a pan-and-zoom camera, small arms fire from the grain elevators. Our own trigger-pullers in the defensive cars—D-cars—were waiting for the right moment. First Battalion began their scramble out of the train and moved for cover. Second Battalion was waiting for their "go" signal from the rear Command Car.

Within a few moments, I could see the enemy start to fall systematically as Third Washington engaged them in some force. I knew though, that there weren't more than a half-dozen of our men doing the shooting. Feed Five had the rear defensive car, along with audio. I watched, my heart pounding, as the cry came in from the rear Command Car.

"RPG!"

The shouts and pandemonium in the rear defensive car, and through the open audio feed of the rear Command Car only lasted a moment until the rocket-propelled grenades hit.

The defensive car took five hits before the rear Abrams and the chain guns found the shooters' locations. The rear Command Car took one grenade, severing our link with the rear of the train. A moment later, Private Martin yelled, *"incoming!"* as the forward portion of the train was targeted. Three violent shocks later, I picked myself up off the deck. Several of the video feeds were blank, I saw, but the remaining feeds showed First and Second Battalions streaming out towards Cozad to our north and south, into the industrial side of the tracks, leapfrogging with fire-and-cover as they went. The D-car chain guns were making hay.

"Men down! Men down! Corpsman!"

The RPG fire ceased, but not soon enough.

13:03 Hours

"Dog Six, back it up," I heard Briggs order the engineers aboard the second train. "Med Team Five, standby for deployment."

"Colonel, you ready?" Jim Schaefer asked.

"Yep. Let's move," I said. Four battalions were in the field in Cozad, eliminating the S.A. in their entirety. Lieutenant Colonel Schaefer and I were heading east to survey the blockage on our tracks.

"Sir, make sure your comm link is active, please," Briggs asked before I put on my helmet.

"Done," I said. "Thanks, Briggs."

"No problem, sir. Battalion commanders are on Three-Echo, with subroutines programmed to contact smaller units."

"Haven't read the manual, Briggs. If I get in trouble, I'll just holler," I said, Briggs of course knowing that I had read the manual

526

on the complicated communications headset, and had tried it out earlier.

Outside, the transportation crews had unloaded most of Charlie Sixes Humvees, with the last one off the train parked near my Command Car. This particular unit had a manned top-mounted gun and was up-armored.   The gunner, and a following support truck were weapons ready. All eyes were looking for targets, weapons ready.

"Care to drive, sir?" Jim asked.

"Hell, yes," I said. "Tired of sitting around."

"Should be a couple hundred yards up the line....the first blockage that is, sir."

"Multiples?" I asked. "Thought we only had the highway bridge down on the tracks. Saw it on the enhanced monitors."

"Oh, more than that, sir, from what the point men out west are saying."

"Great," I said. "No IED's spotted yet?"

"Sir? I can field that one. Sergeant Kinlin, First Battalion, Delta, er...sorry, D Company," he said, correcting himself. The more modern phonetic alphabet, *Alpha-Bravo-Charlie-Delta* was widely used by the S.A. The U.S. forces reverted to *Able-Baker-Charlie-Dog*. "We cleared a hundred meter swath on either side of the tracks and about two hundred meters down the line. Couple squads from Easy Company are clearing further out."

"Thanks, Sergeant," I said. "I appreciate your work out there."

"Years of experience, sir. Three tours in the Raq and two in the Stan. Could really used a Short Bus out here."

"Short Bus?" I asked.

"MRAP, sir. Mine Resistant Ambush Protectant. Look like a short bus, Colonel."

"Pretty much guarantee we'll never have one of those handy when we need it, Sergeant."

"Universal truth of combat, Colonel."

We headed east several hundred feet beyond the lead engine, where the first blockage stopped us cold. The S.A. had detonated an IED and dropped a concrete overpass, blocking the rail line with an impassable barrier thirty feet wide and five feet thick. I headed south of the blockage, around the downed bridge and down the embankment, which was easier said than done with the Humvee side-slipping on the icy slope. A few hundred yards east of the overpass, they dropped one of the rail bridges into the river...the Platte River, I assumed. The Interstate Eighty bridges though, were intact, or at least, hadn't been blown, yet.

"This is gonna suck," I said. "Have any bridge engineers handy?" I asked Jim Schaefer.

"Nope, we sure don't, Colonel. Nor any bridging equipment or heavy equipment to clear any of this."

"Resupply to any unit east of here depending on rail service on this line just ended from this point until we get this figured out," I said just as a rifle round hit the Humvee.

"Not quite secured out here, sir," Kinlin said.

"Ya think?" I said. "We'll get back toward the train and get into town. Sounds like our boys have a few areas swept out."

"D Street by the hospital, as far north as their middle school, everything west of that. East and north of there, well, the civilians are kicking ass up there Colonel, ahead of our men. One of the squads said they were killing the S.A. with shovels and axes."

"Whatever it takes, Sergeant," I said. "Any guess as to civilian headcount?"

"Three thousand if there's a one, sir. Probably more."

528

"Probably no way to get them to let us do the job," I said.

"Not one chance in all of Hell, Colonel."

I drove south, slowly, along D Street, passing dozens of dead S.A., one face down in the snow with a pickaxe buried in his back, his blood soaking the snow and ice. To a man, or an animal, as my opinion of the S.A. line fighter was now defined, the dead appeared to have been beaten to death by a mob. I noticed there appeared to be no civilian bodies.

"Sergeant, the S.A. ran out of ammo, I'm thinking."

"Probably so, sir. Civilians lit out after them and killed who they caught."

"Victor Two," I said into my headset after switching to the right frequency.

"Two," I heard in my ear.

"Estimate enemy remaining," I asked.

"Six hundred plus. Civilians and Dog Company are in pursuit."

"Rendezvous at location Sugar after you secure the area. Victor Five out," I said.

"Jim, how long you think mop-up will take?"

"Two to three hours. First units in are about a third through the building sweep. No completed IED's so far, except at their airport, but a shitload of material to build them, sir. Excavations all along the Interstate, and three arterials. Didn't have time to finish them."

"All right, enough of my sightseeing. Let's see how this hospital looks."

Sunday
December Third
13:50 Hours

The hospital appeared to be remarkably intact, like most of the town, unlike many of the other towns we'd seen, either through pictures or first hand. No electricity of course, but there were cars and trucks in the parking lot, most showing that they'd been driven recently. Fifth Battalion men were in place all around the hospital, in their snow camouflage. I parked the Humvee in a normal parking stall, just like anyone, pre-War.

"Looks in good shape," I said.

"S.A. was only here in force for a day or so. Didn't have much time to make it like home," Schaefer said. "Between the Marines and that gang from Texas, I don't think they had much time at all."

We climbed out of the Humvee, and were met almost at the curb by a half-dozen medical types.

"Colonel Drummond, Third Washington," I said, introducing myself to an elderly man. His name badge was illegible, or it was to my eyes anyway.

"D.C.?"

"The other end. The state."

"Welcome to Cozad. Larry O'Connor. I'm the managing director for the hospital."

"Good to meet you, Mr. O'Connor. What can we help you out with?"

"Surgeons, nurses, supplies, electricity, food. That'd be a start. You've already got some of your corpsmen and doctors working inside."

"We'll see what we can do about more supplies," I said.

"Already on their way, sir," Jim said. "Supplies and most of our corpsmen. We've also got two medical cars on the trains that include full surgical suites."

"Don't have the staff to use them," O'Connor said. "Statists took all the supplies and every doc and nurse that wasn't hiding someplace."

"Now that Cozad is back in the United States, supplies and utilities will be more regular, I suspect. What's your population here, Mr. O'Connor?"

"Around three thousand. About five before the War."

"How're the rest of your supplies? Food in particular."

"Again, what wasn't nailed down..."

"Got it. We'll see what we can help out with. How about your city leaders, police chief, and all? Where can we..."

"Dead. All of them. First to go. Pastors and priests were the next."

"I'm sorry. Seems to be the pattern of the S.A.," I said.

"Killing children seems to be as well," O'Connor said.

"Unfortunately, yes, that too."

"Colonel, if you have chaplains, we could use them here. There are a hundred broken hearted families up at the middle school....trying to identify their dead children."

"Jim," I said. A chill went down my spine.

"On it, sir."

"What happened, Mr. O'Connor?"

"C'mon inside. It's marginally warmer in there."

We filed into the darkened hospital foyer, lit with several of Third Washington field lanterns, and passed the body bags of fifteen Third Washington men killed in action. The foyer was packed with people, many wounded. I saw down the hallway a row of bloodstained gurneys. We headed to the administrative area of the hospital, littered with files and overturned furniture.

"Men, lend a hand while Mr. O'Connor and I meet," I said to our two security men. Jim Schaefer was talking with Second Battalion's commander, working on clearing the eastern side of town, and moving north. The last of the S.A.'s mechanized capability in Cozad was running hard north, a single tank, I was picking up on my headset. A Russian-made T-90 variant. *'Front-line main battle tank.'*
We sat in what was left of a small conference room, out of the commotion in the corridors.

"The S.A. gathered up most of the kids and used them as leverage against the city. We don't know what else they did with them. When the Marines were on the horizon, they told everyone to stay in their houses and that if they were on the street, they'd be shot on sight. The night before the Marines and the Texans swept through, most of the S.A. faded away east," O'Connor said.

I sat there, leaning forward on the table, as he continued. In my headset, Second Battalion was credited with destroying the T-90 variant and its crew. Secondary explosions aboard the tank prevented any detailed look at the wreckage.

"The kids were put into a secure room at the school. That room is all concrete, part of the tornado shelter. No way out. They threw in grenades. Dozens of them."

I felt sick. "My God," I said quietly.

"God had little to do with that, Colonel. They're nothing but butchers. Soulless, heartless, mindless butchers."

I tried to gather my thoughts, struggling to find words. "We'll do what we can, Mr. O'Connor, to get some help here. Our brigade has seen what they can do. They slaughtered more than fifty thousand soldiers in Colorado a couple of weeks ago. We helped retrieve their bodies."

O'Connor was shaking. "I cannot believe that men could do this to each other. The senselessness of it all," he said, voice trailing off, tears coming to his eyes.

Later in the afternoon, I visited the school, a typical American middle school, which in the future would be mentioned in the same hushed tones as Beslan, Treblinka, Auschwitz. There are sights that words just cannot describe.

I'd asked volunteers to serve at the school in remains retrieval, and had more than two hundred men respond. Twenty-five were selected. Along with representatives of the city, they retrieved the remains of the children, most unidentifiable. They were gathered and placed in a common grave on the grounds of the school. The burial service was one of the most emotionally powerful events of my life. I had to pour myself back into my day job to relieve my mind of what I had seen.

17:40 Hours

"Sir, we have one of the Marine units on secure line, I'll patch you through to your station," Private Kittrick said with some excitement. The comms guys had been working on getting some sort of communications going since the attack on the satellites, and repairing the damage to the secondary communications array at the rear of the train. Two of our techs were wounded when an anti-tank round penetrated the car, but did not detonate.

"Understood. Thanks, Mr. Kittrick," I said, putting on my headphones, and taking my attention away from the computer screen with the loading reports for our wheeled vehicles. The work was a good distraction.

"Secure channel, sir. You'll be speaking with the second in command."

"This is Colonel Richard Drummond, Third Washington."

"Colonel, I'm Major Stevenson, First Marine Expeditionary Force."

"Major, how're you standing? Are you and your men going to be able to hold out until reinforcements arrive?"

"S.A.'s holding their own, sir. We're keeping them in check along with our Army friends from Texas."

"Supply status?"

"Thin, sir. Could use a resup. We've had no contact with command most of the day."

Perhaps he didn't know about the satellites being knocked out, I thought. "Satellites are down, Major. S.A. took them out. Regarding resupply, we're working on that right now. S.A. dropped a bridge down onto our track and blew a bridge over the river, so our train isn't an option for the immediate future. Trucks are being loaded with everything they can carry and will be on the way by twenty hundred. What's the status of the highway up to Grand Island?"

"Other than what's left of fifty or sixty S.A. tanks and trucks and their dead, it's clear, Colonel."

"All right, Major. I'll pass you off to Lieutenant Colonel Atwood. Atwood is head of Fifth Battalion and will be point on the resupply. Wait one," I said.

"Much obliged, Colonel."

"Bryce? He's all yours," I said. Atwood joined the conversation from one of the other communications suites.

Between the two trains, we had sixty Humvees of various models, and twenty trucks loading. Some of our mechanics had also retrieved some civilian vehicles from Cozad, and put them back in running order. Food, ammunition, and medical supplies were being loaded into them by every available hand, with a handful of Humvees remaining in and around town. Those men that weren't loading were working on the river bridge, building a rubble abutment from steel, broken concrete and whatever they could lay hands on. Three local engineers had been found to provide Third Washington an impromptu bridge design…what should take months to do, we required immediately.

The highway bridge was a different story. The smaller pieces were being removed by hand by the men and women of Cozad and our crews. The larger pieces—most of the bridge deck—would have to be broken into smaller pieces and then moved out of the way. Tricks learned from our trained combat engineers would be used for the heavy work. IED's of our own, placed in strategic locations within the wrecked bridge deck, would break the pre-stressed concrete deck into smaller pieces. Multiple draglines on tanks would then pull the pieces out of the way. The damaged track and roadbed would then be rebuilt.

"Mister Kittrick, a moment please," I said.

"Sir?"

"How did you manage to raise the Marines?"

"Uh, we bypassed all military frequencies to establish initial contact, then had the Marines match our frequency on their encrypted gear."

"You just described how you established encrypted contact. How did you raise them in the first place?"

"Well, Morse Code actually, on a shortwave freq."

"And they had someone on the other end listening in?"

"Yes, sir. Comm tech by the name of Juice."

"You know him personally?"

"I've been in communication with him since we hit Colorado. Haven't met him personally. We set up a, well, contingency plan in case our normal channels were unavailable, Colonel."

"Helluva job, Corporal."

"Sir?"

"You just got promoted. Carry on."

"Yes, *sir! Thank you*, sir!"

Colonel Atwood completed his coordination with the Marines, and joined me for a 'dinner' MRE, in my case spaghetti with meat sauce.

"Bryce, I'm expecting that you and your men will be engaged alongside the Marines until we arrive."

"Counting on it, sir."

"Let's do what we can to all come back alive, Colonel. You've got a lot of green troops under your command."

"Been there, sir. We'll do O.K.," he said.

"Hope so, Colonel Atwood. We lost fifteen men today, and experience didn't weigh into their fate."

The last of the gear was lashed down and covered by nineteen-thirty hours, and Atwood's' detachment pulled out almost immediately, drivers and spotters with night-vision goggles and illuminators on the vehicles. The full moon provided some light, with the thin, high cloud cover. Fifteen minutes later, Charlie Six was quiet again, and I made a pass through several of the bunk cars.

The days' efforts had taken a toll on the men, with empty bunks and our dead stored in transport caskets, with an honor guard. Two of our large tent shelters were set up in anticipation of civilian need, but only one was being used, mostly to stage supplies before delivery into the community. Weapons were being cleaned, the off-duty men were mostly resting in their bunks, playing cards, or alone with their thoughts.

On-duty crews were still helping civilians in Cozad with food and supplies to get them through a few days, and picket-line security, ringing the town and the train yard. One of our Abrams was towing the large hunks of the downed overpass from the main track and the siding. I hadn't seen any of our chaplains for most of the day.

Back in the Command Car, two communications techs were working on one of the damaged video displays, while two others continued to attempt to re-establish contact with military units further up the food chain.

"Sir, we've got incoming friendly aircraft, rotary, distance forty miles....make that multiple, Colonel," Private Jenkins said. "Three birds, sir."

"You sure they're friendlies?" First Battalion commander Shawn Miller replied.

"IFF codes check out with current data sets, sir. Two Chinooks and a 'Hawk."

"Sergeant Baumann," Miller said into his headset, "We've got inbound friendlies. I hope for your sake that LZ's ready...."

I listened to Miller's half of the conversation as he chewed a platoon sergeant a 'new one,' and roused several hundred of his men to action. I grabbed my parka and helmet and headed to the door.

"Nice work, Colonel Miller," I said.

"Never hurts to have an LZ handy, even if most of the Air Force seems to be parked, sir. One of these days, today for instance, we might have need of one."

"Captain Shand, hold down the fort. Colonel Miller and I will go greet our guests."

"Yes, sir," Greg replied. "We'll get the mess moving along as well."

"Very good. Thanks."

Outside, a few hundred feet south and west of our Command Car, Baker Company had cleared a large landing zone, and was setting up beacons to identify the LZ to the night-vision gear worn by the helo pilots. We could hear them approach far sooner than we could see them, skimming low along the highway, without anti-collision lights.

The lead helicopter landed straightaway, perfectly aligned with the ground beacon, followed by the twin-rotor Chinooks. The Blackhawk's passengers immediately disembarked and bee-lined it over toward us. The three helicopters engines shut down quickly.

"Colonel Drummond, Third Washington Engineers," I said.

"Commander Daniel Evans. United States Navy."

"Welcome to Cozad, Commander. I'd like to say you were expected, but you're certainly welcome. This is Lieutenant Colonel Miller, First Battalion commander. How many men have you got with you?"

"Seventy-six, Colonel. A whole lot more pretty quick, sir. I've also got orders for you from Command."

"Thanks. Command Car is over this way. We'll find space for the men for the night, and can round up some dinner, I suspect."

"Much appreciated, Colonel. If at all possible, I'd like to sequester them from your troops."

I looked over my shoulder as a non-com barked at the men as they grabbed their gear and double-timed it behind us.

"Shouldn't be a problem, Commander. Looks like you've got a Sergeant Rock back there."

"Einreich. He's the real deal, Colonel."

We walked a little further, and Evans noted the honor guard, and looked a little surprised.

"Sir?" he said.

"Lost fifteen men today, Commander. Twenty-one wounded."

"Sorry to hear that, Colonel."

"Thanks. Seven hundred fifty-five enemy dead, confirmed at this point, a fair percentage of them killed by the citizens of Cozad. With axles, shovels, picks, and baseball bats. You've seen line action against the S.A., Commander?"

"Behind the line action, Colonel."

"Well, when you get back behind the lines, I hope you prosecute your mission with extreme prejudice. Unspeakable things have been done in these towns. Here in Cozad, they loaded a classroom up with kids, held them hostage, and when the Marines showed up, they grenaded them."

Evans said nothing.

We headed into the conference car, where coffee, soup and sandwiches were just being placed by one of our mess crew.

"Have a seat, Commander. How are things outside of direct radio range?"

"We've got some new comm gear for you, Colonel. Four sets, to be precise. That should patch your unit in with Command through ground relays. To answer your direct question though, sir, San Antonio and Houston were both targeted by S.A. ballistic missiles with nuclear warheads. Six separate launches. All were destroyed in flight by airborne lasers, still in boost phase. That rained warheads and wreckage on both sides of the front. Two detonations, both in northwest Arkansas. The team outside is tasked with infiltrating the northern third of the S.A. territory and taking out that capability."

"Know where you're headed, Commander?"

"Yes, sir."

"Not asking, just want to make sure you're not on a snipe hunt."

"We have good intel, Colonel."

"All right then, Commander. Let's get your boys set up and you whatever local intel we can without compromise."

"Thank you, sir. Probably the last warm night my men will have for awhile."

"Feel free to use this as your HQ," I said as the mess soldier came back in. "Sirs, chow's ready in fifteen for the Navy men. Should I bring up more here, Colonel?"

"Up to the Commander, Mister Pierce. I expect the Commander and his staff have some business to attend to this evening."

Commander Evans and his senior staff met in the conference room as the remainder of the SEALS grabbed dinner and would try to get some sleep. Sometime during the night, this group of men would head east for points unknown. Our orders, provided by Commander Evans in a sealed envelope, directed us to proceed to Grand Island immediately and *'stage for large-scale support of up to fifty thousand troops for an extended period of time.'*

I reviewed the orders, as well as several dispatches from Austin on other events *'influencing civilian understanding of the prosecution of the war.'* I tried to wrap my head around that statement, and gave up. The 'events' though, were self-explanatory:

--As I had suspected, the S.A. had distributed, before destroying the military and remaining commercial satellites, video illustrating the Sixth Army engaged in a massacre of civilians in *suburban areas of Denver*, of course refuted by the video from Lt. Susan Kirchener's team.

--Bulk food stockpiles and shipments had been poisoned in several major cities, throwing all bulk food shipments and storehouses into doubt. These included food warehouses operated by

541

several religious denominations, bulk public warehouses operated by government agencies, and commercial vendors. The S.A. published reports that the United States Government was behind the poisonings, in the name of population reduction and generation of fear, creating dependence on the U.S. government.

--Continued sabotage of utilities, refineries, rail lines, and public facilities seemed to be increasing; probably along the strategy of the "swarm" we'd seen in Spokane County.

--The S.A. broadcasts touted defeat of 'rebel' forces throughout the Great Lakes region, pushing through the Dakotas into Montana. Complete fabrication, as the U.S. held the line, well within the Minnesota border. The strategic weapons throughout the Dakotas, as well as bases in Minot and Fargo, were well defended. I wondered how my brother and his family were, in Minnesota. It'd been many months since we'd heard from them.

--Finally, the S.A. broadcasts boasted of reopening New Orleans and Charleston, South Carolina, to State of America commercial shipping, providing *'free access to commerce necessary for the reformation of the State.'* I'm sure that was a surprise to the few thousand residents of the remains of New Orleans, not quite abandoned but nearly so, after the last big Gulf hurricane; and to Charleston, which was deep inside of United States territory.

I finished Austin's incoming, and began my own assignment.

Dr. and Mrs. John Miller
Veradale, Washington

Dear Doctor and Mrs. Miller—

It is utmost sorrow that I write this letter about the loss of your son, Mark. There are no words to adequately convey this loss or the enduring memory of the space in our Brigade that he filled.

Third Washington has been in the field a few short weeks, and during this time, your eldest proved himself to be a natural leader and a man who deeply understood the sacrifices that have been made to preserve this nation and to see it free.

I had the privilege to work alongside Mark in Sterling, Colorado in the retrieval of those lost in the Sixth Army massacre. It was most difficult and challenging work, and it weighed heavily on us all. Mark and I discussed his personal relationship with the Almighty during this work, and I am confident that your son is at peace and in the presence of God.

These words, I pray bring you comfort. For a man of just twenty, he cast a very long shadow on the men around him and the Brigade as a whole.

Respectfully,
Colonel Richard J. Drummond
Commanding
Third Washington Engineering Brigade

I had just finished the last of the condolence letters for each of the men lost, along with the Brigade status report. The fifteen men we'd lost included a West Point first lieutenant, two senior sergeants, a corpsman, and eleven men who had yet to reach twenty years of age. Six were injured when two RPG's hit near their location, the rest were hit by small arms fire before they could find cover.

The Brigade status report would be radioed back to Command, with the condolence letters. The status report gave our current equipment, fuel and supply load (decreasing rapidly), and requests for resupply that might vary from our 'standard' resupply. I wondered, how could there be a 'standard' resupply when even we didn't know what we'd need and when.

The packet from Command contained a slated schedule of troop trains and supply trains to arrive in Grand Island over the next several weeks. The United States was about to go after the heart of the S.A., in the middle of the winter. Third Washington had several options moving east by rail, depending on the progress on the Front. In no case, did our potential routes travel more than another three hundred miles. I heard a knock on my door, and Kittrick announced Commander Evans.

"Commander, get your men all settled in?"

"Looks like we're here until around oh four-hundred, Colonel. We'll head up to Grand Island and hop east from there."

"Pretty good chance you'll see some of our men up there. We sent a slug of our men and vehicles loaded with everything they could carry up there before you arrived. Marines and our friends from Texas were running a little low. They'll need more soon enough."

4 4

Tuesday
December Fifth
05:00 Hours

Two eighteen-hour days were needed to clear the downed overpass from the tracks, and full-time work to then repair the crushed ties and rails, along with the downed bridge over the Platte.

Supply crews meanwhile, had shuttled almost all of Third Washington's supplies further east to Grand Island, where ammunition was being expended at a high rate. Along with our own men, the Marines and the Lone Star troops, California's Golden Bear troops had moved south to reinforce the seriously outnumbered linetroops. The downside of the arrival of the Californians was that they were all but out of supplies when they hit Grand Island. More troops just meant less to go around.

I'd been up for an hour, and got a little exercise in before the day went completely to Hell. Our first dedicated resupply trains were due in an hour. The first would bypass us completely, and follow the Army-reinforced Burlington Northern repair crew up the line to Grand Island. The crew had completed repairs almost all the way to the destination, but it was certain to find more damage closer to town.

The second train was virtually nothing but food, water, medical supplies and 'civilian oriented' relief equipment, along with two hundred relief workers from Oregon. They'd fill in for our departing crews as we moved out. As usual, Charlie Six would move up-line first, followed by Dog Six, after Cozad's supply train was unloaded. While that train was unloaded, a third supply train would pass Cozad and follow us toward Grand Island. Within a few hours after that, large-scale troop trains would follow on.

Grand Island's small airport had been the home of several S.A. units, using the seven thousand foot runway to operate light aircraft used for command-and-control operations throughout the region.

Much of the rest of the city that once was home to more than forty-thousand, according to our advance units on the ground, resembled Dresden in the spring of Nineteen Forty-Five.

Civilians had evacuated to the Dakotas as the S.A. began their retreat from Denver, probably hearing about what was happening west of them. Those that stayed, according again to our own troops, were S.A. faithful. The scorched earth philosophy of the S.A. was carried out as our troops encircled the city, S.A. troops defending the city and the many fires, only retreating when there was literally nothing left to defend. Grand Island was not yet fully secured, but was deemed 'safe enough' for Third Washington to advance, resupply our many troops, and stage for further movement east.

The United States of America paid for that ground with the lives of another fifteen hundred men and women.

05:40 hours

"Colonel, we've got a live one," Gerry McGowan said as I entered the Command Car.

"You've got a WHAT?"

"Prisoner. Caught him north of town. One of our inbound squads saw him out in a field. Nice enough not to try to fight back."

"Where is he now?"

"Five minutes out, sir," one of the communications techs said.

"Who got him?"

"Lieutenant Arkwell's boys. That wild bunch out of Chilliwack, sir," McGowan said. Third Washington had about a hundred Canadians in the ranks. While our own men wouldn't say anything in public about it, the Canadians were fierce. They really wanted to be assigned to a front-line unit, and were first to volunteer for 'point' to a man. Most, I'd noted, were of Scottish lineage, if their surnames were any indication. More than a few with red hair, as well. They enjoyed their work.

"Make sure that he gets here alive, Captain. Got a plan for interrogating him?"

"Yes, sir, but I'd like not to do that while we're in transit."

"How long you figure?"

"Probably a day until Command directs his transport somewhere west or south, unless they want to fly him out, Colonel."

"So you have a few hours to make hay, Gerry. Get on it. You need some additional troops for intimidation, or a few civilians with pitchforks and mattocks, you just say the word. Just be sure you keep him alive enough for San Antonio or Austin to have use of him."

"Thank you, Colonel," he said, heading out of the Command Car, trailed by one of his lieutenants.

"Mr. Briggs, what's the state of the union today?" I asked.

"Sir?" he didn't know what to make of that question.

"Sitrep. News, boy. What's the word?"

"Normal for a civil war, I suspect, sir," he said, finally getting it. "Lot of requests from up-line for supplies, including our units. Looking for evacs for the wounded on the outbounds, but they're short of corpsmen. Wondering when we're going to stage. Overall, sir, they all sound pretty damned tired."

"I'll bet," I said. "Enough days straight in the field and anyone would be. Throw in winter weather and it just gets worse. We looking at any delay on getting underway?" I asked, knowing that he wasn't going to be comfortable replying.

"Sir, I think Sergeant Major…"

"If I wanted Chet Travis' opinion, I'd have asked for it. And then he'd have checked with men in this car on the status of the load out and the engineers up front."

"Yes, sir. Nothing on the boards showing a delay, Colonel."

"Good. Remember that next time," I said.

Gerry McGowan requested half-dozen men, three of whom were multilingual. The prisoner was a mercenary, of European origin, but the Canadians couldn't pin down a country of origin. With luck, McGowan could radio to us his findings. If not, we'd wait until he caught up with us.

The supply train had quickly passed Charlie Six, moving at a good forty miles per hour, about ten minutes past six. At oh six-thirty, we had a green board from all cars for departure, with Charlie Six quietly pulling out of town. The hundred or so miles to Grand Island ticked by, with little to keep me busy, other than things that I really didn't want to do.

Our on-board supplies were ten percent of what we'd need to last two weeks in the field, with no reserve. Bulk meal preparation was down to 'breakfast, lunch and dinner' without any choices of what was served, unless the soldier wished to have an MRE.

"Sir, got some line traffic coming in," Briggs said.

"Trouble up ahead?"

"No, sir. Behind. Two troop trains, about fifteen minutes behind us."

"Supply train status?"

"Unknown, sir. Troop transports weren't supposed to be pulling in for hours."

"Did Cozad's supply train arrive?"

"No sir, or no confirmation on status. With the troop trains, I'd lay odds that the supply train is somewhere behind them."

"Try to run that down. I'd like to know what's coming our way, Mr. Briggs."

"Yes, sir. I'll do my best."

Over the remaining miles, Briggs found out nothing but bad news. Three troop trains would follow us in, somewhere behind that would be our supply train, but not until the troop trains were unloaded and moved back west...there weren't enough sidings or trackage available to stack that many rail cars. At a minimum, we'd be two more days without resupply. Command wasn't just cutting it thin, they had no idea what they were doing to us, and there wasn't one damned thing I could do about it. Our battalion commanders would have to improvise in the whole 'support' aspect of our mission.

Track speeds were uneven moving toward Grand Island, but through the video monitors, we could see the plume of smoke ten miles away, staining the clear, still blue Nebraska sky.

The last of the S.A. troops were no more than a few thousand yards outside of Grand Island, with thirty-thousand U.S. troops between where Charlie Six would stop and 'the line.' General Garcia's communications crews informed us of *'sporadic mortar and artillery fire in the region.'* 'Nothing like that to inspire confidence in your future,' I thought.

With troop trains behind us on the same track, we were going into Grand Island whether things were quiet or not. The fresh troops were needed to push back the S.A. out of range and stabilize the front.

08:41 Hours
Grand Island, Nebraska

"Double-time, you worthless pukes!" One of the California Golden Bear sergeants yelled. The S.A. had concentrated fire on our rail lines as soon as we'd stopped and begun to dismount, and everyone aboard Charlie Six—with the exception of the defensive cars and the trailing communications car--was in the field and away from the attractive target. Rear Comms was providing coordination to Third Washington and other units tapping into our tactical frequencies, and using on-board cameras to spot targets and serve as fire control. The Californians were running to get into the fight.

I'd found decent cover along with Lieutenant Colonel Jesse Casselis Fourth Battalion, Able Company, a few hundred feet from the Command Car. Charlie Six had made it all the way through town to the west side, found a convenient siding among ten to choose from, and had taken three near-miss mortar rounds as we evac'd the train. We were stopped about a mile south of the small airport, now held by the Texans, and sandwiched between the Golden Bears and Third Cardinal from Arizona. Southeast of us, on the other side of U.S. Thirty, a subdivision was afire. Somewhere beyond the subdivisions' trees, were the mortar emplacements. Within the tree line, snipers. Our location, behind an irregular gathering of mostly wrecked warehouses and industrial buildings was out of direct line of fire, with decent earthen embankments and an overstory of thick trees. It reminded me of what the hedgerows might have been like in France, in June of Forty-Four.

"Colonel? General Garcia's wondering where you are, sir," Private Ayers told me. "Your comm gear not working sir?"

"Guess not, Mr. Ayers," I said as I checked the switches and got no signal. "Be kind enough give the General my regards and to pass on that I'm not enjoying the scenery, south of our known last, as a dismounted infantryman. Understood?" I said as another mortar round hit south of us. The shelling seemed to be moving away. A second, then a third, hit east of us, one with a dull *'whump'* sounding much different than the others.

"Yes, sir," he said with a grin, then relayed that through his headset up through the food chain.

"They're at about max range for these shells, sir," A Company's commander, Captain Tealson said. "Not quite six thousand meters." His First Sergeant was twenty yards or so south, looking through his binoculars south, and radioing back to the communication car. "Fifteen minutes at this rate of retreat, shelling's done. We can get some armor moving in then and root out the stragglers."

Before I could respond, two Abrams fired nearly simultaneously, a few hundred feet west of us, toward the southeast. Many seconds later, we heard the impacts, thousands of yards away. Mortar fire was returned, and fell far short.

"Captain, how far can we chase these bastards?" I asked.

"Those tanks use something like three hundred gallons of fuel every eight hours or so, sir. More on rough terrain. Top speed a little over forty miles per hour. From what I heard from the Californians, they're damned near out of fuel, though. And shells."

"What's their effective firing range?"

"About eight thousand meters, sir. Error of margin around thirty meters.

"Thanks. Not the kind of thing I have ingrained into my head."

"Sir?" the first sergeant asked. "You should be clear to proceed to the airport. Lone Star's got a Brad on the other side of Charlie," he said.

"Mr. Ayers, let's go see a General. Captain, don't get your ass shot off," I said.

"Sound advice," he said. "Ditto, Colonel."

Moving quickly, Ayers and I moved as quickly as we could back to Charlie Six, around the lead engine, and to a very scarred Bradley Fighting Vehicle, where four of the Lone Stars had fanned out to cover us.

"Colonel, good to see you," General Angela Garcia said, from just inside the lowered rear hatch.

"General, good to see you in one piece."

"Good to see you, too, along with those trains following on. Might have just saved our bacon," she said as the hatch closed and we headed away from Charlie Six.

"I hear things are a bit thin up here," I said.

"Drastic understatement, Colonel Drummond. We're all but out of ammunition and fuel. If that battalion of yours hadn't shown up when they did, we'd have been done for. Where's that supply train?"

"Somewhere behind the two troop trains that followed us in, ma'am. In other words, I have no idea."

"Comms are lousy out here, even with that gear the SEALS brought us. And the S.A.'s got jammers, so that isn't helping. Another hour or five, and the S.A. would'a taken us."

"What's their strength?" I asked.

"Best estimates, north of eighty thousand within fifteen miles."

I let out a long, slow descending whistle. "One of my Marine friends called that a 'target rich environment,' I said.

"Would be for us, as well, had we the tools we need," she said with some disgust. The Bradley slowed, turned, and stopped.

"Welcome to Camp Grand Island," she said as the rear hatch lowered, bringing in welcome fresh air.

Ayers and I climbed out and looked around at the remains of the small airport.

"We wreck this, or the S.A.?"

"We did. Tank round killed the S.A. Field Marshal and a slug of his staff over there in the building off to the left. Seems he was too proud to get while the gettin' was good," she said as we headed toward a less-wrecked structure. I noted it had been home to the Nebraska Army National Guard, with one of their unit logos, 'The Muleskinners', painted on the side of the building. 'B-Company/ 2-135 Aviation', below the logo of the kicking mule. "Nebraska Guard ran Chinooks out of here, before it hit the fan. Their birds were assigned to Oklahoma, and then Texas. Some of our men are from here, fighting for home and all," she said as we entered the hangar space. "That Chinook crew that came in the other night was one of the local crews."

"Tough way to find your home town."

"Not much left here, that's a fact. The only civilians left were S.A. They either left when the S.A. did or they're now ambient temperature," she said. "In there—that's our HQ for the time being,"

Garcia said, pointing to the second of three large tents inside the hangar. I noticed Ayers was looking quite out of place.

"Soldier, the mess is in that tent, yonder. Go make yourself useful," Garcia said.

"Yes, ma'am!" Ayers said, saluted, and smartly marched to the third tent.

"Good God, Colonel. You've got more kids under your command than a high-school principal."

"Only if it's a small high-school, General."

"Let's get some coffee. And I hope you've got some good news for us," she said as we went inside the Lone Star command tent. I noted there were no computers hooked up, or much in the way of electronics at all for that matter.

"I do have, what is supposed to be the manifest and schedule for the resupply trains, of course that's gone to Hell already today. My men will get the schedule nailed down once comms are back up."

"That'll have to do I imagine," she said as she sat down behind a makeshift desk.

"I have it on a flash drive, and here's the hardcopy," I said, pulling two dozen double-sided, single spaced sheets out of my shirt."

"Won't need the flash drive. Computers were all fried when the satellites went. Techs figured it was some sort of directed EMP burst. Homed in on our electronic emissions and cooked us."

"Saw that up in Idaho. Before the War, General," I said, almost absentmindedly.

"When? How was that possible?" she asked, leaning forward.

"Sorry, Ma'am. It was….mid-October I think. One of our Army recon units had a modified Humvee. Lots of electronic equipment that'd been looking in on a compound that had been stirring up

553

trouble. Whatever they used cooked the Humvees electronics suite. Army and Air Force bombed them a day or two later after their private army killed some civilians. Turned out the residents and their private army were tied to political parties on both sides, as well as American and European banking interests. Command at the time told us that they were tied to the New Republic as well. Happened the same time that Blackburn was capped."

"You had an S.A. base, Colonel," she said. "What happened after you hit it?"

"First, I wasn't in uniform at that point, but that's a minor issue. Attacks ramped up, pretty dramatically as the war started."

"You stirred up a hornets nest. I hope to God you killed it."

"The base was destroyed. Infiltrators were everywhere. They were still mopping them up when I shipped out."

"Colonel, if there's anything in common between places like your Washington and Nebraska, it's that fat cats from elsewhere came in and built their little fortresses and surrounded themselves with their own pissant armies. We've taken out three since we left Colorado. Lotta European money went into building those places and buying hundreds or thousands of acres of land."

"You think these were supposed to be the castles maintained by us lowly serfs, General?" I asked.

"Yeah, I do, Colonel. And that sticks in my craw," she said.

15:20 Hours

Despite Angela Garcia's preference to push the fight hard into the S.A., it was apparent that most of the forces in the field needed rest. Much of the equipment used by the Lone Stars was sorely in need of full overhauls, but that of course wasn't in the cards. The gear used by all of the other line units was only in marginally better condition.

The burned out city came alive with thirty thousand troops fresh to Grand Island, hailing from all over the United States and Canada. Only a handful of units weren't 'Composite' in nature, that is, dedicated to a single task. Most were, with support from units like ours, stand-alone and quite capable.

Most of the new troops were infantry, with mechanized units expected to arrive over the next few days. Grand Island would be one of several jump points East, part of a claw to grasp, then crush the S.A. Many Third Washington troops, including finally Dog Six, enlisted anyone standing around in the offload of the supply trains and the mountains of equipment and supplies were sorted and dispersed.

The Brigade was fully involved in the support and resupply effort of the military, really for the first time not working with a civilian presence. The language was more coarse, the jokes more crude, the orders more pointed, no slack given. Our medical suites were running full up, with everything from working on field-dressed gunshot wounds to frostbite, fractures, and miscellaneous afflictions of war. A solid ten percent of the Texans wouldn't fight again anytime soon, and would be evac'd by rail to hospitals down south.

The support mess tents and rail-mounted kitchens would also be running twenty-four-seven, and still wouldn't be able to get everyone hot food but once, and maybe twice a day.

I'd toured the Third's operations and came away pretty impressed. North of us at the airport, damaged runways were being prepped for repairs, in anticipation of helicopter traffic. Row upon row of Abrams, ancient M113 armored personnel carriers, Bradleys, and too many trucks to count were lined up for needed maintenance and repairs, refueling, and re-arming. Two-dozen fuel tankers were dispersed around the area, with camouflage netting around and over them. Most were filling as quickly as they could from the isolated fuel tank cars, now disconnected from their arrival train. Back in the Command Car, the communications crews were re-working the hardware again, trying to get more communication range. A hundred miles just wasn't going to cut it.

"Colonel, here's the weather report. We did at least get this from San Antonio while we had a bird overhead," Major Ryder said as he handed me a single sheet of paper.

"Any word from McGowan?" I asked, wondering about his interrogation.

"No, sir. I'd lay a twenty-dollar gold piece on Command getting the prisoner by the end of the day though."

"Wouldn't take that bet," I said, reading the forecast. "This ain't good, Gary. Thirty mile plus winds, and snow coming out of Alberta, before midnight. Looking outside you'd never know it."

"Yes, sir. Word's been spread throughout all units to prepare for extreme weather conditions tonight. We've got a few buildings south of us that didn't get completely hammered. One'll house several thousand men, Colonel."

"That big shipping warehouse?" I asked.

"Yes, sir. Georgians are fabbing up some patches in the building to make it a bit less like an icebox."

"All of our tents up and secured, that'll handle some. I'm hoping to God that these new troops have some shelter of their own."

"They do, not as good as the stuff we've got, but adequate, Colonel."

"Did Dog Six get their water heater problems figured out?"

"Transferred the water to other tanks. Mechanics gave up on them for the day."

"How about their solids? They get them dumped?"

"Yes, sir, both trains, blackwater pumped into the local sewage system."

"Good thing they have one," I said. "There anything needing my immediate attention?"

"Well, nothing comes to mind, sir. What have you got planned?"

"Thought I'd head up to the repair shop and see if I can find some trouble. Been a while since I've wrenched and burned metal. Kinda miss that."

"Plenty of work up there, according to the guys in the D-cars. The Texans were looking over our mounted Abrams with an eye to cannibalize them, Colonel."

"Saw the parts and equipment requests. I'm not sure there are that many parts out there to be had," I said.

"One of the replacement commanders said that down at Hood they're crating up stuff right and left. New manufacture. So, maybe there's hope yet, sir."

"Maybe. I'll take a real radio this time, since those headsets are so flaky," I said for the benefit of the communications crews, who were embarrassed by the fact that my battery packs seemed to have a fifteen-minute half-life.

"Won't happen again, sir," Private Briggs responded.

"Good to know. I'll hold you to that, Mr. Briggs."

A half-hour later, I drove a tired Humvee over to the airport, wearing one of my civilian work outfits, insulated coveralls that I'd quit wearing years before as my waistline expanded. Now, back down to a hundred and seventy, it fit just fine. One of my more worn Army-issue parkas and a rabbit-fur hat, and I was good to go. I was flagged to stop at the airport checkpoint.

"Where do you think you're headed, Mac?" a Marine snarled.

"Well Sarge, I hear there's some mechanic'in to be done over there. And seein's that I'm a Colonel, as this here patch illustrates, I figure to go get some work done." He looked over the insignia with a little surprise. "Colonel Richard Drummond, Commander, Third Washington."

"Sorry, sir," he said.

"No apologies necessary, Marine," I said as I drove on. 'Thanks for not shooting first,' I said to myself.

Tuesday
December Fifth
22:00 Hours

Stress cracks, battle damage and worn parts were common on all of the line equipment we were working on. I'd introduced myself to the 'lead wrench' in the Transportation Company, who was under my command but hadn't had the chance to meet personally. At first, he was under the impression that I was there to take charge, and as such, was a little more stiff and formal than he might have been otherwise. Once I told him that I was there to work, and where could he use a hand, he softened up a bit and we discussed things that I had experience with. It was a little like a job interview, with the boss being interviewed by the employee. Short interview, fortunately. There was a lot of equipment to get through.

A half-hour of warm-up on the arc welder and I was back up to creating decent welds on heavy steel. It was rare, pre-War, that I'd had enough 'practice' to keep my skills up. Hobbyist-level repairs didn't lend themselves to honing anything close to expertise or speed.

The Transportation Company used some Third Washington's repair equipment, but had salvaged much more equipment in Grand Island--the arc welder that I was using and the light-reactive helmet were an example. Towed generators were moved up from the rail siding, fueled up and we were in business.

I was tasked with frame repairs and reinforcements on civilian-type trucks used by every unit in the fight. Better-skilled men were working on tank hydraulic systems, electronics and optics systems failures, and replacing reactive armor. A half-dozen of our newer Abrams went up against a single new T-90 or -95 Russian tank under command of a skilled tank commander, and five came back damaged. The sixth was destroyed and her crew killed. They fared better against the German and French armor in the field, according to the tankers, anyway.

Three and a half hours into some real labor, I was called back to reality.

"Colonel, sir? That Texan General's looking for you," Master Sergeant Cramer said after he saw me finish up a frame weld.

"Damn. Just when I was getting back into my stride," I said.

"She's over there, sir."

"Got it. Thanks, Dean. Maybe I'll have the chance to get back down here sometime."

"Anytime, Colonel. You've got a good hand with that stick."

"Thanks," I said as General Garcia approached.

"Hiding in the garage," Garcia said with a smirk. "You men are all alike. Any chance to pick up a wrench."

"Good to get some work done, General. Been a while since I've been able to do something mechanical. I'd forgotten how much I like to weld."

"Need a few minutes of your time, Colonel. You had dinner yet?"

"No, ma'am. Wasn't that hungry. Sounds good now though."

"Meet me in the mess in ten."

"Will do, General," I said.

The mechanics had a wash-station of sorts, including some very Third World quality plumbing into an electric hot-water heater. I made myself moderately presentable and headed over to the Lone Star mess tent.

The weather had really begun to turn, with low clouds coming in from the north along with the cold. The wind hadn't kicked up too much, but it was no night to be without shelter.

General Garcia was seated with a half-dozen of her senior staff, and rose to join me in the chow line when I entered the tent. We were served a couple slices of bread, beef stew, and canned peaches, and had a pot of coffee waiting for us at the table. By the time we were headed back to the table, her staff had left.

"General, what's up, other than the obvious?"

"Honestly, I need someone with some mileage on them to talk to. I'm fifteen years older than the next oldest person in this command. They aren't exactly the minds I need to vent to," she said. "My orders go against my grain, Colonel. We want back in the fight and we're being told to hold fast."

I thought about that for a moment. "No major military engagement in modern times has been successfully fought in winter weather, General. Not to get out of line, but your troops could use some rest. The equipment over in that bus barn is a bunch of patchwork repairs that are wrapped around powerplants that are way overdue for replacement, let alone simple maintenance," I said, not enjoying the stew. It was awful.

"You agree with Austin and San Antonio then? When we're this close?"

"I'm not a career soldier, General. However, what I see are tired men and well-worn equipment, poor real-time intelligence, unfavorable weather, and a thin and precarious supply line that could be disrupted by a single IED under a rail bridge or in a culvert. Substantial gains have been made at the cost of a significant percentage of the men and women under your command and the command of allied units. Significant percentages, General. Fifteen, twenty, twenty-five percent. Unsustainable losses against an overwhelming enemy force," I said. Not what she wanted to hear.

"Don't get me wrong. These bastards need killing more than anyone in recent memory. I just think that the opportunity will present itself on our time, when we're ready, and that a pinch of patience will pay off. They're on the run. That doesn't necessarily mean that it's good for us to keep chasing them."

"If we sit here, we lose the advantage."

"If you pursue them without adequate force, you suicide, General, and even with these thirty-thousand odd troops, you're pushing three-to-one on the downside of the equation. That doesn't spell 'win' to me. There will be time, soon enough, to get back underway. Get these other Guard C.O's together, get them up to speed on what all of these units have seen and what the S.A.'s doing. God knows I haven't seen anything come through Command about anything like a plan to move east from here. Makes me wonder if they know who is where, and with what."

She nodded, looking with tired eyes at the tabletop.

"Angela, you need to get some rest yourself. Pushing yourself too hard does not equate to good decision-making. Get a commander-level briefing going for tomorrow afternoon. We may have Command communications back up by then; we might even have some sort of battle plan, who knows. You'll know though, better than San Antonio or Austin, what these forces are capable of against the S.A. in the field conditions we have now, or will have in the next few days. Ten or twenty-mile gains are done for until this weather lets up. The men can't handle it, the equipment can't either, and we could be walking over the top of a field of IED's and never know it until things go boom. It's down to one to five miles, my guess, on cleared ground, until the weather breaks or until we have travel paths established."

"You're probably right. It pisses me off though."

"Don't be George Patton. Didn't end well for him, General."

"No it did not," she said, pausing, and it appeared to me, finding herself in the uncomfortable position of realizing that she was probably wrong to continue pressing for the current pursuit of the S.A.

"General, do you ever ponder how your own decision-making process works?" I asked.

"I gather information and analyze it and decide. Why do you ask?"

"A logical process. But is the information you gather, factual, or predictive? The reason I ask is that if it's predictive, it's not necessarily factual. I had a fair amount of time to ponder this, laid up after an accident. I did a little introspection into my own decision making process. It was seriously flawed. Here's why," I said.

"If it has happened, it's fact. If it hasn't happened, it's a prediction and not a fact. Weeding out what has happened from what hasn't isn't easy but it is necessary. At least half of what my own decision making process was based on wasn't based on fact. It was based on 'feel'...on 'emotion'....or on 'prediction.' I suppose I knew it was wrong, but it *felt* right. I had that answer all along, but I cannot for the life of me remember where I learned it or whom I learned it from. But I did learn it, years ago, along with remembering the key to the whole thing: Once you learn what the facts are, you need to give yourself enough time to let them sink in and only then can you make a decision. Austin can't do that for you. Neither can the big brains in San Antonio. You need to make your own decisions, here. You shouldn't need to question your superiors, if they're using a sound decision making process, but they're probably not. They're probably not trained to do so. That makes your lobbying effort—and I hate that phrase—that much more critical to the prosecution of the war. You need to make the case for pursuit—or not—on facts. Until you're ready to do that, you need some rest. You cannot make decisions when you're mentally unready to do so."

"Colonel, you sound like my ex," she said, taking a drink from her coffee cup.

"As long as I'm not on the receiving end of a cast-iron frypan," I said. I noticed the winds picking up outside. "General, if you don't need anything else, I'd like to get back to my unit."

"Thank you, Colonel. Dismissed."

And so we waited, to learn the facts, and how to fight a war based on facts.

For two solid weeks, Grand Island was the receiving zone for United States ground forces, and Third Washington was tasked with reestablishing potable water, temporary power, and helping feed and house the masses of troops. We had staged sixty-five thousand troops out of Grand Island, almost all of them arriving by rail, and then within a few days, dispersed them across a two hundred mile long front, mostly by truck. During this time, we were unmolested by the S.A., and found nine civilians alive within five miles of Grand Island. All had been in hiding; all were part of the Resistance. Unlike other towns we'd been through and heard of, there was no sudden influx of civilians after the city was back in United States control.

General Garcia and her Lone Star troops had left Grand Island on December Tenth, accompanied by troops from Georgia and Arizona, and fifteen thousand Regular Army troops. They headed to Manhattan, Kansas, and would be joined by our First Washington....we hadn't heard a single word of where they had been since we'd left Spokane. We assumed they would progress east toward Topeka, and after that, it was anyone's guess. Thousands more headed north, toward Sioux City, Fort Dodge, and Minneapolis, with tens of thousands of men headed to Lincoln and eventually to Omaha. It appeared, although it was never stated, that the U.S. strategy was to put the classic 'pincer' grip around the S.A., backing them up against the Mississippi, and eventually eliminate them. That might work, if forces in the east could capture and hold the eastern side of the river, and then sweep up north. It wouldn't be long before we left Grand Island for the East.

Our communications were marginally better with new equipment and some serious jury-rigging on the part of our communications teams. In fact, they were pushing the equipment to the limit, sometimes with great success. Our short-lived cell-phone experiment was over, until the EMP-damaged equipment could be replaced, along with the satellite network. We were getting by on not quite six hours rest in twenty-four. I was usually getting by on less than that.

We had no real idea on when an 'offensive' might start, the communications between Command and our units was cryptic, probably for good reason. Grand Island's supply stockpiles followed the troops out, to be re-staged down the line. The supply yard was dwindling daily. I wasn't really minding the relatively monotonous work. It didn't involve getting shot at.

"Sir, patrol contact, due east, friendly dismounts coming in," Private Ayers said, passing a slip of paper to Captain McGowan.

"Colonel, that's a Ranger unit," Gerry McGowan said. "One of ours. From Spokane."

"Mike Amberson's unit?" I asked. I noticed my heart rate had increased.

"Sure could be sir. We'll know in a half-hour. They're on foot—we'll get some wheels out there to bring them in," Gerry said, signaling one of his assistants to get transport on the way.

"Do it," I said. I hadn't heard anything about Mike's unit either, since we'd pulled out of Spokane back in November. "How many men, Mr. Ayers?"

"Seventy, sir, plus one civilian," he said. A Ranger company could vary in size, but should be almost two hundred men.

"Kittrick: Get medical ready, and figure out billeting. Gerry, get your intel group together for debriefing, Mr. Ayers, I suspect we're going to need to get these Rangers direct contact with command. Work it out. Questions?"

"No, sir," I heard in unison.

"Good. Mr. Ayers, pull up a map in your spare time and get it on my monitor showing where the Rangers made contact."

"Done, sir. Fifty clicks out, near the town of York, between Interstate Eighty and U.S. Thirty Four. Coming overland, sir."

"Easy Three's patrol point?"

"Yes, sir. Outer edge of the patrol limit, Colonel," he said. Everything east of that point was no-man's land. The S.A. still held Lincoln, and Omaha, that much at least, we knew.

Communications during their return trip in was mostly directed to medical, requesting medevac of several seriously wounded men. The helos that we might normally have had in Grand Island however, were three hours away, shuttling gear to other units.

It took almost two hours to return the Rangers back to Grand Island, which were among the longest hours I'd ever spent.

1330 Hours

"Gerry, direct the inbound traffic straight to Med Two on Charlie; Med one on Dog," I said. "Corpsmen and surgical ready?"

"Yes, sir. Doctor Willitson is prepped and ready. Remaining troops will head into the receiving cars for eval."

"I'm heading out to meet them," I said, grabbing my parka and helmet.

Outside, Sergeant Major Travis met me at the entry stairs. "Colonel, good to see you."

"You as well, Chet. Been a couple of days."

"Northern perimeter rotation. Not much to look at up there though, sir."

"Your men ready in receiving?"

"Yes, sir. Food, showers, clothing, the works."

"Outstanding. Thanks," I said.

"I expect these men will need it, Colonel. Any idea on what they saw for action?"

"Not a one. Rangers are behind-the-lines guys most of the time, I understand. I expect they created some havoc," I said as I heard them approach from the southeast. "Here they come."

Fifteen corpsmen appeared just as the Humvees pulled in next to the two medical cars on Charlie Six, and another dozen or more further west of us at Dog Sixes' med car. The wounded, several on stretchers, were quickly carried straight into the surgical car. At least twenty more men were 'walking wounded', and taken across the tracks to the main receiving area for new troops. At least two corpsmen attended each, some holding IV bags. I noted that one of our troops led a civilian woman over to the evaluation area.

I was looking for Mike's familiar form, finally finding him coming out of the surgical car. He'd helped carry one of his stretcher-bound men in.

"Mike, good to see you," I said. He was almost unrecognizable through the grime and dried blood, and his face was now filled with deep lines and an ashen color. I could not imagine what he must have gone through. It hadn't been a month yet.

"You too, Rick," he said, taking off his banged up helmet. He had a field dressing on his head, above his left ear.

"Let's get you over to receiving and get some warm food. And get that head looked at."

"That and a shot of Scotch," he said.

'Thousand yard stare,' I thought to myself. "I can do that, too. We're working on getting you a comm link to Command. I expect you'll have a long debrief."

"I expect so."

Mike didn't say a word as we headed to receiving. Inside, his men were being swarmed over by corpsmen, food piled in front of them and hot drinks by the gallon. Coffee was not on the menu. No point in caffeine-loading before stand-down.

"We had a hundred eighty men going in," he said numbly, standing and looking over his men, the unblinking, unfocused stare all too apparent. "Seventy coming back, one probably brain-dead. Probably lose two more due to blood loss."

"Over here, Mike. Get some hot food," I said, directing him to a small table out of the way, as one of the men brought a heaping plate of something appearing to be stroganoff.

"Thanks," he said, disassociated from most of what was going on in the room, focusing on the plate in front of him. I'd seen post-traumatic stress before. I'd had it myself. I was wondering if Mike would be dealing with that, or if this was just extreme fatigue. Gerry McGowan joined us, silently. Mike was halfway through his plate, and me through a cup of non-caffeine tea, before he spoke.

"Started out pretty solid. Inserted behind the lines on a low flying C-130, dropped us at little strip near Osceola, south of Des Moines. Found out the S.A. was a hundred fifty miles away at best. Split up into teams, found a substantial resistance force already in place, damned near every farm. Good couple of weeks. Then the shit hit the fan. One of the resistance cells was S.A. infiltrators, reported everything that unit was doing up their chain of command. Started hunting us down, chasing us further west. Twenty thousand S.A. against us. Half of my men were gone in a week. Thought we were doing well to come back with what we did."

"You probably were," I said.

"You met any of them yet?" Mike asked, referring to the S.A. obviously. "I mean, spoken with them?"

"Uh, no. We've been shot at a few times. Never face to face."

"Their line soldiers. They're messed up. Seriously. They're absolutely remorseless. No conscience whatsoever. No care to consequence of action, except to kill absolutely everything in front of them. One of our corpsmen thought they were drugged or something. A couple of their wounded were left behind and we interrogated them before they died. Normally, you gotta understand…they kill their seriously wounded. It's as if they didn't feel pain. Then we captured a few more before we figured out that they let us catch them as bait. Used trackers on 'em. That really narrowed the hunt."

"Mike, this isn't your fault," I said.

"I know that, Rick. But I don't get why they let us go."

"They let you go?" I asked, incredulous.

"Yeah. We were literally out of ammunition. Among our men I'll bet there's not five magazines with anything in them. After that, we're down to knives and rocks. They just melted away one night and were gone. We were holed up for the last stand, figuring hand to hand and that's it," he said, finishing his plate and going after another placed in front of him as if it were the first. "They were gone come morning. Tens of thousands of them, just gone. I don't get it."

"I doubt anyone would, sir," McGowan said. "Colonel Amberson, when you're ready, I'd like to get a more in-depth debrief from you and your men. I believe that our communications crews will have a secure link patched through to San Antonio around fifteen-hundred, depending on the satellite, sir."

"Sure. That's fine," Mike said. "Whatever."

Tuesday,
December Nineteenth
1740 Hours

'A' Company, Second Battalion, Seventy-Fifth Regiment, was thirty-eight percent of it's pre-engagement level, with one soldier, as Mike stated, suffering from a severe brain injury. Doctor Willitson had no logical reason why the twenty-six year olds' heart was beating, with the amount of brain damage. It would be hours or a day before A Company's number would decrease again.

Early on Thanksgiving morning, three companies, including Mike's men were dropped at the small airport of Osceola, Iowa by several C-130's and immediately dispersed per their original mission.

They broke down into platoons and squads, working over the pattern they'd been assigned, adjusting sometimes dramatically, based on conditions in the field.

A Company discovered their first contact as expected, who directed them to several other resistance leaders...but not set up in the 'triangle' pattern of resistance cells—but in family lines, unlike Jess Armstrong's Colorado classic resistance model. The resistance in Iowa was deep, widespread, and well integrated into the normal fabric of the S.A. territory and leadership structure. Mike's men made further arrangements with the resistance leaders to supply them United States radios, weapons, and supplies.

The Army and Air Force discovered, almost by accident, that once United States forces made it through the tens-of-miles of S.A. force protection, that there was virtually no armed S.A. presence. Getting through the line was interesting, but simple. They posed as an S.A. aircraft, on their frequencies, with their IFF codes, on a return mission after inserting S.A. troops in U.S. held land. Pretty ballsy, I thought.

Things went fairly well for Mike's troops until December Third, when the S.A. took out the satellites and Mike's communications protocols were lost. At the same time, the eastern-most troops began to be hunted down, with word reaching Mike through the resistance network far sooner than they could have verified themselves. The lone civilian who came back with the survivors was their last contact, and happened to be a second cousin to one of Mike's lieutenants. Their backup plan, in that eventuality, was to rendezvous near Lenox, Iowa, and proceed west, back through the lines. The hand of the S.A. began to close on them, pushing them further north and west, directing them towards Omaha. The Statists had a sizeable military force at the remains of Offutt Air Force Base. The Air Force had directed a significant attack on the infrastructure of the base, to mixed effect. Army Corps of Engineering standards for construction proved to be pretty well thought out. American weapons used against American targets didn't cause anywhere near the damage anticipated, until specific 'soft spots' were identified and targeted, requiring further missions and accruing further losses.

My read of Mike's mission, without any offense toward my friend, was that it was…stupid. No support behind enemy lines, when the enemy was known for stripping most everything of use. No equipment or transport, for the same reason. Worse yet, no extraction plan or resupply behind the lines. It struck me as all but a suicide mission. The higher ups just didn't understand this enemy. I hoped to God that there weren't many other units behind the lines, so badly supported. I then remembered the SEALS that were also behind the lines…

Mike's debrief, and the compilation of after-action reports from the surviving leadership—officers and men—ran until a little after 1700, when Doctor Willitson recommended that the men get some rest. I offered Mike a shot of Scotch in my quarters before he headed off to get some sleep. While he was finishing his debrief with our staff, including transcription and contact with both Austin and San Antonio, I received his orders. Along with his men, his unit would be furloughed for fifteen days back in Washington. After that, they'd proceed to Fort Hood and await their next deployment.

"Cutty Sark. Not bad," he said, sipping his drink. Despite a hot shower and clean utilities, Mike looked awful.

"Medicinal purposes only," I said, and then paused a little. "Got your orders while you were finishing up debrief. You'll be home for Christmas," I said. "Train heads out tomorrow morning. Two weeks and a day. Then down to Hood."

"More than I expected, for damned sure," he said. His eyes still didn't have their characteristic spark. 'Something in him died out there,' I thought to myself.

"You need this time, you know."

"Yeah, I know," he said before uttering an expletive, and continuing. "You heard the debrief. You heard the sanitary version. Someday, maybe, I'll feel like talking about it. Don't ask, though."

"Hadn't considered it. There aren't many people left in this world, if any," I said, suddenly considering the possibility that there was now, no one who knew, "what I saw over in Sudan. What I did over there, what others did on my orders. I haven't told everyone the whole story. They wouldn't understand, and it doesn't matter anymore, except to me."

"But it changed you," he said, staring through the floor.

"It changed me. No going back. Not for you, either," I said. "Just don't let it destroy you. People ask about my testimony. Why and how I became a Christian. Well, you are the first to know. I didn't have any other place to go. Nothing to look to. I was, well, utterly destroyed. God was there, because there was nothing else. No one else knows that, not even Karen. Too tough to talk about, no one else, except maybe you, would understand. Others, I'm sure, tried to find solace in booze, or women, or some other faith. For me, though, for what was missing in my life, for the forgiveness that I could not get anywhere else, that was the choice I made."

Mike didn't have anything to say, and I understood perfectly.

"Go get some sleep. You're going home to your wife and twins for their first Christmas. You have a lot to be thankful for, despite the Hell you just went through."

Mike just nodded, shook my hand, and left. 'It'd be a long time,' I thought, before he would 'be the same.'

Five minutes after Mike left, Private Ayers handed me a packet as I returned to the Command Car.

"Here's your mail, Colonel."

"No shit?" I said before thinking, looking at Karen's handwriting on several thick letters. I'd written several...and not sent any back westbound with any of the 'official' correspondence.

"No shit, Colonel. Ten big bins of it came in on the Thirty-One."

"Any packages?"

"No, sir. Just letters."

"Many for the men?"

"Well, the bins were pretty damned big, sir. Cubic yard apiece, so I'd say so."

"Excellent. Thanks."

"Sir, Troop Nineteen expected arrival at twenty-three hundred and change," Captain Shand said. "Just came in."

"Swell. You and Major Ryder and his men figure out where in Hell to put them?" There was precious little space in Grand Island that could be called 'habitable.'

"Not yet. They weren't expected for three days yet."

"We're running out of room to park trains. Anyone down south figure that out yet?"

"Not likely, sir."

"Headcount?"

"Three thousand, sir."

574

"I wish, just for a minute, that I had a glimpse into the thought process of Command, or some fricking clue as to a battle plan. Too much to ask for, I suspect," I said.

"Above our pay grades, Colonel," Shand replied.

"Already spread the word down through Third?" I asked. I'd finally gotten it through my head not to go through the minutiae Third Washington's standing mission.

"Fifteen seconds ago. Automated notification, sir."

"All right. Good work," I said, thinking, 'damned command idiots.'

I decided to read my mail, later, in private. It was tough for me to not just rip them open, but I still had work to do.

1930 Hours

"Jeff, how're those Rangers?" I asked Doctor Willitson, both of us grabbing something to eat in the mess tent.

"Shot to Hell, Colonel. Three in critical condition, and we lost one—that head wound. Fifteen with gunshot wounds. Three with compound fractures. Almost all of them dehydrated. Couple with viral pneumonia. Several with intestinal issues. Patched up as well as we can here. We'll evac the worst of them tomorrow, if the birds are ready."

"Should be, unless the weather goes to crap again," I said, noticing a Ranger officer and a stocky brunette at his elbow coming our way. "Three Blackhawks and a couple of Chinooks were going through overnight service in anticipation of evac tomorrow. No one's got more than an eight-hour look ahead on the weather right now."

"Excuse me, are you Colonel Drummond?" the Ranger asked, an older second lieutenant.

"Guilty as charged, Lieutenant," I said, standing. His name stripe said, 'Van Hook'. 'Good Dutch name,' I thought.

"Sir, there's someone you ought to meet. Colonel Amberson asked me to make the introductions, sir."

"I'm guessing that it must be time to meet our civilian. Am I close, Lieutenant?"

"Yes, sir. Colonel Drummond, this is Mrs. Klasena DeJong, or Clara for short. She's my second cousin, sir."

"Mrs. DeJong, quite pleased to meet you," I said. She looked to be in her early forties.

"You as well, sir. Thank you for taking care of these young men," she said, shaking my hand firmly.

"It's an honor, ma'am. This is Jeff Willitson, Third Washington's head doc."

"Doctor, thank you very much."

"Tough men, Mrs. DeJong. I'm confident that most of them will make a full recovery."

"Clara, please have a seat. Can I call you Clara?" I asked.

"That's fine, Colonel, thank you."

"Call me Rick if you like. I'm not exactly regular Army," I said. "I hear that you were part of the Resistance in Iowa."

"Yep, when we weren't hiding in a storm cellar or trying to keep from being looted," she said, looking at the men around the room.

"Pardon me asking, but did you leave family behind?" I asked.

"No, actually. My husband headed up to Pennsylvania in early November on…well, business. Resistance business, that is. Our boys are in the Marines. Last we heard was quite a while ago, but they were in Virginia."

"We haven't heard anything about operations in the East, unfortunately."

"We haven't heard anything, period. Anyone caught broadcasting either disappeared or was just outright shot," Clara said. "Real news is hard to come by, and we didn't know what was real or faked, even on the radio. Oh, and possession of a radio is either a death sentence or hard labor, which is usually a death sentence."

I'm sure I looked surprised by that, although I should not have been. "I'm finding it hard to figure out how to ask this question, but how did you decide to stay, when you could see what was going on with the S.A?"

She paused for a moment. "Pre-collapse, I helped teach courses in critical thinking....mostly for home schools in the area, and of course running the farm with my husband. Our own boys were taught in the government schools, but by the time our youngest was going into high school, we could tell that they weren't teaching them *how* to think. They were teaching them *what* to think, and to *go no deeper.* We began to realize that most, if not all people, once conditioned through years of sameness, display an abundant lack of ability to see a new danger bearing down on them because they just can't recognize it. A fatal consequence of *not being able to think*, but bandaged over by the warm and fuzzy feelings of *what to think.* They look to the past to inventory and analyze, and usually dismiss a new and critical threat because they just don't see it for what it is. They don't have a basis of understanding of what the threat can mean to them," she said. "So they naturally dismiss it."

"It gets more complicated of course, because proper recognition of a new threat isn't enough to protect one from the threat. They have to have the *right response* in reaction to the *correct identification* of the new threat. People are not geared to do both well. One, maybe. Not both. Combine those two problems with the binds that we place upon ourselves to meet our past obligations, and the responses are usually both *too late* and *inadequate* or just plain *wrong.....*,"

"And of course the sooner you recognize a threat, the sooner you can respond..."

"And the less you will be affected by it. We stayed, because most of the younger generation, and a small percentage of the older folks, still know how to think. They know right from wrong. Those people are the core of the Iowa Resistance."

December Nineteenth
2200 Hours

November 27

Dearest Rick—

It's been only five days, and its an eternity. I can't tell you how much I miss you because you already know…..so I'll not write of it.

The big news at the moment is that they've rounded up your four ringleaders of the Samuels gang who'd been released back to the Feds…and then the S.A. They were caught down in Tekoa, moving north in a stolen Whitman County pickup truck. They did not give up, according to Elaine Cross. She didn't go into it, but said that they would no longer be bothering anyone on this Earthly Plane. She gave me the impression that they were expected.

Things are going O.K. here, and the curfew is still in place, and random, so we never quite know when the stores are supposed to open and close until an hour or so before the Army wants them open. Alan and Ron and the new guys are keeping up with demand, but there are more shortages coming without more goods coming in to the area. Alan hasn't said anything much about it, but I can tell he's concerned.

Mom is doing better than we thought she would, but her mental acuity is not what it was before she fell. Sarah and her nursing manager Reba think that only part of it is related to the meds…part of it is almost certainly an age-related condition. Ron has been splitting his time between the stores and supervising more work on what we're calling Serenity House….he's putting in a fence around the front yard today, and has plans to create a fenced back yard for the residents—one has Alzheimer's and wanders. When weather is better, hopefully we'll have a garden space outside for them to enjoy.

Our kids are being pushed hard to get back into their studies…these curfews seem to be a good reason for them to find other things to occupy their time, and I've had to raise my voice more than once. Libby is more persuasive than I am with our kids, and I seem to be more persuasive with Marie....go figure.

We saw your unit on television yesterday...but couldn't tell if you were in the picture.   They talked about the recovery of the Sixth Army and that a Washington State unit was in charge...and we saw a shoulder patch insignia. The tape was from a civilian helping with the work. We then saw the tape of what happened in North Platte. I think we all understand now, why you said you'd volunteer if Governor Hall had not drafted you.

I cannot imagine you in such a difficult place among such tragedy. I do hope that you are taking care of yourself as you should.

Come home to me.
     All my love forever,
           Karen

I read the letter three times, then carefully folded it and put it back in its' envelope. I had three more letters from Karen and two from Carl and Kelly. Rather than rushing through them, I decided to take them one at a time. I thought they could soak in a bit more that way.

I made my way over to the Command Car. Troop Nineteen was coming in early.

Wednesday,
December Twentieth
Grand Island, Nebraska

Second Lieutenant Daniel Van Hook had grown up in Iowa, outside of Pella, before moving to Ellensburg, Washington to attend college. It was near coincidence that he found himself back in Iowa, and managed to play a huge role in getting A Company good intel by almost immediately locating one of the family farms. Sometimes, it is all about whom you know.

The DeJong farm, Clara told me over a very early breakfast of oatmeal and black coffee, had been in the family for a hundred and seventy-five years, with many relatives scattered across eleven counties. Family reunions ran into the thousands of attendees, pre-War. The last one had to be held at the County Fairgrounds, because there wasn't enough room on any single farm to handle them all.

Well ahead of the Second Depression, many of the farms in the region had thinned their herds, dramatically reduced land under cultivation, and in general contracted as they could see the storm approaching. The DeJong clan in particular, was debt averse, and self-financed all operations, and had done so since nearly losing half of their farmland to the banks in the First Depression. With depressed prices, cuts and then elimination of subsidies, those farms that were running on credit went under.

Being fairly far away from a large population center weighed in the favor of most of the farms, well off the highways and main roads. As the collapse began though, anything within a hundred miles of a large population center began to see dramatic increases in city residents, fleeing the Guangdong Flu; running from possible nuclear attack; getting out of the city to 'live off the land'.

The math was simple enough: Most people typically had a half-tank or a quarter tank of gas in their cars, pre-War. Once things started to come apart, refueling was difficult or impossible, and whatever they'd had before things started going down, were 'less' due to their driving around looking for fuel or taking the wrong road or just being wasteful. Most people, it turned out, had a hundred miles or so of vehicle range, with most refugees exiting highways and heading onto frontage roads anywhere from seventy-five miles out to a hundred and fifty miles out. Beyond that, the 'countryside' was relatively unmolested.

Defensive measures in the heartland ranged from enforcement of Rule .308, meaning, hitting any looter or credible threat with a .308 round at considerable distance; to blocking roads with deep trenches; to hiding roads completely by plowing them over. Many of the DeJong families' driveways were long and unpaved. Making them less visible especially when windbreaks and natural vegetation assisted in the camouflage, assisted the preservation of many of their families.

Clara and her husband Gerritt's home was fairly prominent, located on one of the main County roads. It had also been under reconstruction due to tornado damage, never completed before the Second Depression. They made their own adaptations, mostly for looks once the collapse was well underway, by making it look like a burned out wreck. Half of the roof was already off, rafters exposed, siding was missing, windows removed on the second floor. With the addition of black paint, sprayed on above and adjacent to the empty windows and across the soffits in a burn pattern, and on the rafters of course, the place looked from a quarter mile away like a burned out farmhouse. The addition in the yard of old furniture and junk, made it look like it had been looted in addition to being burned.

Inside the house, they'd built a cocoon of sorts, well insulated, well secured, and enclosed by the larger shell. The home was connected through the basement to the large storm cellar, an Iowa requirement. Both were connected to a cistern that collected rainwater from the equipment shed and barn roofs, both metal. Cooking was done only deep into the night on a highly efficient wood stove, and warming fires were kept small in the superinsulated house. Lighting included kerosene lanterns, candles, and propane while it lasted. Refrigeration included using an icehouse, left from the eighteen hundreds.

A ravine to the rear of the house concealed normal foot traffic from the roadside viewer, with livestock kept in a very old barn at the far end of the ravine. It was outwardly decrepit and unused, but was structurally reinforced. The DeJong's dairy goats, hens, and meat rabbits resided there. Once the transient population settled down (either through attrition or through being encouraged to move on), they moved some of their cattle closer.

Most of the S.A. that flooded through the state, westbound, weren't interested in looking around except for food, and food didn't necessarily include food on the hoof...it came from stores. Some farms further away had livestock slaughtered out of sheer malice or sport, but not consumed .They swept through to the larger cities, consumed, and moved on. The S.A. conscripted troops along the way when they could find people. They only burned cities and towns when they retreated. They killed those who resisted at any time, usually quite publicly.

As with any Resistance movement, the primary mission was to disrupt the S.A. in any way they could without getting killed or compromising the larger effort. In the American heartland, this included picking off S.A. supporters, sometimes in "industrial accidents" or through more direct means. In the first few days of 'occupation' (the period of time after the S.A. announced their 'being', and before the shooting war arrived), there were a remarkable number of hunting accidents. The informers were relatively easy to spot, their pre-War political beliefs well-known, making themselves targets along the way. Clara DeJong was group coordinator for a hundred square miles, and had connections to many other cells in the region.

Once the obvious targets had been taken care of, the Resistance helped place their own people in positions of influence, which then allowed them an inside look. Shipping schedules, supply routes, communications protocols were then opened up to the Resistance. The Resistance was well underway in disrupting shipping to the front lines when the Rangers came into the picture. Only a few attacks had been planned and executed, with more on the way, when the tables turned.

Clara didn't know who in the network had been turned, or how. It became immediately apparent though that the S.A.'s Internal Security Force was hunting down the DeJong extended families, with cells dropping out of communication and 'going dark.' Clara hoped that many of her cousins were able to flee south, where the S.A.'s forces were thinner and the lines porous. She did know that some had been captured, with verification that others had been killed.

With her home lost, Clara would ship west with the Rangers, changing trains in Denver and eventually out to California's Central

Valley, where her younger sisters lived. Someday, she might be able to find her husband and sons.

08:40 Hours

"Colonel Drummond, Colonel Amberson to see you sir," Private Kittrick announced in my ear. I'd been talking with two of the battalion point squads, north of Grand Island, where civilians were starting to reappear and move south. One unit reported that the civilians appeared to be starved, and had obviously walked for miles. Transport would be heading north along County roads, somewhat risky, as none of the roads had been cleared of potential IED's.

"Send him in, Private. Thanks," I said. I had only seen Mike for a moment as I finished up breakfast with Clara. He was with his men, barking a little at one of them. I didn't get in the way.

"Sir."

"Colonel, good morning," he said, looking five years younger than he had the day before, clean-shaven, fresh utilities, new boots and parka.

"Morning, Mike," I said, shaking his hand firmly. "How'd you sleep?"

"Like I was in a coma. I blame it on the Scotch," he said, for the first time showing a little of the 'old' Mike Amberson.

"Three fingers in a tumbler can hardly have that effect."

"Might have been more psychological in nature," he said. I noted the bandage on his head was gone, but a number of stitches were quite apparent. "We'll be in transit pretty quick. I wanted to convey my thanks, and the thanks of the men. You've got a great outfit."

"Had good stock when I showed up. Most of Third has served on the Line at some point during the war, or in the sandbox, or in the 'stan. I think they understand what you guys went through better than most any one," I said as Kittrick caught my eye.

"Mister Kittrick?" I said.

"Sirs, Nineteen is three minutes from scheduled departure, just a reminder," he said, a little nervous to interrupt us. "And Colonel Amberson, the evac birds have arrived in Colorado Springs safely." Twelve of Mike's men were aboard, and would spend a considerable amount of time in the hospital and in rehab.

"Thanks, Private," Mike said. "Rick, I better get moving. Part of me wishes otherwise."

"The minority part. Get your ass home to your lovely wife and your children. And take this back to Karen and my two, if you would," I said, handing him a small package.   My own letters, to Karen and our kids.

"I'd be happy to," he said as he stood to attention, and saluted crisply. I returned it, less so, and shook his hand.   "Watch yourself, Rick. Don't overextend. Sure as Hell it will come back to bite you," he said.

"I think I said the same thing to General Garcia not long ago," I said. With that, Mike nodded and headed out of the Command Car, homeward bound. I was in part envious, but knew that our mission was nowhere close to being called 'finished.'   Since I'd met Karen, we'd never spent a Christmas or New Year's apart. This year would be different.

Wednesday,
December Twentieth
10:50 Hours

"Orders incoming, sir. San Antonio," Kittrick said to me as I looked at the weather report. Warming weather, temps in the thirties, and heavy rains expected.

"Decrypt and send them to my monitor, Private."

"Will do, sir."

I'd been expecting them. Our departure orders for 'down line.' Senior staff had a pool going, whether it would be Lincoln, Omaha,

585

or somewhere outside Kansas City. Lincoln had fallen back into U.S. hands, but only after a siege; Omaha was still in S.A. control; as was Kansas City.

It was Lincoln. We were to be relieved by a combined Army and civilian relief unit. The Army unit would come from the Mexican frontier, the civilians from Utah and Nevada. In a new development, Command was telling us other probable future destinations: next, Omaha, after that, Des Moines.

Sixty miles downline, we had "best possible time" to get there.

"Mister Kittrick, it's Lincoln. Two hours we have an inbound with our relief. Get Major Ryder in here, pronto."

"Yes, sir."

Third Washington was already in the early stages of tear-down even before our orders came in. The troop trains passing through were the first obvious sign to the Brigade; the lack of 'recovery' and 'restoration' in Grand Island was another. Third had worked their way out of work. It was time to go.

Grand Island had a civilian population of two hundred and six, half of them relief workers. The city had one unreliably working water system, thirty square blocks of restored electrical grid, no natural gas. Not much left to rebuild.

Thursday,
December Twenty-First
07:40 Hours
East of Grand Island, Nebraska

Departure from Grand Island had been delayed until morning, which gave our relief unit more time to set up and be briefed. Our staff wasn't all that upset about it, either—no one liked running down the track in the dark in territory that might or might-not have enemy roaming about.

Track repair teams had gone ahead of all rail traffic moving east, ensuring that the tracks were safe for travel. Quite a few transport trains—but few cargo trains—had made the run to Lincoln. The previous trains had also been shorter than either 'Charlie' or 'Dog', and quite uneven in their arrivals. Resuming traffic with a predictable pattern might present an opportunity for an S.A. team to 'disrupt traffic', the sanitized version of, 'destroy a train.'

The Battalion commanders and senior staff had finished our briefing meeting not long after oh seven hundred, prior to departure for Lincoln. Our travel would take us through the 'Hobson' rail yard south of Interstate Eighty, where most of the supply trains would stage. 'Charlie' would stage near the University of Nebraska-Lincoln campus; 'Dog' would stage on the northern edge of the rail yard. Two other trains, belonging to Idaho's 'Gem State' Brigade, would also stage in Lincoln. 'Able' at the municipal airport; 'Baker' in another rail yard northeast of town along U.S. Six, the 'Cornhusker Highway.' The Idaho units were moving east from Denver, following us along.

Intel provided by advanced ground crews and limited aerial reconnaissance showed that most of Lincoln was relatively intact. The notable exceptions included almost all of the downtown area, the heavily damaged State Capitol, and many of the freeway overpasses. Aerial images showed the wreckage of hundreds of vehicles blocked by the destroyed bridges, abandoned or bombed, not unlike North Platte.

A quarter million people lived in Lincoln, before the War. The sketchy reports from the city stated that perhaps a third of that number was still present, after the siege, now they were hungry and cold.

Sunday,
December Twenty-Fourth
09:00 Hours
Lincoln, Nebraska

Christmas Eve dawned with hard rains and steady winds, threatening to turn to ice before the end of the day. The rains helped dampen the few fires still burning uncontrolled, and lessened the stench from the dead.

Third Washington had been deployed for less than three days; near the wreckage of a two S.A. trains destroyed by Air Force missiles and guided bombs. Several of the ordnance experts had secured the area around our train, clearing unexploded shells, surface to air missiles, and other materials to safe areas. The S.A. trains were rolling weapons platforms, as well as distribution centers for infantry and armor with all manners of ammunition and fuel. After securing our immediate area and transit paths to our location, the clearing crews went about securing areas hit by U.S. forces, clearing unexploded missiles and artillery.

United States artillery units had targeted S.A. emplacements with 105mm and 155mm shells, systematically reducing them to rubble in a rolling wall of fire. The S.A. then dispersed to other locations in Lincoln, then targeted with very accurate, select fire. Larger, or softer targets were blanketed with multiple-launch rockets, to devastating effect.

The crew from Charlie went to work immediately on setting up our field kitchens and shelters for the tens of thousands of civilians who were still in the city. Most had been without meaningful amounts of food for weeks. What they did not have hidden, the S.A. took, or it ran out as transit into and out of Lincoln was stopped during the siege. Unlike the other towns we had transited, there were no dogs anywhere. I didn't wonder why. I was on my morning 'rounds' and ducked into Medical to get out of the rain. I'd picked up a deep cough, and my ribs were hurting.

"Colonel, good morning, sir," a corpsman by the name of Bartleson said. He was restocking one of the supply cabinets from a recent shipment.

"Morning, Bart," I said. 'Bart' was his nickname. I'd not heard his given name. "Doc in?"

"Yes, sir. Down in Bay Two, doing some sewing on an S.A."

"Thanks," I said. 'S.A.' as a label, stood for many creative labels all of them quite crude and in some cases accurate. I made my way down the container-car, where Jeff was working over a scalp wound. Three soldiers from Idaho had their weapons trained on the young man, who was probably in his mid twenties. He was bound with zip ties, hand and feet, very creatively tying the prisoner to near-immobility.

"Morning, Doc. One of our prisoners soon-to-ship, huh?"

"Yes, sir."

"Has he been through intel yet?"

"No, sir. Fifteen minutes and he's on his way to command though, where they can work him over at will."

"Get that wound in action, prisoner?" I asked.

"No, sir. Abuse after capture," he said, glaring at me with hate-filled eyes.

I turned to one of the men with weapons trained. "Anything to that, men?"

"Caught a bad patch of gravity, sir. Hit his head when he fell against one of our transport trucks. Missed a step on the way up into the back," he replied.

One of the others chimed in before I responded. "Too bad you didn't break your effin' neck, you son of a bitch."

"I was pushed," the prisoner spat.

"Bull…..*shit*," the younger soldier said, drawing out the word for emphasis. "And I saw the way you were shooting. You couldn't hit the broad side of a barn from the inside."

"Right. Like I could miss after getting surrounded by fifty of you arrogant bastards."

"Fifty my ass. Your blind *and* a liar. Eight man squad, you worthless piece of shit."

"Soldier, I assume your C.O. has your after action," I said.

"Yes, sir. Sorry sir."

"No need to apologize. I'm always surprised when any come in alive," I said. "We saw what they did in other cities and towns."

"Didn't seem all that sporting to shoot an idiot with a First War Russian bolt-action and no ammo, especially when he wasn't smart enough to figure out how to use an attached bayonet, sir," the soldier responded. "And I think he shit himself to boot."

"He'll probably do that when they hang him, too." I said, not really caring one way or the other what the prisoner thought.

"All right. He's done," Doctor Willitson said. "Go get him cleaned up, corpsman."

"Yes, sir," the corpsman responded, leading the prisoner and his guards out the second door.

"Jeff, what do you think?" I said between coughs.

"That guy's about as nearsighted as you could get and still tie his own shoes. Wouldn't respond to me of course when I asked him about his eyesight, but he plainly can't see well, which fits the story of the boys that captured that particular nest. I don't think any of them still have glasses or contacts they might have had before the war, and our boys were probably right. Couldn't hit a barn from inside it."

"Hmmm. I wonder how prevalent that is," I said.

"Quite prevalent, I'd think. Pre-War, seventy five percent of adults used some sort of corrective lenses, either contacts or glasses. We haven't seen any of the S.A. dead or otherwise, with either, sir," he said. "The other prisoners are more concerning to me, though."

"How so?" I asked, after a cough that hurt.

"Colonel, I think they're drugged. We've had some communications from the medical researchers at Command, who've been looking into it as well. Hadn't seen it up close and personal until today though of course. That one," he said, motioning to the prisoner that had just left, "I guess he was the equivalent of a platoon sergeant. He can still think, more or less. The others, they've got next to no short term memory. They do not appear to know what they've done, or where they are. They didn't feel pain. Further, it doesn't seem to matter to them. Without short term memory…it's sort of like hypnosis," he said.

"Drugs can do that? How often to they have to take them?" This possibility had never occurred to me.

"They can do that. An engineered drug, say with the properties of midazolam and an opiod, designed for long lasting effect, and reinforced on a regular basis, and you could end up with the S.A. line soldiers we saw today. The drug could create anterograde and retrograde amnesia. They wouldn't remember much if anything. They could take orders without much trouble. Add an opiod and they don't feel pain, have euphoria, and are happy as Hell to be wherever they are, as long as they get their hit. Highly suggestive. Easy to boss around."

I thought about that for a minute, and coughed again. "Damned ribs," I said.

"How long you had that cough?"

"Coupla days, I guess."

"You up on all your immunizations, Colonel?"

"Got an armload and a butt-load back in Spokane. I was pretty current on everything else before the War, for this continent anyway."

Jeff ordered me to peel off a couple of layers, and listened to my breathing.

"Chest pains? Left side?"

"Well, yeah, but I had a slug of broken ribs in August, so that's nothing new."

"Chills? Signs of a fever?"

"Not particularly. Tired a lot though," I said.

"Colonel, if I were a betting man, I'd say you have a mild case of pneumonia. Your heart rate is elevated. We're going to get you a chest film and run some tests."

"You serious? I'm that sick?"

"You checked out for having had the Guangdong this past year, right?"

"Yeah. Knocked me on my butt. Got it early."

"Alpha strain, before the mutations diluted it. Then you're probably a prime candidate for pneumonia. Permanent lung scarring. We'll know after the tests."

"Jeez. I came in here for an aspirin."

"Good thing you did. It'd suck to spend Christmas on an IV antibiotic."

"What's the fix for this?"

"Oral antibiotics, which we have of course. Probably a longer regimen than normal, like ten to fourteen days. In the old days, before the G-Flu, it would take three to five. Compromised immune system and scarred lungs, we're not taking chances."

"OK. What else?"

"Stay inside where it's relatively warm, away from anyone else that's ill. A whole lot of rest. A whole lot of fluids…for a week. I know this'll cramp your style, sir. You won't be on any line unit, you won't be serving chow, you won't be welding up some beat to Hell Stryker. Get Lieutenant Colonel Schaefer to handle the outside work and reviews of the battalions operations. Stay the Hell out of the medical tents, the hospitals, and away from any refugee. They're walking biology experiments," he said before turning his attention to one of the pharmacists. "Howard, set up the Colonel with A-Fourteen, twice daily."

"Yes, sir, Doctor," the balding young man said, turning his attention to the drug storage compartment in the back of the rail car.

"Colonel, you aren't one of those difficult officers that I have to have watched, are you?" Jeff asked, with a slight tilt to his head and a wry smile. "You know, the kind that don't follow orders?"

"Depends, Doc, on if the orders are stupid or not. Yours aren't. Don't worry."

"Good to know, Colonel."

Once the civilians started to come out of hiding, it quickly became apparent that the medical teams had nowhere near enough manpower to address the situation, and we'd reassigned anyone available to assist and go through additional training. In addition to dehydration and starvation, there were hundreds of cases of measles, diphtheria, whooping cough, and dysentery. Doc Willitson thought we might also have patients with significant parasitic infections.

'Dog Six' deployed as planned, more or less, and began to organize from chaos, the remains of the rail yard. Wrecked S.A. railcars and locomotives needed to be cleared, the tracks repaired, all the while under the watchful eye of the ordnance clearing teams, with incoming supply trains breathing down our necks. We needed the supplies to function and to equip both 'Able' and 'Baker' and the many other units in the area; tend to the needs the civilians; and we needed an intact and operational rail yard to and manpower to unload and distribute. I met with a brigadier from California on the second day of our deployment, told him of the cluster that I found myself in charge of, and we had every man under his command at our discretion. Things were beginning to shape up.

"Colonel, crews from the Two Four Nine will have the rest of the main campus on line from rolling power within an hour," Gary Ryder said. "Finishing up fault testing now, and the hospital district is powered up now."

"Good. Thanks, Gary. Second and Third Battalions done with their sweeps?"

"By eleven-hundred, sir. First can then start shifting military and civilian critical care patients to St. Mary's and the V.A. center. Secondary and tertiary care will remain at the University. Are you planning on making a run over there, sir?"

"Nope. Doctors' orders. I apparently am working on a case of pneumonia." That drew looks from everyone in the Command Car.

"Sir?" Major Ryder questioned, obviously surprised.

"I have duty restrictions per Doc Willitson. And meds. And orders to get lots of rest. Find Jim Schaefer and get him back to command, if you would."

"Will do, sir."

Eight hundred of our troops were working the University of Nebraska campus, room by room, to ensure they were clear for civilian occupation. The first sweep through the campus showed many shuttered buildings, relatively undamaged. Some of the data from the administration building showed that enrollment was twenty percent of pre-War levels.

With heat and electricity, the University of Nebraska-Lincoln could house many thousands. We knew that with the rapid progression of the U.S. into formerly S.A. territories, we wouldn't be in Lincoln very long.

I'd taken lunch in my quarters, and been treated to another batch of letters from home. Afterwards, I'd take a nap. Whatever Doc gave me, was obviously knocking me down.   Carl's letter was pretty much all business. Kelly's was as expressive as her personality.

Dear Dad—

I hope things are going OK wherever you are. Carl and I have been working to keep up with Mom, who has turned into a tornado around here. She's going a million miles an hour! We just finished canning a bunch of the squash. I don't think I want to see another butternut for a year.

Both of us are way ahead on our classwork, and we'll probably both graduate early! I know, I have years to go, but it'd be great to be out of school by the time I'm seventeen!

Grandma is doing pretty well, and is getting around in a wheelchair at her house. She said to "give you her thanks for all he's done for my family." She's working on her cross-stitch again, but she's not as 'sharp' as she used to be.

We're going to have the Pauliano's for Christmas, and Mom and Aunt Mary are working on the menu already. We helped them move some more stuff from the Pauliano's place last Sunday, and Sarah said that the hospital would be able to get Joan a more steady supply of medicines for her arthritis. They made us an apple crisp for our work, with fresh cream from their cows! OMG it was good!

We've also been dehydrating some of the apples, they aren't keeping very well. Uncle Alan built a big dehydrator out of a little electric furnace, and it's absolutely amazing. I think we have enough apple slices for years. I wish we had more cinnamon! He built that in the big garage across the street from his house—you know, the one where the house burned?

Mom's been teaching me how to drive the Expedition too. Don't worry, I go slow and it scares me. It's too big. Do you think that someday I can have my own car? Like the Mustang or the Convertible?

596

Aunt Libby, Uncle Ron, Marie and I went over to Coeur d'Alene last Friday. Carl wanted to go but had to work at the church. I didn't know that the big hotel was gone. It was pretty sad. There was a big lake boat though near the beach. Uncle Ron called it a 'lake steamer'. I guess it has a steam boiler? Without gas it's not very easy to get around or across the lake. Probably easier when it's frozen over though. What's an 'ice boat?' And how do you race them?

Mom's hollering that I need to get to bed. I'm praying for you every day—stay safe, Daddy!

All my love—
Kelly

I finished it, another letter from Karen, and put both back in their envelopes. 'I'll have to find time to write more,' I thought, lying back down on the bed. Before I could even shut my eyes, my computer came to life.

"Colonel, sorry to disturb you," Jim Schaefer said through the messaging program. "We've got something you ought to take a look at."

"Be right there, Jim," I said after activating the microphone. 'Swell,' I thought.

A few minutes later, I was looking at the fresh email from Command. We'd have aircraft on the ground by days end...a lot of them.

"How's 'Able' doing on the runways?"

"Runway is good. A couple of the aprons are behind schedule, but they'll be ready, Colonel," Schaefer said.

"Kittrick? How long until the fuel train rolls in?"

"Two hours, twenty minutes present speed, sir."

"Jim, anyone check the fueling from the rail lines to the airport tanks? Or the airport tanks for that matter?"

"Unknown, sir. I'll call over to Able Command and check."

"Thanks. Not real smart to leave this many tank cars full of avgas out in the open."

"Colonel Drummond, sir," a new-to-Charlie comm tech said, "We've got an Air Force Oh-Eight on Secure Two for you, sir."

"Affirm. Secure two," I said, punching up the code for the channel. "Jim, listen in on this."

"Colonel Drummond, Third Washington," I said, seeing Schaefer at one of the consoles.

"Colonel, this is Major General David Rowe at Lackland Air Force Base. Colonel, Lincoln is going to be a forward operating base for close air support operations starting immediately. How are repairs coming? You got a runway for us?"

"Runway's ready for anything up to twelve-thousand nine-hundred. A couple of aprons are still receiving repairs, and we're working on verifying the in-ground fueling system. Rail tankers are coming in this afternoon, General, two hours and change."

"We've got a pair of C-17's that'll be on the ground within two hours. They're carrying mobile air traffic control and short-range drone fire control systems, but we'll need ground power almost immediately. Can you accommodate us?" he asked.

"Affirmative, General. We have power at the airport from one of our rail mounted generators, and will be setting up stationary generating units there and at several locations, for mid-term use."

"All right, Colonel. That's what I wanted to hear. After the first two -17's expect to see a pretty dramatic increase in traffic as aircrews and support come into Lincoln. You'll see traffic from all branches, naturally, and a couple of trains that aren't on your schedule."

"I'd expect that, sir."

"Outbound cargo and passenger aircraft are open for refugees, after military wounded are taken care of, Colonel."

"We'll need to get after that, sir. We have thousands of civilians here, many needing advanced medical care. We have about a thousand wounded soldiers. We're doing what we can, but..."

"Get them on the outbounds and anyone else who wants to go. They'll be in the way or a distraction to our men—you included. There's plenty of room out of the war zone and they'll be better off outta there. Clear?"

"Yes, sir."

"Good job, Colonel. I'll see you in the next day or so. Rowe out," he said, then the line went dead.

I looked over at Jim as he took of his headset.

"Swell."

Sunday,
December Twenty-Fourth
18:00 Hours
Lincoln, Nebraska

Within the space of a few hours, Lincoln Municipal Airport became again, Lincoln Air Force Base. I wasn't aware that it had ever been an Air Force installation, until I'd seen an old-timer who'd worked on Atlas ICBM's when they were stationed locally in the Sixties. It had been home to both Army and Air Guard units before the War. They'd been reassigned to Cannon Air Force Base in New Mexico.

True to his word, General Rowe's C-17's delivered men and equipment that transformed the wrecked airport to a forward operating base for every type of close air support aircraft in the inventory, no matter what branch.

By seventeen-hundred, Air Control was up and running, not far from the wrecked Nebraska ANG buildings, despite the forward air controllers not having a place to sleep that night. Crews from both the Washington and Idaho brigades were assembling housing for the aircrews and controllers, from rail-mounted units nearly identical to ours. Two off-load cranes systematically unloaded the converted containers and shifted to flat-beds towed by semi-tractors, moved them to the airport, and then offloaded each unit with another pair of cranes. The creation of the Air Force Village would probably take a full twenty-four hours, especially getting the utility hookups made. There was plenty of work to go around. I toured the operations of the Gem State and Third Washington in a very old, but low mileage Chevy Blazer that at one time had belonged to a missile complex up in North Dakota. I'd never seen as many heaters in anything painted olive drab. It was nice to be warm.

At seventeen oh-five I was headed back up to the airport with Jim Schaefer for a last look before I sequestered myself. I didn't hear them until they were nearly upon us: three KC 135's in quick succession, perhaps thirty seconds apart, landed and immediately dispersed on the fair-sized apron of the base.

"Nice to see they're starting to get some aircraft in the fight," Jim said. "Really packing them in close.

"They've probably been in the fight all along, just not where it would do any good," I replied. "Or at least, any good for us."

Right after the KC's, the familiar 'hum' of the A-10 Warthog. I gave up counting them after twenty.

"Shee-it," I said, pulling up to the Air Force security policeman for the second time in an hour.

"Good evening, Colonel. Where you headed this time?"

"Off to see your C.O. with Lieutenant Colonel Schaefer here," I said.

"One moment, sir, let me locate him," he said, then stepped away from the truck and spoke into his headset mike. "Should be in Thirty One Oh Seven, sir."

"Thanks, Sergeant," I said with a nod, and drove off. "They've got their Command and Air Traffic Control in those six containers behind the three layers of fence."

"Anti-RPG fencing?" Jim asked.

"You got it."

"So, Colonel, how long you think you'll be down?"

"I've got a two week supply of antibiotics and the Doc will be checking on me as often as he thinks is prudent. He's not messing around. Just consider me an office-bot for the duration. Which, by the way, I will hate."

"I'll bet. You're not the kind of guy to sit on your ass, sir."

"Not so much, no," I said looking over at the runway. "Fairchild Thunderbolt II's. Those have to be one of my favorite aircraft, period."

"The Warthog is one of the best things flying, sir. Every time I meet one of their pilots, I buy them a drink."

"I hope we have a lot of them left…pilots and Hogs."

Colonel Mike Kazmer was a bundle of nervous energy in a five-foot nine frame, simultaneously listening to three different attack missions in mid-execution, giving orders to his command staff, and listening to our situation report. He seemed to take it all in, and asked pointed questions that were relevant to air operations. Transport and converted civilian airliners would begin to evac civilians on Christmas morning.

"OK, Colonel Schaefer, that covers the basics: Fuel, food and bullets. How's security on our approach and departure? How many people with long-guns picking for us?"

I responded for Jim. "Colonel Kazmer, the S.A. disarmed most everyone here. There is no Resistance movement to speak of. There is no civilian presence within two miles of the airport in any direction. There wasn't before the City was re-taken, it's been maintained that way. There are no habitable homes from Interstate Eighty north and west of Highway One Eighty."

"SAM's? Find any?"

"No, Colonel Kazmer. Spent SA-7's manufactured twenty years ago, -14's and -18's. Hundreds. No live weapons."

"Common manufacture?"

"Not hardly. Russian, Egyptian, Chinese, Pakistani. Manufacture dates of Nineteen Seventy-Nine to three months ago," Jim said. That raised Kazmer's eyebrows.

"What'd you find for fixed installations?" he asked.

"Wreckage," I said.

"Can't I.D?" Kazmer asked.

"Six radar locations with six launchers each. There really wasn't enough left of any of them to identify what they were or where they were from, but three Intel officers said they didn't recognize any of it. Secondary detonations at all locations. It appeared they stored spare missiles well within blast radii of the missiles on the launchers."

"Amateurs," Kazmer said, listening to us and his controllers in contact with 'Gunfighter Six' who was engaged over Omaha. 'Six' was an A-10 that had been hit during a run through the SAM umbrella over the city. I'd overheard that the plane had engine damage and had lost both hydraulic systems and had reverted to manual—meaning cable operated—controls.

"Colonel, it's clear you've got work to do. We'll let you get to it," I said as I stood. I was getting tired. Jim stood as well.

"Busy night in a long line of busy nights. Thanks to you both and your men. Good having juice to run these systems, food for our men and a supply line for gas and shells."

"Merry Christmas, Colonel."

"And to you as well," he said, shaking our hands, still listening to 'Gunfighter Six' and 'One', the stricken crafts' flight leader.

Jim and I put our parka's back on, and headed outside. Air Force emergency response crews were ready to respond to 'Gunfighter'.

"This could get interesting," I said to Jim.

"Yeah, at least. Here he comes," he said, pointing north-northeast.

We watched as the anti-collision lights flashed and a single landing light wavered on approach, and touched down without incident.

"Uneventful is good," I said.

"Yeah it is. I'm thinking that pilot's gonna kiss the ground."

"At least," I said as we looked to the northeast, thirty-five or forty miles over to Omaha, where we could hear artillery and see the flashes of explosions.

For the first time ever, I spent Christmas Eve alone. Six chaplains from the Brigade were at several refugee locations for makeshift church services. I'd have been there too, but for doctor's orders. There was little in the way of traditional Christmas celebrations in Lincoln. I read my well worn Bible, and listened to carols being broadcast through our train, Dog Six, and Lincoln Air Force Base. I wrote letters to Karen, Carl and Kelly; Ron and Libby; Alan and Mary.

I reviewed in my mind the previous year, and how different it turned out to be.

Karen and I had planned on a family trip to San Francisco for Spring Break, staying at our favorite hotel off of Columbus, not far from Fisherman's Wharf. I didn't tell her but I'd also planned a nice quiet dinner for the two of us at the Mark Hopkins. I'd made reservations six months in advance. Instead of San Francisco, we finished the roof on the house, and slept inside a house and not a barn, for the first time in months.

Summer would have brought around another family reunion with my brothers, probably without Joe. We'd have golfed at Liberty Lake's north course, water skied behind a friend's boat up at Priest where we'd vacationed as kids, seen a Spokane Indians baseball game on a fireworks night. Instead, we farmed and split wood and built houses and worried a lot.

All the other plans were shelved as well. Building a new deck in the back of the house, adding an above ground pool, finishing the Sixty-Six Mustang for Carl and Kelly to drive to school.

A little before midnight, I shut the lights off and listened as the A-10's continued their sorties.

Christmas Morning
04:30 Hours

I rose early, tired of coughing, and not quite knowing where I was. I didn't sleep well, with the constant thrum of air traffic and all the noises associated with normal operations of Third Washington.

After showering, I flipped on the monitor and reviewed the imagery currently being viewed in the Command Car. It made me fee like a teacher looking over the shoulders of students, to see if anyone was cheating. Two monitors were reviewing weather inbound to Lincoln, others were working on equipment manifests, personnel assignments, supply train schedules, and sorting through lists of civilians requesting transport out of the city.

The latter, in particular I found interesting, as the tech running that station was cross-referencing the photographs of civilians with known database information from before the War. The database was quite extensive, more so than I'd ever realized. We were weeding through the 'civilians', to see if there was a cross reference to any known S.A.

I grabbed my parka and gloves, and headed to 'work', making my way through the slush-covered ice.

"Merry Christmas, everyone," I said to the full Command Car.

"Good morning, Colonel. Fresh coffee?" Major Pat Morrissey asked.

"Absolutely, Pat. The real thing?"

"Courtesy of the United States Air Force," he said, pouring me a big mug.

"Mighty nice of them," I said.

"Considering they're looking to requisition one of Third's machine shops, permanent-like," Pat said, "I'd consider this as part of a buttering-up process, sir."

"When did the request come in?" I asked.

"Little after midnight, Colonel."

"How high up the food chain?"

"Bird Colonel, sir. Name of Harris."

"Anybody from Third comment on this?"

"Charlie's machine shops are running full steam, Colonel, three shifts. Refits of equipment far and wide, mostly tanks. Dog's a little slower."

"Correct me if I'm wrong. They have four shops from 'Able' at their disposal, and they want ours as well?"

"Appears that way, sir."

"Yeah. Not really feeling like Saint Nick today," I said. "When they put a formal request in, send it, and the messenger, straight to me."

"I'll see to it, sir," Pat said.

"OK, now, what's the overnight sit rep?"

"Lost three water filtration systems on our train, two on Dog. Pump systems in the waste tanks are having issues, too."

"I figured the honeymoon would wear off pretty quick. Crews on repair?"

"Twenty-five men on rotation, Colonel. The cold is a bitch."

"And the boys in blue? They've been busy overnight."

"Flyboys have been hammering on the S.A. in Omaha. Lost one plane. Ground forces are closing in, should be entering the central core within the next six hours," he said, pointing at a tactical display on one of the monitors. "They've basically got everything west of a line from the airport on the north side of town to Papillion on the south. Six more transports came in overnight from Arizona and

California, men and gear. Planes are really stacking up at the airport, Air Force says that evac flights will start as soon as the civilian relief forces and ground workers offload—they're inbound right now, probably an hour out. Most of Dog Six is standing down until eleven hundred, they had a freight come in around oh two hundred and were on alert to offload. That one got shuttled straight up to the Air Force instead—munitions—including some new drones, and the boys in blue took care of the offload. Next train's not due until fourteen-hundred. Night shift of Charlie should be coming off duty at oh six-hundred. No news there, most of the men were up on campus in the civilian shelters and med centers."

"Find any S.A. in this vetting process?" I asked, pointing to one of the tech's working over on Suite Two.

"Five. They don't know it yet. We have men there. They'll be removed from the civilian population shortly. We planned on taking them at oh five-hundred."

"Are they together, or separate?"

"Separate," Morrissey said.

"If you do this, will you tip off any other S.A. in the lot?"

"Colonel, sir?" the Suite Two tech, 'Jackson' replied. "We're done with the vetting process across the entire civilian population in the next fifteen minutes, sir. Facial recognition programs are running in every Command Car—all eight between the four trains—most on multiple suites. This suite is reviewing some questionables raised by all other suites."

"You've done this overnight?" I asked, quite surprised. Thousands of civilians were photographed, names taken, and other identification given.

"Yes, sir. Captain McGowan's orders, along with the intelligence officers from the Idaho Brigade."

"Nice work," I said. "Pat, proceed per your original schedule." All civilians had been searched for weapons when they entered the civilian shelters. In the thousands of refugees, the most serious weapon were folding blade knives. No firearms whatsoever.

I reviewed the Christmas Day operational schedule as the time ticked toward five a.m. The S.A. in hiding would be whisked out of the civilian shelters quickly, taken to a secure facility within the perimeter of the Air Force base, and would go through interrogation. Along the way, they'd be strip searched and zip tied.

Christmas breakfast for the civilians would be nothing out of the ordinary, unfortunately. They'd be fed and warm though, and some would evac to warmer climates and safer places. Third Washington wouldn't be 'fixing' much in the way of infrastructure in Lincoln, beyond keeping the University and hospital areas alive for military support.

One of the sergeants from Second Battalion served up breakfast for the Command Car, earlier than we'd expected. Breakfast bagel, with sausage, egg and cheese. Not bad, but not home. I missed Karen's sausage, egg, bread and cheese breakfast casserole....

I put on the headset and microphone, and listened to the tactical frequency as the S.A. in hiding were taken, forgetting that there was probably headset video from each squad. None put up a fight, but exiting the group sleeping area was a little tense. The civilians wanted the S.A. for their own. Within a few minutes, the S.A. were on their way to their new, limited future.

A second cup of coffee later, Pat placed in front of me a stack of recovered S.A. documents that were being scanned and transmitted up to Command. They were an interesting glimpse into the Other Side. Although cryptically written, the gist of the 'Priority Directives' included these choice thoughts:

Doctors, nurses, scientists and engineers were to be captured and shipped East to Pennsylvania, where the S.A. was establishing research and development centers for medically enhancing the soldiers of the S.A. and dramatically increasing the immune systems of the senior members of the S.A. hierarchy. Simultaneously, anyone deemed to be of inferior 'stock' would be conscripted into the S.A. ranks and 'fully indoctrinated into the Sacred Mission of the State.' The 'inferior stock' would be used as front-line soldiers, and were fully intended to be expendable. Those with 'superior social value' would of course be spared.

"Eugenics at it's finest," I said to myself, as I continued reading.

The capture of breeding-age females of course was part of the process, where either they would be selected for breeding based on 'pre-determined genetic superiority' (which seemed a contradiction in terms to me). Those with 'acceptable prime factors' would be directly bred; those without would be artificially inseminated. The report was incomplete, only part of their 'Statistically Superior Creation Effort' was here for me to read. It was sickening.

"Pat, has Captain McGowan read this?"

"Yes, sir. I was reserving passing on his responses until you've read the documents."

"These people are barking mad," I said. "They're getting soundly thrashed on all fronts and they're talking about breeding the next generation from *'genetically superior' people?'"*

"So it appears, Colonel."

The rest of the documents paled in comparison to the 'creation effort'. Machinery and tooling, all identified by location, type, capability and capacity were present in a thick, three-ring bound document. Someone had put significant effort into inventorying, documenting, and locating all of this equipment. All of it was to be seized intact, disassembled by 'Relocation Teams' and relocated to designated R&D centers, mostly in Pennsylvania, although several were in northern Indiana. There was no specific information on 'what' was to be created from the assembled equipment, only that it was 'necessary to ensure the dominance of the State in the prosecution of the War against all enemies.' Many of the directives were signed by their 'president', with the intended recipient being an S.A. General by the name of Arnold Slocum. I saw hand-written notes in the hand of this general, outlining occupation and elimination of *'resources not directly beneficial to the supremacy of the State.'* The document appeared to be a rough draft of orders to his army.

Any equipment that could not be removed was to be destroyed so that 'enemy' efforts could not 'exploit the equipment for use against the State.'

For the first time, I saw in print, the specific instructions to destroy anything and anyone left behind in any 'offensive' that could be 'used against the State and allow the enemy to mount a recovery.

Recovery would be dictated by the State on the State's terms, only after the destruction of enemy population centers.'

I sat there and thought about that for a long time. Only after a second request, did I respond to one of the junior officers requesting that I take a call on one of the secure channels.

"Colonel, you OK?" Major Morrissey asked.

"Yeah, thanks Major. Just thinking," I said as I put the headset on.
"Colonel Drummond," I said into the mike.

"General Garcia, Colonel. Merry Christmas."

"General, to you as well. What can we do for you?"

"You can get to Omaha, pronto. What kind of ETA can you give us?"

"Probably six hours to break down both trains for transit. After that, just best possible time to get to a terminal point, General. Clear tracks, an hour or so." I'd anticipated a move like this, and asked for realistic break-down and ready-to-move schedules from the entire Brigade. These were updated daily. I didn't like surprises.

"I'm putting in the request with Austin right now. I would expect an answer back within an hour."

"Understood, General. We'll be waiting."

"Garcia out," she said as the line went dead.

Morrissey let out a long, descending whistle. "Into the fire, Colonel."

"Maybe so. Get the duty officers up to speed. Not really how I wanted to spend the day," I said, thinking, 'Americans. Killing each other on Christmas.'

Christmas Day
13:00 Hours
Aboard Charlie Six

Third Washington had done the near impossible, in my mind, demobilizing and getting both trains holding the balance of the Brigade in four hours and fifty-five minutes. Part of the time savings was due to abandoning many of the tents and equipment in the field, instead loading up fresh equipment from the replacement stockpile.

United States ground forces were on the verge of taking the remains of Omaha, pounded into submission by nearly ninety thousand troops, hundreds of pieces of field artillery, seven hundred main battle tanks and hundreds of Air Force sorties. The few poor-quality images we'd seen of Offutt Air Force Base reminded me of photographs of a concrete recycling operation. There wasn't a single recognizable structure or piece of pavement that hadn't been blasted.

Third Washington, soon to be followed by other support units, would help feed, house, and resupply the tens of thousands of troops that had passed through Lincoln while we were there. Leapfrogging across the Midwest, we'd eventually either wear down the S.A. and defeat them through attrition, or we'd find our own supply chain tighten around our neck, and find ourselves in a stalemate.

Unlike other destinations for Third, we had no pre-designated staging area to review before we arrived. The largest rail yard in the area was actually in Council Bluffs, across the Missouri River…and still effectively in S.A. control…and bombed to ruin. We weren't able to pre-plan distribution of our assets, have any educated guesses on deployment, nothing. We were going in cold.

Most of the command staff was crowded into our conference car with Second Battalion's commander, Trayvon Chappel, and Third Battalion's Hugh Epstein. We were having a heated discussion on our deployment, not liking any of the potential locations and deployment scenarios. We'd almost certainly be deployed in lowland areas, overlooked by neighborhoods on the higher surrounding terrain, exposed, and without escape.

"Sirs?" Kittrick interrupted, his image appearing on the video screen on the back wall. "Just got this message from command: General Howard is proposing that Third Washington stage near a suburb called Chalco, about ten miles west of Offutt. All lines east into the city are blocked. There's also a small civilian airport about a mile north of the staging area. Fifth Marines control that area, including substantial air cover," he said, punching up the proposed staging location for our brigade on the monitor.

"Thanks, Mister Kittrick," I said, turning my attention back to the men around the table.

"All right, we've got a spot to park and a semblance of security. We just don't quite know what we're getting into yet."

"Safe bet, Colonel, on the following," Doc Willitson added. "Frostbite, dehydration, and all of the other afflictions of battle of course."

"We have no idea what we have for a civilian presence in Omaha, Jeff. Anybody want to hazard and educated guess?" I said as I felt and then heard, something go horribly wrong.

The shock seemed to ripple through the conference car as the train derailed, threatening to roll the train onto her side. We were all tossed out of our chairs, coffee and water and papers thrown to the downhill side, lit by the red emergency lighting.

"Well, *sheeeit*," Lieutenant Colonel Chappel said a moment after we came to rest.

"We're under attack or we've derailed accidentally, and I don't believe in coincidences," I said, getting to my feet on the sloping floor.

"No small arms fire," one of the men said. "That can't be a bad thing, Colonel."

The men in the back of the converted shipping container managed to push the door open, which was now swinging uphill. Daylight streamed into the darkened car, along with the cold. Other than voices outside, there was no other sound. I was last out of the

614

car. It took me a minute to find my Kevlar helmet and get my parka on. I realized my rifle was in the Command Car. 'Damn', I said to myself, realizing that I was armed with a .45, period. I made my way out, moving to the 'uphill' toward the track, and landed on my stomach next to Lieutenant Colonel Epstein, who had his rifle trained on the empty gray horizon. No threat was visible.

I looked toward the front of the train and saw the entire side of one of the lead defensive cars, which was straddling the tracks, but upright. Two supply cars ahead of it were on their side, smoke was rising from where the lead engines should be. Unlike prior trips, this train was assembled with 'pullers' and 'pushers,' meaning, engines on both ends of the assembled train.

The men under my command rapidly barked orders to the Command Car staff, some of who had left their posts, although the Command Car was still on the rails. A dozen of the radio headsets were found, passed around, and Charlie Six was again able to act tactically with acceptable response times within two minutes.

The derailment had severed electrical power and communications to most of the train. With the sudden stop, almost all the men aboard Charlie had grabbed their gear and deployed in rehearsed defensive posture until we could figure out what had happened. Both flanks of Charlie's position were protected against the unknown threat.

"Colonel, you hurt?" Doc Willitson asked as he tracked me down.

"Not so far as I know, Doc," I said. "Pissed off maybe, not hurt."

A few minutes later, Able and Baker Companies, Third Battalion had deployed and secured the real estate forward of the conference car. While they were slowly progressing northeast to the wrecked cars, the men in the defensive car radioed an 'all clear' and a request for corpsmen due to serious injuries. Two of the four men in the lead engines were dead. Doc Willitson and his medics quickly moved forward to the wrecked engines. To the northeast, I could see thin smoke rising from what was left of the small town of Greenwood.

Chappel and I walked up to the lead end of the train as more men were taken from the defensive posture and into their assigned roles, helping the corpsmen with the wounded. The lead engine was on its side, burning; it's back broken from an explosion directly under it.

The second power unit was upright, but smoking. Behind the second power unit, a fifteen-foot wide crater, and fifty feet of rails peeled up and away like a pretzel. Parts of railroad ties were everywhere.

"That was one Hell of an IED," I said, looking over the damage to the lead engine. The massive frame of the locomotive was bowed upward and out, and a three-foot diameter hole through the lower part of the engine. The blast pattern seemed to suggest a culvert under the tracks.

"Shaped penetrator. Big ass shaped penetrator, sir."

"You'll have to school me on that, Colonel Chappel," I said.

"Simple, sir. The bomb is built with an explosive charge beneath a concave form of metal. Bomb goes off, the concave form goes convex with the force of the blast. Think, thin piece of metal instantly formed into a missile, propelled at the speed of the explosion," Chappel said. "But I've never seen one this big."

Dog Six pulled up behind our trailing engines, and radioed ahead to Command that Charlie was disabled and the track blocked until we could clear the rails. We walked around the end of the wreck, a platoon in front of us, as one of our Humvees ran further a field, dismounted troops following.

"Sirs, you might want to look at this," one of the platoon sergeants said, pointing out an object a hundred yards out.

We walked over the scarred ground, where something had blown out of the explosion, carving out snow, slush and mud along the path.

"That's a human torso," Chappel said, looking over the blasted remains, partially cast into what appeared to be a large concrete block.

"They used the culvert for an IED location. Plugged it with concrete on this end to direct the blast upward. Probably one on the other side that we missed," I said, looking at the concrete that reflected the corrugations of a metal culvert. "And they used a body for fill in the concrete."

"I'm not sure I know what to say to that, Colonel," Lieutenant Colonel Chappel said. "Honest to God, I don't."

"I don't know either," I said.

December Twenty-Fifth
19:00 Hours

A rag tag crew of rail workers and Army transport specialists came *from* ravaged Omaha to clear and repair the tracks, using all available hands—many—from Third where we could help. I was not allowed to do much.

Observation posts had been set up a mile out in all directions, as we were a stationary target with idling engines. It's not possible to hide a train, or two, along with the lights and noise of a wreckage-clearing operation.

In addition to the loss of a third of our train engineering crew, we had seventeen other significant injuries, including concussions, broken arms and collarbones, and crush injuries from inside the lead Defensive Car. One of the chain-gun ammunition lockers had torn loose and broken the legs of the gunner. Jeff Willitson and his men had been in surgery most of the day.

The train had damage throughout, from electrical surges that cooked one leg of the power system in our communications car to broken water and waste piping, torqued frames of several rail cars, leaving several cars with doors that wouldn't close properly.

The Omaha crewmen could move the damaged and destroyed cars out of our way and fix the tracks. They could not do so within a timeframe that was viewed as 'acceptable' by my superiors. I received an ass chewing that I viewed as unwarranted, but I could understand the frustration on the part of General Garcia. None of the U.S. ground forces in Omaha could pursue the S.A. without supplies and equipment, which was mostly assigned, to rail traffic on this line, and there weren't enough operable semi-trucks and trailers within five hundred miles to make a dent in the demand. The pursuit and destruction of the S.A. would slow because of this, perhaps dramatically. A supply train coming toward Omaha from the north had been blown apart as well, blocking the northern route.

617

"Colonel Drummond, we've got contact, back end of Dog Six, sir, estimated range two thousand yards," Private Ayers said.

"Whose patrol quarter?" I asked.

"A Company, First, sir."

"Punch me up Colonel Miller," I said. Shawn Miller was usually out with one of the companies, especially at dusk.

"Tactical channel thirty-one Able, sir. Call sign Victory One, yours is Raptor Lead."

"Thanks, Mister Ayers," I said as punched in the communications codes.

"Victory One, what've you got out there?"

"Two on horseback, approaching cautiously. Bolt-action rifles in scabbards, Raptor Lead," was the hushed response.

"Vic Two and Vic Five will make first contact and will challenge at one hundred meters. Video feed should be on Vic Two's channel, Raptor."

"Understood. Raptor out."

Ayers punched up Victory Two's night vision equipment feeds, clearly showing the riders, approaching cautiously but deliberately. I found myself wishing I were out there.

"Ayers, alert all posts that Victory has imminent contact," Greg Shand ordered, looking over at me. I nodded, continuing to watch the greenish images on the screen.

"Yes, sir, Captain," he said, immediately contacting the hundreds of men in the field.

A few more minutes passed as the riders grew closer, and the camera went to a wider field of vision, and the horses wheeled as the challenge was made. Both riders raised their hands as ordered, and dismounted as they were surrounded, and surrendered their weapons.

"Victory, transmit their given identification and bring them to Raptor Lead."

"Affirm," came the response.

Ten minutes later, I met the two riders, escorted by a platoon of security, in the rear conference car. The man was in his mid-fifties, joined by a much younger woman. Both looked fit, clean and in good health. A welcome look.

"Colonel Richard Drummond, Third Washington," I said, introducing myself.

"Pleased to meet you, sir. Dave Barkley. My daughter Amy."

"Have a seat, please. This is Captain Gerry McGowan, our intelligence officer, Sergeant Major Chet Travis and Captain Adam Fillmore, our chaplain," I said, introducing the senior men. "Coffee?" I asked, getting a quizzical look.

"Real coffee?" Amy asked. She looked to be twenty-five or so, and was a 'looker.'

"Yes, ma'am," Sergeant Travis replied.

"That would be wonderful. Thank you," she said as Chet poured two mugs.

"Mister Barkley are you from around here?" I asked.

"Grew up here, Colonel. Call me Dave, please. The rail lines run through our land. We heard the explosion, and debated for quite a while on whether we should make contact. We were scouting when your forward observers identified themselves. We didn't know we were that close."

"Fair enough. Now, if I can ask, where do your allegiances lie?" I asked, surprising him I'm sure.

"Solely with God and the Constitution of the United States of America, sir."

I chuckled a little bit. "Good to know. Thank you."

"You're really from Washington? The state?" Amy asked.

"Yes, Ma'am. After a fashion. We've been heading east for some weeks now."

"Chasing the S.A. back to their hole, I hope."

"Well, that and to fill the hole in after we put them there, yes. Then pave it over."

"Are either of you two hungry, or is there anything we can get you?" Chaplain Fillmore added, another 'good cop'.

"We're OK, but thank you."

"If you wouldn't mind, Mister and Miss Barkley, could you tell us how you, well, are in such good condition, after being behind the S.A. lines for so long? As an intelligence officer I'm naturally skeptical," McGowan said, arms crossed across his chest, leaning back in his chair, body language shouting, 'liars'.

"My wife and I were from Dallas, before the War that is," Dave Barkley said. "And my daughter's last name is Fournier. She lost her husband on *USS Augusta*. She was in Corpus Christi looking for a job, staying with friends."

"I'm very sorry for your loss," I said, Amy Fournier lowering her eyes to her coffee cup. I remembered the thousands of sailors lost in those early days of the Third War.

"When things started to come apart," Dave Barkley said, exhaling, "I suppose not long after the earthquakes up your way, my brothers and sisters and their families decided to get back to home to ride it out. Three of us made it, two didn't. My younger brother was in Florence, on some damned Renaissance tour, never made it back. My wife and younger sister boarded a flight from Hawaii that never arrived in L.A. We thought that EMP took out the plane. We don't know," he said, taking a sip of the coffee. "My sister had multiple sclerosis, and couldn't travel well. My wife flew out to help her.

620

Never made it back," he said, and paused for a few seconds. It could not have been easy, reliving this.

"The farm has been here for a hundred and fifty years, most of that time in the family. We left Dallas with our Suburban hauling a trailer and a Class C motorhome. Didn't have a lick of trouble on that trip."

Amy took over the conversation, as I noticed the 'thousand yard stare' on her father's face. 'Perhaps no trouble on that trip, but there had certainly been enough trouble in this man's life,' I thought.

"The farm is far enough off the beaten path not to have been bothered by any of the S.A. that mattered, and thank God we're far enough away from a highway that they went around us. Anyone that was a threat was killed," she said, quite matter-of-factly. "There were S.A. patrols that just never went back to wherever they came from."

"My husband always knew something was coming, and we were ready for it, or so we thought at the time. The Suburban and the motorhome are both diesels. Danny—my husband—installed radio gear for long-range communications in everything, including the farm. The trailer had quite a lot of our emergency equipment and food, and the motorhome was always ready to go. We'd planned to move back to the farm at the end of his tour," she said. "Plans changed though."

"Again, my condolences," I said.

"Thanks. We knew it could happen…"

"Not really something anyone wants to plan for," I said, hopefully ending the journey down emotionally draining paths.

"Life on the farm has been OK though. There are twenty-six of us, just waiting to get on with life," Dave Barkley said. "Life off the farm, that is. Hasn't been exactly prudent to go too far a field."

"I'd like to tell you that it's all right to do so now, but I can't, yet," I said, looking down at the computer monitor in front of me, shielded from our guests. On the screen were pre-War drivers licenses of both Dave Barkley and his daughter. Their identification at least checked out. "Although we're making progress."

McGowan continued to question them about their life on the farm, their tactical and defensive measures, which received understandably cryptic answers. I thought they both showed remarkable composure over fifteen or twenty minutes of thinly veiled interrogation.

Dave Barkley worked as a civilian aviation mechanic at DFW Airport before the war, while Amy had a degree in elementary education, and was working at a private school, before it closed as the economy soured in the months before the war. They had been talking about 'getting back to the farm' when dollar started to collapse, but held out just a little longer, wondering if it was 'time.' Amy was in Corpus Christi looking for work when news of the *Augusta* came through. Dave quickly went to bring her home, hoping to meet his wife back in Dallas after returning from Hawaii, and then head north to the 'farm.' Of course, she never arrived.

On the farm, it sounded like they had about as good a setup as I could ever imagine, down to geothermal heat coils that helped mitigate the heating and cooling needs; a full machine shop; nearly four hundred acres of farmland; substantial water storage and filtration, all updated over time by Dave and his siblings and their children.

"OK, Gerry. Let's have these folks get on their way. No reason to detain them any longer," I said.

"Can't argue with that, Colonel," McGowan said. "To you both, apologies if I was a little direct. It's my job to find chinks in the armor."

"I understand," Dave said. "It'll be nice to see a friendly flag again."

"You haven't seen the new flag. You might not agree," I said, chuckling a little, which then ran down the description of, and need for, our new flag.

"I'd like to escort you home, but I'm afraid I'll have to have one of the officers to serve," I said. "The men will make sure you'll get home safe and sound. A little dark to be making the trip on horseback without lights, I'd think. I suspect we'll be here for at least another day or five, if you need any assistance."

"Thank you, Colonel. We appreciate your service to the nation," Dave said.

"Mister Barkley, you might be serving the country soon yourself. Air Force is in pretty serious need of skilled aviation mechanics," I said. "You might consider that. And, Merry Christmas."

December Twenty-Sixth
Aboard Charlie Six

A thousand men had worked all night to clear the tracks, strip the damaged cars of anything useful, and monitor overnight action in Omaha.

We were too far away from a highway to mount up an effort to move men and supplies to Omaha, and the weather was working against us in any regard. It was frustrating and heartbreaking, to hear of the fighting in Omaha and the pleas for relief, and to be unable to respond.

The Air Force made a substantial effort to resupply the ground troops with steady flights of C-17's delivering supplies by air, cargo parachutes landing west of the city, where there was little danger of S.A. retrieving the equipment. There was however, danger of surface to air attack.

By oh eight-hundred, Third Washington's 'graveyard' shift was rotating through the breakfast line, and the 'day shift' was in the field helping the rail crews stage the repair operation. I was stuck, with Doc Willitson checking on me, in the Command Car or my quarters—and not liking it one bit. I still had the deep cough, and the pain in my side.

Captain Fillmore had conducted funeral services for the dead rail crewmen, who could not be quickly returned to their homes in the Pacific Northwest. I had watched the brief service, via the helmet camera of one of the men. They were buried with full military honors, despite their civilian status. One day, their remains would be returned to their home cities. One day...

0840 Hours

"Sir, we're getting a skip broadcast from back east. Civilian radio broadcast—our side," Captain Shand told me, distracting me in a welcome way from my letters of condolence to the families of the crewmen. I'd already read the weather report, which would turn from wet and sloppy overnight to a Canadian cold front. Lows overnight would be in the teens, with subzero wind chills.

"Freq?" I asked.

"Shortwave, sir. Five point niner three five, sir. Haven't located a city yet, sir."

"We don't have a cross reference? Try for Nashville. This sounds like WWCR," I said, listening in to the news. "We listened to them a lot when things were coming unspooled," I said.

".....that Baltimore and Washington D.C. have been formally retaken by the United States of America, despite claims by the Statists that they remain in S.A. control. Our correspondents in the area report that in fact, the Capitol was never within S.A. control, with the heart of Washington in firm control of the United States Navy since the evacuation of the city last April Fourteenth. The current Flag of the United States of America now files in the Capitol, a city with a current population that is a fraction of Pre-War levels. Field commanders estimate that there are less than a hundred thousand residents in the city, although it is impossible at this time to confirm this, as most residents scurry for cover when patrols or vehicles are sighted.

Radiation levels throughout the Chesapeake Bay area, from the bombed cities of Norfolk and Newport News to the location of the dirty bomb in Silver Spring, remain significantly higher than safe levels. Correspondent Larry Malone, west of Bethesda, Maryland, reports.

"Dan, it's been only two weeks since we even learned of the half-dozen dirty bombs intended for detonation around the Capitol, only one of which was actually detonated. Crews from the Nuclear Emergency Search Team are credited with eliminating the threat of five of the terrorist teams. The sixth, that was apparently moving to it's target in Washington, it is believed to have originated in Pittsburgh. The enemy managed to detonate their device when a roadblock was set up for an unrelated highway accident. We have no information available on exactly who is responsible for the dirty bomb operation. We do not know if it was domestic or international, although we certainly believe that the United States government fully understands who the responsible parties are.

Cleanup efforts within the Silver Spring area include wholesale demolition of areas within the contamination radius, and the removal of radioactive soil, structures and other material to a landfill. It is estimated that five square miles are contaminated with highly radioactive material believed to include reactor fuel material, materials formerly used in the medical field, and other un-named sources."

"Dirty bomb?" I asked no one in particular.

"Makes me wonder what else we'll learn after the war, Colonel," Shand said.

"History's written by the victors," I said, turning my attention again to the broadcast, 'who may or may not tell the whole story,' I said to myself.

"...Chicago, with the S.A. President and his Cabinet rumored to be moving from city to city. Propaganda broadcasts still boast of the strength of the State of America, despite common knowledge that their military forces are in retreat on three sides," the broadcaster said as the signal began to seriously fade. There were only a few more words before it disappeared into static.

The Burlington Northern and Union Pacific crews did all the heavy lifting, figuratively and literally. They'd sent for a massive bridge crane designed to lift railcars and engines, just enough to get them off the active tracks and conduct rail repairs. The damaged or destroyed engines could then be retrieved by other rail-mounted equipment after normal service was restored. The crew boss stated in our first meeting though, that the damaged cars would probably remain in place for 'a long-ass time'.

Our forward Defensive Car was too badly damaged to either put back on the rails or ever put back into service. All weaponry, useable or not, was stripped out after bulk ammunition, heating and cooling equipment and communications links were stripped. There wasn't much left after the torches were finished with the car. *'Black Betty'* was unceremoniously shoved out of the way with a D-9 Caterpillar, after the crane had moved it as far as it could. The Defensive Car crewmen had named the all of the defensive cars and painted on artwork akin to the Second War's aircraft 'nose art'. *'Betty', 'Rockin' Jenny', 'Smokin' Sarah'* and *'Roxy'* made up the quartet of defensive cars. We would not have a forward Defensive Car on 'Charlie' moving in to Omaha, which put us at a significantly higher risk than we would have liked.

Once the dozer cleared 'Betty', it made quick work....meaning, three hours...of filling in the bomb crater. With the BN/UP crews serving as foremen, Third Washington lay new railroad ties and rails.

"Three hours, max, Colonel Drummond, and you boys'll be back in the fight. We're buttoning up the last of the rails now, we backtrack to the first siding, which is about five miles up the line or so. You get two patched up engines hooked up, and you're good to go. We'll follow you and that second train back into Omaha," the crew boss, a largish Puerto Rican named simply, 'Mario' told me.

"Thanks, Mario. It'll be good to get back in the fight," I said.

"Plenty o'that where you boys're headed. Smoke's thick over Omaha. Not much left I'm thinkin'."

"Maybe not. We still have work to do though," I said.

"Yeah you do. Best letcha get to it, Colonel," he said, shaking my hand and heading out the door.

"That was one big dude," Kittrick said to no one in particular.

"Yeah. Damned near crushed my hand," I said, making a fist to get the blood flowing again.

1240 Hours
Five miles southwest of Omaha, Nebraska

Another deployment, this time with small arms fire on three sides of the train as we disembarked, and artillery and tank fire due west of us. Smoke was everywhere, veiling the massive fires to the northeast. From the maps, it appeared that there was an industrial strip south of Interstate Eighty, which appeared to be ablaze. Downtown Omaha was further east, shrouded in smoke. Offutt Air Force Base was south of that, and also covered.

Third Washington deployed on two rail sidings south of the Interstate, due south of the small Millard Airport, and some brainchild had assigned us the place name of *'Infield Double.'* To the south, the small Papillon Creek, not visible to us from the train. We were 'parked' in what appeared to be a failed business park, with a burning 'call center' building not far away. Further north, bedroom communities. We'd proceeded as far as the rails allowed—the tracks were blocked not more than six hundred yards to the west of us. I thought as I reviewed the deployment zone, that we looked like a good target for a hit-and-run mortar attack. There were dozens of abandoned, burned out cars in the parking lots not far away. Most looked as if they'd been shot up and burned many months before.

A third of the Brigade was tasked with establishing a defensive perimeter and observation posts around the trains and the access roads to our location. The remaining men quickly went to work setting up large scale staging operations for the supply trains now stacked up behind us, and setting up a mile long string of tents and shelters between the trains. There wouldn't be rest for a long while, now that we were back in the game. I was doing my best to do my job and attempt to follow doctors' orders, which seemed mutually exclusive ninety percent of the time.

"Raptor Lead, we've got numbers that impact *Infield Double* operations," Fourth Brigade commander Jesse Casselis—'Hollow-Point One'--told me over secure radio. "Think five large, Raptor Lead." Five thousand of our men, wounded.

"Majors Ryder and Morrissey, my office three minutes ago," I said after punching their radios into the internal comm link separate from my conversation with Lieutenant Colonel Casselis.

"Hollow-Point One, you're south of location Castle?"

"Affirm, Raptor. Steady stream of dismount friendlies met along the way, ETA staged location two units." 'Castle' was Interstate Eighty; a 'unit' was thirty minutes. Casselis and a fair number of his men were traveling in a convoy of our Humvees, looking to meet up with Army units deployed along the Interstate. Major Morrissey appeared in my doorway, followed a moment later by Ryder.

"Understood, Hollow-Point One. Proceed to designated objective. Raptor Lead out."

"Boys, we've got a problem," I said. "Casselis says we've got five thousand wounded and walking wounded headed here, starting in an hour, probably less. We're not ready for them."

Both looked at each other for a half a second before responding. I was looking for answers, not excuses.

"Colonel, we can pull most of the men assigned to the perimeter. Small arms fire is quite a bit farther away than we anticipated on arrival. Cut the deployment to five hundred men. If it stays quiet, cut that again by a third for the next watch. That frees up half of the men in the territory around *Infield Double*," Major Ryder responded.

"Still short-staffed of course, Colonel, but every man in the Brigade has had trauma care training to Advanced level," Morrissey added.

"Task some of your men on where we're going to house them until they can evac. We have a cold front moving in tonight. Expect every square inch of both trains, every tent and shelter, everything we can muster to be dedicated to the wounded and getting everyone fed. If we have five thousand now, you can bet we'll have more soon enough. Expect Third Washington to be outside tonight, or caring for these wounded men. Anyone's that not doing that will be assigned to Supply Fifty-Seven. We're going to need the gear on that train ASAP, and need the train to send back with wounded. Not to mention the food."

1550 Hours

We had nowhere near enough medical expertise to go around, nor enough shelter. The five thousand men rapidly turned into six, and then seven thousand plus. Despite the 'heads up', there was just not enough time to prepare for this kind of influx. Every available man from Third Washington was involved and over tasked almost immediately. My quarters were 'doubled up' with other command officers. I had about five minutes to secure my personal belongings before Captains McGowan and Shand hauled in their gear. A second bunk could pull down from the ceiling. Irregular watch schedules meant that a couple of the command staff would probably be trying to get some sleep at any given time.

The medical cars were all handling surgeries, tents outside of each were trauma and critical care areas, and triage was going on everywhere. The trained medical staff—including our surgeons, corpsmen, and medical staff from other units, worked relentlessly on the wounded. The small airport north of our location was unusable, but the parking lot of the business park made an acceptable landing zone for the string of evac helicopters. Once the seriously wounded were stabilized, they were to be shipped out to points west by air. I had no idea where they'd end up.

In the command cars, Third Washington's communications suites were providing additional capacity to analyze communications throughout the Omaha theater of operations. 'Dog Six' was working on decrypting enemy transmissions, which kept two of the suites busy. The rest of the S.A. communications were 'in the clear' with no codes, phrases, or attempts to disguise locations or place names. All of that information was then fed to the Theater Commander, General Robert Anderson, formerly of Pacific Northwest Command, now located twenty miles northwest from Omaha. General Angela Garcia reported to Anderson. Bob had almost certainly had a hand in getting me 'drafted'. I'd have to think of a way to repay him someday.

At my desk, real-time inventories of supplies from 'Charlie' and 'Dog' were ratcheting down, and back up again, as new material was logged in from the supply train, parked just behind us. Three more trains were waiting to move in, parked miles back on the only available sidings. Once Supply Fifty-Seven moved out, we'd need to task the correct train to move in. We were going through cold weather gear, shelters, food, and medical supplies as quickly as it could be resupplied by Fifty-Seven. Fifty Nine and Sixty were carrying ammunition, weapons, food and limited medical supplies. Fifty-Eight was geared toward civilian needs: Food, clothing, medical, with a small percentage of the freight being weapons and ammunition.

I took a two-mile long walk along and through both trains, reviewing the overall operation, and thoroughly breaking doctors' orders for my pneumonia, but wrapped in a scarf covering most of my face. The mess cars were running full steam, with fresh supplies coming in one end of each car and going out with to the men through the other. On the far end of 'Dog', an area had been set aside for those who had not survived long enough to receive medical care, or had not survived surgery. There were dozens of dead. Four men stood guard over the body bags, set in rows. Our Brigade flag and the new American flag were at half-staff on two makeshift poles. I spotted one of our chaplains as he rose from prayer near the dead.

"Chaplain Rodriguez. Thank you for your time with these men," I said.

"It's my honor, Colonel. I'm afraid we'll have many more soon," he said.

"I am afraid you are right. Where are these men from?"

"Most are from Tennessee and Alabama, Colonel. Their captain—I think he's in recovery right now—said they moved up from the south, straight through Topeka. The rest of their men are tied up in the Kansas City fight."

"How many strong?"

"Company level, sir."

"Thanks, Chaplain. Where's that Captain?"

"Forty three oh-two, sir. Captain Mayfield."

"Thanks. Take care of yourself, Chaplain."

"God's hands always, Colonel."

"Indeed."

Medical tent forty three oh-two held more than a hundred men in various stages of recovery. The tents housing the wounded or those needing shelter, were double-walled affairs, an inner tent that was heated, an outer weather-shell, staked and weighted against the winds. Heat for the tents—inadequate, but better than nothing—was basically waste heat from engine coolant from the generators, circulating through double-walled insulated hoses. Rows of cots filled the tents, with four rows of small but bright LED lights illuminating the general sleeping areas.

I noticed some of our intelligence gatherers were conducting interviews, a couple of them carrying laptops, pointing to map locations and I guessed, trying to determine opposing force capabilities and tactics.

"Sir, may I help you?" a bespectacled medic asked.

"Captain Mayfield is here, I believe?"

"Seventh Alabama? Yes, he is Colonel, but I'm afraid he's sedated at this time. Might be better in the morning, sir."

"Badly injured?"

"Well, no actually sir. Some second degree burns, but the worst news he got today is regarding his heart. He has severe cardiomyopathy. Without a transplant, he's, well, gone. The surgical medics found it first, consulted with a heart doc, and there it is."

"How old is he?"

"Twenty-eight, Colonel. There's a fair chance, the cardio doc said, that it was an infection that did the damage—it could be a side effect of the G-Flu," he said, referring to the engineered Chinese influenza.

"Damn. All right, I'll try to get by tomorrow. I was just curious on how his unit managed to get through."

"Understood, sir. The intel guys have been having a field day."

"Thanks, anyway," I said, not shaking the medics' hand...he was gloved up.

"No problem, sir."

For twelve more hours, the rumble of artillery and aerial bombardment continued as wounded kept arriving. There was little sleep for anyone that night.

December 31
Strauss Performing Arts Center
University of Nebraska, Omaha
09:00 Hours

Omaha's remains were now firmly in the hands of the United States but our forces in Council Bluffs, just across the Missouri, were still under sniper and mortar fire with random RPG hit and run attacks.

Since arriving in western Omaha, Third Washington had served tens of thousands of meals, filtered hundreds of thousands of gallons of water, and treated more than ten thousand combat injuries of all kinds. Along the way, we'd learned that Idaho's Gem State Engineering Brigade had lost 'Able', a sister train of Third Washington's 'Charlie' and 'Dog. Idaho's 'Baker' was damaged, and would be stationary north of Omaha until the brigade could be reconstituted. Idaho had lost nine hundred men in the coordinated attack on 'Able' as it pulled into the northern suburbs of Omaha, in areas thought to be secured. Numerous IED's under the rails were detonated simultaneously, derailing and setting fire to many of the cars, and quickly killing a substantial number of the men aboard. The survivors were then attacked in force as they scrambled from the wreckage before friendly forces could arrive.

We were lucky, again.

University of Nebraska, Omaha presented an intact venue for a major face-to-face briefing of field commanders and support staff of all branches. Before the battle, the performance hall appeared to have been set up for a concert. Outside the building, enemy and civilian dead were lined up on the sidewalk, waiting for burial. I found myself viewing what should have been a disturbing sight as...routine.

A few blocks north of the building were two piles of wreckage that had at one time been Airbus airliners. One appeared to have been converted a cargo carrier, filled with SAM's and RPG's. Many had cooked off in the fire after the crash or forced landing. The second had at least a hundred people aboard. Their remains were still strapped into their seats, the top of the fuselage burned away, starboard wing sheared off. No one knew how they were brought down.

I hadn't seen many of the men and women up on the stage of the concert hall since we'd left Spokane, seemingly another world ago. Bob Anderson noticed half of Third Washington's senior staff, and waved us over to the stage before the briefing began.

"Good morning, General. Good to see you," I said. "It's been awhile."

"Colonel Drummond, I hear good things about your unit," he said before turning his attention to the other men, shaking their hands and then mine. "Good to see you're representing our state well."

"We've had our moments, sir. We've had an interesting run so far."

"You'll have more challenges tossed your way in the weeks to come, Rick," he said quietly, being called to start the brief.

More than two hundred men and women were in attendance, including a fair number of Navy personnel. Other than the occasional F/A-18 and a few encounters with SEALS, we hadn't had any contact with blue-water personnel. Marines, regular Army and Guard officers, dozens of Air Force officers, all ranks, shapes and sizes. Most of us wore dirty uniforms, coming straight from the field. The smell of burning Omaha was embedded in our clothing.

"Good morning. I'm Major General Robert Anderson, formerly of Pacific Northwest Command, of late, assigned to the Joint Chiefs. I have been assigned command of the drive to the east against the S.A. Four other field generals are under my command, including General Angela Garcia of the Texas National Guard; General Bill Monroe, regular Army; General James Wilkerson, regular Army and an outspoken Razorback; and United States Marine General Kenneth Daily, commanding Marine Expeditionary Units now covering three states. Please be seated." A map image of eastern Canada and the United States appeared on a screen behind the officers on the stage.

"S.A. forces are in collapse across fifteen hundred miles of battle front and are concentrating their defenses on the southern Great Lakes area, stretching from west of Rockford, Illinois to north of Indianapolis, and east to Pittsburgh," he said as the map image showed U.S. progress over the past few weeks, a line of red moving against the 'blue' of the S.A. "We have no idea why they are reinforcing this line, to be frank, and further, don't really care. The United States military, along with our Canadian troops, have now completely encircled the S.A. on all sides; with the Northeastern states now back in U.S. control. We have everything from Maine to Maryland, all of eastern New York State, parts of eastern Pennsylvania. Quebec and Montreal were sidestepped, and aren't worth at this time, investing men and materiel. Ottawa, everything north of this line," he said pointing to North Bay and Sudbury, "are in U.S. control."

"Simultaneously, we are seeing violent attacks on U.S. forces in recently taken territory. Think, the Iraq insurgency. The Afghan firefights. The attacks on soft civilian targets carried out by Mexican agents and cartel operatives. Ruthless, ladies and gentlemen, and we're sending all of you into territory where this is a daily or weekly occurrence. We never did find a way to defeat it in Asia within the rules of engagement we were operating under at that point in time. Those rules of engagement do not apply here. You identify a threat, you take it out. There will be no chain of command to run up, approve, and filter back down slowly, while viable targets escape. I repeat. You find a viable target, you engage and destroy."

Anderson outlined projected paths for each of the major military groups, coordinated with Air Force and Army air support units, with the overall objectives projected on the screen. Each units designation was shown in motion, ours in support of fifty thousand troops moving east and north, followed by supply and reinforcing units. Wisely, no timelines were shown—things would happen as circumstance allowed.

The map display showed of course, a smooth, fluid motion of armed units across the fields...nothing ever, ever ran smoothly though. There would be inevitably, attacks on the rails, bridges, roads and the ever unexpected.

The briefing wrapped up in forty-five minutes, allowing us to get back about our business. Third Washington would be one of the trailing support units moving out from Omaha, allowing our depleted resources, and tired men a more leisurely pace than the frantic pace we'd had for days on end.

I had my own ride back to the command car, and the rest of the staff split up and headed to their various destinations. One of General Anderson's men had flagged me down asked for a few minutes of my time with the General, in private. As I waited in the hallway, I helped myself to a couple of shortbread cookies and a bottled Coke, the first I'd had in more months than I could remember. I couldn't remember anything tasting so good.

Our staff was putting together a supply plan for the residents of Omaha, after our departure, not unlike the plans we'd executed for smaller towns, but much more complex due to the damage done in the fighting and the larger population.

Medical staff—greatly supplemented by skilled civilians, doctors and nurses, flooded into the city not long after the last of the major fighting pushed east. Our staff was now back to a more manageable number of routine military injuries, rather than catastrophic triage, field hospital surgery, and evacuation. The survival rates of wounded were now much better than at the onset, and there were far fewer cases where nothing could be done, other than pain management.

"Rick, c'mon in. Have a seat," Bob Anderson said from a small office not far from the main auditorium.

"Thanks, Bob. You think the war will progress that smoothly?" I said, skeptic tone in my voice.

"Nope, but it's good to be optimistic. We have the upper hand."

"I didn't hear anything about the S.A.'s ballistic capabilities. I'm hoping those are no longer an issue."

"Can't talk about that, sorry," he said, saying of course that they were probably still in play. "Impressions overall. What'd you think?"

"From a civilian-as-Army-officer point of view?"

"Absolutely."

"Depending on how they consolidate their lines, and what they have behind them, you could be fighting this war for a very long time. They had time, before the war really started; they had a LOT of time to stockpile fuel, food, weapons, whatever. We don't know what they've got...or, more properly, I don't know. I don't know what exotic hardware and weapons they might have. We've seen French, German, and Russian armor, and very, very capable commanders. We've seen a ton of Russian, Chinese and Egyptian SAM's, and some stuff that my Intel guy can't identify. We had a thousand mortar rounds fired at us in seventy-two hours. They have deep pockets," I said. General Anderson nodded, leaning back in his chairs, fingers interlaced above his chest.

"Go on," he said. There didn't seem to be any new information that he was hearing, nor should there have been, I hoped.

"To look at the S.A. moving into the future, they cannot ever overcome the stigma of what they have done to the people in their paths, unless they are absolutely confident of complete victory and complete control of all people, media, education...essentially having to re-write the history of the war, and kill anyone who posits a different story. Stalin revisited. For them to continue along the process of war fighting they have used to date, that has to be their ultimate end, there is no other possible goal that makes sense. That brings two possibilities to light, for me. First, they still have some unknown and devastating capability that they will use on the United States to destroy us; or second, this is the only thing they know, and even as they collapse, they continue this process because there is no alternative. The latter is more ultimately more dangerous." Bob leaned forward on the desk toward me

"Hmmm. Why do you think that—that some massive attack will be actually less devastating than the continued scorched-Earth strategy?"

"Not more devastating—more dangerous," I said, correcting him. "If they had the ability to attack us in a decapitating manner, they would have done so by now. Maybe that missile attack back at the beginning of the month was their last big shot, I don't know. Now though, we, the United States, is mobilized fully. I don't know their numbers. For that matter, I'm not sure I know ours. But if feels like the math is on our side, and math always wins," I said. "I believe that the 'fight-as-we-die' approach is far less predictable and more dangerous in terms of threats to our, well, our freedom. The true believers strike at any target, viable or not. As things collapse, they spread out through the lines, blend into far-flung society, and become centers of terrorist attacks far and wide. Then they start indoctrinating the 'disenfranchised' and a hundred years from now, here we are again."

"Fair enough. Now, take a few minutes to read this," Anderson said as he slid a file across the desk to me. "I'll be back in about ten minutes. You'll have the gist of it by the time I get back," he said as he stood, and I stood as he did per protocol.

I opened the folder, and found a partially destroyed report, from the State of America. Many pages and halves of pages were missing, some burned, the rest of the document water damaged and unreadable. What remained was still quite enlightening. The heavy hardback cover was embossed in gold. The total report was perhaps three-eighths of an inch thick in the original form. I had perhaps ten to twenty percent of the total report in my hands.

State of America Report on Progressive Element Actions,
Midway through the Twenty Year Plan

Three or four pages at the start of the report were missing, with the text beginning I guessed, in mid-chapter or mid-section.

Currency actions throughout the history of the Movement have always been directed toward the singular goal of gaining initial, and then complete control through individual monetary systems. With dramatic cascade-like action initiated by the Movement over the past decade, including the engineered destruction of three major currencies, the Movement was perhaps a year away from global financial domination. The Caliphate aberration has slowed this progress, but alternative actions are being initiated to overcome this delay. Once that level of control is achieved, Movement authorities have complete control of all meaningful economic transactions and therefore, complete control of all elements of society. The Movement can then continue unabated to shape the future of society as necessary.

Five more pages were missing from the report, printed on a fine linen-style paper with exceptionally good graphic design and layout.

I noted in an odd way, the beautifully designed report was in perfect contrast to the words printed therein.

I moved on to another partial paragraph, part of a page clipped into the document, with notes from an Intel analyst on its probable location within the whole and overall context.

Successful influence by the Movement on Western ratings agencies throughout European and American investment industry resulted in the aggregation of power to eventually control the global finance system and achieve the goals set by our predecessors. With the ratings agencies cooperation, major investment houses fell into Movement influence, and then control, quickly allowing universal control of the financial system..........

Another ten pages torn out. It was frustrating to see bits and pieces of this report, stating some of the deepest conspiratorial theories as fact, and yet not having a full picture.

Re-direction of technological advancements through means of government regulation has been successful in restraining advancements that might otherwise negatively influence Movement progress. Control of many industries in the developed world, Pre-War, was firmly under covert Movement control. Losses through the Third World War and the current American operations have regrettably resulted in the loss of Movement control systems, and post War, we project a period of innovation that the Movement must gain control over. Movement representatives within industry have been responsible for monitoring, redirect, and acquisition; and as often, for control of advancement until managed release benefits Movement goals and objectives. Where these operatives have been lost, new Movement influences must be put in place immediately to quickly regain control and re-establish determined paths to the future...........

The governmental collapse in Europe and the dramatic spread of the radically fundamentalist Caliphate has forced relocation of key parties in the Movement to the United Kingdom, Canada and the State of America. After the defeat of the United States, it is projected that within five years, an invasion of the Continent will consolidate Movement objectives within the State of America, Europe, and the former Soviet Union. Progressive elements at this time are active in China and are aggressively organizing the people into the

Progressive Movement system, rapidly identifying candidates for Organization and consolidation of surviving key industries. Further infiltration into Chinese held corporations abroad is also a stated goal, but resources have not been allocated to pursue this objective.

Destruction of information systems that did not directly benefit the Movement, has largely been through acquisition of competing media outlets, then consolidation and elimination, and resulted naturally in managed output of information.

Control of commercial broadcast frequencies, and the planned elimination of all but digital radio and television broadcasts, was partially complete by the onset of the Third World War. Movement operatives are systematically addressing remaining analog broadcast transmission equipment, with the obvious goal of meeting the Movement's requirement. Amateur equipment presents a larger challenge that will be addressed in the field by operatives on a case-by-case basis.

Having had some direct experience in Spokane County with sniper attacks on our television and radio transmitters, it was chilling to see how the S.A. would pursue our future, given the option.

There was little in the report that held as much gravity as the limited bits of text related to health care.

Central planning and management of medical care Pre-War, began to achieve the stated goal of providing staged care to designated patients who had become vested in society; who had remaining years or decades of productive contribution; who exhibited superior traits identified by the Movement, etc. Conversely, those who had not achieved full productive vestment in society (fetuses, children up to the age of 18, or those identified with physical, genetic or mental abnormalities) were provided alternate management, naturally resulting in separation from what was internally identified as Prime Care Management. The alternative, widely publicized and implemented in the former United States, was called Natural Care Management, and was successfully marketed and implemented across the lower-tier of the population, with beginning results illustrated in a dramatic "savings" in terms of gross costs. Projected implementation rates over a twenty-five year look ahead would have reduced the lower tier population by up to seventy percent across the United States, similar to performance in other Movement nations over the past ten years.

I closed the report, not reading it completely, but thinking about what I'd just read, and took a sip of the Coke on the desk. Bob Anderson came back into the office, and I stood by reflex.

"Still think that there's an 'either or' in terms of threat?"

"No sir, I don't believe that I do."

"Good try, though. The point I need you to understand Colonel, is that the people that wrote that report are not all that different than a whole lot of other people now in the United States. When the FBI analyzed the S.A. leadership and structure, and then put together the connections between the S.A. and surviving United States leadership, well, let's say the white board was a mess of connections. There's a generation and a half, maybe two generations of people that have this type of acceptance of Government Being In Control ingrained in them so deeply that it may well be two generations to get some balance back in the system. Central command economy. That whole health care debacle. The financial control and the destruction of what the Founders defined as 'money,'" he said. "No, this war won't end at when the S.A. is defeated. It will end when the people are educated, and not until then. You won't be a soldier forever. You're one of a handful of people that has a demonstrated perspective that goes beyond rank. Start thinking about what you're going to do after the War. We're probably a couple months away from the end of it."

"Bob, what are you suggesting? I can be thick when it comes to taking advice."

"Once you wrap things up with your Brigade, I think you should consider running for office in your state. You have a lot of what this country needs, and you're young enough to make a difference."

"General, I've been drafted twice in the past year. First to help run Spokane County, and then by Dave Hall for Third Washington. I can't say that I would have chosen either, had I the choice."

"Sometimes, Colonel Drummond, things happen not of our choosing that are exactly right, but cannot be seen as exactly right, until they are viewed from many years distant. Think about it."

December 31
University of Nebraska Medical Center
Omaha
13:00 Hours

My second major task of the day was to meet with several hundred civilian survivors and to outline relief operations after the Army moved east. We didn't have long, and Omaha was as damaged as any city I'd ever seen, mine included. It would be years to rebuild in a perfect world. In our imperfect world, decades.

"Ladies and gentlemen, if you would take your seats, we'll begin," Lieutenant Kittrick announced to the assemblage. Kittrick was my audio-visual geek today, running a PowerPoint presentation on a salvaged laptop. The communications crews had salvaged a couple hundred computers in Omaha and had set them up to run DVD's of our resource library. During their salvage operations, they found only a handful of working AM/FM radios, and no shortwave receivers or transceivers. The computers would be distributed to community centers, shelters, and surviving libraries, and more radios would be shipped into the city.

"Good afternoon. I'm Colonel Rick Drummond, Third Washington. Thank you for attending today," I began.

"I'm not career Army. A year ago, I ran a consulting business in Spokane. On the fourteenth of January, that changed. The Domino earthquake hit the Pacific Northwest, the subduction quake probably also triggering the eruption of Mount Rainier. We lost hundreds of thousands of people. We were also thrown into a situation that most of the population were completely unprepared for. I'm here to help you with some information that we found crucial in getting through a pretty bad year," I said as Kittrick punched up a map.

"So far, one hundred locations more or less, have been identified as potential community centers where these library resources will be located," I said as the map was joined by a list, and the attendees rapidly took notes, I suppose finding locations nearby.

"In Spokane, these locations included pre-Domino community centers and centers and shelters set up after the quake; fire stations, hospitals, and neighborhood schools. In our city, National Guard units were also usually co-located in each neighborhood," I said, hearing some displeasure at that comment.

"Please recognize, that we, like Omaha right now, didn't have enough civilian law enforcement to go around. There was looting. There was theft. Home invasions. People died because they had food. Most of Omaha is disarmed, meaning that it's likely that the people that have weapons aren't necessarily the good guys. The Army will be re-arming you with weapons and ammunition captured as well as new weapons brought into the area. Security forces will train you on their operations, and you'll have to demonstrate basic safe weapons-handling and be of age of course," I said, getting a few chuckles from many of the grey-hairs present, "before you're provided a weapon. As a civilian, my family and some friends sort of adopted our military units watching over our neighborhood. It was a good way to get inside info, take care of the men who're taking care of business, and make friends. You'd be surprised how much influence fresh-baked bread and fried egg sandwiches have, not to mention fresh coffee or hot chocolate."

"The information provided on these DVD's includes thousands of topics. A lot of this stuff I used myself. Some stuff I added to the resource library where I noticed a gap--consider these interim survival resources after most of the military moves out. Basics like shelter. Water. Heat. Food. Cooking and heating with wood, field expedient housing, insulation, air locks and mudrooms, food preservation, communications, and self defense tactics. You'll want to formalize neighborhood patrols with both your civilian and military forces. You'll need to work out communications systems. Radios are hard to come by, probably will be for some time, but we'll see that portable radios are shipped in and distributed. Cellular system is toast. Omaha might be a decade in rebuilding, maybe longer, and the rebuilt city will not resemble the old. We are not what we were a year ago; you will not be in a year, what you are today."

"We have fifteen men from Third Washington to give you some guided tours through the information, and we'll be here until three p.m.," I said as I wrapped up my remarks. "And I commend you all for making it this far."

I spent the better part of an hour talking about various topics, from cooking in a cast-iron Dutch oven to water filtration, improvised insulation to creation of observation posts and neighborhood militias. My voice was starting to go, and I needed a break.

I almost made it to the coffee pot before I was met by a young man, perhaps twenty-five or so, with a young woman, I assumed his wife, trailing just behind, cradling a very young child.

"Excuse me, Colonel? Do you have a moment?"

"Absolutely. Call me Rick."

"I'm Danny Seifert, this is my fiancé Susan. We're originally from Federal Way."

"Nice to meet you. Sorry about your hometown," I said. Federal Way was south of Seattle proper, and was equally devastated. I'd seen the aerial and satellite imagery. "Did you still have family there?"

"Yes, sir. We haven't heard from them since last New Years. We were students here, until it hit the fan."

"What can I do for you both?" I asked.

"We're wondering, sir, if there's a chance we can evac back home. We know that there's probably not much left back there, but we can't stay here and go through much more. It's either west or down to Texas," he said. "We haven't seen much of what was left back home. I might still have family back there, up in Everett. Sue had some cousins in Omak and out near Republic. Can you tell us how things are there?"

"Colonel, er, sorry. Rick," Susan said. "Things happened here that we cannot live with. We have to leave," she said as the baby started to fuss a little, looking at Danny with some expectation on her face. The child could not have been more than a few weeks old. The more the woman talked, the more I could see the trauma just behind her soft, brown eyes.

"Let's go find a little private place to talk. Short answer is, 'probably'. Might be a roundabout path to get you there though," I said as I caught the eye of Kittrick, nodding that I was heading into a tiny office off of the larger conference center. It had two chairs and a small desk, and nothing else.

"Have a seat. Let's talk," I said.

Susan and the baby entered and sat in the larger, more comfortable chair behind the desk; Danny in the more utilitarian chair. I stood against the doorframe.

"OK, this is a little more private. To answer your questions about back home, well, they're messed up of course, but we haven't had a civil war raging about us full-time. The S.A. is still there, or was when I left, using hit-and-run tactics, assassination, intimidation, and out-and-out terrorism. I don't know what the progress is of cleaning them out. I'd suspect that most of them are, or will be ambient temperature if they try anything overt. Everyone of age is armed, and quite a few folks that aren't of age, my kids included," I said. "Boy or girl?"

"Little girl. We rescued her," Danny said.

"Oh. I'd assumed you were her parents."

"No, well, we are now. The S.A. was going to kill her," Susan replied, as she pulled a blanket away from the little girl. The baby appeared healthy enough.

"Why in God's name would they do that?"

"After the crash, classes were pretty much done. Susan worked as a volunteer at the University hospital. I was in food service," Danny said. "And God had nothing to do with it. The Statists identified her parents as subversives, and less than an hour later killed their whole family. The parents were Susan's professors in the teaching hospital before the War. Caitlyn here was their youngest. They killed her older brother and sister as well. Examples to be made. They killed babies because of things their parents did. We need to leave this place, sir."

"What did her parents do?" I asked, ever wanting to know more.

"We have no idea, Colonel. There was never a reason for anything they did."

"All right. I'll see what I can do about getting you out of here. We will have some evacuation abilities, by air and rail. Rail's a bit tougher due to the cold, and we're working on ways to keep standard rail cars warm enough during the trip back to civilization."

"What's it like, back home?" Susan asked. "I mean, really?"

I thought about it for a moment before answering. "A lot of work. Good though, I guess. My family and I lived in a barn for a fair amount of time after the quake, just to stay alive. I didn't want to evacuate south, and am glad I didn't. We farmed a bit, bartered for things, adapted," I said. "Bellingham is a naval port now, because Bremerton's down for the count. The North Sound area—Everett was hit hard, all the way up to Vancouver—will recover far quicker than anything in the Seattle area. The nature of the area has changed that much. The floor of Puget Sound was lifted up in the quake—it's much shallower, and there's massive amounts of debris and ash filling it in every time it rains." I didn't say that he debris included human remains.

"The Governor's a good man. My most recent 'job', if you can call it that, was the administrator for Spokane County. That put me in touch with most other counties in the state. Republic's still there, tough little town," I said. "Phone service was just starting to come back when I was drafted. Electricity has been irregular at best. Took us months to get even irregular power back, but that's a long story. Once you get out of the war zone, it might be possible to forward the names of your relatives to their last known locations, and try to inform them of your status. I'd caution you though, there really isn't a single community out there that takes all that kindly to rootless refugees. They're viewed with suspicion or outright distrust, and have a tough time fitting in when those prejudices are heaped on them. Having ties to the community, even distant relatives, is crucial."

They pondered that for a moment, and then I continued. "Where are you living?"

"Sub-basement. There's a storage room that no one knows about," Susan said, before turning her attention to Danny. "Danny, you need to tell him about the others." He nodded, and looked down toward the floor before meeting my eyes with his own.

"Colonel, there are three other couples and sixteen infants and toddlers."

I was surprised, of course. "That'd be good to know," I said.

"Sir, some had birth defects. The S.A. kills children with birth defects."

I supposed I should have known that, based on what I'd read previously, but I was still stunned by the reality of it. "We'll get you out of here," I said, feeling rage growing in me at the thought of what had been done here. "Any more secrets?"

"No sir. We are though, short on food."

"We'll get you taken care of," I said. "Stay right here for a few minutes. I have some contacts to make," I said, turning out of the room to get one of our secure radios.

"Red Leg Five to Red Leg Lead," I said into the headset.

"Go, Five," came the reply.

"I need to speak with Bulldog."

"Understood, wait one." Bulldog was Gary Ryder, who was coordinating evacuation efforts for the critically ill or wounded.

"Bulldog, Go Five."

"Bulldog, we need to confirm this, but I have two adults and one infant here at the U Hospital, who report that they have six adults caring for sixteen orphaned infants and toddlers, close by. Can you break anyone loose and get them over here?"

"Does it sound legit, Five?"

"It does, but it needs to be double checked. There should be third party confirmation of this story from other witnesses. We're not doing Delta One Three again."

"Affirmative. We'll dispatch to your location."

"Send some food along as well. Five, out," I said, and then picked up a pad of paper and a pen and headed back to the little office.

"OK. I have some additional staff coming over. I need you to list the names of the children and the adults you have in your group, and the circumstances of each child and each adult. We need to verify your story."

"Colonel, is that really necessary?" Danny asked.

"Yeah. Required. We had a bad experience with people posing as folks desperate for evacuation, who were S.A. plants. Lost a plane two days ago. Sixty-five people dead, a hundred and six injured. We're not taking chances, sorry."

Fifteen minutes later, three Army investigators and three civilian aid workers arrived, and I directed them to our guests. Within an hour, all of the children and caretaking adults had been moved to the meeting room, and the other hospital staff was questioned about the S.A. and the children. The children's murdered families were listed as best as possible, which was sketchy in some cases. Food arrived, including a fair amount of child friendly food. I realized that these children had probably would never have some of the foods that we'd grown used to, in the old America. None of the caretakers were older than Danny, who was twenty-three years of age.

"Colonel, we can't find anything linking these people to the S.A., and we have verification on thirteen of the children," Major Ryder said. "Helluva deal," he said, looking at the kids, huddling with the adults in a corner. Both civilian and uniformed adults were holding some of the younger children.

"Yeah. Ain't it though," I said, still pondering the events that put these children in this room.

"We can get them out at sixteen-hundred, Colonel. Of course, that'll mean with the clothes on their backs and precious little else."

"I don't think that'll be that big of a deal. Airliner?"

"Yes, sir. First stop will be DFW. Spend the night there, catch military transport to Salt Lake, then Walla Walla. Civilian network is looking to find relatives of the kids—which will be a nightmare—and try to find surviving family members of the adults."

"Great job, Major. Maybe they'll end up with a happy ending."

"Maybe, Colonel."

Later that afternoon, Danny, Susan and a parade of adults, some walking wounded and a few nurses carried the children aboard a 757.

They were on their way out of the War.

Supply Seventy-One was empty of the incoming load, and would travel west with an honor guard and more than three thousand fallen.

One, I learned while reading the manifest in a spare moment, was the son of Governor David Hall. First Lieutenant Jake Hall was one of the last graduates of West Point, pre-War. The personnel file was classified, covering young Hall's mission status in clinical detail. He had achieved a field promotion, distinguishing himself by saving his unit from being overrun before an organized retreat could take place. That particular fight was near Des Moines. He had been killed by a sniper, while moving between positions that his platoon held, near the Interstate Eighty Bridge over the Missouri. The shot that killed him had come from behind him, an S.A. sniper in hiding, behind the lines. The sniper had not been found.

Before Seventy-One departed, I took a few minutes to write Governor Hall my condolences. No matter what words I used, I felt they failed to express my thoughts. I placed the letter inside the file that would be sent to his parents, a non-classified file, blew my nose, and went to meet the next incoming train.

"Excuse me, Colonel. General Anderson has requested a meeting with you at eighteen-hundred," Lieutenant Kittrick said.

"Confirm that, thanks. Staff invited?"

"General Anderson requested a private meeting, sir. Over dinner."

"Hmm. Thanks," I said, wondering what Bob had to say next. I'd find out soon enough, the meeting was in a half hour. I sat down at my desk, reviewed the status report and dispersion plan for Third Washington, and then the weather. The rain would change again to snow; the moderate temps again would change to bitter cold. By the time we would leave, four days or so out, we'd be in the heart of an arctic outbreak.

18:00 Hours
Charlie Six Conference Room

"General, good to see you again," I said, shaking his hand.

"A little less formal, Rick. I have surprise for you from home. Karen asked that we bring you this," he said as he signaled to one of his men at the doorway. He brought in a large cardboard box, taped up with strapping tape.

"Seriously," I said.

"I had a hand in getting you here, so it seemed fair enough," Bob said. "Late Christmas present, or early New Years, your choice," he said, dismissing the young man who brought in the package.

I cut open the top of the package and peeled away many layers of packing paper and plastic.

"You have got to be kidding me," I said, lifting out a quart jar of tomato soup, then another.

"She said you'd say something like that," he said with a smile. "Soup?"

"Oh yeah," I said. "Taste of home. We should break one open," I said.

"Your wife sent instructions. Dinner will be served shortly. I had to give them the specific instructions, but the galley car is working on it now. This batch," he said, patting the box, "is for later."

"General you know that I only eat what the men eat, right?"

"You're ordered to make an exception. And I've heard a lot about this soup via many channels, so I'm exercising command prerogative and joining you."

I gave in. "Fine. I'll take an order," I said.

"And I've heard that you're recovering from pneumonia. Probably acquired through a few too many nights checking on your men out in some far flung OP. Correct?"

"Three nights in ten days, not consecutive, not much chance of anything bad happening. In other words, I was out there to, yes, check on the men, but keep them awake as well. Doc said that I'm susceptible to lung problems due to the scarring from the flu."

"He's right. You through your regimen yet?"

"Getting there. Halfway through."

"Rick, you didn't have any business running the kind of schedule you did today. I looked over your calendar. You need to ease off or you'll end up as compost."

"You sound like you have experience with this, Bob."

"I wrapped up mine ten days ago, so affirmative. Hated every damned minute of it. And this is my second round," he said as a knock on the door announced dinner, as a young man brought it in. I didn't really take note, as I was wondering how many more of us had the makings of a chronic or fatal disease.

"Cornbread, tomato soup, and what appear to be micro beers, sirs," the young man said, snapping to attention, a moment before I recognized him.

"Private John Martin," I said, finally buying a clue. "What in God's name are you doing here?"

"Fresh out of Basic, Colonel. Assigned to Third Washington as a replacement, sir."

I stood and shook his hand. "John do you know General Anderson?"

"We've met, Colonel," John said as Bob started laughing.

"Happy New Year, Colonel Drummond. Between your wife and Private Martin's family, I've had little peace concerning this man's assignment. My wife, it so happens, relocated to the Spokane Valley last month. It being a small town, word travels fast."

December 31
Aboard Charlie Six
Omaha, Nebraska
22:15 hours

The soup had another fan in Bob Anderson, who excused himself after a second bowl, taking a bottle of homemade Hefeweizen with him. John and I had a chance to talk in private, catching up on his newlywed status for starters.

"No honeymoon, Colonel. Well, except that night," Private John Martin, married on Christmas Eve, said.

"You take what you can get, John. And when we're in private and off-duty, you can call me Rick. Just don't let it slip."

"Yes, sir. Should not be a problem sir."

"Which Battalion are you in? And how is it that paperwork on the replacements didn't find its' way across my computer?"

"Fifth Battalion, Lieutenant Colonel Atwood, sir. I'm not sure about the paperwork."

"Colonel Atwood is a hard-ass. High standards from coming straight out of Helmand Province in the 'Stan. I have no idea why he's with us and not on a line unit...all of our Battalion CO's are sharp."

"I've heard you've seen some action," John said. He seemed much older than he'd been a couple months before.

"A little, yeah. Lost some good men," I said. "You're a trained infantryman. Nothing more dangerous on the planet than a young infantryman. To others and sometimes to himself. How confident do you feel, Private?"

"I can handle myself, sir."

"Seen any live fire training? Sounds of incoming rounds smacking the ice and the mud and flesh?"

"Not flesh."

"A billion years ago, when I was a little older than you, I went through some training probably a little more aggressive than yours. Crawling under live booby traps, live fire over that, mounds of pig carcasses that would be shedding meat and blood and bone, showering us with body parts. Not something you ever forget, especially in summer heat."

"Yeah, we didn't have anything like that."

"That's only because pork is hard to come by and expensive," I said. "John, you know I'm not going to intervene in any assignment that your commanders have for you. There's not a job that I wouldn't do in this entire brigade myself, or one that I'd hesitate to assign to anyone else. Other than tonight, we all pretty much eat the same food; I take an irregular rotation on with the observation posts on our perimeter, and was working my way through a few other jobs as time allowed, until this pneumonia set me back. I take at least half of my meals with the Brigade, not with Command, or with my officers. It sounds all noble. It's not really. These men are my brothers, cousins, sons, uncles. I need every man to be able to depend on every other, no questions. I need them to trust me, as well. That includes me, and includes you. We all depend on each other for our lives. That's the way it is."

"Not a problem, Colonel. To be perfectly honest, I didn't want this assignment."

"Understood. Your Mom's hand is in this, along with my lovely wife. There is not much though, that gets in the way of Liberty Martin, alone. With assistance, an unstoppable force."

January First, Year Two
Aboard Charlie Six
Omaha, Nebraska
02:00 Hours

I'd managed around four hours of uninterrupted sleep, after sending Private John Martin back to his quarters, on the tail end of Charlie Six. At oh two hundred, I awoke with a start, for no apparent reason. Something felt wrong. I called the communications car on the computer network.

"This is Colonel Drummond. Sitrep," I said to the communications officer on duty, a second lieutenant by the name of Breitmann.

"Good morning, Colonel. Our sector is quiet, sir. Sporadic contact twenty miles east, heavy ground contact a hundred miles north. Civilians remain at the shelter, no news there. General Anderson's aircraft departed at twenty three-thirty hours. Supply Eighty-Four is due in around oh nine hundred. That's about it, Colonel. Something wrong, sir?"

"Don't know, Lieutenant. Check contact with all perimeter units, Priority status. Notify me immediately if there is anything amiss. And keep me posted if anything out of the ordinary comes up in our sector or any adjoining sector. Clear?"

"Affirmative, Colonel," the young man said, obviously puzzled.

I was blessed, or cursed with the inability to remember my dreams the vast majority of the time…but over the past year, I did relive more of the distant past than I ever wanted to. I didn't know if my sudden break from a seemingly sound sleep was because of a dream, nightmare, or 'what'. I elected to calm my nerves by re-reading our schedule for the next deployment.

We were now scheduled to depart Omaha on January seven, the next-to-last support unit to move east or north. Leapfrogging along the path of war, Third Washington would trail out of town this time. With five days until we'd pack up for shipment, we were down to fifteen percent of our supply levels for normal operations. Supply Eighty-One through Eighty-Three were supposed to include replacement provisions for Third Washington. They were reassigned and shipped directly to line units, instead, putting our unit on the back burner. Without Eighty-Four, we'd be out of food and basic provisions in less than a week. Command was cutting things close. My repeated requests for fuel and supplies according to Bob Anderson were heard. They just weren't as high a priority as the mechanized and infantry units. Understandable.

By quarter of three, I decided to try to get some more sleep, rocked by the wind against the converting shipping container that served as my quarters.

05:00 Hours

"Colonel, you're going to want to see this," Lieutenant Breitmann said over the intercom. I'd just dressed, after a quick shower in marginally warm water. "Secure channel nine, sir."

Rather than look at it in my quarters, I made the quick trip to the Command Car, figuring that I'd be there soon enough in any regard. I was surprised as I pulled my jacket on as I opened the exterior door, by the eighteen inches of drifted snow against the door, drifts almost completely covering the stairs to the ground. The lee side of the train had four and a half feet of drifted snow. I hadn't seen the windward side. Thankfully, the drifts were solid enough to walk on…and I thought, solid enough to lock us in position if we weren't careful.

"Colonel, we have flash traffic from the Air Command. Downed Navy crew, our sector," Breitmann said. "Plastic Bug went down about three miles southwest, ten minutes ago. Ejection notice, and we're tasked with ground search and rescue. Air Force can't get a bird in the air for the next two hours—they're committed to other missions."

"Plastic Bug?" I asked.

"Sorry, sir. F/A-18. It was coming here after a mission over Des Moines. Pilot reported engine trouble about two minutes before punching out."

"Do we have data on where he ejected?"

"No sir."

"Locating beacon from the pilot?"

"Nothing, sir," another tech said. "And no radar of course," he said as Sergeant Major Travis came in to the Command Car.

"Chet, we need SAR operations for a downed Navy pilot, right now. What can you get moving?"

"Second Battalion is on Alert as of twenty-hundred last. Snow's going to be an issue, sir. It's bad out there."

"Worse for the pilot," I said.

"No argument there, Colonel. I'll get Second moving."

"What's Fourth's status?" I asked, thinking that another Battalion would not be a bad idea.

"Fourth is scheduled for dispersal for daily operations starting at oh six-hundred."

"Retask for SAR operations immediately. Third can run dailies again, and Fifth will go to civilian operations, I said to Sergeant Travis.

"Breitmann, get me the Air Force," I said, getting to my desk. "And somebody round me up some coffee."

Charlie's primary and secondary communications cars were quickly creating the anticipated search teams, despite an undefined search area; determining transport capabilities; and coordinating normal operations with the search effort. For the better part of a week, one Battalion had stood Alert status, rather than working normal rotations across the spectrum of Third Washington responsibilities. The Alert status had come from Command. I assumed that they had good reason for it.

"Air Command on Secure Twenty-Two, Colonel," Breitmann said.

"Very good, Lieutenant," I said as I put on my headset.

"This is Colonel Richard Drummond, Third Washington."

"Colonel, this is Captain Anderson, Air Command."

"Captain, can you give us more information on this downed aircraft? I understand that it's estimated three miles southwest of our location. Can you confirm that?"

"Colonel, it went off radar at latitude forty-one, ten, one point two nine; longitude minus ninety six, eight, fifty-nine point seven eight four. It may be possible that the actual crash site is further west than that location, but doubtful, the aircraft was losing altitude very quickly. We did not have an IFF transponder or any other on-board telemetry for three minutes prior to that time for reasons unknown. We did get a signal of the ejection sequence for the crew right before radar contact was lost."

"Single seat?" I said as Breitmann punched up the coordinates on our mapping software.

"No, sir. F/A-18F, two seater, from Atlantic Fleet VFA-103, the *Jolly Rogers*."

"Understand we have no beacons for the crew, is that correct?"

"Yes, Colonel. Neither beacon has activated. Should be automatic upon separation from the aircraft."

"OK, Captain. Last question—do you have an altitude for ejection?"

"No sir, other than, less than five thousand AGL."

"Given the winds we have out here Captain, that's one Hell of a search area."

"Sorry, Colonel. That's all we have from here."

"Where is 'here', Captain?"

"I'm at Nellis, Colonel."

"Understood, Captain. We'll keep you plugged into command level communications assigned to the search."

"Much appreciated, Colonel. The aircrew is of some importance. Can't elaborate."

"Got it. Drummond out," I said as Breitmann waved me over to his console.

"Breitmann, what have you got?" I asked.

"Wehrspann Lake, sir. Looks man-made. The coordinates match."

"All right," I said as the rest of my senior command staff flooded into the car, along with Second Brigade commander Trayvon Chappel.

"Gents, we have a downed Navy aircraft, two seat model F/A 18. Last radar contact was over this lake, about three miles from here, and Air Command says that the crewmen ejected right before it went off radar. We have no beacons from the crewmen, no radio calls, nothing. Air Command says the crew is of 'some importance.' Take that as you will," I said, that comment generating some glances among the staff. "Two tasks—retrieve the crewmen, second locate and secure the crash site."

"Altitude of ejection, sir?" Major Ryder asked.

"Unsure, less than five thousand above ground level."

"Wind drift will have pushed them a fair piece, Colonel." Ryder stated.

"Estimates?" I asked. "I've jumped out of one perfectly good aircraft, and that was not quite thirty years ago on a calm day."

"Ten miles per hour will drift a canopy a half mile from three thousand feet. Figure they ejected at five thousand plus, add in the thirty mile-per-hour gusts we have, and they could be a couple miles downwind, easy. Assuming their chutes opened, of course," the Major said.

"I'd buy that. So, an oval-shaped search area, centered laterally due south of us," I said, pointing at the map. "Nice even grid of quarter sections of farmland, all the way over to Papillion. Colonel Chappel, questions?"

"No sir. We'll be ready in ten minutes. Have to dig out some wheels. This snow will slow us up."

"We've got maybe an hour and a half before it starts getting light out, and three until sunrise," I said. "Let's try to leave no snowball unturned."

"Snowmobiles sure would be handy right about now, sir," Chet Travis said.

"Anyone run across any?" I said.

"None in operable condition, Colonel. A few parts rigs, the rest were shot up," Lieutenant Breitmann said as he looked at an asset inventory of the Omaha area.

"Thanks anyway, Lieutenant," Chappell said, grinning a little bit at the instantaneous response of the young officer.

Ten minutes later, the Alert staff was ready for departure, assignments for the grid search provided followed five minutes after that by the Fourth Battalion. I'd have liked to have gone along.

07:04 Hours

"Easy Four to Raptor," I heard on the headset. The frequency flashed on my computer monitor, designated solely for communications regarding retrieval of Firefly Two-Nine, the call sign of the downed Navy plane.

"Raptor. Go Easy Four," Kittrick said to the patrol.

"Got the full package, fair condition. Banged up a little in shipment. Two seven east by one one four south."

"Affirmative, Easy Four," Kittrick responded, as I punched in the search grid coordinates. Lavista South High School, just south of Highway Three Seventy.

"ETA thirty-five, Raptor."

"Affirm, Easy. Proceed to Delta Three Three."

"Will do, Raptor. Easy out."

"Mister Kittrick, get me Air Command, and recall those teams not within the search area for the aircraft."

"Air Command will be on Nine, sir. Kellison is already placing the recall, Colonel."

"Kittrick, that's why you get the big money," I said, pleased that his crew was on top of things.

"I'll take that in rare metals, anytime, Colonel. Or, maybe a steak."

"I'll make a note of that."

"Air Command is ready, sir," he said as I switched the frequency.

"This is Colonel Drummond. Your crew has been found. A little worse for wear I understand. Should be back at our location within the hour."

"Damned good news, Colonel. Compliments to your unit. This is Admiral Hendricks, joint unit commander. Have you located the aircraft, Colonel?"

"We have it narrowed down to a couple hundred acre area, sir. There's a very good chance that it went down in a reservoir. I'm not willing to put my men on the ice to find a hole the hard way, Admiral. I'd prefer to have a helo take a look at the surface."

"How deep is that reservoir, Colonel?"

"Around thirty feet or so, Admiral. Something aboard that plane that makes it worth diving on?"

"We'll let you know if that's the case, Colonel. Depends on what the crew says in debrief. Please contact me immediately when the crew reaches your location."

"Will do, sir."

"Air Command out."

"Sir, we've got three more civilian transports scheduled, then we're bingo on evacs," Major Ryder said. "By eleven hundred, our civilian relief efforts are pretty much done. Civilian organizations will be in charge." Which meant, we wouldn't be feeding them anymore, either.

"What's the status on our resup?" I asked, noting his suddenly uncomfortable expression.

"Just heard. Eighty Four has been expressed east."

"Major, we cannot expect to go much longer without a resupply. That includes fuel. We have maybe three days left to keep our water flowing and heat on, if we're really, really damned lucky. We have five days food. Maybe."

"I understand, Colonel, believe me. This decision…"

"Kittrick, find me a commanding General," I said, cutting Gary off. "Dismissed, Major."

"Sir," the Major said, saluted, and left.

Ten minutes passed before I was informed that General Anderson was unable to take my call.

"Kittrick, get me Air Command."

"Sir?"

"Did you not hear me the first time, Lieutenant?"

"Sorry sir. Yes, I heard you Colonel."

Less than a minute later, I was speaking again to Admiral Hendricks.

"Admiral, I'd like to ask a favor of you, if you don't mind...."

January First, Year Two
Aboard Charlie Six
Omaha, Nebraska
07:30 Hours

"No, Admiral, I don't like having to ask another command to see if they can help us out. Stepping out of chain of command isn't right. But I'm also not about to deploy this Brigade without fuel or food, and that's what I'm faced with. I have five days worth of food for three thousand men, if I'm lucky. I have three days worth of fuel, with conservation measures. We haven't had a full resupply in weeks. We will cease to be a support unit without in days, Admiral, and that sticks in my craw."

"Colonel, this is a damned unusual request," Admiral Hendricks said, sounding cold and irritated.

"Admiral, I'm not regular Army. Or Guard. I'm used to getting things done with whatever tools I have at hand, and having to make something from nothing. Well, I'm bordering on nothing here. I'm not going to wait for what isn't coming. If I have to go and get it, I will. So, I'm on the phone. If pulling supplies forward to line units is advancing the war effort, great. But eventually the support units that keep those line units on the move need to catch up to the line, or you end up with a very fragile link back to the world. Shit breaks. The enemy takes advantage. It snows. Would you suggest otherwise, sir?"

"Colonel, you're going to get a royal ass-chewing for this."

"You know, sir, I'm OK with that. I'm not going to see my men go hungry or freeze. If the line units need to slow their advance in order for us to be resupplied, then so be it. It's not like we're the only rear area unit that this is happening to, because I know for a fact that three other support Brigades are in the same shape or a little better than we are. If units like ours don't see resupply, then we have no business advancing out of Omaha. We're done, then, Admiral. Frankly, without units like ours up near the line, I have no idea who is offloading and distributing supplies. For damn sure the line units will not do it without massive waste. I've already seen that here. Figure thirty percent losses, sir. That's inexcusable, sir. We don't have that kind of excess to waste."

"I know that you must have made these same points with General Anderson."

"And most every other officer up the food chain of the United States Army. I'm tired of making the case, Admiral. Either they don't give a shit about what will happen to the line without support of the line units, or they don't give a shit about what happens in the prosecution of the war. It will drag out, we'll lose men in a senseless counteroffensive, tired men and worn out equipment will falter and lengthen the war, and for no reason whatsoever. Am I wrong here?"

"Colonel Drummond, I'll get back to you in an hour on this."

"Thank you, sir. I appreciate that," I said as Kittrick handed me a note. "Admiral, your aircrew just passed our perimeter patrol. Should be at our location within ten minutes."

"Excellent, Colonel. Hendricks out," he said as the secure channel clicked off.

"Mister Kittrick, there are days that this job absolutely sucks," I said as I flung the headset on the desk and grabbed my parka. "I'm heading over to receiving."

The receiving area consisted of two of our converted shipping containers, dismounted and set up in an 'L', with a massive tent that covered both units as well as the space between. Behind one leg of the 'L' were the medical tents for general care; the other was one of several galley tents, both had seen a significant effort to keep the snow from collapsing them overnight. As our work in Omaha wound down, the only two containers that hadn't been re-loaded for shipment down line were these two—without the thousands of refugees or soldiers to feed and tend to, we were running out of things to do, along with our supply stocks.

"Colonel, a little cold to be out here in your condition, don't you think?" Doc Willitson said, looking over his magnifying glasses at me, as he stitched up a soldier's forearm.

"Probably so, Doc. We have some Navy fliers coming in for eval. Thought I'd drop by. What happened here, soldier?" I asked. His arm was a mess. Five inches of sutures from just below the elbow on the inside of the arm, a jagged mess.

"We were on patrol downtown, sir. Caught a hunk of a storefront that was falling over. Lieutenant Carroll said that he thought the wind caught it. Hunk of metal went right through the roof of our pickup."

"Lucky it didn't take out an artery here, Private Lewis. As is, you're done running any weapon right handed for a long while. Another half inch and you'd have been in serious trouble."

"Southpaw, Doc. No problem."

"Not for a week you're not. Neither this arm or it's partner are doing anything but resting. Got it?"

"Yes, sir," Lewis said.

"Best take his orders, Mister Lewis. It's futile not to," I said.

"And yet, here you are, Colonel Drummond, ignoring them."

"Not for long, Doc. Although it does cramp my style," I said as I heard the muffled sound of a Humvee approaching. "Sounds like we have guests."

"Ehrlickson, see to our new assignments if you would. I have about ten more minutes with this. Jacoby, see that Mister Lewis is set up on antibiotics," Willitson said to his staff.

"Colonel, ten minutes or so, and you ought to get back to your quarters. It's maybe fifty degrees in this tent, despite the heaters, and a summer-like ten degrees outside. Not good for you, sir," Willitson said, not taking his eyes off of his work.

"No problem, Doc," I said as the inner tent door opened, and two very banged up Navy airmen entered, tended by four of our corpsmen. They were walking at least, but both looked like they'd been on the losing end of a bar fight. Both came to attention when they noticed my rank, and saluted.

"Colonel Drummond, Third Washington," as I returned the salute. "You boys have a seat. You look like Hell." Both had significant facial bruising, the younger a black eye.

"We've had better days, sir. Lieutenant Commander Michael McAllen, sir. This is Lieutenant Peter Shaw."

"McAllen?" I asked.

"Yes, sir," the Commander answered. "Eldest son of Ryan and Kay McAllen, late of Texas, sir."

"No wonder the interest in your disposition, Commander. I expect your parents are quite relieved you're in one piece," I said. "Doctor Willitson's staff will evaluate your medical condition, and if you're not too banged up, we'll get quarters established for you both outside of medical," I said looking over at Doc, who looked at both men and gave me half a nod. "Meanwhile, I need to talk to an Admiral in Air Command."

"Thank you, Colonel," Shaw said. "It's good to be somewhere warm, sir."

"Yeah, it is. Let's hope we can keep it that way," I said, moving to leave, and both men stood.

"Boys, things are a little more casual in the med tent. Park it and thank God you didn't land in that lake where your plane probably hit."

"Yes, sir," they said in unison.

672

A few minutes later, I was back on the secure line to Air Command. The President's son was safe.

McAllen and Shaw both had what Doctor Willitson said were injuries inflicted through a typical ejection sequence, and neither had any injuries from landing—the snow had seen to that. Per the request of Air Command, both were sequestered away from most of Third Washington troops until debriefing could be completed. Air Command said that a helo would evacuate the men later in the day.

Most of the Brigade shifted gears again, into their pre-search assignments. A significant portion of the men not assigned to either Alert status or normal mission operations were getting the trains ready for movement east. A third of Dog Sixes' personnel cars were having heating issues, and all remaining food had been inventoried and split evenly between the two. Charlie Six, on the other hand, only had twenty percent of her cars with heating, lighting, and water issues.

After seeing to the Brigade's assignments for the day, I joined the two Navy men in the conference car, where a late breakfast awaited me. Both stood as I entered.

"For Pete's sake, sit down," I said. "Pete, no offense there," I said, recognizing the unintentional reference. "Relax and enjoy some fine pre-cooked, pre-packaged, pre-pared food," I said as I again, shed my parka. "We're running low on damned near everything. Sorry we couldn't rustle up something a little more celebratory."

"Sir, if this is pre-packaged MRE food, then the Army's a whole lot better fed than the Navy," McAllen said, followed quickly by Shaw.

"Colonel, this is one of the best breakfasts I've ever had. No apologies necessary," Shaw said. It was then that I noticed that breakfast wasn't what I'd expected at all.

"Sorry, guys. It appears that the galley rounded up something out of the ordinary," I said, checking out what appeared to be some sort of breakfast enchilada in an industrial sized pan. "Let me get the galley chief on the phone."

"Kittrick, get me the galley chief," I said into the intercom. "No, belay that. Send the galley chief in to Conference One."

"Problem sir?" Kittrick responded.

"Nope. Double-time, Mister Kittrick," I said.

"Yes, sir!"

"All right, Commanders. What exactly do we have here, and may I join you?"

"Absolutely, sir," McAllen said. "Seems like a homemade tortilla with ham, egg, and cheese. And that pitcher, Colonel, has real by-God coffee. That one has heavy cream."

"Beats the Hell out of MRE's, which is what we're down to," I said.

"Sir?"

"Our resupply trains keep getting expressed east to the line units. Problem is, that without the support units like Third Washington, the Line doesn't have the manpower to distribute the supplies per unit. Stuff is wasted, destroyed. Texas seems to think that the line units can handle the whole operations and maintenance aspect of war fighting all on their own, while fighting the actual war. Can't happen. You boys can't fly and keep the aircraft in full readiness all on your own. Seems like the Army thinks they can. So, we're running out of fuel and food. A handful of days, and we're out," I said as the galley chief, a corporal, entered.

"Colonel Drummond, Corporal David Velasquez, reporting."

"Corporal, how exactly did you manage this breakfast?"

"Uh, some creative horse-trading, sir. I traded some of our laundry soap and bar soap for this, sir. A trial run with the local population."

"Corporal, I was under the impression that the locals don't have these kinds of resources available. Am I incorrect?"

"Colonel, the more capable people do, sir, and have not really been the recipients of any assistance from Third Washington."

"What kind of volumes are we talking about, Velasquez?"

"Enough for about a dozen, sir. Figured this would be a good occasion, Colonel."

"My compliments, Corporal. Good job," I said, "As long as we're not shorting the other supplies."

"Sir, we have enough soap products to last a solid year."

"Maintain an adequate level, Corporal. Clear trading with your superiors in all cases. Clear?"

"Yes, sir!" he said as he came to attention.

"Dismissed," I said, and the young man made as hasty exit.

"Colonel, are all your corporals eighteen or nineteen years old?" McAllen said.

"A fair percentage, yes. We have a pretty well balanced percentage of green-as-grass soldiers and very experienced non-comms and officers. I'm damned lucky to command them," I said as the intercom beeped. I picked up the headset and punched the 'activate' key.

"Drummond here," I said.

"Colonel Drummond," Captain Shand said, "One moment, sir. We're waiting for an uplink to San Antonio."

"Very well," I said. I figured that it was time to be chewed out from On High.

"Gentlemen," I said as I hit the 'mute' key, "Excuse me while I get my ass chewed for going to your commanding Admiral to try to get food and fuel." The two officers looked at each other, raising eyebrows, and looked a little uncomfortable.

"Colonel Drummond," the instantly recognizable voice said, "This is President McAllen. I understand that your Brigade retrieved my son this morning."

"Yes, sir, Mister President," I said, more than a little shocked. "He is at present, enjoying breakfast here in our conference room. Would you like to speak with him, sir?"

"Yes, Colonel, if you don't mind. I also would like to inform Lieutenant Shaw that his wife has been informed of his recovery, and that she will be waiting for him when he returns."

"I'm sure that he will be happy to hear that, sir."

"One more thing, Colonel. I hear through a roundabout way that you're itching to head east."

"Sir, I'm not itching to head east, but will do so when possible. I'm itching to have enough food and fuel to stay a viable unit. We're down to days worth of food and fuel, and Army Command is shifting our supplies east to the line."

"That will not be a continuing problem, Colonel. You have my word."

"Understood, Mister President, and my thanks for this."

"Armies march better on full stomachs, and fight better with full magazines."

"Amen, sir. Here's your son, sir."

"Thank you, Colonel. I owe you one."

"No sir, Third Washington owes you," I said, taking off the headset and handing it to the Lieutenant Commander. "Commander, you might be prepared to discuss the loss of your aircraft. I think the

Commander in Chief might want to know how you totaled a fifty million dollar aircraft," I said with a grin.

Shaw replied first, "Wrecked Dad's plane. You're hosed, Commander."

McAllen scowled a little, and put the headset on.

"Shaw, you're with me. Let's give son and father a little space," I said.

"Yes, sir."

Shaw donned his parka as I grabbed mine, and we headed over to the Command Car for a few minutes.

"So, Lieutenant, if you can, tell me about your mission over Des Moines."

"Nothing classified, sir. Straight bomb and go. Command and control targeting—we were tasked with taking out the communications links back to Chicago and points east. Damn it's cold out here," he said as we reached the door of the adjacent car.

"Successful?"

"Yes, sir. No doubt about it."

"What happened to your aircraft? Were you hit?"

"Small arms fire. The S.A. has a shi...has a lot of SAM's they're putting up, but if we go in low and fast, we've a better chance of getting through their perimeter and can then prosecute. We were hit on the way out. Had a few minor thrust issues but nothing major until we flamed out—no warning. No master caution, nothing. Everything died. Not exactly comfortable going from fully functional to dead stick in ten seconds, Colonel."

"I assume you've been told that neither of your personal locating beacons activated."

"No, sir," he said with a questioning look, "I did not."

"The aircraft ejection indicator was the last known point of you and Lieutenant Commander McAllen. Telemetry for the last three minutes of your flight, including IFF, also was not transmitted."

"Could have taken some fire into the avionics, Colonel. That might explain it."

"You're both damned lucky, Shaw. And before I forget, the President said that your wife would be waiting to meet you upon your return."

He stopped in his tracks, on the way back to my desk in the back of the Command Car. "I haven't seen Amy in six months, sir."

"Apparently all you need to do is to get shot down with a distinguished aircraft commander and survive, and magic comes your way," I said. "Where's she been since you last saw her?"

"Norfolk, sir."

"Your lucky day, Mister Shaw," I said.

"Yeah it is, sir. Sometimes I forget how lucky I really am."

"You're still young. There'll come a point where you wake up every single morning, and realize right off, how lucky you really are. Maybe for you that'll be tomorrow."

January Twelfth
Aboard Charlie Six
Van Meter, Iowa
14:30 Hours

Third Washington progressed across the terrain east of Omaha at a painfully slow pace, fixing wrecked trackage and stopping in virtually every town along the rail line. It seemed we hit every township south of Interstate Eighty, taking four days to reach Des Moines, barely a hundred and forty miles from our Omaha start.

Both trains that moved the Brigade were showing wear and tear. Our main drive units had been changed before we left Omaha, but Dog Six had lost heat and power to a full thirty percent of the personnel cars, as well as heat to both defensive cars. Charlie had lost heat to fifteen percent of the cars, and power to five percent. In Des Moines, we planned to switch cars around between the two, to balance out our losses. Spare parts might catch up to us sometime, hopefully before the War ended.

I found myself becoming uncomfortably accustomed to the sight of the burned out farmhouses and collapsed barns, slaughtered livestock frozen to the snow covered ground. The small towns were particularly pathetic, the once-vital heart of a county or township, in failure before the war just due to the ease of transportation to bigger cities...which was the death knell to many small town businesses. The S.A.'s heavy bootprints reached every small town along our route.

Most were hit hard and fast, but much of the population who'd survived had fled to the hinterlands long before the S.A. forces arrived in force. The S.A. in retreat took little time to strip the light industries and the sparse businesses in these towns, instead they burned them to the ground, along with the schools, courthouses, libraries, and churches. Homes were ransacked, mostly for food and clothing.

Our inability to proceed east 'per schedule' was not of our making, but more of the work of the S.A. in destroying the tracks ahead of us. Two companies of Third Washington were advanced east on track inspection and repair, along with half-dozen trained railmen. As our delays mounted, word spread among the civilian population about the Brigade and our supplies. The further east we progressed, the larger the population, the greater the need. Van Meter, Iowa, was such a place.

Pre-War, Van Meter was home to around a thousand residents or so, but this day, there were five times that, crowding into the shattered little town, as we were waiting for the ten miles of track to Des Moines to be repaired and cleared. One of the supply trains that had passed us by heading east, was now being loaded with refugees, carrying anything they could to keep warm on the trip west. Most of the cars were unheated. Stacks of unused equipment were piled near the siding, and troops from Third were busy retrieving the gear and setting up shelter tents, which had been tossed off the supply train without care. The people wanted food, but ignored the insulated shelter tents that were also aboard the supply train.

"Colonel, Mayor Farman is ready to meet you in receiving," Corporal McDowell said. McDowell was the communications whiz of Dog Six, often able to revive equipment long after the technicians had tossed it for scrap.

"Thanks, Corporal," I said as I made my way to the newly assembled receiving tent. Willitson's medical staff was completely overwhelmed with the rush of civilians, almost all women. I knew instantly that horrible things had happened here. Whispers had been spreading through the Command staff since right after our arrival.

The tent was heated with steam-driven radiators, connected to the generating units on the trains. Each radiator had men, women and children huddled around them. Part of the receiving tent had been screened off, and I took a look inside.

"Colonel, this is Mayor Tina Farman," I heard from over my shoulder as I looked at the rows of blankets strung from ropes, to create semi-private cubicles.

"Madam Mayor, nice to meet you."

"Thank you, Colonel. You people are a godsend."

"Let's go find a quiet space to talk. I think we'll have one of our logistics folks with us in a minute," I said. "We'll try to get as much done here as we can before we ship east."

"Moving some of these refugees out will be a start. The S.A. did their best to strip us clean, and then they moved to Des Moines, and the people from Des Moines and Chicago are now flooding us. We just don't have anything left to give."

"Four additional supply trains will be headed east within the next day or so. When they're coming westbound, refugees will be able to head west."

"That's a little bit of the problem," she said as Captain McGowan joined us.

"This is Captain Gerry McGowan, intel. Gerry, where's Major Ryder?"

"On the horn, sir. He won't be able to make it," McGowan said. For Ryder to miss a meeting like this, he had to be dealing with a real cluster.

"Mayor Farman, you were saying?"

"Most of the refugees we're getting first of all, don't want to leave, and won't lift a finger. The worst of it though is in that room you were looking into a few minutes ago."

"What's going on in there?"

"Rape victims, Colonel," she said as she gripped the table in front of her, barely containing her rage. "That bastard General Slocum told his men to rape every female they could lay hands on. No one is prepared to deal with this, Colonel. There are two hundred and fifty women in there and more that we can't yet find."

"Ma'am, I don't know what to say," I said. "I had no idea."

"Colonel Drummond, no one does," she said as I sat there for a moment.

"We'll do what we can, ma'am. I'll try to get some help from the west."

"I'd appreciate that," she said, taking a sip of coffee from a chipped Third Washington mug. "Now, these refugees. What can you do about them?"

"You said that they're not willing to do anything, ma'am?" Gerry said.

"Citiots. City-idiots. Waiting for the government to take care of them. If we don't do anything, they steal from those that are doing things, absolutely anything is fair game. If we provide for them, they bitch that it's not enough or not good or whatever. There is no pleasing them."

"We don't have time for this, Mayor," I said. "These people are late to the party. They need to figure out that what is here is all there is, and they can take what is given them and be happy or get the Hell out of town on their own, and not come back."

"You feel free to tell them that, Colonel. I tried and damned near had a riot on my hands."

"From a handful of people, or all of them?" Gerry asked.

"These things always start with a handful, Captain. Stirring the pot."

"'It does not require a majority to prevail, but rather an irate, tireless minority keen to set brush fires in people's minds,'" I said.

"Who's that from?" Mayor Farman asked.

"Sam Adams, talking about the other side of the equation," I replied. "What do you have left for law enforcement?"

"You. That's it."

"Weapons?" Gerry asked.

682

"Maybe some shotguns, nothing owned by the City. We didn't have a whole lot to start with. The S.A. came and took everything, even trap guns."

"Get yourself a town Marshal and a bunch of deputies. We'll get them armed. Anyone that steps out of line, lock 'em up. If you can I.D. the agitators before we ship east, point them out to our men and we'll have a little chat with them," I said. "Your utility grid is shot, Mayor. How are you going to keep people warm here, and water safe?"

"It's not as bad as it seems. Power's off, all right, but that's because we pulled eleven transformers down before the S.A. got here. Our citizens were more or less ready for that. The refugees were the ones that weren't of course. And if we put things back together too soon, they'll never leave," she said.

"Interesting tactic," Gerry said.

"I wouldn't worry as much about the refugees not staying as I would about hypothermia and the spread of disease. There will be plenty of military around for a long time. You're on one of the primary rail lines to the front. That's not going to change."

"Colonel," one of the corpsmen interrupted, "Doctor Willitson would like to speak with you ASAP."

"Be right there. Thanks," I said. "Mayor, we'll be talking. Gerry, in lieu of having Major Ryder here, see what you can do about getting power back up."

"Yes, sir," he said as I stood and excused myself.

Fifty feet away, Jeff Willitson was washing up after two hours of surgery.

"Doc, I see you're doing your time in Hell today."

"You got that right, Colonel," he said. I noticed the bloodstained floor, and pile of stained surgical utilities in a laundry bin. "We need large scale evac of these women, and we need it now, sir. We cannot deal with this with what we have on hand. We just can't do it. I lost three of them in the past hour. We'll lose more, I guarantee it, if we don't get them out of here. I don't mean rail service, Rick. I mean air evac, and a lot of it." His hands were shaking.

"I have no idea what's available, Jeff. I'll get on it though,"

"We have kids in there, Colonel," he said, looking down into the still-running sink.

"I know, Jeff. Give me a few minutes to get something going," I said. I'd never seen Doctor Willitson as shaken.

I made the way back to Dog Sixes' Command Car, which happened to be closer than the primary car in Charlie. Other than the damage inflicted weeks earlier, the cars were identical.

"Ten-hut!" one of the sergeants said as I entered.

"At ease. Who's your duty officer?"

"Lieutenant Kramer, sir," the Sergeant said. He looked a little surprised, as well he might.

"Here, sir," Kramer said, standing from his location at communications suite three.

"Mister Kramer, get me in touch with the Air Force, Air Mobility Command."

"Yes, sir. I'll patch you through to the Deputy Commander's suite."

"Fine," I said, moving back to the vacant desk and formulating my request for evacuating civilians.

"AMC on Secure Four, sir."

"Thanks," I said before putting on the headset. "This is Colonel Richard Drummond, Third Washington."

"Major Arnstein, sir. What can we do for you, Colonel?"

"Good way to start the conversation, Major. I'm in Van Meter, Iowa. I have several hundred critical care civilians needing evac, pronto. Rail evac isn't going to cut it. Nearest airport of size is Des Moines, and it's a wreck," I said, explaining to him the nature of the injuries inflicted on the victims. He was quiet for a moment on his end of the line.

"Pulling you up on the map, sir. One moment," he said. "You're south of Interstate Eighty. Depending on the condition of the road, that could be used for evac.....affirmative, sir, C-130's can handle that highway. You'll need to clear the highway from One Sixty Nine—that's just north of DeSoto, to the first overpass to the west of that," he said, then providing me exact coordinates for marker beacons at both ends of the improvised airstrip. "One moment sir. My C.O. would like to join in the communication."

"No problem, Major," I said as a note was handed to me, in Jeff Willitson's handwriting.

"Colonel Drummond, this is Colonel Stack," the female voice said.

"Colonel," I said. "Can you estimate the number of evacuees?"

"Three hundred to start with," I said, reading Jeff's note. Expect at least double that. The majority female, most were victims of unspeakable brutality. Our staff is unable to attend to the magnitude of this, Colonel. We're losing patients by the hour."

Silence on the other end of the call. "Colonel Stack?"

"I'm here, sir," she said. "We can handle around seventy patients per aircraft. Five aircraft are being dispatched from Omaha at this time. Expect arrival of the first transport at the coordinates provided to you by Major Arnstein within the next hour."

"Much appreciated, Colonel. Given what I know about what's happened here, you will likely need a lot of help down there, ma'am."

"Understood, Colonel. Stack, out," she said as the link went dead. I sat there for a minute, wondering what kind of beasts we were fighting.

"Colonel, would you like some coffee?" one of the techs asked.

"Nope. I'd like to have an S.A. soldier in the sights of my rifle. You let me know if that kind of opportunity comes up," I said.

Touring Van Meter with Lieutenant Colonel Atwood, we could see the path of the S.A., like the proverbial tornado through a trailer park. Every small business had been destroyed. Five days after Des Moines fell, six or seven days after Van Meter had been nearly destroyed, some buildings still smoldered.

"Ever feel like you're just watching the same terrain on a different day?" I asked as the January rain spattered against the Humvees armored windshield.

"Yes, sir. Had a lot of days like that in Afghanistan."

"This is going to sound trite, but is this worse, or better than over there?"

"Way worse, sir, for me at least. These are our countrymen doing this to each other. We never saw brutality on this scale over there. Honor killings among the Muslims, sure, which are senseless. Nothing like this. It just doesn't seem to stop. Destruction for no reason."

"Until this mess, I'd never been in a real war zone. One that's been declared at least. I'd seen wholesale murder of innocent civilians, but I've never seen wholesale brutality for brutality's sake," I said, remembering Sudan.

"Evil unleashed in the world, Colonel. Nothing but."

"Yeah," I said, noticing the wreckage of a museum of a long-gone baseball player, noted for pitching three no-hitters, once upon a time.

19:50 Hours

"Mercy Two Six, this is Mercy command, cross at twenty knots at three four zero degrees," I heard through the headset.

"Two-six," was the reply.

The next-to-last transport was on the ground, the last on approach. Once word got out that transports were evacuating the victims of the S.A., things in Van Meter started to come unglued. Refugees rushed the evacuation convoys, demanding to get priority. Third and Fifth Battalions both fired warning shots to keep the refugees restrained. During those encounters, several ring-leaders were identified and separated from the crowds, their separation taken with indignity, many demanding, and then pleading, that they be allowed to stay 'with their families' and 'their friends'. No family members came forth though, nor friends. By eighteen-thirty, less than a dozen of the most vocal were cooling their heels in two empty supply cars on a siding, not far from the galley cars.

"Mercy Two Six, on terra firma. Thirty seconds to ramp," said the pilot.

The 'ramp' for Two Six was the westbound lane overpass at the east end of the Interstate Eighty landing strip, marked with infrared beacons and few normal lights. The patients staged there, along with a planeload of medical personnel from the Three Seventy-Fifth Air Medical Group. Pre-War, the Three Seventy Fifth called Scott Air Force Base Home, but had evacuated to Dyess down in Texas. Mercy Two Five was on the eastbound lanes, almost ready for departure.

As each aircraft taxied toward the overpass, they would turn a hundred and eighty degrees, and lower their rear access ramp to allow quick loading of each litter into the aircraft, never shutting engines down. Once each plane was loaded, they would immediately take off for Omaha.

Once Two Six was away, the remaining medical personnel and Third Washington would take down the tent shelters, and head to Van Meter. The medical team would provide greatly needed assistance to Jeff's worn-down men.

687

"Colonel, the detainees are in debrief with Captain McGowan's teams. They should be through initial stages by now. The Captain wondered if you'd like to sit in on one," Sergeant Travis said.

"Not a chance in Hell, Chet. I just might get myself in trouble if I were in a room with one of those self-centered bastards."

"Understood, sir," he said with a smile. "Wouldn't do to have our C.O. in a court martial."

"Yeah, probably not."

January Twelfth
Aboard Charlie Six
Van Meter, Iowa
23:30 Hours

I was an hour or so late for bed, wrestling with the present and the soon to be. The Soon To Be was winning.

Third Washington had been tasked with progressing immediately south and east of Des Moines, essentially sprinting across the state toward Burlington and the small town of Fort Madison. All surviving bridges across the Mississippi, from Dubuque to St. Louis, now numbered two. One at Keokuk, Iowa, another at Sabula. Every other bridge, whether it was rail, highway, or foot, had been destroyed. If there were S.A. forces on the west side of the Mississippi, they were trapped. If they could somehow get across, they would do so without mechanized units.

Third was supposed to ship east by oh six hundred, as is. The sprint—a relative thing on a train—would be possible due to undamaged tracks between Van Meter and Fort Madison, with the track already checked for IED's. West of Burlington, Composite Group—composed of Army and Marine units---had fought a major battle with the S.A, before the Air Force destroyed the remaining bridge, cutting off the S.A. Twenty thousand enemy were trapped, fifteen thousand of them died fighting. The remainder was wounded or surrendered, with a handful—perhaps a hundred—trying to escape across the Mississippi. Third would stage near Fort Madison, southwest of Burlington, both had bridges targeted by Air Force precision munitions. We were tasked with munitions and heavy equipment retrieval, moving from Fort Madison north. Two trains back, behind a munitions train that would head north, would be a train comprised mostly of flatbed rail cars and mounted cranes. Third would serve as the tow truck operators to retrieve damaged and destroyed U.S. tanks, and to work with explosives experts to safe up live shells and to permanently disable enemy tanks and heavy weapons.

"Most of the equipment will be down and stowed in an hour, sir. That which of course, we can take with us," Captain Ben Farragut said. Farragut was part of our quartermaster crew.

"Thanks, Captain. Not much we can do about those shelter tents. We probably have enough anyway. Besides, there's always a supply train coming for us, right?" I said jokingly. Ben and I had had too many conversations about stretching our supplies. Simple math usually said otherwise. "What's our supply status?"

"Ten days fuel, fifteen of food, with scant fresh goods. Medical is, well this is an average, about forty-seven percent of full-on. Water treatment capabilities are sixty one percent between the two trains; Dog is clearly in trouble there. Mechanics did manage to revive heat in a number of Dog's abandoned crew cars, and they're now on a par with Charlie."

"That's some good news for a change. Did they figure out how to keep them going?"

"Report said that some were more prone to basically vapor lock due to poor castings of the steam piping. A couple were losing pressure due to cracks in the pressure system. Two had damage from small arms fire that had gone undetected."

"Hmm," I said. "All right then, get some shut eye when the gear's stowed. Tomorrow will be a long-ass day."

"Yes, sir," he said as he stood and left the conference car.

"Private Houston, what's the weather at our destination?" I hollered down the Command Car, rather than to try to check it myself. Satellite data was quite sketchy. I dragged on my parka and cap.

"Last reports were at twenty one hundred, sir, thick fog and temperatures in the low thirties."

"Thanks," I hated fog, especially in this part of the country. It seemed colder and more penetrating. "I'm turning in—See you boys in the morning," I said as I left the car.

"Good night, Colonel," one of the sentries outside the car said.

"Good night, Private. Stay sharp—big day tomorrow."

"Will do, sir."

My quarters never looked quite as good as they did that night. I was dead tired, without the promise of enough sleep ahead.

January Thirteenth
Aboard Charlie Six
8:40 Hours

"Sir, we're good to go on your command," the rail engineer in Charlie's lead engine said over the intercom. "Dog Six as well, sir."

"Roll out, Mister Edwards," I said, a moment later feeling the train begin to move.

"Lieutenant Kittrick, I know this is early to ask, but when do you expect communications back on line?" I asked. We'd lost the uplink to both Command and Composite Group during the night from Charlie, but Dog still had active communications.

"Not yet, sir. We have a couple techs on it now. We do have a hot link between Charlie and Dog though. There's a little delay in the data feed, but we are in touch..."

"More or less."

"More or less, sir," he said. "And Colonel? That short haul that came in had mail for you. It's there on your desk sir."

The 'short haul' was a rail tug that had hauled food for Van Meter and a little for Third. 'It would be nice to read one of Karen's letters,' I thought. I looked at the envelope, only five days past.

My late breakfast today would be coffee, canned juice, and a 'breakfast' MRE, either an 'apple maple rolled oatmeal' with hash browns and bacon, or a 'sausage patty' with hash browns and bacon. I chose the oat version, all else being equal. The galley cars were going through major service while on the go, with the entire Brigade relegated to MRE's for at least two meals. Once we arrived in Fort Madison, the galley chief expected to be back up in full operation within an hour or so, with all of the deferred maintenance problems addressed during this run across Iowa. The galleys had many of the same problems as the other crew cars, compounded by constant use and high demands.

We'd been delayed twice in rolling out of Van Meter by conflicting reports of track readiness down the line, and then further pleas by some of the disenfranchised refugees, demanding that we improve upon the well being of the refugees in general. A few more instigators were found and separated, and I had a few more minutes with the Mayor before departure. She'd hand picked a number of people for the new police force, and our Armory had provided Van Meter two dozen old-style M-16's, a like number of shotguns and M-9's, and fifty thousand rounds of ammunition, total.

"Sir, if you'd care to pull up Secure One One on your monitor, you might see something interesting," Kittrick said.

"What do we have?" I asked as I flipped the monitor to life and punched in the correct security code.

"Real time mapping of Air Command operations sir, from an AWACS tracking action over St. Louis. Blue tracks are SAM's. No enemy aircraft. Red are ours."

"That data on the right is the number of SAM's in the air? Good God," I said. It varied between fifty and two hundred at any given time.

"I believe so, sir."

'Unsustainable,' I thought. The two dozen Air Force aircraft in the vicinity—and some were drones—were nowhere near the blue shield of SAM's fired at them. I moved the cursor over one of the red aircraft designators and was able to pull up the aircraft type, call sign, and an acronym for weapons remaining on board. Most were B-52's from Minot, probably pounding S.A. emplacements with cruise missiles or GPS guided weapons. They orbited St. Louis at a comfortable distance, as the SAM's, probably shoulder fired, tracked randomly and seldom came close.

A massive flare of something—donut shaped—spread over east St. Louis, eliminating many of the SAM's in that area.

"What the Hell was that?" I asked.

"No idea, sir."

"Can you patch in the AWACs frequency?"

"Sorry sir, we don't have that ability at the moment."

The 'void' created by the detonation, whatever it was, had to be more than a mile in diameter. Occasional tracks from SAM's crossed the void, but nothing originated within it.

January 8th

Dear Rick—
I hope this finds you safe and warm and well. We've seen three days in the thirties so far this year, so here's hoping that this is a sign of things to come!
As I wrote earlier, we had a nice New Years celebration with Ashley and the twins and the Pauliano's....but I have sad news---Joe passed away last evening in his sleep. I heard from Don a little while ago, and was already going to write. There wasn't anything particularly wrong, and he was in the best spirits I've seen him in years just last week. Don said that Joan is taking it well. Carl and Kelly are both taking it hard—the Pauliano's were like another set of grandparents of course. We're going to the funeral in a few hours. Joe will be buried not far from your parents.
There is other bad news, unfortunately. Two blocks south of our store, there was a house fire night before last, and a young family died, along with one of the firefighters from Station One. The fire inspector said that it was probably hidden damage to the chimney that started a fire in one of the walls. The new medical examiner said that they probably died of smoke inhalation—the firefighter died

when he entered the house and fell through the floor into the burning basement. All flags are at half-staff, and Libby and Mary and I will be helping at the memorial service next week.

We are doing OK, but missing you terribly....it is all we can do to keep up with the place and keep the status quo. Tackling anything beyond that is almost out of the question. Ron and Alan seem to be feeling the same way. The trading stores are doing well, and three new stores should open up by Spring, including one near Fort Overbeck, one near Fairchild, and one near Felts Field. Pacific Northwest Command said that the other stores in the area were trying to take advantage of the military, and we competed for a concession for all three—we won, but I didn't want to tell you that just in case we lost—No harm no foul! Mary and I will be putting together a staffing plan—and we're going to employ as many of the Army spouses as we can. I think you'd approve. Most of these girls don't have ANYTHING to make their homes with, and as you well know, the Army doesn't pay much!

I had better run—it's time to rouse our children and get them moving about their day, and it's bread-making day! It's still not yet sunrise. Even the dogs are still sleeping.

> *All my love forever—*
> *Karen*

Someday, I hoped that all of her letters would catch up to me, to fill in the many blanks in between the letters that I did receive. I'd miss old Joe—he was a good friend to anyone, no matter the age or race or condition, had a quiet wisdom and uncommon good sense. Another good man, gone Home.

On the ground near Fort Madison, we would meet up with a company-sized Marine Recon unit and the remains of an Army artillery company, both north of Keokuk. The artillery unit was a straggler, having seen numerous breakdowns in their equipment after being pounded by the S.A., and would cross the Mississippi when the last of their repairs were complete. The Marines had seen heavy action and were trailing behind to gain some rest before going on point again with Composite Group. I noted in the report, that they'd lost forty-seven percent of their officers and just under sixty percent of their line soldiers since hostilities began. I also noted that their field commander was not happy that they were pulled from the line, even for a few days. 'Not happy' being a relative thing, I read his non-redacted communiqué to command, filled with creative uses of expletives when describing those that ordered Recon Twelve to stand down.

It would take around four hours to make the hundred and seventy-five miles to Fort Madison. Battalion commanders had given the orders to have all weapons cleaned during the trip, and other than the defensive cars, everyone stood down to get some sleep. We'd have a lot of work to do once we arrived. Someone in the rear communications car had improvised a connection from several iPods to the internal communications channels, similar to the commercial airliners before the war. Four channels of playlists were on rotation, none of which I cared for.

Outside the train, despite our lack of windows, our external cameras showed us the towns of Monroe, Pella, and Oskaloosa, civilians wandering about the streets, some running toward the trains that wouldn't stop, a few uniformed soldiers to keep them back. The towns looked in better shape than most we'd seen. Karen had a cousin that lived in Pella years back. I remembered the neat-as-a-pin town square, the many Dutch influences on the town, the incredible food we ate there. Was it twenty years ago already?

I spent a little time reading some of the readiness reports on the Air Force, as imagined by the S.A., captured and decrypted by one of the Composite's intel algorithms out of thin air. Most of the report was blather, perhaps correctly interpreting only one thing, the effect off massed surface to air missiles on deflecting close air support missions.

Another report intercept seemed to be more grounded in reality, talking in frank terms about the S.A.'s inability to meet the nutritional needs of their population, beginning as soon as the coming June. The report, prepared by someone who almost seemed to know what they were talking about, stated that without dramatic changes in the ability to import food from the West (meaning, the United States) and from other 'non-affected areas', large scale starvation would come to the majority of the S.A. states. Resources within the S.A. were not directed toward food production, but toward seizure of manufacturing abilities and storage of technology with the 'hope of advancing the State through technological breakthroughs unforeseen by the United States.' The notation at the bottom of the intercept said that the report was written in late November, and that the report had been heavily redacted before being completely deleted from official record. Unofficial versions had surfaced outside of official channels, and a new version created for public distribution. It was wholly different than the honest attempt to wake up the S.A. leadership. It was two weeks newer than the original report.

"...acquisitions of basic food stuffs and expansion of State regulated farms and dairies continue throughout the mid-West, with further expansion plans in the Mississippi and Ohio Valleys..."

This, as they were beginning the collapse and as U.S. offensives were stripping them of these lands. By the time the report was written, it would have already been too late to do anything meaningful regarding farming, planting and livestock production. Non-farmers just imagine that beef and grain and poultry can be made available on command. Farmers know differently of course. Farming and livestock production is a combination of luck, skill, weather, and Providence.

I could not fathom the disconnect between the reality of the S.A. soldier on the ground, fighting the United States military, and those that would look at verifiable facts, and re-write them for their superiors, rather than to upset their superiors. Rather than disturb the planned Utopia under State Rule.

The painful lesson that would be learned again, would first hit the civilian population within the diminished State of America. Last of course, it would hit the leadership. I was certain that the leaders were not starving, had everything they could desire in terms of material goods and physical pleasure, and that this would remain so as long as they desired it so, simply because they desired it, and that those around them benefited from the culture of fear that substituted for leadership. I was also sure that the leaders of the S.A. had never studied history.

Those that are most wrong, are also those that hold onto their wrong beliefs, until the very end. Pride is a difficult thing to swallow, and freedom an impossibility to control, for those that choose to be free.

January Thirteenth
Fort Madison, Iowa
Aboard Charlie Six

The sprint across Iowa had been a little more trying than I thought it would be, the last fifty miles illustrating burned farmhouses or towns, with a few scarecrow civilians and probably no supplies. The S.A. continued to demonstrate their ability to emulate the locust swarm.

A continuing threat of surface to air missiles by the hundreds effectively kept normal Air Command ground-support missions in a stand off position, and hindered their ability to effectively target the S.A. in an agile manner, except with drones of limited capability and increasing rates of failure....and the result was the field of damaged heavy armor nearby. The reality was that the U.S. Army and Air Force were fighting with worn down aircraft and inexperienced replacement crews. It was catching up to our Brigade of course as well. When real-time mattered, the satellites couldn't deliver, or the effectiveness of numerous enemy anti-satellite missions proved their effect. Recon was spotty. The scale of air support needed was completely beyond Air Command's ability to deliver, due to the hundreds of sorties needed daily to meet everyone's demands. Not all problems could be addressed with massive hammer blows...surgical strikes were needed, and almost impossible to execute.

Thin U.S. forces held the bridge at Keokuk, and all points south. That bridge had been the last point that the S.A. crossed, as Composite swept north and east. Composite Group was moving east and north, from that point, as all bridges across the Mississippi between Keokuk and Davenport, far to our north were gone. The vast majority of the Composite, almost ninety-five thousand men and thousands of trucks, tanks and artillery were already across the Mississippi south of us, in pursuit of the S.A., headed toward Bloomington and Champaign...eventually Chicago. I'd learned that everything east of us, from the Illinois line roughly over to Cincinnati, was now in U.S. control.

Third Washington would begin our work at Fort Madison, but within a week, we'd be heading over the Mississippi ourselves to support Composite moving north.

Fort Madison, according to my intelligence file, was a few miles north and across the river from Nauvoo, Illinois. It was the home to the oldest military garrison on the upper Mississippi, dating from before The War of Eighteen-Twelve. The town itself was above the banks of the Mississippi, on the northern edge of a floodplain that stretched eight or so miles southwest, about two miles wide, obviously carved by the river. The pre-War satellite images of the plain showed that it was ringed by tree-covered hills, and bisected north to south by Highway Sixty One, and cut again by the rail line to Kansas City. The Air Force had considerately taken destroyed the Fort Madison Bridge, along with many others across the river, which enabled the destruction of the S.A. armor and forced infantry south to the few remaining crossings of the river. Fort Madison also was the home of the Iowa State Penitentiary. I'd read that the inmates, to a man, were executed by the Iowa State Militia, rather than risk their release…a repeated event at many maximum security prisons.

Hundreds of Humvees, tanks, and Bradley Fighting Vehicles had been towed or dragged to the railyard in Fort Madison, for the train-deployed crew following us to repair and refit, or haul back West for repair or reconstruction. Charlie Six and Dog Six would have no more than two hours to deploy before a train hauling twenty-four refitted Abrams and uncounted other vehicles would arrive from Kansas City. Plans changed quickly on the rails, often it seemed, in conflict with each other. The offload began at fifteen-thirty, after we'd figured out a staging plan.

By seventeen hundred, offload and setup was complete for both Charlie and Dog, and recon of the battlefield north of Fort Madison would start at first light. From initial reports of the fight, the S.A. threw everything they had at the U.S. forces, eventually abandoning most of their surviving heavy equipment well before the Air Force took out the bridge crossing. The Brigade was working through the 'dinner shift', that on a good day took a couple hours. I ate with the squad from Second Battalion that had helped clear Sixth Army in Sterling. First Sergeant Jones and I had worked some difficult hours together. I'd made it a point to try to check in with every squad, once in awhile, but this one was a little more on my mind than most.

After dinner, I headed up to the far end of Dog Six, out to the farthest observation point with the relief watch, and back down to the far end of Charlie. The thick fog that had covered our progress for a hundred miles was still with us, limiting visibility to hundreds of feet at best. It was irritating and taxing on the men, who had to split their duties at observation posts that had almost no observation ability. The fog also muffled sounds, putting an additional strain on the men.

2100 Hours

"Colonel, here's the latest from on-high," Gerry McGowan said as I entered the darkened Command Car, handing me what Texas thought our schedule should be. In typical Command fashion, the pronouncement was made without on the ground intelligence, made wildly optimistic projections on the ability of Third Washington to create order from complete and utter chaos.

"That good, Ger?"

"They want us to mobe in forty-eight hours, sir."

"They DO realize that we actually haven't done any work here yet, right?" I said, reigning in some unwarranted anger.

"As usual, sir, I don't think they care what we've actually done, versus what they have expected us to have accomplished by now. Also, that Mechanized unit is running late, estimated time of arrival, twenty-three hundred."

I uttered several expletives, and read the orders, and said a few more, before the Command Car door opened and closed quickly.

"Sirs, we have company," Captain Shand barked, hearing traffic through his headset as the communications techs scrambled into 'alert' mode. "Marine unit has heavy contact with enemy. Our side of the river." Orders immediately went out to all Third Washington troops and the few hundred unattached troops.

"Well, *shit*," I said. "That, I didn't see coming," my adrenaline level kicking up dramatically. I picked up the headset and tuned to the south end recon and observation frequency, listening in on the

Marines as they fought off what seemed to be a very large attack. "Kittrick, map me friendlies on the terrain model."

"Twenty seconds, sir."

"Faster would be *way* better," I said. All troops in Third Washington were deploying in support...to where was the next question. The Marines were near the junction of Highway Sixty One and Highway Two Eighteen. South of them, an Army artillery unit, a few miles from Keokuk. We were on the northeast end of a crescent-shaped plain, a little more than two and a half miles wide at the greatest. The Marine contact was at the southern end of this plain. To the east, gently rising terrain, wooded, overlooking the broad plain. Several large farm-industrial plants just south of the county road—'Jay' Sixty Two, the rest appeared to be farms.

"Done, sir," Kittrick replied as I looked over the screen and the current locations of Charlie and Dog and the three thousand men under my command. Greg Shand, Gerry McGowan and I quickly sketched out a deployment plan, against an unknown force.

"Battalion Commanders, this is Colonel Drummond. Marine Recon Twelve is in heavy contact with enemy forces, approximately four miles southeast, Highway Sixty-One observation post. Gentlemen, we need to flank whatever S.A. forces are out there. First and Second Battalions, you will proceed east by whatever means possible—best possible time--to deploy on the ridge just west of Highway Two Eighteen from the Sixty-One Junction to due west of New Boston. Third Battalion, from New Boston to County Road 'Jay' Two Sixty-Two. Fourth and Fifth Battalions will move east then south across the Fort Madison Plain to enclose the S.A. forces. We are recalling an Army artillery unit to support the Marine unit in this engagement and requesting reinforcements. Upon contact, do not engage unless you are fired upon. We are to determine the size of this force before taking action, and contain them. Drummond out."

It took nearly an hour to fully deploy Third Washington in the field, using our own trucks, transports, and our two Abrams tanks, and two dozen shot up but drivable salvaged trucks and a few Bradleys. Our tanks were held in position south of both Charlie and

Dog, intended to protect both the town of Fort Madison and our train.

During most of that time, the Marines were engaged. Probably against better planning, Jim Schaefer stayed in 'Charlie's' Command Car while I went afield, setting up a mobile command post between two Humvees, between First and Second Battalions, uphill from the area where the S.A. was believed to be, perhaps a mile away, near a Federal-style two story farmhouse on 'Valley Road.' The house looked to have been built not long after the First Civil War.

By twenty-three hundred, we knew we had a serious problem.

"Colonel Drummond, Gunnery Sergeant Delaney is here," Kittrick said, not taking his eyes off of the monitor, but listening intently to the tactical frequencies of our picket line.

"Very well, Kittrick. Thanks," I said as the tent flap opened.

"Colonel," Gunny Delaney said, snapping to attention and saluting.

"At ease, Marine. Sit rep," I said, returning the salute.

"Substantial enemy presence, sir. Some thousands, at a minimum. By the enemy muzzle flashes, we had a target rich environment."

"Interesting way to look at it....you're getting lit up and you call it a target rich environment?"

"Yes, sir. Emptied five mags and they kept coming. Evac'd up the road and the Brads stuffed a few hundred rounds their way. That shut 'em up for a while. Won't be for long, though, sir. We can hear them down there."

"Sergeant, are we talking a thousand, or ten thousand?"

"Colonel, I'd have to lean toward the higher range. If we were talking hundreds—which is almost certainly what we killed, the rest would've turned hind end and melted off. They just piled over their dead and kept coming."

"What do you have for recon around the area?"

"We're down to thirty-eight, sir, although fifty-five are wounded and still able to fight. Eleven KIA. The rest are moving up from Keokuk, but it'll be awhile before they get here."

"Colonel," Shawn Miller interrupted, "We can get more intel only one way, and that's moving closer in and infiltrating. We don't have enough night vision equipment that's operational." The Third Washington night-vision gear issued to us was given to front line units long before.

"Pretty ballsy, Colonel Miller," I said.

"South end—Fourth and Fifth Battalions—have had no contact at all. They could be three miles away. Sir, I'd suggest sending advance elements south and east until they make contact. Same thing with the other units. Probe a little bit."

"Colonel Miller, we could be seriously outnumbered here, and we're at best, lightly armed," I said. "Kittrick, report on ETA of reinforcements?"

"I have that, sir," Corporal Martin said. "Rather, I have relayed the information to Command. They replied with 'several hours at a minimum,' Colonel."

"Shit," I said. "Sergeant, where is the enemy at present? Did they advance or retreat after action?"

"Retreated, sir. Estimate three hundred meters from the engagement location."

"They leave their dead behind" I asked.

"Yes, sir."

"Shawn, get some of your men and some from Second. Not many....retrieve some of the dead, get their clothing. Execute your infiltration," I said, seeing Lieutenant Jenkins—from the communications staff of 'Dog Six' perk up at the suggestion.

"Colonel, if I may?" Jenkins said.

"Lieutenant?"

"Sir, we have four dozen remote sensors that will allow tracking and targeting of human targets within a two mile range of our receivers. If First and Second Battalions men place those sensors around or within range, we'll have a better idea what's out there."

I'd forgotten all about the sensors. They were intended for small unit defensive use, basically an electronic picket line that would identify friend from foe.

"Get on it, Lieutenant. This works, and I'm buying you a steak dinner after the war," I said. "Sooner, if we find some beef on the hoof."

January Fourteenth
Valley Road at Highway Two Eighteen
West of Montrose, Iowa
01:30 Hours

It had taken an hour and a half for the infiltrating soldiers to complete their mission, wearing ragged S.A. clothing and openly carrying the hodgepodge of weapons. The S.A. was pushing out on their own, probing the defenses of the Brigade, without fully engaging us. During the wait, more equipment and a dozen more communications techs arrived and set up their field equipment. We were certainly not in a position to attack until we knew what we were up against…and even then, we were likely outnumbered and outgunned. The train carrying the Abrams tanks still had not arrived, nor had we heard from it.

"Sir, that Army artillery unit is on location and awaiting orders," Corporal Martin said.

"Have them stand by. Should these bastards break out toward the bridge at Keokuk, they're the last stand. Understood?"

"Yes, sir….One moment sir. Got something from Austin coming in," he said as Gunnery Sergeant Delaney came into the tent. His clothing was in tatters, boots mismatched, and he was carrying an AK-47 with a cracked stock, taped up with duct tape.

"Spill it, son," forgetting that he had to decrypt on the fly.

"Composite is eighteen hours away conservatively, sir. We might get another couple thousand men coming up from Kansas City by rail by then. Air Command might be able to get some support if the weather clears. Bad storm west of here, moving in tomorrow early morning. Zero viz over target, way below minimums of the fly-guys weapons systems right now."

"All right, so we're on our own, which is about the worst thing we could expect. The S.A. isn't going to sit there for eighteen hours. Fine. Not a real big surprise at this point. Gunny, your men got the sensors in place?"

"As best as possible, Colonel, while trying not to get shot."

"Lieutenant Jenkins, fire it up. Let's have a look at what we're up against," I said. The topographic map of the area, showing our 'friendly' positions, tanks, and other U.S. equipment. As the field sensors came alive, we could see what we were up against.

"Gunny, I can see what you mean about a target-rich environment," I said as someone else in the tent let out a long, descending whistle. "All right, lets hear it from boots on the ground."

"Zero noise or light discipline. Guys sleeping on brush and scrap. Muddy, nasty ground down there— still frozen up here of course. Caught a glimpse of what was probably their HQ. Group of three or four tents about here," the Gunny said, pointing to the flat-panel display, with heartbeat signatures, moving outward in a radial pattern. "No signs of civilians or women for that matter. Poor morale by the looks of it. Warming fires made of whatever they could scrounge, they're not taking care of their weapons. Maybe five percent of them are in actual tents. Most are outside or under tarps or ponchos. There are a shitload of them and that's their advantage. They also have at least a hundred tanks on this end, probably more north. Couldn't tell. Lined up nice and straight, crews camped under tarps between the tanks. If we had a few A-10's and DU shells, we'd light their asses up," the Gunny said, referring to the super dense depleted uranium shells. "They must have five semi-trucks full of shoulder-fired SAM's, though, sir."

"Sergeant Travis," I asked my sergeant-major, "What've we on the south end?"

"We have troops deployed to an east-west line along Two Sixty-Two, sir. Point men believe they are within a hundred and fifty meters, Colonel. No heavy equipment on that end anywhere in sight, although there are at least two large industrial facilities ablaze approximately a mile south of our line. They have a very porous line, our men moved beyond their outer perimeter before we realized it— enemy is not positioned well. Pulled back to the highway to consolidate."

"Excuse me, Colonel," Kittrick said. "We have contact with the train from Kansas City. Dog Six has contact, sir. Secure fourteen Charlie, Colonel."

"Damned good timing," I said. "I hope to God they have ammunition with those tanks."

"Downloading their manifest, Colonel," Kittrick replied.

The rail line from Kansas City cut diagonally across Missouri and Iowa, bearing northeast to Fort Madison, where it followed the Mississippi for a mile or two, then turned north. I spoke with the Captain in charge of the mechanized unit, and brought him up to speed on our situation. The train was halted at the Highway Two Eighteen crossing a couple miles south of us, and the tanks deployed. Their commanding officer was pleased to inform me they were fully armed, but would not go into detail until we met in person.

"Sir, this is Captain Gibson, Fourth Infantry Division, Second Brigade, Sixty-Sixth Armor Regiment."

"Colonel Drummond, good to meet you, sir."

"Captain, I've read a little of your manifest. A few minutes in the conference room, if you don't mind," I said, motioning him over to a folding table in the middle of our impromptu tent.

"Not at all, sir."

"Gerry, got a few minutes?" I asked.

"Yes, sir. Absolutely."

"Captain, tell me about the M1A1-N, if you would."

"Absolutely, Colonel. They're nicknamed the '*Nightmare.*'

We cobbled up a battle plan from scratch and quickly put things in motion. The Abrams 'N' Models would deploy on high ground south and west of the S.A. encampment, and on the plain behind our point units north of the S.A. Their movement would be masked by the sound of the big diesel electric locomotive engines, running at high throttle but stationary, along with every single engine that Third Washington could muster.

I hoped to push the S.A. back through a little bit of fear, disrupt their sleep, and put them on the defensive long enough for the Nightmares to gain their positions...and then shut everything down. Randomly, we'd order certain units to start up, rev their engines, move a little, and shut down.

We were favored with a slight breeze from the west, but the low clouds and fog kept our positions well hidden from the S.A. below us, compounded of course by the night. I ordered field kitchens set up not far from the line, to make sure that the men would at least have some hot food before the counterattack. I had ulterior motives with the kitchens as well.

We'd either win the day or lose everything, here. It really didn't matter that we had no more than a few more days' worth of food for the Brigade and the Marine survivors of the S.A. battle. I also suspected that the S.A. was out of food, fresh water, and knew they didn't have adequate shelter or foul-weather gear. I hoped that the aroma of beef stew might waft its' way through the S.A. troops, barely a mile away.

"Sir, we're receiving a request from the S.A. field commander to meet at our headquarters at oh four hundred hours. I believe sir, they're going to ask for our surrender," Captain Shand told me.

"Let them come on in," I said with little hesitation. "Field commander and not more than one escort, unarmed. More than that and no one gets through. Got it?"

"Yes, sir."

"OK. Now, get the word out to shut down all non-essential equipment, and in forty-five minutes, fire it all back up—not the Nightmares, though, and remember not to let stuff sit at idle. Make them think we're moving stuff around for the last time, getting ready to move on them. For now though, I want it quiet. Calm before the storm. Now, a little change in plans for the command tent, everyone," I said loud enough for everyone to hear. "Everyone in the tent, every soldier from the point where the S.A. commander crosses the line to this tent: I want you in clean, new utilities. I want food at every workstation, coffee, the whole thing. I want a dozen men along the path to this tent to be eating a nice, fat sandwich for the S.A. to see. Eat as much as you like, and leave some on your plates. I want these bastards to think that we're swimming in new equipment, have plenty to eat, and are so well supplied that we throw him off his game. A little theater for our guests. Questions?"

"None, sir," Major Pat Morrisey said.

"Good. Preparations for the counter continue as planned then, and execution as scheduled," I said.

It would be an elaborate ruse, and would work, or we'd be making noise for nothing, the first engagement for the Nightmares would fail, dawn would come, they'd advance up the hill, and eventually overwhelm us. I hoped, again, to throw the S.A. into confusion, with two hundred running diesels, hoping they'd think they were tanks moving into position. Some of that was partially true. I really just wanted them on edge with no rest. They would find out soon enough.

Promptly at oh four-hundred the advance line unit, well camouflaged and only a hundred meters from the S.A. lines, signaled the approach of two individuals, carrying kerosene lanterns. Two hundred meters further along, they were searched for weapons, and then directed along a rather difficult climb up the muddy, snowy hillside, which was neither the easiest nor the most direct route. Their original course though, would have taken them directly to a parked Nightmare. Per my orders, the men that escorted them in, those that weren't in weapons-ready mode, were enjoying ham sandwiches on rye, with spicy mustard. I would have enjoyed seeing the theater.

A few moments later, the S.A. commanding general and a captain stood in the "field command center" for Third Washington. I hovered over Corporal Martin's workstation, which illustrated the S.A. positions. Other data were not displayed for the moment.

"I'm Colonel Richard Drummond," I said, not shaking the hand of, nor saluting, the S.A. officers.

"I'm Major General Ames Arnold Slocum. This is Captain Jamal Blankenship. Let me cut to the bone here, Colonel. You are completely outnumbered and at dawn will be wiped out. I am here to demand your immediate and unconditional surrender."

I laughed a little, holding it back out of 'respect.' I noted that both of them were poor poker players, and their eyes moved around the space, taking in the troops in their smart uniforms, the food at the workstations, as I had hoped.

"I'd expected as much. General, it is at your request that you walked through the American line and into my headquarters. It is at my request however, that you surrender unconditionally and immediately. With that surrender in my hand, I can assure you that you'll live out this day, although not too many more days based on what the S.A. army under your command has done across the Midwest. Places like Van Meter, Iowa, in particular. Without it, I can guarantee that you will not. I might just shoot you in the balls, and then your head myself. God knows you have it coming."

"You dare threaten me, Colonel? With this pissant force, you think you'll defeat the numbers and the technology that the State of America has amassed? We've all but defeated the Air Force's ability to continue their harassment with our umbrella of missiles. We've shot down thirteen planes today alone. We have uncountable numbers of ballistic missiles and the ability to use them at will. We own the day, Colonel. Your Army training should have by now pointed out the hopelessness of this situation."

"Just to clarify, General. You and your captain here, did walk into this command center of your own free will, that is correct?"

"Of course. To demand your immediate surrender."

"I don't surrender to murderers, you stupid son of a bitch," I said as a half-dozen Californias were leveled on the pair. "Find them a nice, cozy place to sit and watch their defeat." They were immediately placed face down on the ground, hands and feet bound with industrial-grade zip ties, and roughly placed in two chairs about ten feet from the main display screen that we'd be monitoring shortly. They were then strapped to the chairs. "And by the way, General Slocum, I'm not regular Army. I'm not even old-school National Guard. I'm a civilian who got drafted to help turn bastards like you into compost. To reiterate, I'm well more than half-tempted to put bullet in your head right now. Commanders who order children to be killed with grenades shouldn't be shown one iota of mercy. And if someone wants to prosecute me for that, I'm just fine with it."

"I demand that we be released immediately, Colonel. We came in here under a flag of truce. No way in Hell will you get away with this. My men will come after you and hunt you to the ends of the earth."

"I've seen what the State of America First Defense Force did, across four states. Your troops. Your command. Your orders. Your responsibility. You will now begin to pay for your actions and those of your government. I don't recognize any sort of truce with you, Slocum," I said, before turning my attention briefly to Weapons Specialist Andrew Jameson.

"Jameson. Light them up," I said, not taking my eyes off of the General's bound form.

"Sir?"

"Was I unclear, Mister Jameson?" I said, maintaining my glare. The two S.A. officers were now plainly worried.

"Need a few more minutes sir to complete the targeting, sir…to guarantee maximum effectiveness in the sweep," Corporal Martin answered for Specialist Jameson. "Lotta live targets out there, Colonel, and of course equipment."

"Fair enough," I said. "General, your troops shot down three armed or unarmed drones in the past twenty-four hours, and one manned aircraft in the past seven days. No other United States aircraft has been shot down. Your ballistic missile launches have been successful in that they made it off their launchers, and then they had holes burned through them during boost phase, courtesy of the Air Force. Maybe you're believing your own propaganda," I said. He sat there and fumed.

The main display screen came alive in three dimensions. The plain terrain model showed the icons of the S.A. troops, scattered to Hell and gone on the plain below us, blue targets on black. The Third Washington and regular Army troops were in red, the M1A1-N's in green, with a light green overlay showing their effective field of fire.

"What in the Hell is this thing? A damned video game?" the well-fed, sweating Captain Blankenship asked us.

"The end of your Army," I said flatly. They didn't express any additional worry at my statement.

"Ready, sir," Jameson said.

"Gents, if either of these animals make a move, shoot them someplace painful," I said. "Don't kill them though. I'm thinkin' I'd like to see them swing from a tree on Constitution Avenue," I said, not taking my eyes off of the display. "Unless we find a convenient tree or light pole around here, first, after a meeting with a judge advocate general."

"Absolutely, Colonel," A sergeant said. "And thank you for the honor, sir."

"Slocum, you see this field of blue? Those are your troops. We track them by their heart signature. This view is provided to us by a series of sensors, linked to our communications matrix, as well as to our weapons targeting systems. Our troops infiltrated your lines and placed them there, earlier this evening. The red, well, those are the good guys. That'd be a rear-area support element known as Third Washington Engineers, part of the Transport Command, numbering around twenty-nine hundred men, and the survivors of the previous S.A. engagement, some fine Marines. Call it three thousand and change. The purple symbols are various tanks, trucks, Humvees, generators, and other noisemakers designed to disturb your troops, or scare the shit out of them. Those bright green symbols are twenty-four highly modified Abrams tanks, slang name is the Nightmare.

The overlapping light green color is their effective field of fire, blanketing the entire S.A. encampment."

"You think twenty-four tanks are going to take out the S.A. First Regular Army? You're seriously delusional," Blankenship said, almost spitting it. "We'll have your balls for breakfast."

"Nightmare teams ready," I heard on the console speaker, from the lead tank commander. *"Nightmare one-three, charge coupling reset, three seconds to nominal...One-three ready. Nightmare fire teams have a green board."*

"Jameson, execute Sunburn."

"Sunburn team, execute, execute, execute," he said into his headset.

The screen instantly illustrated the effect of the Nightmares, as all twenty-four fired in their pre-programmed, coordinated pattern. The terrain we had hastily selected above the S.A. position gave the Nightmares complete battlefield vision, and the range was well within the capability of the Boeing-modified, General Dynamics platform.

The battlefield was immediately divided into triangles of overlapping dark stripes, slowly sweeping across the field of fire. The implications of the dark stripes were not immediately apparent to Slocum and Blankenship. Within seconds of the initial activation, the symbols denoting the individuals of the S.A. army began to panic, running from the invisible weapon, in any direction but the one that was killing them. We could hear, and feel the detonations of S.A. weapons, and wild fire coming from their troops...firing at the invisible enemy. Five minutes later, it was over. There were no blue symbols left. Secondary explosions, probably from tank rounds and missiles, continued.

"This is some kind of trick," Slocum said.

"Not hardly," I said. "Count of enemy dead, Martin?"

"Eighty-six thousand four-hundred and twelve, sir," the Corporal replied, generating a startled movement from Slocum. I suspected he knew to the man, how many he had under his command.

"Survivors?"

"Zero, Colonel."

"You want to surrender, or do we turn you loose for the Nightmares to work you over?" I asked the lone remaining S.A. troops for miles.

"This is a trick. You couldn't possibly have done what you've said. You're lying!" Slocum said.

"No, we're not. Come first light, we'll show you personally. Maybe by then the stench will lessen in the cold. Until then, you are to be treated as a war criminal. Sergeant Carruthers will be more than happy to see that you're taken care of appropriately. Strip 'em naked, throw them in a box. Keep them from committing suicide, Sergeant."

"Sir!" Carruthers said, nodding to his men to remove the two from the command tent. A minute later, I gave the command for the majority of the Brigade to safe weapons. There wouldn't be any more fighting any time soon.

"Jameson, put me through to Austin," I said.

"Yes, sir."

"And pass the word, Army artillery, Mechanized, Third Washington and Marine Recon units stand down until oh-six-hundred, excepting Delta rotation," I said. Delta was the oh two-hundred to oh six-hundred skeleton crew and basic guard patrol. "Have an honor guard ready at dawn to raise the colors. There will be no celebrating. Clear?"

"Yes, sir. Clear," Corporal Martin said.

A minute and a half later, I was on the line with the duty officer in the command car, and then patched through to Theater Command.

After breaking the news, I walked back to Charlie Six, alone.

Battle of Fort Madison Plain
Twenty-Fifth Anniversary

The farmhouse was modest, nicely restored and well-kept, and it was nice to have some time alone with my thoughts. In the many years since the S.A. army was defeated, I'd had the chance to travel to much of the nation, but not once had I visited this part of Iowa. The weather was not unlike that January day. With misplaced concentration, it would not be hard to find myself back on the battlefield. I was pleased to see the old Federal-style house restored.

My security men knocked on the front door, which I then answered, not quite dressed for the commemoration. I still had an hour until I was expected outside. I was not unwilling, at seventy-one years, to go outdoors in twenty-degree weather despite the risk.

"Sir? Mr. McKenna is here for his interview," Tim Crawford said.

"Thanks, Tim. Please show him in. I'll meet him in the living room. Ought to make myself more presentable."

"Sir." Tim replied as I headed back into the guestroom to get my tie and dress jacket. A few minutes later, I joined the *Sun-Register* reporter. He stood as I entered the room.

"Please, sit," I said. "No need for the formalities, Mr. McKenna."

"Thank you, sir, for your time. This is a rare opportunity."

"What's your first name, son?" I said. I had the right to call him that, I thought. He looked like he was maybe two years out of Iowa State.

"Jefferson, sir."

"Good name. May I call you Jeff?"

"Absolutely, sir," he said, relaxing five or six levels.

"Good. Call me Rick."

"Thank you, sir."

"Good. Now, fire away."

"Yes, sir....I have a number of questions obviously, but I'd really like to hear what your thoughts are on the single, biggest change in the Federal government, pre-War and post."

"Good way to dive right in," I said with a chuckle. "I'm not sure that I can come up with a single biggest change, because there were so many, and the accrued Reconstruction efforts caused a fundamental reset of the Constitution, through several channels. In short, we are closer to living within the Constitution of a hundred and seventy-five years ago. There are some changes though, that I think will help the durability and resiliency of the Republic far more than anyone gives credit."

"What would those be, sir?"

"The elected leadership being term-limited under the Twenty Eighth Amendment, which also eliminates the potential for any influence of any elected Federal official by any enterprise, public or private, under penalty of law," I said, sounding more like my professor-lecturer self than I might want. "Of course, it also eliminates the ability of 'congressional staffers' to be employed for more than eight years total. Those unelected staffers wielded far too much power and were accountable to no one, way back when."

"Before you were born, Jeff, Hell, before I was born, Representatives and Senators, and probably Presidents as well, were bought and paid for. Republicans on one side of the aisle, Democrats on the other, not like today, where they are seated by state, regardless, and formal party affiliation is all but illegal. Industries, agencies, non-governmental organizations, individuals...if they had the money, they could find a way to buy what they wanted, either through direct influence or party affiliation. Under the table at first, with winks and sly grins and with what they used to call 'pork barrel' projects, where one elected would pass a law that benefited another elected, in exchange for the similar favor. Judges legislating from the bench, using their power to subvert the Constitution, the legislature, and the will of the people. By the time the War started, it was in the open, The corruption was complete, and the greed unabated....along with the grab for power. The staffers wrote the legislation, most of the time without having the Congressmen read it. Multi-national corporations operated outside the bounds of both morality and law. They corrupted foreign governments, positioned our own to defend their business interests at the cost of the lives of our men and women and civilians. Once the lines were so completely blurred, once ethics were completely and openly ignored, the *socialisti* could easily game the political system. These days, you try to influence a Federal official, or most State officials, and you're doing hard labor for ten years minimum. Downside of that, is that some Senators and Representatives feel they all but walk on water, but their paycheck is meager, by design. That Senator from New York, can't remember his name, proposed that Congress be outfitted with Robes of State or some such nonsense. 'Designed to be appropriate to the high office and dignity required,' I recall his motion. At the time I made an offhanded remark that the last thing we needed were more priests of the law. The Congress is set apart. It is set, not above, but to serve the citizenry. We also have strict Constitutionalists serving on the Supreme Court....must not underestimate that."

"We studied the origins of the Reconstruction Amendments pretty thoroughly of course, but it's different hearing the personal experience," he said, directing his comments toward the small media recorder on the coffee table.

"I wasn't always an elected official. Matter of fact, I tried pretty hard not to be. Back before the War I was in private enterprise, making money, enjoying life. Like everyone else, I was increasingly pissed off about what they were doing to our civil rights, and frustrated that what The People really wanted was not only ignored, but ridiculed by the people we elected! The life you live today simply cannot be compared fairly, unless you really know how bad it was before the end."

"I suppose not, sir."

"There are plenty of resources of course, us fossils and everything you find on Verimedia. But as usual, I digress."

"Government growth," Jeff said, referring to another amendment.

"The stripping away of the ability of the Federal leadership to grow as a malignancy, consuming everything around it. It can't do that, by Constitutional amendment, because the Federal Government, excluding the armed forces of course, can no longer grow beyond the average of the most populous states' selected employee count. The Federal employees, to put it simply, cannot, by Amendment, ever outnumber the selected public employees of the largest state, let alone all states combined. Do you know how much of a difference that really is, numerically or by percentage?"

"I'm...afraid not sir."

"Pre-War, there were two and a half MILLION Federal employees and a massive dependency infrastructure that kept almost twenty percent of Americans dependent on the Federal Government. Hundreds of thousands of departments, many administrations, bureaus, and Cabinet level directorship of areas never intended or dreamed of under Federal control by the Founding Fathers. Now, there are less than a hundred and fifty-thousand employees. Total. The more they *could* grow, the more they *did* grow. The Federal Government created dependency systems that ignored Constitutional limitations. Research the concept of Federal Social Security—you'll see what I mean. The States are in much more control of the Nation than they ever were twenty-eight or fifty and probably a hundred years ago. States Rights under the Tenth Amendment were fully restored and ensured, I believe, with the passage of the Twenty-Ninth Amendment. Arguably one of the largest and most dramatic changes ever put in place in the history of the United States."

"Your idea, it's been rumored."

"Nope. But I was in the room," I said flatly. "Seriously. I'm not the author of that thought. Senator Garcia's through and through. Wish it'd been my idea."

"The *Frontier Years*," Jeff asked.

"The Rebuild, some called it. Others called it the Great Cluster," I said with a little smile, omitting some colorful language from the label.

"I'd heard that from my Dad," he said. "He was a laborer out West."

"Rough work. Wildly underappreciated," I said. "I'm not sure who coined the term, first of all. Wasn't any of us. The tasks we were initially faced with were just so staggering in scale, it was hard to understand it all. Part of it was the mental adjustment of a much smaller population. We lost so many—more than a hundred million Americans alone. What was left, that which wasn't destroyed in the War, well, we had more 'built' for a lifestyle that no longer worked. It couldn't be maintained. It started with that. Understanding how many people we had, what kind of country we wanted to live in, and move on from there. There were parts of the Midwest that were without utilities for years, thanks to the S.A. and their EMP's and outright destruction. Entire counties were abandoned, and not really repopulated at rates anywhere near what they were pre-War. Twenty years of reconstruction in New Seattle alone, and we're not close to being back to what it was. Roads gone to pot, bridges washed out or collapsed....stuff wasn't built to last in the first place, it was built to have a short lifespan and get built again...roads in particular, but major public buildings and homes as well. The time and effort to restore what was there before the War just didn't make sense."

"The controversy about property ownership still goes on," Jeff stated.

"It does. It will for eternity, nothing we can do about that. Almost impossible to track down the rightful heirs on property all over the nation that was abandoned, of course, with many of the old records destroyed. That which was abandoned, was reclaimed by the respective states and in most cases homesteaded. No one expected the outright indignation from the agro-chemical industry at the reversion of all those mono-culture super-farms back to the states, and the threats and lawsuits and such. The land was sitting. No fuel and not enough equipment to farm. Damned few farmers. The nation needed food. The fact that Iowa decided to be the first to break up the Ag monopolies was the floodgate that allowed reasonable-sized, highly diverse farming to be reintroduced to the United States. An unpopular Supreme Court decision from the viewpoint of corporate America. Again, an underappreciated event in the course of modern history."

"I'd like to come back to the corporations in a moment, but first, sizeable amounts of land were never put back into productive use. Do you see in the future, another Settler expansion into those areas?" he asked, referring to the land-lottery that took place seven years after the War ended.

"Sure, if it makes sense. There is a fair amount of land in this country though, that had no business coming under the plow. Once upon a time, during the early days of the Frontier work, I was accused of being an 'environmentalist', which I found a little insulting. That my primary goal was to keep Man off of the land and that it would revert to Nature. I couldn't be farther from it actually. I'm a conservationist first….the appropriate use of the land and water for productive use, and the preservation of that which, by adverse use, would cause the land to be damaged, destroyed, or cause the destruction of other lands. My definition, not one you'll find in a dictionary."

"Some say, sir, that the farming and resettlement policies are overly restrictive."

"Subjective view, either way. Like I said, plowing up all the land on either side of a river, leaving no buffer to protect water quality, then spraying fertilizers and herbicides and pesticides on the genetically modified crops is no way to do anything except create runoff filled with mud, chemicals and nutrients that don't belong in rivers. I like to fish in water that's not full of some stuff that's going to kill me. It's not too much to ask to have people use common sense when it comes to working the land," I said. "GM crops were a disaster to the ecology of the planet. Unfortunately there's no going back now that they're out there. The terminator stuff in particular, spreading to other varieties, cross breeding, and then self-eliminating," I said. "We lost wheat as an entire species. All that is left are the genetically modified remains. The grain is different now. That shouldn't be forgotten."

"When it comes to resettlement policies, they are much more restrictive than pre-War settlement patterns. Main reason is that no one ought to be building in a floodplain, or in some other naturally-inclined hazard area that will endanger the structure, its owners, or the land, or other people. The fact that 'no one ought to' translated, in the old days, into, 'We got flooded out. Pay me to build a new building in the same spot.' That stuff doesn't make sense—so it's not allowed to happen, most of the time. Some States allow it, most don't. No one provides insurance against stupid decisions, though. Same reason that out here, where tornadoes happen, that new buildings are engineered to handle them, more or less. The money's already being spent, once. Build to last and build smart."

"OK. You mentioned Corporate America. Can you shed a little light on your view of the new corporate limitations?"

"Well, not new anymore. If it's an American corporation, it's based here. It produces here, it is taxed here, it ships from here, and the money it makes its' shareholders stays here. It hires Americans and documented aliens here. If they're an international corporation and they want to do business here, they form an American corporation and follow the rules of an American corporation. If an American corporation wants to work off shore, they do it as a subsidiary corporation, working under the laws of the respective nation, but by American law the subsidiary can never be larger than the parent corporation. And it never pays more than ten percent corporate tax, ever. The Byzantine tax codes of old allowed...no, encouraged, the domestic corporation to have most of its' production off-shore, didn't pay taxes on it, much if not most of the time, essentially, practices like that destroyed American heavy industry and crushed innovation and drove intellectual capital away. The re-writing of the rules for corporate behavior included all of that and much more of course. I think the preceding are the most important points, because they've caused the flood of industrial innovation and business that we've seen over the past eight years. For the creation of this system, we were called fascists. I advised a certain young

Senator to revisit the definition and get back to me, after I told him to shove it," I said. "That Senator was also advised to review what happened to the vast majority of Pre-War Congressmen, because he was heading down the same road they did. Most of them were strung up or shot. The Liberty Tree at the Capitol Reflecting Pool is a real place. Tyrants swung from it. I was there."

"The creation of National Sales Taxation."

"You have no idea how good you have it these days, Jeff. You buy a new item, you pay NST on it. You buy a used item, you don't. You trade for something, you don't pay taxes on the trade. You don't pay tax on what you make. You don't pay property taxes in the same manner that we once did. You don't pay taxes on earned investments, because you'll pay taxes when you buy something with the earned investments. You don't pay the Federal government, the state you live in does, based on purchases. You don't pay taxes when you buy gold or silver, because those are a form of currency. The Tax Reformation Act was as much about *simplifying the tax structure for the taxpayer* as it was about *limiting the amount of money that the Federal Government can lay hands on*," I said with particular emphasis.

"We, ahem, unemployed a lot of accountants and tax attorneys. We created a fifteen percent national sales tax, and are using no more than ten in the operations of the Federal Government, and a hunk of that goes towards reserves. Property taxes of course are set by the local jurisdictions and the States. The excess taxation collected by the Federal Government, up until a couple of years ago, was a strictly guarded secret of course, but that cat's out of the bag."

"Debt payback," McKenna said.

"Absolutely. It will take time to pay back those nations that invested in the United States, that which the former government repudiated. There is relative peace in a lot of the world today, and trade is prosperous in the U.S., because we are making good on debts incurred, despite all of the troubles over the decades. With the money we pay back, they rebuild, they invest, in their own nations and sometimes in ours. Without the confidence of other nations in the ability and the dedication of a nation to honor its' obligations, there can be no basis for international trade, or alliances, or even basic relationships. There is trust now, where there was none."

"Pax Americana," the young journalist asked, finally getting to the meat of things.

"A wonderful notion. The fact that the United States of America has grown up and avoids foreign entanglements is at least as important as the Dis'sembler." I noted his shock has he started back in his chair, mouth dropping open a little.

"I'm surprised, sir, that you brought that up."

"Worst kept secret since Jimmy Carter told the evening TV viewers and our enemies all about the Stealth Fighter. Why not talk about it? The fear of the thing is at least as effective as the impact of its employment. Besides that, it's allowed the United States military to be sized appropriately, namely for the protection of Americans abroad, commercial trade, and our continental interests. *Pax Americana* means something radically different now, than it meant when I was your age. It didn't work under the old meaning. It seems to, now. We don't pick fights, no one picks fights with us. We don't go pulling someone's privates out of the fire or try to 'build nations' anymore."

"Would you mind me asking about the DisAssembler? I have…"

"I opened the door. Your notes and this recording will be cleared of course prior to any distribution, per the Witness Agreement."

"Absolutely, sir."

The Witness Agreement, adopted not long after the defeat of the S.A., required anyone serving in the journalism racket to report honestly, equally, and fairly, as verified by the electronic Verimedia Witness and a disinterested observer, through the electronic images and audio being collected. There was no such thing as a biased reporter any longer, which released the journalist to the creative efforts of telling the truth in a compelling manner. In my case the Witness Agreement would also have a Federal review, in case some confidential information, perhaps better-kept than the M-DisAssembler, came out.

"It's been eleven years since Station Liberty was established, and twelve since near-space was cleared. For years it's been rumored that the Dis'sembler made that possible," Jeff stated, "but no one talks about the Dis'sembler in any detail."

"Come February, the Freedom of Information Act will likely confirm that for everyone. Twelve years, since Liberty went up. FOIA covers all that, including the MDA."

"But use against earthbound targets, instead of its intended mission...." He said, afraid to continue.

"My idea. Yeah."

"Sir, I have to ask this. Do you not have a difficult time reconciling the use of such a device..." he asked, before I cut him off.

"Weapon, son. Call it what it is."

"OK, sir. The use of such a weapon against targets on Earth?"

"Nope. Hard-hearted bastard that I am, no. The Molecular Dis-Assembler was created to effectively and safely clear near-Earth space of orbiting nuclear weapons parked there before the War. The impact of that Soviet weapons cluster splattered all over the Urals was ample demonstration that the device's deployment couldn't wait, and that was three years after the International Space Station de-orbited, dead crew and all, scattering their remains and the station itself over five thousand miles of burn-in. Further, it was impossible for the United States, or any other nation, to ensure the successful orbit of any satellite due to the space debris and remaining orbiting weapons. The Dis'sembler eliminated the debris over a six- month period. Without it, safe space travel would have been impossible for generations. Maybe forever. No Space Station Liberty. No bases on the Moon. No manned missions to Mars."

"OK, I understand, but, you haven't fully answered my question, sir."

"No I have not," I said as I stood, and looked out the window. "Jeff, you're twenty-something years old. Not far from here, I had three thousand men and change under my command, and we defeated a far superior force with a weapon that was much more cruel and crude in implementation. On my order, twenty-four tanks burned to death eighty six thousand four hundred and twelve State of America soldiers and conscripts within minutes. Burned them alive. In some cases it appeared, burned them in half, searing their wounds, keeping them alive a few minutes longer until another pass made sure they were dead. They never saw the weapon that killed them. They didn't know where to run, because they were enclosed in a pattern that had no escape. Their ammunition and fuel exploded in the heat, the truck tires exploded around them. Their plastic rifle stocks, and then the metal barrels and receivers melted into their flesh. After that, we were called the *Sunburn Brigade*, not *Third Washington Engineers*. I cannot imagine the minutes of Hell those men were subjected to. Do you have any idea of the smell of such an event? Of the cost of the event in terms of human destruction?"

"No sir."

"No, you don't, Jeff, and I hope you never have to see something like that," I said with a shaking voice. I'd noted that as I aged, I could not hold back the emotions of events such as this. It broke me up, perhaps proving to me, that I was still human on occasion. "Although, I hope to God the Creator that no one ever forgets what was done here, or in any of the towns destroyed so that an almighty State could exist anywhere on this earth. Millions died so that the powerful could stay powerful," I said, taking a drink of coffee before continuing. "And yes, I'd do it all over again if need be. We killed the S.A. that day, but it took two and a half more years for the killing to stop." I noticed out the window, another car coming in the distance.

"The DisAssembler has been used to eliminate targets that posed a direct, immediate, credible threat to the United States of America, and her territories. That might mean an individual. It might mean a pirate ship. Might mean an inbound aircraft carrying something or someone bent on our destruction that the military cannot address as quickly and effectively through conventional means. Could we have helped England against Argentina? Sure, we could have. We could have stopped the Chinese from taking all of Central Africa. Could we take the Caliphate out of Europe? Sure, and right-quick. Are we going to? No. Bailed Europe out twice, got screwed for it in the end, and got the bill to boot. We'll never see those cathedrals of Europe rebuilt. Notre Dame, a pile of carved stones with a mosque built on the remains, like the mosque at Cordoba, Spain. They could have converted it like they did to the church that became the Mosque of the Rose in Istanbul. Instead, they just tore it down. Hundreds of other masterpieces of architecture, blown up by the Caliphate. Pretty good chance you'll not hear any more detail than that. You will not hear it from me. I will say though, that had I had such a weapon available here, I'd have used it, for the sake of those we killed as well as those of us who buried the dead. I would have much preferred to see the barren earth with the fine coating of the molecules of vaporized men and their weapons, than horror of hundreds of acres of seared flesh and mounds of unexploded ordnance."

"Let's change the subject, if you don't mind."

"No, I welcome it, Mr. McKenna."

"How's your health been?"

"Pretty good for an old fart," I said, relieved for the subject change. "Seriously, not too bad. Heart meds, arthritis, knee rebuild. Hearing gone to Hell. All the joys of being over seventy."

"You've been hospitalized a number of times this past year," he pressed further.

"Yep. Pneumonia, double pneumonia, and walking pneumonia. Did you hear I had pneumonia?" I said with a smile. "All three bouts are the result of the Guangdong flu and lung scarring from back then. Doc said it'll kill me if I'm not careful. My wife ensures that I am more careful than a male of my age might want to be. I don't feel my age most days."

"Your retirement."

"Enjoying it immensely," I said. "Karen and I have been doing our best to spoil the grandchildren as our primary occupation. Some

726

time in New Seattle, but mostly in the home area, few weeks at the lake each year. Occasional trip to San Francisco to see our niece and nephew and their families. Lecture a little now and then at the University, where I think they tolerate me. Give a sermon once or twice a year at the home church, where they also tolerate me."

"From what I hear sir, there is standing room only."

"That's overly generous, I'm sure. Bad nights for sports or media. I think my secretary makes sure of that before she schedules anything. And I make it a point to give a sermon at Christmas or Easter, when they pack 'em in anyway, if I am indulged, of course."

"Ever think of going back into public service, sir?"

"I'm in public service every day, Jeff. I just don't get paid for it."

"You and your predecessors have refused to serve but a single term."

"Absolutely. Get out while you can and get on with life before government sucks it out of you. If you ever get elected, you'll understand what I mean," I said as I heard the door open. Jeff, being a very-well mannered young man, stood immediately.

"Ma'am, I'm Jeff McKenna. I'm a reporter with the *Chicago Sun-Register*. Pleased to meet you, Mrs. Drummond," he said. Karen was looking her beaming self, silver-blond hair tucked under her fur hat.

"Thank you, Jeff. You as well. My husband spinning yarns and talking farming?"

"No, Ma'am. I'm afraid I've been steering him in other directions."

"The unseemly and disreputable, then. Politics, if I'm not mistaken, right?" she said, taking my hand.

"'Not to be spoken of in polite company,' I believe my grandfather once said," Jeff replied.

"Wise man. You should take his advice," I said.

"Hon, you ready?" Karen asked. "The kids will be here any minute."

"I thought they'd have had enough of my speechifying."

"Nonsense. This is important."

"It is, just trying to maintain a sense of balance. This place can be overwhelming," I said. I could feel it, they were almost tangible, the memories.

"Jeff, care to join us?" Karen asked.

"I'd be honored, ma'am."

"Nonsense. Can't have you walking all the way over to the memorial. It's a mile off and it's snowing," she said.

I grabbed my overcoat and hat, necessary but not liked, and we made our way out to the hybrid Lincoln. A few silent minutes later, we were on the dais, Karen holding little Charlie on her lap, bundled up against the cold. I was joined by a dozen of my men from Third Washington, and hundreds more in the audience.

Introductions followed, and brief remarks by Christine Schimanski, the senior Iowa Senator, and Chief Justice James Carlton. Jim served with Mike's 'A' Company Rangers. Chris Schimanski's mother-in-law had been Clara DeJong. Clara had passed on not long after Chris and Clara's son Jakob were married. I had the privilege of reading Scripture at her funeral. Like many I'd known, we lost her too soon.

I was next...I heard, but didn't listen to my own introduction. As always, I spoke without notes.

"Good morning, and thank you for inviting me to the dedication of this memorial. It is not without powerful emotions that I stand before you here today, even surrounded by family, friends, and those

728

that put up with me as their commander," I said, looking over my shoulder to a few smiles.

"It has been my honor to serve the citizens of the United States of America in one fashion or another, for more than twenty-five years, of those, four years and six days in uniform. Twenty-five years ago this morning, three thousand men under my command defeated a much larger force on this field of battle, now remembered properly as hallowed ground. On my order, eighty six thousand four hundred and twelve Americans died here. Those men, and others like them were responsible for the deaths of more than two hundred thousand fellow Americans across the Midwest, and untold damage on those they left alive."

"Third Washington, Recon Twelve of the Fifth Marine Expeditionary Task Force, a handful of SEALS and regular Army soldiers participated in this action. I would like to speak of this, in terms that may not have been explored over time."

"On that early morning, we stood wildly outnumbered in every respect. The decisions made by the State of America commanding general saved Third Washington at the cost of his own life and the lives of his entire command. They could have easily swarmed up that hill," I said, pointing behind me, "and killed us all. They could have moved south, and destroyed the five pieces of artillery were still operational. Five. They could have moved north, beyond the Memorial Grove there, and wiped out everyone else. They didn't because they were not fighting for a nation, they were fighting for men. Others would dispute me here, but there are few precious few men that are worth fighting for," I said, pausing for effect. "The decision of the State of America commander changed both the course of the war and the face of the United States of America, forever."

"There are ideals embodied in a nation such as ours that are worth fighting for, even at my advanced state of decay," I said, getting a few quiet laughs. "Those of us with six or seven decades behind us and less than one or two ahead, should fully realize the sense it makes to have the older generation fight, and not the younger. These young," I said, waving to my children and grandchildren, "are the future of this nation. I pray to God that the examples we have given them will provide ample education on how over time we can destroy a nation, and that the leaders of the several States are wise enough to not throw our future before cannons."

"The losses of these men—husbands, fathers, sons, brothers, uncles—touches every single citizen of the United States. Virtually everyone knows people that served in the S.A. army or was killed by them. The bitterness of this civil war will burn for decades. There was no North versus South in this war. There was though, in the most honest sense of the words, good versus evil. For a few precious decades we may enjoy this respite from evil, although it reigns in many other nations around the globe. It will return to this continent, I have little doubt. For a few precious years, we are at peace. For these years, we will treasure our time with our children, working and playing and learning and teaching them to not repeat our mistakes."

"What we lost here though, should not be forgotten to history, we must mourn it as we mourn the losses in our own families. We lost the creative energy and the momentum of a generation. We lost doctors, lawyers, teachers, writers, scientists, researchers, builders, painters, playwrights, and the products of their lives. We owe it to these men, however we view the guidance of their leadership, to remember what they could have given this nation, and what we have lost as a nation as a result of their deaths."

"For a few minutes, before we traveled here to this dedication, I had the honor of spending some time with a young reporter. He asked me a number of good questions, and I answered without much in the way of forethought, but I answered honestly. There is one thing though that occurs to me, that should be an addenda to the answers I gave. Jefferson McKenna down there," I said, pointing to the second row and embarrassing him somewhat, "asked me about the single biggest change in the Federal government pre-and post-Second Civil War. Jeff I suspect will have my answers sketched out in the evening *Register*. What he didn't ask, but what I would like to add as an answer, are the biggest changes to America pre-and post-war," I said, a gust of fresh January air catching me a bit by surprise.

"This is a nation of laws. It is a nation that again can be viewed with virtues. Its people have a right to be proud. We once again are the goal for millions around the world, the shining beacon of freedom…not just this land, but the very *idea* that is our nation. Our children study our history, our Constitution, the causes of our collapse, the progress of reconstruction. We have people who can think, which I'd like to add as an aside, Clara DeJong, Senator Schimanski's late mother in law, would be most proud—she taught critical thinking to homeschoolers long before it was stylish to think for ones' self," I said, getting a few more laughs.

"We have returned to a sound monetary system, and are paying those that invested in our former form, regardless of whether they view us an enemy or a friend….the United States is indebted to those nations, we will fulfill our obligations. We again have our own industry, we are self-reliant, we have morality-based self-determination. We are Citizens of the Several States first and we are citizens of a larger nation. While my heart breaks for what we have lost here on this battlefield and on dozens more, my spirit soars at the prospects for the future of this country."

Applause, building slowly, and the crowd began to rise, and to continue their applause, before I held up my hand to hush them.

"I stand here today, broken from what happened here under my command. I pray to God that no other American commander, anywhere, ever has to face the decisions we did that night. Thank you, and good day," I said, backing away from the lectern, turning toward the huge flag, rising from half mast to full display, as those on the dais stood as well, also turning toward the flag. I came to attention and salute as bagpipes played *Amazing Grace*, followed by twin trumpets playing *Taps*, the horns in soft echo.

The applause rose again as the notes faded, Karen, then Kelly and her husband to my left, Carl and his wife to the right, grandkids all around.

"Let's go home," I said giving Karen a squeeze and a kiss. "We've a long way to go."

www.ingramcontent.com/pod-product-compliance
Lightning Source LLC
Chambersburg PA
CBHW030918020726
47498CB00001B/17

* 9 7 8 0 6 1 5 4 0 0 7 8 5 *